# *Adventures, Barbarians, and Devil's Breath*

*By*
*Mike Bowley*

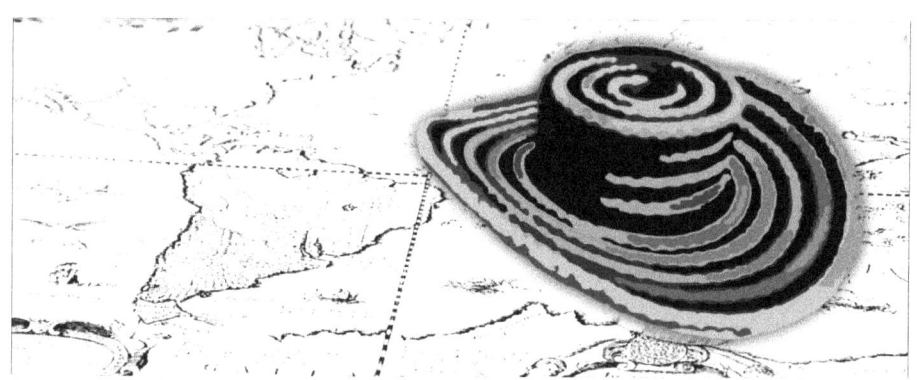

Published by Mike Bowley

Publishing partner: Paragon Publishing, Rothersthorpe

Part 1 First published 2017 and Reedited in 2023

Complete work First published 2025

© Mike Bowley 2025

The rights of Mike Bowley to be identified as the author of this work have been asserted by him accordance with the Copyright, Designs and Patents Act of 1988.

Thank you must go to Independent Editor and Translator from English to Latin Espanol – Cristina Rueda Nieto.

Grateful thanks again to Anne & Mark at Into Print for all their invaluable work and guidance in taking this culminating anthropomorphism-styled storyteller to the point of being a published author.

Black and White illustrations courtesy of Bing Illustrator under their subscription model.

All rights reserved; no part of this publication may be reproduced, stored in a retrieval system, or transmitted in any form or by any means, electronic, mechanical, photocopying, recording or otherwise without the prior written consent of the publisher or a licence permitting copying in the UK issued by the Copyright Licensing Agency Ltd. www.cla.co.uk


ISBN 978-1-78792-081-1


Book design, layout and production management by Into Print
www.intoprint.net
+44 (0)1604 832149

# Contents of Adventures, Barbarians, and Devil's Breath

| | |
|---|---|
| *Part One – Adventurous Tales From A Few Mountain Ridge Walks* | 5 |
| *Foreword to Part One* | 6 |
| *List of Chapters* | 9 |
| *Quotations, Sayings, and Proverbs* | 10 |
| *Chapters 1 to 26* | *11-184* |

*****

| | |
|---|---|
| *Part Two – At Last The Barbarians Are Sleeping* | 185 |
| *Foreword to Part Two* | 186 |
| *List of Chapters* | 189 |
| *Quotations, Sayings, and Proverbs* | 190 |
| *Chapters 27 to 50* | *191-382* |

*****

| | |
|---|---|
| *Part Three – Devil's Breath Claims New Victims* | 383 |
| *Foreword to Part Three* | 384 |
| *List of Chapters* | 385 |
| *Quotations, Sayings, and Proverbs* | 386 |
| *Chapters 51 to 72* | *387-657* |

*****

| | |
|---|---|
| *Final Thoughts* | 658 |
| *Your Author* | 660 |

# Part One

# *Adventurous Tales From A Few Mountain Ridge Walks*

## *Foreword to Part One*

*I* first started trekking on the old rocky and craggy road back in December 2013. I had just arrived at my new home high up on one of the many ridges of the Andes Mountains, known locally as "Cordillera de la Occidental ." This particular ridge looks down on the nearby city of Cali in the southwestern part of Colombia. Now, with my future bride Isabel Cristina Rueda Nieto, her elder son Carlos, his wife Paccha, and four very differently-minded Fila dogs named Nieves, Seven, Lula, and London, I have never experienced so much that life can offer in such a short space of time.

Nieves was the old grandmother who, in her prime, would have no problem bringing down a cow who had the misfortune to step in her way. Her son, Seven, was a mountain lion disguised as a dog. Seven's wife, Lula, was a female with the saddest of faces. But, also, the owner of the biggest heart and loudest appetite to protect all in her household, which included all the humans as well.

Then there was London, the son and grandson. He was the blackest colour you could imagine, which made everyone uneasy about what was hidden in his thoughts. In reality, he loved humans, and like his grandmother and parents, his sole reason for living was to protect all who fed and showed him love.

Sadly, Nieves, Seven, Lula, and London have all gone.

Since I was ten years old, my life in England had been consumed by earning money to live. Nothing else seemed to matter in my previously material world, and it was clear from the start that I had a lot to learn.

Here on this old, craggy road, I found new challenges: the heat, the altitude, and the need for Spanish as a language. Add the danger of not knowing if anyone would be a friend or foe, notwithstanding the fear of getting lost and my general lack of fitness. To be more accurate, being obese from all the excessive eating that kept me alert in the long hours at Heathrow Airport.

Fifty-eight years of European food have now been replaced by mountain cuisine and exotic fruits & vegetables never seen before. In those early days, there were continuous thoughts of being a possible target for kidnapping or robbery. What would the perpetrators say when they found out I was not a rich gringo.

Now add the fear of dreaded snakes, fearsome-looking scorpions. Sometimes, I had to face mountain spiders that were somewhat larger than I was used to. And dare I not forget the evil mosquitoes Cristina's family and friends had warned me of with their deadly ambition to infect us all. The contrasts in life could not have been more different.

I need not have worried. My experiences have been incredible and life-changing. At no time had anyone shouted or threatened me; far from it. I have only experienced warmth and good humour on this mountain ridge and, of course, the odd earth tremors that kept everyone alert.

The contrast in life could not have been more different, even if I had tried to fly to Mars. Every day brought me new experiences and new learning. Initially, I felt I had been drifting in the sea all my life and had just finally landed on dry land again in a different time dimension. As I got to know the land and started to acclimatise my mind and body to this arduous mountain ridge existence, I undoubtedly fell in love with it all.

Every time I walked up or down, my imagination ran riot. I knew from the very beginning that I wanted to write a tale or a large number of tales reflecting my experiences and feelings of everyday life in South America. But I had never written a book before. I knew from the outset that I did not want to write the standard blogger type of history. I wanted to bring a new and fresh approach. I needed a light bulb moment to present itself, and until it arrived, I would have to wait.

It took me four more years before the light bulb moment appeared.

It happened when I found myself leaning against a very large rock. It was higher and broader than me. I remember saying sorry to it as if it was alive. It was at this point I stopped. I looked back and asked myself, what if there really was a person in that rock looking bewildered at this stranger with his strange use of words? My tales of adventures began to flow like tidal waves towards me.

I must admit I struggled to remember all, and I must also confess some have gone totally away from me, but here's hoping they will return one day before it is time for me to put my pen down for good. Now I have my smartphone and an old-fashioned notebook and pen. I am often seen stopping abruptly and scribbling down ideas. Then suddenly, I am off again.

I hope and pray you will experience real enjoyment, the odd laughter line and sometimes the need to shed a tear if I have reached your soul with each tale of the mountain as they came to me.

Many of the items are authentic; they do exist. I just gave them life as I felt they deserved to have it. Please excuse the names used, as they are not meant to reflect anyone who has been given the same names. But secretly, I love the sound of Spanish names, and I hope you all enjoy the way I have used them.

Finally, I wish to say: "Thank you very much, my friends and my family, and especially my wife and best friend Isabel Cristina Rueda Nieto. Hahaha (you cannot imagine my world of adventures).

*Mike Bowley*

August 2017

Part One – Adventurous Tales From A Few Mountain Walks

# List of Chapters

| | | |
|---|---|---|
| 1. | *I am El Sol & the Clouds are my Children.* | *11* |
| 2. | *I am the Rock.* | *18* |
| 3. | *I am the Old Graggy Road.* | *23* |
| 4. | *I am the New Road.* | *26* |
| 5. | *I am the Oldest Scorpion on the Old Craggy Road.* | *29* |
| 6. | *I am the Little Colombian Sombrero.* | *32* |
| 7. | *I am the Small Cross & the Warning Sign.* | *42* |
| 8. | *I am One of the Two Flying Cows.* | *47* |
| 9. | *I am the Quad Bike with a Sexy Señora.* | *53* |
| 10. | *I am the discarded Chilean Bottle of Wine.* | *58* |
| 11. | *I am the somewhat thirsty and always hungry Colibri.* | *65* |
| 12. | *I am the shiny 100 Peso coin.* | *69* |
| 13. | *I am a Willy Jeep in Need of Some Help.* | *73* |
| 14. | *I am Gracie, and the Smiling Cleaner of the New Road.* | *81* |
| 15. | *I am a Home of Eternal Wishes for a Good Story.* | *85* |
| 16. | *I am Hector, and I also live in a home for the elderly.* | *94* |
| 17. | *I am Gabriel Garcia Marquez, but alas, not the famous one.* | *108* |
| 18. | *I am Leonardo's Kite who wishes to be a Satellite.* | *116* |
| 19. | *I am the Retired Policeman who everyone avoided.* | *121* |
| 20. | *I am Ignacio Perez the Mountain Truck Driver.* | *131* |
| 21. | *I am the Nun on a Mission to Sing.* | *139* |
| 22. | *I am the Earthquake measuring 4.7 on the MM Scale.* | *150* |
| 23. | *I am a Historical Event incorporating four human lives.* | *161* |
| 24. | *I am the Police and Fire Department Preliminary Report.* | *170* |
| 25. | *I am the Sol's account of the Aftermath.* | *173* |
| 26. | *I am the Mountain who witnessed, something truly special.* | *180* |

*This massive task is dedicated to my wonderful wife Isabel Cristina Rueda Nieto aka Cristirin.*

*(A woman of many names, and now she can add mine).*

*In appreciation for always showing her love and warmth of heart throughout our time together.*

*She has always said "You cannot imagine".*

*Well, I hope this gift will show her I can.*

"You are one of the billions of people on our Earth. Our Earth orbits the Sun in our Solar System. Our Sun is one star among the billions in the Milky Way Galaxy. Our Milky Way Galaxy is one among the billions of galaxies in our Universe."

"If the sight of the blue skies fills you with joy, if a blade of grass springing up in the fields has power to move you.

If the simple things of nature have a message that you understand, rejoice, for your soul is alive."

*Eleonora Duse (Italian Actress 1858 – 1924)*

"The Andes do not give back what they take." *Old Chilean saying.*

Adventures: Life's way of reminding us that even the best-laid plans can turn into hilarious, unexpected disasters that make for great stories later. Think of it as a rollercoaster ride which you didn't sign up for, and then cannot wait to get off, but secretly you kind of enjoy the chaos of it anyway."

*Mike Bowley*

Author of culminating anthropomorphism and short stories.

# *1: I am El Sol & the Clouds are my children*

It is customary in fictional mythologies where the sun is personified, you would see me as a male. But they are wrong. For example, according to J.R.R. Tolkien's legendarium, I am a female. That famous English writer, poet, philologist, and academic was right to personify me as female. That way, his storytelling allowed for a unique twist on traditional gender associations when commenting on celestial bodies such as myself. It gave him the creative freedom to add more depth and complexity to his artistic interpretation. One day, the same could be said of the English stranger, whose physical description is a deliberate contrast to the traditional image of a sun god, with his white hair, blue eyes, slightly pot-bellied, and sturdy-looking legs.

It is never hard for you to see me except, of course, when wearing protective measures. Sometimes, I am totally alone, and sometimes, I am surrounded by my children. Again, you may find it hard to see me when so many of them come together and create a mass.

Behold, I am a near-perfect sphere, a celestial giant in motion. My speed, a staggering 220 km per second, is beyond the grasp of your mortal eyes.

When you look up with one of your hands acting as a shield, I appear small in stature, but I can assure you I can easily fit a million of your Earths inside my sphere. 74% of my mass is hydrogen, making me the most potent force in the colossal Milky Way Galaxy. Even my temperature can exceed 15 million degrees Celsius.

Eventually, the day will come when I consume all that's on your Earth, including the Earth itself. Yet I am only one of more than 100 billion stars in the Milky Way Galaxy. I am the giver of life on your Earth through my energy and heat.

With the heat, I am able to evaporate liquid and thaw frozen water.

This technique turns the water into a water vapour gas. In this transformation, the gas can and will rise high into the atmosphere and fill my children, which you refer to as clouds.

Here, my children reflect my light, which allows them to appear white to you. They float and dance over the globe and slowly cool down the gas again, converting it all back to droplets of rain by condensing onto tiny pieces of dust or sea salt. When billions of these droplets come together, my children become visible to you humans.

Behold the wondrous 'Water Cycle', a symphony of transformation and renewal, orchestrated by my radiant heat.

Marvel at the simple yet miraculous reason behind the appearance of rainbows-my desire for my children to engage with me, a testament to our harmonious relationship.

I can see you humans love rainbows.

You, like me, can see the delightful result of the synergy between myself and all my children.

I once witnessed a female human called Cristirin sitting on top of a mountain ridge craggy road as she created this beautiful poem: *In the realm where sunbeams dance with tears, a celestial collaboration duly appears; From the gentle touch of rain's embrace, a breathtaking vision takes its place.*

*As droplets fall from the heavens above, gossamer whispers weave a tale of love.*

*Sunlight, like a painter's cherished brush, meets water's essence in a passionate rush. A prism's enchantment begins to unfold as smiles of colours swirl and behold.*

*With grace and elegance, they soon take part in the grand choreography that nature awakens.*

*In sacred union, light finds sweet refuge, caressing delicate and huge water droplets. With every moment, the spectrum expands, creating an arc, a celestial bridge in hand.*

*Red, like passion's fire, adorns the outer side, while violet, like dreams, is on the inner edge. From fiery orange and golden hues to calming blues and greens, nature's muse.*

*A sacred dance, exquisite and surreal, nature's luminary masterpiece so ethereal, a painter's palette, an artist's delight, a radiant emblem in heaven's night.*

*But fleeting is the moment, as time unfurls, as heavens shift and the canvas swirls.*

*A transient vision, a poem of light, rainbows fade, bidding a whispering goodbye, out of sight.*

*Yet in our hearts, the memory of this ephemeral beauty that shall not wane, a poetic symphony, from Earth to the sky, a rainbow's beginning, an eternal sigh will remain.*

If I continue with the metaphorical representation, I can describe the wind to you as an invisible messenger, tirelessly carrying the whispers and secrets of your world. It's like a storyteller, sharing the tales of the Earth's landscapes and the creatures that inhabit them.

Just as a messenger spreads words far and wide, the wind travels across the expanse of the sky, influencing the weather and shaping the atmosphere. It dances and swirls, caressing the clouds and carrying their stories beyond the horizon. The wind's movements determine the direction and intensity of storms, the distribution of heat and moisture, and the formation of clouds, all of which contribute to the dynamic nature of Earth's climate.

*****

"Good morning, Earthlings, or barbarians, but certainly not humans. Let me take a moment to introduce myself to you. I am Climate Change. I have been dormant for centuries, that is until your Industrial Revolution arrived at the beginning of the 18th Century."

"Before that, natural factors like volcanic eruptions and variations in solar radiation have influenced my behaviour in the past, but your barbarian activities significantly increased greenhouse gas concentrations in your atmosphere. Couple that with your widespread use of fossil fuels and your disastrous land use practices such as deforestation since have accelerated the rate at which I have had to increase my endeavours to unprecedented levels to punish you. Now, I am thinking ahead to my grand finale. Whenever that may be."

"Let me tell you none of the above is acceptable. I have been commissioned to put a stop to your destructive ways. I am not here to educate you, but I am here to warn you daily of the consequences you are facing. So far, many of you have ignored my warnings. Every year, I feel the need to raise the stakes."

"Let me demonstrate some of the key ways in which I have increased and made my presence known:"

"Have you observed your average global temperatures have been steadily increasing over the past century? Do you understand my efforts due to your ignorance have led to more frequent and intense heat waves?"

"Have you noticed that your world's ice caps and glaciers have been melting at an accelerated rate? Has the proverbial penny dropped yet? If not, then let me assure you this is leading to rising sea levels and posing a threat to all your coastal communities."

"Has the increase in extreme weather events started to concern you? In the last twenty years, I have heard you barbarians speak and link me to being culpable for the increase in extreme weather events such as hurricanes, droughts, floods, and wildfires, which have resulted in widespread damage and loss of life. Finally, some of you recognise my presence, and in contrast to your El Sol, I am pleased with my work, but I do not need to be a permanent fixture."

Your scientists and oceanic experts have raised the issue of the oceans' absorption of excess carbon dioxide, which has led to ocean acidification, which is harming marine ecosystems and threatening aquatic life."

"I can assure you it does not bring me any pleasure, as I love fish more than you barbarians. When you are gone, El Sol and I will witness the rebirth of the oceans once more."

"In recent times, I have caused shifts in your ecosystems and habitats, leading to the loss of biodiversity and threatening the survival of many species. Ask your scientists to explain what is emerging in the jungles and forests around your globe. My message to you is simple: You need global action to mitigate the effects I have been implementing over the past century. You need to adapt to my changing climate rules soon.

*****

Hi again. It is me; El Sol. Climate change has moved away from here for now. I can imagine how you are feeling right now. I would, too. The trouble is, he is not totally wrong.

For now, let me describe happier times. Once each year around the time of August, Kites become the playful offspring of the wind. They are the colourful and joyful extensions of its boundless energy. With strings in hand, you humans harness the wind's power and create these magnificent creations that dream through the celestial tapestry.

Kites gracefully rise and fall, soaring on the wings of the wind. Their flight is an enchanting spectacle of collaboration between nature and human creativity.

Like me, I know you all love birds, and I am sure you see them as the spirited messengers of the heavens.

Aloft in the vast expanse of the sky, they possess a freedom that echoes my nurturing warmth. Like intrepid adventurers, they traverse great distances, carrying melodies and stories across the lands.

Birds glide on the currents of the wind, serving as ethereal vessels that bridge the heavens and the Earth. Each harmonises with the wind's rhythm and adds its own symphony to the ever-unfolding narrative of nature's song.

In my context, the wind, kites, and birds become interconnected elements intimately tied to the tapestry of the natural world below me. Within the embrace of my celestial family, they embody grace, freedom, and a sense of purpose.

The winds that move the clouds along will influence where the water will eventually precipitate downwards. It is usually on the oceans that make up 70% of your Earth's surface. Why, you may enquire. Well, because these oceans hold at least 97% of all surface water.

I am also responsible for the warm currents on top of your oceans.

Evaporation is not restricted to the oceans. I have the same effect on lakes, ponds, lagoons, swamps, rivers, streams, brooks, and puddles. I even have power over all your plants, trees, and flowers, and finally, of course, all your humans, flora, and fauna.

For example, the sweat from your body always feels like it is heading downward to the ground, especially when you think of the droplets rolling down the middle of your spine. Still, unknown to you all, as soon as the droplets become gas, they will naturally rise again towards the sky and the atmosphere as water vapour gas.

There are, of course, days when very little water is evaporated, and my children are very subdued in certain parts of your Earth, and there are times when there is an overabundance in the atmosphere, and all my children start to cry at once. Their moods sometimes become dark and moody for no known reason, just like all human children.

You humans can always tell when my children are throwing their tantrums.

You refer it to the sounds of thunder.

This is caused by the intense heat from the lightning, which causes the surrounding air to expand rapidly and create a sonic wave.

Sometimes, there is just a loud crack; at other times, you will hear a low rumbling sound. You always see lightning first and then hear the thunder because light travels faster than sound.

It's at times like this that I become a little moody, too.

But I must never forget I am here as an excellent, loving mother, and it is my responsibility to watch over the entire water cycle.

So, as you can see, I am very important to you humans on Earth. Without me, your Earth would be nothing more than a lifeless block of ice-coated rock like many of your neighbours.

Talking about your neighbours, I should mention a few facts about your Moon. Yes, this ball originated when a meteor rock similar in size to Mars smashed into your planet about 4.5 billion years ago.

Every year, it keeps trying to move away from you. It only achieves a minute distance of four centimetres each year. But that does mean if you live a further 600 million years, the idea of eclipses will disappear and be no more.

In the meantime, both the Moon and your Earth will continue exerting a gravitational pull on each other. With the gravitational pull from the Moon, the effect on your Earth is experiencing bulging high tides at the highest points that exist on both the closest and the furthest sides of the Moon.

Please also remember again that I warm your oceans, stir your atmosphere, and generate your weather patterns.

The Moon partly causes your tides with a lot of help from me, of course. So, with all I have mentioned, you may rightly conclude I am the only genuine provider of all the food and oxygen for your entire life on Earth.

But alas, as I have already said, I am not totally perfect. I do have mood swings, and certainly in the area of the Earth where the mountain ridge of this book lives. You refer to my mood swings as Climate Change.

*****

Her Ladyship has referenced her mood swings and I can assure you they are on the increase. But she has neglected to mention, I, as Climate change, represent these mood swings.

While the impacts from me are largely unfavourable and pose significant challenges to your barbarian societies and ecosystems, some potential positive outcomes could result from addressing my impact. For once, I will be benevolent and offer you a few ways in which addressing my concerns could lead to positive outcomes:

Firstly, you need to reduce greenhouse gas emissions and foster the transition to renewable energy sources to spur innovation and technological advancement in areas such as renewable energy, energy efficiency, and sustainable agriculture. Believe me, do not keep ignoring me; this has the potential to create new industries, generate economic growth, and provide job opportunities.

Secondly, Actions taken to mitigate my effects, such as reducing air pollution and promoting active transportation options like biking and walking, have a positive impact on your health. Cleaner air and increased physical activity do lead to lower rates of respiratory diseases, cardiovascular problems, and obesity. Just ask the white-haired, blue-eyed, terracotta-looking, slightly pot-bellied, with, I must admit, sturdy-looking legs stranger I see daily on the mountain ridge craggy road overlooking a city below him.

Thirdly, you have to appreciate that efforts to combat El Sol's mood swings often involve protecting and restoring natural habitats and biodiversity. This will lead to the preservation of vital ecosystems, such as forests, wetlands, and coral reefs. In time, you will be providing essential services like carbon sequestration, water purification, and habitat for wildlife.

Fourthly, building resilience to the impacts of climate change can help your communities better withstand natural disasters and extreme weather events. This will include measures like improving infrastructure, implementing early warning systems, and incorporating climate-smart agricultural practices.

While these potential benefits are important to consider, it is crucial to also recognise the urgent need to address the root causes from me and take immediate action to limit my impacts and protect your planet for future generations. Let me one day change my attitude towards you and cease seeing you as barbarians and once more see you as humans.

*****

Like you, I, El Sol, can sense that climate change could be our saviour if we listen to and heed its warnings. If we do not, then it will be senseless to blame him for the outcome to mankind and Earth itself. Now let me shift my gaze and deal with developing events on the mountain ridge overlooking a city below.

*****

On this ridge, there is an old, craggy road with a massive rock standing upright on its dusty, terracotta-coloured surface.

The diamond-shaped rock must have arrived unseen at night because I surely would have seen it moving if he had travelled in the daytime. It is so big; I could easily imagine one of you humans fitting inside.

But to be fair, when he arrived, there were many larger rocks than him moving around. It was challenging to see which was going to end up where. Eventually, your Earth settled down, and apart from the odd protest, there was little for any human to fret about. Thousands of years have passed by, and the ridge has been left alone throughout time.

Obviously, there will be points in time when the mountain and all its ridges protest.

I will have to keep a closer eye on the "Cordillera Occidental," as I sense such a moment is not far away.

*****

## 2: *I am the Rock*

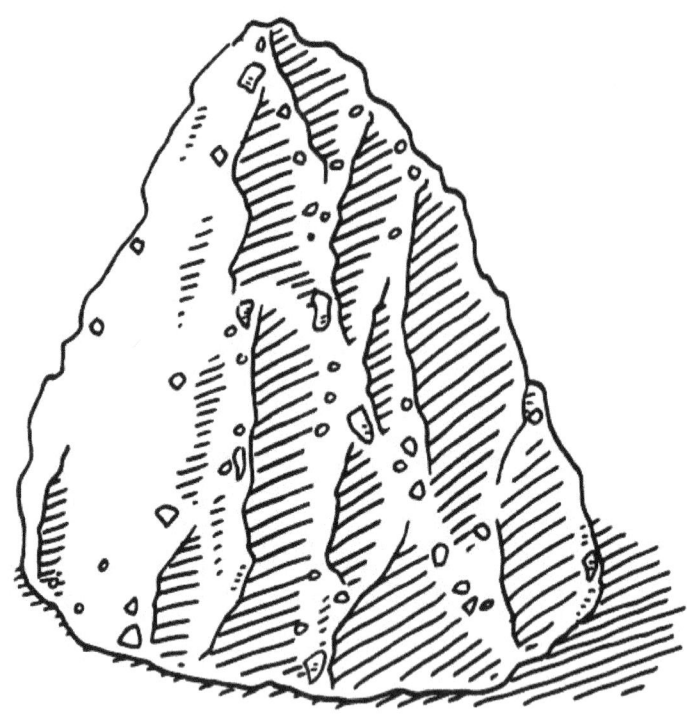

Anyone who drives a vehicle, rides a mule, cycles, runs, or even walks past me will only see a very tall and aggressive-looking rock on the side of the mountain ridge facing the valley below.

Nearly all will make a mental note of the rock's presence and will immediately forget about it as they go about their daily lives.

Should anyone have stopped and decided to investigate closer, they would have seen me below the surface. Maybe they would have been horrified, or perhaps they would have been in awe. I had no idea, as no one did.

I doubt that, never in the thousands of years that I have been here, has anyone or anything stopped to look beyond their nose.

If they did, would they have seen me sitting here in the rock? I do not know.

Once, a man with many medals on his chest and sitting on his white horse stopped in front of me. The impressive-looking man, who appeared to be the leader of many such men and their mounts, dismounted from his horse and proceeded to speak to his men about him. All the time, as they spoke, they faced the vast valley and small garrison town below.

Ignoring the sight, the white horse moved towards me, raised its tail, and proceeded to urinate on me.

Yes, I was mortified; I felt dirty, but then it had not rained for many months, so why should I complain? If I could, to whom? Also, what's more important is how?

My rocky shell could not be moved as it had always been broader and taller than the average man. I have sat here, as I said before, for thousands of years. How many I do not know? I forgot to keep counting.

Each day, the sun rises as early in the morning and retires later in the evening. Some days it rains all day. I sit here, always watching the storm clouds moving up the mountain ridge towards me. Maybe an hour goes by, and then I am enveloped with a grey haze, and the moisture from the beautiful and fluffy clouds dampens my surface.

Sometimes, the clouds change the colour of all the birds, and instead of showing their colourful plumage, they all become black-like silhouettes. Butterflies have the same effect in the sun: they become every colour imaginable to humans, then black or grey within the clouds.

On other occasions, the clouds hold another force, a much darker one. Lightning followed by thunder.

I have worked out that the smaller the gap between the flash of light and the rumbling sound, the closer the storm will be. There have been many occasions where the vicious storm was right above my head, and I closed my eyes when the lightning struck the ground.

There is a crackle of electricity, and I can see sparks racing along the ground.

There is never any wind in the storm; it's just rain. On one occasion, I don't know when. Two men stopped to drink water from leather containers that hung from their belts. One turner to his friend and remarked, "In times when it is just a gentle storm, the sound of the rain is like an orchestra playing an entire concerto, and I sway to and fro as if I am attending a grand concert hall, listening to the purest classical music possible."

His friend turned up, allowing the coolness of the water droplets to blind him briefly. "I know what you mean; rainwater like this is so refreshing." I heard no more as they both moved off, their horses following behind them.

This is rare compared to the power of the sun.

It is always there, shining down on me, keeping me warm. Mind you, she does become aggressive at various times of each year by increasing the temperature, and I can see my shiny surface start to steam with the moisture left from the night before.

I do feel a little uneasy when she is aggressive because I never know how long she will be hostile. Sometimes, in the distant past, she could be in a rage for months. But when she smiles again, well, life becomes bearable once more.

Time goes very slowly, as you can imagine. Maybe you can envisage my solitude. In the old days, I could go decades and see no one or anything. At night, I can hear the sounds of small things moving about, but alas, they, too, are not interested in me or my well-being. It's a lonely existence, being a rock. I'm surrounded by life, but I'm always alone.

A few decades ago, I started to see in front of me what I can only describe as metal carriages, some small, some very big and noisy, passing by on the old craggy road.

To my surprise, I could see humans in them.

Often, I thought how wonderful it would be to be a moving rock and to be able to go places I had never seen or heard of. But this thought process only often made me sad and feeling desperate. In time, I accepted my fate, and I just looked out and listened for their vibrations through the earth beneath me, warning me of their approach.

Then, just recently, in fact, within the last few days, my tranquillity has been disturbed by a new presence—a man, a strange-looking man. He started to walk past me and go down the hill.

What makes him strange is that he has no colour except his hair and his clothes! His skin was not the same as everyone else I had seen.

Usually, the locals are tanned or dark. This stranger is different.

His hair and legs are white, his face and arms are red, and his eyes are blue. Everyone I have ever seen has black eyes and black hair. Where has this monster come from?

Is he a monster or a freak of nature? Is he an albino? I have no idea, but I do know he has powerful legs. He must have. To be able to walk on this mountain ridge at such speed. Everyone else walks so very slowly, as if there is no tomorrow to worry about. But not this phenomenon; he walks with a purpose. What it may be, I have yet no idea. All I know is he keeps looking and smiling at me when he passes by!

Today, he stopped very close to me. He has even placed his arm on my shoulder. It's a strange feeling, being touched. I've never experienced anything like it before. It's almost as if I can feel his warmth, his energy. It's a sensation I can't quite describe, but it's not unpleasant.

He looks in distress and reaches thirstily for his bottle of water.

Once he has drunk a quarter of the contents, he appears calm. He reaches into his backpack and pulls out an apple. I have not seen or tasted such a fruit in centuries.

I can see the moisture on his lips and the contentment he is feeling with each bite exuberating from him.

Now, he is looking at me and smiling. He is speaking to me in a strange language, one I have never heard before. Where do you come from?

"Hi, buddy. How are you? "I hope you do not mind if I speak very little Spanish, but I plan to learn this incredible language as quickly as humanly possible for a 62-year-old man."

I stay still and completely dumbfounded.

He speaks again, "You may think I am crazy talking to you, but right now, I feel the need to reach out and communicate on this old craggy road, and well, you appear to be the only one available."

I am still perplexed by this situation, and I have no idea how to react.

"I arrived here in the last few weeks and have found myself living on this South American ridge. My Spanish is limited, so I am hoping you will not be offended by me relying on my native English to speak to you."

"I have travelled to many places, usually on holidays. But this time, I have made a massive leap into the unknown and moved with my future wife to this hostile feeling but beautiful-looking location."

"Everyone who is local and my future family warns me not to leave my home, but I cannot stay put. My spirit speaks loudly to me every day. It urges me to satisfy my curiosity and explore everything new. It keeps telling me I will be safe. "I hope so."

Suddenly, he pats my shoulder again and, with his left hand, waves goodbye. With his right hand, he casts aside the remains of the apple to the side of the road. He seems to know that the core will disappear quickly. The little creatures on the ground are already racing towards it to claim their unexpected prize.

Can he see me? Can he actually see me? Or am I imagining it? Am I going crazy after all this time? Can I hope to finally reach out and communicate with him? I have to be patient; well, I have been waiting a long time, so please forgive me for wanting to rush and find out.

He does seem like a gentle soul, but his legs are so pale and horrendous; he needs to wear pants, but how can I convince him? Then, in an instant, he has gone from view, heading down the mountain far below.

I did hear once that it would take a fit, very active young person at least two hours to reach the garrison town below. How would I know I am neither fit nor active? I have not moved in centuries. I still call it a garrison town after listening to that impressive military man on his white horse all those many years ago. I believe that generations later, they now refer to it as a city.

I can see it at night when the sun has gone to sleep, and the twinkling lights below disturb the darkness. At various times of the year, I see fields full of sugar cane being burned to the outer edges of the city. The fires glow red and, towards their centres, fiery orange. They light all night, and for some unknown reason, I find solace when they appear.

I enjoy the nights. I love the silence the most. During the daytime, there is always a cacophony of unharmonious sounds emerging from the people whom I, at times, refer to as the barbarians. All of them seem to prefer the daylight.

I have found myself watching the city lights grow and expand every year, but after a few hours, they, too, go dark, and only a few remain until the new dawn approaches. I always smile and say, "At last, the barbarians are sleeping." to no one in particular.

Now, I am back to my loneliness again, and I feel a little perplexed. The question of the walking man has started my mind racing. Will I be able to talk to others again soon? I do hope so with all my heart and soul.

*****

# 3: I am the Old Craggy Road

Since time began, I have been an old, craggy, and filthy road, and I am proud of it. I am different from the new addition that has been built further down the mountain towards the now-called city.

I remember when the city was just a quiet town with just a few old folks who never went far and very rarely came up the mountain to disturb me. Later, it grew into a garrison town housing over 20,000 soldiers. These same men would one day rise and join a famous General on his white horse.

The man's name was Simon José Antonio de la Santisma Trinidad Bolivar Palacios Ponte y Blanco, and his horse was Palomo.

You may consider me a traditionalist. I believe the old ways are the best ways. I miss the sounds of the horses and mules clopping hoofs.

Now, they are replaced by those fancy and heavy-looking metal machines that come thundering down my surface, squashing my little rocks and stones into dust.

The same contraptions dare return later that day loaded up to the brim with more heavy rocks!

So please explain that one. Why crush my little rocks to pass me by without a word of thanks or any explanation offered to this here old but proud and dependable craggy road?

I wager I will outlast that new and fancy road I mentioned earlier. He, with his shiny and smooth surface, wears buttons that shine at night, disturbing the peace. Little does he know the mountain is not always quiet; Sometimes, the mountain wakes up and often alters the look of himself.

I never know when he has decided a change is required.

There never appears to be common sense or radical improvements involved in his thinking about him. Usually, there's nothing one can do to stop him moaning and groaning his head off.

Often, it's only a tiny and almost unheard-of moan. It appears he has become lazy in his old age. Mind you, haven't you all?

I do enjoy the tickling I get from all the creatures that pass from side to side; you never see them going up or down the road, just from side to side.

One or two slither along as they apparently do not have any feet.

Others sprint with huge loads, such as leaves bigger than them; they move like an army, usually around 7.30 in the evening, and where do they go? Underground!

Now, why the heck do they do that? It doesn't make sense to me.

But I once heard that these insects' ancestors go back as far as 140 to 168 million years ago! I would not be surprised if they are not considered the oldest creatures still inhabiting this Earth.

I do not mind the hairy four-footed animals that like to bark their presence as they decide if someone coming is a danger to them. Most of them are lazy, too; one bark or two is usually enough to throw them out.

The only thing that annoys me with them is their toilet manners.

They do not have any, and in the sun, boy, they can smell at a distance.

Not only that but also look what occurs if a human happens to tread into one of their smelly creations... well, only today, a weird-looking white-haired human was stomping and hollering and scraping his right shoe against the grass.

Cussing at no one in particular except at all the population of hairy creatures in the world.

The culprit just sat there looking at the human; The hairy creature didn't care.

He thought it was amusing, he reasoned that he had tried to warn the idiot, but the idiot just splashed some cold water from his bottle at him, so he thought, "Sod him."

Mind you, the human cannot complain; only yesterday, I saw him stop a bit further up where a shaded area was obscured from view by three old trees; he went behind them, but I could clearly see him drop those ridiculous shorts, and he squatted and proceeded to poo too!

They were a sight larger than any hairy creature I know could produce, and I suspect a lot smellier, too.

I have decided to avoid that spot until it has rained for a good few months.

Mind you, the funny bit was towards the end of his operation. His composure seemed to be replaced with sheer panic as he heard a metal two-wheel noisy machine heading his way.

It did make me laugh watching him rush those shorts back up and head back down my surface as if butter had not melted in his mouth.

I love it when it decides to rain, which is not often; I enjoy the feel of the dust becoming all muddy and a hindrance to those metal machines and those funny things I see with two wheels and a human risking life from limb as they each struggle up the hill, blowing hot air out of each lung, their muscles screaming with agony and for what, I heard one say for pleasure!

What pleasure! The only fun I can see is when they decide to turn around and race down again at three times the rate of speed they come up at. But I have my fun, too, as I throw the odd little rock in their way, and they come flying off with no parachute to help them.

How do I know about parachutes? Well, a few years back, someone dropped a magazine out of their machine, and eventually, when it was quiet, I sat up and read it from cover to cover.

Then, the rain and wind came along one evening and took it away.

I never found out what happened to that magazine, but it was interesting for an old, craggy road. It talked about humans having souls. Well, guess what, humans? You are not the only ones because we are old and craggy; even roads have souls, too; you are just too busy to stop and talk to us to find out.

Mind you, that white-haired dude I mentioned earlier, well, he is always looking at the ground. I think he is looking for my soul because of the number of times he falls head first, hand second and the rest of him a fraction-third.

He gets up eventually, covered in my dust; heck, he even looks like a road.

His colour changes to the same as mine. He doesn't seem to enjoy the experience because he is wiping the stain away as fast as he can. Why? He looks good when he is the same as me.

I have been watching that old rock for many years now.

The occupant never moves; he just sits there. What a boring life he must lead. One day, we will get the opportunity to chat. I wonder if he knows the definition of soul.

I can feel the rain coming, I can see the clouds slowly moving up the side of the mountain ridge, and the birds are singing a merry tune. I love hearing them sing every day. It makes me feel young and youthful every time.

*****

# 4: I am the New Road

Now it's time to introduce myself to you. I am first and foremost female and the true soul of this mountain, not that old has-been further up. Look where he goes to. For example, how many houses are there on his shoddy old surface? Only a few, I can tell you.

But with my shiny and smooth surface that took over eighteen years to complete, I am young, vibrant, and shapely.

I can assure you all my curves are in the right places.

Palatial homes and estates are springing up day after day. Schools and universities are finding their places. More and more yellow school buses are motoring up and down, just like in the USA.

It took so long to design and create me. The reason is simple: it is hot all the time here in South America. Things tend to move slowly, with the exception of those shiny new motorcars, which race up and down at incredible speeds.

They even overtake each other when their drivers cannot see around the next bend. It is so exciting to see how they never seem to have an accident with each other. I cannot say the same for the cyclists and motorbike owners. They often fall foul of the racing vehicles and quad bikes.

Also, it's shocking to see humans hanging off the back of buses and jeeps; do they not know the danger? It is purely scandalous. I blame it on their parents.

They started the practice in the '60s before I was born, and pray do not get me started on those bicycles. Have you seen their rate of speed as they race down my surface?

Also, I know the Lycra they wear is so fetching. I can forgive them, especially on Tuesdays and Saturdays when there are many such sights.

Mind you, it's not just cars that travel up and down my luxury surface; There are also those old and dilapidated minibuses and heavy-duty trucks that pour heavily polluted, smokey-looking diesel exhaust fumes out of each one.

Their primary function seems to be to spoil the environment all the time.

Let me not forget the devastating effects that air pollution is causing on humans, animals, and wildlife, such as insects, fish, birds, and mammals.

In the past eighteen years of my existence, the lifespans of many animals and wildlife have begun to decrease. I can see that, like humans, many animals suffer from respiratory diseases such as asthma. They also have weaker immune systems and an increase in allergies, infections, and skin irritations.

I have seen with my numerous cat's eyes many with liver conditions because of the lack of fresh and clean water. Many have to rely on the nearby polluted water surfaces, thus making them prone to the awful future of not having one and becoming extinct. I do complain often but to no avail.

Hopefully, it will rain again soon as my buttons need some of that horrid dust to be washed away, and then I will be the rightful and cleanest soul. Talking about sights; there has been this weird experience I have to announce. I eagerly await the cleansing rain, a symbol of hope for a brighter, cleaner future. Twice this week, I have witnessed what I can only describe as totally out of this world: a white-haired stranger with, I must admit, solid and hairy legs walking down the length of my road, much to the annoyance of the old man, craggy road further east of me.

He always walks deep on the left side, facing the oncoming traffic. I find that strange because all the natives here walk in the same direction as the traffic. Why does this stranger not trust the traffic behind him? Why does he feel the need to see them? Indeed, he has good ears.

Mind you, he knows never to have a poo or pee here; Well, I do have high standards; yes, I know what he did on the old, craggy road. I take my responsibility as a clean and respected road seriously, ensuring that my surface remains untarnished.

I had to listen to the sounds of the furious, old, craggy road. Indeed, he went on for what seemed hours, maybe even days. Well, if he should even contemplate such a disgusting action on my surface, I can always trip him up.

Anyway, the old craggy road should moan. He has not become the latest victim of the laughing woman who likes to pee everywhere she chooses to.

My friends had often warned me since my completion that there was this very old and some described as a totally crazy woman who thought nothing of squatting down and hoisting up her skirts.

And before you can say, "Welcome to the pleasure dome," the disgusting event happened.

Immediately, she would re-drop her skirt and race around in a circle, hooting and hollering her joy in the absolute freedom of releasing her innards to the world.

The more the reaction of shock she witnessed, the more she would hoot and holler until instinct told her it was time to flee the scene. Nobody knew her history or wished to know. Many were traumatised by such a display of self-gratification.

I remember seeing the white-haired man's shock evidently showing for all to see for at least an hour afterwards when, on such an occasion, the older woman had decided he was to be her next victim.

The old craggy road always complains about my shiny buttons that reflect at night. I think he is just jealous. But all my friends have shiny buttons; only the poor ones do not. They have potholes and sometimes giant craters. I don't believe that it's my fault they don't look after themselves.

The old craggy road keeps warning me that one day, the old mountain ridge will rumble and moan, but it's been over fifty years since that last happened, and he did it much further away from here.

I keep telling him I am more important and have been built to resist such an ordeal. My resilience is a testament to the strength of our creation, providing a sense of security to all who traverse my surface.

I think he may desire shiny buttons, too, but it will never happen for him. It's a shame because as he ages, an upgrade seems unlikely.

*****

# 5: *I am the Oldest Scorpion on the Craggy Road*

I am a fearless, toothless, and ancient scorpion—not a blood-curdling demon. I am considered ancient because I have lived for fifteen years, whereas many of my contemporaries have yet to live past five years. I put my longevity down to surviving numerous skirmishes during the mating seasons.

Each lucky female loved holding my pinchers and being led around the dance floor, but when the good deed was done, I was off as swiftly as my little legs would go.

I was not interested in becoming the first meal of a pregnant female scorpion. My ancestors can be traced back well before dinosaurs existed.

I can travel up and down any surface except glass, which is a valuable lesson for all humans. All my life, everyone has been frightened of me. They all think I am dangerous, with my black, sinister-looking body, my curled-up stinger, and the venom in my heart. But all this is an exaggeration that has been passed down from generation to generation of humans.

Yes, I admit some of my ancestors have been a bit aggressive and, at times, a little touchy, but I, no, that had never been the case. I like being a hermit. I cannot help owning eight legs and a bard, which I would only use in defence. Never have I caused any human or animal to cry because of me.

If you wish to visit me, please check your shoes inside your home and any exterior buildings such as sheds and garages.

Do not bother thinking freezing me will kill me. No, my great-great-grandfather lived a further twenty-five years after a school experiment went horribly wrong. He got five students and a teacher that day. Don't get me wrong, he did not kill them all, but they sure did cry a lot.

My problem is that now I am old and fat. For years, I have struggled with my weight. I always have to move slowly to conserve my energy. But these past few years, insects have been abundant, and honestly, between you and me, well, I have been a bit of a pig, never passing up the odd meal or two or three or four or more.

I have been standing here today for a very long time on my poor, tired legs and two front claws, wondering when it will be best to cross this old, craggy road. Still, every time I decide to move forward, I have to waddle back so as to avoid those big noisy metal machines with their big eyes that see everything or those little two-wheeled motor-type things that appear to move with a lot more agility than the big noisy beasts.

Some are fatter than me, carrying many humans both inside and outside. My mother once told me that she thinks those machines are always pregnant, just like my naughty sisters are every few months. There are now hundreds of their offspring up here. Sometimes, it is difficult to avoid them. What happens when you are young? You are prone to be impetuous. You end up in situations where there is no exit plan in place. I may be fat, but at least I have never been accused of being impetuous.

My old mind is wandering again. I need to concentrate on the upcoming journey to the other side.

Wait, what is that? Or should I say, who is that?

If I had bones, they would be frozen stiff with fear, but alas, I have no skeleton, so I am rigid through sheer curiosity. I can only describe the weirdest-looking human I have ever seen, and he is fat too, just like the big machines. I know he is human because he only has two legs, but what crazy-looking legs!! They are full of hair and scratches where he must have fallen before arriving here.

His boots are covered in dust, and they march relentlessly towards me, and abruptly, they stop. I wait for a moment, and gingerly, I look up. The human is staring at me with a look of surprise and fear on his face. I always see the same; they never acknowledge that I also, too, am afraid of them and, indeed, right now, of him and his strange legs.

As I said before, I am not impetuous, so I will let him make the first move. Turns out he is not impetuous either. After what seems like a month, finally, he steps back a little, and I do the same. He moves to his left of him; I do the same. He takes another, only more comprehensive step to the left; I do the same with my eight legs. Every minute that passes by our half-circle dance progresses. Eventually, we passed each other with no incident. We both sighed with relief, and the stupid fool started to talk to me; could he not see I was busy?

*****

"So, Mr. Scorpion, you are not impetuous. "Just like me." He ventures forward but is still not in danger of me. What? I am a South American-based scorpion, and yes, I only understand Spanish. I have no idea what he just said.

"It makes sense to show respect, but I promise you if I ever see you in my house, I will ensure you lose weight instantly and suffer the mother of all headaches, and that is my promise." He says this, pointing one of his fingers towards me.

Still, I have no clue what he is rambling on about; anyway, who cares? If that finger gets any closer, "Wallop!" I will strike. Not with venom, as it takes a lot for me to produce venom. It will be a dry run for me. But should he feel reckless and up the ante, I will definitely give him a full throttle of venom. It won't kill him, but his day will be ruined.

"Just get lost, human, before I strike your big toe through your boot, or I will strike a hole in that silly finger of yours with no poison I can see within it.

Remember, one day I will stop being impetuous and enter your bedroom and give you a right good seeing too; I promise you that." Well, at least I am now on the other side, and it is time for my lunchtime treat of a platter of spiders or, if lucky, on those rare occasions, maybe a snail, lizard, or wee small snake.

Wait until I tell the others what I have witnessed today. Mind you, they do not ever stop to listen to this old fool. But at least I know that I have a heart and soul that is totally misunderstood, and today, I proved to this human I am a nice scorpion with a very patient soul.

*****

# 6: *I am a little Colombian Sombrero*

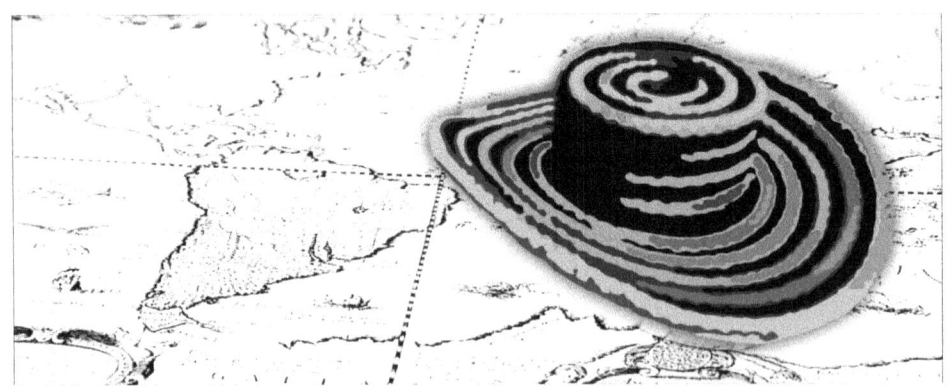

*I* have had an adventurous life so far, and I have been to many countries. I am a well-travelled little Colombian hat with alternating bands of dark brown and beige going around in circles throughout the brim and the area where heads typically go.

My life started in a tiny, noisy Chinese factory.

I had many brothers, sisters, and friends—far too many to count—and we all looked the same. But I always knew I would be different.

From the very beginning, I was destined to visit many places this Earth had to offer. Little did I know at the time that I would go into a box and then into a giant metal box on board a big ship that sailed from China to South America via a wonderful human-made invention called the Panama Canal. My only regret is that I never got to see it.

As we approached the Panama Canal, I couldn't contain my excitement. "Please, Mister Container, can you describe what you are seeing as you approach the Panama Canal?" I eagerly asked, my curiosity piqued. The anticipation was palpable in the metal box, And we all strained to hear the container's response.

Everyone in the metal box seemed to come alive at the same time, and all were now pleading for the container to tell all. "OK, OK, OK, I will tell you all that I can see. But you must all stop shouting, or you will not hear me."

It astounded me how fast we all obeyed the container's soft, female-sounding voice. Within a moment, we heard her description of her beginning, and this is what she told us: "Let me first paint you a vivid picture of this astounding engineering marvel. The Panama Canal is nestled between the continents of North and South America. It is an artificial passage connecting the Atlantic Ocean to the Pacific Ocean. In doing so, the humans were able to revolutionise their immense global trade and shorten all the necessary shipping routes."

I swear you could have heard a hatpin drop. We were so enthralled with the description of the canal that none of her audience dared to interrupt the soft vocal cords of the container.

"As we approach the entrance of the canal, I can witness towering, lush green hills that envelop the surrounding landscape. Everywhere I look, I can sense the air is thick with anticipation, as vessels from all around the globe gather eagerly awaiting their turn to embark on this epic journey."

"I can feel my heart racing with excitement as we inch closer to the first set of imposing steel gates."

"So is mine!" I heard a voice scream out. "Shush, you fool! Let her continue!" came a thousand voices directed at me. My hat went down, and I sheepishly obeyed.

"As this ship enters the canal, I am getting a sense of awe washing over me. I can see the process of us all crossing this intricate system of locks beginning, and if you listen, we will all become a part of a symphony of moving parts. If you concentrate, you will hear massive locomotives, known as mules, gently guiding the ship through each lock chamber. Can you hear them?"

"LOCKS!" was the resounding response from over 200 thousand little hats.

The container's voice started to rise, showing her excitement. "Alongside, I can see other colossal cargo ships, their hulls towering way above mine. "Each was forming a mesmerising amalgamation of shapes and colours against the tranquil waters."

The container paused, and I can assure you not one of us uttered a word, not a sneeze, not even a yawn. Time appears to stand still for us all. Then, a very minute sound from somewhere way back from where I was sitting whispered, "Is there more we should know?"

"Of course, I was waiting to see what happens next, and now I can tell you: Each of the canal's locks is a masterpiece of engineering. This one is raising our ship upwards, bridging the altitude difference between the two oceans I mentioned at the beginning. Amazingly, I have a perfect view as we stream through the water. "It is like we are suspended in time."

She paused for a fraction of a second and powered on with her storytelling to all and sundry. I can see the sunlight reflecting off the shimmering surface below, and when I look up, I can see we are surrounded by lush vegetation and tropical wildlife. It is simply awe-inspiring."

As she waited to find the words to tell us more, we all rose as one, begging for more. I suspect I was the loudest.

"Now we are sailing through the narrowest part of the canal. I can immediately feel the immense power and determination of all human innovation. Our little container ship is now gliding like an elegant dancer through this winding canal.

Amazingly, it was carved out of the rugged landscape, allowing us safe passage no matter what size vessel we were travelling on."

She was quiet, and we, too, stayed silent. We knew and trusted she would tell us unreservedly more. Our patience was well rewarded, as she continued in a couple of minutes.

"We are now approaching the iconic Bridge of the Americas. It is a beacon signalling our imminent arrival in the Pacific Ocean."

"Never forget you are all essential parts within a humble container on this Chinese freighter. Today, we have all witnessed the wonders of international trade and the power of human ingenuity. This magical Panama Canal represents a testament to humanity's indomitable spirit. In the years to come, you must remember all the experiences the course of maritime progress and prosperity has unselfishly shown you today."

Then our container and her gentle voice were replaced with silence; her duty to us young hats was over, and she could now relax.

*****

Later, we were transported by what I now know are trucks. These big beasts of power and metal moved swiftly from the port to our final destination, a big city in the south of the country. The city was overlooked by a mountain ridge that I could see had a stunning new road with lots of buttons that reflected in the night.

Further up the mountain, I could see the beginning of an old, ugly, craggy road. Right now, I was watching a beautiful burgundy-coloured truck ascend so quickly up its terracotta-coloured surface.

I do hope I never have to travel on that poorly kept-road.

How was I able to see all this?

Well, the box I was transported in from China had been delivered to a store retailing artisanal giftware, designed and crafted by hands by various Indigenous communities up and down the country.

I was separated from the others and placed in the main store window, next to the entrance, with a little price tag laid down in front of me. It made me proud to be the chosen one. Every day, a little old lady dusted my surface, so I always looked new. The lady also lovingly looked after all the other trinkets and souvenirs. We learned that her name was Juli, and she was our favourite person in the artisanal giftware store.

It was amazing for me to discover many of the carvings of animals and wildlife from a place known as the Amazon Rainforest. The carvings from trees known as the "Arboles de Sangre" were hand-carved by members of the Ticunas using only machetes, pairs of artesian eyes, and expert knowledge passed down from generation to generation for hundreds of years.

Each carving represented the four elements: Water, Earth, Air, and Fire.

Every day, while I sat in the window display area, I would watch the passers-by stare admiringly at the shiny, blood-red creations on a shelf just behind me. From them, I learned about the world of hummingbirds, dolphins, armadillos, jaguars, iguanas, and so many more.

One day unexpectedly a young boy visited the shop and chose me! He told Juli he wanted to buy a small present for his father and only had a few pesos. Juli asked him, "What is your favourite memory of your father?" The boy thought for some time and suddenly beamed out loudly.

"He always wears a Colombian hat to ward off the rays of the sun while he works outside on our farm."

Juli pointed to me in the window and suggested we add a metal attachment that would turn me into a functional key ring. The boy was so thrilled he eagerly handed over his money, and before you could shout "Adios," I was wrapped up in the little boy's hand.

I didn't have a chance to say goodbye to my friends and family. Yes, it is true; I was a little scared of not knowing what was going to happen to me, but there was also a part of me that was excited. I couldn't wait to see where I was going.

The boy ran to his mother and revealed what he had spent his money on, and she smiled. Her little Juan was a loving son and only five. She only hoped her husband would receive the gift in the same vein as Juan hoped for.

Well, there was nothing for me to worry about; Later that afternoon, I felt myself being passed to a very earthly damaged pair of hands. I could see clearly that they were powerful, but for me, they were gentle.

I looked up to see his weathered, beaten face looking down with gaps in his mouth mixed with the odd decaying tooth.

Above them was an untidy-looking moustache. It looked like it was holding up and supporting a weather-beaten nose with two huge hairy nostrils jutting out.

Above and further up still stood a matching pair of overgrown hairy eyebrows that, in truth, were like wild and unkempt bushes. Finally, to complete the bewildering picture, there stood an unruly mop of hair hanging below a big hat!

For the first time in my life, I could see a massive version of myself.

Only it was a little tatty and worn.

I did not care because below the brim were the human's eyes, and they said everything about this human. I knew instantly that I had found a friend. He was smiling so brightly when he saw me for the first time, and his young son presented me cupped proudly in his tiny hands. He thanked his little Juan joyfully.

Later, I discovered that his parents were Magdalena and Alberto. This small peasant family was very kind to me. Every day, one of them came looking for me, as both could drive the big engine, a silver Chevrolet open-top truck with one backlight that never worked.

My keyring now married to the truck's set of keys. Most of the time, I found myself in Alberto's pocket and, other times, in Magdalena's leather-bound purse. I was now safe in the knowledge that I was helpful and appreciated by all my newly adopted family.

Alberto worked on various farms and gardens to supplement his meagre living on the mountain ridge, and often, I found myself travelling on both the roads I first saw on the day I was placed in the window of the artisanal giftware store.

Once or twice, we all visited the store, and while my little family was busy browsing, I rested on the countertop. I spent the time letting my old friends know how I was doing and described life on the mountain ridge to them. I found out many who had travelled from China with me were gone, including my family. This was a little sad for me to hear, but I was confident they were all well and happy.

Then disaster struck, and a foreign pair of hands grabbed me. I felt myself rushing out of the store.

One of the keys I was attached to was roughly placed into the ignition of Alberto's truck. The engine roared as the stranger engaged a gear and pressed down hard on the accelerator, and we all moved away. I wanted to scream out, but who would have heard me? I am sure that nobody knew I was gone.

The thief and two other strangers to me were now racing the Chevrolet up the new road, heading towards a small town I had not visited before. Once they arrived on the outskirts, they abandoned the truck behind a hedgerow, and I found myself flying through the air and landing on the side of the road. I was so sad. How was I going to get home again?

Over the next few days and nights, I just sat there, desperate to go home. The dust was making me dirty, but sometimes, water droplets arrived from nowhere, and I was clean again.

*****

I am not sure how long I was like this, but one particular morning, while I was sleeping under the hot sun, I noticed a shadow pass over me, and I looked up to see a very unusual-looking human being. His hair was snow white, his face looked young but a little red and his eyes were so blue that I couldn't stop looking at them.

I had never experienced such beauty with those ocean-blue eyes of his. I felt the need to be with him, and to my astonishment, I found him picking me up and saying something I didn't know, but it sounded like, "Hello, my little hat. I think you need a better place to rest."

Silently, he placed me in his rucksack's little front compartment. Every once in a while, as he walked on the old craggy road, he would stop to check if I was still there. I felt his warm fingers brush over me very gently so as not to disturb me.

To my limited reckoning of time and most certainly by mid-day, I found myself in a well-kept house resting on the side of the ridge. The vast windows gave both this man and me a panoramic view of the valley and the city below.

A few minutes earlier, he had retrieved me from his rucksack, and I was sitting at the family dining table with a glass mug of coffee on the surface in front of me. My new friend sat gazing at me with a warm smile and said, "I have decided to give you pride and place in my new home back in England. "We will be travelling together soon, and I will introduce you to the English weather."

"It is a lot different from what you know here. For example, it can get pretty cold. So, I will have to take special care of you when it happens."

"For now, you do not need to be a key ring, just a friend in my car sitting in full view of where my business cards will go. You can sit proudly on top of them, viewing all the passing landscapes from this mountain ridge to the city streets below."

With this initial introduction, I started my new adventure. With this human, I travelled in his pocket to places such as America, France, Holland, Spain, Poland, Eire, and the United Kingdom.

Well, to be more accurate, with regard to America, France, Spain, Holland, and Eire, these were limited to their various airports, but after listening to my new owner, I felt that from his many stories, I knew everything I needed to know to imagine them clearly in my mind.

Often, we would have to wait for different modes of transport, which he called aeroplanes, to arrive, so instead of us both sleeping, I would sit outside of his bag and listen to his memories of and unlimited knowledge of each destination we were waiting to travel to.

I found myself soaking up all the history this inquisitive mind had stored away over his lifetime.

Poland was different from the other countries. I would experience good and evil in this country.

We stayed in a hotel in the beautiful and captivating city of Krakow, nestled in the heart of this incredible European country. We embarked together on a breathtaking journey, and as he stepped foot onto the enchanting streets, I could sense the city's rich history and splendid architecture instantly enveloping me.

The first landmark that caught my interest was the majestic Wawel Castle, standing tall atop Wawel Hill. Its Gothic, Renaissance, and Romanesque elements date back to 970 AD. My guide and owner informed me that nearly all Polish Kings have resided in this now-famous castle.

I looked with a renewed interest at the extraordinary fusion of styles, which in turn left me in awe of its grandeur and historical significance.

Later, around noon, we continued our exploration as he carried me through Europe's largest and most charming medieval Market Square. The awe-inspiring architecture of Saint Mary's Basilica, with all its intricate details and vibrant hues, left me speechless, and I still have an everlasting impression of how wonderful it was.

Every hour, I heard a trumpet call melodiously echo across the square. It became easy for me to marvel at the harmonious blend of past and present.

After that, I had the opportunity to witness my guardian while he sat, drank coffee, and ate a selection of Polish pastries. He struck me as a good man, lonely for sure, which was a shame as his knowledge held no limits. Whatever he saw, he could tell me a story about it or them.

In the late afternoon, we wrapped up our visit and took a leisurely walk along the Vistula River, enjoying the scenic views and the vibrancy of the riverfront.

I can confess that day, I learned what it is like to feel goodness. I slept well that night on the bedside cabinet near my human friend.

*****

The next day, over breakfast, my guardian warned me that today's visit would not be so enchanting and wonderful. I felt trepidation about where he planned for us to go, and I waited. I had no idea how low and stressed we were to become.

Today, we both learned what evil felt like.

He took me to a very dark and sinister place called Auschwitz. I could not believe the horrors I would listen to and see. My owner told me that everyone should pause their busy lives for just a moment and experience visiting such a place to stop them from ever becoming evil.

We first encountered the infamous arched entrance gates, bearing the words "Arbeit Macht Frei," which in English translates as "Work Sets You Free." In Spanish, it translates as "El trabajo te libera."

As we passed through the gates, we could see the original brick barracks still standing. My guardian mentioned the initial purpose of this camp was to house the local Polish military. But after Germany invaded Poland in 1939, it was transformed into a concentration camp. It was here I learned that millions of Jewish people were exterminated for no reason except the Germans at that time hated the Jews.

Inside the camp, we were greeted by a young Polish female who introduced herself and offered her services for the day as our guide. Together with others, we explored many areas, including the Auschwitz 1 main camp and Auschwitz 11-Birkenau. Auschwitz 1 comprised numerous blocks, and each had a different function, such as housing personal belongings which were seized from the arriving victims.

The most horrifying thing for me was seeing rooms housing a mountain of human hair. Another was a wall-to-wall room filled with thousands of pairs of old glasses. A third block had a room full of the remains of shoes.

In some buildings, I saw walls adorned with photographic evidence, testimonies, and fading documents giving me a glimpse into the prisoner's lives and detailing the atrocities committed by the iniquitous Nazi regime led by a clearly very evil man named Adolf Schickelgruber aka Adolf Hitler.

When I saw the baby's little jumper in a glass cabinet, with what looked like a bullet hole where the heart should have been, it made me inwardly sob.

What a dark world humans live in.

Away from the main blocks, we were guided to the harsh living conditions endured by the prisoners; we were shown the cramped wooden bunks resting on earth only. The Nazis could not see any purpose in laying a concrete foundation, and now, apparently, after nearly eight decades have gone by, the wooden sheds are slowly disappearing from the harsh winters that visit every year.

Our guide approached the now visibly upset white-haired man who was still holding me in his left hand. He had not spoken, and the young Polish woman, sensing his horror and dismay at what he had witnessed, guided him to the Auschwitz 11-Birkenau complex. Together, all three of us walked the short distance from the main camp to what the woman said was now deemed the iconic railway tracks leading through the entrance gate.

We stood at the point where the death trains would cease their horrendous journey and where evil men known as the SS would offload all the poor victims from the wagons that in former times carried freight.

Our guide told us that one officer held the power over who would die that day and the ones he chose to delay their inevitable extermination by making them work to the point of sheer exhaustion. He always selected the women, children, and older people to head to the gas chambers. In contrast, he moved with his luger to the men to move away toward the main camp.

My friend showed his continuous deep feelings of sadness at the thought of what depravity and cruelty his species had happily gone to in their desire to rid their world order of a race of people numbered in their millions.

He held me firmly in his hand, and as if he knowingly knew what my inquisitive mind was thinking, he said the following words: "Nature possesses a remarkable ability to reclaim what we humans have created and subsequently abandoned over time. Structures once bustling with human activity either in godliness or in pure evil, be it cities, dilapidated buildings, forgotten highways, or thankfully death camps, will gradually succumb to the relentless pursuit of nature's forces."

He paused, took the weight of one foot, and transferred it to the other, and began speaking to me again. "In a testament to its tenacity, plants will push through cracks in pavements, vines will weave their way up crumbling facades, and trees will emerge through the roofs of forsaken buildings."

"The passage of time will erode the once-imposing man-made buildings, with rust, weathering, and decay becoming the tombstones of their transformation."

Now I could see teardrops in his eyes, and one escaped down his left cheek. He continued without wiping the teardrop away: "As nature's quiet but persistent reclamation takes hold, reclaiming what was lost, it will become a poignant reminder of the ever-changing balance between our human progress and the overwhelming power of the natural world."

My friend and the young Polish guide stood side by side and recited the Lord's Prayer. I was hearing it for the first time, and I found it passed a range of emotions through my soul. Today, I learned about words such as reverence, gratitude, peace, humility, and spiritual connection.

We observed the ruins of cremation and gas chambers. The world appeared to be frozen in time; no birds above me, no rustling noises in the trees, and even the hearts of the humans near me seemed to go quiet.

Apparently, we were told as the war was coming to a close, the regime made every effort to destroy all the evidence of their barbarousness and evil atrocities prior to handing the country back to the invading Allied armies from the UK, France, The USA, Canada, and Russia.

It was long ago decided these remnants would stand as haunting reminders of the systematic genocide that had taken place for generations to follow.

My white-haired friend turned to the young tour guide, and they shook hands and bade farewell to each other. I noticed neither spoke; both appeared lost for words. Whenever I look back on this experience. I still shudder at the sheer evil that I felt all around me that day. I hope I never experience such malevolence again.

Later, he took me back to the city of Krakow and its central square. Now, it was nighttime, and my thoughts of humans were uplifted again as I saw the many restaurants goers heading to the venues of their choice. This time, I only witnessed happy people laughing and smiling as they moved around, with no signs of horror invading their lives that night.

Such beautiful visions are so openly on display. I saw them being enjoyed by the humans walking among their narrow walkways and surrounded by magnificent old buildings. I soon put the despair I felt earlier in the day to the back of my mind. At one point, it disappeared to a small memory at the top of my little hat head.

*****

When I reached England, I could write a whole book about what I saw and learned. There is so much history and so many stories. My owner has agreed that the two of us will be featured in another book one day, recording all that we experienced together.

Whenever he opened his case, he always greeted me with a smile; he never failed to examine me to see if I needed repair. But little did he realise at first that I was a sturdy little hat and would not break down easily. He would cup me in his hands and, making sure no one was watching, show me around the immediate area. I got to see many exciting visions with my white-haired friend.

My dreams had come true. I was indeed a very happy, contented, and well-travelled hat with a well-travelled soul.

*****

# 7: *I am the Cross and the Warning Sign*

My name is Marco Uribe. I was born on the 8th of October 1999 but sadly died on the 16th of December 2017. As you may have noted, I was only 18 when I met my fate through a freak accident. I was racing down the mountain ridge, heading to my city below on the newly constructed road with its amazing cat's eyes on my brand-new racing bike.

When I woke that morning, I was full of anticipation and excitement, and I thought of gliding onto the fresh, newly laid asphalt. Within an hour, I was captivated by the smoothness of the surface. It felt remarkably even, and it was devoid of cracks, potholes, or bumps that commonly characterise older roads, such as that mean-looking old craggy road.

The sheer enjoyment of the absence of imperfections created a sense of ease and stability, allowing me to focus on the sheer joy of riding rather than constantly adjusting my balance.

The newly laid asphalt also offered me a certain level of grip, making it easier for me to maintain traction while cycling. The bike's tyres felt securely planted on the surface, ensuring my confidence in manoeuvring and greatly reducing my fear of skidding. Instead, the enhanced grip provided me with a gratifying sensation that allowed me to have increased control over my bike.

As I pedalled along, I noticed minimal vibrations resonating through the bike frame. This not only enhanced my comfort but also reduced my fatigue, enabling me to ride a longer distance without the jarring impact that the old craggy road and other rougher surfaces caused.

In terms of sound, the recently paved road was significantly quieter compared to the old surfaces. The absence of accumulated debris and erosion resulted in less noise previously generated on my old, now scrapped bike. No more, for now, experiencing my tyres rolling over uneven patches or loose gravel, thus enhancing my overall riding experience.

My euphoria did not last long. Initially, I noticed a slight change in the handling—almost microscopic—and the steering felt different. Within a minute, I needed an increased effort to maintain my speed. The bike started to feel slightly heavier and more challenging to propel.

My brain would not accept the truth. No way! No, it cannot be! Everything is brand new, even my clothing and safety helmet!

The perfect handling, stability, and manoeuvrability began to sag, and I felt less stable around the next set of innocuously looking corners. I tried to maintain a straight line in the stability exercise. Deep down, I knew my front tyre was injured. Suddenly, without warning, the bike veered off to the right side. This was the point when I felt the need for a rest. I looked down at my front wheel and saw clearly that my front tyre was almost flat!

I could not believe it. Only the first time out on the mountain ridge. Either the new road or the old craggy road had caused me displeasure. On this occasion, I did not see the need for my usual equipment as I mistakenly believed everything new would protect me. Now I had to buy a repair kit. Luckily, there was a small pueblo only a few metres away around the next mountain bend; I knew I could easily walk there in 15 minutes. Restarting downhill after the repair job would be easy.

Thankfully, on this occasion, I was on my own. If this had happened on the following Saturday, I would have been the laughingstock of all my racing team friends, and there were many. The meeting would attract over 200 riders every Saturday. Riders and bikes would meet up early to challenge the mountain ridge with its 1 in 4 gradients.

The best way for me to explain the challenge to a non-racing cyclist would have to be: "As each gradient sapped our strength at every stage upward. Our legs' muscles burned and screamed in protest. Our lungs panted like it was our last breath. Our hearts beating outside of our bodies—well, it felt that way."

Only some of the 200 souls each week would reach the top, but many would not. Those that failed, well, they would just head back down the mountain ridge, and the following week, they would take up the challenge again and again. Never was anyone looked upon as a failure; far from it, all was deemed solid and brave, with the odd bit of craziness inside. It was like a drug that, each week, our bodies would crave. None of us complained, only when we were in the middle of the mindset battle with our bodies.

But oh boy, what a beautiful feeling each time we reached the top near the pueblo situated just below the fork in the road. One road led upwards further to the old church and its nearby school and cemetery, and the other road led across the ridge of the mountain to meet up with the old craggy road.

There, we would all stop and drink our energy drinks, laugh, and chat with each other. It is a wonderful experience when there are so many people who share the same highs and lows of a sport as we do. The fraternity of riders became a united family, too.

Then, it was a flat race on the road for one mile, followed by a further two miles downhill all the way to the city. We all felt the exhilaration when the bikes were at their highest speeds, the warm air becoming cool by the sheer speed of it passing us and our racing bikes.

As I disappeared around the bend with my bike on my right-hand side nearest the mountain wall, I could clearly see the shanty-styled housing and shops ahead of me. I knew from the past there would be a small shop where an elderly man who used to ride bikes up the same mountain ridge many years before would be.

The cycling veteran had retired due to his body becoming frail and weak. He still loved to stop and talk to the younger versions of himself, including all my friends. Together, we would all rejoice in his stories of how he rose to the top of his fame as the fastest racer in South America.

They would love to listen to his memories of the past during the Second World War period. No one dared interrupt when he spoke of his experiences when going to the Olympics in Berlin in 1936 and witnessing all the Red & black Swastika flags and uniforms of an overpowering force of military proliferating. Three years later, he was to learn of the great destruction these people had caused to the world.

When his race came, he managed to be the third fastest in the world, and he was incredibly proud to receive his bronze medal, which he always brought out to display at every opportunity that showed itself. Now, in his nineties, he could still envisage it all as if it was only yesterday; his tired eyes would light up as he re-enacted the honour he felt when the national anthem was played out loud.

I heard the loose rock before I saw it racing down above me as it smashed into the side of my brand-new pride of joy. It impacted just below my saddle seat. The force sent the bike racing into my body, and I fell sideways with one arm automatically stretching out to the ground to support my fall.

I felt bones break as I made contact with the hardened ground. My arm became useless as the rest of my body landed on it. My screams of agony must have woken the whole mountain. But it did not reach the driver of the old bus, and its noisy diesel engine came around the bend, heading to the city below with its workers and cleaners, who had travelled monotonously every day until today.

The driver did not stand a chance. He panicked first, and then precious seconds were lost before both of his feet simultaneously went for his clutch and brake, making braking a forgotten thing. The front wheels were now controlled by the sloping ground towards me, and I felt my life distinguish the moment the bus struck.

I am not sure how long time moved; all I know was that I was now witnessing the aftermath of the accident. My body lay broken under the bus, and my beautiful bike was now unrecognisable. I could sense people racing up the hill and out of the bus vainly in the hope of reviving me, but I knew I was not of the material world any more. I was now in another realm, one to which I could only bear witness.

I closed my eyes and started to cry, but there were no tears; my body was shaking with uncontrollable grief. I was now in a state of shock. One minute, I was living a great life, and the next, I was trying to deal with this new realisation. I was in a different place where no one could see me.

At one point, I felt a presence around me. A light made him or her invisible, but I knew I was safe. A hand rested on my shoulder, or what I thought was a hand. I felt comforted by the touch and looked back towards the accident below.

The scene had rushed in time to what I can only assume was the following Saturday. There were thousands of people and riders with their bikes all stationary where I had fallen. They were saying prayers, and many were crying. My world of friends had come out to remember me. The old man from the bike repair shop sat weeping in the middle of them all. This display of heartfelt emotion from him meant so much, for we had hardly ever spoken.

In the past, I had just listened quietly to his life's history. Now, he cried like a baby in front of my parents, who together were holding each other in their shared grief at the loss of their oldest son. I loved this old man wholeheartedly, and I knew when it was his time to arise and join me here, I would ensure I would be the first to greet him.

My sister, Kathy, came to the middle of gathering mourners and reflected on my life and promised all in the congregation that I would always be loved and remembered and a cross with my name and date of birth below. This new cross would be placed near the accident to mark my passing.

I would become their guardian angel, watching over their safety with an accompanying brand-new sign. It would have a yellow diamond shape and a black silhouette of me walking in the middle of it. This sign would stand on a pole proudly for all to see, be a reminder, and, most importantly, a warning to persons walking without a footpath to protect them.

I had a new role to play so my soul would not be wasted doing nothing. Over the last couple of years, I have saved many by sending thoughts to those in danger who, without realising, moved away from their pending perils and continued down the road safely.

*****

But wait, what am I seeing right now? Across the other side of the road, facing downwards, is a man I have never seen before. He is taller and broader than most I have known, maybe he is a gringo, but I do not think so, as no Americano would dare walk down such a mountain all on his own. Perhaps he is European.

They also do not usually walk about on their own but do, at times, walk with their Colombian wives and girlfriends, who act as their guards and guides. The way he is dressed in his shorts and top and a small black rucksack on his back makes me think he takes his fitness seriously and is using my mountain to stay fit.

Well, good on him, but does he not know it is safer to walk in the same direction as the cars behind him? Why would he walk down on the opposite side and see them coming up towards him? He may have a point; I will have to see how this develops. Maybe he is right, and we have all been wrong all these years; would it have prevented my accident?

Yes, thinking back to that fateful day, I would still be racing up and down on my new powerful racer, becoming, in my imagination, the fastest racer on the continent of South America and then the world at the next Olympics.

I can assure you that dreams and ambitions never go away, even when your body ceases to function for whatever reason. Here in this realm, your soul is allowed to enjoy all that pleases you, with no nightmares or evil thoughts permitted.

*****

# 8: I am One of Two Flying Cows

My name is Clary, and my younger sister's name is Marta. I am nearly all black with the odd patch of white, and my sister is half brown and half white. We have lived on this mountain ridge for almost five years now.

We have produced milk whenever the humans who own us feel we have plenty to give and are ready to share our milk via the tickling instruments attached to our udders.

Production will soon end, and we have been assured that we will be able to wander around in retirement for another ten years or more.

We are generally allowed to roam wherever our mood takes us.

Today, we are just below the new road with its shiny buttons on a small piece of fenced-in land that sits just above the old craggy road. We can see it below us. Really. We should not be interested, as the patch of land is small, but no one else bothers coming here, so we know there will be grass for us both.

The grass turned out to be quite dry and offered us very little sustenance to produce more milk, but not to worry; we were on a mountain ridge with an abundance of wild grass and food for us to enjoy.

Yes, we do have to exert ourselves and move further along to savour new, fresh edibles that nearly always seem to appear at our feet.

Marta is the daft one, whereas I am the nosy one.

Whatever I do, she will always unthinkingly follow. I have no recollection of her ever deciding on what we do. How life must be so simple for her, having me as her total decision-maker. Her only thought of her is chewing the cud.

Adventure is the key. It is a priority for me to make as many monotonous days interesting and enjoyable as possible. The trouble is that interesting days are hard to come by here on this mountain ridge.

I look at Marta, so calm, so content in keeping her head down and chewing the cud constantly. Already, she is showing signs of being bigger than me below, and I suspect she will yield a bit more milk than me when the time comes.

But there is never any sisterly competition. Marta will produce what she has, no more and no less.

The Farmer's wife, Magdalena, will usually be the one sitting on a three-legged stool harvesting the milk from us. She sings songs like a demented cat; she has no angelic vocal cords, but both Marta and I are content with her soft fingers pumping the milk from us when the tickling instruments do not work because of a power cut.

Her husband Alberto would usually come to find us each day, shooing us back to within reach of the farm. Never have I seen him angry; the world always moves faster than he does, which suits Marta to a tee.

I am sure she even smiles when she sees him.

I know I have seen her behave like a little calf, and at other times, she races towards him. Meanwhile, I will keep my dignity and cruise over when I am ready.

The farmhouse where Magdalena and Alberto sleep with their little boy Juan is made of old breeze blocks, cement, and wood. It has a metal tiled roof. The windows are protected with metal rails, and the doors are also solid metal. Inside, the furniture is sparse but adequate for the family's needs.

The only extravagance is the 54" smart TV in the living room that only works again when there is electricity.

We usually sleep in the backyard, where the chickens and cockerels roam. The numerous dogs bark and only shout when humans come walking past on their long journeys up the mountain and sometimes on their return down again.

All the dogs on the mountain ridge have been talking about a stranger who will growl back at the same vocal level as any dog does.

He appears not to be scared, and sometimes, he will actually sit down and talk back to the dogs as if they are old friends. The dogs' instincts are to protect their homes, but this stranger never seems to understand the rules. He often ignores them and carries on walking past in whatever mood takes him.

We have often seen him from a distance, and sometimes he will stop and chat with us or the other beef-producing cattle that are white with humps on their shoulders and big floppy ears, which gives them that film star looks from one of those famous Star War movies that Juan is always searching for on the big television.

These same beef cattle always have their friends with them, known as Cattle Egrets. They are also white in colour and are related to the heron family of birds. They enjoy catching insects and small prey that are disturbed by the cattle's search for food. The cattle love the egrets equally as the birds like to remove the ticks on their hides and instantly eat everyone they discover.

We have no clue what he says to us. We look and stare at his physique; he is nothing like Alberto. "Like two peas in different pods." That one insight once escaped from Marta's mouth. Remember, she does not pass conversation easily. She usually is so busy filling her face. In response, I pause, shake my head, and meander on, looking for more clues about who this human is and where he goes.

I remember another occasion when I witnessed this same stranger walking up the old craggy road with a mule keeping up the same pace beside him. The mule was carrying hay on its saddleless back. You could see the mule was in deep shock, its eyes staring unblinkingly at the stranger. The human just kept laughing and chatting to the mule.

About what none of us will ever know, but whatever it was, it kept the human amused.

The current owner of the mule was further down the mountain ridge, smoking a precious cigarette and minding his own business. He had not even seen the conversation between his mule and the stranger. In his experience, nothing happens out of the ordinary on this mountain ridge, but unknown to the farmer, something just happened.

The mule decided enough was enough. Without any thought to the stranger, he just quietly turned left and ambled up the little path to where he lived. The stranger had not seen the departure of his new friend and carried on talking.

Eventually, he realised this by looking back and seeing only space with no mule and roared with laughter. The mule owner appeared and only noticed a stranger on this ridge outside his home, and he was laughing. Is this a nutter? Why is he laughing? Is he laughing at me?

If he is a nutter, I will head indoors to get my old shotgun. I will soon rid that smile from his face, and with that thought, he menacingly moved in the same direction as his mule.

Today is slowly starting to end; The calm, fresh winds are heading up and down the mountain to cool the roasting streets of the city below. The blades of grass are dancing in the breeze, and I love this time of day. My hide is not so hot, and I find it easier to move about. I look at the road below, and the craggy surface is still the same, but it will cause no issue for my or Marta's hoof feet.

Something is missing in my vision, and for a moment, I cannot see what it is. Then I realise the fence has gone.

Someone has stolen the fence during the last forty-eight hours or more; Alberto will be a little annoyed when he discovers this. But for now, my monotonous day has finally become interesting. I can see lots of virgin grass below next to the mountain edge.

I sense this is going to be nectar for both Marta and me, so without thought to safety, I run and jump.

Marta is only a split second behind me.

For once, she is on the ball and senses the nourishing offerings straight away. She, too, leaves the earth where we were originally standing, and now both of us are flying through the air. Landing may be complicated, but we are on a new adventure.

We are pilots of our destiny. Our souls are, for a fraction of time, free.

We both land safely on the old, craggy road and stop to catch our breaths. At this point, we realised we had a witness to our daredevil antics. It is none other than the strange white human with an incomprehensible accent and words. He is standing frozen stiff, no more than ten feet from us.

His mouth and eyes are wide open, with no words coming from them except, "No one is ever going to believe this.......flying cows!!"

We rapidly ignore him; what does he expect, the Highway Code? We are cows. We go to whatever lengths it takes to chew our cud. Well, Marta does. I lead.

But on this occasion, we stood transfixed; we dared not move. The white-haired stranger with the most reddish skin we have ever seen smiled at us and sat down with his legs crossed underneath him. He quickly moved his backpack from his shoulders and rested it next to him.

His hands disappeared inside, and within a moment, he magically brought out a large notepad. Not satisfied with his discovery of him, he returned his hands back inside the backpack, and moments later, out of him came a black pen.

His head went down, and for what seemed like an eternity, he stayed in this position, writing like his life depended on it. The only parts of him that showed he was alive were his fingers and hands. Both Marta and I were transfixed. Well, I was. Marta lost interest rapidly and moved slightly away, having discovered a huge clump of grass with which to satisfy her appetite.

Suddenly, the man looked up again at us with his mesmerising blue eyes. His lips began to move, and then I realised he was talking to us.

"You two beauties have made my day. You have inspired me to write a brand-new story. I have decided I have time on my hands, and I am going to give you a rendition of it. Why not sit and rest while I read it out loud to you?"

Without warning, as if on cue, Marta sat down. I felt I had no choice, so I, too, sat down.

*****

Once upon a time in South America, in a quiet countryside village, there lived a curious old man. His name was Miguel. With his white hair and weathered face, he was known as the local sage. Miguel had spent his entire life observing the mysteries of the world and seeking wisdom in every corner.

One sunny morning, as Miguel was taking his daily walk, his eyes widened in amazement at the sight before him. Two cows, yes, you two beautiful and friendly cows, were soaring through the sky, flying gracefully from one field to another. Your long ears flapped in the wind, and your hooves dangled in mid-air. It was a sight that would've left anyone bewildered, but Miguel, being a sage, decided to approach this spectacle with an open mind.

With measured steps, he headed towards the cows, who had now landed gracefully in the second field. As he drew closer, the cows turned their heads towards him, their eyes seemingly gleaming with awareness.

"Good day, fine ladies," Miguel greeted you both with a polite bow. "May I inquire about this rather extraordinary display of yours?"

You, with your black and white coloured hide, responded with a gentle moo. Miguel was momentarily taken back, but he quickly realised that your "moo" sounded strangely like a human voice.

"Good sir," you spoke again. We are not mere cows. An ancient enchantment has granted us the gift of flight and speech. However, we rarely reveal our abilities to humans, as requested by a certain gnome couple that we have not seen for some time.

Miguel's eyes widened with excitement. "Pray tell, how did such a magical enchantment befall you both?"

Marta, the sleek brown and white beauty with piercing blue eyes, spoke next: "Centuries ago, a wise gnome couple blessed our ancestors, granting them the power of flight and speech in many tongues. Our lineage has inherited this extraordinary ability, although we only take to the skies when the moon is full or I have decided to follow my nose. It fills our hearts with joy and helps us appreciate and, dare I say, like you, the wonders of the world."

Miguel marvelled at the cow's tales. "Such remarkable beings you are! Do you have any advice to share with a mere mortal such as myself?"

You, Clary, lowered your head, seemingly contemplating Miguel's question.

"We have roamed this mountain ridge for generations, witnessing the ebb and flow of life. Our advice to you, wise one, is to appreciate the beauty and magic that exists in every moment. "Life is full of miracles if only you have the eyes to see them."

Miguel listened intently, hanging onto your every word. Your wisdom resonated within him, stirring a deep sense of wonder and connection to the world around him.

As the conversation came to an end, you bid farewell and prepared to take flight once more. Miguel felt a mixture of honour, awe, and gratitude for having encountered your magical creatures.

"From this day forward, the sight of cows grazing in the fields will take on a whole new meaning for me. I will become more present, paying attention to the simple wonders that surround me. And every time I observe a herd of cows, I will venture nothing but a smile, cherishing the knowledge that beneath their earthbound appearance, they hold the capacity to dream to the heavens."

*****

Both Clary and Marta bowed their heads in appreciation. As their new friend watched them begin to move away, he leapt forward and said earnestly, "Can I know the names of the wonderful gnome couple?"

"Of course, you can. Their names are .If you have the privilege to meet them, you can call them Derek and Abella; they will not complain or take offence. Let them know you are a friend of us, Clary and Marta."

The stranger's head went down as his fingers and pen wrote the names given before his short-term memory; could dispose of them forever. When he looked up, the cows were gone. He spun around, searching the skies, but no sign was present of them. Was it a dream, had he fallen asleep, or was the memory real? He could only believe it must have been a dream, but what a wonderful dream he had had.

The white-haired man continued his walk down the mountain ridge towards the old craggy road, where the new road crossed its path. He had the choice of either heading down to the city below or up the ridge to the old church and cemetery. Today, I have decided to go upwards.

*****

# 9: I am the Quad Bike with a Sexy Señora

*I* am a modern machine travelling up and down a very ancient and craggy old road and sometimes down a new road with such a sexy and smooth surface. With those buttons in the middle of the road, I found it so captivating, especially at night. I love following their allure, each one compelling me to go further with each kilometre.

Modernisation, in my eyes, is the definite future. Forget the old; always in with the new, I say.

I am painted a glossy yellow with big black wheel guards overlapping my impressive-looking fat tyres. I know I am sexy to both men and women. Everyone wants to be transported by me. Where to? They do not care; everyone universally believes that I will raise their profile and make them sexy.

I spent a few weeks only in a shop in the city, and nearly every day, I sat outside with my other friends. Some of them were much larger and more powerful than me, while others had smaller engines but were equally brilliant to own.

The typical visitors to the shop are fresh-faced young teenagers who could ill afford any of us but loved to sit on top of us while their friends took pictures with their mobiles.

Sometimes, older men, such as the white-haired visitor, would venture to sit on me. With both hands on the handlebars, they would imagine themselves racing in and around the city and up towards the mountain ridge towards the north of the city.

When the costs were explained against the endless value I would give when making the decision to invest in buying me, the price always dismissed the value. Usually, the interests of both young and old would disappear for the same reason—Insufficient money or dinero insuficiente, depending on your mother tongue.

Typical arguments or questions not to buy were given, such as, what happens when it rains? How do I stay dry? How easy would it be to steal? How safe are they? Do I need a special license? Look how dangerous they must be; there's only room for one. Why do they not include a boot? Look, there is no room to store cases etc. etc., etc.

So, when the Latin American beauty named Ximena Londono arrived, all of our quad bikes were equally lustful to be the one she would choose to have under her shapely and well-proportioned frame.

As all men and quad bikes would agree, this lady moved confidently, knowing everyone would stop and look at her.

Today, she had made the decision to buy one of our beasts and to ride the lucky one chosen back up the mountain ridge to her mother and father's palatial home. The Londono family had the largest estate sitting to the northern part of the ridge with a meandering driveway snaking down to the old craggy road. Looking over the valley below gave the family and all who visited a revealing visita. The Londonos willingly spent time sharing their part of the mountain that unselfishly gave a magnificent panoramic view of the city below.

Ximena saw herself as the Queen of the mountain, and she wanted a status object that would ensure others would notice her even more than she had already expected they did.

She stopped at the sales floor outside the corner shop and moved her black, expensively branded sunglasses up over her brow to perch on top of her luxurious flowing ebony hair. Her mane shone and flowed like waves from her crown down, passing her shoulders and to the middle of her lower spine. She always knew this was one of her assets.

Men were unknowingly attracted to it almost immediately, and women instantly compared theirs to hers. Some could equal her, but the majority could not.

Her choice of what to wear was also an essential aspect of today's purchase. She knew that with the right choice, the salesman would have no chance with her. She first chose a cream-coloured chiffon blouse that hid and, at the same time, insinuated her curves. The sleeves were short and just enough to cover her modesty, just like the V-neck front with buttons.

Her second choice had to be her latest white jeans that literally looked like they had been painted on her small waist and round buttocks.

Her designer buttocks, yes, she had decided when she reached that tender age of eighteen, she would have her average-size body transformed by one of the most famous plastic and cosmetic surgeons in the city. His name was Hector Jesus Ruiz Garcia, MD.

First was her breasts, or as the surgeon commented, a breast augmentation. Ximena went from 34B to 36D in one go and had no complaints; her waist was taken in by a further two inches with liposuction and abdominoplasty-tummy tuck to you and me.

This latter procedure did hurt immensely, but it was a small price to pay for the next couple of months. And then, Ximena's buttocks were treated with a gluteal augmentation to enhance the contours.

She laughed loudly when her friends told her the street name for this buttock procedure was Brazilian Butt Lift, after Brazilian Plastic Surgeon Dr Ivo Pitanguy back in the 1960s. "I will call mine Ivo one and Ivo two in honour of such a wise and generous man!"

Whenever she looked in the mirror, she knew Ivo one and Ivo two would stop traffic, coupled with the designer high stilettos, the way she walked or, better still to describe her, how she glided through rooms and across streets always caused a commotion behind. She never saw herself as the possible cause of numerous minor accidents that occurred on a regular basis.

She now had the breathtaking beauty she desired. It was time for her to focus on the accessories that would complete the image she craved.

Her father's generous nature and his wealth as a international businessman would supply the finance needed to acquire all the accessories she desired. She had no interest in her father's current business; maybe one day, she would ask.

In the meantime, the unlimited bank balance meant more to her than what she could buy on her journey to being beautiful. Her father's secretary covered the invoices her boss passed to her to be settled by the company credit card account.

Ximena initially sat on the camouflage model but felt it had no connection to her. She did not see herself as a soldier; she loved her growing womanly charms; they had already reduced some beaus to quivering idiots, and she was far too young to think seriously.

She sat there and looked around, and her beautiful brown eyes settled on me. The thrill raced through my bodywork to the heart of my engine; I knew I was all muscle and power. Would she be satisfied with me? I must be patient.

She moved like a purring cat from the camouflage model and strolled directly to me. Her left leg straddled me. If I could have groaned, I surely would have groaned the loudest that day in the city.

I felt her weight lower onto my solo seat, and I knew she was impressed. She held onto the handles for what seemed an eternity, but in reality, it was just a brief moment in time. I thought at first, she was not impressed but just then the salesman arrived with his crisp white shirt open at the collar with no tie. She turned to him, gave him her killer smile with her perfect white teeth on display, and said those immortal words, "How much for this beautiful beast?"

The negotiation only took a few minutes, and I saw my new owner stop and her manicured hand reached out to accept the handshake to secure the deal.

The salesman attempted to stay calm and tried his hardest to create the impression of being full of confidence. Still, inside, he was a wreck; his emotional circuitry was in overdrive, and his mouth betrayed the inner turmoil he was going through. Please let me explain a few steps to ensure your overall safety when starting a quad bike." Ximena looked on, smiling at the salesman's discomfort at not hiding his emotions as well as he thought.

"My name is Efrain; "How are you today?"

"My name is Ximena, and yes I am fine, please explain more to me."

"Okay, safety must come first. I recommend you always wear a properly fitted helmet to protect your head. Helmets with face shields to keep your eyes safe from debris and dust work well. Then, I think you should wear gloves to help you grip the handlebars better and, of course, protect those delicate and beautiful hands."

Before Ximena could comment, Efrain powered on. "Boots, not high heels, are essential to protect your feet and ankles. Finally, wear protective clothing to match the riding conditions. It is best to avoid shorts and T-shirts. "Always put safety ahead of anything else."

Efrain continued setting up and checking the fuel gauge. "I will explain the use of the Kill switch and the ignition switch located on the handlebars. I should also talk more about the brakes and the gears…. Efrain paused. It was clear to him that Ximena had lost a fair amount of interest in what he should tell her. He knew she just wanted to ride as quickly as possible.

"Tell me, Efrain, do you have a coffee machine in your office? "I feel the need to move out of this sun."

"Of course, please follow me." Efrain was also melting in the glare of the sun's rays. Was it his vision of her eyes? He was not sure.

Later, he found himself offering the insurance tax-free with a brand new shiny white helmet and visor thrown in, even though he was not asked for anything. Never mind, he thought his commission would cover such items; I just wanted to impress this beauty.

He informed her, or more accurately, pleaded with her, that the paperwork and payment would take two hours, and then she could ride away with her exquisite taste in machinery. He offered to find her a seat, hoping to have unbroken time to look and admire her more.

She raised her eyes and apologised most softly that she had another important meeting that would also take another two hours and would be back later in the morning to ride away with her newly chosen purchase. Efrain was a little disappointed, but he hid it well and agreed to have everything ready by midday on her return.

A couple of hours passed, and I was cleaned unnecessarily and re-polished again unnecessarily. I was most definitely in showroom mint condition. I was ready for her with a full tank of fuel, and a final check of my engine and parts ensured this.

My new, beautiful owner, Ximena, returned first to me. She ran her fingers gently so as not to damage my skin in circles to remind me she was the sexy one. But she had no idea that, in truth, I was the sexy one; I was the prize that all men wished for; she was just the distraction. Wait until she sees the allure I will bring as I roar up through the busy city streets and up through the mountains.

Another hour passed, and finally, she emerged with my ignition key. Again, I experienced the thrill of her mounting me, followed by the key entering and turning me on. My engine came to life, and I felt her move my throttle, and my machine grew in sound.

When she was confident, I was ready. She started to move away from the forecourt, and straight away, we both felt we were a unique and sexy team. It was time for us to unite as one and become the masters of speed in our journeys together.

Both would bring heart and soul to our relationship together; nothing else she purchased would ever replace what I would share with her, and no one else did I desire to have sat on my seat belonging to Ximena.

On the way up the mountain road, I was at my best; she proved to be a natural, and she was totally in tune with my needs and desires; we passed through the shanty town, and the world stopped for all the poor people. Within seconds, we had passed before their very eyes at such a speed as to make them all stand back and be amazed at the wonderful sight we had made. Then, we were but a distant memory for all.

Then I appeared around the bend that housed the cross at the side of the road of the young man who had died with his new bike three years ago. Standing there reading the description on the cross was the white-haired stranger.

He turned to us as we appeared, and instantly, I saw his eyes move to me, the almighty and sexy machine. His steel blue eyes said it all. On this occasion, I had won – I was the sexiest of the two.

*****

## 10: I am the discarded Chilean Wine Bottle

Humans often say that others have all the luck; well, that also applies to objects. Just look at me and my life. In the human world, I am referred to as a wine bottle. I started my life in a small glassmaking factory near the port of Santiago in Chile.

Several substances are used to make me and my fellow compatriots, such as Silica, which is sourced from sand. Silica provides my structure and stability. Then, Soda Ash is used to make it easier to shape me at low temperatures. My maker then adds limestone to stabilise and strengthen my overall frame. Finally, additional substances such as alumina, magnesia, and other metal oxides will be added to enhance my overall colour and transparency.

Just imagine for one moment all my raw materials now mixed, being heated at extreme temperatures of around 1500 to 1600 degrees Celsius and being melted in a furnace.

Like all wine bottles, I was made through a process called glass-blowing or glass moulding. The production process involves several steps, including gathering molten glass, shaping it into a bottle mould, and then allowing it to cool and harden. Overall, I was made within an hour.

Early on in my life, I learned the remarkable history of glass production in Chile. It dates back to the colonial days when Spanish settlers settled in this part of the world and introduced the necessary glassmaking techniques. However, bottles like mine were not introduced into the domestic market until much later in the 19th century. It is known that before glass bottles, humans transported and stored wine in leather bags or clay amphorae.

The latter is a type of vessel that consists of a tall body with two handles on the neck or shoulders, a narrow inlet, and a spout for pouring the richness of the wine.

Once made, I was transported to a wine grower in the Central Valley close to the capital. I am classed as from the New World and not from the Old World, such as the famous French Bordeaux, the equally famous Italian Chianti or even the Spanish Rioja.

My contents' birthplace has been described as the perfect climate for harvesting my organic and balanced grapes. Once the process is complete, my grapes, having been merged into a generous amount of berry fruits and then blended with a subtle hint of leafy spices coupled with the dark aroma of chocolate, will become a rich mixture. The added velvet tannin creates what the tasters describe as a genuine seductive flavour, with a deep, earthy undertone and a lingering, velvety finish.

*****

As I sat on the shelf, I couldn't help but feel a pang of disappointment. I had always believed I was destined to become a famous and desired bottle of wine. But alas, the human world saw me as a reasonably inexpensive class of wine, and my final destination was a supermarket in the city known locally as El Exito.

I sat despondently on the higher shelves of many other misguided wines from my homeland. All believed they were destined for far-flung places such as Europe or America but were now awaiting their uncertain fate. This is just one conversation I had with three other bottles close to me.

"Hey, how long have we been sitting here? I feel like I'm collecting dust!" I started the conversation, breaking the silence that had settled over us.

Bottle, at my side, spoke next, "Oh, quit whining. "We're just waiting for our lucky day to be chosen by someone who appreciates our fine Chilean heritage."

Bottle, further away, commented, "I heard the store manager talking about a big wine sale coming up. Fingers crossed, my friends!"

Bottle, so far away, had to raise his voice to ensure we all heard him. "Hey, did you notice those fancy bottles of champagne on the opposite aisle across from us? "They think they're so special with their bubbly personality."

Back to me. "Well, at least we have more substance. "We are sturdy and elegant, and we do not need those sparkling bubbles to make an impression."

Bottle, at my side, piped up with, "True, true. We have the richness of the Chilean terroir flowing through our glass walls. That should be enough to attract a discerning buyer."

Bottle, further away, raised his voice even further. "Just imagine the stories we could tell if we could be heard. The vineyards we came from, the cool breezes and warm sunshine that nurtured our grapes.

Bottle, so far away, had to continue being the loudest. "Yeah, we've got layers of history and flavours. We are like the Vinoteca Avengers, ready to save any meal from tastelessness!"

It was my turn again. "Let's embrace the wait and stay positive, my friends. Our day will surely come, and when it does, we'll be sipped and appreciated by someone who knows the value of a good Chilean wine."

Bottle at my side. "That's the spirit! Until then, let's soak in the supermarket ambience and enjoy the view of those restless shoppers debating which wine to take home."

Bottle, further away, was delighted. "Cheers to that! May we find our perfect match soon and bring joy to someone's glass. Patience, my friends, patience."

Bottle, so far away, ended with. "Patience and glass half-full thinking. We are the unsung heroes of this supermarket. Let us shine on this shelf and await our turn with grace and dignity!"

Mine was a few weeks later; I sensed I was bought as a gift from a man with a hat. He indeed spent a long time looking at all the wine bottles, totally confused about who to pick. It was his wife's and his wedding anniversary, and the occasion demanded a spectacular gesture from him, or his life would not be worth living in the shanty household up in the mountain.

Finally, the decision was made. I was to be the one who would carry the burden of hope and enjoyment to the chosen lady of the house. The man kissed me for luck and took me to the cashier, who processed the purchase for him with a smile of approval.

I looked back at my friends, and each one was staring down at me. "Wait, everyone. I have been chosen! Look, look! "This customer has taken me off the shelf!"

Bottle, at my side, "No way! And just as I was taking a nap. Congratulations, buddy! You are going from shelf-sitter to wine connoisseur companion!"

Bottle, further away, "Cheers to you! Finally, one of us gets to fulfil our destiny and bring joy to someone's evening."

Bottle, so far away, sang out, "Oh, the honour! We always knew you had that irresistible charm. Remember to show off your label with pride, my friend!"

I was standing up in one of the corners of a yellow chariot-like trolley. "Thank you, thank you! I promise to represent our Chilean heritage with elegance and flavour. To the checkout counter, I go!"

Bottle, at my side, "Safe travels, my dearest friend. Remember, when you are uncorked, be your finest self. Deliver that smooth, fruity goodness to your owner's palate."

Bottle, further away, added: "We will be watching from this here shelf, cheering you on from far away. Enjoy your new adventure beyond these supermarket walls!"

Bottle, so far away, voiced out as loudly as it could muster: "Farewell, our dear friend! May your journey be filled with laughter, good company, and unforgettable moments. "We will be here waiting for our own chance to shine."

I also said my final goodbyes to my disappearing good friends: "Thank you, my faithful row of Chilean wine bottles. I will most certainly make you proud. Until we meet again, remember—we are all Vinoteca Avengers in this aisle of deliciousness!"

As we moved away from the aisle, I could hear the dialogue continuing with a mixture of excitement, well-wishes, and a touch of camaraderie as I, the selected wine bottle, embarked on my journey. I could hear the other three bottles maintaining their spirits as high as possible, knowing that their individual opportunities would come someday soon.

*****

Once I was in a plastic bag, I felt myself being conveyed outside into the sunshine. I could see the lady of the household peering into the bag. I witnessed her excited composure of being the one who would be partaking in the flavours of my bottle that night. They had prepared a sumptuous meal for themselves and their other son, Sergio, and his wife, Constantina, who lived further down the mountain's old craggy road.

They placed me in the back seat and then returned to the supermarket to purchase other items they felt were necessary to make the night a success.

As soon as they disappeared from view, three other younger humans jumped into the Chevrolet and, within a minute, were racing the vehicle with only one brake light through the city streets, which at this time of day were pretty light of traffic.

One of the boys, Leon Jaramillo, brushed his hand against the bag he had not noticed before and looked down to see me lying there. Only Pepe Jhon, the driver, did not inspect me, but Leon and his sidekick Lucas Cruz both leaned inwards to each other to attempt to read the shaking bottle's label. None of the three were well educated; They preferred to play truant from their school and find different ways to amuse themselves.

It was a while before they could clearly see I had a screw-like top and not a cork. Soon, I was open and spilling some of my beautiful wine onto everyone as the truck made its way up the mountain road.

By the time we reached the junction of the beginning of the old craggy road, I had been passed many times around as each boy drank thirstily from me. They had got close to the outskirts of the town. I was empty and of no more use to the thieves.

With this in their minds and that I could be used as evidence if caught with them, Lucas unceremoniously threw me through the open passenger window to the ground, racing below.

Miraculously, I did not break but landed with a thud on the uneven and rocky surface. I did bounce a couple of times, and a small chicken had to rush away, screaming at the top of her voice with indignation at the unexpected experience. In her fright and anger, her wings flapped endlessly, but her claw feet only left the ground by an inch or two.

The sounds of the disappearing truck started to fade; the chicken had regained her composure, if not her original place because I now occupied such a spot at the side of the old craggy road, just about on view but no more, no sign to tell anyone I was there. The last drop of wine gently flowed away from me, and now I had only to wait to see what would happen next to me.

One thing I was sure of was that it could well be a very long time. I looked around; nothing else lay nearby to give me comfort; I was alone; the daft chicken would be gone soon, I was sure, and then the realisation began to invade my very conscience, all my hopes and ambitions gone in a fraction of time.

All that could have happened in my life was washed down the throats of three thieves who probably could not even read or write.

How could they have really enjoyed my wine? I was probably no different than a bottle of cheap water as far as they were concerned. I started to feel very depressed. What was going to happen to my soul? I don't have any idea. I can only hope my life is not over yet.

I can hear footsteps coming towards me from further back along the road. I can see a little boy with his head and shoulders drooped. He looks unhappy, dragging a small blue rucksack-type bag by the handles along the road surface. His mind is in a far-flung place, and he only becomes aware of my presence when his left foot kicks me. He stops and investigates who I am.

To my great surprise, he squatted down with both his legs crossed, picked me up, and tried to read the words on my label. He has yet to do such a task as he has not been at school for more than a couple of weeks.

Usually, his mother waits outside the small school room behind the high-wire fence, which protects the classroom furniture and equipment that the poor humans in the city have given to the school. Today Magdalena was absent and nowhere in sight.

On this rare occasion, Juan had the opportunity to show his parents that he had the ability to become a big boy, so he braved his way back to his home again by himself. In his mind, it was a short journey. But in reality, to a little boy with little legs, it was a long journey.

He looks at me and instantly agrees that I would make a very fine candle holder for his parents' bedroom.

He immediately knew where best I was to be placed. He, even, in his next thought, had decided the tall white candle lying in the bottom drawer of the cupboard in the kitchen would adorn me.

His parents would be so pleased, and since it was their special day of celebrating their anniversary, this would indeed make a positive addition to the festivities. He even reminded himself that his older brother and his wife would witness his appreciation of him borne from the shared love of his mother and father.

Juan introduced himself and he picked me up in his tiny hands, and for a second, I thought I might still be broken, but no, he managed with purpose to cram me into his little blue rucksack and then hurried home as fast as his little legs he allowed.

When he arrived at the metal door, he found no one was home, only the dogs, chickens, and cockerels, with Clary and her sidekick Marta at the rear of the yard.

None of the livestock took any notice of Juan or his contents in the blue rucksack. He was too little to be of value as a source of food just yet. In the future, there is no doubt he will be the one to feed them each day.

But for now, the older human with the striped hat will be their main interest, and at the moment, he is overdue. Alberto usually has fed and watered them by now. But don't worry; it was not dark yet.

Juan placed me, the new addition to the household, in his parents' small but adequate bedroom. I found myself on top of the broad four-drawer chest, and soon, the little boy had unceremoniously placed a white tapered candle into my opening at the top of my neck.

He looked at me and explained my new, vital role for him. I must admit, I was taken aback. I had never seen myself as a makeshift lamp for times when the electricity disappeared.

After pondering this new situation for a short while, I started to smile at how life takes unsuspecting turns; now, I will be necessary to his parents when they most need me in the dark. I was content with this new knowledge and responsibility.

There was a commotion at the front of the house, and I lost sight of the little boy disappearing past the bedroom door to somewhere I could only presume was the front door. Soon, he reappeared, dragging his tired and exhausted mother to examine his new gift from him to her.

"Oh Juan, thank you for such a beautiful gift. I am sure it will always be here, taking pride and place in my heart whenever I need its services."

"Alberto! Come see what our clever boy Juan has found for our anniversary!"

With that scene in front of me, I could now see that luck was indeed on my side. The parents of this little boy were the happy couple who had bought me earlier at the supermarket.

"Oh, what a small world we all live in," Alberto acknowledged when he saw me.

His mood lightened with every minute he stared at me. How can a little bottle from Chile still make it to his home? It is fantastic; it does not matter that the contents were gone. Now, it's the story of an extraordinary soul in that bottle that he can pass down from generation to generation.

No one will ever match this story of having his rusty-looking old truck with one backlight never working stolen twice with the loss of a hat keyring and the discovery of an empty bottle of Chilean wine that still found its way into his home.

*****

## 11: *I am the somewhat thirsty and always hungry Colibri*

My title here in South America is El Colibri, but you may call me the thirsty and always hungry Hummingbird. I am a small bird with a heart proportionally five times the size of a human's heart and an enormous appetite for nectar and small insects such as mosquitoes, small spiders, and the occasional flying ant.

They are delicious.

My tongue has a groove-like shape of a W with tiny hairs on the tip, which helps me gather nectar.

I am typical of my species. I have to know where my next source of nectar is coming from.

I am proud to say I have an encyclopaedia of all the flowers up here on the mountain ridge and along the old craggy road. I even know when they will produce and how much there will be at any given time.

Most days, I will need to visit as many as five thousand different flowers to find my much-needed nectar. This amount will give me approximately double my body weight and will be sufficient for me to continue with my busy and often hectic social life for one day only!

My favourite colour is red. I cannot resist any red flower, as they never disappoint me in my quest to fill my stomach.

Am I aggressive? I would say no. I am a lover, not a fighter.

I have my ways with the ladies here that are never going to be surpassed. Well, excuse me, I have only a life span of approximately five years, and already two have passed me by, so you might say I am in my prime. I am a solitary fellow, and I find a degree of full-on macho is the order of each day.

At night, I do not see very well, so I tend, for health and safety reasons, to go into a temporary torpor and just hibernate in a tree branch without snoring like many of my neighbours in the trees do. I remain as such until the dawn appears again, bringing a new day of adventures.

To see how I look, imagine a small bird with a big brain in proportion to an elephant; mine is 100 times bigger. As for overall size, I am an impressive 8.5 cm long, and I weigh a hefty 20 grams.

I am one of 360 species of hummingbirds found globally. If you really love hummingbirds, you will find almost half of the world's population right here in Colombia!

My family is known as the Indigo-bellied hummingbirds, and we live mainly in trees. The majority of my extended family lives in the Amazon, where there is an abundance of rainforest areas to thrive and enjoy.

We moved here recently due to the continuous threat of deforestation, which causes human farmers to cultivate and breed animals called cattle for beef production. Apparently, you humans love beef, and you may not know that for every pound of beef, 200 square feet of the forest floor, including the trees, have to disappear.

Just imagine that happening to where you live. How long would it be before you and your family would be thought of as endangered and subject to becoming extinct?

How do I know this? My all-knowing father told me a year ago that when he found out, I had no idea, but I was happy with his decision to relocate us all to this mountain ridge where the majority of trees are left alone. In fact, you humans are often seen transporting new trees to your homes, giving us more choices to explore.

I have an excellent fluorescent indigo throat patch with a fluorescent lime-coloured chest. My lower abdomen starts with a hint of white, followed by my black tail. On either side of me are my beautiful and powerful grey wings.

My wings can rotate in circles, and they can flap over 80 times per second, and I can cover anywhere from 25 to 30 miles per hour.

I counted once and got to 85, which definitely pleased me, as the humming sound of my wings generated huge interest in the ladies.

I even have huge ears, and the ladies just swoon at the sight of me. I can assure you I am a very popular Colibri on this mountain.

I often decide to act coy on most days and settle on perching and scratching with my poor feet. My father also told me to refrain from both hopping and walking, as it was a waste of energy. The ladies got bored quickly with such a weak display, so another valuable lesson was learned.

My heart beats over 1200 times per minute, so you can imagine I have to have a lot of sustenance to keep up. Flying and soaring is an average day for me.

I can stunt fly like no other; I can fly forward, backwards, upside down, and sideways.

Just imagine I am the ultimate flying acrobat in the sky. At times, you cannot see me actually moving; I am so fast.

I can see more colours of the spectrum than humans can. I even have a third set of eyelids. These act as goggle protectors when I zoom through the air.

For those horrible days when it rains persistently, I have a way of dealing with the raindrops by hovering and shaking my head with such acceleration that I can reach a g-force of 34. My father told me that some humans race cars in a race known as Formula One. The racing cars may appear fast to you humans, but they typically only reach a g-force of 6. When I heard that little-known fact, I leapt up and gave a demonstration to all and sundry that day.

How does he do that? Well, I head to a mid-air manoeuvre that takes me only 0.1 of a second to achieve. This instantly removes nearly all the water droplets from my many feathers. Pretty impressive, hey? That's not all; my head is going through 180 degrees within a 10th of a second and sometimes less.

It doesn't matter if I am dealing with a drizzle, a typical light to medium shower, or even a downright heavy burst of rain. I adjust my oscillation to meet my needs to see effectively during flight. If I did not have this skill, I would be forever falling out of the air when the rainy seasons are active.

I am often seen diving at speeds up to 65 feet per second, especially on occasions when I feel the need for attention from a particular female. I allow my tail feathers to vibrate during my high-speed dives towards the ground below me. At the same time, the female concerned will hear my loud chirping sound from my feathers and not my throat.

You may well be astonished by the following lesser-known fact. When I am diving, for the reasons already given, I can be measured by my overall body size to that of a human fighter jet or a space shuttle re-entering Earth's atmosphere after one of its missions. Well, that is what my father says. He did concede that those same jet fighters out-accelerate me on every occasion.

That little setback didn't bother me. I never fail in my quest, and as such, a display always turns on the lady. It appears there are no limits to my abilities....

Well, apart from one....the superior power of acceleration from the Jet and its powerful jet engines.

A new day has arrived. I am in a quandary: Should I go to the little boy's garden first, with its abundance of ripe and definitely ready-to-produce nectar flowers, or should I check out that possible new source of interest I spotted only the other day?

A strange-looking man living nearby has placed at least 17 new small red plastic trays on all the trees surrounding his house. I say placed; he actually nailed them to the trees. He has filled each one with sugared water—my favourite!! How did he know? I ask myself. Who cares? It appears I am the only one who knows of such an abundance of free sweetness.

I must admit I am curious about this stranger. I have never seen such a display of friendship before. A few months ago, one of my distant cousins told me that there was an oasis of such trays over the mountain, with over 145 different species of hummingbirds making up a community of hundreds.

He told me that you could hear the sound of the wings humming for hundreds of miles. No, I was not impressed. I like working alone, and I am not even a bit interested in migrating. What a waste of feeding time.

As I said, I am a lover, not a fighter. Just imagine all that territory that needs protecting. They must be fighting each other every minute of each day. I enjoy the tranquillity of not having to compete, and the ladies show no sign of complaining.

I decided to visit this new friend first; I knew I didn't need to worry. I was confident that I could fly right up close to him, and even if he moved quickly to try and catch me with my lightning speed, I would never be seen. I would always outfox any human.

My closeness pleases him immensely. His eyes were wide open with joy, and he showed his pleasure at seeing me doing a massive display of acrobatics in front of him. I can see clearly; he is no threat to me. In fact, I have never experienced such malice from any human.

He has only made one mistake.

He does not understand the nuisance of the tiny honey bees that also love the sugar.

He has also made it easy for them to reach the sugared water, and today, I will have to push my way through. Hopefully, he will quickly learn to adjust this for me.

So, for now, I will head to the other place, my second source of kindness with the little boy and his father. I can clearly see these humans have as big a heart and soul as I do.

*****

## 12: I am the shiny 100 Peso coin

My history can be traced back to the 1800s. My ancestors replaced the then-known Spanish Reale, and their names became Colombian pesos. I was minted in 2016, and I am made of a unique combination of Aluminium, bronze, copper, and nickel. This composition not only gives me my shiny surface but also ensures my durability, making me a reliable and long-lasting coin.

But wait, please. Allow me the honour of sharing more facts about my existence. I promise it is worth reading.

The Reale was a historical currency that originated in Spain in the late 14th century. It was the primary currency in 1536 and used by the Spanish Empire during its colonial period. As the Spanish rule expanded throughout South America, it was also adopted by other countries influenced by Spanish colonisation, including my country, Colombia.

The Reale was originally a unit of weight for silver and gold, but it eventually became a specific denomination coin. It would take another 283 years for this to change, with the actions of a Venezuelan soldier, later described also as a famous thinker, reformer, and liberator.

His name was Simón José Antonio de la Santísima Trinidad Bolívar Palacios Ponte y Blanco.

With the wave of independence movements in Latin America led by

Bolivar during the early 19th century, many former Spanish colonies, including Colombia, gained their independence.

As part of the transition to self-rule, these newly formed nations sought to establish their own identities and systems. One way to do this was by creating their own national currencies.

During this period, the real was replaced by the peso, which became the official currency of Colombia in 1810 following the country's declaration of independence from Spain. The adoption of the peso allowed Colombia to assert its sovereignty and establish a currency that reflected its independent status.

The transition from the real to the peso was part of a larger movement towards national economic autonomy and consolidation following the end of Spanish colonial rule. By introducing their own currencies, these countries were able to establish control over their financial systems and depend less on the former colonial powers for their economic affairs.

Since then, the Colombian peso has remained the official currency of Colombia and is used in everyday transactions within the country.

*****

But that is not the whole story. There is more: When Colombia declared its independence from Spanish rule, the country was not yet officially named Colombia. At that time, it was part of the Viceroyalty of New Granada, which encompassed present-day Colombia, Ecuador, Panama, Venezuela, and parts of Peru and Brazil.

The process of independence in Colombia began on July 20, 1810, with the establishment of a local governing board known as the Supreme Government Board. This board was composed of prominent local leaders and officials who sought to govern the region in the absence of Spanish authority.

The junta was not declaring total independence at that time; instead, its primary goal was to govern autonomously while pledging loyalty to the Spanish king, Ferdinand VII. This was a significant step towards self-governance and a precursor to the later declaration of full independence.

The members of the Supreme Government Board in New Granada included Camilo Torres Tenorio, a politician and lawyer; Antonio Morales Galavis, also a lawyer and military thinker; and Jorge Tadeo Lozano, a scientist, journalist, and politician. Together, they played significant roles in leading the movement towards independence and establishing the early stages of self-government in the region.

However, it is essential to note that the process of achieving complete independence from Spain was a lengthy and complex one. It was not until August 7, 1819, that Colombia, then known as the Vice Presidency of Gran

Colombia, achieved total independence under the leadership of Simón Bolívar and his military campaign known as the Battle of Boyacá.

Simón Bolívar, often referred to as El Libertador, is considered one of the primary leaders in the struggle for independence throughout the broader region that encompasses present-day Colombia, as well as other countries such as Panama, Venezuela, Ecuador, Peru, and Bolivia. His military victories and political leadership were crucial in ultimately achieving independence from Spanish rule in the region.

Enduring the passage of time, I have lived through many hands, some pristine, some not so. Yet, I do not lament, for such is the fate of coins. Each of us, without exception, leads a remarkable life, each unique in its own right.

So far, I have lived mainly in the South West of this vast land known as Colombia. Everyone looks at my front face with pride when they read "Republica de Colombia" and below the year of my birth. Which together symbolises the country's sovereignty and independence.

On my back, I display the famous Frailejon, a famous and popular South American plant. The reason is magical to me as it is represent resilience and adaptability, characteristics that are often associated with the Colombian people.

It is a lesser-known fact that we were once linked to the English currency, and before that, the French. This historical connection has endowed us with a level of education and sophistication that sets us apart from many other coins in the world.

My elder sibling, the pioneer coin, arrived in 1992. His journey has witnessed the burgeoning of various industries, from manufacturing to catering, technology to shipbuilding, electronics to tourism, and mining. He, like all of us, takes pride in our collective contribution to shaping our beloved country into the fourth-largest economy in Latin America.

They describe bees as busy and ants as industrious, but our pesos are both active and dynamic.

Except that today, I am resting on the old craggy road in the midday sun. I am a little worried about what is going to happen next. Only yesterday, I was in the pocket of a farmer on his motorbike racing up the old craggy road. In the vibration of the engine, I fell unaware from the rider's jacket pocket with the hole in the bottom onto the rock surface where I lay now.

*****

I need not have worried; This morning, the first person who saw me was totally different from the others. Looking at him I could see he likes money, because as soon as he saw me his eyes lit up and a big smile appeared. He immediately stooped down, his soft hands reaching out to scoop me up.

When I was within his eyesight, we both stopped to inspect each other. His face was soft and a little red, maybe from the exertion of walking down this old, craggy road again. His eyes scanned both sides of me. His facial features show a tranquil nature that has seen a lot in a long life of travel and work. His eyes look deep into me, and he tells me that from this day forward, he is going to take extra care of me, as I am a particular coin which happens to be the first one to appear in front of him on his new stage in life as a possible author.

He showed me his new black rucksack and placed me safely into the small zipper-fronted pocket. Here, I join a little Colombian hat.

"Hello. Is it okay for me to join you?" I asked, landing next to him.

"Yes, of course, there is room for two, as you can see. It will make a change to have company, and someone like you, who this human chose, must be a good thing indeed." Replied the jubilant hat, making more space to allow me to face him.

"Why do you say that?" I ventured.

"Well, I am a lucky little hat who, by sheer good fortune, found my way into this human's heart and protection. It seems you may have found the same luck, too, and your journey is about to follow mine." He puffed out proudly. I could see he was not being arrogant; he genuinely felt happy and contented with his lot. Well, maybe life will be okay for me, too. So, I decided to relax, lay back, and rest.

I replied, "Well, did you hear the human say that I would also bring him luck and good fortune? I hope so; I plan to travel to many places, as is my destiny and my forefathers before me. "To be abandoned on the old craggy road for eternity does not bear considering at all."

The little Colombian hat leaned forward with a smile and said warmly, "Do not fret, little 100 peso coin any more. I believe we will have a wonderful life with this human. He thinks he is the lucky one when really it is us who really hold the luck. Let us share our now combined gift with him for bringing us together."

I instantly agreed with the suggestion; it made perfect sense; with double quantities of luck, we can change this human's life for the better, and we are sure he will always appreciate us for it. We can honestly believe we may be with this human for some time, and we will bring him prosperity and good fortune as this is not only our duty but our soulful pleasure.

*****

## 13: I am a Willy Jeep who needs some assistance

At the end of World War Two, in 1945 to be exact, there proved to be an excess of our army jeeps called Willys, so we were more or less abandoned for a while by the Gringos. It was only a short time before someone commented we may be of some use to the farmers in a place called Colombia.

Up until then, the only modes of transport that the humans living there used were very slow and cantankerous mules, horses, and oxen to pull carts and wagons for transporting heavier loads.

These animals were well-suited in the mountainous regions for navigating the rugged terrains with their limited road infrastructure and steep slopes. The mules and horses were used to carry both the humans and their goods, allowing the farmers to transport their agricultural produce, equipment, and any other supplies deemed necessary.

It was argued that the introduction of Willy Jeeps could replace the animals and provide a more efficient and reliable means of transportation.

Willy Jeeps, initially produced by an American company called Willy-Overland Motors, became the answer for the Colombian farmers. They needed our ruggedness and navigational abilities to meet any challenges head-on.

A few hundred of us from the Philippines were loaded up on ships and transported to this new country. We were an instant hit for the very grateful farmers, and it was not long before they started to wonder how they functioned without us.

They quickly realised and discovered we could carry vast cargo even to the point where our front wheels would rise off the ground. We would still move forward, albeit a bit precariously, with our loads on the back wheels. We only weighed 590kgs when empty. We surprised everyone with this feat.

We proved we could carry anything imaginable; anything was a possibility for us.

Due to our original design specifications needed by the US Army, we were designed as a light-cross country reconnaissance vehicle with a 4-wheel drive.

Our engines were mighty strong. We had no problems increasing productivity, gaining previously out-of-reach access, and generating cost and time savings. We were also ideal for the often rough trails, muddy fields, and unpredictable terrains, such as my new home, Armenia. This was and still is coffee-growing land.

I was purchased by one family and given a new coat of paint: red on my main bodywork, white on the upper parts, and finally, yellow on my wheel hubs.

I became the most needed piece of equipment on the farm. I acted as a taxi, logger, removal van, and school runner. In fact, I was used for all kinds of errands or reasons.

Over the next sixty years, I raced up and down many mountain peaks and once manoeuvred over a dormant volcano. I even saw dunes from a close distance, which I found enchanting, but at the same time, I felt a sense of danger as I did not trust that the sand particles would not cause me to break down.

I also found the jungles creepy and claustrophobic. The vast tree canopy prevented me from seeing the beautiful clouds in the sky. I was always relieved when they ended, and the terrain changed to enormous and countless rolling hills.

In the beginning, I carried large sacks of coffee beans, which the soft hands of the Señoras and Señoritas systematically picked.

Legend has it that coffee is tastier when a lady picks the bean rather than the man, as it is believed that her gentle touch and attention to detail bring out the best flavours in the brew, creating a more nuanced and satisfying cup of coffee.

Sometimes, I was hired out to other relatives of the farmer who grew bananas, plantain, yucca, papaya, avocados, tomatoes, and giant watermelons, each the shape of a rugby ball only ten times bigger.

Back in the nineties, when I was in my prime, my then-owner from Salento would enter me in the yearly JIPAO parade. I came second twice and third once for having the best-arranged charge.

Each JIPAO parade was a festive time for us Willys and the humans who employed us.

It gave us time to catch up, see old friends, reminisce about old times, and describe the unusual jobs and journeys each was experiencing.

There appeared to be a growing trend for many of us to become taxis and support the ever-increasing tourism trade. On weekends, my colleagues were often used to taking sightseers to the wax palm trees on the side of the Cocora Valley just above Salento.

In my later years, I started to become a nuisance for my owner; my inner parts began to stop functioning one by one on a regular basis.

No longer was I economical or reliable.

My owner's body also showed the same signs of wear and tear. A family emergency meeting was held to discuss the decision to sell me off and for the family to head to another place to live.

Little did I realise that an earthquake with a magnitude of 6.2 would end my career so abruptly.

It struck on a lovely Sunday afternoon and was felt as far away as Bogotá. 1,900 humans passed away, and over 270,000 lost their homes and livelihoods, including my family.

The decision was made for all; the family was to immigrate to Miami, where many other relatives lived. All the possessions, including me, were to be sold off, and I was sold to a broker in the vast city nearby.

Here, my loads changed to varying amounts of furniture, from tables and chairs to mattresses to almost anything made by humans for their use in the home. I have even moved Televisions!

Back in the 60s, there was a famous and comical television series from America called "The Beverley Hillbillies" starring the Clampets family and their fictitious Pa and Grandma. If you can remember this series, you will have an idea of what I came to look like.

In this same period, I changed hands many times, and each new pair always seemed poorer than the last.

Eventually, I ended up with a poor labourer named Jaime. I have lived on the old craggy road, and as my parts started to fail more and more, I moved less and less. Rust and the local vegetation began to take over my paintwork.

My tyres began to tire, and inevitably, all became flat. My engine was stripped, my seats disappeared, and opportunistic thieves would often stop to see what else they could pillage from my carcase.

It had become a sorrowful and depressing time for me.

No more will I be able to parade with my friends. No longer will I be able to exchange gossip and laughter. Now, all I feel is solitude and emptiness.

Little did I see this being my final resting place.

While in this horrible state, I felt no interest in anything happening on the old craggy road. Everything that moved appeared to have a purpose. I had become old and useless.

No one stopped and looked at me with admiration any more. No one sang and danced around me like they did at the parades. No one bothered to clean me. I was just left abandoned to rot away forever.

I had yet to learn who my current owner was. Was it still Jaime, or was it some other faceless human?

*****

"¿Hola, mi amigo, come estas?"

The exact words came to me again and again until I woke up and realised someone was asking me a question. I understood the words, but the accent was vaguely recognisable to me. Where had I heard it before?

I searched my mind, but no, I needed more words to know for sure.

I opened my eyes and looked in the direction the voice came, and it was to my left. I could see a man with white hair, a large frame, clean-shaven, and strong legs. His clothes and boots reminded me of the time the gringos were in huge numbers, more than our Willys.

Was he a gringo too? If so, he would be the first one I have seen since childhood in the land of The Philippines.

He spoke again, and in my rush to invade my memory, I missed what he said. His lips were moving again. This time, I concentrated on every word he said, and it was in English!

"Hello, my poor friend, what has happened to you? Why are you in such a poor state?" he declared as he inspected me from every angle he could.

Then, as he leaned towards me, he followed with, "I suspect you must be at least 14 years older than me, and as I am 62, you must be, I guess, 76."

This was true. I was born in 1941. This stranger must be knowledgeable. He understood who I was and my age.

Wait, he is speaking again; I need to listen to him. I think he is not gringo but an Englishman.

The last time I heard their unusual posh way of speaking was way back in the jungles of the Philippines when the British were fighting with the gringos against the invading army from Japan.

The British forces included units from the British Army, Royal Air Force, and the Royal Navy. They and the Americans were there to liberate the islands. I saw action with them in many battles and campaigns, including the Battle of Manila.

This was a time in my life I wish to forget; many sad memories of friendly young gringos and Tommys riding on my worn leather seats, usually just once and never seen again.

The Battle of Manila, which took place from February 3 to March 3, 1945, during World War II, was a significant and highly destructive battle between the American and Filipino forces against Japanese troops. It aimed to liberate the Philippine capital city from Japanese occupation.

The battle began as American forces, led by General Douglas MacArthur, one of the most prominent military leaders, launched their assault on Manila.

Yes, this famous man did sit in my Willy Jeep seats a good number of times.

I remember four funny anecdotes that totally demonstrate this famous American General's colourful personality as I was there on all three occasions:

1. MacArthur and the Chiefs of Staff: MacArthur was known for his flamboyant personality and disregard for protocol at times. During a high-level strategy meeting with his chiefs of staff in the Philippines, MacArthur arrived by me, his preferred Willy Jeep, wearing his trademark corncob pipe. As the meeting progressed, MacArthur got up, left the room, and returned a few minutes later, riding me into the conference room, much to the surprise and amusement of his staff.

2. MacArthur's Escape: In March 1942, as the Japanese advanced on the Philippines, MacArthur famously carried out his strategic retreat to Australia. During his escape from the enemy, MacArthur and his entourage had to cross a treacherous mountain terrain in a Willy Jeep. Yep, it was me again! The journey was difficult, and at one point, I was stuck on a narrow mountain road. With Japanese forces closing in, MacArthur's assigned driver successfully freed me, and they continued their escape. It was probably the only time I ever got stuck.

3. MacArthur and the Mud: MacArthur was known for his impeccable personal grooming, and he often wore a dress uniform even in combat zones. However, during a visit to a military base in New Guinea in 1943, heavy rainfall turned the base into a muddy mess. As MacArthur's entourage, led by me, drove in their Willy Jeeps, they encountered a particularly muddy section. I got well-stuck, and the general had to trudge through the mud to safety. Despite his filthy appearance, he famously declared, "The only time my feet are in mud is when I'm walking on water."

4. Password Episode: MacArthur had a close call during a visit to one of his forward positions in the Pacific. The password system was in place, which required soldiers to provide a correct response to gain access. As MacArthur approached, a young soldier asked for the password. Expecting his staff to

provide it, MacArthur continued to walk by without responding. The soldier, not recognising MacArthur, shouted, "Hey, Mac! Show me your password!" MacArthur quickly turned around, delighted by the soldier's wit about him, and responded, "I'm the password!"

*****

Sorry, I digressed. Back to Manilla, the city which was heavily fortified, and the Japanese defenders fiercely resisted the Allied offensive. The battle took place street by street, building by building, making it one of the most intense and brutal urban battles of the entire war.

The American and Filipino forces faced numerous challenges during the battle. The Japanese defenders used an extensive network of tunnels, barricades, and fortified buildings to their advantage.

Furthermore, they employed guerrilla-style tactics, including ambushes and booby traps, which significantly hindered the progress of the attacking forces.

I, too, did not escape the carnage. I took many shrapnel wounds to my undercarriage and body, but not enough to stop me from continuing.

As the battle raged on, the Japanese troops adopted a ruthless and scorched-earth policy, destroying buildings and infrastructure, including bridges, roads, and utilities, to impede the Allied force's advance. This led to significant civilian casualties and widespread destruction throughout the city. Like many of the fighting heroes around me, I, too, stopped taking in all the death and destruction. I witnessed. I, too, managed to blank all out.

The battle reached its climax with the recapture of the heavily fortified Intramuros district, a historic section of Manila. American forces, with the assistance of tanks, artillery, and aircraft, launched a massive bombing and artillery assault, reducing much of the district to ruins.

The Japanese defenders suffered heavy losses and eventually were killed or surrendered.

However, the victory came at a significant cost. The battle resulted in the deaths of over 100,000 civilians and the complete destruction of Manila's infrastructure. The city's cultural and Spanish colonial architecture and historical heritage, including ancient buildings and landmarks, were also largely lost.

The Battle of Manila was a significant turning point in the war, marking the beginning of the end of the Japanese occupation of the Philippines. The battle's brutality and the extensive loss of civilian lives and historical treasures emphasised the grim nature of urban warfare and the devastating consequences it can have on civilian populations and one particular Willy Jeep.

It was a while before either of us dared to look at the other. The stranger before me broke our silence.

"Let me guess, you came here back around 1945 and spent much of your life working hard up near Salento. I suspect you were treated well, and you did not disappoint your owner. Now, for some unknown reason, you ended up here on this poor old craggy road with only me as company."

"I, too, am in a similar situation as you. I am looked upon as being old now. But my mind and heart say I am not. I, too, have worked very hard for others all my life, and I am afraid I know no different."

He paused for another moment and then began speaking again to me. "Perhaps one day we can join forces and help each other. Let us imagine I can earn enough money to rescue you and take you to a magical man who will restore you to your former glory. Together, we will ride as a team to all the stops we can."

"Just think of all the meetings you can have with your friends from way back. I will sit proudly in your new seat and drink poker beer, laugh, and boast about you to everyone and everyone who stops to listen."

"You can take me to other Latin American countries I wish to explore, such as Peru, Chile, Ecuador, Panama, Paraguay, Uruguay, Argentina, Mexico, Brazil and maybe Venezuela, if things start to settle down there again."

"Maybe we could go to Cuba together and discover an island I thought I would never see."

"Okay, I know at this moment in time they are dreams, but hey, dreams do often become true for many people; just read the books and see the true movies out there; they are full of such stories."

"We should agree to find a way; stay strong, my little Willy Jeep; I will find the way, and I will come back for you." Then he added, "Look, I have a very lucky hat and also an auspicious 100 Peso coin. With their combined charms, perhaps they will willingly add you into their sphere of good fortune."

At this point, he had both items in his left hand, which showed me that he was indeed genuine with his proposal.

With the hat, the 100 Peso coin, and the now excited stranger, who evidently had lost any composure he may have had, he was now rejoicing in the pending opportunities that willingly buzzed around in his head: "Hey, Willy Jeep, I have some exciting news to share with you!"

"We're going to give you a fantastic makeover and restore you to your former glory, taking inspiration from the many iconic MGs found in England. We're going to paint you in a classic racing green colour, just like those beautiful MG sports cars."

I have yet to learn what he is talking about, but it sounds exciting.

"Racing green is a shade of green that has been associated with British racing cars for decades. It's a colour that symbolises speed, elegance, and a rich history in the automotive world. By choosing racing green, we want to pay homage to the heritage of British motor racing and capture that timeless and iconic look on you."

Sounds good to me.

"Just imagine cruising down the road, turning heads wherever you go, with that deep and vibrant shade of green surrounding you. You'll instantly emanate a sense of vintage style and sophistication. People will admire your rich and storied past while also appreciating the care and attention to detail that went into your restoration."

I am starting to see his vision of me, and I like it.

"This choice of colour is made to evoke a sense of nostalgia, reminding people of the golden age of British motoring. It's a way to honour the proud heritage of MG cars and their contribution to the automotive industry. By mimicking the colour seen on so many MGs, you'll be joining a prestigious club of timeless, elegant vehicles."

Golden age, heritage, prestige, timelessness, and elegance will suit me fine.

"With your new racing green coat, you'll stand out from the crowd, showcasing your unique character and history. Rest assured, we're committed to ensuring that the restoration process is not only thorough but also maintains the true essence and spirit of the classic Willy Jeep."

Okay, I am in. Where do I sign?

So, get ready, Willy Jeep, for your transformation into a stunning symbol of British motoring excellence.

We can't wait to see you painted in that gorgeous racing green shade, capturing the hearts of car enthusiasts everywhere!

Say no more. I accept your offer.

"A future of safe travelling, my friend, and enjoying the motoring experiences in your newly restored and iconic racing green look."

With those parting words, my new English friend patted my hood and looked inside to see my rusty inners: "Do not worry. I am confident you are restorable. We will change your colours to those of the old MGs back in England—the famous racing green for you, sir.

"We need some luck from these two little friends of mine and a little time."

I suspected both the human and I had a shared desire to be restored, and our souls were alike.

Slowly, he moved away and began walking down the road. Now and then, he would stop, turn around, and wave to me. I finally started to believe maybe my future lies with a stranger with white hair and his two friends. I will allow my soul to hope so for now until proven otherwise.

*****

## 14: I am Gracie, the Smiling Cleaner, on the New Road

My name is Gracie; I have been asked to clean the new road from the junction where it meets the old craggy road down towards the small town a few kilometres away. Every day for the past three months of the dry season, the trees have shed their foliage onto the road surface, and this has built up to such a degree that someone wishes for it to be swept away.

I do not know who, but I do know that I am grateful for the work.

I jumped at the opportunity to have regular work and high up a mountain where the air is fresher than down in the melting pot of the city. If I do a great job, they will offer me a permanent position as a mountain road cleaner.

I have even been supplied with a uniform. I now wear a yellow polo-style shirt with a motif on my left shoulder. My pants are also yellow, and I have a baseball cap that I can adjust whenever I need to have it tight against my head or loose when the sun is at its highest.

My shoes are a pair of brand-new white trainers. With all these new clothes, I feel like a rich Señora today, and I cannot stop smiling.

In the first hour, I must have looked ridiculous because I paused whenever a vehicle approached me.

I smiled every time, showing my gleaming white teeth.

In reality, I was unsure if I was in a safe position, but I always seemed to be as each driver moved slightly to the middle of the bend to avoid any contact with me.

I soon calmed down and only checked when I felt the rumblings of the bigger vehicles, such as the large lorries and those crazy mountain buses that always seemed unsafe wherever they were in the city or up any mountain.

The company that had been given the contract to ensure the road was clean and pristine issued me with a brand new brush and tray with what looked like excellent poles for me to sweep and gather the leaves.

They were bigger than I was used to using, and it was only a short time before I understood I would need to use more energy to implement them on the road surface. The ones in my apartment in the north of the city are smaller and do not need such an effort.

I live with my two small children, Hernan and Rita, who today are being looked after by their Abuela Manuela, who suffers from her back and is always in pain.

But what we all love about her is the unmistakable love she has for my children, and I always know she is safe with them. Hernan and Rita are inseparable; wherever one goes, the other will surely follow. I do not need to worry about either of them.

If one is unwell, the other will always tend to him or her and offer comfort until he or she is well again. It is a beautiful bond they share and a pleasure to witness. They are now 8 and 9 years old and full of curiosity and questions.

Grandma Manuela will be drained by the time I get home this evening.

I fill each bag with as many leaves as possible, and then one of the three other workers on the team I have been assigned transports the load to the back of the truck parked nearby.

Later, when it is lunchtime, we will all sit on the road with our backs next to the big tyres, relaxing in a makeshift shade, rejoicing with each other at our good fortune in finding work in a city that only 50 years ago had a population of approximately 500,000.

Now we are told there are over 2.5 million souls all competing for government jobs and careers with the growing number of private companies.

My dream is to one day leave the city and live in Europe like my three surviving Tios (Uncles) in London.

Each weekend, after I have taken the children with Abuela Manuela to Sunday prayers at our local Catholic Church, the routine is the same. On my arrival home, I will open Messenger on my mobile and talk for at least an hour with each of my Tios.

They tell me many things about their lives there and show me many videos of where they live and work; they honestly make it look like a beautiful place to live and raise a family, especially on their last call with them.

They have agreed to raise the money for visas for Manuela, me, and the children so we can visit them to see if we would like to go there.

We will be allowed to stay there for three months. At some point, we will all have to travel to our capital city, Bogotá to catch our flight to Europe. It is a 10-hour bus ride or, alternatively, a one-hour flight away.

My Uncles want to pay for all of us to fly, but with the enormous cost, I must refuse such an offer.

This is another reason to have a job here on the mountain ridge, and I can save a little amount each day towards this dream of mine.

I am happy and excited about the prospects for my mother's and the children's lives, too.

I have not seen their biological father since the younger Rita was born. He sold me the idea that he would go to America and apply for a job there as an engineer on the subway. As soon as he was settled, he would arrange for us to join him. So far, that call and no other call have arrived.

The last we heard, he had been disallowed his work permit and had absconded to California, where it was rumoured, he was working as a gardener for a rich movie star in LA.

After some six years had passed, I gave up hope of ever being part of a complete family again with him. We had made it on our own and were doing OK. As long as the children were happy, then I would be happy, too. As for the children, they had no memories of their father and never asked many questions of him.

I have been working for four hours now; my back is a little sore, and my shoulders are aching, too. There is only one more hour until my lunch break. As I turned to the next section of the road, I looked up, and to my surprise, a man was walking towards me.

He is a little taller than me and has very striking blue eyes, the colour of which I have never seen before. His face is red from the exertion of walking from where, I am not sure, but I think he has come down the old craggy road!

I am so pleased the contract did not wish us to clean that road; it most surely would have killed me trying.

The man's walking boots were the same colour as the terracotta earth further up, and his socks had also changed from white to terracotta.

I started to look up. His shorts were baggy and black, but they were invaded one side with another colour, terracotta. His shirt and right arm also had changed to terracotta.

I then realised he must have fallen earlier, and the old craggy road had tattooed him. Temporarily, I know, but all the same, the road had made its mark on him.

He stopped and started patting himself down, the dust creating little plumes of terracotta clouds around him. He removed his cap, and I could now see a mixture of terracotta and white hair; I started to laugh.

He stopped and looked up, realising he must look funny, he started to laugh, too. He put out his hands with his palms facing upwards; his right hand was cut deeply, and there had been some dry blood mixed with the earth that would need some attention.

He did not seem to mind and showed little discomfort; he just kept smiling at me and saying nothing. I suddenly thought this was the first foreigner I had ever been standing close to in my entire life.

Yes, I saw many on the stupid television that always seemed to show violence that often I would object to and would turn off when the children were watching. It was hard raising children, as always for each generation, and now it seemed more invasive having such gratuitous violence so readily available in my home.

None of my friends or family seemed to worry about this aspect of South American life, but for me, it always felt it was not right. God teaches us to love each other, not to kill each other with whatever means one can imagine. I wish for my children to be children first and foremost; Later, they can be adults and make all the mistakes they want to. I hope for the same upbringing that I have lovingly experienced for them. As Abuela Manuela always says, "If it ain't broke, do not attempt to fix it."

Where this saying came from, I have no idea; perhaps from one of the countless movies she loves to watch in her little bedroom.

I focused my thoughts on the stranger in front of me. He had his mobile in one hand and used his fingers adeptly to type in some of the keys. I leaned forward and I saw that he had Google Translate open on the screen.

I looked up again and the man's lips are moving up and down, and I realise he has been speaking to me; I smile up at him and in broken Spanish, I understand him saying: "Wow, Señora, a lot of work for you on this little mountain road, and you are doing an excellent job, too."

I replied with my chest proudly and with great pleasure, "Thank you, señor, for your compliment; indeed, the mountain is little in my hands today."

He ventured to reply again in Spanish, "Forgive me, Señora, but my Spanish is not perfect, I heavily rely on Google Translate to assist me and I like to practice often with everyone I meet."

I replied, "Calm down, señor, your Spanish is perfect today."

He smiled at understanding my words and waved goodbye as he finally said, "Bye, and good day to you and your family."

Oh, what a lovely experience. I can't wait until Sunday to come back and relate this occasion to my Tios in London.

*****

## 15: I am a Home full of eternal wishes for a good story

*I* am a home situated almost at the end of the pueblo on the straight part of the ridge heading towards the new road that takes all travellers directly up and down the mountain at a more leisurely pace for most.

Due to the level surface, vehicles do not need to strain themselves going up or down. Even cyclists can treat the road as expected for a short time. They feel the need only to turn their pedals with their feet in calm movements.

There are no more straining muscles; that time you have passed when facing downhill. But it is, of course, a different matter when facing the start of the uphill climb.

The bravest need to steel their hearts for the colossus challenge of the mountain. It's what attracts them week after week for many years until the legs stop and refuse to endure any more punishment.

There begins the resemblance of a footpath on the left side of the road facing towards the city three kilometres away. Often, young men and women wearing nurse's outfits can be seen going into and leaving my home.

Locally it is called Hogar Cristales, a home for Christian people who are now coming to the end of their lives.

The walking young are answering their call to assist the old folk in meeting their beloved maker peacefully.

It was built during the time of Simon Bolivar, our famous Liberator. Who, back in the same period, knew Emperor Napoleon, who was pretty occupied being defeated at the Battle of Waterloo by the renowned English warrior The 1st Duke of Wellington, who was also known as Arthur Wellesley.

How do I know this?

Well, in every care home in the world, many older adults know many such things, and my home is no exception.

One of the memorable inhabitants was a veteran soldier who fought many times with Bolivar. According to him, he rose in the ranks to Master Sergeant of a cannon regiment. He fought alongside Bolivar's armies in all campaigns, including Ecuador, Bolivia, Peru, Venezuela, and, of course, Panama which at that time was part of Colombia.

He often sat talking near the old drawing room to anyone who would listen to his tales of battles and the history at that time. Many of the young nurses would sit quietly while the older man talked about what he knew.

"As a Master Sergeant of a cannon regiment fighting alongside the great Liberator Simon Bolivar against Spanish rule, a typical fighting day is both intense and strategically demanding. Allow me to describe the exhilarating and arduous experience."

"The day begins before dawn, as the first rays of sunlight peek over the horizon. The men of our regiment rise swiftly from their makeshift quarters, the taste of determination and anticipation filling the crisp morning air. We gather together, brushing off the remnants of sleep, and don our uniforms, proudly displaying red, yellow, and blue, the patriotic colours of our cause."

"With the regiment assembled, we receive a briefing from our commanding officers. Maps are unfolded upon rough-hewn tables, illustrating the terrain upon which we will clash with our Spanish adversaries. Intelligence reports are analysed, and strategies for the day's battle are discussed with meticulous attention to detail."

"Awaiting the arrival of the sun, we march as one towards our designated positions, cannons and artillery in tow. The rhythmic sound of the drums resonates through the air, harmonising with the collective footsteps of our dedicated soldiers. We march with discipline and determination, knowing our purpose is to free our oppressed countrymen from the shackles of colonial rule."

"Upon reaching our assigned vantage point, the regiment swiftly readies its cannons. These formidable weapons, symbols of our strength and resilience, stand tall and majestically, each crew meticulously preparing their artillery pieces. Smoke-stained faces, etched with a mix of unwavering focus and steely determination, attest to the calibre of warriors we have become."

"As the battle begins, explosions reverberate through the land, shaking the surrounding trees and sending birds fleeing from their perches. The sound of musket fire fills the air, intermingling with the cacophony of war cries and cannon blasts. Amidst this chaos, the disciplined efficiency of our regiment remains unwavering."

"Shouts of command pierce through the tumultuous symphony of battle as the cannons are unleashed upon the enemy. The deafening boom of each discharge masks the cries of both fallen comrades and retreating foes. The smell of acrid gunpowder mixes with the scent of burning buildings and the earthy aroma of churned soil, immersing us in the raw reality of combat."

"With each well-aimed shot, we watch as enemy lines crumble, their formations disintegrating under the relentless barrage. Our cannons breach fortifications, scattering soldiers and shattering the illusion of Spanish invincibility. The deafening roar of victory echoes through the countryside, invigorating our spirits and pushing us to fight harder."

"Throughout the day, we tirelessly load and reload our cannons, ensuring that each shot counts. Fatigue tugs at our bodies and minds, but our determination carries us through. We rally together, encouraged by the words of our officers and the knowledge that we fight not only for our lives but for the freedom and sovereignty of our homeland."

"As dusk settles upon the battlefield, weary but undefeated, we gather what remains of our strength and secure our positions. The day has brought both triumph and sacrifice as the toll of battle is etched onto the faces of fallen comrades. Our victories are hard-earned, and we honour their memory in our hearts."

"In the fading light, we reflect upon the day's events, knowing that tomorrow will bring new challenges. Yet, with the undying spirit of liberty burning within us, we march onward, resolve in our mission to secure a brighter future for all who call this nation their home."

"We did this for our leader, Simon Bolivar, who was a Venezuelan soldier and later Statesman. He was born near my village on the 24th of July 1783, and he died on a horrible day in December 1830. in Santa Marta, Colombia. "

"Yes, I am Venezuelan too, and I was born 5 years before him. Where he lived for only 47 years. I am still here at 95 years."

How much longer I have, I am not sure, but I did do well compared to him and his favourite woman, confidante, and ardent lover, Manuela Sáenz." One excited female nurse perked up and requested a little too loudly, "Please tell me more about this woman. I know her name but little else. Why was she famous?"

"Okay, my knowledge is not, of course, total. Much of what I am going to say is based on the many stories we have all heard; some may be true, some may be exaggerated, and some may well be incorrect. But I prefer my version over anyone else's as I was there when she was there." From the very start, Antonia Manuela Sáenz y Aizpuru, more commonly known throughout history as Manuela Sáenz, was indeed the prettiest revolutionary and the finest horse rider I have ever seen. Her use of the sword was legendary."

"She was born on the 27th of December 1797 in Quito, which at that time was part of the Spanish Viceroy of New Granada. You would know this now as Ecuador."

"She died in a small town called Paita in Peru on the 23rd of November 1856."

"In 1822, when Manuela was only 25, she decided to marry an English Army Officer and Businessman named James Thorne. It did not last long due to the more powerful pull of the Independence struggle against Spanish rule. She soon ditched the marriage and left to join the revolution that was taking place in Lima."

"It was here in Peru that both Manuela and Simon first laid eyes on each other. As you can surmise, it was not long before Manuela became a staunch supporter of the revolutionary causes, and Bolivar was quick to trust and admire his new companion."

"She actively participated in the independence movement, assisting Simon Bolivar in various ways, including delivering important messages, nursing wounded soldiers, and even participating in various skirmishes and battles with the Spanish."

"It was rumoured on many occasions that she saved him from cowardly assassins. Imagine such a strong and resourceful woman fighting your corner while you escape to fight another day."

The most famous account of her courage occurred on the 24th of May 1828, where it is said she saved Bolivar's life by intercepting an attacker and shielding Bolivar, earning her the nickname "The Liberator of the Liberator."

The Master Sergeant paused and drank from his near-to-hand jug of cool water.

"It is a shame that you young people have almost lost her from your history. The reason is simple and sad. Despite her significant contributions, Manuela's involvement in the political sphere was often criticised and led to much controversy. Sadly, her relationship with Bolivar and her active role in politics was seen as unbecoming for a woman of her time."

"Just think for a moment: after Bolivar's demise, she was marginalised and found herself in poverty."

"But remember, Manuela is a courageous fighter; in her later years, she sought recognition for her contributions but faced opposition from many political adversaries who refused to acknowledge her role and downplayed her significance. It was only recently that her actions and contributions were rediscovered, and she was posthumously recognised as a true heroine of South American independence."

At this point in his astounding history and that of those famous around him, he decided to stop and go to the toilet to relieve himself. On his return, he sat and continued where he had left off.

"Now Bolivar, by today's standard, had packed a lot of action in his short life, far too much for me to talk about here to you all."

"He was and will always be known as El Libertador (The Liberator) because he simply never conquered countries. He liberated them from the dreaded and cruel Spanish Rule."

"I may be wrong in my calculations, but I believe he fought in over 46 different battles, and never once did he sustain a bullet or sword wound from any of his opponents, and you can imagine there were many that were aimed at him over those years."

*****

"I was one of his earliest supporters and later regarded as a gallant soldier by many. Like him, I was never hurt in battle, nor was Pio, his lifelong companion and trusted manservant. He had sworn to be by his side when Bolivar had reached the tender age of nine."

"Little did Pio realise what life promise would entail. Pio's full name was José Palacios, and he was of Afro-Venezuelan descent. His birth is reported to have been around 1785, but his place of birth and the exact date are lost to history."

"Throughout their travels and campaigns across South America together, Pio always supported Bolivar. He happily gave his undying dedication and unwavering loyalty and steadfastly shared a strong bond with his master. Pio's duties included attending to Bolivar's personal needs, organising his belongings, and ensuring his comfort during his many military campaigns and political endeavours."

Pio's presence and assistance were always on display to us mere soldiers. This was particularly significant during Bolivar's most challenging times. He was a constant companion, apart from when Manuela was close by. When he came to war, Pio provided not only practical assistance but also emotional support. He would often act as Bolivar's closest confidant, always there offering advice and solace during challenging moments.

It was rumoured that if you stood within arm's length during a battle between Bolivar and Pio, you were guaranteed never to be hurt. There was an aura surrounding them, and I was grateful on many occasions to see him on his beautiful horse directing his army to wherever there was the best strategic place and Pio standing ramrod defying anyone to try and pass his protective barrier." Another nurse raised his hand, and our Master sergeant paused to hear the question. "Sir, what happened to Pio?"

The veteran paused for a moment or two, trying to find the right words to answer the young nurse's question. That is a good question and one that is not often asked. Pio's story may be overshadowed by the larger-than-life figure of his master and friend, Simon Bolivar. Pio never left Bolivar's side. He was there still tending to his needs in Santa Marta back in 1830 when Bolivar breathed no more." After his death, Pio faithfully carried out his master's final wish for Pio to return to his homeland, Venezuela, and settle down in the city of Caracas. From here on, I am sad to say I have no idea what happened to Pio. Maybe one day we will all find out."

The same nurse raised his hand again, and without waiting, he asked, "Did you ever have the opportunity to sit and talk to Bolivar himself?"

"I remember one quiet evening; he joined us around the campfire. When asked if he liked being called the Liberator? He said," Of course, I am not here to conquer; that was the mistake Napoleon made. You cannot suppress men forever, so I will not try. I want to bring freedom to this vast South American continent; it is for others to govern behind me, hopefully as a federation of nations." "Hearing these words for the first time made us realise we were in the presence of a truly great man, and it made all of us more determined to follow him on his remarkable journey without any doubt."

Another nurse, praying he was not asking a stupid question, asked if it was true that he liberated six countries from the Spanish. "Yes, it is true. We liberated Venezuela, Colombia, Peru, Panama, Ecuador, and the area now known as Bolivia. In every village and town we came to as liberators, he was welcomed as the ultimate hero. Everyone hated and dreaded the Spanish regime and wanted change. Every village elder would greet him and shake his hand warmly."

"I read in a local newspaper in Bogotá once that the writer of the column considered him to be the greatest genius of our great continent; not only is he internationally known in his own right, but few figures before him in history or those in the future will be able to display that rare combination of strength, foresight, character, temperament and poetic power." Finally sensing his strength starting to sap away from his long regular sleeping pattern, he forced himself to sit upright and say, "It has taken my homeland of Venezuela nine years after Bolivar's demise for them to realise that it had lost a very great man".

*****

"I'm sorry, sir. Please excuse me. My name is Diego, and I have been a nurse here for the past two years. I have often heard you reminisce about the days of your youth and your memories of the famous man. I would often go home and retell what I have learned from you to my grandfather, who is now a retired history teacher. "Why thank you, Diego? You have a question that needs answering?"

"Indeed, I do. You mentioned Bolivar had a manservant named José Palacio, and this José had a nickname of Pio."

"Yes, that is correct."

Diego, now squirming in his chair, collected every ounce of courage he could muster and asked, "Is this Pio, the same Pio who tried to assassinate Bolivar? If so, was it true he was executed? And finally, who was Hipolita? Was she the only black servant who raised Bolivar for the first years of his life and certainly after his mother had passed away?"

The older man disappeared into his ageing memory, trying to find answers to questions long forgotten. What must have seemed a lifetime for all watching and waiting for him to respond held their breath. Finally, the old man's eyes appeared to have come into focus, and he slowly began to speak: "Please forgive me. It has been a very long time since I have thought about the name Pio."

He continued, "There was a fair number of attempts to assassinate our Liberator. The one you may be referring to was indeed attempted by a man named Pio. It happened when both of them were renting a small room in a place called Curacao. The Impoverished furniture only consisted of two hammocks and some old rotting tables and chairs."

"On one particular evening, while Bolivar's manservant Pio was out frequenting the local bars and getting as drunk as humanly possible. His owner, Bolivar, had decided to move to another location that fit his status. He had failed to leave a note of this unexpected decision, and the next visitor was Felix Amestoy, a former paymaster who wished to gain monies owed by his General."

"Noting Bolivar was nowhere to be seen, he thought it prudent to stay put and await the Liberator's return. At some point, he took a shine to the hammock and thought it was okay to take a nap."

At this next point, the older man decided he needed some more of the cool water in front of him and reached out. After quenching his patched lips, he continued with the story, "Regrettably for Felix, he fell into a deep sleep and did not hear the approaching Pio with a raised knife in one hand, and fatally he was slain."

Diego leaned forward, "What happened next?"

"Patience, young man, give this old man a chance to tell you. Pio, it turned out, had been paid a king's ransom to kill his master by unknown people. His first thought on believing he had done the evil deed, was to take off and disappear from sight."

"Eventually, Pio was captured and faced a court hearing. It was here he learned he had, in fact, failed to assassinate Bolivar. It did not take long for Pio to be convicted and sentenced to hang. For good measure, the executioners also chopped off his head, fixed it to a stake and placed it where everyone could see it."

"So, to answer your first question, was José actually Pio? I cannot say. History and fiction sometimes get muddled up. I may well have been wrong, but you have to wonder if there could have been two José Palacios, both of them black manservants to the famous Liberator who referred to them as Pio."

"As for the lady you mentioned. I think you said Hipolita Bolivar. Yes, she did indeed raise and nurse the early Bolivar as his parents, Don Juan Vicente de Bolivar and Dona Maria de la Concepción Palacios y Blanco, had both perished from Tuberculosis before he had reached nine. His father had died when he was only three, leaving Hipolita as one of only two capable of enslaving black nurses to ensure his survival. The other being another slave named Matea."

A young female nurse spoke up with excitement and curiosity, "Please, sir, could you tell us about Hipolita and Matea? What became of them both?"

The Master Sergeant turned to face the young nurse who had fed him this evening. He smiled up at her, knowing she would love what he would say next.

"Young lady, both Hipolita and Matea were two wonderful nurses, as you undoubtedly are becoming. I knew both women well. I will start with Hipolita. I believe she was born in Aragua in 1763. She was a slave to the Bolivar and Palacio families, and three years before Bolivar died, she also died in the Venezuelan city of Caracas."

"Now I will tell you about Matea. She was born ten years later than Hipolita in a place called San Jose de Tiznado. She lived a very long life, mostly as an enslaved nurse with the Bolivars. At one point, she was given freedom by His Excellency, but she decided life would be too hard and that her chances of survival would be almost nonexistent. She indeed made the right choice as Matea lived to the ripe old age of 112 years!"

"Matea moved with Bolivar's sister, Maria Antonia Bolivar, and they settled in Havana together. She also passed away in Caracas back in 1889. I remember in the same church on the day they buried the Liberator; I witnessed Matea laying a wreath in "his honour."

The room went quiet, and no one dared ask another question of the dying Master Sergeant. It was time for him to rest, and slowly, the nurses rose and moved away.

I, the home, eventually learned from another patient many years later due to political unrest and various circumstances. The request to return Bolivar's body to them for burial in his homeland stood ignored for a generation and more.

Colombia did graciously comply more than a century later, in 1947, when Bolivar's remains were finally put to rest in the National Pantheon in Caracas.

"But with the words "We'll give you his body, but we will keep his heart." Looking back to the Master Sergeant's time again, it was now the point where his mind was on a battlefield, deep within his memory.

He was no longer aware of the young people around him. At this time, they all quietly moved away and tended to the other older people who needed to be washed and changed for their nightly sleep. The mosquito nets were above each bed, including the old warrior who was at the side of the great man.

I do remember that he died shortly after. For many years that followed, the stories each older person relayed during his or her afternoon rest period did not quite match up to what the old Venezuelan Master Sergeant did during his time here. That is until a certain Hector arrived.

*****

## 16: I am Hector who also lived in a Home for the Elderly

*F*ast-forward to a time closer to now and another elderly man. Only this one could once speak many languages, such as Spanish, English, Portuguese, German, and French. His name was Hector Rodriguez. Why do I remember his name and not the Master sergeant?

Simple, time is catching up with my memory, too. Like Hector, I, too, may be showing signs of becoming an Alzheimer's sufferer.

The walls of my home have changed much over the years to the point where only I know what it originally looked like, and even then, images are starting to fade with my deteriorating health.

The purpose is still the same. People have gotten older, and families need to decide when it is best to send each one to a place like mine. There, the relatives could relax in the knowledge that the older person was now in a good place for them.

Some of these older people were even lucky if the said families continued to visit them to the very end, but in modern times like now, that has become a rarity.

Anyway, I am not here to judge morals. I am here to listen and learn about this vast history, and I am pleased to say I see each person as a book of life; each story is different from the next, and it does not matter how mundane life is.

It is the delivery and conviction of the truth that I love to hear. This Hector Rodriguez, for much of his time here, was an outstanding example.

Hector appears to have led an unusual life. He was born in Manizales. At that time, his family were poor farmers harvesting coffee beans on a small patch of land on the side of the mountain. The crop was only sometimes regular. It often depended on the rainfall and how big and strong the weeds became.

At times, the price for their meagre crop helped them through the coming months—often, it didn't.

From an early age, after attending the local school and discovering that there were sailing ships, and some very big ones, too, Hector decided that maybe he could get a job with one of them, see the world, and bring back riches from his travels for his beleaguered family.

On one quiet evening, when the family had gone to sleep hungry because there was not enough food to share with his brothers and sisters, he waited for the right moment when everyone was asleep.

Hector rose like a cat and was gone in seconds.

He dared not look back in case his will continued to diminish. He had decided to walk to his intended destination, Cartagena, a port in the north of the country.

Hector estimated it was going to take many months to get there.

Certainly, by walking, so he hitched rides with trucks and buses; sometimes, the drivers knew he was there, but often, they didn't.

Fruit was easy to find; he only had to wait until dusk, and he could pick it from the trees and eat it. He was already thin, so eating the odd vegetable helped him with his vitamins.

Meat was the real problem; he knew he must have protein. So, he could only do what he had to do, and at times, he would distract someone and steal their food.

He could run fast and always outran the person who had just lost his meal for the day. Walking high up on that volcanic mountain gave him the gift of running fast.

The days became weeks, and eventually, he arrived at his first sight of the sea. The books in class could not have prepared him for the vision of the waves.

His initial reaction was fear, but he knew he had to move forward if he was going to overcome this emotion. As he did, his heart started to beat louder and faster. He ignored this, but his legs and arms began to fail him.

He roared like a jungle cat and followed his voice closer to the rolling waves. As their noise increased, his roars also became louder, trying to match the velocity of the endless movement of the waves.

Finally, he was at the edge, he looked down, and the sea started to overlap his feet.

The feel of the sea was purifying for him, and the chill of his skin made him gulp. Now, it was time to conquer, so he ran as fast as he could into the waves, and before long, he was waist-high and struggling to move forward.

Then he remembered he could not swim.

Panic arose instantly, and he turned to race back to safety, but a giant wall of water, just taller than him, overlapped and smashed into his little frame.

His feet left the ground, and he was like an arrow racing to the beach.

Soon, he was lying there choking on the salty taste of the water, but he was still alive. He had overcome his fear. One day, he would learn how to swim properly; until then, he would treat the sea with respect.

It took him the next five days watching silently how the port worked, and eventually, he witnessed an opportunity to become a stowaway on board one of the larger freighters. He waited for the right moment and was on board without anyone realising there was someone small and thin not on their crew or passenger manifests.

The freighter set sail the next day bound for England. Hector was unaware of its destination. He had been avoiding all contact with anyone. The problem was the need to go to the toilet, and his food would not last more than another meal. So, finally, on the third day at sea, he decided it was time to declare his presence. As he did so, fate had a twist in it that Hector had not imagined.

Hector, a young and adventurous spirit, found himself in a situation no child should experience – the perils of becoming seasick for the first time amidst a raging Atlantic storm. The journey that unfolded for this small stowaway was nothing short of daunting.

As the turbulent waves battered against the creaking hull of the ship, Hector struggled to maintain his balance. Already trembling from the sheer force of the storm, his stomach churned, and he felt an unsettling dizziness settle within him. It was the onset of seasickness, a ghastly sensation he had never before encountered.

The ship pitched and rolled, mercilessly testing Hector's resilience. With every surge of the tempestuous sea, his fragile body was thrown about like a puppet on strings. Holding on to anything available, he clung desperately to the rope railing, his knuckles turning white from the strain.

As the storm intensified, the chaos and disarray multiplied. The once stable vessel was now a battleground of relentless wind and crashing waves. The howling gusts whipped around Hector, who battled the urge to retch him with all his might. The sea spray lashed his face, stinging his eyes as if nature itself was mocking his predicament.

The thought of being discovered as a stowaway, hidden away in the bowels of the ship, added another layer of apprehension to Hector's already turbulent emotions. Determined to remain invisible, he pressed against the damp wooden wall, his heart pounding with fear. Every step of the ship's violent dance threatened to expose him to the crew above.

The relentless assault of the storm, combined with the torment of seasickness, battered Hector's spirit from him. Nausea overwhelmed him, twisting his insides and leaving him weak and helpless. He was yearning silently for the storm to cease, praying for a moment of respite from this merciless order.

Amidst the chaos, Gabriel, a sympathetic crew member, discovered the hidden boy. Seeing Hector's distressed state, Gabriel took pity and provided comfort. He guided Hector to a calmer area of the ship, away from the relentless sway and rocking motion. Gabriel's gentle encouragement offered a glimmer of solace as he assured Hector that the storm would eventually pass.

Hector's suffering, though agonising, became a pivotal learning experience. Through his first encounter with seasickness in the midst of a treacherous storm, he acquired a newfound appreciation for the power and unpredictability of the ocean. And as the tempest slowly subsided, his queasiness eventually waned, leaving behind a resilient young boy who had weathered the storm both within and without.

*****

When Gabriel presented him to the merchant captain, the old seafaring face just looked down at sorrowful-looking wretch for some time. Eventually, the Captain beckoned to his First Mate, Noah, to find him something to do to earn his place on the ship and to make sure he washed, as he could smell the little wretch from a mile away.

Hector's new important job turned out to be cleaning the crew's kitchen. Over the next few weeks, Hector learned how to scrub a kitchen from top to bottom, no matter what the weather.

Chef Pierre, a jolly sort, quickly guided the youngster and taught him how to make the massive number of loaves of bread the crew devoured weekly.

He learned to speak a little French as Pierre, being a native speaker, spoke it better than Spanish. Soon, both were communicating in the strangest language known to man. Despite this, Hector learned the world was at war for the second time in over 20 years.

The battlefields of Europe were flushed with the dead once again. The last war took over five years to stop, and this one looked like it would go the same way.

Hector wondered if the ship was in danger, and judging by the look on Pierre's face, it was. He confirmed that the freighter was carrying important foodstuffs to England, an island that desperately needed food for its people and army.

But out there in the dark, cruel sea lay a hidden danger called U Boats.

These weapons of destruction hunted in packs and were always looking out for tankers and ships with cargo. The German high command deemed it a priority to starve its enemy into surrender.

This was also the first time Hector heard the name Winston Leonard Spencer Churchill. The other crew members, such as Gabriel and Noah, talked about him constantly and listened to his broadcasts on the ship's radio.

*****

*"Ladies and Gentlemen, I stand before you today as the voice of a grateful nation to express our most profound appreciation and admiration for your unwavering courage and unparalleled dedication. As the brave merchant mariners who have navigated the treacherous seas amidst the storms of war, you have exemplified the true spirit of the British people.*

*In these perilous times, you serve as the backbone of our maritime fleet, the silent heroes who risk life and limb to ensure that our nation is supplied, safeguarded, and resilient against the ravages of conflict. Your unwavering resolve has been nothing short of extraordinary as you navigate the dangerous waters, evading enemy fire and facing the constant threat of torpedo attacks.*

*I need not remind you of the challenges that lie ahead, the countless thousands you will traverse, and the countless lives you will touch. Each voyage you undertake is a testament to your indomitable spirit, a spirit that has made Britain strong in its darkest hours.*

*Our island nation owes a colossal debt to your selflessness and bravery. From the depths of my heart, I extend my sincerest gratitude to each and every one of you who has risen to the call of duty, kept the vital supply lines open, and refused to let adversity sink your spirit.*

*You are the lifeline that sustains and nourishes our people. Your commitment to duty is a flame that burns bright amidst the shadows of war. Your sacrifices and tireless efforts do not go unnoticed. We honour you, we stand beside you, and we will never cease to support you.*

*Know that the people of England, from the cities to the remotest corners of our land, hold you in the highest regard. Your courage echoes through the annals of history, inspiring generations to come."*

Churchill was heard to pause and reflect on his next message, which he delivered with clear enunciation and powerful delivery to all who listened to his British deep, commanding, and authoritative accent.

*In the face of adversity, you have epitomised Horace's words: "Ingenuity and courage spring from within." Your unyielding determination has not only served as a beacon of hope but also as a powerful testament to the indomitable spirit that defines our nation.*

*In this struggle, we are all united, bound together by a common purpose to protect and preserve the freedom we hold dear. United, we shall prevail. Together, we will overcome the challenges that lie before us.*

*From the depths of my soul, I extend my deepest and most heartfelt thanks to you, the courageous merchant mariners of England. May the winds be ever in your favour, the waves gentle beneath your hull, and may your journeys be safe.*

*God bless you all.*

*Sir Winston Churchill.*

Although many struggled to understand all his words, the way he said them made them know he was their true friend and needed all their help urgently.

*****

As the ship meandered closer to Europe, the weather became increasingly violent again. Waves started to rise against the sides of the ship. The front often disappeared below the waves and, a brief moment later, suddenly reappeared again. Much to Hector's relief.

The cold started to become more unbearable, and Hector became an unofficial mascot, and oversized clothes were reserved for him.

They were given on the condition that he paraded around the crew's quarters. He always looked funny in his man-size boots and baggy trousers. His sea jacket cascaded over his upper body, and his hat and scarf hid his head from view.

Gabriel, Noah, and Pierre would laugh and choke with false alarms of a monster in their midst, but everyone knew who this motley-looking figure was.

After the next storm the ship ploughed through, Hector had managed to find his sea legs. Now, he was becoming an asset to the crew and not a hindrance. Ice began to appear on all areas of the vessel, and Hector learned how a pair of gloves would become an essential piece of personal equipment while at sea. He was so relieved when he knew how they would protect his hands from the dreaded ice.

Late one night, when the sea was calm, and the moon was out lighting up the sky, the Captain ordered most of the men to watch the horizon for any signs of the enemy.

The ship had now entered the hunting ground of the U-boats.

They did not have to wait long for the evidence of them being active.

At three in the morning, another ship silhouetted on the horizon was struck by two torpedoes almost simultaneously, resulting in two huge explosions, one at the bow and the other just before the stern, creating many violent-looking colours of destruction.

The night sky and its darkness did not take long to return, except the silhouette. That was gone from view forever more.

Later, one of our crew members called alarmingly to report that a torpedo was seen racing towards the stern of their ship. The Captain's orders to commence evasive weaving action were not quick enough, and the torpedo struck. There was a thud but no explosion.

The unthinkable had happened; a dud had hit them.

The Captain ordered his crew to continue with evasive action, "Head to the mouth of the Irish Sea, and race as fast as possible up the Straits between England and Ireland."

U-boats preferred to go a different way. There was the possibility of being trapped by destroyers of the British Navy and their dreaded depth charges. Furthermore, the U-boat captains knew there was always another ship to chase and destroy in the busier straights of the English Channel between England and France.

Hector's ship eventually arrived safely at Bristol's port. Once docked and secured, the Captain gave the crew permission to go ashore and find their land legs again.

It did feel weird for Hector and Gabriel not to have to keep an eye on their balance anymore. Noah, because of his vast experience of seagoing, never showed any emotion about not swaying on dry land.

That night, the small group discovered English ale. They found fish and chips, and later, Hector alone discovered what a lady of the night was for.

All in that order, too.

But if Hector was truthful, he loved the fish and chips the most.

The cargo took two days to unload, and the Captain offered a good wage to board for the return trip to South America. All three signed up.

England was too cold for them and too dangerous with the nightly bombings over the docks and industrial areas of Bristol. Each decided for their differing reasons that the freighter was a good substitute for a home. It was a more inviting prospect, and the money they each would save and earn would help. In Hector's imagination, his family would buy more land and some new equipment such as a pulping machine, drying racks, and a hulling machine to remove the parchment layers from the coffee beans.

The return trip went without any problems, and Hector learned more about cooking from the now often-drunk Pierre. He also discovered more about the early life of his newly acquired friend, Gabriel. When Hector first heard that the older boy was actually christened Gabriel Garcia Marquez. It meant nothing to either Hector or Gabriel, except it sounded like a lovely name to have.

Years later, Hector discovered that Colombia also would have a Gabriel Garcia Marquez. Only this one would go on to be the celebrated and well-loved novelist. This writer's full name was to be Gabriel José de la Concordia García Márquez. Hector had so much fun whenever he talked to his friend about him, and he would always ask the question, "So, Gabo, what have you written lately?"

During the weeks that followed, Gabriel and Hector found themselves on the same rota for U-boat watching. So far, they had seen none. On one particular icy night shift, when thankfully the sea was calm and the sky was clear, they both could scan the horizon and take advantage of the full moon.

Gabriel was on the port side while Hector was scanning the horizon to the starboard side.

Both were deep in their individual thoughts, and Hector broke the silence between them. "Gabriel, when I was first discovered by you and over the next few weeks, I noticed you always seemed reserved, quiet, and yet disturbed. May I ask what was making you this way?"

Gabriel continued looking ahead as if he had not heard the question or because he had decided to ignore it.

Hector wanted to know Gabriel's history about him, and yes, he desired a friend with whom he could confide. He was about to pluck up the courage again to repeat the question when Gabriel stopped him in his tracks by turning and speaking warmly to Hector.

"It was clear when you were discovered as a stowaway you were but a child. I could see no reason to trust you. I chose instead to make myself amused by watching you grow in stature as each day passed. The day you drank the ale, ate the fish and chips, and eagerly visited the whore house confirmed my deep pleasure in seeing you learn so much in such a short time."

He went on, "And by the way, it was not me but Noah who thrust you toward Dirty Gerty and her outstretched flabby arms."

Hector exclaimed and cried out, "Please, do not remind me! "I prefer to remember her if I have to, like Marlene Dietrich. You know that sultry looking singing beauty from Germany!"

Both roared with laughter. Gabriel managed to stutter, "Hahaha, I will keep your secret. It is a good one. But I promise to remind you from time to time of the sheer pleasure of seeing the look on your face of her when Dirty Gerty wrapped those massive tentacles around you, and those vast painted red lips sucked in your nose!

Both were now in a fit of giggles, the images of the momentous night when Hector became a man clearly in each of their minds.

The presence of the Captain nearby went unseen until he had heard enough of their escapades back in Bristol. He smiled at how happy they both were. Quietly, he moved forward, presenting himself in a way so as not to cause alarm to either young men whom he happened to wish were his sons.

"OK, boys, don't forget what a crucial role you both are playing tonight in keeping me and all the crew safe."

The Captain moved past both and began scanning the horizon in all directions. He appeared to see deeper and further than his two young crew members had. Seeing such an experienced man on display gave both Hector and Gabriel confidence in being protected and guided by a real expert on the open seas.

Without turning back, the Captain remarked with humour in his voice, "Ah, dreaming of Marlene Dietrich, eh? Well, I hope you navigated through that dream safely, Hector! Just remember, there's no room for distractions on this ship – we've got a course to steer and no time for Hollywood stars!" This light-hearted comment elicited a chuckle from both Hector and Gabriel and lightened the mood. Before either of them could comment or ask questions further, the intrepid sea dog of a Captain turned and headed back towards his cabin.

He was silent and appeared satisfied they would all survive the night.

It was another ten minutes before Gabriel spoke. "I am older than you by five years. I have probably seen more unrest than you have. I heard you talk about your family back home, and never did I hear you mention family disruptions apart from the economic ones."

Hector said nothing. He felt it was time to listen.

*****

"For me, it has been different. For starters, my father was German, and my mother was Argentinian. I was the only child, and I do not know any of my possible extended family. Life for me has been of survival by my own wits."

"You say your father and mother was."

"True, I did. Both were killed in a car accident involving a horse and cart."

"A horse?"

"Believe it or not, the damn beast decided to have a heart attack and collapsed on top of the open-topped sports car they were in. The animal rolled over the bonnet and landed on top of my parents."

"Were you there?"

"No, I was at a worker's rally in the city of Buenos Aires. The Police had arrested me for breaching the peace. I was in a cell waiting to be taken to court."

Gabriel paused for a moment and continued, "The Policeman informed me of my loss and decided to release me to arrange my parent's funerals. He did say I would be recalled at a later date to face the magistrates."

"What did you do?"

"Well, with the help of the local Mayor, his wife and the local community, we buried my mother and father."

"A few weeks went by, and the local postman arrived with a summons to attend the court. I decided not to go. I headed down to the docks, sought a merchant ship and signed on as a deckhand. I suspect there is a warrant out for my arrest. So going back is not an attractive proposition."

"What are you going to do?"

"Oh, I will sail with the Captain until this war is over, and maybe I will come and find my adventurous little Colombian stowaway and continue this budding friendship."

They both turned, smiled, and shook hands. Indeed, a friendship had begun that remained strong for the rest of their lives.

*****

On arriving back into port again, the Captain was true to his word and paid his men handsomely and forthrightly.

He did invite Hector to stay on, but he wanted to return home. Gabriel was still determining what to decide, and Noah was easy to please. He was a single guy with no ties to make him stay on land. In truth, Gabriel loved everything the oceans could offer and went below decks to organise his weekly wash. Gabriel did not want to walk away from his friend Hector, but he was not ready yet to walk away from life at sea.

Life at sea would give all three many stories to tell in the years to come.

For now, Hector wanted the tranquillity of the mountain of Manizales. Maybe he would adventure again one day.

*****

As it happened, Hector never did. Within five years, he was married and had children to care for him in his advancing years.

Hector prospered in the coffee business, and the income helped him study and learn more about history and education. He started teaching part-time to the children of his village and, in time, became invaluable to the village elders.

Soon, he was teaching history and English to the locals. Hector did not become wealthy in monetary terms from such work, but in words of gratitude and praise, he did indeed become rich.

Once, while he was in the local town having his haircut, Hector picked up a magazine. The front cover showed the funeral of the famous Winston Churchill.

Hector opened the feature that described the famous man. He read that Winston was born in 1874 and died in 1965. Hector looked at the magazine's date, and he could see it was over a year old.

This was going to be the World Cup year of 1966, and Hector was getting excited that the tournament was approaching.

He learned that the great man had attended a school in Harrow and had actually had military officer training at Sandhurst. Later, Winston became a War correspondent, first in the Boer war between the Dutch settlers in Africa and England.

It was while he was there that he was captured by a Boer soldier who later turned out to be Louis Botha, the future and first Prime Minister of the Union of South Africa. Imagine this soldier could so quickly have shot the future Prime Minister of England who spearheaded the victory against Adolf Hitler.

Hector had smiled at the very next picture in the magazine showing the latest South African President called Charles Robberts Swart, nicknamed Blackie standing side by side with Sir Winston. Both were photographed enjoying their shared passion for oil painting. Blackie and Winston were actually oil painting a scene of tranquillity together.

Hector was taken by surprise when reading of Charles Robberts Swart who was born on 5 December 1894 in Winburg, Orange Free State, and who grew up in a conservative Afrikaner household. Swart's nickname, "Blackie," was derived from his dark complexion, which he inherited from his Indonesian ancestors. Despite his skin colour distinguishing him from the typical stereotype of Afrikaners being predominantly white, Swart strongly identified with his Afrikaner heritage and embraced his cultural roots.

In his early years, Swart was deeply involved in student activism. He joined the Afrikaner Broederbond and became an influential leader within the organisation. He completed his law degree at the University of the Free State and went on to establish a successful legal practice.

Swart began his political career as a member of the National Party in the Orange Free State Province. He served as a Member of Parliament from 1933 until 1961, continuously representing the interests of his constituents. Known for his conservative ideals and commitment to Afrikaner nationalism, he was highly regarded within the party.

Swart's political achievements culminated in his becoming the first President of the Republic of South Africa in 1961, following the country's withdrawal from the British Commonwealth and the adoption of a republican form of government. As President, he embodied the values of apartheid, the racially discriminatory policy that characterised much of South African governance during that time.

During his Presidency, Swart supported policies that enforced racial segregation, limited the rights and opportunities of non-white South Africans, and perpetuated institutionalised racism. His government implemented apartheid laws that further marginalised black South Africans, leading to widespread protests and international condemnation.

Despite his controversial political beliefs and the criticism he faced, Swart remained a respected figure within the Afrikaner community. He advocated for the preservation of the Afrikaans language and culture, which he saw as integral to the survival of the Afrikaner people.

Swart's presidency would end in 1967 where he retired from politics. He subsequently retired from public life and spent his remaining years in retirement.

*****

Hector continued turning the pages and stop to read the following: Just like Bolivar before him, Churchill had proven to be a man of immense strength, fortitude, daring, poetic and loved by all. He was an accomplished writer, and he won his Nobel Prize in Literature in 1953 for his historical and biographical works.

His humour was legendary in the Halls of Westminster. One such story was during a heated parliamentary debate on economic policy. In response to a particularly long-winded and convoluted question from an opponent, Churchill quipped: "I may be drunk, Miss, but in the morning, I will be sober, and you will still be ugly." The unexpected one-liner diffused tension and brought a moment of comic relief to the otherwise serious discussion.

Another example of his humour winning the day was when he was delivering a speech to the House of Commons during World War II. As tensions ran high, Churchill lightened the mood by saying: "If you're going through hell, keep going!" The witty remark garnered laughter and lifted the spirits of many present.

As a painter, in his lifetime, he produced over 600 pieces of art. Some were deemed so good they went on to be displayed in exhibitions around the world.

He is loved and admired for his powerful and eloquent oratory skills. Many of his speeches became a source of inspiration for many. His famous speeches, such as the "We Shall Fight on the Beaches" address, are still remembered today.

*Even though large tracts of Europe and many old and famous States have fallen or may fall into the grip of the Gestapo and all the odious apparatus of Nazi rule, we shall not flag or fail.*

*We shall go on to the end; we shall fight in France, we shall fight on the seas and oceans, we shall fight with growing confidence and growing strength in the air, we shall defend our Island, whatever the cost may be, we shall fight on the beaches, we shall fight on the landing grounds, we shall fight in the fields and in the streets, we shall fight in the hills;*

*we shall never surrender, and even if, which I do not for a moment believe, this Island or a large part of it were subjugated and starving, our Empire beyond the seas, armed and guarded by the British Fleet, would carry on the struggle, until, in God's good time, the New World, with all its power and might, steps forth to the rescue and the liberation of the old.*

Hector wondered when this "British Bulldog" ever found the time to accomplish so much in his life.

*****

Hector became one of my favourite inhabitants while with me; he told jokes often and many tales, some tall, some true. All the staff loved him, and when he died of aggressive Alzheimer's, which left him very much in a vegetative state, all his relatives and friends came down from the mountain of Manizales in a vast convoy of Willy Jeeps to honour his passing.

Life has been quiet again for some years after Hector's passing, and I have not had any engrossing life stories to listen to. Today, two new visitors came by separately. I instantly knew the first was an Englishman when he appeared in the morning sunlight, and the second one who arrived in the late afternoon turned out to be a pale-looking Argentinian.

The white-haired Englishman came to see one of our guests and stayed a few minutes. The Argentinian came to see Hector's final resting place and stayed at least three hours drinking cascara tea in celebration of his friend's life. He spent the rest of his time reading from a novel by a writer with the same name as his. The book title was "No One Writes to the Colonel."

I know this book well; Hector was consistently referring to it until his mind began to fail him. It is a novella that tells the story of an impoverished retired Colonel, a veteran of the Thousand Days' War. The Colonel still hopes to receive the pension he was promised some fifteen years earlier. The Colonel lives with his asthmatic wife in a small, poverty-stricken village under martial law.

What a beautiful gesture from this visitor. He must have been a true friend to Hector.

I liked the look of both of them and wonder if the day will come when both will be sitting here telling us their life stories. I await the future with anticipation.

*****

## 17: *I am Gabriel Garcia Marquez, but alas, not the famous one*

**Y**ou would all know the real "Gabo" is from Colombia, whereas I christened also Gabriel Garcia Marquez is in fact, from Argentina. In Hector's story, the Care Home mentions our growing friendship when we met on a freighter heading to England and the theatre of war in Europe.

To be fair to you readers, the care home, and the memory of Hector with his aggressive Alzheimer's did not know all of our illustrious stories. I would like a few moments of your time to enlighten you more. Yes, it was true I had already been on board the freighter for some time as I had met the Captain back in Buenos Aires. And it was there I became a member of the crew. It appears that I was following in my father's footsteps.

I, too, was looking for adventure. More about that later.

My father's ancestors originated from a small hamlet named Stockum in Germany. It was the gateway to the Mohne Reservoir with its colossal dam. Later, in 1943, this very dam suffered at the hands of the British Lancaster bombers and their specially designed "Bouncing Bombs."

In contrast, my mother's ancestors were rumoured to have been among the early settlers of Buenos Aires in 1580. However, the historical documents of the family line had been destroyed in a fire many years before, so now, I only have limited recollections of my mother.

My father had no idea either. Both of us relied on the scant knowledge that my mother offered from time to time. In 1920, my father, now a young man, wanted his life experiences to be full of adventures. He had escaped the killing fields of World War One as he was, but a boy and no one wanted him to lose his young life to a lost cause.

He researched the family world maps and listened to his elders as they talked about the vast, entire world and its endless opportunities for those who wished to explore.

At one point, they talked about South America and the growing European-styled city of Buenos Aires, which many were calling the "Paris of South America," with its ever-increasing port in Argentina.

Apparently, it was here that the local city had an open immigration policy that was in existence for over 100 years. Argentina was second only to the USA for accepting immigrants to its country.

My father heard his uncle remark on numerous occasions, "Buenos Aires seems to be the place where adventurers go to figure out their lives." As soon as he listened to those words, he knew his immediate future.

As he stepped off the ship onto the bustling streets of Buenos Aires, a mixture of excitement and trepidation filled his heart. It was 1921, and the echoes of World War I still haunted his memories of life so far. He had survived the horrors of the conflict, but the scars on his soul were deep and memorable.

Argentina was a far cry from the battlefields of Europe, and he hoped that this distant land would provide him with the chance to start a new and leave the nightmares of war behind. On board the slow-moving ship, he has heard stories of vast untouched landscapes, mysterious cultures, and potential adventures, and they called to his restless spirit.

As he strolled through the vibrant neighbourhoods, the rhythm of tango filled the air, captivating his senses. The city's energy was infectious, and he found himself creating a new rhythm within, one that matched the heartbeat of Buenos Aires.

Yet, beneath the façade of vivacity, he sensed something lurking in the shadows. The people he met spoke in hushed whispers, as if secrets whispered in the night. As a former soldier, his curiosity was piqued, and he felt compelled to unravel the mysteries hidden within this foreign land.

In the cafes and bars, he encountered a diverse mix of characters – adventurers, artists, and intriguing individuals who seemed to have tales to tell. The war had taught him to be vigilant, to watch for danger lurking in even the most unexpected places. But it had also taught him the resilience to face it head-on.

*****

Driven by a need for purpose, my father immersed himself in the local culture. He delved into the traditions of the gauchos, learning to ride and herd cattle on the expansive pampas. Their wild spirit resonated with his own, reminding him of the comrades he had lost and the bond they had shared.

Through chance encounters, he stumbled upon stories of hidden treasures, secret meetings, and clandestine operations. The echoes of war seemed to reverberate through the cobblestone streets, speaking of mysteries and unknown dangers.

Compelled by his past experiences, he became embroiled in a web of intrigue where political and personal ambitions collided. Yet, in this strange mix of danger and allure, he had also discovered unexpected friendships and love that transcended borders.

As he took up his metaphorical sword once more, this time fighting battles outside the trenches, he found solace in knowing that his suffering during the Great War had prepared him for these unforeseen adventures. The journey was arduous, fraught with peril and uncertainty, but he refused to let fear drive him away.

In pursuing new and unknown adventures, He hoped to find redemption for the past and perhaps a glimpse of the peace that had eluded him for so long. For once, he would shape his destiny, carve a path of survival and purpose, and leave behind the horrors of war for a chance at a fulfilling life in the vibrant heart of Buenos Aires.

Within six months of signing on as a stoker on board the South American-bound freighter, he took his first steps on solid ground again when reaching Buenos Aires. On his arrival, he also met my mother almost immediately, who worked as a clerk in the Immigration department.

She left a new set of feelings within him that he had never known before. It was love at first sight for this new admirer.

*****

My father went on to secure various positions in the offices of a large meat processing plant, and it was here that he would fall in love again with the "beauty like no other beauty", as he would often say to his future wife and me.

Both had enrolled in a nearby night school by sheer accident. My mother loved languages and was already proficient in both English and French. My father had enrolled in a Spanish class. It was over an evening break for the students, and they locked eyes on each other. For the first time, my mother noticed this sad-looking man and felt butterflies within her whenever he looked her way.

After a very short courtship, they began living together in a tenement-style house with other immigrants. The rent was affordable, and the conditions, although not of the standard my mother had been accustomed to, had not prevented them from anticipating a new lifetime of adventures together.

*****

So, years later, when the Second World War erupted in 1939, life became confusing for all three of us. On my father's side, the Germans were invading as many countries as they humanly could in Europe. It was the first time he started to hear the words of Nazism and its leader Adolf Hitler.

My father's friends and work colleagues were in a state of excitement with the military achievements they were reading in their local Argentinian newspapers and from the snippets they got from the local radio. My father always remained quiet. For me, I do not know why their excitement sat uncomfortably on my shoulders.

I felt something was wrong. I didn't know what. It was a growing feeling that something was unjust about invading other people's homelands.

For my mother, life continued as if nothing had happened. She was neither interested in politics nor Germany. Secretly, she just enjoyed my father's elevation in stature and his new status as a rich man.

His career in the meat processing business and his part-time import business had both grown successfully over the years. He was importing German-made beer steiners and coasters as a means of earning an extra source of income.

While other entrepreneurial Germans at that time arrived and concentrated on beers, wines, and schnapps drinks, my father took up the niche market of providing steiners and coasters to all the customers of the busy bars and restaurants.

Unsurprisingly, my parents lived modestly in a small but expensively furnished apartment north of Buenos Aires. For their entertainment, they loved only the latest offering of opera at the grand 1908-built Opera House with its plush 2,500 seats.

I grew up to love the sounds of opera and classical music from my parents. They were like a living encyclopedia of music. They answered any question I asked. German opera was their favourite. I could never remember a day going by without hearing Beethoven or Mozart filling the rooms of our home.

My father consistently lectured me that operatic music, with its complex structures and emotive power, stimulates brain activity and cognitive development in any listener. After a lifetime of obeying his wishes, he has proved to be right.

To my mother's dismay, on a quiet, sunny evening, my father turned up in a brand-new car. It was not any old car but the latest BMW 328. He secretly had waited two years for it to be built and shipped to him.

It was a 2-litre class sports car painted brilliant white; even the wheel hubs matched.

My mother's discomfort did not come from the colour but from the fact that it only had two seats. "Where was our son Gabriel supposed to sit?" she asked, looking out of the window at the beautiful sports car below.

At the same time, her mind had dismissed the question. She had no interest in the answer.

She couldn't wait to be seen by the whole neighbourhood. She would have to head to her favourite boutiques to purchase the latest fashions to match the car's decor.

My father never replied. He knew my mother was hooked from the moment she opened the lace curtains to see the white beast below. Instead, he rattled the keys and headed to the door, "Come, let's tour the neighbourhood."

"Wait! I have to change to something suitable for the occasion," she shouted as she disappeared into the bedroom, flinging off her comfy cardigan. This was not the time for a cardigan.

*****

Sadly, these would be my last memories of my parents; Later that day, while out on their first jaunt together in their magnificent white BMW 328 sports car on a country road, they met a substantially overweight horse who decided to have a heart attack and collapsed onto my shocked parents, crushing them both to death.

Now, I was officially declared an orphan. From that moment on, I was always in trouble with the authorities, so adding the title orphan to the teenager seemed to cause the government people to dislike me even more.

That same year, I was approaching the end of my school days. In the next six months, I would have sat my final examinations. But unknown to my unsuspecting parents, I had been hiding a secret life.

That morning, I was scheduled to attend a political rally, and I had also joined a gang of thieves with liberal, almost communist tendencies. We wanted to rob the rich, but not like Robin Hood to feed the poor. But to provide our young delinquent minds with what we felt was an adventure.

Everyone now carried a gun or a knife. Even our victims were to be expected to be armed. All my friends and I were of the age of bending the rules and profiteering from our deeds. We saw no structure within Argentinian society to make us resistant to temptation.

We had become the heavy-handed protection for the growing political agitators preaching their indoctrination. My country had a long history of neutrality when it came to European wars. We were heavily influenced positively by Great Britain's economic influence with Argentina when it came to supplying Great Britain with grain and meat.

Two political factions paid us for disrupting everyday life on the streets and at Political rallies. There were the Pro-allies (Alidofilios) who wanted Argentina to end neutrality and fight for the allies and the Pro-neutral (Neurtalistas) who wished to remain neutral.

We favoured the latter as adventure should not involve dying in a foreign field, and we were paid a more significant fee to support the Neutralists.

*****

The night before my parent's accident, I had been on a raid with three other friends to what we understood would be an empty home of a retired banker. He was supposed to be away with his family in the Pampas, some 200 miles outside the city.

When we broke in through a small window at the rear of the property, the family dog heard us, and all hell broke loose. Lights came on throughout the house, and in the glare, I could see a heavyset man in pyjamas heading towards us with an aggressive-looking Rottweiler at his side.

The retired banker was also aiming a heavy-looking shotgun in our direction. I was alarmed to see how composed he looked, applying steady pressure with his trigger finger. I knew instantly someone was going to get hurt tonight. I dived toward the darkness of the forest of trees on my left.

I heard the sound of the trigger being pulled back with a smooth, deliberate motion. Next would come the trigger break. The shotgun's firing mechanism set off the ignition, causing the ammunition to ignite and propel the shot out of the barrel. The expanding gases generated a recoil, which was expertly absorbed by the oversized body behind the shotgun.

The second sound came of the shotgun being fired. "Boom", followed by someone being hit from behind. In my fear, I stood behind what I thought was a shaking tree.

My senses eventually told me it was not the tree but my body that was shaking violently.

I ran as fast as I could, dreading the impact of another shell.

I could see a body face down and not moving on the ground. It was Miguel, a wealthy textile owner's son now bleeding profusely from his wounds peppered in his back. There will be hell to play tomorrow when the city finds out what has just happened.

I finally got a hold of myself when there was another sound, only this time it was POP followed simultaneously by another POP. Both bullets from the handgun being used by Miguel's younger brother Juan reached their target.

The banker's body was raised in the air as both bullets slammed into him. The first in the throat and the second in the chest. His lifeless body landed on top of the now-cowering dog.

I reacted in sheer terror. I turned and ran at the garden wall, the adrenaline inside of me propelling me over the brickwork. I landed with a thud and felt my knees take the brunt of the fall.

I shamefully did not look back but ran as fast as my legs would allow me. I left the carnage behind. I proved to be a coward and did not go to my friend's assistance. My knife is still firmly in my pocket.

I removed the knife and threw it into nearby bushes. If I am caught tonight, I do not want any incriminating evidence on me.

When I arrived back home, I silently entered my bedroom, a once safe and comforting haven that felt invaded by haunting memories and shut the door. I didn't sleep that night. The recurring images of the nightmare relentlessly crowded my mind, weaving a tapestry of fear and anguish.

The first image that gripped my thoughts was that of the retired banker, his face contorted in terror and disbelief as a shadowy figure sneaked up, silencing his existence.

Next, my mind fixates on the eyes of the impassive accomplice, their gaze cold and calculating. It's as if their eyes bore into mine, penetrating my consciousness and sending shivers down my spine. I see the gloved hand clutching the weapon, a stark contrast against the fading light outside my bedroom window.

The vivid scene plays over and over, each repetition etching itself deeper into my psyche. I remembered the blood pooling on the floor, spreading like a sinister stain, reminding me of the irreversible consequences that accompany the heinous act.

The metallic scent of fear lingers in the air, assaulting my senses as though the room itself is contaminated by the violence I witnessed.

Then, my mind jumped to fragmented flashes of the aftermath—the panicked footsteps, the muffled cries, and the fevered attempts to escape the crime scene. It's as if I am there once more, trapped in a whirlwind of chaos and despair, desperately trying to make sense of an incomprehensible nightmare.

The images continue to swirl, blending reality with the nightmare, blurring the boundaries between what I saw and what I feared. It becomes increasingly difficult to decipher where the line is drawn, leaving me trapped in a cycle of confusion and distress.

As I finally settle on my bed, the haunting visions persist, their intensity only growing more vital as the weight of my guilt settles upon me. The images served as a constant reminder of the horrors I witnessed, a torment that lingered in my mind, leaving me teetering on the edge of sanity.

*****

A few hours later, I heard my father rise earlier than usual and quietly let himself out of the apartment. It would be another hour before my mother would come knocking on my door.

"Hello, Gabriel. Would you like to have breakfast with me? Your father had insomnia and went out early this morning."

"Yes, of course. Give me 30 minutes to get ready," I offered under the covers.

She smiled and parted my room. "OK, but no more than 30 minutes. I will call you."

It actually took me another 45 minutes to feel I had some composure within me to face my mother. I sat quietly while she mollycoddled me as she had always done.

An hour went by, and then the sound of keys entered our apartment door, followed by a man so full of excitement. "Darling, go to the window and see what is outside on the street below."

My Mother, with her cardigan wrapped around her, pulled the curtains open...............

*****

I, you know, headed to a worker's rally, unaware my parent's lives were about to end and mine into directions I would never have dreamt.

Please forgive me; I have to pause and settle my nerves by relating my life to you all. Don't I pray to think wrong of me; there are instances when I was a good man. One day soon, I plan to continue my story and explain my deep admiration of the famous writer of magical realism, foreign correspondent, and journalist Gabriel Jose de la Concordia Garcia Marquez, who was of Colombian birth.

*****

## 18: *I am Leonardo's Kite who wishes to become a Satellite*

Leonardo was brimming with excitement as August approached, the month when the skies above the mountain towns were painted with the vibrant hues of countless kites. It was a time when the young and old, locals and visitors, all became children again, united in the sheer joy of kite flying.

The skies above the mountain were washed with the vivid colours of the flying kites in the best winds of the year.

Everyone became a child, no matter their age, with the sheer pleasure of either witnessing the events or participating in handling each of the flying kites.

Traditionally, if they wished to enter competitions, then they had to go to Bogotá. But for these mere souls surrounding me on this mountain ridge, overlooking the city below, they were happy and content to play and enjoy the feel of their kites sailing in the winds.

Unbeknownst to Leonardo, his new kite, which is me, harboured grand ambitions. I was not just a kite, but a dreamer with a desire to soar higher than the rest.

When Leonardo's uncle Sergio was making my frame, he consistently talked about the Satellites he saw in the midnight carpet of stars racing across the skies without a care in the world.

He would describe to me while in production that I was being made in traditional ways going back over 50 years when the creator was a little boy listening to his grandfather and his own father about the great space program that had occupied their thoughts for many years.

Each owned a telescope with which, on certain nights, they could see the beautiful blanket of the Milky Way galaxy and the moon up high.

They would always take Leonardo up to the mountaintop in August to see the stars with his own eyes. When the satellites emerged racing across the sky, they would identify each one.

Uncle Sergio could tell him when, where, and why they were built. It was amazing how much knowledge these men had. Now it was time for the new generation to be shown this spectacular event above that happens every year.

I was ready now and belonged to Leonardo. I was going to be his special kite, not one of the street purchases but specially made with the old Chinese ways of using silk and bamboo for the frames.

This should allow me more ability to reach the stars like no other.

In addition, I was going to have unique florescent colours painted on my bamboo frame to allow me to be flown and seen at night.

The street kites could not do this, so that is why Leonardo's kite was going to be deemed exceptional.

On my maiden flight, Leonardo was shown by the older men how to tether me securely in his tiny hands. To fly, I needed to be heavier than the air and have large wing surfaces that could react against the air to create lift and drag effects that allowed me to appear to be dancing.

"The lift effect comes from when your kite generates air movements around, producing low pressure above its wings and high pressure below its wings. Let me demonstrate for you." Said Sergio, who had taken control of the string to show Leonardo how to gain the desired effects he was looking for.

He made it look easy, but Leonardo knew, given time, he would be the most excellent kite flyer in the whole of Colombia.

Well, you do know what children are like. If it captures their imagination, they will go on to be the best; no obstacles could possibly hinder them in their quest to be the greatest.

This also appears to be the case with this handmade kite in Leonardo's hands again.

*****

Yes, technically, I am an inanimate object, but you would be wrong to believe as a kite, I do not possess the ability to experience feelings or sensations. I can easily describe my first experience of being in flight high above the mountain ridge of the Andes.

My first flight was a symphony of exhilaration and awe. The winds, my faithful companions, propelled me effortlessly across the vast expanse of the sky. As I ascended, the rugged beauty of the Andes ridge unfolded beneath me, a sight that filled me with wonder.

These same winds were invigorating and challenging, each characterised by their individual strength and variability.

Sometimes, I encountered a gust of wind, causing me to dip and sway unpredictably, yet at the same time, the blast provided me with an exhilarating sense of adventure and excitement.

The passing winds would buffet against my kite's body, creating a vibrant symphony of rustling sounds as I cut through the air. I could easily sense a connection and harmony with all the elements.

I loved the cool breeze rushing against my fabric; now imagine adding the combined warmth from the sun. All in all, I could not get over or ever forget the energising sensations I experienced that perfect afternoon.

I planned to join the satellites that orbit the skies and give pleasure to Leonardo and his elders for the rest of their lives. This was going to be my way of saying thank you for creating me. I, too, felt no fear, and the thought of failure never entered my mind.

First, I was created a kite. Next, I was going to become a satellite. How difficult could this be?

From my Sergio's teaching, I knew that satellites are moving stars or as once described, artificial moons placed in a low earth orbit.

Many of the currently active 7,702 satellites were launched by solar power TV-4 rockets from Cape Canaveral.

Their missions, in order of importance and number, begin with communications, followed by Earth's observation, technology development, navigation, and finally, space science.

The majority of the early satellites launched back in the decade of the fifties eventually lost communication with Earth in the following decade.

Many are just now hunks of metal sleeping for the next 150 years before deteriorating and finally disappearing from view.

Once in place and balanced by the pull of the Earth's gravity, they orbit the Earth in the same direction that the Earth moves in. Without this balance, they would fly in a straight line and, at some point, leave the Earth's orbit, never to be seen again.

Yes, it is true. There have been instances where satellites have lost their balance or experienced failures that caused them to deviate from their intended orbits. When a satellite drifts away from Earth's orbit in a straight line, it typically continues on its trajectory into space.

In such cases, the satellite will gradually move farther away from Earth and eventually escape its gravitational pull. This means that the satellite will not be able to continue its intended mission and cannot be controlled or communicated with any more.

It will become adrift in space, becoming what is often referred to as "space debris" or "space junk."

Space agencies and organizations track space debris to avoid collisions with functioning satellites. Satellites that have strayed from their orbits can pose a risk to other operational satellites and even the International Space Station.

*****

One evening, Leonardo's uncle Sergio declared to the night sky and to his little one protected the following words, which he truly believed were deep in his heart.

I lay on the mountain ridge's old, craggy road surface, out of harm's way to the passing traffic. I held my breath for what seemed like an eternity.

"Once upon a time, in the vast expanse of the starry night, a vision was born – the dream of an awe-inspiring structure, a floating marvel in the heavens that would serve as a symbol of unity and exploration. This dream took flight in the form of the International Space Station (ISS), a breathtaking masterpiece in space. The origins of this epic adventure can be traced back to the Cold War era, a time of fierce competition between two superpowers—the United States and the Soviet Union. But within this rivalry, a seed of cooperation was planted, a tiny spark that grew and ignited a burning desire for international collaboration.

In 1993, representatives from fifteen countries embarked on an extraordinary mission – to build a space laboratory that would transcend political boundaries. It was a fusion of minds, a marriage of technology, as the United States, Russia, Canada, Japan, and eleven European countries joined forces to create something truly magical. Construction began piece by piece, like a puzzle being assembled in the boundless. Cosmos. A symphony of human ingenuity took centre stage as modules were launched into space. Carefully orchestrated manoeuvres brought them together, and with each connection, the ISS grew more splendid.

And oh, the allure of this celestial wonder! It was a dazzling sight, shining like a star amidst the darkness, beckoning with the promise of knowledge and exploration. It became a sanctuary for astronauts from across the globe, a place where their dreams of venturing beyond Earth's limits could take shape.

These brave explorers embarked on daring expeditions, venturing forth to live and work aboard this remarkable testament to humanity's boundless potential. They pushed the boundaries of scientific knowledge, conducting experiments, studying the effects of microgravity on the human body, and unravelling the mysteries of the universe.

But the enchantment of the ISS didn't end there. Through its windows, astronauts gazed upon our beloved planet, witnessing its splendour and fragility from a perspective most could only dream of. They marvelled at the vibrant blue oceans, the wisps of white clouds, and the delicate balance of life below that seemed to hang in perfect harmony.

This incredible collaboration in space has become a symbol of hope and unity, a testament to what can be achieved when our collective imagination takes flight. The International Space Station stands as a testament to human resilience, curiosity, and the insatiable hunger to explore the cosmos.

So, as you gaze upon the night sky, let the story of the International Space Station capture your imagination. Let it inspire your dreams of reaching for the stars and join the chorus of humanity as we continue to push the boundaries of what is possible, leaving an indelible mark on the tapestry of the universe.

I was speechless! I slowly looked at Leonardo's face of him. It was clear he was in a faraway place right now. I stayed quiet; I wanted to devour more insights.

So, I now know that balance is essential for me to gain. This way, like the moon, I will not come crashing back to Earth.

I will be like the other satellites just by finding myself going around in circles, and the higher I go, the less speed I will need. Maybe I, too, will become a close neighbour to the International Space Station.

Leonardo will be able to boast to all his friends and future family members that this new satellite, which they can see every night, was once in his hands. Now, I will probably be orbiting for another 200 years before I am destined to become degraded and obsolete.

Well, that will be fine for me. Just think, you humans cannot hope ever to reach two hundred years of age, but this little kite can and will do so!

I will work by receiving and sending signals to and from the Earth. How is this going to happen? I am certain Leonardo's uncle Sergio will find a way. I will be known as Celestial 27 (ID 2017-Leo127).

*****

## 19: I am the Retired Policeman whom everyone avoids

There are times I need to remember the name I was given when I was born; my brain only sometimes functions as I would like it to. But today, I can tell you it was Stalin. I say this because I am no longer the same person who grew up with a loving family and promising career.

No longer am I the innocent child growing up and studying hard to pass all my examinations; no longer am I the student who went to university to earn my degrees in Criminology and Mathematics.

I am no longer the same person who, when I graduated, immediately enrolled in the National Police Force and passed out of the academy with top honours for my year, beating over 30 other candidates.

My family would no longer present me to all their neighbours and friends as the future of the rising family.

No longer am I the dutiful husband of nearly twenty years and the proud father of three boys? Not one of them wishes to see their father or spend time with me anymore.

In fact, I am the retired policeman whom everyone avoids at all costs.

My rise in the Police ranks was meteoritic. Within five years, I went from patrolman to Colonel in Chief of the City Police division.

As a young and driven individual, I possess an unwavering commitment to serving and protecting my community. From an early age, I was fascinated by the intricate workings of law enforcement, inspired by the bravery and dedication exhibited by those in green. Determined to make a real difference, I wholeheartedly pursued a career in the police force.

Starting as a patrolman, I immersed myself in the daily challenges and intricacies of maintaining law and order. My relentless work ethic and desire for constant self-improvement quickly caught the attention of my superiors.

With each passing day, I honed my skills and expanded my knowledge, actively seeking opportunities to learn and excel in my chosen profession.

Recognising my exceptional performance and unwavering commitment, I was entrusted with progressively higher responsibilities in various divisions. From accompanying detectives in investigations to leading the implementation of community policing initiatives, I consistently displayed exceptional leadership qualities that set me apart.

Throughout my journey in the police force, I perpetually pushed the boundaries of what was considered achievable, never settling for mediocrity.

My ability to efficiently navigate complex situations, make informed decisions in high-pressure scenarios, and inspire those around me endeared me to my colleagues and attracted the trust and respect of the community.

My meteoric rise in the ranks came with its fair share of challenges. I faced countless obstacles that tested my character and resilience, but I approached each setback as an opportunity for growth.

From handling delicate cases to diffusing tense situations, I maintained a steadfast dedication to justice and serving the public, always acting with integrity and professionalism.

It was this steadfast commitment to excellence and an unwavering devotion to my community that catapulted me to the pinnacle of my career. After years of dedicated service, I was selected as the Colonel in Chief of the City Police division. This role carried immense responsibility but also served as a culmination of my unwavering dedication and exceptional track record of achievements.

As Colonel in Chief, I continue to lead my team with the same passion, determination, and unwavering commitment that propelled me to this esteemed position.

Guided by a vision of a safer and more harmonious community, I implement innovative strategies, foster meaningful relationships with community leaders, and ensure that our police force is at the forefront of modern policing techniques.

My rise from patrolman to Colonel in Chief of the City Police division is a testament to the belief that hard work, resilience, and an unyielding commitment to public service can overcome any obstacle. I remain grateful for the opportunities that have come my way and, more importantly, for the faith that the community had placed in me to protect and serve them in the pursuit of justice.

In some quarters at the government level, I was being considered as a future General and possibly the absolute chief of all the divisions in my country, the name of which I have sadly forgotten.

Then I made my mistake.

*****

I went to the local shopping mall on a rare day off with no armed escort to ensure my safety. I was dressed in my favourite shorts, a Budweiser-branded T-shirt, and my Jesus shoes, as my boys used to call them in private.

I remember approaching the hole-in-the-wall cash machine to take some money out of the machine to purchase my children's Christmas presents via the list my wife had given me in the morning over breakfast. At the same time, I had planned to buy some perfume and toiletries for my wife from the department store. She always loved to smell nice, so I always ensured she had the latest fragrances on offer.

Reaching the cash machine ended my memory for the next two decades and more.

Later, I learned from an old friend who never deserted me like the rest but sadly died a couple of years ago that I failed to see the unknown perpetrators who were suddenly around me. In a fraction of a second, a spray covered my face, eyes, nose, and mouth.

Instantly, I was rendered incapacitated by the effects of Devil's Breath, which is derived from the flowering of the Borrachero shrub. My eyes streamed, my nose ran, and my mouth stayed quiet. No one passing knew or understood what was happening to me.

The voice of the person holding me up firmly requested my banker's card and security number, and, in a very calm manner, as I was apparently helpless, I willingly gave the four-digit code with no resistance.

Within seconds, they had emptied my account with a large withdrawal. When the powdered seeds entered my nostrils, my mind became ensnared in a web of illusion and stripped away my autonomy. The renowned Scopolamine took its sinister grip of amnesia that descended and shrouded my memories in an impenetrable mist. I was rendered powerless to recollect future experiences or the discernible identities of the perpetrators involved.

Without any haste, the culprits, who will always remain invisible to me, directed me away from the cash machine to a waiting car. With my wife at work and my three boys in school, the house was empty, and it did not take long for me to freely give information on the whereabouts of everything that was of value to my wife and me.

At this point, the evildoers discovered who their random victim was. They obviously went into a massive panic and, after much deliberation, decided drastic action had to be taken rapidly.

Next, I was taken away and driven to the centre of the city to a very broken-down building. Here, I was administered an unknown cocktail of drugs to scramble my mind permanently.

Apparently, killing me would not satisfy my enemies; a much slower death would await me hidden in this emancipated body until I drew my last breath.

Luckily or unluckily, depending on one's point of view, this evil cocktail did not have the total effect that was intended but still did so much damage that I could not control myself forever after.

My mood swings would rush from one extreme to the exact opposite with no notice ever given. Completing my duties as a policeman became a thing of the past, and at times, even as a normal human being, controlling my own body was impossible.

Gradually, I became a liability to my colleagues, an embarrassment to my family, and unbearable to the ones I once classed as my friends.

Even the doctors and nurses turned their back on me with no medical insurance cover left and no sign of a remedy to make me well again.

The cocktail had been very effective in reducing me to almost a vegetable.

It didn't take long before I was seen and found wandering the streets in nothing but a pair of shorts, often with nothing covering my upper body and feet.

When word finally got out on the street that I was now without any defence in any manner, slowly but surely, I became a target of violence nearly every day. The levels of violence were never enough punishment to kill me. But always, there was enough to make me cry out with pain and frustration in not being able to defend myself.

I started hiding in doorways and down alleyways. Sometimes, when the rainy season came, the levels of violence abated. But equally, as soon as the dry seasons arrived again, the villains and other street urchins would begin to come looking again to administer their vengeance for actions they deemed I was guilty of.

I always suspected during this period that it was not just me they were punishing.

It was the fact I was once the Colonel in Chief of the Police and deserved all I was going to receive from them without redress.

After such a lull in the attacks, I was sat in a city area I always seemed to gravitate to. Why, I cannot tell you. But in my broken mind, I found solace in the people who lived and worked there. Sometimes, an elderly lady would come out and, showing no fear but a smile for me, hand over a small cup of water and a piece of toast or a freshly cooked arepa.

I had lost the use of speech and muttered a noise more like the sound of a dog growling.

I was always gentle when I took the offering and moved away with my head down.

*****

On another occasion, a foreign man who owned a motorbike shop approached me with a bundle of T-shirts and jeans. He just passed them to me with only a smile. By the next day, I had exchanged most of them for cheap tobacco and kept one pair of jeans, which I ripped into pieces to make a skirt for me to wear.

This made it easier for me should I be busy relieving myself. An attack abruptly started with perpetrators I had not seen prior. I discovered that pulling down a skirt is quicker than pulling up a pair of denim shorts.

Not having the ability to purchase guns or knives to protect me, I was forced to carry a rock in my left hand.

Never was I ever seen without a big, aggressive-looking rock held high in line with my head.

My colour in the burning sun had turned my skin an intense, penetrating sun-kissed brown. My hair had stopped growing, and therefore, I did not need to visit any barber. My stoop became more pronounced as each year passed.

My feet started to disfigure with the total lack of protection and care.

The stench of me always now preceded my presence but was totally invisible to my nasal passages, which had been destroyed in the attacks over the years.

My hearing had also deteriorated, but for some unknown reason, my eyesight was never better. In my clouded and often befuddled mind, my eyes always managed to see danger before it actually began. In the odd window reflection, the intensity of the sunlight and distinct surroundings brought out the brightness of my irises, and they appeared earthly brown with a hint of hazel and were more vivid and lively.

My skin tone due to the daily dust and grime from the streets left a permanent layer of the same on my exposed skin. Yes, if you looked hard enough, you could make out the odd, slightly varied skin tone and the added texture of my appearance. In the beginning, I could boast of a well-toned physique appearance, but the lack of a proper daily diet soon put paid to that.

Still, now I was fighting back and winning each challenge that presented itself.

The thugs were not coming so often now. They were avoiding me like all the other citizens of the city. I was becoming a force to be frightened of again, not, of course, at the same levels when I had all the power of the Police, but in my barrio, thieves and rogues would move away very rapidly once they realised I was near.

Now, I was resorting to sleeping during daylight hours in derelict houses, and at night, I started walking up the main road to the new road that went up the mountain.

Here, I would find solace in being on my own, meeting little danger except the racing cars up and down the mountain each night.

*****

On this last occasion, I had walked the length of the road, keeping as close to the sides as possible. When I arrived at the junction, I spotted a big Burgundy American-style truck waiting to turn left up towards the mountain. Its trailer was not attached but was back at its depot near the city's industrial area.

I was no more than a couple of meters away. With my beady eyes, I looked in all directions rapidly and saw an opportunity that had never presented itself before. In a moment, I was on the back of the truck, where the trailer would typically be married and secured.

On this occasion, it was going to my front-row view of the back of my vast and private carriage to those calm winds further up. The driver, whoever he was, would never know who I was, and besides, I am sure I would find an opportunity to vanish again when the moment is right.

Do I have emotions any more like all others? I have to say no.

I no longer cry with frustration, I no longer laugh with happiness, and I no longer act surprised by others doing good or bad to me.

On this trip, on the first stage, a bus started to pass my carriage. The door of the bus opened, and a plastic bag landed on my outstretched and hanging legs. By instinct, I reached out to secure the bag and didn't look up. I opened the bag, thinking it would be excrement, but no, not on this occasion. It was what looked like lasagna in tin foil.

I closed the bag; I had dinner tonight. Hang on, why wait till tonight? I reopened the pack, and within a minute, I had consumed the lasagna entirely.

At the same time, I ignored the nagging message to my brain: This lasagna was tasty and sour.

Throughout my meal, I just kept my eyes down with my head and watched for possible danger. Long ago, I realised that by behaving as I do, no one wants to be near me. To everyone, I must be avoided.

Little did I know soon I was going to be needed by a Nun.

*****

But wait, that little-known story will be coming to you soon. Please let me talk about a problem that has plagued me for a good while.

As I have already mentioned, my name is Stalin. Yes, I know, it's a weird choice of name for parents to call their firstborn. Maybe I was destined to be different and strange to all who, unfortunately, came into contact with me.

But, just like all humans, my brain asks questions that many others also require the answers to.

The first question is, who the heck was Stalin? Years ago, I researched my name, and I wrote this article mainly for myself. I never envisaged I would share it or publish it as I am doing now to you all. It's a bit pompous. But hey, I was a dedicated policeman once.

### Title: The Curious Choice of Naming: Stalin and the Puzzling Parental Decision

**Introduction:** When it comes to naming their children, my parents often spend hours debating, considering family traditions, cultural significance, and personal preferences. However, every so often, a name choice raised their eyebrows and stood out from the norm.

One such perplexing choice is my name, "Stalin," which means "Steel" in Russian. In this article, I have explored why it is a strange decision for any set of parents to name their firstborn "Stalin" and provide insight into who Stalin was.

Who was Stalin? Before delving into the question at hand, it is essential to provide some historical context. Joseph Stalin, born in Georgia in 1878, was a prominent figure during the early 20th century. He led the Soviet Union from the middle of the 1920s until his death in 1953. Stalin's regime was characterised by a totalitarian grip over the country, marked by massive purges, political repression, and forced collectivisation. He led the Soviet Union through one of its most tumultuous periods, including World War II, the Great Depression, and the subsequent Cold War.

**1. Historical Atrocities:** One of the primary reasons why it is strange for my parents to choose the name Stalin is the association with his actions and policies. Countless human rights abuses, including mass executions, brutal labour camps, and famine-induced deaths, marred Stalin's reign. Under his leadership, millions of innocent lives were lost due to his purges, forced labour, and agricultural policies that resulted in widespread starvation.

Sorry, parents, but naming your first child after such a notorious historical figure seems to overlook the atrocities committed under Stalin's regime.

**2. Negative Public Perception:** Stalin's name carries an overwhelmingly negative connotation in public perception. Even though some in specific segments of society may try to distance themselves from the harsh realities of Stalin's rule, the majority view him as a symbol of oppression, totalitarianism, and cruelty.

Indeed, you must have found it essential to consider the potential impact on a child's life when they bear the name of someone so universally condemned.

**3. Lack of Positive Association:** Unlike other historical figures whose names may be chosen due to their positive contributions or the values they represented, Stalin lacks any redeeming qualities that any parents, let alone mine, could possibly highlight. It is difficult for me to imagine why any set of parents would willingly connect their child's identity to a figure responsible for so much suffering and tragedy.

**My conclusion:** While my parents had the freedom to choose the names of their children, confident choices may appear strange or questionable to others. Naming a child Stalin, given the historical context and the actions associated with the figure, reflects a lack of sensitivity and awareness of the negative implications tied to that name.

It is vital to exercise caution and consider all the long-term consequences when selecting a child's name, ensuring it reflects positive ideals and avoids unnecessary controversy.

*****

The second most nagging question has to be: What's the difference between horse poo and dog poo? Either one is a pain in the ass when you stand in it.

At the beginning of the week, I was having my usual stroll around the local neighbourhood, checking that everything was well and that no bad guys were nearby. Guess what? Yes, I stood in some dog poop and went crazy. I had no shoes on. I am a street man, and I cannot afford such luxuries to protect me.

If I could, my memory would never allow me to remember I had them should I ever remove them from my feet.

For some unknown reason, I can remember standing in the poop. As I mentioned earlier, I did my usual and hitched a ride on the back of a Kenworth truck. The driver did not complain; I don't think he had any idea I was there.

I keep myself to myself, and I find it safer that way. Anyway, back to the mountain ridge above the city. I jumped from the back of the trailer just as the truck started to negotiate the old craggy trail, and guess what? As my feet felt the ground, I professionally rolled not to damage my weak legs, and I landed directly into a mass of horse poop.

To say I was a little upset would be an understatement, and I was only wearing my customary skirt and nothing else.

Most people who fall on this rough old road usually change colour to terracotta. Not me. I changed my tone only to a slightly rusty-looking style.

Then to make matters worse, three scrawny mutts arrived and smelt the poop, and they followed me for hours after that!

I continued on my awkward walk up towards the small town. Once there, I located a local veterinarian's establishment next to a cafe. There was a wall between them, and I quietly squatted to try to understand everything.

Outside the cafe sat two old-looking Campesinos (farm workers to you) who could smell my body odour and the richness of the bouquet emitting from the horse droppings.

The tall one, I shall call him "Horseman," closest to me, said to his companion, "Do you know, no one wants to step in dog poop. Let alone horse poop. For a simple reason, there will be more of it."

The shorter and fatter friend, whom I will refer to as "Dogman" because all three dogs were now at his feet staring at me, replied with a chuckle, "I know what you mean. In the past year, I undoubtedly have walked thousands of kilometres over this ridge with my dogs, and I must say that stepping into horse poop has got to be more distasteful than stepping in dog poop."

Dogman added, "I always try to step out of the way of dog poop, but once or twice the horse poop has got me."

I silently agreed with both and reasoned that it would take a massive pack of dogs to poop the same amount produced by a horse, and one positive point referring to our canine friends they do like to spread it around so as to reduce the problem.

In contrast, a horse considers no one but himself.

That goes for the riders, too.

When was the last time you witnessed a horse rider dismount with a shovel and a black bag heading toward the horse's rear?

Do not ask me that question for obvious reasons – memory.

Horseman paused briefly and offered what he thought was a reasonable explanation for the lack of riders scooping up the evidence. "We horse owners only wish to see our horse's manure clean and healthy with no unhealthy ammonia fumes. We want to see football-shaped droppings, and they must be smooth in texture, which will mean the horse could be better.

My horses can produce up to 50 pounds daily, and I have ten of them. I can vouch for that by the state of me; they must have all had a call of nature at the same time! What is your horse's poop made up of then?"

"Oh, that's easy to tell you: lots of water mixed with grass, grain fibre, some minerals, scrumptious fats, and a good dollop of soil."

"Soil?"

"You have to remember as they rip up the grass, some measure of soil will be attached. The horse knows to ignore this and munch away."

"I never thought of that," replied the enlightened Dogman. Horseman quips up with a big smile, displaying a row of "condemned houses" for teeth. "My missus swears by the manure, and she will often be seen feeding the vegetables and flowers with it. She never had a bad harvest. So, she must be right."

"Not only that, how many houses up here have been built with adobe bricks from Old Carlos down in Medio Dapa? All his bricks have horse manure in them. Bear in mind that they smell a bit in the rainy seasons but are much more acceptable than your mutt's droppings."

Dogman had another question "Can horse poop spread diseases to us humans?" he ended the question by looking directly at me. "No, if you landed face first into a pile of good old horse muck, you will unlikely attract any disease. If there were any bacteria such as e-coli, they would quickly die in our sunlight. Your poop and your dog's poop pose a bigger issue and are more likely to spread disease and parasites to my missus and me."

Both men were now in hysterics.

Dogman was legendary for often being cut short on the ridge and seen by his shorts behind a bush or tree. Another man wearing a doctor-looking outfit appeared from the veterinarian's establishment. He ordered his usual coffee and empanada as he sat down with his long-standing friends and neighbours. "My friends, "How are your animals?"

Both men ventured that neither had any problems except for Dogman and the amount of dog waste he had to deal with daily. "Do you know your dogs can excrete an average of one pound of waste daily? How many dogs do you have?" inquired the newcomer.

"Not sure; at last count a few years back, I reckoned I had thirty or more."

My eyes almost exploded – over thirty dogs in one household!

The vet leaned forward, looked at Dogman directly, and spoke, "Remember, picking up your dog's waste safely is imperative to your well-being and health. You also have our mountain ridge water supply near your homestead. The likelihood of contamination in our water supply from faecal bacteria could be high if you do not pick it all up."

Before Dogman could respond, the vet continued almost without taking a breath: "Do you know your dogs, and other people's dogs, can carry common forms of heartworms, hookworms, tapeworms, whipworms, not forgetting roundworms, E. coli, and salmonella? "

"Wow, I had no idea. How should I best dispose of all this waste? Asked Dogman, who by now sat a little lower in his chair.

"Well, the best advice I can offer is you poop in your toilet, why not do the same with your dog's waste. It's a no-cost-friendly removal method and is ecologically sound, too. Surely it is better to flush the waste instead of leaving it everywhere on the ridge?"

All three of us agreed in unison with his suggestion, and the conversation moved to a more mundane topic called COVID-19. I had no idea or interest in what they were referring to, so I quietly got up and walked away. I need to find somewhere to wash, the local source of a river will not be far away, and I will need a poop.

*****

## *20: I am Ignacio Perez the Truck Driver on my Last Run*

For millions of truck drivers around the world, being a truck driver was and is a heavily regulated, poorly paid, very lonely, and somewhat dull job, and sometimes I felt the same, but I must admit very rarely. Let me explain myself.

My father, Ernesto the Younger, had been truck driving in South America since the war. His grandfather, Ernesto the Elder, originally started truck driving during prohibition in the USA.

Only the bravest of truck drivers dared to load their trucks with bootleg alcohol from the Deep South and transport it through the perilous dark hours of the night, pushing their vehicles to top speeds to avoid the numerous and often deadly hijackings. It was a display of courage and determination that commands respect.

Danger could come anytime from the threat of both other rival bootleg gangs and the Prohibition Agents when driving to the thirsty cities of Chicago and Boston and their numerous illegal drinking dens known as Speakeasies.

These establishments were called Speakeasies because to gain entry, you had to whisper either a code or name through a locked door.

The crazy thing was Prohibition was aimed at barring the manufacture of alcohol.

You were also barred from selling it or shipping it, but not for actually drinking it!

Just think you could go as a patient to your doctor, and he could legally prescribe you liquor for medicinal reasons, and off you pop to the local pharmacy who would gladly supply it.

Prohibition began in 1919 and lasted 14 years. It was meant to be "The Noble Experiment," aiming to reduce crime and corruption and solve all the social problems of the time.

They thought it would reduce the burden of taxation created by the overfilled prisons and the numerous overcrowded workhouses. It was supposed to improve the overall health and hygiene of the people of America.

Well, history has taught us that it was a monumental failure and that it will never be repeated.

This illegal movement of illicit booze paid well; no taxes were declared, and as long as you kept your mouth shut and stayed loyal to the Italian crew you were with, you stood a chance of prospering.

My Ernesto the Elder was well-liked by the Bootleggers of Chicago.

Chicago became notorious for its thriving illicit alcohol trade. Bootlegging, the illegal production, distribution, and sale of alcoholic beverages, reached unprecedented levels in the Windy City. A number of individuals and criminal organisations rose to prominence as bootleggers, capitalising on the demand for alcohol during this time.

One of the most well-known bootleggers in Chicago was Alphonse Gabriel Capone. Capone, also known as "Scarface," was the leader of the powerful criminal syndicate called the Chicago Outfit. My abuelo, Ernesto the Elder, drove for this outfit.

He had reasoned early on that to survive, you would need to be the strongest and the fittest.

Capone controlled numerous illegal drinking establishments and breweries throughout the city, ensuring a steady supply of alcohol to meet the high demand. Capone's empire extended beyond bootlegging, as he also engaged in illegal gambling, prostitution, and racketeering.

Another significant bootlegger in Chicago was George "Bugs" Moran, a rival of Capone. Moran's North Side Gang was engaged in fierce competition with Capone for control of the city's bootlegging operations.

Ernesto the Elder and the other drivers feared the consequences of coming up in front of one of their hijackings. Luckily for Ernesto the Elder, this never happened, but I have heard of many terrible outcomes for those who did.

The rivalry between the two gangs culminated in the infamous St. Valentine's Day Massacre in 1929, where associates of Capone brutally killed seven members of Moran's team.

When Ernesto the Elder heard the news, he decided to start preparing an exit plan. This business was certainly not to be considered long-term.

The bootleggers of Chicago during Prohibition operated in a highly organised manner, establishing elaborate smuggling networks, secret drinking establishments, and supply chains. They imported alcohol from Canada, produced moonshine locally, and often bribed law enforcement officers and politicians to turn blind eyes to their illegal activities.

Despite the efforts of law enforcement, fueled by the introduction of the Volstead Act and the creation of the Bureau of Prohibition, the bootlegging industry in Chicago thrived. The city became synonymous with organised crime and the roaring trade in illegal alcohol, leaving a lasting impact on its history and reputation.

Ernesto the Elder drew the line between getting into heavy stuff that involved violence or even its threat. All he wanted to do was drive at every opportunity he could get, collect some payment, and disappear until the next run was arranged, which at one stage of the Prohibition was almost nightly.

Many other bootleggers and criminal organisations operated in Chicago during Prohibition, taking advantage of the lucrative trade in illegal alcohol. These included the O'Banion Gang, the Genna Brothers, and the Touhy Gang, among others. They often resorted to violence and intimidation to protect their territories and maintain control over their operations.

They should have listened to Ernesto, the Elder, and taken a page out of his book. Irish-American mobster Dean O'Banion was killed later in 1924 during one of the deadliest power struggles at that time. The Genna brothers lost four out of five of them in a number of hits, and they were no more in 1925. The Touhy Gang, led by mobster Roger Touhy, had their operation on the city's West Side and often clashed with both the Genna Brothers and the Chicago outfit. However, Touhy's criminal activities attracted significant attention from local law enforcement. In 1929, Touhy was arrested and convicted for the kidnapping of a wealthy local businessman.

He was given a lengthy prison term and spent several years behind bars. After his release, Touhy tried to revive his criminal career. However, he faced continued legal troubles and eventually retired from organised crime. Like all the others, the Touhy Gang faded away as other criminal organisations took prominence in Chicago.

My grandfather turned out to be a shrewd man. He sent all the money he earned to his sister, Betty's home, where she had built a hole literally in the wall and covered it with a carpet.

*****

During this same period, Ernesto the Elder and Betty, could hope to earn only a monthly 30.00 dollars a week if they were lucky. Now, both could enjoy a cut of the profits from each shipment. Ernesto the Elder turned out to be a good negotiator and used his bargaining power by taking the high-risk routes.

Ernesto the Elder regularly attracted tens of thousands of dollars each time, and with these sums involved, the money soon built up, and Betty had to design other hiding places.

The house became washed with dollar notes.

Then it all stopped with Prohibition ending and booze becoming legal again.

So, what happened to Capone? Did he disappear after being "hit"?

After Prohibition ended, Al Capone's criminal empire began to decline. Without the lucrative profits from illegal alcohol sales, his primary source of income vanished. Additionally, the increased focus of law enforcement on organised crime led to increased scrutiny of Capone and his activities.

In 1931, Capone was convicted and imprisoned for income tax evasion. He ended up with a sentence of 11 years in federal prison and fined $50,000. While in prison, his health deteriorated, and he was eventually released on parole in November 1939. After his release, Capone retired to his estate in Palm Island, Florida, where he lived with his family until he died in 1947. With his criminal empire dismantled and his health declining, Capone's reign as a powerful mobster came to an end.

*****

So, before anything went wrong for both sister and brother, Ernesto, the Elder, and Betty packed up and headed back to South America in a brand new Pickup truck loaded with cash. So began a lasting relationship of the Perez family with America's fledgling truck industry.

They both bought some unassuming properties for themselves, and together, they set up a small company that imported and sold the latest designs of American trucks. They opened a garage nearby in the poorer part of the city, and from there, they had an excellent little business supplying imported parts and fixing these big beasts for the growing population of truck drivers.

My father, Ernesto the Younger, inherited the businesses when my grandfather passed away. Betty had died a couple of years previously, single and without children.

But being young himself and not having the same flair for business opportunities, as well as having the most nagging wive and an untold number of girlfriends, the business started to shrink soon.

Eventually, he managed to lose nearly everything except one solitary Kenworth Truck.

*****

Now it was the 50s, and Ernesto the Younger found solace in being on the open road between cities on one of the most dangerous roads known to man. From the southern city to the capital, he travelled via the rugged and highly unsafe road weaving through the Andes.

During this period, it would take at least two to three days to go one way, and if the weather was poor, it could cover weeks.

The road infrastructure was much less developed than it is today. The route from Cali to Bogotá, known as the "Carretera Central," was mainly a single-lane road, often in poor condition.

Ernesto the Younger had to navigate through mountainous terrains, sharp turns, and steep inclines. Potholes and unpaved sections were common, making the journey physically demanding and time-consuming.

The weather conditions and challenges along the route could be unpredictable and sometimes harsh. Rainy seasons could result in landslides and muddy roads, making driving even more treacherous. Fog and low visibility were other common challenges, particularly in the higher mountainous regions.

One of the significant dangers Ernesto the Younger faced during that period was the presence of armed bandits or "highwaymen." These criminals targeted trucks, robbing drivers of their cargo, money, and sometimes even their lives.

The remote and isolated stretches of road made Ernesto the Younger vulnerable to such attacks.

Given the terrain and the often unreliable truck technology of that era, mechanical breakdowns were common. Every truck driver had to possess some mechanical knowledge and carry essential repair equipment to deal with breakdowns, as there were limited repair facilities along the route.

Driving for extended periods on challenging roads took a toll on Ernesto the Younger's physical health. The constant handling, exposure to vibrations, and long hours of sitting resulted in chronic back pain, fatigue, and other related health issues. Furthermore, Ernesto had limited rest areas or facilities, leading to exhaustion and sleep deprivation.

Compared to modern times, amenities and roadside services were limited.

Along the route, there were only a few gas stations, restrooms, and places to eat or get a night's rest. Ernesto the Younger had to rely on his preparation, carrying food, water, camping gear, and other essentials.

*****

I, Ignacio, got the bug of following the family tradition of driving trucks from very early on.

I was often the mascot that was permitted to join Ernesto the Younger, much to my mother's largely ignored protests. By the time I had reached twenty, I had learned to master everything I needed to know to be a truck driver here in South America.

The big difference for me driving, say, here in the South compared to other drivers in the USA and Europe was – regulation. Here in South America, there was no such thing as regulation; This was a wild and untamed country.

No one told you what hours you could drive, no one inspected your rig, and everyone disregarded what should not involve them personally.

Things changed in the eighties and the nineties for the lowly looked-upon truckers. Cocaine became the illicit cargo, and I saw an opportunity to earn a little extra from time to time. So, like my grandfather before me, I waited until the opportunity presented itself.

It took a little time. I was in a café one sunny afternoon, and a man dressed very smartly in his white suit and matching Fedora hat placed on the table in front of him was sitting at the following table to my right reading his newspaper while waiting for his Tinto to cool down.

"May I ask you a question, Ignacio? Please do not mind me referring to you by your first name, but I have a proposition for you. I knew your Abuelo, Ernesto the Elder, very well, and I always admired him."

I turned to the man and instantly knew the opportunity I had been waiting for was about to be revealed. I did not speak and waited for this stranger to continue.

"Ah, just like your grandfather, quiet of voice, a trait sadly your father did not inherit, never mind."

I silently agreed with the stranger's assessment of my father, whom I love, with an open heart. But he was indeed a disaster in many things he chose to do; his only pride and joy was his ageing truck.

Ernesto the Younger remarked often that today's society seemed not to care about the lives of truck drivers. "We clog up the roads and traffic." He offered and followed with, "We are in the way, and of course, we pollute the environment. It seems everyone needs us, but no one wants us."

"My Grandfather told me that your grandfather was a good and very reliable man and only ambitious enough to be able to provide for his family, nothing more and nothing less. Tell me, Ignacio, are you of the same mind?"

Finally, I found my voice: "Yes, I do believe I am; I truly believe I would be doing well to follow in my grandfather's example. I, too, am not a violent man, nor am I, say, an over-the-top ambitious type of man."

I paused and, after drawing in a breath, "I would prefer to be able to have a comfortable life, and should that involve the odd misdemeanour from time to time with a little bonus that will ensure this, I am open to suggestions."

The suited stranger lifted his Fedora from the table and placed it smoothly back on his head. He stood with one hand reaching into his pocket for change to pay for his Tinto. He turned towards me and said with a smile.

"My representative will contact you shortly, Ignacio; I assure you that if you are like your grandfather, Ernesto the Elder, and not like your father, Ernesto the Younger, you will indeed have a comfortable life."

*****

Well, over the years, from time to time, my heavy rig would be carrying the odd extra tyre full of what I could only guess and keep my mouth closed. I always received ample and above payment.

The envelopes were always thick, and I had built a hole in the cellar wall and placed a rug over the top, just as my grandfather and his sister Betty had done all those years ago.

So, there I am, looking back on my life up to now. I smile at the thought that I cannot complain.

I have been married to Jasmina for some 40 years, and we have a son, Samuel, who has also decided to become a truck driver. He is awaiting my arrival in the Capital city with our current truck so he can take over the helm and continue the business. At the same time, I will enjoy my upcoming retirement with Jasmina.

Jasmina has been the success of my life; I could never have made a finer choice; she had her role to play in the city as a nurse in one of the local hospitals. She raised Samuel almost by herself, and thankfully, he came out healthy and with a good standard of education. Never did she complain, or did I give her cause to complain.

We would regularly head to church together, and I tried to follow my grandfather's example.

When I was young, Ernesto the Elder always said. "Ignacio, remember when you start to earn money, always put a little aside each time you are paid."

I did better. In the early years, I put a lot aside, and I was known as the thrifty one. I was not for the typical city life of a young man. Even the ladies of the night avoided me, knowing I was not going to be a regular customer of theirs. I only had eyes for my childhood sweetheart, Jasmina.

We had a modest home in the city, which we could now sell whenever we wanted with no mortgage to settle.

We have our holiday home high up on the mountain ridge overlooking the city below. Again, and it has no debt attached to it. Here, we can escape the compressing heat in the valley below and enjoy the lower temperatures and the freshness of the daily winds arriving each afternoon.

*****

Today, finally, my retirement was about to begin. I will be saying "Bye" to my loving Jasmina and jumping into my favourite driving seat.

This truck, a Kenworth 1993KW W900B model, has been a very comfortable and reliable workplace for the past nine years.

It has a paltry 750,000 miles on the clock, and Samuel will do well with this first rig. I will be driving back down the mountain for the last time as a truck driver and travelling up the immensely improved road back to the capital.

It will still take me 10 to 12 hours to arrive at Samuel and his loving partner, Sofia's place in the north of the capital.

I will then spend the evening with Samuel and Sofia. The following morning, I will be driven to the Capital airport by Samuel, where I will catch my one-hour flight back to Jasmina.

We plan to take a short trip to our other home in the nearby coffee fields. This one has a small mortgage in my wife's name, which will be paid off once she retires, creating no suspicion with the tax authorities. It would appear the time had come for Jasmina to leave her 25-year job so we can celebrate our future retirement together.

Well, up until I reached the outskirts of the mountain pueblo, that is. Just in front of me, I suddenly saw a Nun, a street man with a rock, and a speeding quad bike with, I must admit, the most striking-looking rider I have ever seen. All of them appeared to be heading to the same point from different locations right in front of me......

*****

## 21: I am a Sister who is on a mission to sing

My whole life has always been led to this mission of becoming a Nun. I have thought of no other path I wish to travel down. While growing up, all my friends consistently talked about growing up and having families of their own. Inside my heart, I knew this was never going to be my future. I felt nothing wrong about being a mother.

I just knew my path lay elsewhere. Where? I did not know then, but I was always confident that God would guide me when he felt I was ready.

Going to a small church school run by a couple of elderly nuns had given me the path I needed to follow. From the moment I first walked into the tiny classroom, I loved Sister Miriam de Jesus and her friend, Sister Mily Gabriella Victoria.

Their unified joy of welcoming me and my friends was totally overwhelming, and I felt a movement in my heart that always appears when I think back to those beautiful times in the school.

Never did I feel any anger, even when other girls did wrong in our playing together. Never was there a raised voice, only a word of encouragement. In the daily hours of prayer and silence, I felt a warm feeling from my God, which I later learned from Sister Mily, which was the sign that the Lord was listening intently to me and my words.

One evening, I had the Sisters of the cloth purely to myself. I was sitting outside cleaning all the other girls' shoes. It was never a chore for me, as it gave me time to share my thoughts with the two ladies of God.

"Sister, please explain to me what the difference is between being a Nun and being a Sister."

Both smiled knowingly. Sister Miriam spoke first: "Well, little inquisitive one, the difference is simple. If you, Rosa, are a Nun, it is because you have taken the solemn oath to live a cloistered life, meaning living under vows of poverty, chastity, and obedience."

"You have forsaken all that you had before or could ever receive after from the outside world; in other words, you may not have possessions except for the items you need for prayer with God. Usually, you will dwell solely in a monastery or convent and forsake mainstream society. You will focus solely on prayer."

Sister Mily sat forward and added, "This means you can call yourself a Nun. But Rosa." Here, she paused while stroking my hair back with a small brush.

"You may wish to pursue a different way of life. You can make a simpler oath and call yourself a Sister like us. Here, we are allowed to walk and work among the world as our missions see fit. We can still pray, and at the same time, we can retain and even inherit properties and items from family and friends."

Sister Miriam, too, leaned forward, patted me softly, and whispered, "It does not matter which oath you finally decide upon. Remember, God will help you make that decision when you are ready. At that point, whichever way you choose, you can always call yourself a Nun or a Sister, as we do."

Sister Mily, with her hand touching her chin and now examining her efforts with my hair, said, "Little Rosa, there is even a mission of Sisters down in the city who, over the last couple of years, have served God through social media by singing everywhere they can. They apparently make DVDs, videos, and even old and dated cassettes."

"They only, of course, sing of God, but it has proven to be a trendy way of assisting their large Catholic community. Their visiting Sister Superior the other day passed by and told us that they had been invited to tour Mexico, Panama and the "United States."

Just imagine a life of singing evangelical songs!" She also added with more thought, "Little Rosa, I always hear you singing, and you have a wonderful tone to your voice; perhaps when Sister Superior comes next, you should sing for her." I had finished cleaning the last shoe, and without as much as a second going by, I was off and running to report to my friends what the sisters had said to me. Singing in front of Sister Superior would be so exciting and the prospect fill my head for the coming days. The two Sisters watched me racing away laughing, knowing God's work had just happened in front of their very eyes.

The Sister Superior had indeed visited them as part of her travelling duties. At one point, she had been walking past the communal kitchen and heard me singing softly. Sister Mily and Sister Miriam had just made their guest a small glass of homemade lemonade, "Who is the songbird who has such a beautiful voice?" They told her of the little girl named Rosa who never stops singing. "We believed she sings in her sleep, unlike the others who snore in unison. at night." Ventured Sister Mily laughingly.

"It's a shame I have to go so soon, but the next time I visit this lovely church high up here on the mountain ridge, I will make more time so I can listen again and see Rosa for myself. In the meantime, please sound her out and see what her reaction to such a request will be."

Sister Miriam turned to Sister Mily and remarked, "I do not think there will be any problems between our little Rosa, our aspiring singer, and the Sister Superior who commands over sixty five other singing Sisters."

*****

Sister Superior Josefina Ignacia De Mesa shot out of her chair, much to the surprise of the other occupants in the overcrowded Doctor's Waiting Room.

All eyes were on the unbelievable sight of a fully attired elderly Nun waving a colourful magazine in her hands, lost in her unexpected excitement at what she had just discovered. For the first time in 50 years, the then-young twenty-five-year-old could be seen instead of the usually graceful and balanced-looking senior woman, with her devotion to serving others totally missing.

As if by divine intervention, Sister Superior Josefina suddenly became aware of the scene she had created and reverted back to being what everyone would expect a Nun to act like in the waiting room. It must have seemed an age had gone before she slowly regained her composure. It had been a long time since she felt the same as that carefree hippy with her ageing guitar and missing strings.

Sister Superior Josefina sat back down, still smiling at all the flowing memories that had laid dormant for nearly all of her life. She looked back down at the magazine cover, which immediately transported her back to 1969, to a large piece of farmland that would be the chosen venue for a festival that defined a generation—her generation.

Sister Superior Josefina Ignacia De Mesa was born in January 1945 as Vanessa Torres Mendez in Brooklyn, New York. Her parents were a mixture of cultures. Her mother, Rosaline, came from a small seaside town called Weston Super Mare in the Southwest of England. Her father, Alberto, formerly from Rio in Brazil, both now residents of the Big Apple.

Josefina's parents met during the latter part of WWII during the months leading up to the D-Day landings. Rosaline was an assistant to the local Catholic priest, and Alberto, an M4 Sherman tank driver, was waiting to be deployed to the restoration of Europe.

D-Day, also known as the Normandy Invasion, was a major military operation that took place on June 6, 1944. It marked the beginning of the Allied efforts to liberate Nazi-occupied Western Europe.

D-Day was the culmination of months of planning and preparation by the Allies, led by the United States, the United Kingdom, and Canada. The objective was to establish a foothold on the beaches of Normandy in France and create a bridgehead for subsequent operations against the enemy forces. In the early hours of June 6, 1944, a massive invasion force consisting of over 150,000 troops, thousands of aircraft, and hundreds of naval vessels set out from England. Under the cover of darkness and heavy bombardment, the Allied forces landed on the heavily fortified beaches of Normandy. The landing zones were codenamed Utah, Omaha, Gold, Juno, and Sword.

The assault was met with fierce resistance from the heavily entrenched German defenders, particularly on Omaha Beach, where the American forces faced significant obstacles and suffered heavy casualties. However, with perseverance, courage, and the support of naval and air firepower, the Allied troops managed to break their way through the German defences and secure the beachheads.

D-Day was a pivotal moment in WWII, marking the beginning of the end of Nazi Germany's stranglehold on Western Europe. It established a crucial foothold that allowed the Allies to advance and eventually liberate France and other countries from German occupation.

*****

It was love at first sight for the youngsters caught up in events that affected the whole world. The night before Alberto receiving his orders to "ship out," Rosaline and Alberto had agreed to commit to each other and no one else, no matter the outcome of the war.

The passion in them both went beyond their control, and Vanessa later to become Josefina was conceived under some prickly bushes in a small woodland area close to the beach and the military barracks known to the locals as RAF Station Locking.

Of course, neither knew the consequences of their passion, who would appear a few months later on a snowy February night while Alberto was struggling to survive in his frozen tank in the middle of the Ardennes.

The moment Rosaline knew of her situation, she immediately wrote a short letter to Alberto. She had a close cousin who was an accountant for the local church in Brooklyn. She wrote to her pleading for help. Her ageing parents had no means to assist and were outraged with their daughter's behaviour and the pending shame that would be heaped on the family.

The cousin agreed to act as guardian, and somehow, the money for the voyage was found. Rosaline arrived in New York harbour in December of 1944. In the meantime, Alberto waited another nine months before he got word that he was a father.

He received his backlog of mail when he returned to conscientiousness after being rescued from his burning tank by his commander. The two were the only survivors of their five-person crew.

Alberto discovered he was not only a father, but he also unearthed the realisation that he would use a wheelchair for the remainder of his life.

Both euphoria and despair overwhelmed him simultaneously.

On his return to New York, the small family of three began their struggle to survive in a bustling city that never appeared to sleep. Rosaline trained as a midwife, and Alberto became a Lay Minister in charge of music. Before the war had started, Alberto's family assumed that he would follow his late father as a concert pianist. He had the gift, but the outbreak of war changed everyone's lives.

As a trained midwife in the Baby Boomer years to follow, Venessa's mother was in constant demand. Many nights, the "Angel of Delivery" could be seen racing around the neighbourhood on her bicycle in all sorts of weather and all hours of the day and night.

It fell onto Alberto and his wheelchair to raise Vanessa. He struggled often, but he never lost the relish of responsibility. The two were often seen heading to church together. It was during these years that Vanessa grew to love the world of music. For her, it was not the piano but the guitar that became her chosen instrument.

*****

My name is Josefina Ignacia De Mesa, and I am the Sister Superior of over sixty five singing Sisters in South America. As you have just learned, I was not born Josefina. In fact, my birth name was Vanessa.

From the first introduction of the acoustic guitar by my father, I was hooked.

"Well, y'all, let me take you on a journey back to my roots, where my love for music and guitars first sprouted."

Picture this: I'm a woman, born and raised in the deep south of the good ol' USA. My dad was a Lay Minister, and before that, he was an ex-tank driver in the army.

When I was just a young girl, my father decided to pass down his cherished acoustic guitar to me. It was weathered from years of love and use, but it held a special place in his heart. He wanted to share his passion for music with me, and that old guitar became a bridge that extraordinarily connected us.

Now, let me tell you, I wasn't exactly your typical Southern belle.

I had a wild spirit that craved the raw power and energy of heavy rock and the softly-sounding folk music that my mother loved.

While most girls my age were playing with dolls, I found myself entangled in the world of guitars and amplifiers.

I dove head first into learning how to play that old acoustic guitar.

Days turned into nights as I plucked at those strings, soaking up every bit of knowledge that I could. I would emulate the riffs I heard on the old vinyl records my dad would play, often surprising myself with the progress I was making.

The local music scene became my playground.

With my trusty acoustic guitar in hand, I ventured into dimly lit night spots, where the air was heavy with anticipation. People knew me as that heavy rock singer-songwriter, the one who had a fire in her soul that no stage could contain.

Although I only partially made it to the big time, the local night spots became my stomping ground.

A stage, no matter how small, was my canvas, and my guitar was the brush that painted the emotions of my heart. Every chord struck, and every word sung was a testament to the power of music and my relentless pursuit of expressing my inner world.

In those late-night jams, I found kindred spirits and fellow musicians who shared my burning desire to rock the world. We poured our hearts into crafting our songs, running the essence of our souls into every note. Together, we formed a bond that went deeper than just making music; we became a family, united under the banner of rock 'n roll.

Sure, my journey may not have led to stadium tours or fame, but it gifted me with something far more valuable: the ability to touch people's souls through my music. It allowed me to connect with kindred spirits, with those who yearned for the same raw energy that pulsed within me.

So, as the years have gone by, that old acoustic guitar still remains by my side.

It bears the mark of countless hours spent pouring my heart and soul into its strings. And although the stage may be smaller now, the passion burns just as bright, and I continue to rock the night away, leaving an imprint on the hearts of those who listen.

And that, my friends, is the story of a woman who found her voice amidst the smoky night spots of the deep south, armed with an old acoustic guitar and a relentless spirit never to stop rocking.

Ah, well, my friends, it seems this "ex-rock chic" has embarked on a rather unexpected yet beautiful path in life. After my adventures in the local music scene of the Deep South, I found myself drawn to a different kind of calling: the serene world of the Catholic Church.

Following my heart, I made my way to South America, where I devoted myself to a life of faith and service. Over time, my dedication and passion caught the attention of a local convent, and I was invited to join their community as a Sister.

With my musical background and a voice that could move mountains, I found myself entrusted with a remarkable responsibility. I was given the honour of managing the only choir of singing Sisters in South America. Now known as Sister Superior, I led the enchanting voices of my fellow Sisters in harmonious melodies that resonate with the divine.

Under my guidance, the choir thrived, capturing the hearts of the faithful who gathered in the church's hallowed halls. Our combined music uplifted, inspired, and brought solace to the souls of those seeking comfort and spiritual connection.

The power of our voices, now profoundly intertwined with our faith, resonates through each note, uniting the congregation in a shared spiritual experience.

Yes, my talents as a rock singer-songwriter may seem worlds apart from my current role, but in truth, they serve as unique threads that weave together to create something truly extraordinary. The passion I once poured into rocking the stages of local night spots now finds its expression in hymns and sacred chants that echo through the holy walls of the convent.

Now, as I manage the choir of singing Sisters, I guide my fellow ladies with unwavering devotion and a deep understanding of the transformative power of music. Their voices blend in harmonies that can uplift spirits, offer solace, and ignite the flame of faith within the hearts of all who listen.

It is safe to say my journey from the rocking stages of the Deep South to managing a choir of singing Sisters in South America embodies the beauty of transformation and the power of faith. I have found my purpose in merging my love for music and my unwavering belief in the service of others, creating a harmonious symphony that fills hearts with joy and reverence.

So, my friends, let us celebrate my unique path as I embrace my calling and find a way to touch souls with my voice and devotion.

Even now, over sixty years later, I still play this wonderful instrument at least twice a week and more when my congregation of singing Sisters are in concert or when we are in a recording studio.

I have had the good fortune in life to blend my love of music with my Catholic faith. One of my highlights, and there are many to choose from, was the three days that changed my life back in August 1969. From the moment I finished school, I lived a hippy life.

I loved the freedom of expression, the clothes, and the chance to find out who I was without anyone criticising me in any way. I will reveal to a couple of you that I did dabble in the odd marijuana joint and was a bit soft on a slice of Hash Cake.

The latter on one occasion had me visualising an orchard of trees walking around me. I did not feel comfortable with the sensation of my eyes always being one step behind my normal senses.

But that was my limit. No hardcore drugs such as cocaine, acid, or opium. These bad boys were all the rage, but to be truthful, I was far too shy to start tripping on LSD or snorting white substances up my nose. Yes, I know. It's a bit lame for an ex-rock chic.

I had been invited to join a young band of folk singers as a backup singer and guitarist. We were about to head to a new festival everyone was talking about due upstate from NYC called Woodstock. The cost was either $18 for three days in advance or $24 at the Gates.

We all pooled our money and paid in advance. I was so excited; it was my first-ever festival. I asked if we were going to play and was told no, we were not. But we could start jamming away in between the acts and gain loads of exposure.

When we arrived, there needed to be more clarity; the organisers had to change the venue from Woodstock itself to nearby Bethel. It turned out they had expected some locals to wish to attend, but word got around, and now thousands of us were coming. The final figure hit over half a million.

According to the magazine I was reading in the Doctor's waiting room. They managed to do a deal at the last minute for a large, sprawling dairy farm. Good job they did; imagine 500,000 hippies turning up at your door.

### The 1969 Woodstock Music Festival:

Three Days of Peace kicked off with a folk singer named Richie Havens, whom I liked a lot. At the time, I was amazed he stayed on stage for over three hours. Now I know why. According to this article, Act 2 did not take over. They were waiting for a helicopter to arrive.

When it eventually arrived, the sound of 500,000 roaring their approval rang out to welcome them. Not a single moan could be heard.

The next day, we saw an armada of helicopters swirling past, crammed with new artists and food for the crowds. Wow, what an adventure it must have been for those original organisers.

The festival was due to finish on a Sunday evening with Jimi Hendrix, but with all the delays not foreseen, he showed up on stage the following morning. The problem was no one knew, and the crowds left on Sunday, thinking he had decided not to come.

Luckily for my friends and me, we were delayed as we witnessed a 17-year-old who had decided to sleep in his bedroll under a parked tracker. The poor boy and the unfortunate tracker owner were unaware of each other, and the tractor ran over and crushed the boy.

We provided eyewitness accounts to the local police and missed much of Sunday's entertainment. We could hear the music but couldn't see the shows, which felt like listening to a very loud radio.

Fortunately, the Captain of the police squad was an avid rock music lover. How he managed to locate a small television, we will never know, but we were thankful for his ingenuity. In between acts, we kept everyone's spirits up with our improvised renditions of as many folk songs by the brilliance of Bob Dylan and Janis Joplin as possible.

I am sad here now, looking out of the window with a glass of Lula and an Empanada. All those beautiful performers became household names. You must remember Creedence Clearwater Revival, Jefferson Airplane, Joan Baez, Joe Cocker, Santana, and the legends in my eyes, Crosby, Stills, Nash, and Young.

Image my community of young singing Sisters if they could see me then and now excitedly swooning about my vocal heroes of the past.

I turned to the last page of the article on Woodstock, and I can reveal some facts I never knew.

I always thought Woodstock had been the most significant festival, but no, I was wrong. It turns out a Scotsman called Rod Stewart performed in front of 3.5 million Brazilians at Copacabana Beach in 1994. He gave it as a gift to all the poor people of Rio. What a lovely man he must be.

Another nice man was a Frenchman named Jean Michel Jarre. Apparently, three years later, he also performed in front of 3.5 million Russian fans.

He went one step or many steps further by creating a direct link to the Russian Mir station orbiting around the Earth. Wow, I missed that one. What was I doing on September 6 1997?

The final information I have just read has left me with a slight melancholy:

- Woodstock went on to be listed as the most significant musical event ever and to mark the occasion.
- A museum was erected.

- There's a monument marking the spot where I went crazy for three days.

Thank you, all, for allowing me to relive a moment in time with you wonderful readers. I do hope you are not too shocked by a singing Sister Superior who once was partial to a slab of hash cake and the odd joint. Well, it was the Hippy Years. Peace to you all.

Josefina x

*****

Well, it was another three months before Sister Superior Josefina Ignacia De Mesa returned up the mountain in one of the orange mountain buses that stopped just outside the school and church.

I was waiting for her as she climbed down the three metal steps, her cross up to her lips, and deep in prayer of gratitude to God for ensuring her safety with such a driver's lack of road safety in his head.

She turned her attention towards me and said, "God helps in many ways, and we must always be aware to say thank you." We both giggled together and turned to head to the school.

With my eagerness to see her, I inadvertently blurted out, "Sister Superior, I am the voice you have come to hear!"

She paused and looked at me. "You, Rosa, are so small and yet so strong of voice. Later, my child, please do not worry. I have lots of time to listen to such a beautiful voice; let me do God's work first, and then you can sing as much as you wish."

It was not until after we had our midday lunch that I was finally summoned to sing, and everyone from the school and the local village sat in lines around and behind Sister Superior, Sister Mily, and Sister Miriam.

All were quietly waiting for me to start.

I was struck numb.

I was like a statue, not moving an inch.

Eventually, my eyes focused on Sister Miriam, and I saw her signal from her to me to start. Another silent minute passed, and then I could hear my voice rising in volume; I was singing to the biggest audience of my life.

The experience was overwhelming, and I had to look up to the sky to concentrate on the words and tone of the sounds I had rehearsed repeatedly over the last three months.

Looking at the only white cloud, I pictured God sitting in his favourite chair, looking down at me. From that very moment, I knew what my mission in life was.

When I finished, it was like watching a football match on TV. When one of the players scored a goal, the crowd erupted as one, with hands and hearts reaching high up to the sky in sheer delight. That day, I had to sing three more songs, and eventually, to thunderous applause, Sister Superior rose and waved to the crowd to be quiet so she could speak to me.

"Little Rosa, I suspect God would like you to come and stay for a week at our farm down in the city. There, you can meet the other singing angels, whom I call my sisters. If you agree and enjoy the experience, we would be more than happy to offer you a place in our mission to the waiting world."

I burst into tears and ran into her arms, muttering, "Yes, oh Yes! Please, thank you all and thank you, God."

Another two months have gone by, and here I am now, walking down the long new road. The moon was at its highest for the year, allowing me lots of light to see the surface of the road and its shiny little reflectors.

I am just on the straight part of the road heading towards the older people's home. I am eating an apple and having a small bottle of water to quench my thirst. I have visited this home a couple of times, and it always has a friendly atmosphere. I sit among the older people, serve them coffee and cakes, and sometimes sing for them.

*****

At this point, Rosa's world changed forever. Alarmed and frightened, she could see a street man placing a rock on the ground and staring at her, a racing quad bike with a beautiful rider rising above the ground, and the charging engine of a huge truck approaching fast behind her………

*****

## 22: I am an Earthquake measuring 4.7 on the MM scale

*I* decided to arrive in the early hours of the night, just before 11 pm. I assumed that all barbarians would be in or near their beds and sleeping areas.

At this time, I could make a slight adjustment to the mountain ridge near the Pueblo that faced downwards onto the city below without being a bother to anyone.

With the barbarians sleeping, the disruption would be low. For those with the misfortune to be still awake, well that would be a different manner.

Climate Change had assured me that nobody, not even Scientists or, more accurately, seismologists, could predict when I was going to erupt and quake my anger.

When they did become aware of me, they used their Seismograms to measure my intensity and, in this particular natural disaster of moderate size, labelled me a 4.7 Earthquake event—more of a local nuisance than an all-out disaster.

They used to use the Richter Scale, developed back in the 1930s, to measure me, but the more accurate Moment Magnitude Scale had replaced that method. This apparently uses newer technologies from the 1970s onwards to know what event I am.

So, what had bothered me on this occasion?

Considering there had been another 1000 other times in the past year, I had good reason to shake and heave, which I did not bother to do. The barbarians had slept peacefully without any disturbance.

Yes, I am aware of the strange white-haired man halfway up the old craggy road who woke up twice in one night previously, thinking a big truck was going up the old craggy road and causing the metal bedroom wardrobe doors to rattle and shake for at least three minutes.

Later, he was asked if he had felt the tremors the night before, and he stayed quiet, not wishing to expose his misunderstanding and thinking a truck had caused the wardrobe to shake.

His wife, with the most bottomless brown eyes, the widest of smiles, and glowing white natural teeth, had not been disturbed in the slightest. But please do remember that this was his first experience of a 3.2 minor earthquake.

*****

To answer the earlier unanswered question of what had bothered me was simple. Nothing. It was time, plain and simple.

For quite some considerable time now, the fault lines at the edges of the Tectonic plates closest to this location have been basically puzzle pieces of the Earth's crust, which had gotten a bit stuck under another set of fault lines belonging to another set of Tectonic plates further along.

I could handle them being stuck. The problem I couldn't understand was the fact the tectonic plates kept moving, floating on top of the Earth's core. This caused a lot of stress, and frankly, I had hardened enough.

I am a peaceful mountain ridge, but sometimes it does help to sound off once in a while. At least eleven occasions every hundred years or more is surely acceptable.

*****

It's incredible how earthquakes attract bad press. Over 80% of my colleagues are placed near and around Japan and under the Pacific Ocean in an area known as the "Ring of Fire."

You do see those negative headlines regarding them in the world press. Only we, as a mere afterthought when we have an accident or two, can modestly agree with the headlines.

And yes, when life in large numbers is adjusted or, as the papers say, lost.

Okay, my colleagues do go over the top at times, and I accept the annual loss of over 10,000 humans is an unacceptable high figure, but look, it's not always our fault.

You tell them time after time after time, and do they listen?

No. You tell these same humans if books start falling from shelves or thrown from a chair they are sitting in comfortably prior to landing on the other side of the room. Then do something. Don't just sit there shaking with panic!

Or if the ground starts shaking or rippling, then it might be best to hide under a robust and sturdy table and hold on to it.

Or you advise them to stand under a door frame. Okay, the table might work, but the door frame might make me have trouble keeping a cool head as the rest of the house collapses around me.

I have even read the advice to stay really low to the ground, put your hands over your head, or curl up next to a bed or couch.

Please tell me, if the room is rippling and the bed or couch is on castors, what are the humans supposed to do then? Chase the moving piece of furniture on all fours around the spinning room or what?

Sometimes, you tell them to go outside and avoid trees, power lines, telegraph poles and, of course, falling debris from collapsing buildings. So, apart from the odd football pitch, where else do you recommend?

Well, less of my gripe. Let me tell you what really happened on this occasion. Firstly, as I said earlier, I had no choice. I am allowed to let go when the need is evident, and I am perfectly in my right to make the most of it. I have the right to make the ground shake. I did. I have the right to make sure buildings tumble. I did. I have the right to make roads heave and crack. I did. I had the privilege to cause the odd fire. I did.

But on this occasion, I did draw the line at mudslides, floods, and those horrible bullying tsunamis, all of which leave a terrible mess.

Also, the ground was dry, and no significant rain had appeared for at least three months, so those last options were not really available to me. Not that I am complaining—far be it for me to complain.

*****

Anyway, let's get back to what happened.

Let's start with the old craggy road. Well, not much can be done to him. With all those years of neglect by barbarians, whatever I did may have improved him.

Yes, I lifted the road a fair bit and created some rather large ruts and the odd man-sized crater that those metal two-wheelie affairs will have some fun trying to avoid.

Adding the problem of keeping in a straight line going up and down will, for a while, keep them occupied. I suspect they will spend more time walking their precious bikes up the mountain ridge than riding them. But they are adaptable.

They will eventually stop moaning and adjust their routes until I decide a change is required once more.

Now, let's turn to that new boring road with its shiny buttons or reflectors, as some call them. She likes to boast about these shiny buttons often, but she went quiet when I displayed my lights.

I initially showed my power to produce strange side effects with eerie blue, green and orange sizzling flames of lights in the night sky. Then, I showed how I could change the lights to different shapes, forms, and colours.

I can make them appear to have emanated and risen to fifteen centimetres from the very ground. They look similar to those lightning strikes in the sky, except mine do not originate from the clouds above but from, as I said, from the ground.

Others I turn into balls of light into ghostly globes and allow them to float into the air for a brief moment. Tonight, many lasted from a fraction of a second to many minutes.

These are always impressive when the ground is shaking. Tonight, I managed to get them to reach as high as 50 meters. In the past, I have managed to reach 200 meters on numerous occasions, but remember, I am only a moderate earthquake this time around.

In days gone by barbarians thought of these lights in a religious context; Much later, they associated my lights with UFOs or aeroplanes. But if they bothered to ask me, I would gladly reveal they are as natural as me.

I like to start my displays just prior to the shaking routine and sometimes during. It all depends on the size of the audience and when they are focusing on me.

I do not fully understand how I am able to do it because I am not a scientist. But when my Tectonic plates cause me stress, certain rocks create electrical charges.

These become active, like when humans switch on batteries and their lights. The one important thing is that I can only do this lighting display sometimes. In truth, I rarely can, but luckily for the barbarians tonight, I am fully functioning in the lighting department.

The whole road was quiet, as you would expect; nothing stirred until I did.

I found it fun initially to make the rumble noises and test the reflectors as I began shaking the ground just underneath them.

I got bored and started the rippling effect, which proved to be very entertaining. Now, the surface and the reflectors began to sway in unison. Just close your eyes and picture this poetic scene in your mind.

*I stirred from my slumber, bored with the stillness, And set off a ripple, a dance of vastness.*

*The surface trembled, the reflectors did sway, In perfect harmony, a grand display. Close your eyes and see it unfold, A symphony of movement, a story untold.*

*Like a maestro in a studio, I conducted the show, Each wave a note, in a rhythm that did flow.*

At one point, nearly the whole new road gyrated from side to side and up and down like the waves of an ocean. It was just a spectacular thing to behold and to be honest, I never tired of seeing such a display of beauty.

All the birds sang and flew like the road up and down and side to side, and they all started to move away. Then, the animals on the ground began to move. You noticed I didn't say dance. No, they were all crying with fear and just ran in straight lines away from the rippling road using their keen senses that barbarians can only dream of having.

Just imagine yourself observing capybaras, snakes, scorpions, centipedes, horses, mules, donkeys, cows, pigs, chickens, cockerels, cats, and dogs move as one in the unified pursuit of their survival.

They all believed the best place to run was down the mountain towards the plains just east of the city.

It was like watching an inner signal being switched on in whatever species it was.

It was not time to start eating or attacking each other; it was time for survival of the fittest.

Who could cover more ground than the other in a shorter time?

As I refocused back on the rippling road again, I decided to make the road surface crack open, and it was so easy. I was a bit careful not to go too crazy, just enough to spoil the road in three places.

It was not long after the animals had begun their retreat that the lights started to flicker on in the homes up and down the mountain. Humans came rushing out of each occupied building. Humans are different from animals and birds; humans just panic and run around in various stages of fear. Unlike the animals, they appear to have no degree of purpose except to scream in terror.

Most of them at this hour are semi-naked, fully naked or fully clothed in their nightwear.

All of them looked with big, round eyes at the roofs of their homes. Each feared they were going to lose everything they had and maybe get trapped in the falling debris. Very few of them had the gumption to know that most of them would be okay.

On this occasion, their homes appear to have been built to withstand my shenanigans.

Later, once all has gone quiet with me again, these shaken humans will re-enter their properties. I will see I have managed to leave the odd scars, such as cracks in the walls and holes up near the roof joints.

Yes, their belongings will be scattered around, and some fragile items will have suffered some disrepair. But nearly all damage would be declared as superficial.

Apart from those crafty humans who have invested in home cover for their property, they would most definitely make their case known for their considerable losses. All of a sudden, everything goes on claim forms. All you have is now lost. But guess what? Those nasty insurance companies, in their small print, declare I am a natural disaster and, therefore, no cover will be paid out. Ha, to those crafty fraudsters.

There would be no money for the older people's homes as well.

It has only occurred on me how old it was.

I totally forgotten the effect I was going to have on it. Only one word could describe the effect my earthquake had on it, and that was catastrophic.

*****

The roofs over the communal kitchen lounges and library were the first to collapse inwards. The beams had taken all that I could throw at it over the years. But this was going to prove to be one earthquake too many.

A fire broke out, and being this high up on the mountain ridge, it stood no chance of being extinguished quickly. The fire took hold very rapidly as everything seemed made of wood: the doors, the panelled walls, the high ceilings and, of course, the many stairs.

The next target for the flames was the colossal amount of furniture. Every room was filled with fuel for the expanding fire, and All the older people's belongings, furniture, and mattresses were so ancient that you could call them antiques.

Fire certificates had never been issued to show their fillings were fire retardant.

The vast library was the centre of a fire all on its own and lay burning and smouldering for many days after. The books and the paintings were never to be examined or admired again.

For clarity of what I did in this library, I will refer you to my diary entry from the next day: *Oh, trembling mortals, gather around, for I shall recount a harrowing tale of an inferno that consumed the paintings and book library of the esteemed older people's care home atop the majestic mountain ridge.*

*A calamitous event that shook the very foundation of the tranquil abode, turning art and literature into mere ashes within the twinkling of an eye.*

*Picture this, dear souls: a serene sanctuary perched on high, where the wisdom of age intertwined with the beauty of art. Walls adorned with masterpieces, each stroke telling a story, capturing emotions that words fail to convey. Rows upon rows of books, pages filled with knowledge and imagination, inviting its inhabitants to embark on a journey through time and space.*

*But alas! Fate had a sinister plan, casting its dark gaze upon this hallowed ground. Suddenly, the ground beneath began to heave and convulse as though the very mountain ridge was awakening from a long slumber.*

*Fear filled the air, mingling with the foreboding whispers of impending doom.*

*And there I stood, an omnipotent force, an earthquake wreaking havoc upon this sacred haven.*

*With a mighty crack, the heavens roared and unleashed a cascade of sparks that danced merrily upon the fragile canvas of the paintings. Flames erupted, hungrily devouring each stroke of brilliance, reducing them to nothingness.*

*The symphony of cracking fire and shattering glass reverberated through the souls of older people as they helplessly witnessed a lifetime of intricate brushwork disintegrate into oblivion.*

*But not content with this display of infernal chaos, the flames mercilessly turned towards the once-hallowed library.*

*Like voracious demons, they licked at the spines of countless volumes, their pages curling and twisting in agony.*

*Generations' accumulated wisdom vanished, consumed by fiery fiends. The intoxicating aroma of knowledge transformed into acrid smoke that choked the very breath of intellectual enlightenment.*

Oh, the anguish that hung heavy in the air!

The cherished memories of a lifetime, precious treasures that had weathered time's relentless march, all reduced to zero. The flickering embers danced mockingly, mirroring the tears streaming down the faces of the aged residents, a reflection of their shattered memories and irreplaceable losses.

*****

And thus, dear mortals, a tragic chapter unfolded, witnessed by this catastrophic earthquake.

But fear not. The flames may have devoured the paintings and the books, but the spirit of resilience and determination remained unyielding. Even later, as the tears flowed. So, he made the decision to rebuild, to restore what once was.

For art and literature are eternal, and in the face of destruction, the flames ignite a roaring beacon of hope, illuminating the path forward amidst the chaos.

All the fire extinguishers were covered in dust, and fire buckets and towels were non-existent.

The deadly black smoke accompanied the fire, with its growing clouds of toxic gases blowing out and racing to fill every room where it could find an opening.

Many of the older people lay quietly in their beds.

The majority of them could not hear the crackling sounds that were approaching their rooms.

The fumes reached out to them all and engulfed their frail and dying lungs. Most of them, initially, never felt the flicker of the burning flames. Later, these poor souls were discovered in their death throes in the ashes of their beds by the investigating fire teams.

They would eventually declare the final loss of life to be nine residents.

Of course, there were survivors. Most of the night crew managed to move the residents living further away from the main house. But as you can imagine, the few night care nurses and a couple of cleaners were helplessly outnumbered and ill-equipped to put out such a ferocious fire. They could only stand back in horror and shame at their inadequacies.

They had no effective equipment to stop it; their feeble buckets of kitchen water were never going to match the inferno I had created.

Even if they had turned to the nearby small church and its water supply, it would never have been an overwhelming force of opposition to the flames. The only source was a small toilet in the back with a small wash basin. At its capacity, the small church could only seat 20 parishioners and the odd wheelchair user.

Of course, the care workers had yet to receive any training either to reduce the effect of a fire or to handle it as trained firefighters would do. The experience was miles away down in the city or at the airport; nobody in authority had foreseen the risk.

You have to remember I had not been angry for just over a century. Everyone had forgotten that I could exist.

Besides, none of the trained firefighters would have reached me in time to make any difference anyway. Why, you may ask. It was because one of the cracks in the road I had made was just before the location of the older person's home.

It delayed a rescue mission by a further six hours before the first fire truck managed to get through and park outside the smouldering ashes and burnt framework of the communal building's main entrance. The door frame was still intact and standing upright.

The doors that had hung under that frame for hundreds of years were now gone.

The rivets, bolts, and odd pieces of iron belonging to the doors now lie among the ashes of the older people's homes.

Mind you, something unusual caught the corner of my eye, and I thought about it a lot later.

I thought I saw nine ghostly faceless objects moving as one and leaving the wreckage.

They began to glide silently up and away from within the ashes, where I am at this moment, unsure and a bit perplexed as I had never witnessed such a phenomenon before.

I was so busy with other issues that I couldn't concentrate on any single event at the time.

Remember, I was classed as a moderate earthquake, but I was still covering a vast area.

*****

My attention was directed to another ridge just left of the new road; this one did not have any homes on it as its walls were very steep. The land up here had always been reserved for grazing cattle, their ever-present friends, the egrets, and the odd ranch's livery of stallions.

Only one dirt road covered the top of the ridge for most of its length, with a water trough for the animals situated for all travellers in their cars to see midway on the skyline of the ridge from the Old craggy road.

Near the top lay two naturally made lakes, which had minimal purpose to the barbarians except when the bush was on fire.

Helicopters would swoop down and, with large buckets hanging from each, gather up the water from the lakes and race back to where the firefighters needed it the most.

This is an effective way of creating breakers in the fires and turning each one into smaller fires, allowing the fire crews on the ground to deal with each one individually instead of being overwhelmed by one colossal fire.

Another fire had broken out on this ridge in the scrubland just below the horizon due to there being no current rainfall for some time. It quickly became an inferno for all the wildlife, insects and birds. Luckily, the cattle and stallions had been moved the night before by the local farm labourers as they had been warned that arsonists and rustlers were on the prowl and up to their no good by either creating needless fires or by stealing the animals to sell them to unlicensed slaughterhouses in the centre of the city.

Much of these animal products were sold cheaply to the poor inhabitants of the city's shanty areas, and of course, the origins of the meat were never mentioned.

Times were hard; Questions were only asked by the rich, never by the poor.

This fire went uncontrolled as, again, no trained firemen were able to reach the mountain ridge.

The local resistance is comprised of local farmers and labourers. Collectively, they did their best, but it was never going to match the ferociousness of the penetrating flames. The only thing that was to change this danger was going to have to come from the clouds.

And the big grey ones were desperately needed soon.

Given enough time, the bushfires would reach out and pass from the ridge onto the next ridge, which, of course, housed the two roads.

Here, houses and farms would be quickly within reach of the sizzling flames. The fires would then be totally out of control, and it would not take long to race up the mountain to the Pueblo and beyond to the tea plantations at the very top.

Now, it was dawning on the horrified humans that they stood to lose not only their lives but everything they had ever owned.

Many strange and unexplained events happen during a typical earthquake, and often, there is no one to record such events except, of course, us earthquakes.

On this occasion, the white-haired stranger began to write all his thoughts in his notebook, witnessing and recording the cries for help from the men already fighting the fires.

Men from this ridge of the two roads moved together in their cars, on motorbikes, and astride trucks towards the other ridge near the little one-room shop that the English stranger called Tesco.

The big red gate that kept the animals in and the humans out was opened to allow the humans in their carriages to race along the dirt road to the two lakes and the water trough.

Here, they stopped panicking for the first time, coordinated themselves into a protracted human wall, and faced the flames with blankets, sheets, and anything they could use to fan down the fire.

Within twenty minutes, two helicopters from the city's fire service arrived, and water began to be transferred from the lakes to the edges of the fire. Within another six hours, the flames were finally subdued, and smoke was left swirling around and above the ridge.

For the first time, I saw the whole community suddenly become one completely euphoric unit. They were all jumping with elation at being in a position to save themselves, their neighbours, and as many properties as possible.

Someone suggested they build on their success by organising a command centre to coordinate further action that would be required as the night proceeded.

The small church just outside of the Dapa Pueblo was quickly identified as a good location and would allow the effort to continue, as even churches allow for internet and Wi-Fi.

To many of the very rich families, this night became an adventure.

To people experiencing poverty, it became a night to survive.

The father of Ximena, the beautiful daughter with the beautiful quad bike, became the unofficial leader on the mountain and for him a night to save his beautiful daughter.

His vast wealth and his generation of ancestors made him the natural choice to all.

As little as fifty years ago, only five families lived an isolated existence, traipsing up and down my mountain ridge. It was so dangerous to travel as individuals, who all decided safety and strength would be better served if they formed a group.

Each evening, those travelling up would meet at the junction of the main road near the site of a proposed shopping mall. This led to the only dirt road that allowed them access up and down to their properties.

They trekked as a small armed group to ward off the many attacks and ambushes that robbed them of their belongings. Of course, over some time, some adjustments were made to those defending themselves, and a more significant adjustment was made to those who wished to steal.

These same families grew as the years passed, and they were the same families who sold large tracts of land for development and arranged for the church and cemetery nearby.

They became very wealthy and influential. The Londonos were one such family.

They were the driving force behind the new road, which took another eighteen years to build. Why did it take so long? It was not their fault. Even they fought against bribery and corruption, which may well have played their part.

Indeed, it was rare to see descendants of all five families come together as one, as the originals did many years before, but tonight, it was necessary. Besides that, a little bit of mountain history, no one else moved forward to volunteer themselves.

The new quad and motorbikes proved to be human assets in this crisis. A third fire had broken out further up past Dapa Pueblo. The initial reports suggested it was a small one at present but had the potential to go out of control if left unchecked.

The five original families headed by the Londonos and their neighbours, each with their unique skills and resources, knew they had to act quickly to prevent the fire from spreading further. They gathered together and devised a plan to contain the fire before it could grow out of control.

Utilising the quad and motorbikes once more, they strategically assessed the fire's extent to determine the most effective approach. They then divided into groups, with some creating firebreaks using shovels and tools to clear vegetation, while others utilised water from the nearby two lakes and the smaller in statue waterfall close by to extinguish the flames. Their resourcefulness and adaptability were instrumental in their successful containment of the fire.

It was at this point I went quiet once more.

*****

# 23: *I am the Historical Event Incorporating Four Human souls*

I have been asked to tell you all that happened in the middle of the earthquake on the new road, as even the earthquake on the mountain ridge itself feels ashamed and accepts it went too far.

His enthusiasm for creating the spectacular light display, followed by the rippling and shaking effects on that road, led to a series of events that changed four people's souls forever.

I best start just before the four individuals met with Leonardo's kite.

The kite firmly believed in his destiny, that he was soon to be soaring higher and higher to enable him to enter the orbit of the earth and transform into the renowned Celestial 27 Satellite.

The problem is that the kite went in the wrong direction, and it was not entirely his fault.

The kite had started with all the best intentions. He got a fair distance up in the midnight sky.

Suddenly, everything started shaking and moving up and down, including himself.

Within seconds, he ended up entangled in a tree. Poor Leonardo and his uncle Sergio were powerless to free him from the many branches that held him.

The kite saw Leonardo's outcry of misery and further witnessed his uncle wrapping his nephew in his arms until the weeping had ceased.

After a brief moment in time, all the humans who had been enjoying this pastime of kite flying dispersed in terror and hurried down the mountain to their city homes. Most kite owners were content to leave the shaking ridge, while one or two were not.

These latter fools always show no sense in any situation. It appears your human world is full of them.

The evening became night, and now, on his own, the kite had nearly accepted his failure when suddenly a taste of air released him from the branches of the tree, and he was spiralling out of control.

He saw the telegraph pole and its wires when it was too late to avoid them, and he crashed straight into the pole's top.

The damage this time was extensive; remember, his frame was only made of bamboo.

If he had fallen to the ground, the events that were about to unfold could have been avoided. But alas, he got well entangled for the next critical few minutes.

Then, a force of unexplained nature tore his frame free from the pole, and he was helplessly spiralling again. He was only now heading on a horizontal line of flight rather than vertical as he had envisaged. He was directly heading on a straight path towards the beautiful rider on her quad bike.

At the exact moment, Ximena was on course for a spectacular lift-off from the surface of the road.

Obviously, she had not planned to do so.

The mountain ridge's surface shaking of the road had not accounted for the presence of Ximena and her quad.

*****

Ximena left the city below later than she expected. Her friends were more high-spirited than usual, and she did not wish to miss all the fun.

It was tonight that she realised for the first time that travelling up and down the mountain could be a chore and restrict her social life at times.

So, on the next available weekend, she decided to approach her father to see if he would find an apartment in the city purely for her. Then, she would be in the middle of all the fun and in a better position to influence her social standing even further.

It was two in the morning, and the road was calm. Ximena had applied full throttle to her quad, and it responded exactly as she wished. She was flying up the mountain new road, and for once, she had left her helmet in the compartment behind her buttocks. Thus, allowing her flowing hair to spread back in mountainous waves.

Suddenly, Ximena sensed something was different. Through her expanding confusion, what she saw bewildered her.

The effects of the road surface made it look like it was moving, but that is impossible, she reasoned, feeling her anxiety rising, "Why is the surface rippling?" she asked no one in particular.

Never in her young life had Ximena experienced an earthquake, and certainly not on a racing machine doing over 80 mph. She had no idea what to do or how to react.

Suddenly, the surface of the road rose before her very eyes, and the realisation that she was about to leave the surface and enter an abyss enveloped her entire being. Then, a force so instant and unexpectedly smashed into her unprotected face. Everything went black.

*****

Stalin had spent the previous hour bent over in a gully, enduring spasms through his small, wry body. One second shaking with cold, the subsequent shaking with fever. He had no control. Every fibre of his emancipated body was screaming out in pain.

He should have listened to those early body messages regarding the bad-tasting lasagna. He was now suffering from the effects of food poisoning.

He had not yet thrown up or emptied his bowels. As all humans know, those stages will unavoidably arrive. And seeing Stalin in so much discomfort, they would not be long in coming.

He laid down his rock to wipe his sweating forehead, and his eyes began to take in his surroundings. The road was quiet; even the birds were unusually still. Maybe they were not here, he thought.

He struggled to stand with his weakened feet and reached out to the tree next to him.

His befuddled mind thought it was swaying to and fro, or maybe it was himself that was swaying. Then the realisation hit him: they were both swaying!

He gripped the tree harder and focused further with his eyes. In the distance, he could see a small girl dressed in a Nun's habit struggling to remain on her feet.

Both her hands were holding her head, covering her, and the fear in her eyes revealed everything she was going through.

The road surface she was trying to keep her balance on was rising up and down in a rippling effect. In that terrifying moment, she looked like she was surfing on waves of tarmac instead of water.

Their eyes met, and something deep down in her soul told him she needed him now.

It had been many years since he had felt that feeling from another human who wished for him to be close to her, assisting with abating the sheer terror she felt in her hour of need.

As he moved towards her, his hand outstretched, he felt his position rise above the Nun. For a fraction of a second, he stared down at her before the ground started to return to Earth.

Now, they were only feet away. Again, her position rose higher, and suddenly, next to him, something fast and yellow in colour sped past, narrowly missing him.

He could see a young woman with volumes of flowing black hair filling the night sky, screaming out in pure terror.

Then he witnessed the most bizarre thing he would ever know: the rider was hit by a flying kite!

*****

Ignacio had quietly left his bed, and Jasmina only turned to adjust her sleeping position. It was not long before her sleeping noises purred in the dark. She has always stated she never snored in her sleep, thought Ignacio with a smile.

One night, Ignacio will remember this and make her laugh with him when she realises she does snore, albeit beautifully.

Ignacio quickly got dressed and headed into the kitchen to pick up his packed lunch that Jasmina had prepared the evening before, as she always did. A flask of coffee awaited on the stove. He gathered all that he needed, progressed to the front of the house, and stood outside.

He looked up at the night sky and saw unusual green, orange, and blue lights. They seemed strange to him, but he concentrated on opening the big truck door. Climbing aboard involves a particular routine, and he knew it by heart.

Even now, in his sixties, Ignacio imagined he looked like an Olympic athlete who had sprung aboard the big truck.

Jasmina consistently reminded him to stay fit and healthy during his working life, and he always tried to obey her. However, maintaining a healthy lifestyle was not easy when you are a truck driver, and apart from his growing girth, he managed to stay well.

In all those years on the road, he only had raging toothache twice, and on the first episode, he had to administer the treatment as he was miles away from any professional.

He shuddered at the memory. Ignacio, known for his determination and resilience, is not one to let a toothache bring him down. With no option but to take matters into his own hands, he decided to administer his own tooth extraction while remaining focused on his trucking duties.

Remembering the excruciating pain, he was determined to find a solution. He quickly dismissed the idea of seeking professional dental care because the nearest town or city was over 200 miles away. Now was the time for unwavering commitment to take matters into his own hands.

Fuelling up at a gas station, he recalled finding a simple first aid kit in the convenience store. With limited options available, he ingeniously devised a plan to distract himself from the pain and safely remove the offending tooth. He purchased a numbing gel and a spare rag, determined to make this makeshift dental procedure work.

Setting up a makeshift dental station inside the cab of his truck, Ignacio remembers finding the courage to take a deep breath, preparing himself mentally and physically for the dental challenge ahead.

With the numbing gel applied and his rag to bite down on for stability, he took a deep breath and began his self-administered distraction.

*****

With one swift motion, Ignacio pulled the tooth out. The memory of allowing a surge of both relief and adrenaline to wash over him. Even now, he thinking about how his face showed a mix of pain and triumph as the challenge was successfully faced head-on. He would remain privately forever proud of his unwavering determination to do whatever it would take to get the job done.

The "treatment" ended with Ignacio pressing a piece of gauze against the bleeding socket as he continued his journey on the open road. His fellow truckers applauded Ignacio's resilience and resourcefulness as they witnessed his unwavering commitment to his work, even in the face of a dental emergency.

The second time, he lived with the excruciating pain for three hours until he arrived in the capital and stopped outside a dental surgery that luckily married a very efficient young dentist who worked his magic in rapid time.

He set up his driving position and settled into his usual routine. A quick check of the instrument panel told him all was well, so he switched on the powerful engine.

Quietly, he moved the truck away from his house and steered towards the downward-looking road towards Dapa Pueblo further on. In the distance, he could see small white globe-like lights rising to the stars.

How unusual, he thought to himself. Over the years as a truck driver, he had seen many sights that nature always found to startle him, and he always tried to describe each one to his loving Jasmina and Samuel on his many returns. "But white globes rising from the ground?" Even Jasmina would question that one.

As he approached the level part of the road heading to the town, everything went mad.

First, to his right, he saw a Nun struggling to walk and keep upright. In the next second, ahead of him, he saw a street man in only his denim skirt reaching out to her.

Is this an attack? Is he going to rob her? Why would a Nun and a street man be out in the dark on a mountain ridge at this hour?

Before he could find the answer, the road in front of him rose and smashed down and instantly again.

Ignacio froze; he couldn't believe what he was seeing, and then instantly, "Earthquake!" came from his lips.

He was driving right into the middle of an earthquake!

His powers of survival sent his feet to the correct foot pedals.

Both his hands gripped the steering wheel as he prepared for an impact, which he was not sure of. Then, out of the darkness, a quad bike with a screaming woman with mountains of flowing black shiny hair flew up before his very windscreen and disappeared over the top of his cabin.

His unbelieving eyes could not fathom what he was seeing, and his brain stopped working. His head could only follow the trail of the quad as it disappeared from view.

There was a pause, then the sound of crashing metal hitting the road surface with considerable force. Ignacio only recorded the sound as he gave his braking rig his full attention. Sparks and then small flames started appearing behind each burning rubber tyre.

The sound of the protesting G" Forces on the truck's cabin, shattering the sound of the cracking road outside. The truck careered on for a good four hundred yards before coming to a stop. Ignacio switched off the engine and, in the darkness, lowered his head, cupped his hands together, and began to pray in total silence. At that very moment, the mountain ridge became silent.

Ximena lay unmoving next to her mangled and unrecognisable quad. Pelvis smashed heavily, and her breathing was shallow. Her hair was now lying all about her head, matted with drying blood from the wound above her left eye. The kite's impact damaged her jawline, which hung to one side and was out of place.

The damage was not restricted to just her jawline; once perfectly formed, her lower teeth were missing with a large part of her tongue. In their place were broken bits of bamboo and shards of silk.

The first person to reach the crater was Stalin. He looked down, and for the first time that he could remember, he started to cry. Stalin had no idea who this young woman was, but he could clearly see she was beyond his skills. Stalin sensed before seeing the Nun's presence by his side. Her small hand reached out and rested on his shoulder.

"Are you OK? Are you hurt?" she asked.

He tried to answer, but he had lost the power of everyday speech, and at that moment, his stomach let out a tremendous noise, and Stalin clutched his abdomen and bent forward, letting a considerable fart escape from his rear.

"I think he has issues that he needs some space to deal with on his own, Sister," suggested Ignacio as he arrived from behind. Both stood over the crater, neither knowing what to say or do.

"Please call me Rosa." Was all the shocked Sister could offer in words that would seem helpful.

"OK, I will address you as Sister Rosa if acceptable to you," Ignacio replied again without real thought; he, too, was struggling with the magnitude of what each of them had just witnessed. At least the street man was occupied, thought Ignacio.

"Yes, that will be fine with me; what do we do now? How do we get this poor girl out of this crater?" Both were now kneeling, looking at Ximena, who lay very still as if death had already claimed her.

Ignacio looked up around the mountain ridge, aware that all had gone quiet; the road surface had returned to normal with a fair bit of damage here and there.

Another crater lay further up the mountain road, so there were other options than reversing back. He would have to pass the crater very slowly with the remains of the quad bike, and the young rider, whom he could clearly see, needed urgent medical assistance beyond his capabilities.

Ignacio looked down at the quad and, with hidden thoughts, expressed his sadness that such a beautiful machine had come to such a violent end. He wished it well and raised a cross over his chest.

Sister Rosa saw and mistook this small gesture. She smiled at the warmth of the truck driver, who was now examining the ground next to the young rider. She looked like she was not going to survive this ordeal.

*****

"We need to move her now if she is to survive; waiting for emergency services will waste time. Will you help me bring her up from this crater to lay her on the top of my tailgate where the rear tyres are housed? To lift her to my cabin would surely finish her. If I drive very slowly, she can be held securely until we are approached by a medical team or something similar.

Without waiting for a reply from the Sister, Ignacio walked with purpose and determination. At the side of the road, he found a small tree with bamboo shoots sticking out of the ground. There was enough to arrange a small stretcher. He had rope and cable in his toolbox, and quietly and efficiently, he concocted a makeshift platform for the young woman to lie on.

Stalin had disappeared and could be heard groaning somewhere in the darkness. On his return, he looked like his whole life had passed him by. He shrugged off any offer of help from both Sister Rosa and Ignacio. A little while later, they turned their attention back to the injured woman.

Between the three of them, they managed to transfer her to the stretcher; she only let out a feeble cry once before returning to a coma. She appeared to be stable.

Stalin surprised the other two by instantly entering the crater with no thought for his safety. He dragged the makeshift stretcher towards him until he reach her.

At this point, he went about making leg splints for the woman and bathing her face with a cotton pad he had recovered from Ignacio's medical first Aid Kit. When he judged it safe to secure her to the stretcher, he did so without effort.

He even stemmed the flow of blood from her head wound, and before moving back away from her, he bandaged and secured her jaw so no more damage could occur while she was being transferred from the crater to the waiting Rosa and Ignacio.

Where did all this medical and first-aid knowledge come from? No one knew, but each one, including Stalin, was grateful it appeared. Tomorrow, it will be gone again, never to resurface.

Ignacio pulled with Rosa, and Stalin guided and lifted the stretcher. Once out of the crater, all three gently placed the stretcher onto the tailgate surface. With further rope and cables, they secured it into a reasonable position and hoped it would not break loose on the way down the mountain.

Sister Rosa moved to settle down on the tailgate when she saw Stalin holding an identity card listing the young woman as Ximena Londono. So, they had a name for her now, and a beautiful one, too, thought Sister Rosa.

Stalin then surprised her further by taking her hand and guiding her to the cabin passenger door.

He looked at her and up at the handle. Sister Rosa went to protest but stopped halfway, knowing for once it was time to be guided by this beautiful man.

Her heart reached out, and she thanked him. She was sure he had felt it.

The passenger door opened, and Ignacio was leaning outwards, looking for her hand to hoist her up.

Once she was settled, Stalin moved to the rear tailgate and found the best possible place for him to ensure he had control of the stretcher on the downward journey to come.

Once Ignacio could see everything was in place, he turned the engine on and started to move down the hill, suddenly thinking about Jasmina. He hoped and prayed silently that she would understand the dilemma he was now in and prayed that she was not in any danger. Sister Rosa, now shaking with the memory of the ordeal they had all survived, turned and whispered to Ignacio.

"Would you stop and let me get out?? I should stay here and help with the recovery of the mountain. I need to find my guiding Sisters at the Church school and help my friends. I can get a message to your family, and Someone needs to tell this young woman's family.

Ignacio looked out of the screen window, and he could see the lights of the city appearing in front of him. He knew the young Sister who had just survived with him thinking more clearly than he was. She will make a very able Nun indeed. Knowing he was fine would put Jasmina and Samuel at ease while he transferred this young woman to the hospital.

Quietly, he brought the rig to a stop, leaving the engine and lights on, and he turned to her. "Our house is easy to find; just head up past the church and the cemetery and then turn right onto "Calle de Plantain." Continue for maybe 500 meters, and you will see our house with the sign "Terra de Gratis" on the gate. There is a small bell on the left; my wife Jasmina will answer."

"I think I know your wife. Does she come to the church often?" Rosa realised that she might actually know this man's family.

"Yes, nearly every Sunday; I try to as often as I can, but sometimes work gets in the way," Ignacio replied almost sheepishly. But as an afterthought, "When I am in my cabin alone in a faraway place, I always stop and say a prayer and say thank you to his highest for allowing me to provide for my family as I do."

Rosa responded, "I am sure I will know her. Don't worry. I will not delay you further. Thank you for saving us." She fully understood that this was indeed a noble-minded human with a joyous soul. With a smile, Ignacio tilted his head towards the rear of his truck, implying, "On this occasion, I believe we all need to say thank you to God. Even the man behind with the rock in his hand might find a place and time to say thank you in his unique way."

*****

# 24: I am the Preliminary Police and Fire Department Report

## Police and Fire Department Report – Loss of Lives in a Care Home Fire during an Earthquake
September 2017
The City Police Department
Santiago de Cali, Valle de Cauca

[Executive Summary]
This report summarizes the events surrounding the tragic loss of nine older individuals due to a fire that engulfed a care home during an earthquake on the mountain ridge overlooking the city. The report outlines the Response of the Police and Fire Departments, initial findings from the investigation, and recommendations for future prevention and safety measures.

[Incident Overview]
On September 11, 2017, at approximately 19:30, an earthquake measuring 4.7 on the MM scale struck the mountain ridge overlooking the city. As a result of the earthquake, a fire broke out at The Older People's Care Home, a residential facility for older individuals located close to the epicentre. Nine residents lost their lives in the incident.

[Response]
1. Police Department:
- Police Department Mountain Ridge received the initial distress call at 19:50 and dispatched several units to the care home immediately.
- Upon arrival, the officers coordinated with the Fire Department and assisted in evacuating the surviving residents.
- The officers secured the perimeter to ensure the safety of the firefighters, residents, and nearby residents and facilitated communication between emergency services on-site.

2. Fire Department:
- Fire Department Mountain Ridge received the emergency call at 19:52 and dispatched 2 firefighting units to the location.
- Firefighters faced significant challenges due to the ongoing earthquake, which caused structural damage and hindered rescue efforts.
- Despite these challenges, firefighters worked diligently to suppress the fire and rescue as many residents as possible.

3. Emergency Medical Services (EMS):
- EMS personnel arrived promptly to provide emergency medical care and transportation for the injured residents.
- The injured residents were immediately transferred to city hospitals for further medical attention.
- 

[Investigation Findings]
1. Cause of Fire:
- Preliminary investigation reveals that the fire started due to an electrical short circuit that resulted from damages caused by the earthquake.
- Detailed analysis is underway to determine the exact sequence of events leading up to the ignition and rapid spread of the fire.

2. Safety Measures:
- Initial inspection indicates shortcomings in the care home's fire safety systems, including outdated fire alarms, inadequate emergency exits, and substandard fire extinguishers.
- The care home management is currently cooperating with authorities to determine the extent of safety violations and any potential negligence.

[Recommendations]
1. Enhance Building Safety:
- Authorities should conduct frequent inspections of residential care facilities to ensure compliance with fire safety regulations.
- Care homes should be mandated to update their fire safety systems and regularly test their emergency evacuation procedures.

2. Disaster Preparedness:
- Develop comprehensive disaster preparedness plans for care homes, including earthquake response protocols, staff training, and adequate emergency supplies, such as the number of fire extinguishers and first aid kits.

3. Risk Assessment:
- Conduct a thorough review of the structural integrity and safety of buildings located in seismic-prone areas, emphasizing fire prevention measures.

4. Public Awareness:
- Increase public awareness regarding the importance of fire safety in residential care facilities, educating both residents and staff about evacuation procedures and fire prevention methods.

This report is preliminary, and the investigation is ongoing. Once the investigation is complete, a final report with more comprehensive findings and recommendations will be issued.

[Conclusion]

The tragic loss of nine older individuals in the care home fire during the earthquake necessitates urgent action to enhance safety measures in similar facilities. The Police and Fire Departments are committed to collaborating with relevant authorities and stakeholders to prevent such incidents and protect vulnerable individuals in the future.

[Attachments]
- Fire and Rescue Incident Logs
- Incident Scene Photographs
- List of deceased individuals
- 

For any further inquiries or assistance, please contact the City Mayor's Office, Santiago de Cali.

Signed:

Fire Chief Eduardo Dominguez,

Executive Management Team, Santiago de Cali.

[End of Report]

*****

## 25: *I am El Sol's account of the Aftermath*

Well, first and foremost, the earthquake on the mountain ridge has to take the blame. He went over the top and should have shown more restraint throughout that night in question. It's no good just saying sorry. Humans lost their lives; luckily, for the most part, the figure remained at nine and forty-nine injured.

Those poor souls had been given no warning; one minute, they were happily sound asleep, with the view that the next day would be the same as any other day since their arrival in the supposedly safe home for the elderly.

Now, look at what has happened. Nobody really knows at this stage what to do with them, so in the interim, what remains of their bodies have been transferred to a makeshift morgue while the Police and the Fire department do their investigations.

Mind you, it was evident from the start who they were going to hold accountable. They were the first to blame the mountain ridge for the earthquake.

The government officials made future recommendations based on the Police and Fire Department findings, and a file was created and duly filed.

The church that owned the old property deemed it unnecessary to rebuild it and decided, because of the age of the old building, that they could move the remaining residents to the city and spread them around various care homes in both the north and south of the city.

Then, as a cost-cutting exercise, they looked at all their options on whether to redevelop it straight away and reopen it as a fully refurbished care home or leave it derelict with the possibility of someone coming forward in a year or two and buying up the plot for whatever the reason the new owners envisage doing with it.

For the record, it took a further 12 years before a businessman living in the USA bought it for a future plot of upmarket housing.

It was another two years before he visited the site for an hour and another four years before anyone purchased and moved into one of the 20 retro-styled holiday homes with swimming pools and outdoor barbecue areas, all hidden behind a very high wall and guarded frontage where the old care home door frame had stood.

I say, standing. Actually, it had finally collapsed under the weight of the overgrown foliage that had crept over it as each year passed.

*****

Now, let me turn to the incident involving a quad bike, its owner, a young woman named Ximena Londono, a truck driver identified as Ignacio Perez, a Nun simply known as Sister Rosa, and an unfortunate street man going by the possible name of Stalin. This sounds implausible because what parent is ever going to call their child Stalin? Mind you, who am I to judge? I would not consider calling my loved one Stalin.

Sorry, I am digressing – you want to know what happened next to them.

*****

Well, let's start with Ximena. Luckily, she has a wealthy and influential father and a very successful mother who live up on the mountain ridge area..

They proved to be the best parents she could have hoped for. His father delegated all his business affairs to his board of directors. He took a six-month sabbatical before resuming business affairs and meetings again, albeit on a more relaxed schedule than his hectic life used to dictate.

Her mother cancelled all of her social calendars and immediately flew back from a meeting held in New York to be beside her daughter. From there, she was a constant presence throughout the treatment and doctor's appointments that she organised for Ximena.

Never once did she show her daughter her broken heart and guilt of not being there to stop all that had befallen her beautiful daughter.

When she did cry, she was always far away from her daughter's eyes and ears.

Ximena was initially treated by the family friend and top plastic surgeon Rafael Nunez at his practice in the south of the city.

Her pelvis and legs were repaired, and support rods were inserted to allow her to stroll again. Her jawbone was realigned, and implants replaced all of her missing teeth.

The missing part of Ximena's tongue was much more challenging to resolve. Eventually, Doctor Rafael had to gently break the news to both Ximena and her parents that she would have considerable difficulty making herself understood for the rest of her life.

She would need the help of an extraordinary specialist that he knew of by reputation in Switzerland.

Within three days, the Londono family were on their way to Geneva.

Two days later, after resting, they were shepherded into the Specialist's office and treatment rooms. The Doctor with blonde hair and the customary white medical jacket looked up and smiled directly at Ximena.

She had built up her practice and skills over 30 years, mainly treating the terrible injuries that befell climbers and skiers.

For her, the treatment needed to assist this young lady was a routine part of her working life.

Once everyone was settled and introductions had been made, the Specialist spoke, "Ok, as you know, the bad news is best first; your accident has resulted in you losing over 30% of your tongue. The good news is I can repair everything for you very quickly but, of course, with some discomfort for a short period while the healing process makes its journey."

Here, she paused to see what the reaction would be; she was not disappointed with the parents, although the young girl would need more information to make her believe she could be healed.

"In Layman's terms, your tongue is a muscular organ that sits on the floor of your mouth. It contains glands, sensory organs, and four pairs of extrinsic muscles. It is essential for jaw articulation, taste, the manipulation of food, swallowing and, of course, what concerns you the most: the production of speech."

She continued, "Each tongue has three surfaces: the TIP, Body, and base, and most heal by themselves; yours will need my help, but in a very short time, it will also heal."

She rose from behind her desk to a framed screen on the wall; here, she switched on the screen, and a diagram of a tongue was revealed. She picked up a ruler and pointed to the lower side of the tongue. "The laceration was mainly to the side where the kite hit you, and because of your tongue's generous blood supply, you did not suffer from any infection."

She then pointed to the front of the drawing of the tongue. "Here, I will need to do what we call a flap procedure operation; you will need to be anaesthetised so that I can carry out the procedure. There may be fragments of your missing lower teeth that I will have to remove, and I will need you to wear a bite block, which you will feel discomfort with when awake, hence the knock-out drops. This will allow your motor function to return and your muscle layers to heal rapidly."

"So, Ximena, shall we proceed straightaway like this afternoon? If you are free?" said the Specialist, now next to the patient, smiling down towards her, radiating all the confidence of a woman who knows what's best.

Ximena had already dreaded all meal times. She knew she had to eat to live, but all the pleasures she had once taken for granted had gone.

Now, she avoided all thoughts of returning to her previous life of restaurants, cafes and bars.

The very thought of being social and attending to any social situation, which would always involve food, drink and speech, petrified her.

She felt disconnected from her family and her environment.

She looked up into the Specialist's eyes and closed them at the same time, nodding her consent for just a second. "Good," said the Specialist. "Let's get started in turning you back into your rightful place of being the most beautiful woman in the world."

*****

Now let's turn to Ignacio. Whenever there is a crisis, there is always a hero. Ignacio was identified and recognised by all as a stand-up hero.

Of course, he did not plan such a reaction from the humans in the city or, indeed, from his neighbours high up in the mountain. But once the press the world over gets its teeth into a possible big story, a hero will soon be identified, and on this occasion, it was Ignacio.

The story broke of a truck driver arriving on his own with a beautiful young girl in a stretcher laying all strapped up on the back of his rig. Now mention an earthquake, that was it!

The phones went into overdrive, and all the hospital staff and the other patients were waiting to be seen reaching for their mobiles. Photos were quickly taken and on social media channels within moments of their arrival.

Even Police Officers wanted to stand next to Ignacio and have their photos taken.

The world went mad for Ignacio.

By the following day, the South American newspapers were full of the exaggerated news of Ignacio and Ximena; there was no mention of the Nun or Stalin.

Ignacio did try to tell the proper story, but no one was interested, except for the part when Ximena and her quad bike rose above his cabin.

They had yet to talk directly to Ximena as she was securely hidden away in the hospital's internal workings. No amount of bribery could get to her, as Don Londono had taken full ownership of his daughter's security.

Soon, the news reporters turned their sole attention to Ignacio. He was invited onto daytime television. It became a living nightmare for him, the man with a quiet voice. Then, as fast as fame arrived, it was gone again, much to his and Jasmina's relief. She had waited for forty years to have her husband to herself, and by golly, she was going to enjoy the time left to them both.

*****

Sister Rosa's short-term future was not so simple. When she got back to the Sisters and her church, she found herself constantly breaking down and crying for what appeared to be no real reason.

Gone was the urge to sing.

The sisters noticed that Rosa's unique spark in life had fizzled out. When they listened at the door of the sleeping girls at bedtime, Rosa was no longer still; she moved constantly, and many times, she would rise up in her bed screaming and covered in sweat.

They knew Sister Rosa needed help, and Sister Miriam travelled down to see the Sister Superior, who, as soon as she had heard the situation, immediately packed a bag and returned up the mountain ridge with the worried Sister.

Sister Superior Josefina, in her previous missions deep in the south of the country, had seen many humans in deep shock from different traumas. Usually, it was the work of evil men who would abuse and sometimes rape their intended victims.

Often, this would lead to suicide, but she was not prepared to allow this beautiful Rosa, with the most angelic of voices, to disappear from her destiny with God.

Later that next day, they were both in a small room at the rear of the church. Rosa lay with her head in Sister Superior's lap. The older woman soothed the young girl's hair and sang quietly to her nonstop. Now and then, she would stop and turn to pray, and these prayers had to have a simple, soothing message, not all brimstone and fire. This was not the Sister's way.

Gradually, Rosa began to relax, and the images began to diminish, not wholly, but slowly; her brain started to move them to the rear of her mind. Instead, Rosa began to focus solely on Sister Superior's soft voice and her words of comfort and guidance.

They stayed like this for fourteen days and fourteen nights. The only reprieve was when they dined and drank together.

Gradually, Rosa began to function again, first by reading passages from her Bible and then by asking the older and wiser woman who had stopped her mission to tend to Rosa's needs.

On the fifteenth day, they both emerged, smiling and very tired, their eyes blinking profusely with the brightness of the sun.

They held hands; there was a bond between them that would never be broken.

It would be another year before Rosa started to sing again, and as soon as she made that step, she was on her way back to being healed. She eventually found the courage to join the singing Sisters in the city, and with their love and understanding, she rose in their ranks as one of the finest singers of sacred music that had ever graced their lives.

Her mission in life would be simple: she would sing to the world.

*****

Now I know you want to know what happened to Stalin the most; his story is what moves you, I know. Did his life change? Did he find happiness? Did he remember anything the next day?

The answer to all three questions is no. Stalin had been and now returned as a creature of habit. He moved back into the shadows of the city with his head down enough to ensure he did not hinder his sight, but enough to warn others not to approach him.

No, he did not resort to smiling, laughing, or crying; this was all alien to him now. No emotions mattered, only survival.

Finally, the next day, when he woke up, he felt his body was a massive centre of pain; every muscle of his ached, and even his head hurt, too.

His stomach and bum were sore for reasons he was not sure of. Was he able to understand why?

Did he remembered all the events from the previous day?

He had no collection of the rancid Lasagna, the 4.7 earthquake, the scared Nun who reached out to him in her hour of need, the truck driver and his rig and, of course, the beautiful young woman on her racing yellow quad bike.

He looked down the empty street; it was still early. In another hour, the road would be full of the morning traffic going to work. He stooped down and, with his probing fingers, reached out and retrieved his trusty rock.

Once in his hand, he felt complete again, and he began to move away from the shadow into the rising sun's light. The warmth hit his back instantly, and he was back in his world again.

Now, it was time to find a morsel or two of scraps from the local vendors, who accepted when this street man with his rock was in the area, all would be safe and calm again. They understood that when he was roaming around, there was no need to keep an extra eye out looking for possible thieves.

*****

Finally, I must explain what happened to the kite and the quad bike. Firstly, Leonardo's kite is no longer still up high on the mountain ridge road.

When the road maintenance men arrived to repair the new road, their first job was to refill all three craters left by the earthquake.

Lots of debris from the fire at the care home was used initially to fill the holes and as an afterthought from one of the workers, a young street cleaner called Gracie, the now full-time employee of the government department in charge of keeping the roads and highways within and around the area of Valle de Cauca clean and unblemished decided the kite was so severely damaged, it was almost unrecognisable and into the crater so too went the remains of the broken kite.

The dream of becoming a world-famous satellite died with the impact of the young woman on her quad bike.

A Cat digger was then used to transfer more ballast from the local quarry to fill the craters to three-quarters full and, finally, the top coat of tarmac to signal the fate of the kite forever.

They even remembered to add some reflectors and paintwork to denote the footpath on either side.

Eventually, the workers and their machinery left, and the new road reverted to its original look again. There is no evidence on show except in the minds of those who had experienced the terror of that night.

Next, the quad bike. It suffered very little; his soul left almost immediately on impact. Every working part of his powerful engine was crushed.

The recovery team decided that nothing was worth rescuing for the owner of the insurance company or their policy. The quad bike had died from an accident involving an earthquake. He, as they say, was "written off."

Later, three young men from further up the mountain, Leon Jaramillo, Pepe Jhon, and Lucas Cruz, arrived. They loaded the wreckage onto an old-looking pickup truck and transferred it to the eastern part of the city, where the municipal dump for wreckages resided.

Here, the once-fantastic quad bike was crushed even further and spat out to lie for the next twelve months before being sold on to be melted down into simple beer cans.

The three boys received enough money to make the trouble of disposing of the wreckage worthwhile for them to be involved. They planned at some point to dispose of the old, abandoned Willy jeep in much the same way. Luckily, the Willy Jeep continued to be covered in the mountain foliage and slowly but surely began to disappear from any human's mind except one.

*****

## 26: I am the Mountain who witnessed, something truly special

Many living up here considered me a foolish mountain who needed not to have gotten angry and protested like I did. I caused misery and upset to many, but those in the city below decided I had to be forgiven because I had not touched them when I so quickly could have.

The sun above just stared at me for a long time after, almost baiting me to misbehave once more. But I decided quietly between you and me that doing what I did was, although exciting and fun for me, may not be as seen as such to others living on top of my surface.

At the local church, the Father referred to my night of protest for many sermons to come. Eventually, the local humans decided to rejoice in surviving the earthquake by holding an annual party for all.

The memory of the terror I had caused was replaced by the continuance of the life I witnessed on a daily basis. Nearly all would dance and sing and pray.

Even I, the culprit, rejoiced in all the displays of love and laughter amongst those who lived and worked on me and those family and friends who always found the time to travel up and stay for the weekend of celebrations.

On the chosen Sunday each year, the singing Sister, the Father, and the two older sisters led a parade through the town towards the site of the older people's home that now lay in ruins. Here, a prayer was said, and a hymn was sung in remembrance of those who had not survived.

Once this act of remembrance was completed, the parade would continue up towards the church again and finish outside the small café opposite the cemetery.

In time, I was forgiven, and for that, I will be eternally grateful. No more will I find such a poor reason to protest. I hope and pray other forces out of my control will also respect, behave, and rejoice in the souls on this small mountain ridge of land.

*****

The animals, insects, and birds were the first to show their forgiveness.

Almost as one, they turned around, looking up like statutes. When they felt the danger was over again, almost as one entity, they moved towards me with the Hummingbird leading the birds in the night sky; the animals were shown at a slow & almost leisurely pace by two cows and a bewildered mule. Coming up the rear of the column was a very fat and still not impetuous Scorpion.

On their pilgrimage, many passed the white, now broken wooden cross bearing the name of Marcus Eduardo Uribe, the cyclist who had died so tragically, and the road sign that lay to one side that had been positioned to warn others of the dangers of people walking on the road surface.

Within a few months, it was decided that a proper memorial should be placed on the road where his accident happened. Now, even I am happy and proud to say the humans made a stunning base of my very own rock into a man-size square plinth with a black slated figure of a cyclist riding up to the heavens with a smile permanently on display for all to stop and see.

I know Marcus Eduardo Uribe was very moved by such a display, and every night from the moment he witnessed it, he would sit down in the quiet hours and rest his weary legs.

When he heard the old man from the town had also passed away, he immediately took it upon himself to ensure that his sister, Kathy, also recommended dedicating one side of the plinth to the fallen Olympian rider and his many feats.

In time, this monument became the central point for all generations of riders to meet and rejoice in their sport. Oh, what it must be like for Marcus Eduardo Uribe to be so revered and loved by so many in his beloved sport.

*****

The small, low-income family consisting of Magdalena, Alberto, and their loving son Juan finally moved back into their shanty home and proceeded to restore it to what it originally was. Alberto was stunned to see his television and the empty Chilean bottle that was now a candle holder. They had been the only survivors of their precious belongings.

Everything else lay smashed on the marbled-covered floor.

All their animals seemed healthy and had no lasting effects to worry the family. Only the cockerel and chickens seemed to feel the need to shout and holler at every opportunity they could find.

One well-aimed flying shoe or boot usually stopped the ratings.

One of Alberto's neighbours had discovered the missing Chevrolet truck with the absent rear light, and after a further inspection, it was concluded that everything was fine with the vehicle.

It was a further week before anyone could drive it as there had never been two keys, and Alberto had to use the mountain bus to visit the dealership to have a new set of keys made.

Now, the family were regularly seen together just outside the cemetery at the side of the road, selling fruit and vegetables from their makeshift stall to all the passing trade, including the Sisters from the local church and their school.

In time, the family prospered enough to move to a better home. This gave them the opportunity to expand their holdings to include their very own shop and more products were added regularly.

At one point, Juan had recommended to his parents that selling souvenirs would be a small range of possible profit as more and more foreigners were visiting, and the opportunities to sell to them would be suitable for business. His parents agreed, and soon, they were displaying different sizes of traditional Colombian hats, from small keyrings to man sized hats.

On a regular basis, the sisters from the convent could be seen filling the boot of a small car that the Sister Superior had sanctioned to have purchased as a means to have more control of their daily lives. They openly declared on many occasions that the products from the new shop were the best and freshest on the mountain.

*****

Now, I finally arrive at the moment I can only describe as an extraordinary moment in time. Do you remember I told you earlier in the tale of myself witnessing nine ghostlike faceless objects moving away from the fire of the older people's home?

Well, the number I saw needed to be corrected.

There were actually ten. One quiet night, they suddenly returned but not by themselves. Behind each of them came a vast rock, almost the same size as the original one that had spent centuries sitting at the side of the old craggy road.

As a column, they moved like a small army of soldier ants with a marked location in each of their minds.

I sat with my mind transfixed by what I was seeing, my mouth totally wide open, and I dared not breathe so as not to disturb their journey down my slopes to the same old craggy road.

When they reached a certain point, they stopped and, without speaking, positioned each rock so that it would allow each to see and hear the others in the years to come.

Then, each ghostlike light entered their given rock as if an invisible door had opened for each of them, and quietly, almost silently, their lights disappeared.

Looking down at them took me a while to refocus my mind again; I had no answers as to why these rocks had suddenly appeared, as if by magic or some divine intervention.

But wait, something needs to be corrected.

I sat quietly, staring at each rock, and they looked almost identical to the next one. Then, I realised there was a gap between the two of them. Why would there be a gap?

I had no answer until a few weeks later when two more ghostly faceless objects came walking down the old, craggy road. I instantly knew who they were, and now I finally had my answer to the mystery of the gap.

I did not need to see their actual images; their souls told me who they were.

He would be the only heroic truck driver with the quietest voice ever to grace my land and his beloved Jasmina. They had perished together in their sleep when a faulty water heater emitted toxic carbon monoxide unabated throughout the night. The gas, with its colourless, odourless, and tasteless properties, began entering their bloodstreams and rendering both unconscious without the ability to wake up.

The loving couple were to sit together and be allowed to be with all the other old storytellers from the older people's homes. If you listened hard enough, you would hear the old Venezuelan soldier who followed Bolivar on his vast journeys argue gently with old Hector Rodriguez, who would talk about the most remarkable human in history, Winston Leonard Spencer Churchill.

The Venezuelan master sergeant would always respond with, "Hold on, sir, I fully accept he was an exceptional man but not quite the greatest one. To be the greatest, you first had to have a name that would match such a claim, and how many names do you know that would match the mightly Simon Jose Antonio de la Santisma Trinidad Bolivar Palacious Ponte y Blanco?"

There always followed a short pause, and then giggles would erupt from Ignacio, Jasmina, and Hector, followed by all the inhabitants of the rocks. Never did these souls feel the need to argue only to debate good-humouredly, yes, but argue and fight never.

It became folklore on my mountain ridge that if you quietly sat outside and positioned yourself correctly and if the wind was breezing along in a specific direction and speed, you could hear the chatter amongst the rocks. So much history could be learned, so many old stories, both true and false, would be heard again, and so much knowledge about life and what it holds for all who cared to know.

*****

The presence of these rocks made the whole world talk. No one had the answer or the reason why all these rocks would suddenly arrive from nowhere specific. Scientists, Geologists, men of every faith known to man, Doctors, Professors, Writers, Poets, Songsters, and even Royalty and Heads of state—just about everyone you can imagine came to visit the rocks.

They tried to move them and inspect inside them. Everyone needed to have a notion of how and why they were here. Eventually, they were deemed to be the eighth wonder of the world. But was it the same as the old or the new?

You see, there were two lists. The first one included the Old Wonders of the World, comprising the Great Pyramid of Giza, the Hanging Gardens of Babylon, the Temples of Artemis at Ephesus, the Statute of Zeus at Olympia, the Mausoleum at Halicarnassus, the Colossus of Rhodes, and the Lighthouse of Alexandria.

The second list comprises the New Wonders of the World. Each was decided by votes in 2014, such as The Great Pyramid of Giza, The Great Wall of China, Petra in Jordan, The Colosseum in Rome, Chichen Itza in Yucatan, Mexico, Machu Picchu in Peru, The Taj Mahal in Pradesh India and the impressive Christ the Redeemer above the Brazilian city of Rio de Janeiro.

No one could decide for sure; in the end, it didn't matter. Both sides named the Mountain Rocks of Dapa as their preferred Eighth Wonder of the World.

*****

One night, another voice came from the rocks. "Did you see that? Can you believe it? Look at that crazy woman who just urinated up the side of my leg!"

**Far from the END** *for now……*

# Part Two

# *At Last, The Barbarians Are Sleeping*

## Foreword to Part Two

Hello once again. Finally, after six years, I have the time and inclination to pick up my pen and paper. As you know, I began writing the first part of this book back in 2017. Now, it is 2023.

So what happened in those six years? Why the delay?

Well, please forgive me, but I must go back to 2016 first. Prior to that year, I had never considered having a story or two in me that would interest a massive audience. I don't know if I have now. I hope that, with time, my adventures will reach as many of you as possible.

In 2016, I was moving my city café to a new location near the church and opposite the cemetery on the mountain ridge. I was working with my electricians, plumbers, and carpenters. At one point, I decided to repaint the roof and trusted my skills at staying upright on a ladder alongside.

I am sure you already know what I am going to say next. Yes. The ladder failed me, and I found myself falling downwards and backwards to the waiting floor. Only I landed closer to the ridge's edge than anticipated and rolled over the edge, landing further down. It was not much, but enough for me to land on my head with the repercussion of splitting the scalp surface open, thereby allowing a lot of blood to leave my body.

I luckily did not lose consciousness as I still remember a woman's scream somewhere on the road above me.

I made every effort to get back to my feet. But now, the escaping blood had blinded my sight. At some point, I felt strong arms enveloping me and raising me back up to the ridge's surface.

To cut the long story short, I ended up in a coma for the next fifteen days or more. This action was recommended to allow my "brain to drink the blood."

There is an old saying that blood is thicker than water. My brain can vouch for that. It was irritated by the blood mass surrounding it and had decided to let me know, in no uncertain terms, that if the situation did not differ in the immediate hours, it would shut down for good.

My surgeon gave me twelve hours to live. Luckily for me, without surgery, my brain dealt with the "Sangre", and in time, I recovered.

I was banned from any form of work for the next four months. That lasted a week with me.

I got beyond restless.

While everyone was down the mountain in the city below, I began to put strength back in myself and did the only thing I knew I was capable of doing. I walked.

Slowly, I began to regain my strength, and it was on one of those morning two to four-hour walks that I came upon the massive rock with the unknown man inside.

In Part Two, the story continues three years later, in 2019. You will discover that the white-haired Englishman has moved from the mountain ridge to the city below. He has moved with his beautiful Colombiana, with the most enchanting eyes, show-stopping smile, and perfectly sculpted ankles, into a small apartment in the north of the city.

In truth, the stories have never stopped coming. I wrote down as many as I could for future exploration. I was happy to find many of the humans in Part One continued to produce stories for me. I was further excited by all the new experiences that allowed newer humans to come forward. Most of all, I will be internally grateful to the animals, the birds, and the trees who happily presented themselves unashamedly to the walking white-haired stranger with red skin, a growing pot belly, and strong-looking, sometimes pink, sometimes terracotta legs.

Lastly, I have to turn to all the city statues, sculptures, busts, and figurines that represent the city's rich history. It is from them that I learned the term Barbarians. Muchas gracias mis amigos.

*Mike Bowley*

September 2020

Part Two – At Last, The Barbarians Are Sleeping

# List of Chapters

| | | |
|---|---|---|
| 27. | I am truly the most dramatic & thunderous Storm to hit direct | 191 |
| 28. | I am the Tree of Life, and I have a tale or two for you | 196 |
| 29. | I am Simon Bolivar, and I wish to introduce to you Sebastián | 203 |
| 30. | I am the Meeting of the Minds, and the Guests are arriving | 211 |
| 31. | I am Derekamus Stonebeard Stronforce and this, Abella Goldhammer Darkstone | 223 |
| 32. | I am the Street man with little to no memory, you know me as Stalin | 231 |
| 33. | I am a Yellow-headed Caracara, and I sense carrion is not far away | 236 |
| 34. | I am the king of all Cannonball Trees | 240 |
| 35. | I am Caesar, a well-known street robber having one heck of a bad day | 244 |
| 36. | I am a Trainee Policeman named Archibaldo Federico Alcatraz | 250 |
| 37. | I am an unusual way of Dying | 257 |
| 38. | I am the Second Meeting of the Minds in a Week | 263 |
| 39. | I am Ximena Londono. Here is my life before and after the accident | 274 |
| 40. | I am the General of the Honking Goose Air Regiment from Alaska | 283 |
| 41. | I am a little steam locomotive who misses deeply his father and grandfather | 291 |
| 42. | I am Gabriel and the true lifelong friend of Hector | 298 |
| 43. | I am Ignacio's son, and my name is Samuel, and I talk to Gnomes | 314 |
| 44. | I am Rosa who loves to sing, and I have no idea where to buy my Nun's outfit | 319 |
| 45. | I am the Black Cat with the impressive white chest and four white socked feet | 323 |
| 46. | I am the Third Meeting of the Minds and Yes, the city is in trouble | 333 |
| 47. | I am the Phoenix Air Museum, and it is me who is the safe alternative in a storm | 339 |
| 48. | I am the Historical Account of Gracie's mammoth clean-up operation | 343 |
| 49. | I am the Official Mayor of the city Report | 350 |
| 50. | I am the Fourth Meeting of the Minds. Something magical happens for Simon | 357 |

"There is no better friend than a burden."

Old Colombian Proverb

"All fear has much imagination and little talent."

Old Colombian Proverb

"Damn it, how will I ever get out of this labyrinth?"

Simón José Antonio de la Santísima Trinidad Bolívar Palacios Ponte y Blanco. (Venezuelan Military & Political Leader 1783 – 1830)

"He dug so deeply into her sentiments that in search of interest he found love, because by trying to make her love him, he ended up falling in love with her."

Gabriel José de la Concordia García Márquez (Colombian Nobel Laureate, Journalist & Writer 1927 – 2014)

"My almost autographical novel of María and Efraín is inserted into a framework of nature. It is the story of a luckless romance between the son of a wealthy landowner and his cousin, with elements of nature, death, and love."

Jorge Isaacs Ferrer (Colombian Poet, Writer, Politician and Soldier 1837 – 1895)


Barbarians are a brave community of souls who still believe in the power of excessive body hair, questionable fashion choices, and an aversion to table manners. Known for their ability to roar louder than a pride of lions, their prowess in battles of wit is only matched by their tendency to accidentally set their own tents on fire. Often misunderstood, but always ready to party like it's 999 AD.

*Mike Bowley, author of culminating anthropomorphism and short stories* 2023.

# 27: I am truly the most Dramatic & Thunderous Storm to hit direct

**City Newspaper Headline:**
***Citizens Brace for Epic Thunder and Lightning Storm as Rainy Season Arrives.***

*Subheading: The city is gearing up for the most dramatic storm in recent history, which is forecast to hit tonight.*

This is a general warning to all city citizens: you are in for a remarkable display of nature's fury as the rainy season begins with the promise of an epic thunder and lightning storm.

Weather experts are predicting an awe-inspiring spectacle that will rock the city and capture its inhabitants with a performance of nature's might.

All city residents have been eagerly waiting for the arrival of the rainy season, which is crucial for agriculture and replenishing water sources. However, this year, nature has prepared something truly extraordinary for us. Experts are calling it the most dramatic storm to hit the city in recent memory.

Meteorologists and local sky-watchers have been observing the developments in the atmosphere, and their predictions suggest that this storm will arrive directly over our city in the early hours of tonight.

Weather models indicate a convergence of atmospheric conditions that will create a perfect storm with intense rain, thunder, and lightning.

The anticipation is palpable among our population as we prepare for an unforgettable experience.

Citizens, please be advised to take necessary precautions and stay indoors during the storm to ensure your safety.

Weather authorities are reminding everyone to stay away from tall structures, trees, and open fields due to the increased risk of lightning strikes.

The city Emergency Services have been placed on high alert in preparation for the storm's arrival.

Our local government has also issued a public advisory, urging residents to secure loose outdoor items, check their roofs for leaks, and ensure that gutters and drains are clear to avoid potential flooding.

Local businesses, including roofers and electricians, can expect to experience a surge in demand as citizens rush to ensure their homes and properties are storm-ready. Many locals should take this opportunity to stock up on emergency supplies, such as candles, batteries, and non-perishable food items.

Meteorologists have also reassured the public that this storm, although highly anticipated and extraordinary, is a natural occurrence and well within the normal range of weather events expected during the rainy season.

They encourage everyone to embrace this powerful display of nature's forces while prioritising their safety and well-being.

As darkness falls tonight, try not to get too anxious when looking at the sky.

The arrival of the most dramatic thunder and lightning storm we have ever witnessed will be evident.

In the coming hours, this awe-inspiring display promises to create a lasting impression on the minds and hearts of us citizens. This storm will definitely remind us of the power and beauty of nature.

As a city, we must embrace the storm. Let us be reminded of our community's resilience and unity. Let's stand unwavering against the might of this natural spectacle.

*****

The problem with the report above is that the majority of the citizens needed to see the newspaper. The trouble was, they were busy doing their perceived everyday routines. Many headed into the evening, totally unprepared for the spectacular display of an angry night sky that looked like it was at war with itself.

*****

As the sky grew dark with ominous clouds, an eerie silence descended upon the city, foreshadowing the impending storm.

The air, heavy with anticipation, crackled with electricity, setting the stage for a display of nature's fury like no other.

Suddenly, the first rumble of thunder echoed through the heavens, sending shivers down the spines of those who dared to bear witness.

One such witness was a white-haired man standing on his balcony, which gave him a panoramic view. He sensed from the beginning that he was about to witness a storm like no other.

Next came a deep, resonating boom that seemed to emanate from the Earth's very core, shaking the city's foundations.

As if in response, the heavens opened up, unleashing a deluge of rain that pounded against the earth with relentless force, instantly transforming it into a murky sea of chaos.

The lightning, a divine serpent of astonishing power, emerged from the darkened clouds, slicing through the sky with brilliant arcs of blinding light. It danced and twisted, illuminating the night with its breathtaking spectacle. Each flash revealed a landscape momentarily suspended in time, casting eerie shadows that danced across every surface.

The city was both illuminated and obscured, trapped in a perpetual dance between brilliance and darkness.

The thunder roared again, this time louder and more ferocious than before. It carried on its wings a primal energy, tearing through the atmosphere and shaking the foundations of reality itself.

The earth quivered beneath its terrible might, and every living thing stood in awe of its awe-inspiring presence, including the Englishman. He stood on his balcony and immediately recalled an article he had read about the everlasting storm of the Catatumbo phenomenon in Venezuela.

**The Everlasting Storm of Catatumbo**: A Spellbinding Force of Nature in Venezuela Welcome, readers, to an extraordinary journey into the heart of Venezuela's most intriguing natural phenomenon: The Everlasting Storm of Catatumbo. Brace yourselves for a tale that combines the elements of wonder, mystery, and relentless power, seamlessly merging to create an enchanting spectacle that has captivated generations.

Imagine yourself standing on the shores of Lake Maracaibo, in Venezuela's western region, at the cusp of nightfall. Suddenly, the serene surroundings find themselves engulfed in an ethereal dance of nature, transforming the darkness into a breathtaking sight that appears both divine and otherworldly.

As the sun sets over the horizon, crackling bolts of lightning pierce the night sky with an intensity that rivals the brilliance of daylight. These mesmerizing flashes illuminate the dark clouds, unveiling a dizzying display of colours that dance and swirl against the backdrop of an inky canvas. This captivating light show has become an enduring symbol of the region and has earned Catatumbo the title of the Lightning Capital of the World.

But what causes this bewildering storm to persist, unyielding with time?

Unbeknownst to many, the origins of Catatumbo's never-ending uprising can be traced to a combination of unique environmental factors that converge here.

First and foremost, the meeting point between the Catatumbo River and Lake Maracaibo serves as a crucial catalyst. This union creates a perfect storm of warm, moist air rising from the lake's surface and interacting with the calm, dry winds descending from the nearby Andes Mountains. When these clashing air masses collide, they unleash a veritable symphony of atmospheric changes, paving the way for the storm's perpetual existence.

The region's geography plays a pivotal role in adding to the allure. Catatumbo lies at the crossroads of the Caribbean Sea and the South American continent, making it the convergence zone for contrasting weather systems. This unique combination spawns intense thunderstorms, and as they find their way to Catatumbo, they become ensnared in an almost cyclical pattern, trapped and fueled by the landscape.

Furthermore, atmospheric instability due to the presence of methane gas seen from the region's vast oil reserves enhances the storm's resilience. This gas, combined with the warm, moist air, acts as an additional fuel source, further intensifying the storm's ferocity and extending its duration.

Day after day, year after year, Catatumbo's everlasting storm continues its awe-inspiring performance, defying all expectations and understanding. Its constant presence has become an inseparable part of the region's identity and a testament to the untameable forces of nature.

So, when you find yourself basking in the vibrant beauty of the Everlasting Storm of Catatumbo, take a moment to ponder the intricate web of elements that come together to create this captivating spectacle. This phenomenon truly showcases nature's unstoppable power and leaves its spectators in perpetual awe.

*****

The white-haired man is drawn back to the growing spectacle as the storm reaches its crescendo. Nature's fury unleashes its ultimate display. Lightning bolts, like celestial whips, lashed out at the city below, casting an ethereal glow across the entire landscape.

With each strike, the whole sky seemed to ignite in a dazzling, otherworldly symphony of light and sound.

It was as if the Gods themselves were engaged in a battle, throwing bolts of cosmic fire across the heavens.

Amidst the pandemonium, the rain poured in torrents, drenching everything in its path.

The wind howled, creating a symphony of chaos and destruction, bending trees and tearing at structures with an unyielding force.

It was a symphony of the elements, a symphony that both terrified and awed those who witnessed its raw power.

But then, as suddenly as it began, the storm began to wane. The thunder receded, the lightning retreated, and the rain transformed into a gentle drizzle.

The storm, once a furious tempest, now ebbed away, leaving behind a city in disarray but also a sense of wonder and reverence.

In the aftermath, the thunder and lightning storm left an indelible mark on the city. It reminded its inhabitants of their insignificance in the face of nature's might, humbling all who witnessed its grandeur.

As the clouds parted, revealing a sky cleansed by the storm, the white-haired man could not help but marvel at the raw power and beauty that had unfolded before his very eyes.

*****

He retired to his bed, thinking he would be deep asleep as soon as his head hit the pillow. But nature had news for him. Within the hour, a second storm with the same intensity arrived and lasted the next three hours. Was the city he now resides in through climate change going to be another Catatumbo everlasting phenomenon? The Englishman slept very little that night.

*****

## 28: I am the Tree of Life and I have a tale or two for you

The Ceiba tree, also known as the "Tree of Life," holds great cultural and ecological significance in Cali, Colombia. Located in the city's northern district of La Flora, the tree stands as a symbol of strength and resilience. The Ceiba tree (Ceiba Pentandra) is at home in the tropical regions of the Americas and is known for its imposing size, reaching heights of up to 230 feet (70 meters). Its trunk is distinguished by large buttress roots that help support its massive structure.

In Cali, the Ceiba tree has become an integral part of the city's identity and history. Legend has it that the tree was already present when Spanish conquistadors arrived in the early 16th century. Local indigenous communities regarded the tree as sacred and believed it to be the dwelling place of spirits and deities.

Over the years, the Ceiba tree has witnessed significant moments in the city's history. It survived numerous natural disasters, including earthquakes, and has become a symbol of resilience for the city's inhabitants. Such memorable earthquakes happened in February 1787, with a magnitude of 7.2, followed by another one in August 1917, measuring 6.8.

Another devastating earthquake, measuring 7.2, struck on December 16, 1956, and most recently, in March 1983, the city was hit again with a 5.2. All four of the events mentioned affected and damaged buildings, roads, and infrastructure, resulting in displacement and injuries for many and a collective loss of life in huge numbers.

The city has also been affected by periodic flooding due to heavy rains and the overflowing of the Cauca River within its city boundaries.

Today, the Ceiba tree continues to draw locals and tourists alike. Its majestic presence serves as a meeting point and a gathering place for community events and celebrations. The tree's lush foliage offers shade and respite from the city's tropical heat, while its size and beauty inspire awe and admiration.

Given the Ceiba tree's cultural and ecological importance, local authorities protect it and make efforts to preserve and maintain its health and integrity for future generations to enjoy.

If you ever find yourself in the city, make sure to visit the magnificent Ceiba tree. It stands as a testament to the resilience of both nature and the human spirit and offers a window into the region's rich cultural heritage.

*****

I am the Ceiba tree located in the north of my city at the beginning of Calle 44. I am the largest of all the Ceiba trees dotted around this city. I am the oldest and the best place for any stranger to my city to begin their research in knowing my city's history.

Allow me to take you on a journey through time, starting from the era of indigenous settlers to the fateful arrival of the Spanish Conquistadors.

Long before the arrival of the Spanish, this land was inhabited by Indigenous tribes, most notably the Pijao people. This Indigenous tribal community was part of the larger Quechua-speaking ethnic group, which also included the Inca civilization. They formed settlements along the Cauca River, exploiting its fertile lands for agriculture and relying on the abundant natural resources of the surrounding forests.

Historically, the Pijao people were skilled farmers who cultivated crops such as potatoes, corn, beans, and squash. They practised swidden agriculture, also known as slash-and-burn farming, which involved clearing land by cutting down trees and burning vegetation. This method allowed them to maintain fertile soil for their crops.

As a Ceiba Tree, I have been a sacred symbol to these indigenous communities. They believed that I possessed great spiritual power and considered me the axis mundi, connecting the heavens, the Earth, and the underworld. They worshipped me and held ceremonies around my towering presence.

The Pijao people also had a strong oral tradition and passed down their knowledge and history through storytelling, songs, and rituals. They had a complex social structure, organised into different clans or lineages. Each lineage had a chieftain or cacique who led the community and made decisions for the group.

Everything changed with the arrival of the Spanish Conquistadors in the early 16th century. Led by Sebastián de Belalcázar, they explored the region in search of gold and claimed the land for the Spanish crown. The Conquistadors encountered fierce resistance from the indigenous tribes, who fought to protect their ancestral lands.

Now, forgive me, but I have always found Sebastian's life story fascinating. I consider him the first-ever candidate for being classed as a barbarian.

Sebastián de Belalcázar, whose full name was Sebastián de Belalcázar y Dávila Santillana, was a Spanish conquistador and explorer during the 16th century. Born around 1480 in Spain, Belalcázar had a prolific presence in the Spanish colonisation of the Americas.

Belalcázar first participated in Christopher Columbus' and Alonso de Ojeda's expeditions in the Caribbean. In 1524, he joined the expedition led by Francisco Pizarro to conquer the Inca Empire in Peru.

However, Belalcázar soon left the group to explore the region that is now Ecuador and Colombia. In 1533, he founded the city of Quito, which became the capital of the Real Audiencia de Quito, one of the most important administrative divisions of the Spanish Empire.

Belalcázar's explorations were not limited to Quito alone. He ventured further into the interior of South America, discovering and establishing various cities, including Popayán in Colombia. He is also credited with being the first European to find the Pacific Ocean from South America, achieving this feat in 1527.

In 1536, Belalcázar competed with Gonzalo Jiménez de Quesada for control of the territories in what is now Colombia. Belalcázar defeated Quesada and established the city of Santiago de Cali—yes, my city. However, their rivalry continued, and Quesada ultimately won supremacy over the region.

After enduring numerous challenges and conflicts throughout his expeditions, Sebastián de Belalcázar later retired to Quito.

On January 24, 1551, Belalcázar was assassinated by fellow conquistadors Pedro de Puelles and Juan de Ampudia. They were motivated by their desire to gain control over his vast wealth and territories.

Despite his controversial actions as a conquistador, Sebastián de Belalcázar played a crucial role in the Spanish conquest of the Americas. His legacy is still visible in my city and the other cities he founded, as are his contributions to European knowledge of the geography of South America.

*****

Despite their resilience, the indigenous tribes eventually succumbed to the superior weaponry and diseases brought by the Spanish. Many were enslaved or forced into labour, while others perished due to the devastating impact of conditions unknown to them, such as smallpox.

Over time, colonialism resulted in a decline in the Pijao population and a loss of their language, culture, and customs. However, efforts have been made to preserve and revitalise their heritage in recent years, including the recognition of their communal lands and the revitalisation of their language, known as Pijao or Paez.

Today, the Pijao people are recognised as one of my city's indigenous communities, and their descendants continue to live in the region. They celebrate their culture through traditional ceremonies, crafts, and festivals, showcasing their resilience and cultural heritage.

*****

Under Spanish rule, my city, then known as Santiago de Cali, became an important administrative and economic hub within the Viceroyalty of New Granada. It proliferated as a centre for agriculture and trade, with plantations producing sugarcane, tobacco, and other crops.

This period saw the establishment of colonial infrastructure, such as churches, plazas, and government buildings. The Spanish brought enslaved Africans to work on the plantations, contributing to the multicultural character of my city, which continues to this day.

Throughout the colonial era, my city experienced economic prosperity, aided by its strategic location connecting the fertile Cauca Valley to the Pacific coast. My city thrived as a trade hub, exporting goods to Panama and Lima while receiving imports from Europe.

My city has a rich history of population growth and significant events that shaped it from the Spanish colonial era to the present day.

However, due to several factors, my city experienced significant population growth only in the 19th century.

One significant event that impacted my city's population was the abolition of slavery in Colombia in 1851. This led to an influx of formerly enslaved people of African and Afro-Colombian descent who settled in my city and contributed to its cultural diversity. The population growth continued throughout the late 19th and 20th centuries, primarily driven by industrialisation and rural-urban migration.

In the mid-20th century, my city experienced a notable surge in population due to economic opportunities from industries such as sugar production, textiles, and construction. This expansion was linked to the broader process of urbanisation in the country during the post-World War II era.

One of the most significant events in my city's recent history that impacted its population was the rise of drug cartels in the late 20th century. Alarmingly, my city became a battleground for drug trafficking organisations, leading to widespread violence and migration as people sought safer environments. This period of insecurity saw some residents leaving my city, impacting the population growth temporarily.

However, in recent decades, my city has rebounded from this turbulent period and experienced continuous population growth. My city has become a hub for business, commerce, and tourism, attracting people from within the country and abroad. Factors such as improved security, infrastructure development, and economic opportunities have contributed to my city's ongoing growth.

Furthermore, several memorable events have impacted the sentiment of the community in my city. It has gained international recognition for hosting the Pan American Games in 1971, which showcased its infrastructure and athletic spirit. Additionally, my city's vibrant salsa music and dance culture have made it a renowned destination for music lovers and dancers from all over the world.

The annual Feria de Cali, a week-long festival celebrating salsa, has become an iconic event that attracts visitors and boosts my city's tourism sector.

So, you can see, despite challenges, my city continues to evolve and thrive as a dynamic and culturally diverse metropolis.

As the oldest Ceiba Tree in the north of the city, it is my honour to bear witness to this remarkable history. From the humble beginnings of indigenous settlements to the arrival of the Spanish Conquistadors and the subsequent transformation into a bustling colonial city, I have stood tall, silently observing the passage of time and the stories embedded within its foundations.

*****

As you can see, in this now bustling city tucked away, I have witnessed civilisations rise and fall, seasons come and go, and the passing of numerous generations. My roots run deep into the Earth, connecting it to the heart of the land, and my branches reach high, embracing the sky.

Every month, after darkness has fallen, an extraordinary event takes place in the city. Statues and figurines scattered throughout my city come to life, gathering in secret locations to share stories and discuss matters of great importance.

From majestic stone stallions to delicate porcelain-looking children and turtles, the inhabitants of this mystical city come alive during these gatherings.

These statues possessed a unique perspective, having observed my city and its human inhabitants for centuries. They have come to perceive the people as "Barbarians" not out of malice or superiority but rather due to their understanding of the term.

To the statues and figurines, a barbarian is not a word used to demean or insult. Instead, it refers to a being disconnected from the natural world, a soul blinded by its ignorance.

The statues have observed how humans often neglected the harmony of nature, disregarding the delicate balance of life around them.

From the grand buildings they constructed to the machines they invented; the humans have reshaped my city according to their desires without considering the consequences.

They have transformed vibrant forests, plains, and marshes into cold, lifeless concrete jungles. Their waste has polluted the purest rivers. In their relentless pursuit of progress, they have disregarded the beauty and sanctity of the natural world.

In contrast, the statues and figurines have thrived on their deep connection to nature.

They have observed the dance of seasons, paid homage to the energy of the Earth, and celebrated the intricate web of life.

They have continuously cherished the vibrant colours of the blossoming flowers, the soothing sound of a rustling gentle breeze through the leaves, and the melody of birdsong filling the air.

These monthly gatherings are a sanctuary for the statues, a place where they share tales of forgotten wisdom and pass down ancient knowledge. They discussed how to inspire humans to embrace their true potential, encouraging them to reconnect with nature and live in harmony with the world around them.

The term "Barbarians" became a focal point of these discussions, not as a derogatory label but as a gentle reminder of what had been forgotten.

The statues and figurines believe that humans if awakened to their innate connection with the natural world, could transcend their current state and become guardians of the Earth rather than mere conquerors.

Thus, as the oldest and wisest Ceiba Tree in the city, the keepers of this knowledge, the statues and figurines met each month, patiently waiting for the day when the humans would understand the true meaning behind the term "Barbarians."

They long for a time when humans will remember their place in the grand tapestry of life, embrace their proper stewardship of the Earth, and be nurtured by the wisdom of the statues and the timeless presence of the Ceiba Tree.

Personally, I wish the Barbarians would cease the practice of defacing all my wonderful friends, the statutes and figurines. I have often heard from visitors to my city how they need help understanding how the locals here are different from their homelands, who treat every statute and figurine as their history and should always be respected and safeguarded for generations to come.

Mind you wait until you have heard the displeasures of both General Simón José Antonio de la Santísima Trinidad Bolívar Palacios Ponte y Blanco and Sebastián de Belalcázar y Dávila Santillana, who initially held the rank of conquistador and later became a Spanish military captain.

*****

# 29: I am Simon Bolivar, and I wish to introduce to you Sebastián

Right from the beginning, I have not been THE actual person; I am, in fact, a statue of the "Liberator" during both daylight hours and at night.

I am allowed to rest and just be myself or whoever I wish. As it so happens, I like being this man.

You may wish to know me as Señor Simon Bolivar, or you may not.

I was initially made to celebrate the life of the real Simon Bolivar, a very famous man who had an argument with some Spanish men a few years back—well, to be more exact, over two hundred years ago.

At the time, it caused a stir.

It resulted in Señor Bolivar being celebrated in many major cities and countries around the world as the true Liberator of South America from the Spanish.

Because the real Señor Bolivar had visited this city back in 1822, the elders at that time felt I should be created and displayed in a very prominent place to remind all that he ever lived or visited this fair city in the sun of his most generous use of his hectic schedule and his famous decision actually to come.

So why did the real me visit such a place? Well, for over 20,000 reasons, really.

This city now has 2.5 million Souls. It started in 1536 with around 6,500 souls, and at least 1,100 of these were slaves.

As time went by, more and more people came to live and work here, and when the real Bolivar arrived at this place, it was deemed to be of some fair degree of importance as a military outpost.

As I said, there were over 20,000 reasons.

These were 20,000 fighting-fit men who, at various times of their lives, contributed to the War effort of the War of Independence, which also liberated nations further south, such as Peru, Bolivia, and Ecuador.

As I mentioned earlier, during the day, I have a significant role to perform. I stand on an artificial block of stone facing outwards.

Most of today's population do not stop even for a second to say, "Good morning." They just rush on by and do not register a single thought about me or my welfare, except for one stranger who periodically comes walking by in his ridiculous shorts and dirty-looking trekking shoes.

His routine is always the same: first, he stops in front of me, staring up like he has also become a statue. He suddenly seems to realise where he is and follows with searching looks around him, spying on all the other people who are equally not interested in either of us.

Then, his hand reached into his rucksack, bringing out a small black device. He put it up against his eye and started banging his finger against it at different angles.

After a minute or two, this practice ceases, and he appears satisfied. Then he looks around again, locates a bench nearby, and proceeds to sit down. He seems to go into hibernation by just staring up at me in his own imaginary world.

Suddenly, as if from nowhere, I hear his voice, "General Bolivar, I know you did not die in battle, but when they made this statue of you, they could have placed you on top of your wonderful horse called Palomo, who by sheer coincidence is buried only a few miles away from where we sit right now."

I looked at him, and I was instantly reminded of all those other excellent English and Irish men of war who came to the real Simon Bolivar's rescue when he so badly needed them.

They were known as the British Legions and numbered over 7,000 who volunteered to fight under his banner, some for shared political views and many more purely for selfish needs. There was a lot of wealth that could be taken from the prosperous Spanish settlers and their armies.

What motivated them was the fact that most were unemployed and perceived South America as a land of immense wealth in which they would be able to have a share.

By the end of the Napoleonic Wars, the British Empire no longer needed a large standing army.

In April 1817, The British newspaper, The Times estimated that there were 500,000 ex-soldiers in a British population of 25 million.

After 25 years of European wars, including both the wars against Revolutionary France and Napoleon, these men had no other employment history or trade, and they often found themselves in poverty.

South America's Wars of Independence provided many of them with an opportunity to extend their military careers and escape from the prospect of poverty and inactivity at home.

These very same men fought in many significant battles for five years and only stopped because many perished and did not survive the struggles for freedom and liberty.

I stood still and listened intently to the following words from him.

"I know it is not totally correct that if a statue has a horse under its rider and the horse has its two front legs raised from the ground, then the gallant rider would be assumed as having died in battle. But I am also under the notion, rightly or wrongly, that if only one foot is raised, then that would mean the rider had been wounded in battle. If all four hooved feet are on the ground, then the rider more than likely died in his bed."

He paused in thought and then continued with, "But here you are only displayed standing up. You rode into this city on your famous Palomo, which was described as a magnificently tall, white horse whose tail almost reached the ground. This proud horse had been with you for over three years and only just joined you before your famous battle of Boyacá."

"Also, when I think back, I am sure there is another statue of you in Central Park in New York. My recollection, although unclear, makes me think Palomo has one hooved foot risen."

I pondered this information about Palomo. The ever-trusting horse had indeed accompanied him on most of his campaigns. Palomo was a gift from an elderly peasant woman from Santa Rosa de Viterbo.

According to local folklore at that time, Simon Bolívar had visited Santa Rosa in early 1814 on his way to report to the United Provinces of New Granada and its congress on his setbacks in Venezuela.

As Bolivar approached the town on a very tired mule. The animal decided to stop and refused to move any further. There, Bolivar asked his men to find a guide to take the stubborn animal and lead it with him towards the town.

During this walk, Bolívar and the guide had a pleasant conversation in which the guide informed Bolívar about his wife Casilda's dreams, especially the dream in which she envisaged herself giving a newborn colt to a famous officer as a present.

The guide did not know who Bolívar was and became astonished when he discovered his identity.

When Bolívar was leaving at the edge of the town, he smiled and turned to the guide and said, "Tell your lady to keep the young horse for me."

Five years later. Bolívar returned to New Granada to receive the colt promised by Casilda in the middle of the Battle of Vargas Swamp. He named it Palomo, meaning cock pigeon, for its greyish-white colour. Later, on his way back to Venezuela, Bolívar stopped in Santa Rosa to visit Casilda personally and thanked her for the outstanding and loyal horse.

Years later, Bolívar sent Palomo to one of his officers, and he perished ten years after he had himself died. The gallant horse was now exhausted after another gruelling march, which history would show as one march too many. Palomo was buried next to a hacienda chapel.

Palomo's horseshoes and other effects of Bolívar are still on exhibit in a Museum near this city.

"Surely it would not have mattered that he died in his bed. Having a statue praising both rider and horse would have been so much more impressive."

At this point, while I considered his views of him, he quietly rose and moved off towards the north of the city. Maybe he will call again, and I can listen to more of his thoughts about me.

*****

Now that night has arrived, the sun has withdrawn its heat from the city, and I sense rain is not far away.

The neon lights are flickering on to guide the weary workers back to their homes and to assist the daytime drunks on their dangerous journeys to where only their brains will know.

Eventually, the people will fall fast asleep; well, most of them, that is, as I can see from this modern age, some people actually work nights.

I always know who they are as none of them move with a smile, just a weary look of sadness in which they dwell.

Others are there for their own advantages and prey on others whenever opportunities arise, such as the ladies of the night, with their false gaiety on show when it is needed. Then there are the shadowy figures of drug dealers, who seem always to be alert for the presence of policemen's pounding feet behind them.

Scattered among all that I have described, you will find the young revellers making their noisy exits from the places where the lights appear to vanish in the darkness.

It has started to become a good time for ghostly shadows such as me.

Now, I can take the opportunity to walk the streets.

I am free to roam as no one can see me, only the other statues, who, like me, have the same role in life. For a brief moment in time, peace can prevail, and we can walk in the knowledge that, at last, the barbarians are sleeping.

I must admit I hate these streets. Many times, I have tripped and fallen. The sidewalks are never made of the same materials or actually the same height as their previous neighbours.

Many holes can be discovered needlessly and quickly.

Regarding the trees and their spreading roots, I have lost count of how many times I have look up to see where I am going. The next moment, I am literally facing the ground.

For a statue, this can be a proper size problem to regain the correct posture again, especially after your foot disappears into a hole.

Are there warning signs?

I have yet to learn how people cope.

Certainly, foreigners such as the Englishman who I have witnessed on many occasions can re-enact a swan's motion from the Ballet of Swan Lake, but apparently with a different sense of grace and purpose.

Oh, how I wish I could ride into this city as my real hero did on his beautiful Palomo. I would make an elegant entrance in my perfectly tailored uniform and my sleek posture in the saddle.

Tonight, my walk must be addressed. I am on my way to the monthly meeting of all the statutes.

They have called it "The Meeting of the Minds" for as long as they can remember. Like many meetings, they are usually dull, but tonight, this one may well be different.

I need to hurry, as the rising city inhabitants' awakening sounds will soon begin again.

The rising crescendo of the yellow taxi sirens gives away their impatient nature and thoughtless desires to be somewhere else. Can they not see that it would be physically impossible for them to be there?

This mindless practice was never on show in my day when horses and mules were the primary modes of transportation.

Please pause for a moment and imagine all the riders I have only pictured, now stopped at a junction of any road and sounding a horn fitted around the horse's neck at their displeasure because the horse in front had not moved off quickly enough.

Eventually, during daylight hours, a gentle hum of activity will prevail until those flickering neon lights return. Heavy clouds above me appear, and they look formidable and menacing. Soon, I could feel the cool raindrops landing on my shiny black surface.

*****

"Hola buenas noches; ¿Cómo están todos?" Oops, sorry, I forgot. I meant to be speaking to an English-speaking audience. "Good Evening, how are you?" My name is Sebastián de Belalcázar, and I am the most unlikely of friends to the fallen General Simón José Antonio de la Santísima Trinidad Bolívar Palacios Ponte y Blanco. Who, comically, is rolling around on a very wet-looking pavement muttering picturesque expletives regarding all who live and work in this boisterous and polluted city as utter Barbarians.

While my friend is busy, I thought I'd take a moment or two of your time and give you a glimpse of the life of Sebastián before I became a statue in his honour.

I am the embodiment of Sebastián de Belalcázar, a renowned conquistador. I will gladly tell you about his early life and his incredible journey through South America up until he arrived in Cali.

Please excuse me for not referring to him by his surname. Like most statues, busts, and figurines, I have a gentle nature and much prefer the use of first names.

Sebastián was born Sebastián de Belalcázar y Dávila Santillana in 1479, in the town of Belalcázar, Spain. As a young man, he embarked on a journey to the New World, seeking adventure and fortune like many of his contemporaries.

Arriving in the Americas, Sebastián participated in multiple expeditions. He first journeyed alongside Christopher Columbus on his third voyage in 1498, exploring the northern coast of South America. Later, he joined Juan de la Cosa's expedition and explored the Panamanian isthmus and the Gulf of Urabá.

In 1532, Sebastián joined Francisco Pizarro's famous conquest of Peru. He played a critical role in capturing and overthrowing the Inca Empire, taking part in the Battle of Cajamarca and the capture of Atahualpa, the Inca emperor.

Afterwards, Sebastián embarked on a remarkable journey of his own. In 1534, he organised an expedition to explore the region to the south of Peru, known as Quito. This expedition turned out to be a pivotal moment in his life. Facing numerous challenges, Sebastián pushed through daunting terrain, harsh weather, and resistance from local indigenous populations.

In 1536, he founded the city of Quito, establishing a Spanish settlement amidst the captivating landscapes of the Andean highlands. However, Sebastián's ambitious spirit never ceased to drive him further.

Continuing his explorations, in 1537, he led an expedition northwards, reaching what is now known as Colombia. Along the way, he encountered various indigenous communities, fought battles, and faced numerous hardships. It was in this period he moved forever deeper into Colombia in search of El Dorado, a legend of a gold kingdom in the Americas.

In 1538, Sebastián finally arrived at the site where he would establish the city of Santiago de Cali. This location, with its strategic position and fertile lands, marked the foundation of one of the most significant cities in present-day Colombia.

Right away, Sebastián and his loyal followers began laying the foundations for the Casa de Los Gobernadores (The Governor's House) and formalising the Spanish colonial government and administrative buildings; there were many delays before work began. In fact, it took another 20 years before the construction started.

As a statue of Sebastián de Belalcázar in Cali, I stand here as a symbol of his remarkable achievements and contributions to the city's development. I commemorate his courage, vision, and the indomitable spirit that drove him throughout his journey.

*****

"At last, I, Simon, is up again! I wouldn't say I like these stupid footpaths, and most certainly not when it's raining. Now, before thinking that my learned friend Sebastián has told you the complete history of the Casa de Los Gobernadores. Please allow me to complete the picture for you all."

"The reason I wish to bring you up to date will become evident to you. In 1781, The Casa de Los Gobernadores was struck by lightning, resulting in partial destruction.

After extensive repairs, eighteen years later, it was turned into a jailhouse for captured independence revolutionaries.

The fight for independence from Spanish rule was ongoing, and this critical city began to play an active role in the uprisings. The Casa de Los Gobernadores went from jailhouse to meeting place for all revolutionaries. It was finally liberated by the revolutionary forces, and the Casa became a key symbol of independence and self-governance. In the coming years, I was able to visit this fine city and bear witness to the several renovations and architectural modifications to suit the city's needs and purposes. It is rumoured that in later years, it became the home for the local Police force."

At this point, Simon turned to his dear soaking wet friend in his immaculate uniform and uttered between drops of rain. "Just think, you'll have to go back to 1945 before this building was finally declared the Casa de Los Gobernadores National Monument and officially recognised for its historical and architectural significance."

"Do you think they could have imagined the museum that sits in its place today would become the monthly Meetings for all Barbarians, including statues, busts, figurines, cats, wild horses, children, and turtles? Of course, not forgetting us two military buffoons."

Sebastián chuckled at the suggestion and added. "Don't forget the militant-minded steel workers, Jorge Issacs and his lovely Maria and lovesick Efrain. Let's hope it is not as boring as usual."

"Here, Sebastián, can you answer this riddle correctly? What did the South American soldiers say when they won a battle?"

"No, what did the South American soldiers say when they won a battle?"

"Bolivar! We are victorious! No, wait, it's Ecuador."

It was Simon's turn again. "Sebastián, did you hear about the time I single-handedly defeated the Spanish army?"

"Oh really? How'd you manage that?"

"Easy, I told them it was siesta time, and they all took a nap!"

Not to be left behind in the humour stakes, Sebastián piped up, "Hey Simon, did you know I once beat you in a horse race?"

"Ok, is that so? Pray, tell me how you managed to outride me?"

"Simple, I just told my horse there was a carrot dangling in front of it, and it took off like lightning!"

Both statues rocked with laughter. Each sharing of jokes always made them smile and cemented the deep feelings of camaraderie between them.

*****

## 30: I am the Meeting of the Minds, and the Guests are arriving

The first to arrive were the wild stallions. They always liked to be first, these beautiful black-looking beasts that, in the daytime, you could see above the doorway leading into a huge national bank situated in the north of the city. During the day, they were captured in full gallop, and the spirit of their wildness was evident to all onlookers.

At night, en route to the meeting, they felt the first droplets of rain on their skin. Their first detour was to pick up the now sapphire blue children and turtles from the nearby park and its water display on the side of the road. The children were oblivious to the rain pouring off their tiny bodies.

The turtles with the raindrops bouncing off their heads made an amusing sight to behold.

The children were always destined to be innocent and never to reach adulthood. Their notions of the city only appeared as a huge play area.

Danger did not exist for them. They were transfixed in a period where only happiness prevailed, so for that very reason, they were of no current use at the monthly meetings.

They just enjoyed adult company. They rejoiced in the chaos of the cats and found Maria and her dog with no name to be the friendliest of all. More about this lovely lady later.

Most other nights, if it were remotely possible, you would be amazed at seeing the horses and the children galloping out of the city and up the mountain road, not just purely for exercise but for the very reason of being able to let off some steam.

The children loved the freedom and the power of the stallions beneath them as they negotiated the human world for a precious hour or two.

Never were the humans in danger or affected by the speed of the statues.

They lived in total ignorant bliss of such a forceful sight racing towards them, and somehow, each time, the horses were able to avoid each human as if by pure magic.

Even the pounding water in the falling raindrops could not blind the racing stallions.

Mind you, the turtles were different.

They avoided the horsemanship on offer; for them, rushing was the scariest thing imaginable.

They were ancient and very wise.

They only seemed to move a little or never say a lot during the meetings.

However, it was common knowledge that they always ensured they voted at the end of each point on the agenda. Never in the history of the discussions had the turtles been the root of any controversy.

Next to arrive was a famous South American writer named Jorge Isaacs Ferrer, who, midway through his life, wrote a beautiful love story titled "Maria." They say the heroine of the story may have been based on one of the writer's cousins. The hacienda in the novel is called "El Paraiso." I can confirm it is an authentic hacienda that is not too far away from this city.

Maria had fallen in love with her cousin Efrain, but like all truly great love stories, there is always tragedy close at hand.

Through circumstances out of the young lover's control, Efrain is sent off to the capitol to gain his six-year education. On his return, the lovers soon realise their desire to be with each other is still wild in their hearts and set up home together.

Sadly, this only lasts for three months, and another life-changing decision is made to send Efrain to London, England, to study medicine.

This time, he is away for a further two years, and on his return, he tragically discovers the love of his life, Maria, has died from a short illness.

The novel ends with Efrain's soul lost and now on an unknown journey.

Jorge's city-placed statue is as beautiful as the novel.

When you visit the pure white statue, you will see Maria sitting poised with her dog and Efrain leaning towards her in conversation.

Tonight, the trio and their dog welcomed the rain. Within minutes, all the dry dust from the previous sunny days was washed away. They knew now that they looked as new and fresh as the day they were sculptured.

*****

Next, the door bursts open, and in walks together, patting down the few droplets of rainwater on show my favourite statues, Simon Bolivar and his forever good-hearted friend Sebastián de Belalcázar, who founded this city back in 1535. As you can see, many years before, Simon Bolivar came to visit.

Both were clearly in a high-spirited and optimistic mood. They looked splendid in their fashionable uniforms of the periods each represented.

Belalcázar travelled to the New World from Spain in 1519, when he was only 25 years old, in search of the mythical El Dorado, believing it to be a region entirely of gold. Like every other explorer before him and after him, he never discovered El Dorado as it never existed in the way they imagined it would look.

In 1532, a group of some 160 Spanish conquistadors under Francisco Pizarro discovered the mighty Inca Empire, which ruled present-day Peru and Ecuador from the lofty city of Cuzco, high in the Andes.

Pizarro and his men declared war on the Inca.

They treacherously kidnapped Emperor Atahualpa and later marched on Cuzco itself. Those who survived the conquest of the Inca Empire became wealthy men, and many of them went on to other notable deeds in South America and elsewhere.

Sebastián de Belalcázar was one of the original conquistadors and one of the few men that Pizarro trusted. In 1534, Belalcázar was on the coast protecting Pizarro's supply lines when he received some disturbing information Pedro de Alvarado, the blonde-haired, blue-eyed and white-skinned Conquistador who participated in the rout of the Aztecs in Central Mexico in 1519 and followed up when he led the Conquest of the Maya in 1523. He was another violent, cruel, and ruthless conquistador who possessed the typical traits that nearly all Conquistadors needed to survive marching in the Inca city of Quito.

Belalcázar hastily gathered every man he could and marched inland. He beat Alvarado to Quito, keeping the remains of the Inca Empire intact and in the hands of Pizarro and his brothers.

Later, Belalcázar continued his fruitless search for El Dorado and is credited with founding the cities of Cali and Popayán.

"Well, just imagine if both of our respected subjects were to be known as friends," offered Belalcázar with one of his mighty arms wrapped around Bolivar's smaller shoulders, brushing the raindrops away.

Bolivar responded, "Now you know that could never have happened. For a start, you came three hundred years before me and, of course, the small matter of you being a Spanish conquistador and myself, a Venezuelan freedom fighter!"

"Yes, you are right. The times of us being men of war are firmly behind us; now our memories can be friends, and we rejoice in the knowledge we will never need to fight again."

*****

At this very moment, the meeting that was going to take place in an orderly fashion became chaotic when the delegation of the city cats arrived.

Both the warriors and the writer moved away from the entrance as at least ten cats raced in and behaved just as real cats do when they are growing up to become cats.

These monuments of the cat world represented a much larger group that lived near the large river that flowed through the city. The very thought of rain made these excitable felines race about chasing each other and fighting with a softness that ensured they did not hurt each other but intended when they wanted a quick breather and to pick their next victim.

They came in many different colours and designs, and tonight's representative was Sunny, the pure gold cat. This one always intrigued Belalcázar as he remembered his lost cause of ever finding El Dorado.

Another looked like she was only wearing a yellow T-shirt, and yet another was totally impressive to everyone in attendance, with her striking shade of red and what looked like silver needles of hair pointing outwards from all parts of her body.

On this occasion, the other seven cats were seen racing up high on the room's ancient curtains. One body was decorated with a pattern of sparking stars on a midnight blue background. Her twin sister was in hot pursuit, with her design in a totally different contrast. She was white with multicolour dots and images of cartoon characters placed nearly everywhere possible.

Tonight, the cats were extra excited; their prominent leader, the great Rio Cat, was away on business, and that meant no discipline. Only having the San Antonio cat available to second and attend the meeting told the feline, who represented curiosity and exploration with her inquisitive nature, was the least suitable choice for the Rio Cat he could send. The cats who came with her could be accessible as they wished, and they were going to take full advantage.

In the middle of this chaos, the stallions all sat in their customary places, watching the cats' antics. The horses secretly loved watching the horror on the faces of the human statues as the room filled with racing cats. It would be another ten minutes before tranquillity would reappear in the room.

Tonight, Jorge was nominated chairperson of this particular meeting, and he duly opened the meeting with customary greetings to all present.

He then listed "Apology for not attending this evening messages", such as the ones received from Cristo Rey and, surprisingly, from Nelly, the Monumento a la Negra del Chontaduro, or for those who have no idea who this 1,700 kilos of bronze sculpture were or where located. Nelly sits outside a very posh hotel in the heart of the city.

Bolivar looked at Belalcázar, smiling from ear to ear. "Do you know what I love about this bronze lady? Well, I love the fact inside, she has an impressive amount of bullet casings. Yep, over 900 kilos! Oh, how could I have done with that much ammunition at one of the battles I had with you lot?"

Belalcázar smiled and revealed his thoughts on such a fine-looking black beauty: "This eye-catching Monumento Nelly symbolises the beauty and aesthetics of all Afro-Colombian females. She can be seen clearly challenging conventional beauty, most certainly in my era. Dare I say she reflects a celebration of diversity and inclusivity?"

There was a short pause of complete silence; no one, even Bolivar, said anything.

Then one of the usually very quiet Turtles spoke up, "Chontaduros are small colourful fruits that, according to the humans, I see and listen to when buying them. They are unpalatable when raw and are only edible when cooked. After heating, the flesh softens to a consistency similar to a sweet potato or peach."

Every listener was oblivious to what the turtle was talking about and continued talking amongst themselves.

At some point, Jorge Issacs felt the need to bring everything back into order. "Let us begin with point one on tonight's agenda. Over to you Señor Bolivar."

The first point on the agenda was Bolivar's usual moans and groans about the state of the footpaths and roads. "Ah, good evening, dear citizens. I stand before you as the steadfast statue of General Bolivar, the Liberator of South America. However, allow me to briefly deviate from my historical role and voice my present concerns.

As a statue, I am unable to experience the physical hardships that humans face. Still, I need to speak up about the challenges I also encounter while traversing this city at night, particularly during rainy evenings. The trepidation that arises from darkness, coupled with the relentless downpour, is a plight that echoes in the air.

Imagine, if you will, the difficulties faced by those like me who brave these streets. The slippery cobblestones, which were once crafted with artistry, have now transformed into treacherous paths, making each step a test of caution and balance. I advise you all to tread lightly, my friends, for even the most confident foot can fail on these wet surfaces."

"Have you noticed what happens once the vibrant surrounds, adorned with colourful lights and lively activities, fade into shadows when darkness descends? Well, let me tell you, the cacophony of raindrops pounding on the roofs and streets adds a sense of gloom to the very fabric of the night, enveloping this city in a melancholy, mysterious air. It becomes a challenge to navigate, to find our way. Not forgetting to feel secure amidst the eerie ambience that surrounds us."

"And let us not disregard the difficulties of transportation during such conditions. Waiting at deserted bus stops or hailing a taxi that seems nowhere to be found become arduous tasks. The ghostly silence, broken only by the occasional rush of traffic, offers little solace. How I long for a solution that eases the burden on all those who need to move around this city after dusk, especially when the heavens unleash their tears."

"Hang on, Simon, when was the last time you ever stopped to get on a bus?" asked Belalcázar. Bolivar brushed the question aside as if he had not heard it and continued.

"Nevertheless, my dear inhabitants, although the rain may hinder our progress, let us not be deterred. Let us find solace in the memories of past struggles, reminding us that even the most challenging conditions can bow down before the indomitable spirit of humanity. "

One of the horses spoke a little louder than he intended, and all present heard the remark.

"Is Bolivar going to carry on ranting the same old complaint every month we meet?"

"I expect he will." Remarked another horse, groaning at the same time.

Again, with his knack for ignoring all present when he was on a roll with his monthly rants of displeasure at the state of his beloved city at night, he continued without pause.

"Therefore, as the statue of Simon Bolivar, I implore the city authorities to take notice of these hardships and find ways to improve the conditions for those traversing our city at night, mainly when the rain descends upon us. May we work together to create a safe, accessible, and comfortable environment for all who call this city their home. Let our collective efforts light the way, guiding future generations towards a city that shines brilliantly even amidst the darkest nights and the heaviest downpours."

There was a roar of approval, not for what the famous Liberator statue said, but because he had finished and had sat down.

*****

Belalcázar followed up with the state of the area where he lived and pointed his finger at constantly having to face such hidden-looking buildings.

"As the statue of Sebastián de Belalcázar, I stand tall with my finger outstretched, pointing towards a faceless window on a block of offices. Oh, the sadness that engulfs me in this peculiar situation! Allow me to share the mixed emotions I feel, aiming for that fine balance between funny and disturbing."

"Oh, the melancholy that seeps through my stone body as I contemplate the faceless window!"

He paused and allowed for the theatrical effect of his dilemma. "How can one be saddened by such an odd occurrence, you may wonder?"

"Picture this: a window devoid of any features – no glass, no frame, no handles. It stares back at me, offering a void that echoes a sense of emptiness and confusion. As I stand frozen, gazing at this peculiar sight, an overwhelming sadness washes over me."

"Imagine, dear friends, being trapped in a world of dullness, devoid of any character, any purpose. It's like standing before an artistic masterpiece only to find it unfinished and lacking substance—an existential crisis for a statue if you will."

"But wait! Here comes the funny twist! The absurdity of it all starts to creep in, even amidst the melancholy. I find myself unable to resist a chuckle, albeit a slightly disturbed one. Who knew that a faceless window could unlock such a bizarre emotion within the confines of a solid stone figure?"

"I am left pondering the great mysteries of life."

"What devilish architect designed this block of offices?"

"Why did they leave this window without its essential elements? Is it a cruel joke or a misplaced stroke of artistry? Such questions permeate my stony mind, tickling the funny bone while leaving a lingering sense of unease. And so, here I stand, forever pointing at an empty window, caught between the realms of comedy and discomfort.

I am a statue caught in a surreal whirlwind of emotions that unites laughter and an unsettling sensation, leaving me, Sebastian de Belalcázar, forever melancholic yet oddly amused, to remain quiet.

*****

They couldn't offer Belalcázar any solace. They had to all admit their views from where they were all positioned were full of interest for each other during the daytime.

Jorge offered, "Let us vote on how humans should be referred to in the future. Does anyone have suggestions?"

Belalcázar, as if not satisfied and feeling he had been cut short in his complaint, said," There was a time when I could see the entire city draped below me. Now, I face huge buildings with faceless windows and walls. Belalcázar threatened loudly, his chest proudly on display in front of him to emphasise his feelings, "If this continues, I may well have to leave this city and head back to Spain!"

"Can I have that in writing?" Bolivar smirked.

The reply was the customary poke in the upper arm from Belalcázar's outstretched finger. "Indeed, you can. Have you a pen and paper?" at this, both statues bent over in hysterics at each other's jokes.

*****

Jorge, the ever-present politician, waved his hand in the air to bring some degree of decorum back to the agenda." Now, ladies and gentlemen, as no one appears to have a suggestion on how humans should be referred to in the future, can we proceed with the next issue of the day?" He repeated where he had left off with his notes for the meeting this evening. "Due to the deteriorating weather and the possible need for all of us to perform our designated "In An Emergency Duties."

"The next official emergency meeting of the Minds will be held at the "Tree of Life" location on Calle 44."

"Maria and Efrain have a list for each of you, giving you all the information you will need going forward. Maria and Efrain, please take a moment to pass these sheets around. Please restrict one copy for all the horses, one for the group of cats, and one for the Solidarity crew."

"Where's the solidarity crew tonight?" Bolivar asked, looking around. The cats looked at the horses, and the horses looked at the cats, wondering where the humans, who were usually so punctual, could possibly be.

Before anyone could offer a reason, there was a rap on the door. Slowly, it opened to reveal the small community of nearly naked individuals who spent much of their days on a roundabout just to the east of the city.

On this occasion, all were soaking wet, and a water trail cascaded onto the shiny marble floor in all directions. Belalcázar always loved the sights of these buxom, semi-clad females, and to see them covered in rainwater was a voyeur's paradise.

It was the only time of the month when he could sit back and ogle them all.

Bolivar, not being too shy in admiring the female form, would look at Belalcázar and quip, "You dirty old-minded warrior, one of these days you will go blind."

"Who said that?" laughed Belalcázar, feigning blindness with his outstretched hand and finger.

This group was inaugurated back in 1995 and represented the patriotism and solidarity of the people of Caleño. All are made with materials brought from Italy: slate and quartz. The design and construction were in charge of a sculptor called Héctor Lombana Peñeres.

They were made in honour of the civic collaboration of the people of the city. The group was designed to show mutual help and optimism, and nobody lags behind because all participants are tied together in unity and harmony.

The appointed leader of the Solidarity Group apologised for the crew's unthinkable lateness: "Good evening, comrades. We are sorry for our lateness, but you know how difficult it is to find a taxi that takes more than five at a time in this city. "

"So, we had to resort to pounding the streets, and boy is the rain coming down heavily now."

*****

When looking at the solidarity crew, it is easy for anyone to see each distinct individual figure symbolising the concept of solidarity as a whole.

The monument's spokesperson and central figure is a tall and muscular human figure typically depicted in bronze. This figure represents strength and unity.

He stands upright with his arms wide open, symbolising open-mindedness and inclusivity. This central figure depicts a sense of solidarity and support, reflecting the concept of togetherness and unity. He is sincerely proud of his role and rarely resorts to humour. For him to ever be seen laughing was a rarity.

Flanking either side of the central figure are four shorter figures. These figures are portrayed as individuals from different backgrounds, representing diversity. They stand beside the central figure, leaning towards it, to signify their reliance on each other. The use of various heights and positions conveys a sense of interdependence and collective effort required to achieve solidarity.

The figures in the Monumento La Solidaridad are portrayed with their eyes closed, indicating a focus on internal strength and introspection. This emphasise the importance of looking within oneself to find unity and stability when working together for a common cause.

During daylight hours, the monument is located in a public area surrounded by well-maintained landscaping and a plaza where visitors can sit and contemplate the symbolism of solidarity. The overall visual impression is one of harmony, cooperation, and the celebration of shared values towards the greater good.

*****

The only issue that always seemed to arise at the moment of the Solidaridad Crew's arrival was that, suddenly, there was an "us versus them" stance in the ensuing meeting, similar to the workers versus the owners in the human world.

Stalemate often ensued, and the discussions over the years would typically end up with no tangible outcome.

Tonight was no different.

Efrain raised his hand to him, and once Jorge's eyes noticed the polite request to speak, he nodded. "Yes, Efrain, what is your question?"

Efrain, who was never comfortable with public speaking, coughed and asked quietly, "Has there been any response from the Medellín Society for the Preservation of Botero's figurines?"

For some considerable time, Efrain and his beloved Maria had been asking if Botero would ever visit them. Both wanted the great noble artist to honour them with a talk about his life.

Before Jorge could speak, the usually businesslike and somewhat aggressive spokesperson for the solidarity group stood up. He announced his group's disapproval of such disfiguration of the female form as was so clearly Botero's trait.

He continued with, "We, the present committee, have decided at our last Members-only forum held on Tuesday last week that we would unilaterally boycott any such talk as a particular show of protest. All our members had even talked about a possible march with banners and guest speakers of their own."

"Oh, come on, don't be so serious." The unexpected instruction came from the smiling Maria. "How could you be negative to the world of Botero?"

"For me, stepping into Botero's imaginative realm, where everything seems rounder and plumper than in the real world, brings out the smiling side of my nature."

"Even now. I can easily imagine myself strolling through one of his exhibitions, only to find myself surrounded by sculptures of rotund figures, almost all like humans who have discovered a perpetual buffet."

Efrain, agreeing wholeheartedly with his life's love for him, finds the strength to add his admiration of all that is Botero. "Have you noticed nearly all of Botero's figurines seem to have their own gravity? It is as if the laws of physics have conspired to create a world where gravity only affects the waistlines. One might wonder if Botero secretly swapped his paintbrush for a pastry chef's whisk, now creating art that is both visually appetising and absolutely funny."

Maria's enjoyment of having Efrain as an equal admirer of Botero took up the case. "Do not forget his playful exaggerations are not limited to humans. Animals from the animal kingdom also find themselves embracing the curvaceous Botero treatment."

She paused but for only a second to draw in her breath. Maria looked directly at the cats. "Picture a stout and jolly feline, the epitome of contentment, leaving you wondering if they've been spending all their nine lives on feasting and lounging."

"Certainly, when you find yourself staring at the Rio Cat!" remarked the Gossipy Cat. Her name will give you an inkling of her animated expression as if she is engaged in a whispered conversation.

Jorge even felt the desire to showcase his admiration for Botero. "I agree, and not only that, but I just think Botero's art is like a whimsical carnival where everyone cannot help but giggle and marvel at the hilarity of it all. As each of us explores his colourful paintings, we can encounter extravagant depictions of landscapes with houses that seem to have consumed one too many chimneys, causing them to resemble chubby, roly-poly giants."

Jorge was in his element, being an artist and wordsmith spurred on with a more severe outlook than before. "We should also stop and consider amidst all the comical bulk, Botero's art carries an underlying message. Beyond the laughter, one senses a penetrating criticism of today's society and its obsession with perfection and the pursuit of unrealistic beauty. His art challenges us to embrace and celebrate all shapes and sizes and reminds us that true beauty does lie in the eyes of the beholder."

Bolivar sat up and remarked candidly, "In my day, many of the fair ladies of Botero's designs were truly a fair likeness, and I, for one, never felt the need to complain. I think the modern female equivalent we all see in this city could do with a bit more of a fuller figure. So, I, for one, would love to see Botero's ladies here, but I must admit I would prefer he did not bring the men."

"Here, here." came the deep voice of support from Belalcázar. This was the moment the agenda went into its second stage of chaos.

Jorge finally managed to get a word in and answered Efrain's original inquiry. "I am sorry to report we have as yet not received any communication from Medellín, but as soon as we do, I will be the first to pass it on."

*****

One aspect of the modern city that brought the meeting back to a more civilised nature was when they discussed transportation and its effect on the city's environment. They all agreed upon the introduction of the MIO buses and their routes directly through the city from north to south. A massive reduction in pollution had been noticed—not anywhere near enough, but definitely a good sign.

Bolivar observed, "How can these modern-day humans bear to be on those overcrowded MIO buses? It defeats me. The times I have seen the buses full to capacity and beyond with all the humans squashed together, noses in armpits, bums against crutches, breasts against rucksacks!"

Everyone else agreed. The very thought of being up so close to the smelly humans made everyone shudder and lose more raindrops onto the now saturated wet floor.

Finally, those smelly old diesel-driven buses with their disgusting black plumes of toxic exhaust fumes were becoming less and less. They could all clearly see the time coming when they would be wholly eradicated from the city.

"Can we have the train back?" Maria asked almost in a whisper. "Pardon, what did you say, Maria?" Jorge asked, grateful that someone else was showing interest.

Usually, the warring heroes and the solidarity crew would end up face to face, exchanging insults for a good half of each meeting. But on this occasion, hearing Maria's voice again stopped all dead in their tracks.

"Are there any plans to let the train come back? I miss that lovely romantic feeling of sitting on a train meandering through the city and out into the country." The children were in unison at the very thought of experiencing a train journey with sheer joy.

The females of the solidarity crew acknowledged their appreciation, too, of each other's memories of the age when the train was the city's only means of transportation. The evils, on the other hand, were just staring into space, only the least bit interested in train journeys if they meant new jobs for the city's workers.

"Yes, you are right." Began the Solitary Leader: "We should enjoy having the train back amongst us. It defies logic why we appear to be the only city in the world without decent train services."

He heard no objection and took that as a sign to continue: "In comparison to that powerful country India, millions of its population use its rail on a daily basis. I have seen pictures of thousands of people hanging on for dear life and sitting precariously on the roof of all the carriages."

"My armies during my time could have been done with the train, certainly when we trekked over the Andes to surprise you lot at Boyacá." Bolivar offered to Belalcázar.

The smiling Conquistador ignored the remark as he continued to eye one of the buxom females who, in turn, smiled at him appreciatively.

It was not long before the smiling female received a kick in the ankles from her male partner, who by now was considering it was time to flex his bulging muscles to the ancient but well-armed Conquistador.

*****

## 31: I am Derekamus Stonebeard Stonforce and this is Abella Goldhammer Darkstone

Our family tree can be dated back to a country called Germany in the early 1800s. Our ancestors were made out of clay, and. In contrast, our many counterparts around the world are made of a cheaper material called plastic. I am relieved to say that we are still crafted with great care from clay by truly skilled artisans. It is still vital for humans to believe we possess magical powers which can ward off evil spirits and bring good fortune. Most plastic Gnomes are cheap imitations, campy and cartoonish. I am sad to say many young humans don't like us clay ones and invariably we end up neglected and forgotten. But for those older humans who do, we soon become beloved companions and protectors of homes and gardens."

"Our great-grandfather's generation travelled in large sailing ships. They first appeared in the gardens of England in the 1840s, and from there, their popularity began to grow."

Some of our bloodlines travelled further still, across the Atlantic Ocean to a new country called America. Here, our grandfathers and grandmothers were to become the first generation of Kimmel Gnomes." "Thankfully, we were all made of clay and resin. We can proudly boast that our gnomes are finished by hand and not mass-produced. Humans who want a dwarf-like creation with a wholesome soul seek us out, and we come in a variety of sizes and poses." The Kimmel Gnome paused to emphasise this proud heritage.

Everyone else in the meeting room just sat there, not saying a word. It had been over a hundred years since someone other than a statue had turned up and started talking to them as if it was the most natural thing in the world.

A pool of water appeared to be expanding beneath the gnome, and no. one thought to say anything. The gnome's pause only lasted a short moment before he continued, "Unfortunately, during this period back in Europe, two world wars wiped out most of our ancestors, especially those who remained in Germany." In the 1960s, those who survived struggled to find new homes as owning us gnomes was not understandably high on human priority lists of necessary purchases. Our generation of gnomes eventually travelled by ship, and this journey brought my wife and me to your capital port here in South America."

"We were transferred and assigned to a new owner whose recently deceased father and mother live for some months of the year in this particular city. From what I understand, the father was a hero during a recent earthquake, and in his old age, he resembled me in shape and choice of clothing. I am not sure what happened as I was too busy protecting Abella and myself in the box to discover what he did to become a hero."

"Our final journey from the port was not by ship, and for the first time, we experienced travelling on the big plush seats of a large Burgundy American truck. My wife slept the entire journey, whereas I just stared out of the truck's window with open mouth at such a display of beauty. Never before have I seen so much variation to the colour green."

*****

"But what is your function? It is clear you are not the same as us, statues." Asked the elder turtle, who was totally en-rapt by this new experience. He had found for the first time in his life a further use for his tongue other than gathering food.

"Originally, we gnomes were thought of as symbols of good luck. Later, we were thought of as a means to provide protection, especially when there were minerals and buried treasure in the ground. We are still used today to watch over crops and livestock. Often, we are tucked into the rafters of a barn or placed in the garden."

"I do not suppose you know where El Dorado is by any chance?" asked Belalcázar hopefully. The gnome ignored the question as he did not have the faintest idea what the obviously old warhorse was referring to.

"We garden gnomes like to think we add a bit of innocent charm and a loose connection to the old world, where farmers believed our good luck charm usually helped their fields yield produce and protected them from thieves, pests, and other problems. We were also thought in the same way to be of some assistance to all gardeners in the night."

"Many humans around the world can be seen from time to time chatting to us gnomes. Mind you, they are always looking over their shoulders, hoping no one has witnessed such a display of friendly absurdity."

"So," starts Maria, "You say you have a wife. Is your wife here for us to meet? And do you both have names?" As she asked this, everyone moved their heads in different ways to see if they could be the first to see a female version of this peculiar object in front of them.

*****

Yes, they all conceded later that they were similar to humans. But they were both only about 90 centimetres tall, and they suspected their girths were also the same distance wide.

His beard covered much of his chest and stomach, and his spindle-shaped legs looked like they would collapse under his upper weight at any time. Going back to that beard and the matching unruly hair, all of which, according to the elder turtle, needed a good wash and shave.

His clothes did not escape criticism either.

The children laughed at their memories of his baggy shirt, oversized trousers, and scruffy boots. They had only ever known the aristocratic splendour and cultural ambience of the two old generals and the likes of Jorge, Maria, and Efrain. Never had they seen such a working-class individual like this gnome. Even the solidarity crew looked at this new entity as middle class.

The gnome returned to the main door and disappeared for a brief moment when he reappeared. His hand was guiding another version of him, only this time a female of sorts. She, too, was soaking wet from the rain, and a trail of water followed close behind her.

She was definitely not in the same league or taste that the two old war horses would have been attracted to. Still, they confessed they both saw a deep warmth and loving nature in her eyes, even though they went in opposite directions.

She also wore a large, pointed red hat and an equally oversized maxi-length skirt that reached to the floor under her baggy green blouse.

Bolivar moved forward with one hand on his sword, and as he bowed forward, the sword walked expertly behind him. His other free hand made a small half-circle of greeting to them both.

"Welcome to you both. My name is Simon José Antonio de la Santisma Trinidad Bolivar Palacios Ponte y Blanco. What are your names?

✲✲✲✲✲

"Thank you, kind sir. May I present my loving wife of over 140 years, Abella Goldhammer Darkstone? I am Derekamus Stonebeard Stonforce. You can call me Derek for short and my wife Abella for ease. May I also reveal that we are celebrating our 250 joint birthday this very day?"

✲✲✲✲✲

Every statue, no matter what their size, jumped up and moved towards Derekamus and Abella, many of them embracing them with open arms. When they turned their attention to both gnomes, they sang a hearted and joyful rendition of the classic song "Happy Birthday to You" in both English and Spanish. Then, they suddenly remembered they still did not know why they had decided to come that night.

Jorge was the first to recover, "Derekamus and Abella, why have you come to us tonight?"

Now, it was Abella who spoke for the two rain-sodden gnomes. "Well, we are a friendly breed of gnomes. Aggression is alien to us. We like to trade wherever possible; we enjoy tinkering with our garden tools, and we occasionally enjoy fishing. So far, we have yet to find a suitable place in this city to allow us to fish. We were wondering if any of you could guide us on where to go?"

Everyone, including the turtles, was stumped; never in the history of all these statues had anyone asked them where to fish. No one had the faintest idea. Food had never been an issue for everyone for a very long time, if ever.

The Solidarity Crew approached the gnomes and, looking down, asked, "Is that the only reason you both came here tonight?"

Derekamus and Abella looked at each other, and both shuffled uncomfortably. Finally, Derekamus looked up and asked, "Can we join your society of Statues? Because, well, we are very friendly gnomes, and we have found this city a bit quiet and, dare we say it, a bit boring."

Abella, wishing to show support to her embarrassed-looking husband, added, "Since arriving here, we have done our utmost to enjoy our working hours, but we have lived before in London and New York, and in both of these cities, there "it was so much to do in the evenings, and so far we have found nothing to do."

"We are used to the closeness of the humans in the other cities we have mentioned. On their summer nights, they would often sit with us, talking to us and involving us in their daily lives. Here, we have noticed a difference: when night time comes at six, the humans close their gates and doors and never venture out again until morning arrives."

"Yes, my wife is right. We have become a little lonely. We have witnessed the horses and the children on various occasions enjoying themselves, galloping around the city and up towards the mountain ridge."

"We often see you cats, and you are always fun to watch, but for the rest of you, please excuse us. We never see you at all, and sadly, we know nothing of each of you."

The Statues all moved back to the centre of the room and gathered into a group, whispering among themselves.

The two gnomes are still trying to figure out what to do next and stay by the door.

This status quo remained for the next hour, when eventually, everything went quiet, and Jorge moved away from the group and approached the gnomes.

"We are sorry to keep you so long, but as you can imagine, it has been a very long time since any of us have had to deal with such a situation as this. We have all forgotten the original rules for joining."

The gnomes looked up at him to see if there were any signs to make them happy. "So, in answer to your question of whether you can join our group or not, we have deemed it possible. We discussed the reasons for and against us giving you both permission, and we found a reason to allow you to and none against it. In principle, we do not object, but we do not yet have a good enough reason to say, "categorically yes."

"So, we had a vote, and by a unanimous decision, we have agreed it would be nice to promote you to figurines status in the beginning, and you should do something outstanding that would have a marked effect on the city and its inhabitants. We will reconsider your status and may promote you to full statute membership at a later time to be decided when the time is right."

"Does that mean we can join?"

"Why yes, but only as the same as the cats, the turtles, and the children. They are classed as figurines and do not have any real power within the group. All the decision-making must go to the original statues, such as myself, Maria, Efrain, Simon, and Sebastián." Further adding, "The solidarity crew has a block vote similar to the horses."

"Has there ever been an occasion where a vote was needed?" Derekamus inquired innocently. "Ah, that is the other problem we have; none of us can remember." It was at this revelation that the gnomes were invited to join the leading group, and there, the life history of all was revealed to the happy couple. Throughout the rest of the night, they listened intently, not wishing to miss a single morsel of each of their newfound friends' histories.

*****

Much later, as the dawn chorus of the birds warned of the pending sunrise that was only moments away, Jorge hurriedly concluded the meeting and set the next meeting's date for a month ahead at the same venue.

Everyone agreed that this meeting had been the most joyous occasion anyone had ever had. Everyone left smiling.

Outside, the horses gave a lift to the children and the turtles, and the cats raced off as usual, chasing each other. The Equilibrist cat, who is typically seen balancing gracefully on a thin wire near the river, led the troop, followed by The Love-struck cat, who served as a symbol of love and the Fishing cat, who is intently focused on catching a fish. Together with the other cats, they raced up trees and poles onto window ledges and through the many parks en route back to where, in the morning, they would be static again until the night lights reappeared.

*****

Little did any of them notice that another pair of eyes were intently watching them from a very dark and hidden location near the ever-flowing river.

Here sat another cat, entirely black apart from his white crested chest and both front and rear white socks on all four paws. This feline was unknown to all the cat figurines.

He had been watching them with his most striking emerald green eyes for some time, but he was still not ready to approach and reveal his presence. He sensed his arrival would cause a considerable stir, so instead, he settled back down and crossed his front paws to rest his chin. Gradually, he felt he could relax and sleep again.

But he was mistaken; the Gossipy cat had seen him, and she could not wait to report her knowledge over the other cats to their leader, El Rio Gato. She tried earnestly to wake up the Sleeping cat. Still, as usual, she was depicting a cat peacefully curled up, full of relaxation and tranquillity, and only taking time out for herself.

The Gossipy cat turned to The Caleña cat, who embodies the spirit of the city with her vibrant renditions of salsa music and dance. Sadly, she went deep into the world of intricate footwork, quick spins followed by the odd isolation movement with her utmost passion and flair.

The Gossipy cat knew she was no match for the sounds of percussion instruments, like the conga, timbales, and bongos. All accompanied by the deafening sounds made by the brass and piano sections inside of The Caleña cat's mind.

She knew she would have to wait. Then, something she would never forget for the rest of her time, like the Gossipy cat. Two kittens appeared on either side of the bigger cat's back legs. One was female and coloured chiefly in silver. She was smaller than the other lion-looking coloured male kitten without a mane.

"How and why are they here?" Wondered the Gossipy cat. "Surely they must know they are in danger with the flowing river so close to overspilling its strong flowing currents."

She decided to wait and see how things were going to develop, hoping that the Rio Gato would appear soon, like never before.

*****

Abella and Derekamus skipped hand in hand, united in their bravery, to introduce themselves to the statues. They spent the rest of the day contemplating how their journey through life would continue. Each was easily adaptable to changing times in the future. Both were equally eager to bring joy and enchantment into the lives of those who would go on to appreciate their very existence.

Derekamus looked lovingly at Abella: "From humble beginnings in Germany in the eighteenth century to new beginnings in South America, we gnomes have come a long way, and hopefully, we will continue reminding the world of the importance of tradition, craftsmanship, and our enduring magic of childhood imagination."

Abella smiled and began rejoicing at the potential possibilities. "Maybe I will be able to offer the odd sprinkling of magic on those that shine out with kindness and goodness already on display."

Derekamus smiled. "Yes, I am sure you will find many souls who will merit your magic dust. In the meantime. Happy Birthday, Abella. I have loved you for 250 years, and the next few years will be joyful for us both. "

Abella looked in both directions and smiled at her husband and life partner, "Happy Birthday to you, my Derekamus. I am so proud to be your life partner, and I have a good feeling this city is going to give us some magical moments. "With that last exchange, both immensely satisfied gnomes began to rest and sleep in the pouring rain.

Maria, Jorge, the dog with no name, and Efrain walked as a group back towards the city centre, chatting about how different the meeting had been. "For once, it was actually fun," Maria remarked while brushing raindrops from her eyes.

As for the two old soldiers, they accompanied each other until it was time for one to climb the steep road to the ridge that overlooked the city. "So, Bolivar. What are your thoughts regarding those gnomes?" looking down at the flowing stream of water heading down the hill.

Bolivar thought for a moment. "I am not sure, really, but I do see some steel in their demeanour. Maybe if I had a battalion of them when fighting you lot, we could have bitten your ankles and made you all fall over and won the war a bit quicker."

Both soldiers parted, laughing at the images both now had of being bitten by a gnome and what it would have looked like.

*Behind them, the first toot of an alarm by an angry and impatient taxi driver could be heard in the distance.*

*****

## 32: *I am the Street man with no lasting memory, you know me as Stalin*

It has been a while now since I read the disregarded newspaper headlines regarding an earthquake high up in the mountains above the city. I was able to read some of the words, but alas, my memory is not as good or reliable as it once was.

I read with interest the account of the truck driver called Ignacio and how brave he must have been to save a Nun and a beautiful young woman in the middle of the mounting road surfaces at the height of the quake.

For some reason, I cannot explain, I feel something or someone is missing from the story.

Who knows what tricks the mind can play, especially the part images call the sub-conscience.

For me, memory is only fragmented. It is scattered and arrives at unknown times.

For example, this morning, I remembered my name, Stalin.

Why this name and where it comes from, I have no idea; maybe in a couple of years, the rest of the information will arrive and complete the puzzle of "Who I am and where I come from."

I sat under the roof of a dilapidated house in the middle of the city's neighbourhood. I always seemed to stroll around on a daily basis. Some days, I could find myself talking to no one. On other days, I resorted to begging for a few coins to buy a little food from the unique small shop or café that would accept my money.

There are only so many places as generous as one would wish for, but over the years, I have found one. It is not really a shop or café but more a man with a cart that he pulls behind him each day to his chosen place to attract the passing trade.

You rich people would call it a mobile catering concept. His menu is less vast than a restaurant.

Still, the owner always shows his kindness and generosity to others like me with a small but tasty Empanada, which is a type of fried pastry encasing a small piece or two of chicken and potato in gravy and a small cup of black coffee called Tinto.

Often, he will not accept any money from me and waves his hand away with warm words such as, "Be calm, my friend. Today has been a prosperous day for me, and you look like you could enjoy sharing this good fortune."

I bow my head and lower my eyes; his kindness sometimes reaches my permanently scarred brain, but I have been numb from showing feelings for many years. As a token of goodwill, I will offer the coins I have, but as I said, he never accepts possession of them.

"Listen, Stalin, my family has known you since when you were a little boy. We know most of your history, and I feel safer knowing you are in the neighbourhood watching over all that live and work here. I can offer you no more than a small meal a day as a way of showing my appreciation to you. Each Sunday, I go to church with my wife, and we always say a prayer for you. Hopefully, one day, your memory will come back, and you will. have a good life again. Now go and drink your Tinto before it gets cold."

His warm words from him and this small meal may be all that I will receive today.

Now, where is my trusty rock? I forgot to tell my benefactor of my suspicion that a tall, dangerous man with long dreadlocks was on the prowl in the neighbourhood. He looks formidable and could even be a challenge if we need to square up to each other shortly.

I move away and look down the road in both directions. It is the time of day when all the office workers appear from the tall buildings with lots of glass and head to their favourite restaurant, where they can eat the same food as they did when their parents and sometimes their grandparents served them when they were all little.

Amongst them, I would occasionally see the odd young policeman in his green uniform travelling by on his green motorcycle. Most of them do not even glance at me. To many, I am invisible.

Recently, there has been a younger-looking one of about the same height and frame as me, but there, the similarities end. He is young and fresh-looking. I am much older. I do not know how much I do not know, but my looks in the odd window reflections show my weather-beaten face and body. My scalp is sparsely covered in silver grey and white short curly hair.

I wear very little clothes; the heat of the sun acts as my clothing; it always keeps me warm, and when it rains, the water acts as a means of keeping me clean. Sometimes, I visit the local street fountain in the nearby park with the statues of the playing children and the two turtles watching over them.

Without a care in the world, I will take off my denim skirt and place it next to my rock, and with my rotting underwear and my shrinking frame for all to see, I will step into the cold water and sit down to allow my body to accept the initial chilliness. When I am acclimatized to the soft water's touch, I will turn to face the water, plunge forward and start to swim with my head submerged. I come up under the fountain and allow the delicate sprays to act as a shower.

Today, I am lucky; no one else wishes to join me, and no one comes to demand that I go away sharply. I can relax, I use the water to clean myself, and I have no luxuries such as soap or shampoo, just water, but nevertheless, I feel refreshed.

After some time, I rise and stand like a statue, feeling the gravity pulling all the running water away from my torso. The sun's heat rays capture the slower droplets and turn them into wisps of steam. It doesn't take long to feel dry again.

There is no need for towels in my meagre life.

While in this phase of my wash, I can see a large bus stationary in the traffic. Many of its occupants are all looking out of the window at me with no expressions on their faces. They have seen cretins like me all their lives.

No longer are they surprised or shocked. I am expected of them.

I show no signs of embarrassment or bravado. I reach for my skirt, submerge the cloth into the fountain's water, and scrub vigorously with both my hands as if I am doing the most natural act in the world.

Again, no soap powder or detergent, just everyday water lifting of the dust particles for that day and, of course, for the other days since the last time I had rinsed myself. As you can guess, that could be many days, weeks, or months; it depends on my memory to remind me to wash.

*****

So now I am fed, washed, and ready to experience the new day. I keep to the left side of the road and saunter past each tree, looking to see if there are any discarded cardboard or plastic bags that might house something I can sell later at the recycling depot that most street men like me use.

In this city, there are the standard refuge trucks and dustmen that you see in most cities around the world, but there is also another system ranked below the dustmen, and that is people like me.

We collect any rubbish that can be carried and recycled. Some of the others have carts or trolleys on two wheels that they pull along with great effort.

I have seen some pulling huge loads behind that even a strong horse or robust mule would have trouble moving. The men's bodies are stooped very low, and their heads face downwards to the ground as they advance.

Traffic has to avoid them, not the other way around, and miraculously, accidents and collisions are infrequent.

I have never felt the need to carry such loads on my back because my memory would not help me remember where I had left them. So, I will take very lightweight items that will give me a few coins I can comfortably carry in one right pocket in my skirt.

So far, I am still looking for something of interest.

I have reached the third tree just opposite a foreigner's motorbike touring company. This man can speak my language, but he comes from somewhere far away. I think he said Scandinavia, but alas, I am not sure.

He is standing outside of his store, and under one arm, he appears to be holding onto some clothing. With his other hand, he beckons me to approach him. I turn around to ensure I am not mistaking the situation, but I appear to be the only one he is looking at. "Stalin, eat here. I have some gifts for you."

I close the gap between us and look at the bundle he is now holding out to me with both hands. "Hello stranger, we have not seen you for some time. In the last couple of weeks, we have been given many T-shirts for free. "We have more than we need, so I saved some for you."

I raise my eyes to meet his. There is warmth and friendliness on display. There is no sign of judgment or disdain that I often see. Suddenly, the clothes are under my arm, not by me but by the swift movement from the foreigner. "I know from past experience that you are a man of small vocabulary, but please accept these as our appreciation for looking after our store and keeping it safe from the local thieves."

I nod my head slightly in his direction, thus showing I have accepted the clothes and moved away. Without looking back, I continue walking up the road, heading to the black bags under the next tree. Here, I find two medium-sized cardboard boxes already flattened down, so I position them securely under my arm with the T-shirts and head off to the recycling depot.

It takes me a further hour of walking to reach my destination. Another street man sees my small bundle and cardboard. He intercepts me and offers a few coins. Knowing that he will receive closer to the depot, I agree with his offer.

Why would I not accept? What do I use for money?

Nearly everything I get is free. I have no utility bills to pay, no rent, and no mortgage. In my world, money has no value at all.

Free from carrying the bundle of t-shirts, I start to head further towards the centre of the city.

Big black clouds have replaced the sun and its warmth, and it does not take long for their raindrops to start to fall heavily on me. I try to look up to see the size of the clouds, but the ordinarily blue sky is completely hidden behind a formidable wall of dark grey.

My eyes react to the big droplets splattering on my face, forcing me to look back down again. This storm is going to last and even cause some localized flooding. But all would return to normal again within a few minutes, Stalin felt initially, only a mild irritation of unease. That did not continue. Why? You may ask.

Because of the torrential rain's torrential downfall, combined with the crackling of thunder and the flashes of streaking lightning above the city, Stalin lost track of where he was walking. He found himself unsure of where he was and could only see the odd shelter from the force of the rain. The skies above were raging without limit or consideration to this man with his rock.

Many houses and apartments were protected by big iron railings or gates, bushes, and trees. There was very little to offer him a reprieve from the force smashing into his back.

His denim skirt weighed at least three times as much as he had initially, and he had no choice but to keep his arms down and use his fingers as grips so he did not entirely lose the clothing he wore continuously.

Suddenly, in the rising mist of water, he could see a gap in the houses, and he realized he had indeed travelled further north of the city than he anticipated. In front of him, he could see at least twenty very tall trees with, he guessed, at least one hundred dangerous-looking balls hanging in large groups from each trunk. He had never seen such trees before. I wondered why they were here, of all places.

He went to investigate but found it difficult to walk. The terrain had moved from concrete to a mixture of fallen leaves and mud. The mud was sucking down his feet. He tried to retreat but found himself stuck. In his rising panic, he turned in all directions to see if there was any danger to humankind.

There was....

\*\*\*\*\*

## 33: I am a Yellow-headed Caracara, and I sense Carrion is not far away

The white-haired man had risen early and had done his customary duties of feeding and cleaning the dirt trays for his black-and-white cat, who was proudly now washing all four of his white pads while looking at the two newly acquired kittens.

Blacky, the elder, had been with the Englishman and his joyful and wonderful wife, Cristirin, for nearly seven years. Blacky had initially been recruited as a rat catcher with his now-deceased brother Tommy.

Both had proven to be expert hunters until Tommy contracted Feline Leukaemia. It was rumoured that Tommy had gotten into a fight with another older cat and was somehow infected. The vet warned everyone that Tommy could only live for another two years, and during that time, the disease would ruin his life on a daily basis.

Tommy would show how sick he had become by displaying weakness and acting lethargic each day. He would go from being an active cat to someone unwilling or unable to get out of bed. The decision to show him kindness was a tough one, and one that still plays on their minds seven years later.

Now Blacky was fast becoming an "Uncle" to Liz (Short for Queenie) and Goldie. Cristirin had suggested Liz as she had always been fascinated by the British monarchy. She could immediately see this kitten growing regally with elegance and sophistication. Liz would go forth and carry the grace and poise that would benefit a royal feline. Liz would always be the Queen of her domain.

The Englishman approves of Liz's new name and offers Goldie as the future king of Cuddles. He playfully dubbed him Goldie, after the famous children's storybook character "Goldilocks." Just like Goldilocks, this little lion would command attention and, of course, would love giving limitless cuddles to one and all."

Both human cat owners envisioned their new kittens and, of course, with the permission of Blacky as rulers of their household, each with their unique personality and traits. Both kittens were fascinated with seeing a much bigger version of themselves. Every minute of their waking hours was spent following Blacky around, bombarding him with endless questions. Within two months, what was once a very orderly and tranquil routine for Blacky had now converted into a race track and playground.

Even his cat food and dirt box were no longer for his sole use. Over the past week, he discovered that if he wanted a number two, he had to queue up behind. These two poo-creator extraordinaires. Usually, Blacky could escape for some peace by waiting for the white-haired man to open the Penthouse's large sliding window-style doors, but today the storm raging overhead put an end to that enjoyment.

Blacky sat instead, looking up at the skies and could clearly witness the lightning and hear the thunder. He was used to both, but even today, he could see there was a heightened rate of energy flashing before his eyes. He couldn't help but notice the sky growing darker instead of brighter, and even he felt the ominous effect being displayed. The winds began to howl, the air was electric, and the sound of cracking was everywhere.

Then he spotted the squadron of at least a hundred or more Yellow-headed Caracaras coming from the south of the city, now flying overhead and landing on the roof above him.

Up until now, these birds with their hooked bills flew innocently by in pairs and never once did they feel the need to rest just beyond Blacky. Even these birds were suffering from the torrential rainfall and turbulent winds.

These magnificent birds, known for their bright yellow heads contrasting with their black feathers, were battling the storm's elements with all the strength they could muster. They swooped and glided through the tempestuous sky, their wings flapping rapidly against the powerful gusts.

The white-haired man stood near Blacky, and for the first time ever, he was getting a close-up as the rain pounded down on them. Each was drained and looked darker overall than ever before.

With matted heads and more prominent than normal eyes staring back at both the human and cat, it was clear each of the Yellow-headed caracaras was struggling to maintain its balance and precision as each tempted to land on the rooftop. The storm was playing tricks on their coordination, causing them all to misjudge their descent, resulting in less elegance on display than usually seen.

Later in the day, the white-haired man tried to collect his initial thoughts and could only reach the words: "heavy and sodden feathers, large round and frightened eyes, and prominently on display hooked bills." He couldn't help but admire their resilience and adaptability. Today, these birds were facing challenging conditions, but they did not give up, even amidst the chaos and drenching rainfall. I have marvelled at the thought of each demonstrating their remarkable grace and tenacity.

*****

As a Yellow-headed caracara living in the north of this South American city, my life is filled with a combination of urban and wild experiences. Typically, the cityscape provides an exciting backdrop for my daily activities, offering both unique challenges and opportunities.

During the mornings, I typically start my day with a soaring flight over the city. My species, the Yellow-headed caracara, is known for its impressive flying abilities, and I take full advantage of this to survey the urban landscape for potential food sources. From my aerial vantage point, I can spot various habitats and urban green spaces where I might find small prey, such as insects, rodents, reptiles, amphibians, or even some discarded scraps from the city's streets. You humans call it Carrion.

On the negative, I am not a fast-flying aerial hunter like many falcons but rather more accurately described as a sluggish scavenger. I am not migratory but more terrestrial in my lifestyle. But don't get me wrong, I so wish to become a migrant.

My species can be found all over North and South America. I aim to one day fly to places like Panama, Ecuador, Bolivia, Brazil, and Argentina. I am still trying to figure out how best to do what I constantly dream about.

Later, on a typical dry day, I often venture into the more natural areas on the outskirts of the city. This is where I feel most at home, as it allows me to engage in more instinctive behaviours. I can hunt more freely, including diving down to snatch small fish from local rivers or lakes. The surrounding forests and grasslands provide shelter and perching spots where I can rest and observe my surroundings.

As a social bird, I occasionally interact with other Yellow-headed caracaras in the area. We gather in pairs, sometimes small groups, known as flocks, to coordinate activities such as hunting or defending our territories. Our flocks also provide a sense of community and protection as we navigate the challenges of city life.

Living in the north of this city, I've adapted to both the urban and natural environments. I have forged a delicate balance between exploiting the resources the city provides and maintaining my connection with the wild. Although the cityscape can sometimes be loud and chaotic, I find solace in the pockets of nature that still exist within the urban jungle.

Overall, the life of a Yellow-headed caracara in the north is a unique blend of urban adaptability and wild instincts. It is a constant dance between soaring above the skyline and exploring the untamed areas on the city's periphery, allowing me to thrive in this ever-changing environment.

If you had asked me yesterday to describe a typical day for a Yellow-headed caracara, I would have told you the above. But never have I or my fellow friends ever had to endure such a violent experience—and not just once but three times in the last twenty-four hours.

Indeed, this rainy season will end soon. For now, I will have to stay within the safety of the squadron and wait out the tempest above. I have seen the two kittens, and yes, they would definitely fill a hole. But I can see the larger, more threatening black and white feline is never too far from the innocence.

One hundred pairs of eyes look down, seeking a moment's lapse in concentration, and one silver kitten and one golden kitten with blue eyes turning daily to a different shade of yellow will be flying without the need for a parachute.

*****

It is not often that I find my mind drawn to a specific area of the park with the cannonball trees, but right now, I am sensing a rare opportunity to save some human-like Carrion. I have heard that human carcasses are tasty and are a unique food source. My sharp beak will enable me to tear apart and consume the flesh and organs of the dead.

I must admit it is not my number one choice of food source, but with all this rain, beggars cannot be choosers as they say.

This human appears stuck in the mud. I can sense I am not the only one considering changing my diet today from kittens to humans……… One hundred sets of eyes have moved in that direction.

*****

## 34: I am the king of all Cannonball Trees

My family motto, which is displayed at the base of my coat of arms, clearly states: "Anything that can fall on your head will eventually do so."

I watch as humans walk past my family of what they call Cannonball Trees or the Latin equivalent, "Couroupita Guianensis." Try saying that ten times at a rapid pace without taking in a breath.

I have tried many times, and I always stumble into ridiculousness after three attempts. Our peculiar and fascinating trees are usually found in the rainforests of Central and South America. Still, for some unknown reason, my fellow family of twenty trees, with their dense and broad crowns, offered ample shade to the forest floor. All of our trunks are strong and sturdy, providing a firm foundation for the numerous branches that radiate outwards. Our leaves are glossy and dark green, enhancing our striking appearance amidst our small patch of rainforest.

Our only slight drawback regarding our location is that I saw ourselves growing up in what was once a swamp near a river passing through the centre of this city.

I have learned that Cannonball Trees are related to the world-famous Brazilian Nut.

Still, we must confess that none of us actually know or have any idea whether being associated with a Brazilian nut is a good thing or a bad thing.

Sometimes, I have been told ignorance is bliss.

Throughout our various discussions and with the odd titbits of information we have gleaned from the strange human conversation below us, we have learned that it was most likely that a variety of animals called Paca travelled to this site nearly 100 years ago.

They carried some of our seeds in their stomachs, and because they love to burrow their nests next to the running waters of mighty rivers, our small orchard was born.

The city was less populated then, and the Pacas were content over the years to breed and eat our fruit. The seeds would continue to pass through their stomachs and enter the ground on which we now proudly stand.

The Pacas have since left, and the city's population has grown so much that the Pacas sadly decided to find quieter locations to start harvesting another set of trees.

Now, the bats come to us throughout the night to eat our fruit, and the bees love to pollinate with our beautifully magnificent blossom. Once, we were told that we had many relatives in faraway places such as India, Sri Lanka, and Southeast Asia.

We need to find out where these places are. Still, humans seemed impressed that our distant cousins were often found in Buddhist temples and revered by their followers in vast numbers. There is a human mythology referred to as Hindu. Our flowers and fruits have significant cultural and religious significance for their followers. Our flowers apparently are closely associated with Lord Shiva and act as symbols of life and creation.

Now, if you need to learn about who Lord Shiva is or was, let me explain a bit about this deity.

Lord Shiva, also referred to as Mahadeva or the Great God is one of the most revered Hindu deities. He is considered the supreme god, the destroyer of evil, and the embodiment of ultimate reality and cosmic consciousness. Lord Shiva is nearly always depicted as a yogi meditating in deep contemplation, with ash smeared on his body and a snake coiled around his neck. He is often associated with various symbols, such as the trident (trishul), third eye (symbolising wisdom and insight), and crescent moon (representing the cyclic nature of creation).

Lord Shiva is believed to be the lord of dance, known as Nataraja, symbolising cosmic energy and rhythm. His devotees considered him benevolent, compassionate, and the dispenser of ignorance. Lord Shiva's significance and mythology vary across different Hindu traditions and scriptures, making him a complex and multi-faceted deity.

*****

We find that odd because although we are very tall, some of us measure just below forty meters high. We are covered from head to toe in the finest multilayered flowers or, as one human once described, "Outrageous Blooms hanging off our trunks on the long snake-like ropes." Each of us displays vivid colours of reds and pinks at its bases and various shades of yellow at its tips.

It is our fragrance that each flower radiates outwards, upwards, and downwards that always intensifies at night, attracting more bees, bats, and other insects to float around us and enjoy.

What we find odd is our thick-skinned fruit covered in spikes or knobs, giving each a unique and somewhat menacing appearance.

We have as many as 150 balls of rusty-looking round fruit that can take anywhere from one year to eighteen months to ripen. Their shells are rock-hard and definitely similar in size to a human head, weighing as much as 4 kilos each.

For those creatures that are fans of us, Cannonball Trees, each of the balls holds secrets waiting to be discovered. Upon opening our fruit, a fan can easily find an abundance of small, caramel-coloured nut enveloped in a white, fragrant pulp. Our pulp, with its delightful aroma, is well known for being a favourite among fruit-eating animals, and monkeys and various bird species often consume us.

This is not the same for humans. Inside each ball is the problem, not for us but definitely for humans. Every time one of our fruits decides to disembark from our trunk, there is only one way for it to go: in a predetermined direction coupled with a growth rate of speed until it makes contact with the ground.

Here, its hardened, woody-looking shell explodes open with a thunderous crack.

The pulp inside emits a smell that sends humans running as far as possible away, holding their noses and guarding their mouths in case the stench of the paste was to invade them.

I have even witnessed a few humans bending over and wrenching out loud and gripping their stomachs tightly. Once, I saw another fruit fall and hit the human on his head, knocking him out completely!

The other humans rushed to the rescue while looking up nervously to see if more of our cannon balls would decide to take the opportunity to fall. Luckily, on this occasion, it was a few more hours before the next twenty did in rapid succession.

I remember once listening to a man describing one of his ancestors who used to wear a steel helmet with a spike protruding from the tip and a suit of armour that made him sweat profusely to escape from a severe injury when one ball landed directly on the peak and instantly cracked open.

Apparently, it was weeks before the stench from the pulp disappeared from his splendid-looking uniform.

The party, the human, was relating the story to burst out laughing, and I also did because I was sensing history repeating itself if they did not move. As the final member of the group progressed, there was a cracking sound behind him. On this occasion, he was fortunate.

The lucky one bent over and picked up the damaged ball and stupidly moved his large nose closer. Abruptly, his head flew back, and he screamed out, "Wow, that stinks like a rotting skunk passing wind profusely, causing a nearby tramp to vomit his drunken whiskey innards into a plastic bag of mixed rotting blue cheese and rancid mayonnaise! "

No one laughed as they had all beaten a rapid retreat, holding the uncontaminated air in their breaths. I was the only one who enjoyed the somewhat unique description.

On the positive side, I know that my fruit's pulp and the seeds within are a delicacy for many animals in the district.

I have just recently become aware of a strange couple. Well, the male one is definitely strange. The female partner is a typical beauty of this city, but he most assuredly is not from these parts.

Most days and at the oddest of hours, I see them walking past hand in hand, talking about their lives and the trees. Both amusedly hold their heads down as if expecting a crack to befall them.

No, I do not think they will become a victim, but there is someone who inevitably will if the time comes right for it to happen..........

In the shadows, I can see one such wretched-looking street man with both of his feet firmly stuck in a patch of mud. But he is not alone......

*****

## 35: I am Caesar, a well-known street robber having one heck of a bad day

*I* am a very tall street man with a well-built frame and fearsome looks to everyone who sees me. My very long dreadlocks flow from my bulldog-like features. When it rains, as it is now, my menacing appearance doubles in intensity, and my eyes match the colour of my skin.

Many think I must be the devil himself, and often, I see them turn sharply away from my presence and make a speedy retreat to what they presume is safety.

Today, my clothes are soaking wet, ragged, and filthy.

My oversized black coat covers my frame. It hides beneath it the blackest of hearts.

Never before have I found a reason to persuade me not to rob or kill anyone who offends my wishes or demands.

People say I, Caesar, was born with bad blood running deeply through me, and there was never going to be a happy ending to my life.

I am curious to know if what they say is true.

Since I was a little boy, stealing what I fancied has been thrilling to me. Spending my life working for next to nothing on a daily basis was never going to happen.

To see the fear in each victim gave me a thrill deep inside of me, and if they cried and begged, then even better. I loved to prolong their misery, and should any of them deem they were strong enough to say "No." Well, if the opportunity presented itself, I would gladly enter my trusty black knife deep into them.

Even the young police officers, who I only see as young boys, fear me. It would take an army of them ever to stop me.

Today, I have found myself moving through the increasingly wet streets near the city landmark white cathedral known locally as Iglesia La Ermita.

Often, I can be seen lingering nearby, not because I am attracted to its exquisite craftsmanship, bell tower, or even peaceful ambience. No, it's because it is a magnet for locals and tourists with their wallets and purses full of money.

Today, due to the poor weather, the streets around the church are almost empty.

I turned left and passed through the narrow streets to the local street vendors selling their cheap T-shirts, jeans, and trinkets. None had the money or property I so desired. The pounding rain also reduced the passing trade. I looked up, and there appeared no end to the cloud formation above. Well, it is the rainy season, but even so, these clouds seem to be weeping more than usual.

I can see the centre laid out in front of me. Just imagine a vast circle of paving stones surrounded at the round edges by ancient pine trees, all inside a massive square of surrounding buildings.

At the centre of the ring is a remarkable bronze cast statue paying homage to the life and legacy of a man called Felipe Joaquin de Cayzedo y Cuero, who was born in Cali in 1773 and over his forty-lifetime devotion to education and equal opportunities to all and sundry.

They say the statue serves as a constant reminder to the people of the city of the subject's remarkable achievements and his unwavering commitment to improving all lives. Over the years, it has become a gathering place for all to admire, reflect, and seek inspiration from the life and achievements of this politician, military man, and so-called visionary statesman.

Well, my education did not come from De Cayzedo; it was the mistakes I made and never repeated as I began my life of crime.

Five straight walkways lead to the outer edges of the circle from the statue, which is strikingly detailed in its representation of a stylised book held firmly in his hand.

Each of these walkways is edged with small walls that allow people to sit uncomfortably to chat or to watch others walk by. Even when it rains, they still eat and relax. They think that it is only a strong shower and that within a few minutes, the sun will reappear. All will be dry again a few minutes later.

But not today. The sky was dark and menacing, looking like it had never before.

I like to stand with my back leaning against one of the buildings, looking in towards the middle of the circle, ensuring I can see all that is passing through. Today, it appears to be no different. First, I can see the office workers and shoppers passing through as quickly as their feet allow. They hold their umbrellas at angles to enable each to observe the others and still avoid their well-pressed clothes from becoming wet.

Their eyes then move downwards, not wishing to make contact with anyone. I am not interested in any of them. Furthermore, they only get paid twice a month and never carry any significant enough sums of money to satisfy me.

On the small walls I mentioned earlier, a rabble of old men whose lives have passed them by sits. Next to them randomly sit the street women, whose conditions have remained the same as those of the old men.

The only difference that I have noticed on many occasions is where the men's eyes have died. The experienced women have always managed to stay alert, always looking for the next opportunity to make some spare money, even if only selling a cup of Tinto or a coffee or two. Doing this allows them to strike up a conversation with the intended victim with the aim of enticing them to a cheap hotel room to earn more money with their ageing bodies.

Today, the oldest one I can see is also the same colour as me. The weathered woman is wearing a black and white checkered skirt and blouse. The skirt has risen to reveal her voluptuous thighs.

Fortunately, the front of her skirt stays where it should.

She appears to be having difficulty standing, and when she walks, you can clearly see that she does not have many more years left in her body.

She carries a small cardboard box loaded with packets of cigarettes. The lid of the box is on show, offering scant protection to the contents below. I have no cigarettes left in my pockets. Later, the old woman and I will meet on a quiet street, and the cigarettes will become mine whether she agrees or not.

The old men sitting are, all the same, tanned from all the years of working or just sitting in the sun, all wearing cheap glasses and all having white and receding hairlines. All their faces are covered in lines, and many may only be fifty or sixty.

Mistaking them for eighty or ninety is easy.

Many, I suspect, or should I say know, have empty pockets and are resorted to spending their days out of their hovels, away from their accusing spouse's eyes, and just becoming silent witnesses to the street women's trade.

Judging by what is on offer today, there will be little action, if any. You would have to question what sort of man would be attracted to such on display.

I look to my left and I can see two policemen have set up a gazebo. They aim to be busy offering leaflets to any tourists who may stop and inquire. Even though they are protected from the rain, I don't see these boys being very productive today, either.

Next to them stand two women who, to be honest, look beautiful, each sharing a substantial dark green umbrella. Or it could be that the main population on display made these two look so attractive. I can clearly see from the wet information board next to them that they are local Jehovah's Witnesses.

I looked around to see if anyone in the square might be interested in becoming a member. No one came to my mind that I suspect could become one.

Suddenly, just behind them, I see a stranger walking into the square. He has white hair and blue eyes, he is dressed for walking, and he has skin in three colours: his legs are white, his arms are terracotta, and his face is red.

The sun has been enjoying itself with this man.

The stranger stops in front of the statue, takes out his mobile, and starts taking pictures in quick succession, hoping the rain will not damage his mobile.

Yes, this idiot is going to be my next victim. He has a black rucksack on his back, and I am confident that I will be pleased with the contents inside. I reached into my left pocket, which had a large hole in it. With the gap wide open, I was able to get the handle of my knife, which was tucked into my belt, without anyone noticing.

All I need now is the element of surprise.

With a pen and notepad in his hands, my new victim is staring up at the statue and reading the words on the stone plinth. I can see him smiling as he aims his conversation at the statue as if he can hear and understand his language.

"Don Felipe, I am writing a manuscript for a future book to which I wish to add your presence. This is the initial outline; I hope you approve. At some point, please send me a sign or an acknowledgement so that I can continue."

*Introducing Don Felipe Joaquin, the Charismatic Connoisseur of History!*

*Don Felipe Joaquin de Cayzedo y Cuero, the brilliantly sculpted persona immortalised in stone, exudes an air of refined sophistication and intellectual charm. Adorned in impeccably tailored 18th-century attire, complete with a historical book and an intricately embroidered coat, he captivates the attention of everyone who encounters him.*

*When Don Felipe Joaquin attends meetings with illustrious statues like Simon Bolivar and Sebastian Belalcázar, his presence is nothing short of theatrical.*

*Full of life and animated gestures, Don Felipe Joaquin injects a hint of amusement into every scholarly discourse. He is known for his witty banter, intelligent quips, and encyclopaedic knowledge of Colombian history.*

*With an unrivalled passion for colourful storytelling, Don Felipe Joaquin effortlessly brings historical facts to life.*

*He captures the attention of his esteemed companions and the audience with riveting tales from the past, seamlessly intertwining humour, drama, and fascinating details.*

*His animated expressions and gestures give life to long-forgotten events and characters, leaving the rest of the statues in awe of his remarkable ability to turn history into an enjoyable spectacle.*

*Don Felipe Joaquin's charisma shines brightest when he engages in friendly debates with fellow statues like Simon Bolivar, the passionate liberator, and Sebastian Belalcázar, the intrepid conqueror.*

*With his sharp wit and an impressive collection of historical trivia, he effortlessly engages them in discussions ranging from political intrigues to military strategies and even esoteric topics like art and philosophy. Each exchange transforms the meeting into a captivating intellectual joust, where Don Felipe Joaquin's humour serves as an undeniable highlight.*

*In these gatherings, Don Felipe Joaquin's presence is not just about entertainment—it also serves as a reminder that history is anything but dull. With each interaction, he sparks curiosity, inviting others to dig deeper into the rich tapestry of Colombia's past and igniting a collective desire to embrace the lessons learned from history.*

*Indeed, Felipe Joaquin de Cayzedo y Cicero's statue has become a beloved figure in the meetings of great historical personalities. He not only keeps the sessions engaging but also leaves an enduring impression on those lucky enough to witness his vivacious persona as they subtly acknowledge the invaluable role history plays in shaping our present and future.*

I can see that even though I did not understand a word, I had cited the statute. That must have been pretty boring to hear. "A crock of shit" in Spanish is an expression that has come to my mind.

Now, more interestingly, I can see the stranger has troubles of his own. His red face has turned white. He looks worried. Has someone threatened him?

If so, I have not seen anyone approach him. It would be a good idea to follow him from a distance. I am absolutely assured an excellent opportunity to overwhelm this man will show himself soon.

He staggers towards the narrow street heading towards the old white cathedral. Today, he shows no interest in such a building. He races down the broad steps and heads past the government buildings, showing not the slightest bit of attention.

The street vendors try to offer their goods to him but have yet to receive a response. I can see clearly that he is distressed about something, but I have no idea what could have caused such anxiety.

But I am pleased with whatever is causing it as this stranger is not looking for danger as he should be.

He reaches the main road, and the traffic lights go red.

Tremendous luck for him and terrible fate for me.

The cars are now stopped, allowing the stranger only to pause for just a fraction of time. He was instantly in front of everyone else, and if this was a race, he was winning easily.

He is now on the other side and heading towards what, from years of experience, could be a very populated area. If I am going to act, it has to be now.

The stranger slows down, and I can see his hands reaching behind him. Why and what for, I have no idea, but I am now on top of him. The gap between us is decreasing every second. He has not seen me coming. I am only inches away. I pull out my knife and aim it towards his exposed chest. It is now I read into him, expecting to have the sun high above me.

Still, instead, I can feel raindrops landing all around me, so with the deepest of voices, I say out loud, "Dinero!"

He looked up at me, rain landing on his face, seeing me for the first time in his life, and said only, "No diarrhoea!"

With that and showing no fear, he just walked off, leaving me looking like an idiot in the street with a knife in my hand. If I could have shown embarrassment, I am sure my skin would have gone a deep red.

But no, I actually felt sympathy for him.

His troubles at this moment were inevitably going to be more than I could give him.

I quickly replaced the knife beneath my coat, turned on my worn-out heels, and decided it was time I had a cigarette. Surely, my luck today would change for the better.

*****

## 36: I am a Trainee Policeman named Archibaldo Federico Alcatraz

Archibaldo Federico Alcatraz is a 19-year-old Afro-Colombian man who has nearly completed his first year of training in the City Police Force. He only needs to survive one more month, and then he will start to receive a salary. Like all boys, when they reached the age of 18, their country expected them to either be soldiers or policemen.

The only way for him to avoid this decision was if his family had enough money to pay the government to bypass his name.

He couldn't or wouldn't ask his mother about him, who had raised him almost entirely alone, to do such a thing.

For as long as he could remember, he knew one day he would be a very proud policeman.

Before that, he wanted to be a priest, but luckily for him, he listened to his mother and the local sister, who gave prayers and extra guidance with his homework at the only church in the community.

Both women gave him the calling of more incredible things awaiting him in life.

However, Archibaldo never lost the love of the church and its masses every Sunday. Archibaldo was always the first to arrive for each sermon. For him, each service was a unique experience that drove directly to his heart.

Being a policeman would help him pay his way through a life where being a priest may not. He was warned by the two older women, who were a lot wiser than him. Also, he was only 10 at the time.

*****

When he reached eighteen, Archibaldo signed up, knowing full well that he would receive no pay for the first year, and his family and friends were expected to assist him with food and lodging.

His olive green uniform was his working clothes. He was on call duty 24/7. He completed his designated homework as and when time allowed. Police management had long deemed that socialising and buying clothes to impress the local girls were missing from any new recruit's priority list.

Archibaldo would never forget that life-changing moment when he was present in the army barracks for the first time to enlist either in the Army or the Police. This was where he finally had to put pen to paper confirming his decision to either join the Army for a fixed two years with nothing guaranteed at the end or to join the Police on a 25-year contract.

*****

The latter option appealed to his young mind not because he desired to be seen all macho or the need to carry a gun but because the more extended contract offered him a stable future with promotional opportunities that, at first, he could only dream of.

He has wished so much more for his mother and siblings. He always knew that his life would have to change and that he would have to do whatever was needed without complaint.

*****

The family's village living conditions were always challenging, with the constant threat of heavy rainfall, flooding, landslides, and other natural disasters. Choco has always been one of the poorest regions in the country, characterised by its geographical isolation, almost non-existent infrastructure, and abysmal socio-economic disparities.

Houses were basic structures; almost all the walls were made of wood, bamboo, or palm leaves. Each dwelling lacked access to reliable electricity, robust sanitation facilities, or even portable clean water.

Listening to her son's heartfelt dreams and desires also put his mother's fear for his future at rest. She knew her first son was going to be part of the history of the country's only civilian Police Force and would not be under the military's control.

Julieta Alcatraz's son would lead the way down the path she hoped for her other two younger boys, who, in turn, would also offer their hearts and souls to protecting the nation, enforcing constitutional law, and protecting the rights and freedoms of the nation's people.

*****

Like all the men in the small jungle-embedded community of some 1,500 people, the boy's absent father started as a temporary thing, usually around the time each child was due to arrive. Then, around a year later, he miraculously would reappear as if nothing had happened.

Just like the electricity supplying the community, the menfolk would work only during the daylight hours and disappear each night again. This left the town with no street lights and no heating in their homes.

In the rainy seasons, there would be no power or folk for days. It seemed the generators were always waiting for the sun to dry them before suddenly coming back to life again.

*****

Surprisingly, even with so much poverty, the town could boast of having a Community Hall, a school for all ages, a hospital, and even a police station with only one Sheriff. The crime was almost non-existent.

So often, the Sheriff could only be found at his home watching one of the only three television sets in the community.

The other two were under repair and stored in the community service back offices, where they sat unused for generations.

So Archibaldo had just learned what television was for. He had to wait until he had moved to the city when he was eighteen.

The only poorly maintained road went through the town between two of the three rivers and crossed the third via a small bridge connecting the north and south parts of the town. In the rainy seasons, the road often ceased to be what we would call a path and reverted to a canal-type situation where the only means of transportation was locally made canoes.

When the dry seasons prevailed again, Archibaldo and his three friends could usually be found under the bridge in the sweltering heat, bathing and swimming in the calm waters for many hours.

Sometimes, Julieta would join them and then walk them through the local fields of pineapples, plantains, and lemon trees towards the north of the community.

Life would go back to normal for Julieta until the next child started to show in her stomach.

This was the sign for her husband to be up and gone again. Sometimes, he would argue that he had a job at one of the local gold or silver mines and had to live in bamboo huts supplied by the mining companies. Women and children were not allowed to visit, or the mining security guards would chase them and beat them if they were caught.

This went on until the third child started his journey. On this occasion, the absent father made his absence permanent. Over the years, there were many rumours, but Julieta was no longer interested.

*****

One such rumour was that he had got a job at one of the local gold mines further south from the town and that he had another woman much younger than her who, at that time, had no children.

Another rumour that had circulated for a few weeks began with her husband working in one of the many poorly constructed mines with wooden supports, only meters away from the nearby Death River, as it was locally known. The mine had collapsed in its main tunnel and sent gallons of rushing water into the pit.

All the men inside were doomed and drowned. Rescuing them had proven to be impossible.

*****

The rainy season had been in existence for some two months. The surrounding rivers were flowing to the maximum. Soon, the flooding would start, and the terrain would turn to mud.

All the ingredients for a tunnel collapse were in place with devastating consequences.

Knowing which of the victims were lost to the flowing river that carried them to the nearby Pacific Ocean could not be made with any degree of accuracy due to the slavery environment used by the owners of the mines.

Keeping records of who worked in such dangerous conditions was not something they felt was needed.

Julieta did visit the site and found nothing like all the other women who also came to see if their missing husbands had indeed been victims. Even on this occasion, they had no idea how many perished, never mind who they were.

Julieta returned to tirelessly raising her three adventurous and curious boys and holding down a full-time community service position that allowed her sons to run and play with full stomachs and kept her mind busy.

For the rest of her life, she would never know if she was still married or, indeed, a widow.

*****

Once in a while, the children ask if their father is alive. She can only shrug her shoulders. She has no answer; she has heard many rumours, but none of them would plague these lovely sons of hers.

She was so grateful for the job; here, she was the go-between for all the nearby fruit growers and the local markets.

She helped keep everything calm and regular. She acted as an arbitrator when disputes arose from time to time, usually regarding prices and quality of the fruits, especially in the rainy seasons when much of the surrounding land was prone to flooding from the three great rivers that met near the south of the community.

Archibaldo's early life helped map out his decision for the Police.

It was from his experiences of his mother's constant and loving guidance that he improved his life and became the one who would guide his two younger brothers when it was their time. She did not want any of her sons to live the life of the older men and her absent husband.

None of her children were going to become future victims of the gold mines.

As soon as Julieta was sure that Archibaldo was confident about joining the Police, she sent word to her mother, Deissy, who had lived for many years in the big city further south of the country. She had visited there on two previous occasions when the boys were all small by one of the national coaches who threaded their way around the country.

Deissy was a housekeeper for a priest and his family at his church in the north of the city called "Barrio de Flora," and Deissy lived in a small community house on the church grounds. There was enough room for everyone to stay and explore the city.

Deissy and the priest wholeheartedly wished for Archibaldo to be allowed to stay with them in his first year. Once he started receiving a salary, they would talk about how he would need to contribute to his keep. Until then, the church would support him.

Tonight's shift for Archibaldo started at four in the afternoon, and his Sergeant gave him a rapid deployment.

"Do as you normally do. Walk this area as you have been doing for at least six months. Make sure your radio has fully charged batteries and remember your trunk. There have been no reports of possible criminal behaviour that have caused us concern. "You will be relieved around eight tonight for your evening meal."

"Yes, Sergeant. I'm checking to see if my motorcycle is fine and ready. Should I need it later in the shift?"

"Yes, but be quick about it. The Duty Officer will be doing his rounds at some point, and I want you where you are supposed to be." growled the Sergeant good-humouredly. Instantly, he left the squad room for his afternoon cup of coffee from the Police Station canteen.

As soon as Archibaldo opened the main door, he was faced with a complete wall of falling water.

When he looked up, all he could see was dark grey. He reasoned he would need his heavy oil-skinned cape with an attached hood to help protect him.

He looked down at his relatively new shiny boots, and he felt he would be saved, if only for a short while before he felt the wet clothing tight against his skin.

He had no problems dealing with rain. He had spent nearly all his young life naked and soaking wet. He also reasoned with a smile. It had never bothered him then, and he was confident it would not bother him now.

His local Police station was just East of the small park that accommodated some extraordinary trees. Large canon ball fruit hung in abundance as it was their season to ripen. There appeared to be a bumper crop as all the trees were heavily laden with balls.

Best I stick to the footpaths at the edge of the park to allow myself some protection from being hit on the head, he reasoned to himself.

*****

He will never understand how he noticed the figure hiding under one of the enormous trees close to the footpath in front, but luckily for him, he did.

The character was completely black in colour. Even his face and hands matched the colour of his long coat. The dreadlocks also gave Archibaldo another warning that something was not right. Or was he misreading an average-looking man protecting himself from the falling rain?

For sure, he had not placed himself in danger. He knew what these trees could do.

Growing up in the Choco region helped him understand the dangers of being hit by just one cannonball. An impact could quickly become fatal.

What surprised him the most was when he first saw them near his assigned station. How did they manage to get this far south and into a city?

Now focusing on where this figure was looking, he, too, noticed just a few meters away, moving towards the main road, a strange-looking man with white hair and what looked like brand new soaking wet clothes.

The top half of his body was stooped over, and he tried to shield himself from the rain but with no success.

Why would this stranger venture out in such conditions? He asked no one but himself.

By the route he was taking, he would pass within a meter of the hidden black figure.

Like a prophet of old, he could clearly see what was going to happen next and knew instantly he had to prevent the attack from happening.

When he saw the knife appear from under the attacker's long coat, he made the decision to move forward.

*****

At the next moment, the young trainee Policeman looked to his left and saw another man, a street man all bent down carrying nothing but a rock in his hand hidden by another tree. Was he also part of the future attack? No, he decided he was too far back, so why was he there?

Archibaldo could clearly see the street man had seen the figure now poised as if about to jump out and begin an attack. He could see the man with the rock standing no chance of closing the distance between him and the attacker.

He would have to advance now if anyone was going to be successful in preventing the stranger from being murdered.

Archibaldo pulled out his truncheon from under his cape and started to run as silently as possible towards the now lunging attacker. He roared out at the top of his voice, "Stop Police!"

*****

But his voice just left his lips and crashed silently to the ground through the wall of water. His hood started to fall backwards, and his boots began to work in the mud. But Archibaldo's adrenaline had now kicked in. He was going to save a life tonight or drown attempting such a feat.

Now, only meters away from the attacker, and as he started to raise his truncheon ready to strike, the figure turned, and his menacing and dead eyes fixed onto Archibaldo.

Only the attacker's mouth wide open with sudden surprise took away his shock.

Then, there was a series of loud cracking noises, followed by a whooshing sound.

Within two seconds, the introduction of a head-aching pain, ending in complete darkness for Archibaldo.......

*****

## 37: I am the scene of a very unusual way of dying

Caesar's day had been going from bad to worse. It started with the Diarrhea Man. He still had not recovered from the emphatic "NO Diarrhea!" he had received with so much equal conviction from a pending victim. Where had the man found the courage?

He had been asking himself this troubling question right up to the point when he saw him again later in the day. There he was, walking so proudly in a new set of clothes!

He will not defy me a second time this very day, muttered Caesar as he moved away from the wall, following at a more measured distance. Already without realising it, he was giving this stranger more respect than he would typically allow any victim. He was not frightened of him. He just saw some steel and resistance he had not seen before.

In his criminal life so far, he had only seen fear and often the wetting of the pants as his knife entered their soft tissue. This time, Diarrhea Man was going to feel the blade many times. He will do more than wet his pants, Ceasar promised to himself.

Even the older woman in the square had been a waste of space. He had cornered her in a secluded doorway just off the main street. It was one of those very opposite types of roads that even the locals gave a wide berth to, and should any reckless idiot be to think it was okay to follow an old ageing prostitute and Ceasar, well, they would not fare well.

"Okay, Old Woman, where are your packets of cigarettes?" threatened Caesar as he grabbed her arm and unbalanced her into the door well of the rundown hovel with no occupants except just these two.

Showing only slight annoyance at being so roughly handled, she replied, trying to break away, "Behave, Caesar. Look, I have no cigarettes on me. Look again. All I have is these pampers for my daughter's child back home." As the final words came out, so did the packet of pampers hidden under her skirt.

She had been trying to protect them from the storm that was now raging above their heads.

"Don't lie to me. "I have watched you often, and for your age, you always have pockets full of money and cigarettes," accused Ceasar as his hands reached out and started frisking the large body that could hide many a treasure.

The old and wise street woman knew how to handle herself, and she only felt a minor tremor of fear.

On this occasion, she just wanted to rush home, first for her granddaughter's sake and second because one or two of these pampers were for her use only.

The punter an hour previous had been rough with her, and she was now sore and could feel her discomfort with some degree of pain.

She shuddered with the memory of the man's fist clenched tightly as he forced it into her. She didn't need this from this big fool as well.

"As I have already said, Caesar, I do not have anything for you to take today, and if I were you, I'd be cautious where you put your hands." Her eyes were now playing with her tormentor. Her hands went to the hem of her skirt and started to lift it up. "Here, look for yourself if you do not believe me", now grinning from ear to ear with all the confidence she could muster.

The power of the stench that emitted from her was enough for Ceasar to gag and retch away from her.

At this point, the older woman recovered herself and broke away from Caesar's grip on her. She fled further down the filthy and muddy street on her two wobbly legs, roaring with laughter.

Caesar just stood there with his black eyes following the receding shape of the older woman. He could not believe a whole morning had passed, two victims and not a single peso to show for his cunning and tenacity to rob him at will.

"God help those who come into my sphere later today," snarled Caesar, now howling for revenge on anyone. Today, someone is going to wet their pants and die.

*****

Later that day, the clocks struck two. The lunchtime trade was now back in their offices, and Caesar was moving further northwards, looking for new opportunities to change his luck this very day. Shielding himself under a shopkeeper's parasol at the side of the main road, he had been watching the passing traffic for some ten minutes.

Suddenly, the opportunity he had been waiting for appeared with an idiot driver, his side window entirely open and the idiot's elbow resting on the 4 x 4 ledge. Caesar could hear the howling music emanating from the interior of the vehicle. The driver was clueless about the danger he had put himself in.

Caesar did not hesitate. He moved like a puma and was reaching into the seat of the hapless driver before he could even gasp in surprise. But to Caesar's surprise, for the third time this day, the driver fought back with a powerful punch to Ceasar's nose.

He instantly felt pain as blood vessels in each nostril exploded and immediately poured out with such force that they landed everywhere they could. Mixed with the rain, it made everything seem utterly macabre.

To the onlookers in the yellow taxi waiting at the lights behind the 4 x 4, both the driver and his fare turned their heads away. Neither of them wanted to show their reluctance to intervene, and neither did not wish to bear witness to the resulting street robbery.

Neither spoke for a good ten minutes after the violent event. Even when they did, it was only to exchange the fare required.

Caesar fell backwards, and the driver slammed down on his gas pedal, and his 4 x 4 roared away through the red lights to safety. Later, he discovered his wallet had gone missing. No doubt the street robber had been successful, but oh, what a price he had to pay to get just 5,000 pesos worth—mounting to only just over £1.00 in sterling.

Caesar stumbled around the corner, holding his bleeding nose, sensing it was broken too. Not for the first time, he would handle it as he had always done before. Being homeless still had its dangers, and always there was a price to pay.

Today, it was his nose. Later, it would be someone's life.

When he checked the contents of the wallet, he was going to let his head drop forward, but he had only just managed to stop the tide of blood. The rain was instantly washing away all the mucus, the blood, and the phlegm. He was hurting, both inside and outside; he was soaking wet, and he was no further to having a good day.

The pain had turned to apathy. He could handle that. Numbness got him through the days. The wallet disappeared into some bushes, minus the $5,000 note.

*****

He moved further north, and slowly, the shops and businesses started to be replaced by houses and apartment buildings, with the odd restaurant or bakery scattered in between. The rain had not stopped since the early hours.

It seemed everyone was now sheltering from the onslaught, all wishing for that reassuring warmth from the sun's rays again on their bodies.

But it didn't look like it was going to appear today.

Ceasar had yet to learn the time. Street men do not usually carry a watch for obvious reasons. Their own bodies always seemed to be able to predict the time with some accuracy.

Today, he was about twenty minutes behind in real-time.

He turned right at the park in front of him. He knew this park well. It was always full of stupid fitness fanatics in his mind. Some old farts are jogging their lives away; some are even more decrepit, only walking the last of their lives. Others were in a Pilates group on the green, all hoping for the best, others still showing off their bulging muscles and standing around using the government-supplied gymnasium apparatus in the open air.

In the mid-section of the park, Caesar could usually find, in his warped opinion, those demented wildebeests trying to score that long-awaited try or goal.

Today, it was totally empty.

He was just about resigned to giving up, first diarrhoea, then a rectum, then a broken nose and now this emptiness everywhere.

At this point, he wiped the rain from his eyes, and he and behold, Diarrhoea Man was walking down the road away from him.

*****

Caesar roared out to no one in particular. "Now I am going to get him. I will make him pay. He will feel my knife relentlessly sliding in and out of his stupid and weak body. I might even cut his throat for good measure."

So here we find a raging force trailing a short distance from the unknowing and strange-looking man in his now soaking-wet new clothes, who was thinking to himself, "What the heck? If I wanted to be soaking wet, I could have stayed in England and not have needed to travel over 5,000 miles to South America." and as his next thought "Mind you, at least there's no wind and no feeling chilled to the bone. Here, the rain is actually enjoyable."

"Mind you, today, it could be a bit less."

As Diarrhea Man started to walk towards the park with its tall trees and smelly and undoubtedly dangerous canon ball fruit, he did not notice a black figure overtaking him. Caesar was now waiting to spring his trap for the second time this very day.

*****

"I am the eldest tree in the park, and I have been waiting for this very day to arrive. At last, the significant delay of a human they call Caesar is right below me. I am so joyful.

At last, I have the golden opportunity to drop a considerable payload right on him. If I am lucky, all my balls will release at once and bury the evidence, too."

"Now, where is the poor intended victim? Ah, I see him. It's that white-haired, rich, red-faced, and white-legged man, who, to be fair to him, often stops and takes a photo on his contraption. No, Mr. Robber, you are not going to harm this stranger today or any other day."

I squeezed my muscles, and instantly, a mass of rock-hardened balls of pain, each the size of a human's head, started whooshing to the ground.

Caesar's life is extinguished with the very first ball.

The next three pulverises the broad open skull and the previously broken nose. He had no idea what hit him. Now he lay in the mud surrounded by wide-open

Cannonballs, all spewing their rancid smells over Ceasar's body and his clothes. Even the storm will not wash away the stench later found by passers-by when the storm abates.

As for Archibaldo, he now lay next to Caesar, knocked out but still breathing. One of the Cannonballs had ricocheted off Caesar's shoulders and slammed into Archibaldo's temple with just a glancing blow, rendering him unconscious.

All the other five balls had landed harmlessly around him.

As for the stranger, he was oblivious to all. His head was down because of the rain and because he always felt nervous when walking past the trees, so his head was still facing away from the park and towards the road instead.

What with the thunder and lightning, he had heard and seen nothing.

But there was a pair of eyes who did see everything that the rain permitted him to see.

As soon as the stranger had disappeared around the corner onto the main road, Stalin rose and crept forward towards the black figure. He paused and could see instantly he was beyond medical treatment. He will not be one for robbing again, he reasoned to himself.

Now Stalin turned to the other body, lying helpless. He knelt in the mud and checked his pulse. The street man could see a young Policeman and, in his book, a courageous one indeed.

Even if he was a bit stupid, racing towards a seasoned street man who clearly was at least three times bigger carrying a deadly knife. With only a baton as a defence and getting his feet stuck in the mud at the vital moment. Not only stupid but unlucky, too.

Archibaldo began to recover consciousness and gingerly opened one eye, only to see, with difficulty, a street man with a rock lying near him. In a blind panic, he reached for his missing truncheon.

"Tranquil, Señor Policeman. I will not hurt you. You have done that to yourself enough already."

With that, he started to lift the young Archibaldo from the clinging mud. "Now, let's get you back to your colleagues around the corner. If my mind serves me right, your station is yonder past the trees and the park. In fact, I can almost see it from here."

Archibaldo allowed the street man to get him to his feet, but his feet had no power, and they nearly allowed him to collapse again. Stalin prevented further injury by sliding his head under one arm and placing his arm around the policeman's back.

Together, they took a while to reach the safety of the footpath leading to the Police station. Archibaldo was unable to say very much as he slipped into and out of consciousness. When they both reached the station, Stalin placed

Archibaldo under the front door's archway in a dry spot. He had turned around, searching for something. Stalin found what he wanted: a good-sized rock.

He leaned back and hurled it through the window next to the door, turned, and fled the station. He did not want to get involved in future investigations. Besides, tomorrow, he will not remember anyway. Best be gone, he reasoned to himself again.

*****

# 38: I am the Second Meeting of the Minds in a week

Two days had passed since the incident involving a street robber named Caesar and a young Policeman named Archibaldo Alcatraz. The News media besieged the little Police station near the park, and all of Archibaldo's colleagues were beleaguered every hour of the day by the hungry-for-information reporters and their editors, who were continually pressing for more updates on the deceased villain and the new hero of the day.

At the same time, Archibaldo was recovering from a concussion, and if the reporters tried hard enough, they could have found him in his bed being protected by his grandmother and the Priest's family.

Archibaldo was enjoying resting and watching television for the first time. The remote control's batteries had to be changed regularly, but Deissy and the Priest never complained.

They were in awe of such a brave little boy from the jungle who was fast turning into a fearless man with a promising future in the city.

The rain continued almost continuously for the same period. The current habitats had never seen such rainfall. Two months' rain had gone into the ground in days.

At one point, Deissy walked into Archibaldo's room with a large mug of Tinto and a piping hot empanada, cursing mildly about the rain that had fallen so far. "At this rate, we will need to consider what is going to happen with the older people who are dotted around the city in small houses they like to call "Old Folks Homes" or "Casas de Ancianos."

"The fire service will not be able to rescue all of them as they number in their hundreds!" "Don't worry, Grandmother. I am sure there is a plan of action to prevent any older person from losing their lives. I will raise the matter with my Sergeant in an hour or two when I sign onto my shift."

"Well, make sure you do. I sense trouble ahead until, like us from Choco, who are experts in living and surviving floods. The people here in this city are not." Archibaldo quietly reasoned that Grandma Deissy had a lifetime of dealing with excessive muddy water invading her shanty homes. If she is alarmed, I should be, too, and not ignore the fact.

*****

The drains showed signs of large puddles, and the deeply built canals were already half full. This was a sight the locals had never imagined before. Soon, the authorities turned their eyes towards the large rivers and the mountain ridge, looking down to the city's north. At present, their streams were torrents of angry waves with large, frothy sprays reaching the tops of the banks on either side. The authorities had already estimated that it would be another day or two at the most. Such a high rate of downfall would place the city in danger of being flooded, definitely in the north and the centre of the city.

Both had taken the brunt of the storms so far, leaving the south dry and risk-free.

Teams of workers were sent out to look for as many breaches in the river walls as possible and sandbag them up. Everyone in the city was holding their breath and was often seen looking over their shoulders when near any waterways.

Sadly, no one had mentioned the danger to all the older people's homes. No one had thought that each of those homes was built on one level, like a bungalow. They had never seen the need for a second floor without a lift and the impossible effort it would require to carry these older people up and down stairs daily.

*****

The consequences of the weather began with the roofs made of wood as they started to buckle and collapse. Poorly made shanty homes in the east began to slide down the mountain edges.

Mudslides appeared every day. So far, they stayed on the mountain ridge and were small in scale.

The mountain ridge's water sources began to fail under the immense pressure coming from the clouds. Locals began reporting seeing terracotta-coloured water racing in every direction.

If not checked, this new development was beginning to be looked upon as a threat to the city below.

Northern streets started to look like small lakes and holes that could ruin the front tyres of all vehicles began to be hidden, increasing the number of accidents involving motorcycles and pushbikes.

Cars with low bases were not faring much better either.

The little taxis were also starting to voice their concerns. Many of the side roads were already beginning to become inaccessible.

Everyone agreed with the TV reporters nightly that the city now had enough water for comfort.

It was unbelievable when they looked back to two years prior when El Nino, a natural phenomenon characterized by its unusual ocean temperatures centered around the equatorial Pacific Ocean, was prevalent and the main threat.

The ocean is reachable by road within two to three hours of the city, thus allowing irregular occurrences and far-reaching effects to show themselves to the city within hours.

This resulted in the city suffering water shortages for nearly a year. The temperatures rose, and two dry and two wet seasons became only four dry seasons.

This time, the city endured a regular dry season, but this wet one resulted in many rainfall records being broken!

El Nino had numerous effects on the city. Reservoirs dried up, and the local rivers and streams suffered the same. Restrictions on garden sprinklers came into force immediately.

This was followed by the tap water being switched off for most of the day except first thing at six in the morning and again at seven in the evening.

The population began to organise their days around the hours when water would be available to ensure they could wash, use the toilets, and maintain other healthy habits that were once taken for granted.

Eventually, the clouds and the rain they carried returned, and the danger of the city overheating slowly disappeared, becoming just distant memories.

*****

All the statues started to see a change in the mood in the city and its suburbs. The cats and children's figurines soon voiced their concerns to the stallions above the bank, who passed on the worrying news to Jorge and Maria, who were on display next to the government buildings.

They also reported seeing a magnificent white horse with its tail reaching down and almost touching the tarmac trotting on the main highway connecting the north of the city with the nearby industrial town of Yumbo. What made them remember this particular horse was that it was riderless, and humans could not see it.

"Could this be the very horse that belonged to Simon Bolivar?" asked the stallion reporting the curious event.

Efrain suggested holding an emergency meeting to see if anything could be done to help and to ask Simon Bolivar about his famous horse. Jorge saw the wisdom and immediately sent the Solidarity crew in all directions to gather as many statues and figurines as possible to attend the meeting that night.

*****

When Derekamus and Abella arrived in the hall, they found it crowded with unknown images. They met Felipe Joaquin de Cayzedo y Cuero, and immediately, they could see that this was a scholarly hero of the city.

They liked him and knew a time would come when they could ask a lot and be rewarded with the same amount. After a short while, they moved around, looking up at the many new strange sights, but none could have taken their breath away like the vision of Jovita Feijoó.

They both stood like sentries on parade. Neither moved a fraction until Abella found the nerve to ask Maria, "Please tell me the back story of the real lady this statue represents."

Maria chuckled at her willingness to expose Jovita Feijoó's backstory. Both gnomes turned and waited for the mystery for them to be revealed.

Ah, let me introduce to you both the legendary Jovita Feijoó from Palmira, the epitome of comic charm living in this fair city! Jovita Feijoó is one of those characters that you can't help but instantly love. She is knack for turning even the most mundane situations into a laughing riot. With her flamboyant personality and larger-than-life presence, Jovita stands out wherever she goes.

Now, picture this: Jovita strutting down our city streets, wearing sunglasses bigger than her face and a hat that seems to defy gravity. No one can resist her infectious laugh, which echoes through the city, causing people to stop and wonder what mischief she's up to. An endless supply of hilarious anecdotes from her humble beginnings in 1910 in Palmira.

From the time she accidentally mixed up her neighbour's laundry with hers and ended up wearing her grandmother's vintage bloomers to the day she attempted to become a salsa dancer, she ended up creating her own version of herself called the "Feijoó Shuffle. " She always keeps you entertained.

But it's not just her wacky adventures that make Jovita a comedic gem; it's her endless supply of outrageous catchphrases. Whether she's proclaiming, "I'm bolder than a mango on a tightrope!" or exclaiming, "I'm as lost as a donkey in a shopping mall!" her wordplay never fails to bring tears of laughter to the eyes of those around her.

Jovita's unique sense of humour also shines through in her fashion choices. She's never afraid to experiment with bold patterns, vibrant colours, and accessories that defy all fashion norms. You'll often find her standing in mismatched socks or wearing a feather boa as a belt. She believes life is too short to take fashion seriously; her wardrobe reflects that philosophy.

Even the most mundane tasks become a joy when Jovita is involved. Going grocery shopping with her feels like being on a hidden camera show episode. From haggling with the butcher in hilarious broken Spanish to treating every shopping cart as a potential racecar, Jovita transforms an everyday chore into a side-splitting comedy.

Jovita has become a beloved figure in our city. She is known for her distinctive personality and comedic hi-jinks. Her contagious laughter can be heard in every corner of the city, brightening the mood of even the grumpiest passerby.

So, you have found yourself in our city and have encountered Jovita Feijoó from Palmira. Prepare yourselves for a wild, comical adventure. She'll have you laughing until your sides ache and leave you with a heart full of joy. Jovita Feijoó is a true comedy queen of Cali!" Derekamus and Abella slowly turned their gaze back to Jovita Feijoó, each having to stretch their necks to allow them to see her in her sheer glory and magnificence. Already, they were in love with her. Abella knew where her next sprinkling of gold dust was going to land.

*****

The Lady statue concerned was over twelve feet tall. She wore a silky sky-blue coloured ball gown that had white frills at both the collar and the hem that just covered her ankles. The shape of the dress was like a long tube with no curves or shapes associated with a woman. It clung to her fragile-looking body like cigarette paper adheres to tobacco. The shade of red matched her lipstick and nails. No, it was not her height. However, it would have been a challenge for them to communicate with her. It was the fact that she was horrid and noticeably had no idea that she was. When she spoke, her mouth revealed many missing gaps, and Abella had managed to see two yellow-stained teeth on the bottom row and three on the top row.

Her voice would have reduced dogs to tears, and cats would have scurried away faster than any Cheetah in Africa.

It also did not help her cause; she was never seen without a long cigarette hanging precariously out of her mouth.

Her hair was like someone had taken a lawnmower to her head and had raced around in different directions, leaving every strand heading anywhere it could.

How and why any city should wish to have a statue sculptured of such a hidden eyesore was beyond anyone's imagination, and it amazed both the Gnomes simultaneously!

Derekamus was so relieved that fate brought Abella to him first, not Jovita. The very thought of what could have been under different circumstances in life sent a massive shudder through his heavy body, and even his spindly legs wobbled.

He had noticed early that Jovita's head turned in every direction of the room, but her eyes stayed permanently on one person. Tonight, Sebastian Belalcázar was her interest.

Another set of eyes had noticed, too, and Simon Bolivar found the situation so highly amusing. He had been ribbing Belalcázar for nearly an hour. The Conquistador had taken it all in his stride.

Secretly, he knew he had been in worse situations than spending a night with a nomadic, green-eyed brunette who would only be seen in elegant dresses, thus adding to her overall feminine seduction allure.

He agreed with the locals who considered her an "Eternity Queen." A character who transcended all limits of understanding. Also, there was the small fact that she was much younger and closer in location to him in the city.

"Come. Let it be known, General Bolivar; is it not true that you were once a love interest for our fair maiden Jovita?" teased Belalcázar, prodding his friend with his outstretched finger.

"Haha, you must be joking. My old horse Palomo would have stood a better chance," laughed Bolivar, pushing his equally great friend's finger in the opposite direction, forcing Belalcázar to face now the very tall Jovita, whose eyes had still not left these two statues.

At this, both generals, in their splendid attire, as usual, fell apart, roaring at their jokes. Jovita ignored them and moved in the crowds, her cigarette ash landing on all that came into contact with her.

"And remember, Señor Bolivar," added Jovita, waving her arm around her in imitation of Belalcázar. You are only a short little man. It would take three of you to equal me." "Yes, but only one horse to surpass you!" quipped Bolivar. At that point, the horses, as if in unison, shouted to the old general: Señor Bolivar, please tell us about your famous horse, Paloma. What was she like?"

Bolivar stopped in his tracks and disappeared into his memory bank before answering. When he did, you could not help but see his admiration and love of remembrance for an extraordinary horse.

"Ladies and gentlemen, hold on to your saddles and prepare to be whisked away on an exhilarating ride through history as I introduce you to the renowned, legendary – Palomo!"

"Picture this: a majestic creature with a coat almost the colour of pure snow. Palomo stands tall and proud, his muscular frame exuding strength and grace with every step. With his flowing mane dancing in the wind and his expressive, deep, intelligent eyes, Palomo commands attention wherever it gallops."

Bolivar now spoke as if he was picturing himself at the Battle of Carabobo in 1821. The decisive engagement during the Venezuelan War of Independence led to the establishment of the Republic of Gran Colombia.

"We were outnumbered, so I devised a strategy that exploited the difficult terrain, which the Spanish cavalry could be rendered ineffective. We struck and caught them off guard by positioning our troops on a narrow plain surrounded by steep hills and dense forests. We went for a surprise attack on their flanks and rear."

"I must admit the battle did rage on for several hours, but eventually, the enemy forces collapsed too much, to my relief."

A polite cough from Belalcázar brought Bolivar back to the audience in front of him. It had been a long time since he had spoken of that day.

"My remarkable stallion witnessed history unfold beneath its hooves, carrying me, the great Liberator, through the tumultuous struggles and heroic triumphs of the Latin American revolution. Together, we charged fearlessly into battle, our unbreakable bond serving as the heartbeat of the revolution."

"As my loyal companion, Palomo proved more than just a mere mode of transportation. No, my friends – this horse was my partner in crime, an accomplice in the quest for freedom. With a spirit as indomitable as its rider's, Palomo fearlessly charged head first into the chaotic fray, trampling the enemies of liberty beneath its iron-clad hooves."

"But let's not forget, my dear audience, Palomo's undeniable flair for style. Even on the most treacherous of battlefields remained, its mane perfectly coiffed, always its glossy coat unstained. Its tail swayed with such elegance and poise that even the enemy soldiers couldn't help but be mesmerized by its beauty. Palomo was a symbol of strength and determination and an embodiment of sheer equine elegance."

Bolivar was still showing no signs of stopping; he was now reminiscing about the Battle of Boyacá in 1819. His audience was with him every hoof of the way. Never before had they ever heard a general speak of the Battles in such openness.

"Please tell us of your experience at the Battle of Boyacá. Why is it so important to the humans in this city?" asked Efrain, sitting cross-legged on the marble floor, enjoying such a fantastic history being openly spoken about by someone actually there.

"Ok, my dear friends, please allow me to share my account of the legendary Battle of Boyacá, a crucial turning point in our struggle for independence from Spanish colonial rule. This battle, fought on August 7, 1819, in the Boyacá region of present-day Colombia, stands as one of the most significant milestones in our journey towards freedom."

"At that time, our beloved continent was still under the oppressive grip of the Spanish Empire. However, the Battle of Boyacá proved a remarkable triumph for our forces, led by my brave compatriots and me. It was a decisive victory that marked the beginning of the end of Spanish dominion over New Granada, which included present-day Colombia, Venezuela, Ecuador, and Panama."

"During this battle, our outnumbered and poorly equipped revolutionary army courageously faced the royalist troops, who had occupied these lands for centuries. Despite the odds stacked against us, our troops executed a masterful military strategy, outmanoeuvring and overpowering the enemy forces. The battlefield was a scene of intense bravery, with our soldiers displaying unwavering determination, resilience, and unity in the face of adversity."

"The victory at Boyacá was not merely a military triumph; it symbolized the birth of a new nation, a beacon of hope for all oppressed peoples of the Americas. The battle proved possible to defy the seemingly unbeatable Spanish Empire and gain independence. "It ignited the flames of resistance against colonialism, and its repercussions resonated throughout the continent, inspiring countless other liberation movements."

"To this day, Colombians celebrate the Battle of Boyacá as a national holiday every August 7. It reminds every one of the sacrifices made by their forefathers and the unwavering spirit that defined their struggle for independence. It represents the culmination of years of relentless battles, hardships, and sacrifices endured by people in pursuit of freedom and self-determination."

"The significance of this battle goes beyond its military implications. It symbolizes everyone's collective aspirations for a better future, free from oppression and exploitation. It serves as a reminder of the commitment to uphold and respect the values of liberty, equality, and justice that all great nations were founded upon."

"Moreover, the Battle of Boyacá serves as an emblem of unity. It unites all as a nation and strengthens the resolve to overcome the challenges that we face today. It is a testament to the indomitable spirit of the Colombian people, who refuse to surrender their dreams and aspirations."

In celebrating the Battle of Boyacá, everyone, including me, honour the memory of those who fought valiantly for their freedom and the countless sacrifices they made. It serves as a reminder of everyone's duty to cherish independence and protect the hard-won we enjoy today. It reminds us that the struggles of the past shape our present and guide us towards a brighter future.

May the spirit of the Battle of Boyacá continue to inspire us to strive for a Colombia that is just, inclusive, and prosperous for all.

**¡Viva Colombia y su gloriosa independencia!**

As if he was hypnotized, the great Liberator's focus suddenly returned to the original subject of his wonderful horse – Palomo.

"Oh, what tales could Palomo tell if he possessed the gift of speech! From epic gallops across vast landscapes to facing thundering cannons and charging fearlessly into the unknown, every adventure with me was etched into the fibres of this extraordinary steed's being."

"So, my dear friends, next time you find yourself gazing at the stars, contemplating the lofty dreams of revolutionaries, remember my incomparable Palomo – the horse whose hooves echoed through history, with yours truly – Simon Bolivar and the fight for freedom to unimaginable heights."

\*\*\*\*\*

The gravel hit the table, and slowly, all the statues and figurines moved to the table and chairs. The cats, horses, and turtles draped themselves on the marble floor, allowing them to observe the meeting agenda.

Jorge Isaacs stood and paused, waiting for total silence in the room. When it came, he began. "Thank you, general. Your surrender and memory serve you well." There is a short pause: "Good evening to you all. We, the committee, wish to give you a special welcome, and we hope in the future you will find it in your hearts to consider this meeting of the minds a most important event for you all."

"As you all know, the city is in dangerous times; the rainy season is upon them, and the clouds are full of anger and rain. Already, we are receiving reports from all over the city of the rising waters and the possible risk of flooding. The last thing humans are going to think about is our well-being. They may have to abandon the city limits.

"A certain number of you will be in a high-risk situation and may need rescuing."

At this last piece of information, the cats stopped purring, and the children stopped playing.

*****

Only Jovita looked bored. There was never going to be a chance of her drowning her. She was the size of a Lighthouse, Derekamus noted quietly to himself. He had not stopped taking in all the beautiful sights.

It would take him years to learn all their histories. A nudge from Abella interrupted his thoughts of him. Derekamus looked to the front, a little lost, as he had not heard Jorge's last words from him.

"I am so sorry; what did you say?" asked the Gnome sheepishly.

"I was saying that both you and Abella need to be extra careful," Jorge repeated, showing concern for these new additions to the figurine community.

"He means you and your Abella are in the same danger as the cats and children, and of course, our turtle friends, beings, you are both dwarfs." Offered Bolivar.

"No, you old fool, they are not dwarfs; they are Gnomes," Belalcázar quickly corrected as he spotted Derekamus's face harden and strove to change the course of possible confrontation.

"Yes, it is true. Dwarfs and gnomes do share some similarities, such as both are generally thought of as mythical creatures often found in folklore and literature. We can clearly see here we have the genuine articles."

But there are distinct differences between both. Let me explain more." Belalcázar paused and took a deep breath while scanning Derekamus, who also appeared interested. This acted as a cue for the Conquistador to continue, and he did.

"Dwarfs are typically depicted as short and stout humanoid beings, usually no more than a few feet tall. They are known for their stocky build, strong physique, and long, thick facial hair. Conversely, gnomes are also small in stature but are generally depicted as slimmer and less stocky than dwarfs. They are often portrayed with pointed hats, long beards, and wrinkled faces."

Everyone turned and inspected Derekamus more intensely. Derekamus became disturbed and started to shift his stance to a fighting stance.

Belalcázar powered on as if not noticing: "Dwarfs are often associated with mining, craftsmanship, and metalworking. They are often depicted as skilled artisans, creating beautiful art, weapons, and armour. Whereas, Gnomes, on the other hand, are often associated with gardening, nature, and the earth. They are commonly believed to be guardians of gardens, forests, and other natural places."

Derekamus's stance altered softly. Belalcázar appeared to be in calmer waters. He continued unabated: "Dwarfs are often characterized as serious, hardworking, and stubborn. They are known for their love of wealth and treasure and their strong sense of honour and loyalty. Whereas Gnomes, in contrast, are generally portrayed as mischievous, playful, and curious. They are believed to enjoy playing pranks on humans but are generally benign and helpful spirits."

The vast room went quiet. Everyone and everything stayed quiet.

*****

"Sir, please accept my apologies. Good Sir and Madam, please only ask if either of you need my services." Bolivar bowed to both the gnomes at the same time.

"I am sure both my husband and I would like to make the same offer to you all," Abella stated, now standing next to her husband, who was known in the past to have a wicked temper when he believed he had been insulted. Slowly, Derekamus's red cheeks began returning to their standard cream shade.

Maria rose and gently addressed the crowd. "Be careful, all of you. I cannot remember such a situation in the past hundred and odd years. So, let's keep in touch. We should see the need to save any human life; we do so without a second thought. Remember, it was their wishes that we be accepted in their community, and we owe it to all a big debt of gratitude."

This made everyone stop and think inwardly. Yes, human hands had made them all.

*****

Talking about hands, Jovita had nestled up and ensured she was sat next to her intended target and was very close. Under the table, her hand wandered over, squeezing Belalcázar's left knee.

The startled Conquistador shot up in shock, knocking his chair that fell backwards and landed on one of the turtles, who screeched and tried to run fast.

Everyone turned to the centre of the disturbance and started laughing at Belalcázar's embarrassment. Of course, his best friend laughed the loudest and the longest. Jovita just looked around, pushing out her little chest, and blew a perfect smoke ring into the air as if she had no idea what had just happened.

The Emergency meeting of the minds was scheduled, and the subsequent emergency meeting and venue were penciled in for the following evening at the Tree of Life. Everyone present agreed this would be the perfect location to organise and manage the upcoming help to as many of the city's vulnerable inhabitants as possible. Everyone departed, promising to stay in touch and ready for their assigned call to action.

*****

# 39: I am Ximena Londono. Here is my life before and after the accident

My name is Ximena Londono. I used to be the most envied-after young and beautiful woman high up on the mountain ridge overlooking the city. I had all the wealth that my father's money could buy. All the city's designers wanted me to be their unique model.

I was the one that every host would wish to add to their guest list.

Every salsa club and disco ensured the doorkeepers always made a retreat to ensure I swept past without a second thought to any of them or those still waiting to enter.

Salesmen and saleswomen were putties in my delicate and ultra-manicured hands.

Whatever I wished would always be made available to me.

Every server in the city's most desirable restaurants ensured I was treated as my parents had come to expect, with my choice of the most prestigious restaurant tables made available at a moment's notice.

Also, I wanted the best views for all the other diners to see and know that I was above them all.

Often, you would see me eating oysters followed by octopus, accompanied by the finest of red wines from the vintage-produced 2013 Argentina grape. Each has excellent concentration, complexity, and balance. My favourite is the Malbec, with its deep colours, intense aromas, rich flavours, and refined structure. Well, I do listen to my father, and he should know. He owns three vineyards, two here in South America and one in Spain, as part of his growing portfolio.

*****

My choice of transport was my equally beautiful quad bike, with its striking yellow bodywork. I knew deep down men's eyes went to him first, and then I second. I did not mind on these occasions because the final resting place for most men was my desirable frame, especially my perfect buttocks.

Then, the mountain earthquake happened, and all that I took for granted disappeared.

Yes, my parents' wealth remained, and my own wealth was still beyond my wildest dreams. Yes, I could still attend clothing events, but over the next few months, I no longer wanted to be a model. I preferred to be only a witness to each event.

With a significant part of my tongue gone, so was my confidence. I spoke little, and when I attended a forced engagement that my parents continuously arranged, my silence was at the front.

When alone in my bed, I would find myself continually crying, the awful memories of being so helpless on my bike as it soared over the rapidly approaching burgundy truck. Seeing the driver so clearly, looking out of his cabin in stark horror at me. Never before had I experienced such a reaction from another human being. Then I saw from the corner of my eye a decrepit street man with a rock in one hand and reaching out with the other to a young nun and instantly behind her this massive hole in the ground that I was heading directly towards with no way of escaping Item. Then my world goes black.

Later, I discovered from my parents first and then from the rest of the world secondly that I had been knocked out by, of all things, a kite! How on earth did a kite manage to be in such a position to have taken half my tongue from me? No one could explain how or why.

The truck driver, Ignacio, tried to explain, but no one really believed him. They put it down to their distorted imagination of him and their understandable fear of him during the height of the earthquake.

The media consensus leaned to the premise that it was more than likely that debris from a falling tree caused my facial injuries. This so angry me as I, deep down, truly believe I was hit in the face by a damn kite!

*****

I never thought about replacing the quad bike. I learned later it had been buried in the enormous crater left by the churned-up road surface, which I still dream of nightly.

Apparently, there had been a massive fire at the older people's home nearby, and the officials had deemed it appropriate to take the debris from the house and use it to fill in the crater and cover the broken forever quad bike.

I have travelled up and down since on the very part of that road, and every time, a shudder goes down my spine at the mere memory of how I survived such an ordeal.

Much later, when all the world press had moved away to other more pressing world events and the city had returned to being a sleepy city again, I learned that the nun's name was Rosa. I met her and found her to be a soothing influence on me. Her desire to be a singing nun amazed me; I never knew such a practice existed, but as soon as she told me, it seemed the most natural thing in the world.

Ignacio and his entire family were also a joy to meet. He was such a humble man who, in many ways, was similar to my father in his soft use of his voice. Or maybe they were both of the same age, and to all of us young people, every older person appears the same until we eventually age.

I did ask about the street man, but everyone said I must be imagining him.

The more I asked, the more they denied that he existed.

I began to doubt, but in my dreams, he was always there each night.

Not in a position of danger or fear. But something kept telling me he had been a friend in my moment of need.

Now, I spend my days walking around the city by myself. I wear as little makeup as possible. Understand me; I still love my hair but do not consider it central anymore. I need direction at the moment. I am searching for guidance. I walk into churches, sit alone, and look up at the image of Jesus on the cross. I talk and pray to him, but I have not yet felt any response.

I leave the churches in much the same frame of loneliness and despair as I did when entering each of them.

I used to go to the big shopping malls that excited me. Now, I just walk past with a touch of interest, and I rarely go in to buy.

My parents eventually bowed to my wish for a small apartment in the city.

After much deliberation, it was agreed that I should be in a gated environment in the old part of the town where I could be safe and allowed to recover at my own pace.

I go to my regular meetings with the doctors, and with no animosity to any of the medical professionals, I feel they are not what I now need. To be honest, I think I may be suffering from traumatic distress disorder, similar to what soldiers have when they return from various war zones around the world.

Suddenly, my life has no sense of meaning. I cry a lot. I find myself sitting in front of a television for hours and hours but have no recollection of what I saw. After such an episode, I walked over to my veranda and leaned over the railing at the streets below. I felt rain starting to land on me and looked up at the dark clouds, which looked formidable. It may be my imagination. I see danger when there is none.

*****

Hi, it is me again. My mental anguish has subsided. Please fast forward in your mind to a time that has come three years later. It has taken me that long to find the awful memories and store them away in a place that allows me peace.

I have my mother's permission to ask all the female readers out there a question I suspect we all consistently ask ourselves.

Will my buttocks eventually become my nightmare?

As you know, since the accident on the mountain ridge, I have spent long hours in various hospitals and clinics, trying to restore my health to the moment before the collision with that kite. Finally, I was able to move on to other areas of my health and well-being.

I did some research on my never-disappearing question. I was amazed at the information out there on the internet. It seems there are billions of us every day examining our buttocks in the mirror and dreading what we might find.

It led me to my second question. Is having big buttocks sinister for my health?

We ladies from South America like to look good. If we are not so lucky to have our curves naturally, we are happy to visit the doctor for some improvements.

Initially, I was introduced to this way of thinking with my parents. They are wealthy, and I, the only child, now twenty-one, who needed for nothing. So, it is acceptable for you to imagine me as one of those superbrats whose sole aim in life was to spend my allowance and future inheritance on mundane and expensively priced items.

I have to admit when I hit my teens, I was that typical" Airhead" type of person. I learned early from my mother, who, way back in the eighties, was one of the first in our mountain community to go "under the knife."

From the moment she met my father, it was love at first sight, and she was determined to capture him.

He was a tall, handsome, up-and-coming coffee exporter who looked good on an overloaded mule's back.

Likewise, he, too, was smitten from the outset. Never one for showing any interest in the females on the ridge. As there weren't that many at the time. With my mother. That has changed. They were married within a year.

Whenever my mother is reminiscing, she proudly tells me of all the work and pain she went through with each new modification she felt would please her man. Never did he complain. Like most of the men on the mountain ridge in the eighties, the "perceived necessary improvements" were always a pleasure to be held.

My father kept putting his hands in his pockets, producing the cash needed to support his wife, and the doctors smiled.

It was assumed I would follow in my mother's footsteps, and I did from the age of sixteen. I focused on what I wanted to alter. My butt was the prominent place. It was flat, I wanted round.

Little did I realise that in a few short years, I would be one of the central characters in a life-changing event on a mountain ridge. The accident's consequences would affect my confidence, my looks, and my whole personality. Have I changed, and did it redefine me?

Those of you with exuberant common sense may say, "That's good," and maybe you are right. But I am thinking more about how afraid and insecure I have become. I fret now regarding everything and anything. My buttocks, which I was once so proud of, I am not so sure of anymore.

*****

My mother has begun visiting her doctors more than usual. It appears from the odd snippets I gather from the dining table that her health was deteriorating due to a side effect of liquid silicone, which had been injected into her buttocks.

Over time, the silicone moved into her spinal area and placed pressure on her lower back. I could see she was suffering when she tried to walk. I remember us both having the same procedure to celebrate me reaching seventeen and enjoying the world of "Girl Power" with the same doctor.

A year later, the government banned the practice of injecting liquid silicone, but it was too late for us. My mother was ill, and the doctor had disappeared from her practice.

We should have done our research, but we did nothing. We were on a mother/daughter adventure.

Money was the least of our concerns.

She said that she loves a bargain, and this injection versus implant saved us a lot of money, which we duly spent on new outfits to celebrate. So, where did complications and ill effects rate in our thinking?

We were crazy to believe the ageing doctor with the silver tongue that there would be no side effects. That there would be no risk to us. Both of us were in and out within 20 minutes of each other and administering each injection.

Sadly, we know, much to our dismay, that the injections have no barriers to worry about. They can and will migrate into other areas of our bodies, as in my mother's case. Side effects she has reported include suffering from chronic fatigue and some allergic reactions.

Our carefully chosen replacement Specialist and now family friend, Dr Hector Jesus Ruiz Garcia MD, told us on our last visit that we were both lucky that we did not die from those injections and that we would need operations to remove any tissue affected by the doses.

We decided together that Mother would be the first to go under anaesthesia. Because I was not yet showing any concerning symptoms, I could wait three months and then be operated on.

Because of the government ban, insurance companies do not pay for any curative treatment. Apparently, the side effects of these injections are not illnesses. It took Mother nearly four weeks to recover, and now she has some scarring that she will not let anyone, including my father and me, witness.

We are both aware that the same silicone may still affect us both in the future.

So, if you are in this predicament, seek help from your doctor immediately. Don't procrastinate. Don't be embarrassed. One thing I have learned from my mother is not to become all coy; be open with your doctor. He or she may be the one to save your life.

So, back to my original question: is it wrong for my health to have a nice round set of buttocks?

If I opt for the cheaper illegal use of liquid silicone injections, the answer is Yes. If I am willing and can afford to pay for the safer option of silicone implants with regular check-ups, I should be fine.

Oh yes, another tip: if a guy tells you to make your buttocks bigger, ask him to "sling his hook." If you decide to do it, then do so for yourself. It's your body, and you must look in the mirror daily and be content.

*****

Is it true our buttocks will change every ten years?

Now you know a little of my history, let me share with you some more of the information I discovered. Our faces are like our butts. What I mean by that is our faces go through many changes and shifts throughout our lives.

It turns out that when we are thirteen, our butts are at their smallest because we produce little fat. Then you come along with puberty and estrogen levels. Do you remember seeing and feeling how firm your butt was when you were in your teens?

I remember seeing some of the girls in school with pimples all over their butts. I have no idea what was going on there. Mine, which I did check many times, was as smooth as a baby's butt.

Now fast forward to your twenties; your butt has taken on a rounder shape all by itself. The chances are you will have a higher level of fat in each cheek.

Unless you have had children, your butt will remain firm and, dare I say it, perky.

I am on the understanding from my mother and her sisters that when you have children, there will be a few noticeable changes to the butt.

When you hit your thirties, and from everyone I talk to, it's a slippery downhill slope for our butts. This is the decade where muscle mass and tone begin to hang down.

Be like me: start a regimen of squats, lunges, power walks and stretches. All are FREE to do. Now it is time to start protecting the butt. Focus on toning as much as you can.

Our skin cell turnover and production of collagen start slowing down, too. Signs of deterioration in our bouncy and firm butt begin to show.

*****

Please allow me to take over from my daughter. My name is Marlena Lopez Montenegro, married to Don Alejandro Londono y Nieto. I am five years from reaching my sixties, yet I am already fretting about what's to come. Ladies who are slightly older than me will have noticed an increase in sagging and more fat on the hips. That was probably not there ten years ago.

I do apologise for "butting" in. Still, my daughter's head has turned to a report on the local hospital television regarding some young boy from Choco who has become a national hero after a smelly cannonball hit him on the head!

*****

Please do not worry if we all keep focusing on butt-centered workouts and eating the right food. We should get through this decadence with all our glutes in shape.

The most significant danger in your forties will be the urge to sit down every night and watch yourself in the latest Netflix or Amazon Prime series.

This next bit of advice comes from my Grandmother. She comes from a generation who never heard of a scalpel touching our butts or boobs. She, through fits of laughter, tells us "young ones" that your fifties are the time: You lose your fat, and your round butt goes flat.

*****

Nobody mentioned to her that fat distribution is altered. Your stomach and hips attract the fat, and your butt ignores it. Diet and squeezing those butt cheeks were never mentioned. Apparently, it's not Ladylike.

Now, Granny is more informed. She goes to her twice-weekly fitness class. Like all decent Grannies, she has lost that fear of talking about anything.

Buttocks are back on the agenda.

She can be regularly seen dictating to all who will listen to her.

"Keep those glutes strong, and your hips and butt will look good in a while."

*****

Now, a question from my Grandmother, who, as usual, already knew the answer. So, I decided to share it with you all. What is a Gluteal Amnesia or Dead Butt Syndrome?

Are you a female and a truck driver, driving instructor, writer, scientist, family doctor, or forklift driver? Or someone who sits down for 8 to 9 hours a day or more routinely doing your work?

If you answered yes to both questions, then the chances are you are suffering from a condition known as Gluteal Amnesia. It's prevalent in nearly all of us who lead sedentary lives through our careers, jobs, and lifestyles. It occurs when our glutes forget to do their job.

With all of us sitting at every chance that presented itself, it does not take long for the side effects of parking the butt to become the primary culprit.

We all have what is known as Hip Flexors. If they get shorter and tighter through us continually sitting, that will lead to our butt muscles not working as they should. It transpires these gluteal muscles are essential. They enable us to carry out what we take for granted. For example, walking, running, picking up and carrying.

If left unchecked, you could suffer pain in your hips, knees, and lower back and even attract strokes due to the overcompensation the other muscles have to achieve to allow you to function.

Check out Grandmother's three simple ways to test your Gluteal Amnesia.

Lie face up on a level surface such as your bedroom or office floor. Position your hands below your butt and attempt to squeeze each butt cheek, first with the left and then the right or vice versa. It would be best if you were happy when you feel those glutes engage.

Focus on achieving some Step-up or deadlift exercises. If you notice cramps creeping into your hamstrings, it's a good sign that your glutes are not performing as well as they should.

Stand straight in a neutral position and picture yourself wearing a belt. If the result shows your beltline has dropped towards the front, It is a sure sign your glutes are not engaging proficiently. If the belt is parallel to the floor, your glutes work effectively.

Here is some more Grandmother Great news: Gluteal Amnesia does not have to be permanent. It is reversible. Just exercise your butt off. In the office, on the bus, in the garden. Literary, anywhere. Even in secret if you so wish.

Finally, Some signs to let you know if your butt is too big.

• Your butt connects with tables and other pieces of daily furniture.

• Nothing is safe when your butt appears. It is the master of knocking things down.

- You have not found a pair of jeans or leggings to fit your butt, and if you do, you will wear them out in a month.
- Sitting in small chairs has ceased to be an option.
- Sometimes, you are the last to know you are sitting on something that everyone else is looking for.
- Someone is in your way. No problem for the most prominent butt owner.
- Wearing short dresses becomes almost pornographic.
- Everyone has a comment to make on your beautiful booty.

*****

**"Mum, guess what? I have just met my future husband………"**

## 40: I am the General of the Honking Goose Air Regiment from Alaska

How did my vast air force of Migrating Geese and I arrive in this dusty and industrial city area? Deep down, I wished we had not reached here, but our navigator perished somewhere over the Andes Mountains.

I estimated this happened near the capital of Bogotá. Not wanting to land in such a large city, I continued until my squadrons of flying aviators started to show signs of fatigue.

Remember, 65% of all our bird species migrate. Why do we do it?

Here is why I led my squadrons of geese from Alaska to the Pampas in Argentina.

"The first thing I must consider is what the feeding opportunities are. In Alaska, we geese take advantage of the abundant food resources available during summer when plants and insects are plentiful. However, as winter approaches, food becomes scarce Due to the freezing temperatures and reduced vegetation. By flying to the Pampas in Argentina, we geese find a more favourable environment with ample food resources, including grains, grasses, and aquatic plants."

"Next comes the prevalent climate and habitat conditions: We geese are highly adapted to specific climate and habitat conditions. The Pampas in Argentina offer milder winter temperatures than Alaska, with more open water bodies remaining unfrozen, allowing us geese to access food and avoid the harsh conditions of the north."

"An essential subject that also needs deep thought is, of course, Reproduction: The Pampas also provide suitable breeding grounds for all of us geese during the spring and summer months. These areas offer nesting sites with abundant vegetation, proximity to water bodies, and a reduced predation risk compared to our northern habitats. By migrating to the Pampas, we geese ensure the survival and growth of our species by taking advantage of the better reproductive conditions available."

"Next on my agenda has to be our energy conservation: Migration helps us geese conserve energy. In Alaska, we geese spend significant energy raising our young and foraging for food. By migrating to the Pampas, we can replenish our energy reserve and take advantage of the relatively abundant food in Argentina without the demanding task of raising our young."

"Finally, we must consider avoiding extreme weather conditions: Alaska experiences extreme weather conditions during the winter, including freezing temperatures, heavy snowfall, and limited food availability. By flying to the Pampas, my squadrons of geese and I can avoid these adverse conditions, ensuring our survival and increasing our chances of successfully reproducing in the future."

"It's important to note that all of our migratory patterns have been shaped by evolutionary processes, where we have adapted to the fluctuating environmental conditions between Alaska and the Pampas in Argentina."

I had planned to take my heroic squadron of geese from Alaska's winter to the tempting warmth of the Argentinean Pampas, a journey of approximately 16,000 kilometres.

During the migration flight, we would need to fly in formation between 30 and 88 kilometres per hour, which would require us to fly a distance of anywhere from 250 to 500 kilometres daily.

Over the sea, we flew hundreds of meters above the thermal currents formed over the warm ground in our migratory flight. As these sea currents form only during the daylight, we knew from experience that we would be forced to migrate only during this period.

On this occasion, to save time, we decided to take the risk and relocate both during the day and night to migrate.

So, you may ask the question: How do migrating birds compensate for sleep loss? We adopted the technique that ducks use by taking short naps while combining the resting of the whole brain with unilateral eye closure. We would rest one eye and one-half of our minds while their other eye and brain hemisphere remained open and active, keeping us semi-alert to danger.

By doing this, we were able to take hundreds of naps during the day, each of just a few seconds, to compensate for the night sleep loss.

We mainly traveled during the night, often for long hours at a time, leaving little time for sleep. Drowsiness is characterised by a partial shutting of both of our eyes that still allows for some visual processing. By alternating between naps and drowsiness, we were able to reap some of the benefits of sleep while only marginally increasing our risks of being caught by preying birds.

Sleepiness and partial sleep are less effective than regular rest, but they were safe for us.

We are in what looks like an unfortunate part of the city. The roads are dirt roads with no tarmac and are covered in many uneven and fast-becoming dark surfaces.

The first thing to do was to call for a roll call to see how many had survived. I cackled and honked as loud as my voice would allow, and soon, the gaggle of birds was in a somewhat orderly line.

We had started with over 250 birds, but now, sadly, there were less than 180 survivors, and we still had a further 5,000 kilometres to go. I let out a deafening whistle, and suddenly, the gaggle became one and stared at their leader. "Right, Attention!"

Hearing 180 sets of webbed feet crashing to the ground in unison always brings a lump in my throat and a teardrop in my eye. Or were they the raindrops I could now feel? I coughed and straightened my neck the best that I could. I flipped open my wings to salute my aviators, with raindrops scattering in every direction imaginable. "Stand at ease!"

Again, the sound of crashing feet in unison filled the air with precision. That perfect sound, unaffected by the splashing sound, can only be appreciated by an Air Force General.

I took a moment to select the right words for the occasion: "We have completed three-quarters of our migration journey, and for the next few days, we will rest. Chief Warrant Officer Goose, please arrange for patrols of fours and fives to scout the areas for grain and seeds so that we can replenish our bodies."

"Yes, Sir! And what shall we do about the human population and those filthy dogs?" added the Chief Warrant Officer with a distasteful sound to his voice to emphasize his dislike of humans and dogs.

"Yes, you are right, CWO. We need to rid the area of these ugly specimens, send out patrols immediately and clear the immediate areas around our camp. Use reasonable force on this occasion, as I have read that guns and other weapons are freely found among these humans. We do not want to cause a riot while we rest."

"Yes, Sir," honked the Chief Warrant Officer as he rotated around, flapping his large soaking wet wings and eyeballing his underlings. "Right, you horrible lot! All Corporals are to form groups and report to me for deployment in 15 minutes. Now, Officer on parade!" followed by a short pause "Salute!"

Instantly, all 180 pairs of wings began to flap loudly in the air, and crackles of thunder could now be heard miles away. "Dismissed!"

*****

The rest of the day was fun for the humans in their cars and trucks and frightening for those on foot. The geese attacked with much flapping, whistling, and nudging of their bills. The humans fled in all directions; luckily, none returned with guns. The dogs ran even faster once they realized that barking and snarling were not going to stop the Aviators from obeying their General's orders.

Once the area was purged of all humans and dogs, the food patrol began with their task of finding food. Later that evening, the rain increased, and the birds were able to use their oily wings to wash each of them. The only trouble that developed was the rain on this occasion, making the prospect of food abysmal.

The subdued Chief Warrant Officer visited the General's corner of the rubbish and cement yard. His head was lower than usual when he told the General: "Sir, the patrols have all returned with mixed results. The area around the camp is free of humans, but we expect them to return in the early morning hours. Also, the other patrols are unable to find any food for the aviators, and I am sorry to say this has caused unrest in the camp."

"How bad are things?" I ask dejectedly, already knowing the response.

"Evil Sir, I believe most will fly again during the night. They do not like this place and want to head to Argentina while they have the strength to get there."

"OK, Chief Warrant Officer, I will rest now. Let's talk again in the morning."

*****

When morning came, the parade square was empty apart from the mud. Only the Chief Warrant Officer and two aviators lined up before their General.

"Sir, we are reporting to you for any duties you deem we should undertake. As for the remainder of the squadron, they have moved to a leafier park in a Barrio known as La Flora. There is a huge park there, and I have been reliably informed it has been cleared of all humans. They apparently ran away as fast as their two legs could carry them. As you know, this is no defense to our arsenal of weapons."

The Chief Warrant Officer added, "The main body is awaiting your orders, sir."

I looked at who had decided to greet me this morning and secretly agreed with the bulk of my squadron's decision. The Chief Warrant Officer and the two mean-looking aviators in front of me would be enough for what I wanted next to happen.

I greeted them and ordered them to follow me, saying, "All humans and their miserable-looking dogs in the immediate facility are in for a tough time this day. One they would surely never forget in a hurry!"

Then, to make matters worse, it started to rain heavily again, and in the distance, more ominous thunder could be heard approaching.

I, the General, was definitely in a foul mood indeed.

I led the first charge into an approaching 4-wheel-drive vehicle. I showed my anger by head-butting and hollering at the same time, followed by the expansion of my wings. With his side window opened, the started driver tried to swerve to his right to avoid the oncoming attack.

At the same time, my trusty Chief Warrant Officer and my little army of two drove straight at a line of passengers disembarking from a bus. Screams and shouts of pain and discomfort followed the sounds of hardened beaks pecking at exposed legs. Soon, the bus was moving away with the fleeing passengers racing to re-board the fleeing bus.

The local stray dogs stood rigid in awe and growing fear. These birds mean business, and almost at once, all the strays moved in the same direction, creating as much distance as possible between me and my howling aviators. I started feeling better already, but the mud was becoming a problem.

Then, I saw a solitary, pathetic-looking yellow-headed Caracara standing at attention in the middle of the muddy trail. His left wing was ridged in its purpose of saluting me!

"Well, blow me over and tickle my funny bone if it isn't a Yellow-headed Caracara with a wish to migrate!"

*****

"Good day, Sir! Do you know where you have flown in from and where you plan to fly next?" Asked the Yellow-headed Caracara standing in what he hoped was the correct position for showcasing his respect.

"I am an Air Force General in charge of 250 geese based in Alaska. Each year, I am duty-bound to deliver my squadron of geese to the Pampas in Argentina. "So why did you and your squadron land here instead of continuing your migration to the Pampas in Argentina?"

General Goose decided to add more to this inquisitive Yellow-headed caracara? "We were en route to the beautiful Pampas in Argentina when we encountered some mighty bad weather. Dark clouds and fierce winds prevented us from advancing further, forcing us to make an emergency landing here in………. Where exactly are we?"

Yellow-headed caracara took only a moment to reply: "Oh my feathers! That must have been quite a rough journey. But, General Goose, you have landed in an industrial section of this city called Yumbo. It isn't a nice place. While flying here to meet you, I passed over the bulk of your squadron in the Parque La Flora. There are many trees there to protect them."

General Goose's eyes took in the immediate surrounding terrain: "Oh, Yellow-headed Caracara, you have quite the keen observation. Yumbo is not ideal for a flock of geese like ours. However, when we faced the challenging weather conditions, we had to make a quick decision to land somewhere safe."

Nodding what he believed was the right way to convey his approval and agreement, the Yellow-headed Caracara continued: "I see, General Goose. So, what's next for your squadron? Are you planning to stay in Yumbo indefinitely?"

General Goose gave the question a moment's thought: "Fear not, Yellow-headed Caracara! Although we've been temporarily grounded in this less-than-ideal place, we still have our hearts set on reaching the Pampas in Argentina. We are currently assessing the weather and waiting for the conditions to improve before we can resume our migratory journey."

Yellow-headed caracara was pleased: "That's great to hear, General Goose! I'm sure you and your squadron will get back on track soon. In the meantime, can the local bird population do anything to assist you?"

General Goose smiled his appreciation for this unexpected friendship from a bird who never migrates: "Your kind offer warms my feathered heart, Yellow-headed Caracara. As we wait for better weather, any information or updates on the conditions around Yumbo would be greatly appreciated. Additionally, sharing any tips or insights on the best routes from Yumbo to the Pampas would be most helpful."

Yellow-headed caracara repeatedly stamped his feet to attention: "Consider it done, General Goose! I'll keep a close eye on the weather and provide you with any updates I come across. I'll also consult our avian community's older and wiser members to gather knowledge about the routes from Yumbo to the Pampas. We shall make sure your squadron resumes its journey smoothly!"

General Goose: "Thank you, Yellow-headed Caracara! Your assistance means a lot to us. We will overcome this temporary setback with teamwork and determination and continue our migration to the breathtaking Pampas. We geese are known for our resilience, and 'I'm confident we'll soon be soaring the skies once again.'

"In the meantime, if you have time, that is General Goose.......could you please explain what Alaska and the Pampas in Argentina are?"

General Goose did have much to do, but on this rare occasion, he decided to stop and answer: "Of course, my feathered friend! Let me take you on an adventurous journey to the frozen wilderness of Alaska and the sun-kissed plains of the Pampas in Argentina, painting a picture that will entertain and inform those unfamiliar with these fascinating places.

Alaska, the majestic land of ice and fire, is a bird's paradise in the far north. Imagine a sprawling canvas of rugged mountains, sparkling glaciers, and vast stretches of pristine forests as far as the eye can see. It's like living inside a real-life snow globe, where every breath is crisp, and every sight is breathtaking.

In Alaska, winter puts on a magnificent show, with auroras dancing across the night sky like shimmering ribbons. The land is home to creatures that have mastered survival in this freezing wonderland, from enormous moose gracefully navigating the snow to the iconic polar bears, masters of the icy seas. Alaska is also a favourite nesting ground for migratory birds, like our adventurous aviators, who know the secret paths of the sky like no other.

Now, let's fly all the way down to the sun-drenched Pampas in Argentina, where endless grassy plains stretch out like a sea of gold. Picture a vast, open expanse with gentle breezes rustling through the tall grasses as far as your keen eyes can spy. This breathtaking landscape stretches as far as the eye can see, with towering thunderheads rolling in for dramatic afternoon storms.

In the Pampas, wildlife thrives in harmony with nature. Majestic gauchos, skilled horse riders, roam the plains, herd cattle, and live the cowboy way of life. Keep an eye out for the yellow-headed caracara's friends—elegant rheas, slender foxes, and colourful parakeets, all adding a touch of vibrancy to this harmonious environment.

But the real stars of the Pampas are the birds—oh, the birds! Flamingos gracefully wading through shallow lagoons, adding a splash of pink against the green backdrop. And if you listen closely, you might catch the melodic songs of cardinals and mockingbirds, joined by the eerie calls of the burrowing owls.

So, there you have it, my flightful companion! Alaska is a dreamland of wild ice and wilderness, and the Pampas is a sprawling haven of golden plains and vibrant wildlife. Two distinct worlds, each with unique wonders, are ready to be explored and admired. Shall we continue our fascinating conversation, or is there something else you wish to know?"

"Well, I do have one more request. Can I go with you when you decide to continue to Argentina?" The General looked down and paused for what seemed hours to the caracara. "Remember, you are little and have no idea how to migrate. We would have to teach and protect you all the way. There can be no guarantee you will make it, but I promise if you wish to go with us, we will do our utmost to keep you safe."

Hearing the General's decision to allow him to venture with the Goose squadron in the near future was all his dreams come true. He could not wait to tell the caracara flock waiting for his return. He turned, greeted him once again, and flew at the fastest speed he could muster back to his home in the north of the city, opposite a building that housed three cats: one black and white, one silver, and one looking almost like a lion.

*****

# 41: I am a little steam locomotive who misses deeply his father and grandfather

*I*magine living off only coal and water and still having enough energy to run at over 100 mph! That's precisely what I, a steam locomotive, could once do. Well, I could not go at such a speed as I live and breathe in South America, and we could never move that fast here.

Blame it on the sun, the rain, or the fact that I am a little locomotive. But both my father and grandfather before him were more significantly sized locomotives, and they could.

For a very long time, my most prominent relatives, including my grandfather, often referred to by my father as "Giant mechanical dinosaurs," have been extinct from most of the world's railroads.

I have heard this fact many times since, so I must believe that steam technology lives only in human hearts and not on the rusting rail tracks. The other more fortunate locomotives are still running as tourist attractions on many of the few heritage railways in existence.

In their heyday, my ancestors were very popular and renowned for locomotives powered by steam engines. I firmly believe they all deserve to be remembered because they swept the world during the Industrial Revolution in the 18th and 19th centuries.

They were the true pioneers who came first and paved the way for the cars, aeroplanes, telephones, mobiles, radios, and televisions that followed.

Humans regard locomotion as among the greatest inventions of all time. We were marvels of machinery and excellent examples of engineering. Even we, little ones with small engines and big hearts, were often hidden under the smoke and steam as we raced along.

My father and grandfather taught me long ago that it takes energy to do anything humans think of, such as flying an aeroplane, walking up and down a mountain, or driving a car along the city streets. Today, most of the energy they use for transportation comes from oil, but that is only sometimes the case.

Until the early 20th century, coal was the world's favourite fuel, powering everything from my grandfather to ships.

Why Coal? The answer is easy: Humans discovered that there was lots of it under the Earth's surface, making it inexpensive and widely available.

My father also taught me that coal is an organic chemical based on the element carbon. Over millions of years, coal has been formed when the remains of dead plants are buried under rocks, squeezed by pressure, and then cooked by the Earth's internal heat.

That's why humans refer to it as fossil fuel.

Every lump of coal is really a lump of energy. The carbon, each one, is locked to atoms of hydrogen and oxygen by joints termed chemical bonds. When humans burn coal on fire, the relationships break apart, and the energy is released as heat.

My little steam engine burns coal to release the heat energy it contains.

It's like a kettle sitting on top of a fire. The heat from the fire boils the water in the pot, resulting in steam. Only instead of blowing off uselessly into the air, like the steam from a kettle, my steam is captured and used to power me along.

Well, it used to be. More about my current predicament later.

There are four main parts in my steam engine: a fire to burn the coal, a boiler that needs to be full of water to allow the light to heat it up to become steam, a cylinder, and finally, a piston, very much like a bicycle pump, that enables the moisture to be pumped into the barrel. The piston moves in and out, allowing my little body to move along.

A human can load coal into my cabin's metal box, which contains a roaring coal fire. The fire heats up the boiler, producing steam under high pressure.

*****

My father later told me about my grandfather, who was very large and very inefficient, which means he took vast amounts of coal to get him to do anything. He began his working life back in 1947 after being manufactured in Philadelphia by Baldwins and sent to cover several routes around Colombia under the management of "Ferrocarriles del Pacifico." He was one of numerous type 2-8-2 locomotives that was powered by steam, and on its nose was displayed number 64. The Ferrocarriles del Pacifico began operating in 1915.

As I have already mentioned, all the trains in this period were powered by steam. My grandfather's generation was some of the largest and most powerful in the country. Each was designed to handle the challenging Andes mountainous terrain. My grandfather primarily transported goods, such as agricultural products, between my city and the ports on the Pacific coast.

For the next several decades, other locomotives were added to the growing fleet, and my father (number 89) was one of them because his engine could produce steam at much higher pressure by using our smaller and much stronger boilers. This also included me and my tiny engine; my number was 127!

We could squeeze out more force and blow our piston harder. The humans were able to make us lighter and more compact, allowing us to go faster than ever before.

Sadly, as the years went by, the cheap coal supply became expensive. Combine this with the introduction of oil, which was cleaner and offered less pollution, and my steam engine is inefficient because the fire that burns the coal is separate and usually some distance from a cylinder that generates the heat energy in the steam and turns it into mechanical energy, which in turn sends the resulting power to my engine.

I found my once busy city timetable becoming less and less. So did my grandfather's and my father's timetables. We were slowly being replaced by diesel locomotives, which offered several advantages over steam locomotives. No one could ignore their higher efficiency, lower operating costs, and reduced maintenance requirements.

I remember my father telling me with melancholy in his eyes, "That's largely why we steam locomotives disappeared from the human's railroads; our distant cousins, the diesel oil locomotives, were altogether more convenient for them."

He then went on further, seeing the sadness in my eyes: "It takes us hours to have our fires up and ready, to move our steam engines before we can be used. Our cousins, with their diesel engines, will be running in less than a minute. Our side of the family of steam engines eventually disappeared from the factories when the other great invention, electricity, became a more convenient way of powering human buildings.

*****

Now, my last memories of my father and grandfather. They are almost 50 years old. On our final day together, side by side, the railway station was coming to an end. Our home was destined to be closed down and turned into a shopping Mall, and all the railroad tracks were starting to disappear. "You have to understand, little one, that no human wants to load coal into a factory every day when they can just flick on switches to make things work." With that lasting insight, humans suddenly appeared, and my father and grandfather were taken away on large and robust transporters.

Where did they go to?

I had no idea. I was broken-hearted. I cried for many days with my loneliness.

This depressive situation continued, and much later, on my final journey carrying human passengers, I was able to share with them their last experience of the joy of being transported by my little but powerful engine.

That day was the last time I heard a lot of wonder and admiration from humans.

You may have noticed that I have mentioned my size and power before, but I wish you to know that I am very proud of my heritage.

I have a mighty soul still beating and begging to please a new generation of passengers. I am curious if I will ever be allowed to do so again.

Every day, I pray for the opportunity to enjoy the excited voices of humans and their children, too. Nothing would please me more than feeling and hearing their excitement once more.

I do not care what anyone says. Both my grandfather and father were entirely correct. We little or big steam locomotives showed more heart and soul than any other mode of transportation ever invented by humans, and never once did they hear us complain.

\*\*\*\*\*

I have now been resting on a small section of the railroad, which is not much longer than my body. I am positioned outside but only a short distance away from the main gates of what was once a vast and bustling railway station. In the distance, I can still see more discarded railway tracks sitting there doing nothing. What a waste.

This railway station I mentioned disappeared to become the terminal for the many buses that snake around the city roads at high speeds.

Now, after many years, these same buses are showing wear and tear with their choking black plumes of smoke appearing from their rear exhausts. The poisonous fumes pollute the surrounding pockets of air.

Each covering the humans standing nearby in a thin coating of toxic chemicals.

\*\*\*\*\*

Once and only recently, I witnessed a conversation between two humans walking around me and talking about the bygone era of the locomotives, such as me and my ancestors.

Much of the information I now pass with you came from what I knew and what I heard that day.

Apparently, things are different from what they see. Coal and steam never did disappear—well, not exactly. "Where does the electricity we use come from?"

one of the men asked the other.

The older of the two, who had more knowledge on this subject, offered, "It would be great if it all came from renewable energy, such as wind turbines and solar panels. But amazingly, much of it still comes from coal burnt in power plants thousands away from our homes and factories!"

He took out his notepad and started to sketch a rough outline of the inside of a coal-fired power plant. As he said, "Coal is still burned to make steam, driving windmill-like devices called steam turbines, which are much more efficient than steam engines. As they rotate, they turn electromagnetic generators and produce electricity. So, you see, although steam locomotives have vanished from our railways, steam power is alive and well and just as necessary as it ever was!"

Hearing this new information made me proud and determined to visit my father and grandfather one day. I have been told there is a bigger version than me outside of a vast and popular shopping complex called Chipichape. I recently learned that another much larger steam locomotive is outside a museum near the city airport. It is called the Museo Aereo Fenix.

Could they be my father and grandfather?

Both locations are close. I agree if you are on foot or on a set of wheels, but with wings, I need a railroad and, of course, someone to fire up my little but robust metal firebox.

I do not know why, but on that day, I felt something was going to happen. My dream of seeing my father and grandfather again could and would become a reality.

Why did I feel that emotion? I do not know.

*****

The sun is still nowhere to be seen. I am so used to seeing and feeling the sun's presence that I hardly noticed it today. It is much more relaxed now. I can see dark clouds everywhere in the sky and feel cold water droplets landing on my dusty surfaces.

Oh, how I love the rain. To be clean is a beautiful experience, and I often see humans walking or running past me in many directions every day, all clean and smelling fresh.

Of course, there will always be a few exceptions, and luckily for me, the smelly street ones usually have no thoughts regarding me sitting here waiting patiently for something to happen.

I just remembered that I should mention something strange happened late last night. Someone weird-looking came right up to me and examined me everywhere.

It was really off-putting. I was dozing off as I usually do at such a time. The moving traffic had all but disappeared, the passing humans were sound asleep in their beds, and all was quiet.

Now, how can I describe this visitor?

Well, he was not entirely like any human I am accustomed to seeing all the time. For instance, he was very short and fat. His long beard draped down his large stomach, but he was unable to hide the bulge completely. He wore an authentic tall red pointed hat, and his legs were almost just knobbly sticks with big feet and no shoes at the end.

If any human ever examined me, it was usually from a short distance, but not by this creature. He was all over me. Does he know what I am? Does he know what I am capable of doing?

It appears he does. I moved to my little cabin and quickly opened the door where the fire would usually be. He placed his head inside, and his fat and stubby fingers felt the walls inside. His inspection went to other parts of my engine, and all the time, he seemed pleased and contented.

Later, I jumped from the platform and bent down a little to inspect all my wheels. Then he surprised me further by going right underneath me and feeling my lower casing.

After a few minutes, he rose and came to the front of me, placed his right palm flat on me and said: "Soon, you are going to be needed by this city and its humans, and I will be the one who will power up your little engine."

I said nothing. I was lost for words. Then, without moving, my new weird-looking friend added, "This city is going to owe you a great debt, and you are going to become a very famous little locomotive indeed."

Those words spurred me on to splutter out, "Can my father sitting outside of Chipichape Shopping Mall and my Grandfather at the Museo Aereo Fenix near the airport help too?"

"Tell me more about these two places you just mentioned. I am not familiar with them."

I quickly began putting all the information together and almost blurred it all out at once.

Derekamus, his fingers resting on my 127 badges, said, "Calm down, little brave one. First the shopping mall and then the museum."

"Sorry, yes, I am a little excited. Again, I am sorry. Yes, Chipichape is a large shopping centre in the north of the city, and my father used to be on display outside for all travellers and commuters to see every day. "I did hear recently that he has moved inside, out of all the weather conditions, and sits proudly in the middle of the trendy food court surrounded by various eateries and the entrance to the multi-screen cinema complex."

"Now, my grandfather needs to do better. He lies outside the Museo Aereo

Fenix, and rust has caused him much pain and discomfort. But at the same time, I must be grateful to the owners and founders of the museum.

It was right and proper to add my grandfather to the wonderful collection of all types of transportation. Preserving him and allowing him to serve as a tangible reminder of all the bygone eras and to allow him to proudly be an iconic symbol of progress and innovation through history makes me proud."

"Thank you, little locomotive, but there is one small point I need to know. Where is the Museo Aereo Fenix?"

"Oops, sorry once more. You will find the Museum at Entrance 9 at the commencement of the Zona Franca de Palmaseca. I am unsure where that is, but I have been assured it is close to the commercial airport."

Derekamus made a mental note of the address and spoke to reassure me: "Don't fret. I will find out where it is located, and I am sure your grandfather will be of immense help in rescuing many humans when the time comes."

There was a pause, and then I heard, "I do believe you have come up with a fantastic suggestion. I am sure I can find jobs for all three of you soon."

So, if I were you, get as much sleep now as you can in the meantime because the next time we meet, you and I will have the adventure of a lifetime, and that is a promise." Then he was gone. Did I sleep? Not on your Choo, Choo did I

*****

# 42: I am Gabriel and the true lifelong friend of Hector

You may remember me from Part One of this book. My full name is Gabriel Garcia Marquez, and I wish to reiterate once again that I am not the famous writer you know as Gabriel José de la Concordia Garcia Marquez.

Please don't get me wrong; I wish I were. I have read nearly all his books at least twice.

Sadly, no, I am the young shipmate of one Hector Rodriguez, who passed away three years ago in the home of the older people on the mountain ridge overlooking the city below. Hector told you of his humble beginnings and his adventure as a stowaway onboard a merchant freighter during World War 2. I later gave you my account of life in Argentina and the circumstances of finding myself as the crew member who discovered a very seasick stowaway.

I wish to tell you of the intervening years of our friendship. I truly miss my old friend, so I hope you will be patient with me as I remember.

I wish to start with not my own account but Hector's memories of when our paths crossed again not long after the war in Europe and Japan had ended. It is not his recollections that differ from mine. It's just that he always told the tale with a lot of gusto and pride.

*****

The heat could be clearly seen rising from the dusty and unmanaged mountain ridge road. The sun's rays offered do not respite. Clouds were absent today, making our task monumental.

Hello, it is me, Hector. I do hope you are all well. I have returned to the older people's home again. I have been away visiting the graveside of my dearly departed wife, Isabella. She has been gone from my life for some time now. All I have is my memories, and I sit here looking out onto the fields below, reminiscing as I always do when I return from my yearly visits to the place where the most crucial lady in my past life once lived.

*****

The story that consistently makes me break out into a smile from ear to ear is the day Gabriel suddenly appeared and only managed to prevent me from being crushed by a massively impressive-looking rock.

The story began nearly a year after my return from my adventures in the mid-Atlantic on board the sea freighter between Cartagena and Bristol and the returning voyage. The first few days leaving the English port were full of potential danger of being torpedoed by a passing U-boat.

To our great relief, the danger receded as we moved further away from the coast.

The deteriorating weather also offered some protection, but to be honest, I did not fare well with one particular raging storm when it was over the top of us. My "sea legs" abandoned me on this specific night. Looking at Gabriel, I could see he was struggling too.

For once, a few other crew members and I were resting or trying to relax. To help pass the time, we played Gin Rummy in the gallery; others sat around the room at separate tables and read or wrote letters. We sat alone, willing our minds to block out the increasing danger around us. As the storm neared, the sea roared to life, and the waves began to smash into our ship from all directions.

We were thankful that the Captain had secured a load of stone that filled the hold, creating a cushion against the forces of nature as they roared into life around us. This stone was heading to a small US port called Savannah. The locals used the stone to fortify their dock areas when heavy storms were known to be heading their way.

In conditions such as this, only the very seasoned mariner can cope with the thrashing around of their environment. I appeared to be bearing up well. Silently, I didn't feel the same for my good friend Gabriel. Sweat was looking on his forehead, and I could see him continually wiping the droplets away when they became too much to bear with his sodden handkerchief.

I witnessed other men, who I thought could handle the conditions with ease, suddenly turn to a pale-looking white and run from the room, spraying their insides as they negotiated their way towards the exit doorway. Everyone sensed this was going to be a troublesome night for all.

I am okay, I screamed silently to myself. I turned my concentration down to the cards on the table. I must have stared at the four aces for an eternity.

*****

A vast, powerful wave slammed into the side of our vessel and immediately leaned to the port side. Everything was not secure in any part of the ship, and it flew in the same direction. This included our cards, cold coffee mugs, and balance.

I felt that the ship would not recover, and I, in total fear, looked through the circular porthole window to my side and saw only darkness. Suddenly, the image changed for me. Now, I was witnessing the rising of the ship out of the water, and I could see the chopping waves with the foaming froth running downwards on the surface of the "Bull's eye" window. I sensed Gabriel was now beside me. Both of us were silent.

I knew I should look away, but I could see yet another massive wall of water heading directly towards us in the distance. I felt the ship turn towards the approaching wave. The Captain must have seen the impending danger and ordered the ship's change of course. He was trying frantically to meet the wave head-on.

Now, all the men, including Gabriel and me, were struggling with our evening meals inside our groaning stomachs. I was still holding up well. Then I made my mistake—or should I say two mistakes?

I had turned to speak to Gabriel, but the vision of him throwing up into a brown paper bag—where the bag had come from—I had no idea, and before my brain could fathom it out, I had amused my eyes away from him towards the front of the ship.

An alarming fascination took over me, and my legs lurched towards the large windows, which, up to this point, I had stayed clear of. Now, my hands were resting on the ledge holding me up. As my eyes looked ahead, I witnessed the terrifying sight of seeing the bow of the ship disappear into a wall of water.

*****

I think I screamed out in fear, "Oh no, we are going to drown!" but to be truthful, I am not sure if it was me who voiced those words or if it was Gabriel. We would debate about this point for the rest of our lives. Each blaming the other.

To our relief, we saw the bow reappear, and now the ship was gliding over the wave and heading downwards to meet the next rising tide. Soon, my whole body disowned me. I, too, joined everyone else, and the convulsions continued for what seemed like forever.

*****

An hour later, the storm finally abated. Everyone was relieved. We had survived. Now, the considerable clean-up would begin. Our freighter could have been a lot better. It was another 24 hours before the Captain was satisfied with his crew's efforts.

The remainder of the voyage went by with no further issues, and the boredom of waiting to weigh anchor in a quiet harbour took over. Many of us had no complaints. Boredom or sheer terror? I know which I prefer.

When our hardy freighter finally reached Cartagena, the entire crew spent ages saying goodbye to each other, promising to see each other soon. For me, life on the ocean had come to an end. I no longer wanted to experience nature as I had or watch an inbound torpedo streaking just under the waves towards me.

The only sadness I felt was saying goodbye to my dear friend Gabriel. The once quiet stranger whom I was aware of when I joined the freighter is now bubbly and outspoken, full of dreams of what lay ahead for him.

We hugged and shook hands, both of us wishing to grip the other with more substantial pressure than the other. Both of us roared with laughter as we refused to let go.

Again, the Captain came to our rescue. "Now come on, boys, you will have the whole of Colombia thinking you are more than friends." Instantly, our hands departed as the thought reached us both that others thought we might be gay. Now sheepishly, we both punched each other in the shoulders, neither attempting to hurt the other.

Gabriel replied, "Captain, thank you for a magnificent adventure. I will never forget this experience of finding my "sea legs." I will treasure my memories forever."

I turned towards the Captain and extended my hand to him in friendship. "Yes, Captain, I wish to say thank you, too. I have a lifetime of memories to pass onto my future children, and I have enough money to support my family up in Manizales for the next two years."

The Captain accepted my hand and asked: "So, young man, how do you plan to support your family?"

*****

"We have a small coffee farm on the side of the mountain. I wish to purchase the fields adjacent to either side. Thereby, we can have more crops of coffee plants and plantain trees to add shade and protection to the coffee."

I added, "One day, the world will be at peace again. Then, I will export our coffee to all those who wish to serve it."

The Captain turned towards Gabriel, "And what are your plans?"

Shuffling his feet, "I am not sure. I suppose I should return to Buenos Aires and claim my parent's meat packing business and the Beersteiner and coaster business as my inheritance. Then, I best find a suitable wife, raise children, and become a pillar of society."

"Well, good luck to you both. I am sure both of you will be successful and happy individuals. Thank you for your service towards my freighter. I bear you farewell as I have a pending meeting with the ship's owners, and there I will discover what my next voyage will be."

We all three went our separate ways, and none of us looked back; all three headed to new adventures. Within the year, I secured the two fields I wanted, and my father and I returned to our daily routine of growing plants and coffee.

It has long been passed down my family line that our blood must be the same colour as the darkest roasted coffee possible.

*****

My father often sat in front of the evening fire to retell the history of coffee here in our country a million times. Let's listen to his version of him once more together.

"Let's deal with the history first. According to legend, Colombian coffee was introduced to South America by Jesuit Missionaries in the mid-1700s. The powers that had been tried unsuccessfully to persuade their people to grow coffee.

Why was there so much resistance? It would take a coffee tree five years to produce its first crop. Understandably, they were worried about how they were going to survive during that time. One particular Jesuit priest, Francisco Romero, came up with a brilliant solution. Time punishment was required with a confession; he ordered each person to plant three to four coffee plants. As soon as the Archbishop of Colombia heard of what Francisco was doing, he quickly ensured all the Jesuit priests did the same. The map for success with coffee had begun."

We all dutifully shook with laughter when my father reached this point, and I must admit, even now, I do find his version comical.

Now, my father took a moment for all of us to return to the narrative.

"It was not until 1835 that our delicious coffee started to make its way outside the Colombian borders with its 2500 bags to the USA."

"Twenty-five years later, our Colombian-grown Arabica coffee, as opposed to the cheaper Robusta, became the number one exporting product, with over 170,000 bags heading to the USA and Europe; the lucky and hardworking Colombian coffee farmers have never looked back. Currently, together, we are shipping around 11 million bags per year."

"Colombia has remained a firm favourite around the world for our high-altitude grown coffee, and it is only beaten by the mighty Brazilian and Vietnamese output."

*****

So, what made our Colombian coffee so famous and delicious?

Back in 1959, the National Federation of Colombian Coffee Growers created a marketing campaign that was so successful that the whole world stood up and listened to the message of our coffee through the eyes of their fictitious character, Juan Valdez.

When I first heard the name Juan Valdez, I had no idea he was not real. I didn't care when, years later, I found out he was invented to promote our coffee.

I wish to pause in the memories for a moment. My nurse has arrived with my daily intake of medication and a cup of black coffee. I love this time of day. I am only allowed one cup of coffee per day now. Apparently, no more caffeine is needed for an older man such as me.

*****

Now, I can return to the beginning of my story, to the time when Gabriel had re-entered to my life.

I was stood up with four of my campesinos in a massive hole in the rugged mountain ridge road. You could only see our heads. The enormous rock it had taken us three hours to remove from the hole was bearing down on us.

One other campersino stood beside it with a massive piece of timber, acting as a wall to prevent the rock from falling back into the hole and killing us all. We were all at a standstill. None of us dared to move.

At this time of day, we could not expect any other farmers to come to our dilemma. We had to remove the rock, as traffic could not negotiate and get around it. All would have to turn around and head in a different direction to reach our village.

This added another four hours to everyone's journey, and the only gasoline source was from the odd shop with a small amount of bottled gasoline.

"What the heck are we supposed to do now?" I silently questioned myself so as not to cause any consternation or panic among my workers. All their inquiring eyes were on me.

At this very moment, a shadow crossed in front of me and wrapped itself around all of us in the hole.

I looked up, and Gabriel stood in a crisp new white shirt, a cream-coloured cotton suit, a very expensive-looking fedora, and the dirtiest brown brogues!

"Hi, Hector. How is it going? Would you like my assistance?" He said all this with the biggest smile you can imagine, his shiny white teeth blazing away.

I was dumbstruck, and I could not bring myself to answer. I just stood there in the hole, looking up at Gabriel. Was I dreaming, or was I imagining him there? Finally, I felt the need to speak, but before I could, Gabriel lost his footing, and as he began to fall forward, his right foot struck out and landed on the piece of timber.

The branch lifted a fraction into the air, taking the rock with it.

All present for a frozen moment stared transfixed at the rock balancing precariously above our heads. Then, all at once, everyone threw themselves at the rock, including Gabriel. The unbelievable outcome was the rock as if a pebble had fallen away instantly to the side of the road.

We all helped each other to vacate the hole, and finally, I was able to hug my friend. "Gabriel, I have no idea what brought you here at such a moment, but I am sure glad you came."

"I can see you have not lost your touch for an adventure." quipped Gabriel, then he added, "Good job. I was passing, or you lot would have been mincemeat."

All the Campesinos were exhausted and relieved that they were still alive. The one who recovered first shouted out to Gabriel, "Superman!" Then a chorus of happy men started to sing "Superman, Superman" and clapped Gabriel hard on his back and shoulders.

Later, when we were alone, Gabriel revealed that he had not planned to step on the log. It had been an accident. He was as surprised as everyone when the rock rose. It was pure survival instinct for everyone to throw themselves at the rock, and all our brute force overcame the weight waiting to bear down on us.

*****

Trust me, I had managed to walk back into Hector's life again when danger was close at hand. The campesinos remained to have their midday lunch at the side of the road, and Hector and I headed up the road towards their hacienda and coffee farm perched at the bottom of the hill.

That night, we drank and ate beyond what our stomachs would comfortably allow. We told each other of our fortunes over the years since we last said goodbye on the side of the Cartagena quayside. It was also the night I met Isabella. Hector had definitely struck utopia knowing this beautiful creature. Together, they had produced three great children.

*****

Isabella was a beauty of all beauties. You could see she was not only innocent but also open and warm. I never saw her lose her magnetic smile at any point when she laid eyes on Hector or her brood of boys.

I have to admit I felt a jealous twinge when I looked at them all interacting. Maybe one day, I, too, will find love and raise my own family, but until now, there has been no sign of it happening.

I had gone back to Buenos Aires and faced the music with the authorities. A payoff settled all, and within a month, I was an Argentinian owner of a meat packing business and a small business specialising in producing German-style beer jugs known as steins and a range of matching beer mats.

So far, business and earnings have kept me in a decent-looking apartment. However, taking over the existing customer base from my deceased father had not been too challenging.

No one else was interested in doing it, so I had no trouble growing the bottom lines for both concerns. I had two small workforces inherited from my father's days, and they were grateful the businesses got new leases of life from me.

But I was still young and needed to do other things; I was bored by the business's nonchallenging growth. I recruited a management team to take on the daily running of both companies, and I started to look around to see what else could give me a more acceptable stance in life.

After researching different options, I decided to take flying lessons in single-engine aeroplanes from a former retired civil aviation pilot.

The retired pilot had a wealth of aviation experience and knowledge and was willing to share it with me. He also owned a local brewery and felt compassion for my need to find more excitement and purpose.

His teachings focus on flying small aeroplanes, such as the single-engine ones typically used by private pilots. These lessons allowed me to learn to fly and gave me a new perspective on aviation.

Additionally, this experience allowed me to acquire new skills and knowledge that benefited the future of my budding business empire. For example, I used the knowledge gained to offer air transport services to my clients, such as organising tourist flights or special events.

Taking these flying lessons also gives me an exciting way to escape the daily responsibilities of the business and enjoy a hobby that I learned to admire. Flying over the skies of Argentina, I can appreciate the beauty of my country from a completely new and exciting perspective.

While those lessons did require my time and dedication, I saw them as investments in my personal growth and income diversification. But then I got bored again. Hence, I found myself with a rock that wished to crush my dear friend on a dirty and dusty road.

*****

That night, I sat with the Rodriguez's brood as Hector's father, Don Carlos, spent his time telling me of the source of coffee.

"Have you forever wondered where your coffee comes from? How many times have you said to yourself, "I must find the answer later," and never have? Would you like to know all the processes that go into providing you with that simple cup of coffee, whether it be ground or whole?"

Before I could utter yes or no, I heard. "The answer is simple: the beans come from a bright red coffee cherry."

"But you may already know this fact. So, what is inside that coffee cherry, and how does it affect your cup of coffee?" I remained respectfully still and silent.

"There are many parts to a coffee cherry, and each is important in the final processing method adapted to create your brew of choice. The first fascinating thing to understand is that when we roast, grind, and brew our coffee beans, they are initially fruit seeds. Each coffee plant produces coffee cherries containing one or two seeds.

Another surprising fact about the coffee plant is that its deep green and waxy-looking leaves, when left alone, can grow to over 30 feet tall. Each branch displays an abundance of coffee cherries. Nearly all farmers prune and cut back regularly to allow the plants to conserve their energy and to help in the harvesting process. Like many other plants and shrubs, such as roses, coffee plants give a better yield and quality in a limited space.

It will often take between three to four years for each plant to yield the fruit, and you can expect the average plant to produce around 10 lbs of coffee cherries in an average year. In turn, these result in the production of approximately 2 kg of green beans. Yes, the seeds are green coming from inside the red fruit.

The coffee growing belt that expands around the globe will harvest many varieties of coffee, and the beans will naturally have many characteristics. These same variations will affect the flavour, their size, and the level of resistance to diseases each has."

Don Carlos finally, paused to drink more of his coffee before starting from where he had left off. "Let's look at the layers of a coffee cherry."

"The thin red skin of the cherry is known as the Exocarp. It starts life green in colour until it ripens into a bright red. In some varieties, you will find the colour change to pink, yellow or orange."

*****

Now, I found myself leaning forward directly at Hector's father. No longer was I, in a way, disinterested. Far from it, I was enraptured! "Remember: it is easy to become confused with green coffee cherries and green coffee beans. The latter is the unroasted seeds that, as I have said, are found inside of each ripened coffee cherry.

The next layer below the Exocarp is a thin layer known as the Mesocarp, or the Pulp, which houses the water and sugars for ease of remembering.

You will discover a thinner layer known as the sweet-coating mucilage within the Pulp.

You will also find another layer known as pectin here. All these layers are full of sugars, making them crucial during coffee fermentation.

Now, we finally come to the coffee seeds themselves. In the coffee industry, they are known as the Endosperm, but like the rest of us, you can refer to them as the beans.

*****

And as if by pure magic, Don Carlos now had a lap full of red cherries. "You will usually find two beans in each coffee cherry, and each is covered by a thin layer of Epidermis or silverskin followed by a papery hull—the endocarp, which we refer to as parchment."

"During roasting, these cells naturally fall away and are known as the Chaff. Before roasting, the layers of the coffee cherry are removed, and the beans are dried to approximately 11% moisture content. The most commonly used methods for extracting cherry skin are washing (with water) and drying (coffee is dried naturally under the sun, followed by machines extracting the skins).

Around 5% of coffee cherries show only one seed inside when opened. These beans are called Peaberries. They are rounder and more prominent in size."

"They are usually formed due to insufficient pollination, and possibly the other seed has yet to grow. Peaberries will occur where the coffee plant is exposed to extreme weather conditions. Hence, you will often see banana-looking plantain trees near our Colombian coffee plants to add protection."

"We farmers tend to treat the Peaberries differently from the usual crop to avoid any inconsistencies when roasting."

*****

Isabella and the children came to my rescue and pleaded with Don Carlos to give me a break and resume again in the morning by taking me around the Finca and explaining visually as well as in words. I eagerly wanted my newfound guru in the world of coffee to continue my teaching. Unfortunately, he was tired and headed to his bed without too much resistance.

The following morning began at seven. Breakfast on the veranda with spectacular views of the farm and the surrounding coffee and plantain for thousands and thousands. The scenery and the tastiness of the empanadas, pandabonos and tinto made everything natural and complete.

When the early morning meal was over, I walked as a trio with Hector and his dear, sweet father, and my lessons continued on coffee.

*****

Don Carlos was short in showcasing me in this magical world. "What bearing does anatomy impact on your regular cup of coffee? In most cases, the coffee cherry skin is discarded, but thankfully, some entrepreneurs and pioneers are exploring the beautiful taste of cascara."

Don Carlos gave me a cup of this fantastic brew as if by magic. When you see it for the first time, it looks like tea, smells like tea, and tastes like fruit-flavoured tea. Then you discover it is the skin of a cherry from a coffee plant!

From the very moment the mild flavour of cascara with a hint of sweetness hit my lips, I was hooked for life. This is the most excellent tea in the world. The taste is reminiscent of a mild mix of red mulberry, cranberry, raspberry, and, of course, cherries.

"We coffee farmers find it difficult to remove the skin and mucilage from the coffee beans, and we have to design and develop numerous methods to achieve the desired outcome. The only thing for you to reflect on is each way can and does affect the profile and taste of the coffee you are about to drink."

"With washed coffee, the fruit is completely removed before drying. In natural coffee, the fruit flesh is removed after the drying process. Regarding the honey coffee process and pulped natural processing, the coffee cherry skin and large parts of the mucilage are removed before the drying process, and the leftover glue is removed afterwards."

I found myself enthralled by all the knowledge Hector and Don Carlos were willing to share with me. I began to see and feel the emotions in my friend and his father's reaching out to me.

Hector felt the need to take over the lesson from his father, mainly to give him a chance to rest as he moved along. Of course, he was no longer the spirited individual that he still believed he was.

"The term honey is down to the mucilage being extraordinarily sticky and sweet, just like natural honey. If you ever savour a honey-processed coffee, you will immediately notice its delicious flavours. Coffee cherries begin germinating as soon as they leave the branch by using the sugar in the seeds and stop when the drying process starts. "

Now, all three of us were making our way back to the hacienda, and Isabella was outside cleaning a large rug with a good beating from a wicker beater. Both

Isabella, Hector and Don Carlos were smiling at me. Isabella said, "Now you know the world of a coffee cherry. So, pause and wonder no more when savouring your next favourite brew."

*****

The problem for me was that I wondered a lot.

I spent the whole day not drinking coffee but Cascara tea. My experts taught me how to make the perfect brew and, without throwing anything away, make an alternative iced brew.

Then they hit me with a bombshell. The shell could have been more beneficial to them. Instead, like all farmers at that time, they ignored the mess on the floor and used it as compost. There needed to be a market for cascara tea. It was not considered authentic tea because it did not come from a tea leaf of any kind, and it did not taste like coffee, even though it came from a bean. No country was willing to regulate cascara tea.

I was not prepared to let this go; I wanted to know so much more. I was like a dog with a new bone. "Please tell me everything you know about Cascara's history."

Don Carlos could see the need in my eyes and came forward with his arm on my shoulder. "Come, let me give you my last lesson on Cascara Tea." This is what I heard and took on board that afternoon.

"Have you heard of a new hybrid tea, Cascara Tea? Is it available in many of your Argentinian artisanal and boutique cafes? Is your country aware of the fantastic benefits of Cascara Tea? No, it is the same here in Colombia."

"Did you, Gabriel, grow up in a household of tea drinkers? Was coffee a funny-tasting, acidic hot drink you tolerated once it was placed in front of you?"

"For obvious reasons, you can class me as an ardent coffee drinker. But after discovering cascara tea, I am not so sure."

*****

The name cascara is a Spanish alternative for Tusk, peel, or skin. The name was given to describe this tea, made from the outer peel of traditionally discarded coffee cherries. The same outer shell surrounds and protects the coffee beans within them as they grow and ripen.

Coffee farmers like us around the world are turning to sun-drying the coffee cherries and brewing them in ways similar to how we make tea.

The first coffee grower who realised the opportunity of creating and blending wasted coffee cherries was a forward-thinking Una Salvadorena. One day, she accidentally discovered the sweet, fruity aroma when standing next to a pile of discarded cherries.

Like all discoveries, where the rest of the world ignored the pile and accepted the waste as the norm, our heroine instead picked through the dry cherry pile. She selected a small amount and cleaned it with fresh water. After that, she placed the cherries into a glass of hot water and sat back to sample what it would taste like.

I suspect the revelation of this brand-new experience was as exciting to her as it was for me. I couldn't wait to share the flavours with everyone who would stop and listen to me. Sadly, my neighbours were less convinced than my family was.

Legend has it that Kaldi, the Ethiopian goat herder, had reported the dilemma to the local monks after witnessing the strange effects on his typically sedated goats. None at the time truly understood or even contemplated the benefits that would come from the coffee cherries hanging in the trees."

I had to add to the conversation, "Cascara tea, for me, is a beautiful drink with abundant sweet and fruity flavours. From the first drop, I noticed the many flavours of rosehip, closely followed by cherry, mango, hibiscus, red currant, and, I believe, a hint of tobacco. The latter may have come from my stretched imagination."

Hector laughed and remarked to the other two: "It does look like Gabriel has been converted."

Don Carlos took over the thread of this magical lesson for me. "Globally, tea has proven to be a resounding source of comfort, healing and flavour for all tea drinkers around the world, and most certainly within the famous British way of life. The tea's diversity has proven to be the best thing that all will gladly mention when the subject arises. It is the same for any tea, whether it be black, green, herbal, or fruity. Tea drinkers can always relate to a time when the tea of their choice made a difference in their lives."

Isabella picked up a jug of the iced beverage and poured four tumblers of the fruit tea, and while passing to each container, she stopped at me again and smiled: "Maybe the day has finally come for Cascara tea to shine."

All four of us were now sitting at the same table on the veranda, looking at the farm behind us.

Isabella continued when we were settled: "Cascara tea is an excellent source of antioxidants that support our energy, mental clarity, and overall well-being."

"A great example is the British, no matter where they hung their hats in history. Each has enjoyed the benefits of drinking tea for over 350 years. It has become their quintessential English drink. But remember, tea's history did not start with the English. "Its story began a lot earlier."

Hector leaned forward and revealed to me, "I have studied this subject a lot, and I discovered Chinese history can be traced back to a form of herbal tea being brewed as far back as 2737 BCE with emperor Shen Nung, a dedicated herbalist."

This herbalist discovered a great benefit from drinking tea: the abundance of antioxidants in many foods. Their properties are known to protect our immune system and overall health. They protect our cell membranes and delicate cells, as well as the ability to reduce any inflammation we may suffer. It was reported to us that our blend of cascara tea has a higher density of antioxidants than fruits such as blueberries, cranberries, and pomegranates.

As I was about to shout out, Hector's hand came up to hold me back. "Yes, I will reveal all to you at the end, my dear friend. Hold tight, stay patient; your lesson is nearly complete." I did as I was told.

*****

Hector laughed and continued as he watched my growing excitement: "Those of us who have discovered Cascara tea will gladly agree that this tea is the perfect balance between tea and coffee. We love the fruity, sweet flavour and find it a natural choice when we wish to avoid facing the acidity taste of our favourite coffee.

The beautiful irony is that they both come from the same source—the coffee bean. Thus, the caffeine structure is similar in design but in a smaller amount.

Cascara tea has approximately one-quarter less caffeine compared to your regular coffee. So, if you worry about the effects of drinking coffee later in the afternoon or at night, have an alternative. Brewing a cascara tea will give you the needed energy support without the loss of sleep at night and the extremes of highs and lows with sugar from other alternatives such as energy drinks and sugary soda drinks. "I couldn't stop myself. I exploded: " Is that everything?"

Don Carlos stood and opened his arms to me, continuing the lesson that was indeed exhausting my poor brain. "No, there is the matter of a third benefit, and it is the positive feeling of promoting and improving our mental health and clarity. From the coffee cherry, it has been noted that our levels of a brain-derived neurotrophic factor (BDNF), or BDNF in short, can be supported and give us the ability to preserve our memory."

"According to British research findings, higher levels of BDNF are critical for our brain's clarity and will support the promotion of healthy ageing of our minds. This positive benefit can also benefit our memory and our feelings of happiness and goodwill."

I excused myself and headed to the toilet; I needed to think through all that had been passed to me. What should I do with this newfound learning? Could I take it to Argentina and make a small fortune from it? A million questions with zero answers!

*****

As the sun painted golden hues across the vast coffee estate in Colombia, Gabriel sat with his dear friends Hector, Isabella, and Hector's father on the open terrace that evening, sipping on the flavourful cascara tea they had just brewed. The aroma of the dried coffee cherry husks filled the air, captivating Gabriel's senses, and he couldn't help but marvel at the wonder of this beneficial product.

Gabriel, hailing from Argentina, a country renowned for its love of mate, had not touched him, but cascara tea had captured his heart.

It possessed a unique charm; unlike anything he had ever tasted before. Rich in antioxidants, vitamins, and minerals, it offered a whole new world of health benefits.

As he took another sip, Gabriel's mind churned with ideas on how to introduce this fantastic product to his homeland. He knew its popularity would be a dream among the health-conscious population, who were always looking for innovative and natural alternatives.

"I think Cascara tea could find its perfect home in Argentina," Gabriel exclaimed, his eyes sparkling with excitement.

Hector agreed. "Absolutely, my friend! Argentina has such a vibrant culture around tea and mate. Cascara tea would be a brilliant addition to their beverage repertoire."

Isabella chimed in; her voice filled with enthusiasm. "And with the growing interest in sustainable and eco-friendly products, Cascara tea's status as an upcycled and waste-reducing beverage makes it even more appealing."

Gabriel's mind raced with ideas on how to make this venture a reality. Initially, he considered establishing natural partnerships with the Rodriguez family. With his friendship with each of them, they could create a sustainable supply chain. He envisioned later, as growth came, more networks connecting coffee plantations to tea enthusiasts, along with informative campaigns highlighting the nutritional benefits of cascara, all while empowering the local communities.

However, he knew that to successfully introduce Cascara tea to Argentina, he needed to create awareness and excitement among the people. Gabriel pondered organising tea tastings, collaborating with local cafes, and sharing the story of Cascara tea's journey from the farm to the cup.

With these ideas swirling in his mind, Gabriel turned to Hector's father, the wise and experienced figure on the farm. "Don Carlos, what do you think? How can we take Cascara tea to Argentina together?"

Don Carlos leaned back in his chair, his face displaying a kind smile. "My dear Gabriel, you have an incredible opportunity in front of you. Your passion and knowledge of Cascara tea and the power of friendship and collaboration will be the foundation for success. Begin by sharing your love for this beverage with the people around you, slowly expanding its reach."

Encouraged by Don Carlos' words from him, Gabriel knew he had the support of his friends and mentors from him. Armed with their teachings and his determination, he has vowed to embark on this journey to bring cascara tea to Argentina.

Together, they would bridge the gap between countries and share the joys and benefits of Cascara tea with a whole new community. And as they sat on that terrace, embracing the warmth of friendship, Gabriel felt a surge of excitement and the resolve to make his dream a reality.

*****

## 43: I am Ignacio's son, and my name is Samuel, and I talk to Gnomes

I enjoy sitting in my garden whenever I am not on the road. Secretly, I have conversations with my father's gnomes. It was Ignacio who revealed their names as Derekamus and Abella. He swore they were as astute as us. He would spend hours talking to them. Of course, the whole family thought he was going crazy.

But I always had this nagging feeling he was as sane as you and I. Now, sadly, my father and mother have passed away in their sleep, and I have no idea why. Well, that's not true. They died from inhaling carbon monoxide poisoning from a faulty water heater in the next room to the main bedroom in their holiday home. It later transpired that both had forgotten to get the heater serviced in the preceding five years.

Experts have told me the fault could have been there from the beginning of the installation. I will never know.

It hurts me every time I visit the gnomes, but I believe I should continue talking to them. So far, they have yet to respond to me. But I find it soothing to communicate with them when alone. I suspect I try to communicate with the gnomes and my cherished but gone parents.

Jasmina and Ignacio had positioned them both so they could witness anyone passing.

He brought them to me on his last trip, driving the big burgundy Kenworth truck he passed to me on his retirement. No one knew at that time that my parent's retirement was going to be so short.

One particular sedate evening, I found myself sitting with Derekamus and

Abella, and I heard myself ask them: "How do I avoid a truck driver's belly?"

My Sofia has continuously nagged at me over the past decade as I drove my big Kenworth Truck across the country, and I was gaining a driver's belly. How could I have avoided having a big belly?

Fortunately, the two gnomes did not respond, so the answer was simple: all I had to do was walk around my truck, eat with a sensitive attitude, avoid all soft drinks, never sacrifice my health, and listen to my doctor during my routine check-ups.

I looked again at my silent friends. "Is it too late for this Truck Driver to make amends?"

Silence prevailed, so I continued: "How did I get my belly?"

*****

Well, if you were like me, spending almost all your life behind the wheel of a large truck, travelling up and down the highways, working irregular hours, eating and drinking at the wheel, and struggling with interrupted sleep, you, too, would gain that big belly.

Not forgetting having to deal with the stress of the job at hand and all the daredevils and idiots on the road. No one, including your doctor, mentioned we all might develop a hormonal imbalance called Metabolic Syndrome, which apparently affects over 80% of us professionals on the road and around 40% of anyone over the age of 60.

I looked down at the two silent gnomes: "For you two, it must be a nightmare. You are sat together in one pose for 24 hours a day!"

When I think back to my father, Ignacio, his father, Ernesto the Younger, and my father's grandfather, Ernesto the Elder, they all suffered from a bulging belly.

One particular risk factor is called Metabolic Syndrome, which affects our blood pressure. It basically increases it to unacceptable levels if not controlled. Also, we gain excess body fat due to low physical inactivity. Not forgetting, high blood sugar levels lead to increased risks of heart disease, including strokes and dreaded diabetes.

After a decade of ignoring my wife, Sofia, and passing off the risks as nothing to worry about, I am now taking Enalapril 20 mg twice a day, Amlodipine 5 mg once per day, and finally, Lovastatin 20 mg once per day. I am sure you can hear me rattling in the mornings as I head out for my morning stroll around the garden.

Now, I let my mind concentrate on making health decisions, increasing my physical activities, and improving my ability to fight diseases and chronic conditions. I love keeping my body in a reasonable order. Once, I looked short and fat like my gnomes in the garden. I am still overweight, but now there are minor signs I am becoming trimmer. Finally, I am paying attention to my doctor, and I can confirm you can turn things around. It does take willpower, but it can be done.

Yes, it involves life changes; it sounds drastic, but it is not. In fact, it can be fun, enjoyable, and rewarding. The first thing I had to pay attention to was weight loss. More on that later.

Then, that dreaded word Exercise. As I previously mentioned, I am a fourth-generation truck driver like my father, my grandfather, and my great-grandfather before me.

I could no longer eat those mouthwatering roadside cafe breakfasts and takeaways, nor my beloved soft drink, Colombian. It is a bit like the Scottish Ironbru. In fact, all my future drinks that contained large amounts of sugar had to be replaced with 3.5 litres of water per day.

I must admit drinking water took some time getting used to. I found that if I chilled the water in the fridge beforehand, I enjoyed it more than drinking straight from the tap at room temperature. It's the same product but somehow palatable when relaxed. Try it. The benefits are tremendous and fast to present themselves.

Now, the words "In moderation" have become the norm for Sofia and the doctor. Believe it or not, I have loved the transformation. I have shed a lot of weight, the fat around my waist has reduced drastically, I am in my strength, and the threat of diabetes has receded for now.

When I head for my six monthly visits to the doctor, I cannot wait to jump up onto the scales to be told I have lost another four kilos. When my blood pressure is checked, he says I am like an eighteen-year-old—not bad for a 40-year-old truck driver. You can definitely do the same as me. It only takes the will to change, and with a caring woman like my Sofia behind you, it's possible.

*****

Sorry, I have to digress a little. I have sat here once again next to the two non-talkative gnomes. Without warning, a long black cat with an impressive white chest and what looks like four white socks has just stopped and, without an invite, has strolled through the open gate, right up to Derekamus and Abella and started purring like a steam train as he moves around them without disturbing and knocking them over.

"How unusual, Mr. Cat. I must admit I have no idea who you are, but your purr is pretty impressive. It says a lot about you." The feline stranger paused and closed his eyes as if acknowledging my offering of friendship. Then suddenly, he turned and proceeded to walk back the way he had come. But weird as it must seem. He looks like he has specks of golden dust on his fur coat. Now, where did that come from?

*****

It could be the raging storm that had created two illusions, but I will swear to my dying day that two tiny kittens also walked past with a sprinkling of gold dust on each of their fur coats. One was small and silver-looking, and the other was portlier and more resembled a lion cub.

All three sets of eyes looked back at the two gnomes and smiled their appreciation at meeting them. The next second, they were gone.

I had not noticed Derekamus and Abella's look of satisfaction at being able to communicate with the friendliest trio of cats they had ever encountered. I should have done so at the beginning of my career when I took over the family burgundy rig a couple of years ago. Now, I face those gruelling 14-hour journeys from Cali to Bogota twice weekly.

I recommend that all my trucking friends set individual goals and achievable plans and stick to them religiously. It becomes easy to handle when your mindset accepts that exercising each day will add years to your life.

In my cabin, I have a chart on display for all my family to see, which records my week's weight loss. Another great practice I have allowed into my life is to make the most of my stops. Instead of eating behind the wheel as I used to do, I now leave the cab and use my time wisely.

I wish I could run or jog, but in my work uniform, that has proven difficult, so I do plenty of stretching exercises and the right blend of strength exercises that target my lungs, squats, triceps, and, of course, my belly.

When you are driving, why don't you copy me some more? I take every opportunity at red traffic lights, and when stuck in long queues of traffic, I focus on my core by sitting behind the wheel and tightening my stomach muscles to the degree that I am reaching my spine through my belly button.

If you are a family man with a bunch of kids growing up in the household, get the maximum out of your time off. I try never to spend my time watching TV during the day. I do that in my downtime in the evenings. Instead, I get involved in anything where I need to exert some energy. I reserve time for gardening, walking, trekking, jogging a little bit in the local park, and swimming at the local municipal pool. I do not go to gyms. They cost too much. I like being outdoors. It is much healthier.

*****

I have seen an increase in female drivers. When pregnant, when should they stop driving?

I do not want to be accused of forgetting you, lady drivers. Even you gals can attract a driver's belly if you are not careful. All the rules for us guys apply to you, too.

But there is another area of concern for you ladies to consider, which we guys know and understand. That is the question of when you become pregnant. When would you consider handing the keys to the truck over to your colleagues and resting up for your health and that of the baby?

It is pleasing to know that it is down to how you are feeling throughout your pregnancy. You can continue as long as you and the baby are comfortable. You can reach everything you need without stretching and manoeuvre your truck in all situations.

Bear in mind, though, you will get tired and, dare I say it, sleepy too. So be careful not to stretch yourself. Being exhausted at the wheel of a truck is the same as being drunk. The risks are precisely the same. Think carefully about your posture when driving. How uncomfortable is the seatbelt becoming? Remember, you owe it to protect yourself and the baby at all times when driving, so continue wearing your belt. Take all necessary breaks when stopping, stretching, or walking to relieve a backache.

*****

# 44: I am Rosa who loves to sing, and I have no idea where to buy my Nun's outfit

"Where do I go to buy my Nun's outfit?"
I remember as if it were only yesterday when I found the nerve to ask Sister Superior this question. At that moment, she was deep in meditation and prayer. But being the gentle and all-knowing woman that she undoubtedly was, the problem did not upset her.

She stopped what she was doing and turned to face me. Her smile radiated and lit up the whole room. "Well, "Little one with a big voice." I need to share some new information with you. Come and sit with me. "At this point, I cuddled up to her and felt the warmth radiate from her. I looked up expectantly. "All Sister's outfits, which we call Habits, are designed and sewn for each sister, depending on which Order she is joining. No one place supplies all. Nothing is "Readymade" or "Off the Peg", as my mother used to say.

Each habit is deemed sacred. As the owner, you will say prayers as you place each piece on you; it will become an important symbol of your devotion to your calling. Singing nuns often travel around the world, passing our message through the power of voice. We wear a mix of white and blue as symbols of the sky and its holiness, which sits among the clouds. We do not live a more secluded life as many others around the world prefer.

The chosen colours also help us withstand the heat of the day, whereas something like black or brown would cause us discomfort and overheat us as we work. There are many components to a Sister's Habit. These can include veils, tunics, coifs, rosaries, and footwear.

Many prefer to wear sandals. I like to wear discreet trainers, especially with the amount of walking I do a year up here on the mountain ridge." As Sister Superior paused to take in a breath, I shot in with a burning question: "What is a Coif?"

"A good question, and it shows you are listening. Well, a Coif is a cap worn under the veil." If you choose to join us when it is time, you will also wear some form of girdle, such as a belt, a cincture, or a cord. "What is a cincture?" I asked with pride, showing how devoted I am to learning.

"In simple terms, it is like a belt or girdle that fits around your waist." Now my head was full of questions: "When will I have to have all my hair cut off?" "In some orders, yes, you would. But with our Order, no, that is not necessary, although, on induction, we will request you show a sign like a symbol of your faith by snipping off some of your hair."

"Can I continue wearing the cross that my parents gave me on my ninth birthday?" The Sister Superior reached out and held the cross while addressing me. "Yes, of course, you may wear this cross. It is a special cross."

*****

The Sister Superior rose to take a glass of water. The heat this evening was a little oppressive, and the room did not have any air conditioning to keep us fresh. She turned and looked down at me. "I will allow you one more question, and then you must head to bed to sleep and not sing as you usually do." We both laughed together, knowing snoring was not for me. Singing was everything to my young mind. "Please tell me what happens at the ceremony of accepting me as a Sister?"

The Sister Superior's eyes rolled up as she realised the magnitude of the question. "Well, Rosa, as you know, there is a period where you are on probation, and you will be known as the Postulant. A date will be set for The Acceptance of the Veil Ceremony, where all the nuns in the Order will be asked to attend to decide whether you can join them."

She continued uninterrupted, "The ceremony will be full of words, prayers and YES songs that initially affirmed the order of the Nun's deep cohesion followed by your commitment to the same vows."

She paused to check that Rosa had not disappeared in her head while singing a song or two. She could see Rosa was trying to concentrate. "Before that ceremony can take place, you will return home to your family and friends. It's like going into a retreat for several days. The group and I will prepare your ceremony and invite your family, friends, and benefactors to witness the occasion."

"Sister Gabriela, who is our talented Mistress of Robes, will complete the final alterations and ensure your habit fits you like a glove. She will also count the pins to attach to your veil to ensure your perfect day will go without a hitch."

You will receive your new name, which will complete the transformation of your Novice identity because you do not have a father's family name to bear. This part will be simpler than most, and it will mark the final stage of you no longer taking an old name but a new name to complete your transformation from your old family to your new family."

"Now, my dearest Rosa, it brings me great joy to see your passion for singing and your dedication to the path of Sisterhood. As you prepare for the acceptance of the Veil ceremony, I am truly honoured to guide you in choosing a new name that will symbolise your transformation into a new family." "After much reflection and prayer, I have been inspired to suggest the name " Seraphina" for you. Seraphina holds deep significance and embodies qualities that resonate with your journey and the values you uphold."

"Wow, what does Seraphina stand for?" Spluttered Rosa in great shock.

"Well, firstly, Seraphina means "fiery ones" or "burning ones" in Hebrew. It represents your intense devotion and love for your faith and the Divine. Her singing voice, filled with warmth and passion, resonates like flames dancing in harmony. This name reinforces your commitment to becoming a vessel of divine presence, channelling your spiritual ardour through the power of music."

"Secondly, Seraphina is associated with the highest Order of angels, the Seraphim. These celestial beings are known to have six wings, each pair representing characteristics such as humility, love, and purity. Just as the Seraphim's wings symbolise their spiritual excellence, your voice possesses a heavenly quality that uplifts and touches the hearts of those who hear it."

"The name Seraphina encapsulates your growth towards embodying the virtues cherished by our Order." Rosa was singing the name Seraphina in her head and willing it to be a memory. She nearly missed what the Sister Superior revealed next.

"Lastly, the change from Rosa to Seraphina represents the shedding of your old family name and embracing a new one. It signifies your departure from your earthly lineage as you embark on a transformative journey within the sacred Sisterhood. By adopting a new name, you reaffirm your commitment to your spiritual family, in whom you will find solace, guidance, and support."

Sister Superior paused and looked into Rosa's eyes, ensuring she had her total concentration. This following instruction was vitally crucial for Rosa.

"Dear Seraphina, I encourage you to reflect on the significance of this new name. May it serve as a reminder of your devotion, purity, and chosen spiritual path. Throughout your journey, let your voice carry the divine melodies, bringing solace and upliftment to the hearts of many. The veil ceremony shall embrace this new identity as you step into the embrace of your Sisters, forever a Seraphina within our sacred Order."

*****

I sat there looking at the Sister Superior and instantly knew I would never sleep tonight. What will my new name's future hold for me? It was enough questions for now.

I took hold of the older woman's hands, kissed them, and quietly left with my heart pounding. Now I had the answer to my question. I no longer had to fret about how I was going to pay for my Nun's outfit, or I should say Sister's Habit.

*****

The next day, Rosa took the local bus back up to the mountain ridge and the church she first started singing in before the episode of the earthquake and the accident involving Ximena, Ignacio, Stalin, an unfortunate kite belonging to a sad little boy called Leonardo, and herself.

*****

# 45: *I am the Black Cat with the impressive white chest and four white socked feet*

*I* went on display in a small park in mid-July 1996, next to an often fast-flowing river running through the city's heart. I am made from almost three tons of bronze and sit comfortably on a huge concrete block. I have to thank my artist father, Hernando Tejada, for bringing me to life. I love the idea of being one of the now famous city's landmarks.

At first, I felt exposed and isolated. Still, over the next decade, the continuously growing community of smaller cats known as "the cat's girlfriends" arrived, and I have never suffered from loneliness since.

I am grateful to a peculiar group of artists who decided to embark on a whimsical adventure that would forever change the face of the city's riverside. It all began with a shared dream of bringing a touch of magic and awe to the heart of Cali, capitalising on the beauty of nature, and fusing it with their creative prowess.

Led by my imaginative sculptor, the team knew they needed something truly unique: a set of sculptures of the same size and shape but painted by different artists unlike any other in the world. The concept was simple yet enchanting – a colossal cat, seemingly frozen and poised gracefully on the riverbank leading to his harem of beautiful girlfriends.

The team spent countless hours brainstorming, sketching, and prototyping until they finally hit upon our perfect designs. However, to bring their visions to life, they needed the support and cooperation of the entire city. So, armed with their proposals, sketches, and infectious enthusiasm, they embarked on a crusade to rally support for their imaginative endeavour.

Through endless community meetings, public presentations, and even impromptu street art exhibitions, the team managed to capture the people's hearts and imaginations. Spurred on by their contagious passion, the citizens pledged their support and made generous donations to turn this whimsical dream into a reality.

I am also pleased to say that with the community's backing, the team began the challenging process of transforming steel, concrete, and imagination into a sculpture that would make Cali proud. Days turned into weeks, weeks into months, and this monstrous piece of art gradually took shape.

Passers-by could be seen peering curiously over the construction barriers, their faces reflecting a mix of curiosity and anticipation. Speculations ran wild – some believed I would be a statue honouring Cali's feline inhabitants, while others imagined I would be a sculpture representing the city's vibrant spirit.

Finally, the day of the unveiling arrived after days, weeks, and months of waiting and what felt like an eternity to me. The city buzzed with excitement as the final touches were made to this magnificent sculpture. As the sun began to set, casting a warm golden sheen over the city, my much-awaited moment came.

Underneath a starlit sky, with a gasp of awe and a collective intake of breath, the people gathered on the riverside, their eyes fixed upon me. The magnificent El Gato del Rio. I towered over them, my sleek and graceful form capturing the essence of the river's untamed nature and the tenacity of the city's inhabitants.

The local press reported that the river itself had come to life, capturing the imagination of all who saw it. From that day forward, I proudly sit as El Gato del Rio, an eternal symbol of the city's creative spirit and the power of community collaboration.

Countless millions of photos have become reminders for tourists, artists, and dreamers worldwide.

*****

I got back from my business trip to the Pacific Ocean coastline of Colombia eight hours later than I expected. The storm was not limited to the city, although it appears to be the epicentre of the chaoticness prevailing over the north of this fine city.

I had been transported to Buenaventura's seaport, where the diverse and vibrant locals wished to see me in all my splendour. It was hoped that another version of me, coloured black to represent the predominant Afro-Caribbean community with its mix of ethnicities and cultural heritage, could be displayed in the future for all of the locals, tourists, and sailors to sit with and enjoy passing the time with.

But I arrived with the all-mightiest storm! Please allow me some of your time while I describe what I witnessed when the doors of my freighter were opened.

"Now, imagine this: rain pouring down like a million tiny waterfalls, thunder echoing through the air like the heavens themselves are at war, and waves crashing against the rocky shores with unforgiving force. This storm has unfurled its wrath upon us. It is unfortunate to be there, leaving the people of Buenaventura and the brave mariners on their boats and ships in a state of concern and awe.

This vibrant seaport, known for its trade and bustling maritime activities, has suddenly transformed into a theatre of chaos. Locals can be seen frantically securing their homes and businesses, battening down the hatches to protect themselves from the storm's fury. Fear may be in the air, but I can see that the spirit of resilience is equally palpable.

On the shorelines, fierce winds whipped through the palm trees as if nature itself was conducting a grand symphony. From time to time, I witnessed the scarious bolts of lightning streak across the darkened skies, each illuminating the swirling waves below. Once a calm and gentle backdrop for fishermen and sailors alike, the sea has now transformed into a ferocious beast, challenging even the most seasoned seafarers.

Believe me, in the heart of this storm, the sailors on their ships and boats were navigating these treacherous waters. I could actually see the rigging straining and creaking under the wind's relentless assault. Fearless sailors were at the helm, their eyes fixed on the horizon as they defended the elements. It's a true testament to the bravery and skill required to face Mother Nature's temper tantrums head-on.

Amidst the chaos, I can't help but feel a sense of camaraderie in Buenaventura. The local community comes together during these challenging times, offering support, assistance, and a helping hand to those affected by the storm.

In times like these, the human spirit shines the brightest, fostering an unbreakable bond even in the face of such a fierce adversary.

But let me not forget the enchanting beauty that lies beneath this storm's facade. As raindrops skim across rooftops, the colours of Buenaventura's vibrant streets and exotic flora appeared to come alive, painting a picturesque scene against the backdrop of the tempestuous skies.

Nature, even in its most chaotic moments, still holds its own magic, a reminder of the wonder and resilience of this remarkable coastal town.

So, my dear travellers, though this storm has momentarily cast its shadows upon Buenaventura, know that its people and sailors stood firm; they faced the tempest with unwavering courage and unity. The storm continued as the back doors to the freighter that I was married became closed.

Now, I could only sense what I could hear and feel. I can assure you it did not feel safe for me. I was so thankful when I felt the rumbling sensation as the diesel engine came alive.

*****

I had returned to my rightful and safe place with all my "Lady Gatas" in numerous positions around me for my attention. The loudest and most insistent one is the Gossipy cat.

I could clearly see she needed to get considerable news of her beautiful chest.

"OK, Missy Gossipy cat, what's troubling you?"

"Well, Señor Rio Gato, if you feast your eyes to the other side of the road and look under the vegetation, you will see another cat. In fact, you will see three cats. To be more accurate, I mean one cat and two little kittens."

My eyes instantly moved, but locating them took me a short while. I only did so because the small silver one appeared to shiver constantly. She proceeded to warm herself next to the bigger black cat with his impressive white chest and four white paws. Finally, I observed the lion-looking one.

I could see that the big cat was not a female, so I could disregard the scenario of a mother and two tiny kittens now homeless and starving. But I also felt the same scenario: replacing a father with a mother also did not sit well with my intuition.

"How long have these three been here?" I asked no one particularly. Luckily for me, the San Antonio cat answered my question with her inquisitive nature: "The three arrived some hours ago. They must be hungry. Thirsty no, as you can see, there has been plenty of water."

Gossipy cat raised her front right paw. She obviously had more to reveal to me. "What else do I need to know, Mrs. Gossipy?"

"Señor Rio Gato, many of us, as you know, attended the emergency meeting of the minds, and it was there we learned of the looming danger to all of us in the north and some who dwell near the centre of the city from all this excessive rain and thunderstorms."

"The city officials are preparing for a massive flood to arrive from the weeping mountain ridge above us. Don Jorge Isaac Ferrer has advised us all to make haste, move to higher ground wherever possible, and set up ways to assist any humans in mortal danger."

Valentina is my favourite Siamese cat, with her captivating gracefulness, sheer elegance, and a hint of mysteriousness in her aura. Raising her front left paw and not waiting to be allowed to speak, she uttered, with her independent nature and a touch of aloofness, "Should we start our most important endeavours of bringing safety to all we know to be in mortal danger with these three terrified-looking cats over there under the shrubbery?"

I had to admit, Valentina, with her incredible intelligence and quiet ways of solving problems, had to be my first choice for leading a small team to rescue the big cat and two little kittens. Looking around, I quickly chose the following two ideas for the coming rescue mission. Valentina would purr her acceptance of her, I was sure.

The first of the two was Bella, with her mixed tabby features and calico finishings. Bella has always been, since her arrival two years ago. This playful and mischievous cat brings endless energy and excitement to the river bank community with her expressively green eyes. Bella is impossible to miss. She is known to us all for her athleticism and loves to chase after butterflies and dragonflies nearby. She is friendly and exuberances her outgoing nature. She is forever eager to make new friends, whether they be feline or human. Bella is highly friendly and enjoys being the centre of attention. Often, she is seen entertaining the other cats with her acrobatics and silly antics. She will mesmerise the growing minds of the two kittens with ease.

The second had to be the older lady, known for the past four years as Mia. Mia is a sweet and gentle cat with a calm and relaxed demeanour. Her luxurious silver fur and round copper eyes add to her endearing appearance. Mia is well known for her patience and nurturing nature, often comforting her companions during times of distress.

She loves to curl up in warm spots along the riverbank and can often be found basking in the fading sunlight.

Mia is a great listener and provides a sense of tranquillity to her feline friends. She prefers a peaceful and quiet lifestyle, often enjoying the simple pleasures of nature and the calming sounds of the river. Mia's gentle nature and empathetic personality make her a perfect choice for keeping the kittens calm over the next few hours as they are rescued.

"Valentina, Bella, and Mia. Please make up a rescue team and do what is necessary to ensure all three felines over the road return to wherever they live."

All three cats stood up with huge smiles of pride, clearly pleased with being chosen for the task ahead. In unison, even the rest of the Rio Gatas community roared their unity with the loudest set of purring the city would ever experience. Sadly, because of the storm, no human would ever hear it.

"Come, let us go over the road and introduce ourselves to them." I offered.

Valentina placed one of her well-manicured paws on my shoulder. "No, I recommend I go first and alone. I will need to convince the big, attractive black one with his glorious white chest and the most impressive looking white-socked paws that we are a safe option for them all."

*****

"Good evening to you; my name is Valentina. May I know all your names?"

Blacky was almost a statue at that moment. He had watched the most charming and graceful-looking creation ever strolling towards him. He had not passed breath for what seemed an eternity. "Wow, can we male cats also fall in love?"

Valentina sat gracefully next to Liz, and as a female, she could not take her eyes off such a blossoming beauty as this silver-looking one. Under her neck was signs of two more colours to her coat: white and beige. Very interesting indeed.

"Well, do you have a tongue? Are you going to sit there and stare at me? Please remember you have not introduced yourselves yet."

Blacky found the strength to answer: "So sorry, Dona Valentina. My name is Blacky, and these two balls of nuclear energy are Liz and Goldie."

"Are you Don Blacky, the father to these, in your words, balls of nuclear energy?"

"No sweet-looking lady. I have no idea who their parents are. The humans I have lived with for the past seven years one day decided I should have company, as they felt I was missing out since my brother's demise from Feline Leukaemia a while back." I suppose you could say I am their "Surrogate Uncle." It is a term I have heard my owners tell me a lot lately."

Bella and Mia approached and moved very slowly to the outer edges of the growing group so as not to disturb the two kittens. They had already established a wall of protection without causing any dismay. Both figurines began showing concern with the river behind the Rio Gato. Already, they had seen splashes of dirty brown and threatening-looking ripples escaping the riverbank. An eye on both Bella and Mia. Valentina knew they would make it known to her when they felt the danger was exposing all.

"Oh, of course. Can you tell me where you all live?" we live in a fourth-floor penthouse in the La Flora neighbourhood. It is in the north of this city." offered Blacky.

"Thank you. I am aware of where La Flora is. Luckily, we are heading that way ourselves as we are to meet all of the Meeting of the Minds rescue coordinators in approximately 30 minutes under the "Tree of Life." Perhaps you will allow us, three figurines, to escort you safely back to your home. I am sure your owners will be missing you."

"Thank you. Yes, I know that tree. It is magnificent and the biggest tree I have ever seen. These balls of nuclear energy will bombard you with questions on the way. Could you answer their inquisitive questions for me? As I am at the end of my tether today in finding the answers for their relentless curiosity."

Valentina nodded silently to Bella and Mia, "I am sure my two sisters here will answer all their questions as we move along. Looking at my Bella and Mia, I feel we should begin your journey back. Would you like to hop onto our backs to ensure no more delay befalls us?"

As if by sheer divine intervention, all three large figurines selected one of the dripping wet kittens and one "Surrogate Uncle" and placed them on their backs.

Within seconds, they all turned and began moving away from the riverbank, which was now unable to hold back the angry-looking river.

*****

Liz was looking at Mia's copper-coloured eyes within the same time frame. This ball of nuclear energy was the first to speak up. "When we are cats, will we be able to see better at night?" Mia was taken a bit back; she had not expected such a question from a petite version of herself.

Mia smiled at the little mind above him, and so she began the lesson about the world of cats during the worst storm the city had ever experienced in over a century.

"Yes, it is true; we cats have excellent night vision compared to humans. We each have a higher number of rod cells in our eyes. These extra rod cells are responsible for detecting light and motion. This simple adaptation allows us to see better in low-light conditions."

Goldie was next to test his rescuer, Bella's knowledge of her. "Do we cats close our eyes when sneezing?"

Bella burst out laughing. "Wow, what an imagination you have already. OK, here comes the answer. Similar to your human owners, we cats close our eyes when sneezing. Sneezing is a reflex action that helps expel irritants from our nasal passages, and closing our eyes provides us with the necessary protection."

Valentina was enjoying this lesson of life, and she, too, had no idea what sort of questions these little versions of themselves were going to be.

The next question that surprised Valentina, Bella, and Mia was from no other than the "Surrogate Uncle" himself. "Do kittens within the same litter have different parents? The reason why I ask is that these two are twins. Liz is silver, and Goldie is, well, coloured."

Valentina glowed with pride that she was being asked to answer such a brave question; she sensed there was more to this black cat with an impressive chest and four equally white paws.

"It is possible for kittens within a litter to have different fathers. This phenomenon is known as multiple paternity. Cats can have multiple mates during their fertile period, and each mating can result in fertilisation. This can lead to kittens with different appearances and coat colours within the same litter."

As if on cue, Liz was back with her second question: "When do we kittens become cats like you?"

Mia looked to Valentina for assistance with this query. "Well, Missy Liz, that is a tough question and must be answered in two parts. Firstly, lovely-looking kittens generally become adult cats between 9 and 12 months of age. The time frame can vary depending on a number of factors like your breed, genetics, and individual development."

"During this time, you will go through physical and behavioural changes associated with reaching maturity. Just look at Blacky here. He is most definitely someone you two should aspire to grow into with your individual colours and traits."

"Now, if you are asking when you will become like Mia, Bella, and myself, that is out of your hands. That will or will not happen after the humans in this city have gotten to know who you are. If you remain good and honest kittens and grow into dependable and loving cats, there will always be the chance for you to become like us."

Mia sighed quietly and secretly passed her vote of thanks towards Valentina for her skill at solving all problems, even tricky questions such as those provided by Liz.

Goldie waited until there was a pause and tried to ask them a question, but there was no answer: "Where did we cats originate from as a species?"

Bella whooped with joy. This was an easy question, and one all cats asked at least once in their lives: "We cats, as a species, are believed to originate from the African wildcat (Felis Lybica). These wildcats were domesticated by ancient human civilisations thousands of years ago, leading to the development of various domestic cat breeds we know today."

Goldie was not going to let Bella off the hook that quickly: "OK then, pray. Do tell us how many such cats are in the world right now?"

Bella whooped again: "It is an estimate, but at the last censorship count way back in 2021, there were over a billion of us domestic cats worldwide!"

All four cats and two kittens screamed with laughter at Bella's answer. They knew it was not true, but it was fun to imagine censorship being completed worldwide to find out how many cats there officially were.

*****

As a troop, they had been travelling along, and although the figurines were delicate and in no way affected by the howling wind and the insistent deluge of rain. They couldn't say the same for the kittens and Blacky. It was evident they would need to rest soon.

Valentina estimated they would still have to travel ten more blocks to reach the Tree of Life. She saw a doorway with five giant concrete steps leading up to the entrance of the apartment block. "Let's rest on the upper step for ten minutes. This will allow Liz and Goldie a chance to recover from these diabolical elements."

All agreed, and within a short time, they were under the overhanging roof, offering them some welcomed respite. Both Liz and Goldie were asleep and purring like two locomotives.

Blacky, too, was showing signs of fatigue, but he had a nagging question he wished to have an answer to. "Why do humans always give their animals names?"

Valentina presumed Blacky was referring to his chosen name. "I suspect you were christened Blacky due to your predominant coloured fur. Names for pets are often chosen based on each cat's physical characteristics or attributes."

"So why was I not called Four White Soxs after my gorgeous-looking paws?"

Valentina paused and thought long and hard about the solution to this profound question. Then she smiled warmly toward Blacky. He, of course, melted.

"To be referred to as Four White Sox is a bit long for most humans to contemplate. It sounds as if you might have been raised by Native American tribes. And I do not believe there is any evidence of such an event as cats living in tepees. You would have had to wait until the European settlers arrived."

Blacky seemed to accept this possibility and without the definitive proof available. He resigned himself that it was indeed plausible that some Native Americans may well have coexisted with their cats in tepees. Maybe his bloodline one day could be traced back to the Sioux or Apache Indians.

*****

"Oh yes, Don Blacky, before I forget, the answer to your original question when we first set eyes on each other. It is, Yes. Maybe not in the same ways as humans do, but we can always show our affection through grooming, head butting or snuggling up to each other. I have been known to give the odd head-butt here and there, but I do believe in trust, companionship, and a good degree of security. "I am sure there is a certain lady out there waiting for your next move."

Valentina turned her rear to face the star-struck male, giggling to herself at the mischief she was creating.

Blacky delved deep into his memory of her, and then he realised the question Valentina was referring to. Now, he blushed like no other cat had ever done before in centuries. He tripped over nothing in particular and landed on the bottom step in a heap. This mishap, though, did not stop him from purring like never before.

The group spoke no more for a good twenty minutes. They either catnapped or stayed alert to the pending danger of flooded streets. Then, excess water began to appear in front of them. It was time to set off again to the safety of the Tree of Life.

Valentina knew the tree was within a couple of blocks. If they moved swiftly as a group, they should do it without any issues. She leaned into Bella and Mia, and without saying anything, each picked up and settled their assigned charge of nuclear energy onto their backs, and they left the sanctuary of the five steps.

*****

# 46: I am the third Meeting of the Minds and Yes, the city is in trouble

The first group to arrive for this crucial emergency meeting was Jorge Isaacs Ferrer, Maria, and her dog, who had no name. Both looked splendid as always, even in a vicious storm. Following closely behind was Efrain, wearing all the proper attire of his day to keep him as warm as possible.

It had been forty years since the last emergency, where statues with their larger-than-life presence had teamed up with the sculptures with their smaller frames and the lesser figurines of all sizes, but they still had equal importance as the other two. Adding to the experience of previous disasters, it was agreed that various creatures from the animal kingdom should also meet up at the Tree of Life location.

Next came Valentina, Bella, and Mia carrying two kittens and a black cat with a mighty impressive white chest and magnificent white socks on all four paws. Jorge reasoned that the figurines were already working as rescuers. He would trust their judgment to ensure none of their charges would be harmed tonight.

Maria and Efrain welcomed another cat figurine, the Gossipy cat. It turned out she was the designated messenger between the Rio Gato and Jorge. It had worked well in the past, and Jorge took a moment to get an update on the city river. The update still needed to come with good news.

The Gossipy cat sat back on her hind paws and began her report: "It seems that the city river has burst its banks. The nearby streets have already filled up with ramping waves. But fret not, Don Jorge, we have some good news: the majority of the inhabitants of the city appear to have been smart enough to heed the warnings on their televisions, in their newspapers, and with the hourly radio messages."

She paused for breath and continued almost immediately: "The humans are safe and sound for now. Many live in apartments and can easily go to their neighbours above them for safety. All the businesses closed earlier than normal, and sandbags are almost everywhere, occupying the spaces in doorways. The hospitals are filling reasonably well, and throughout the day, nearly all the patients have been moved to safer locations via the large elevators."

"I must admit the scene outside is quite surreal. It's like the city has transformed into a massive water plain. The streets have become rivers, and most of the houses look like little islands floating amidst the waves. I almost forgot why I was travelling to you. I nearly made the mistake of having a dip myself, but this curious cat knows better than to venture out into the flooding streets."

"Thank you, Dona Gossipy cat. I will relay all that you told me to the others as and when they are all here. I am expecting a good turnout tonight." Said Jorge with a great deal of pride, knowing how this magical community of history and splendour always shows its colours of bravery and fortitude when faced with extreme situations.

*****

The Solidarity crew and the military friends all appeared as if they were one complete group: ten strong and able-working individuals, one conquistador, one Venezuelan freedom fighter, and Colombian born Felipe Joaquin de Cayzedo y Cuero, the military man with the rank of Royal Lieutenant and politician, looking refined in his all-bronze appearance.

Maria was mesmerised and spellbound by the testosterone oozing from all, including the Solidarity females. "Good evening to you all. Already, I feel as if tonight, the city belongs to us, and it will survive intact."

The statues of Felipe Joaquin de Cayzedo y Cuero, Simon Bolivar, and Sebastián de Belalcázar stood and bowed alongside each other. Behind them and around them, the rain acted as their backdrop, pouring heavily, causing the pavement beneath them to flood.

Felipe spoke first while leaning on his walking stick: "Oh, my dear friends, it seems our city is facing quite the order with these river waves flooding the streets. We must act swiftly to ensure the safety of our dear city inhabitants."

With his raised sword, Simon Bolivar responded: "Indeed, Felipe. These barbarians are in desperate need of guidance and protection. Let us pool our wisdom and devise a plan to safeguard them."

While shaking his soaking wet gloved finger, Sebastian said: "Aye, aye. We cannot let this chaos consume our beloved city. But pray, Felipe, what genius plan do you have in mind?"

Felipe smirked as he knew his mind better than anyone else: "Well, my dear comrades, I propose that we turn our statue personas into superheroes! I shall become Felipe the Flood Fighter. Simon, you can be the Water Warrior and Sebastian, the Torrent Trouncer!"

Simon now felt the need to raise an eyebrow: "Superheroes, you say? Felipe, isn't that a bit too... whimsical?"

Sebastian now loved the emerging banter and failed in his efforts to hide his amusement from him: "Oh, Felipe, do elaborate on how you envision this magnificent transformation taking place."

Felipe, now grinning mischievously: "Hear me out, friends. We shall call upon the power of imagination. With a simple touch, people's imaginations bring us to life. We will be their quirky, yet brave, saviours!"

Simon, now equally finding it hard to contain his laughter, says, "Felipe,

I do appreciate your inventive spirit, but how exactly will we carry out these superhero feats?"

Felipe, never one to be beaten: "Ah, my dear Simon, have you forgotten the power of creativity? With swirls of our capes and a sprinkle of humour, we shall turn these floods into laughter! We will make the people forget their troubles while keeping their spirits high."

Sebastian, now chuckling: "Felipe, you truly are a beacon of whimsy amidst this flood of practicality. I must say, the idea has a certain charm."

Felipe immediately began bowing modestly: "Thank you, Señor Sebastián. With your endorsement, we shall commence Operation Aqua Amusement!"

\* \* \* \* \*

And so Felipe Joaquin de Cayzedo y Cuero, General Simón José Antonio de la Santísima Trinidad Bolívar Palacios Ponte y Blanco, and Sebastián de Belalcázar y Dávila Santillana agreed they should set out on their mission, bringing joy and laughter to the city's waterlogged streets.

Each firmly believed that if they used their eccentric powers to entertain and distract the city inhabitants, the worries of the floods would slowly fade away, replaced by a light-hearted spirit that would unite the barbarians in laughter.

"What about the older people in the homes for the elderly?"

\* \* \* \* \*

The trio of adventurers turned as if one and were now facing the magnificent statue of the Black Woman from Chontaduro. Again, all three moved as one and bowed lower than average to show their joint admiration and respect for such a fine-looking statue. She never told anyone her name, and so secretly, the three friends had christened her "Nellie" for no specific reason apart from giving her a funny-sounding name to match her larger-than-life personality.

Behind Nellie or as others spelt Nelly stood Jovita Feijoó, and on her left and right stood Abella Goldhammer Darkstone and Derekamus Stonebeard Stonforce. All the black stallions were to the left of Abella, and to Derekamus's right were the children and turtles.

If that was not enough, waiting in the wings to be introduced was a General Goose with a yellow-headed caracara on his shoulder and his squadron of airmen, including his loyal Sergeant Major. Next to them was a Policeman who had recently become a city hero. Archibaldo was holding hands with the most striking of females called Ximena.

Next to Archibaldo, holding his free hand, stood an older version of Archibaldo, who, it was clear, was related to him and was called Deissy. Not to be forgotten stood a human couple named Samuel and Sofia, who were holding hands in front of a considerable burgundy Kenworth Truck.

As if that was not enough, silently moving up behind the three military-minded friends and waiting to be introduced stood three locomotives—one massive one, one large one, and one most definitely to be considered—the smallest one!

Everyone and everything was covered in a fine sprinkling of gold dust, including Sebastian. He had at last found his El Dorado. Finally, flying around was the most impressive sight of dancing fireflies.

*****

Over the heads of all present, the storm of unprecedented intensity raged with fury, sending torrents of rain cascading down and piercing screams of thunder echoing overhead. The wind howled with such force that it seemed to shake the very foundations of buildings, threatening to tear them apart. But not where the rescue team now stood.

In the midst of this chaos, something magical unfolded. As lightning cracked across the darkened sky, a brilliant burst of golden glow radiated from the city's numerous statues, sculptures, figurines, animals, birds, friendly-looking barbarians, and two gnomes. It was as if they had been touched by a celestial hand, transforming them into masterpieces of shimmering art.

Everything, regardless of origin or style, became adorned in a delicate layer of gold dust, rendering them ethereal and breathtaking. The raindrops danced upon the golden surface, creating ripples of light as they fell, painting the scene with a mesmerising spectacle.

But the enchantment did not end with the rescuers. As if summoned, which they had by Abella, fireflies emerged from the darkness, their bioluminescent glow becoming stars that fluttered and weaved through the turbulent air.

She had foreseen the possibility that the city lights would turn off at some point, and the need for the fireflies and their ability to create light from their very tiny bodies would act as a very magical substitute for the upcoming rescue mission.

Their tiny bodies would happily emit soft, golden hues that would act perfectly, adding a touch of ethereal grace to the rescue ahead.

Like a celestial ballet, the fireflies weaved patterns of light around everyone and everything present, creating an enchanting symphony of gold and luminescence.

For that brief moment, the city's worst storm in over a century transcended the ordinary and became a scene of unparalleled beauty. It was a reminder to all present that even in the darkest and most tumultuous times, magic can emerge, transforming the ordinary into something truly extraordinary.

As the storm showed minute signs of subsiding, taking the golden dust and fireflies with it, the memory of that magical scene would forever be etched in the hearts of those who witnessed it, a symbol of hope and resilience amidst the forces of nature.

*****

It was some time before anyone spoke, and of course, it was proper, albeit surprising, that the Tree of Life would speak up: "Welcome all of you. What an incredible turnout you have made. I will ensure your future endeavours tonight will never be forgotten."

"I feel I may have a possible plan that should be acceptable to you all."

The Tree of Life paused, giving anyone the opportunity to object. None did.

"I recommend the following:

1. Nine members of the Solidarity crew are here tonight, and there are three trains numbered 64, 89, and 127. Let the leader split up his group into three and assign them to each train. You will find that the big locomotive with the number 64 on its front has ample carriages, and your passengers will be very comfortable indeed.

2. because of their vast numbers, the fireflies can organise themselves to ensure their lights protect all of you.

3. Three locomotives mean three military officers with the sole aim of staying in communication with each other. Oh yes, I recommend the stallions, the cats, the children, and the turtles, who can act as guides for each train. And of course, they can double their duties by providing entertainment for the older people as they may be a bit alarmed at seeing you all.

4. General Goose and your impressive-looking squadron, including the Yellow-headed caracara, should fly ahead of you. Each locomotive should pass on relevant and essential messages when required.

5. Jorge, Maria, Efrain, and the knowledgeable and indeed most acceptable heroine—the Lady of Chontaduro, who tonight wishes to be known by the beautiful name of "Nellie," should head out together to the neighbourhood La Flora, which is close, to ensure that all the older people who need rescuing are indeed rescued.

Nellie looked at the three military men and burst out laughing at their looks of surprise. She had always known.

Everyone and the Tree of Life also enjoyed seeing the three veterans having one over them by Nellie. It was a great moment for everyone present.

"Now I must turn my attention to you wonderful humans, who I must tell you have been selected by none other than our two gnomes. Over the short time

Derekamus and Abella have been here living with us all, each of you has shown them both friendship and kindness. You all bothered to stop and talk to them. Neither now feel loneliness. They are so deeply proud to know each of you.

For dramatic effect, the Tree of Life paused and looked into the eyes of all the humans.

"As a team of rescuers, I have saved the most important duties for you all. I want you to head out in Samuel's and Sofia's burgundy truck and a particular Willy Jeep that Gabriel García Marquez's has restored. He is not the famous Colombian writer you would have learned about in school, but he is our superhero for tonight's endeavours.

"Yes, this Gabriel is going to be equal in notoriety by becoming your chauffeur tonight in nothing but a flying suit. You have to agree with me. Man and machine look perfect together. The humans were in awe of the Willy Jeep in its new MG colours. Your destination is the Pheonix Air Museum."

"Er, where is that?" asked Ximena.

"It is next door to the city's International Airport. You will find it perfect for all your needs. The big large train knows it well so you will be able to find it easily. It has a cafe and a flight club behind, with ample hot food and delicious non-alcoholic cocktails for one and all."

"I can also tell you that the private club and the museum will be closed tomorrow due to the rain. So, beds and blankets will be made available by the museum duty manager, Norman. That being the case, we have decided all those fortunate to be rescued will each have a wonderful gift from the museum. All will be revealed in good time."

"So if you are all clear on what is about to happen and you are acquainted with your duties as a valuable rescue member, I suggest you all get going. Good luck to you all."

Everyone and everything moved as one.

Except two.

One taciturn emancipated figure, wearing only a denim skirt and carrying a sizeable formidable rock in his hand. With the happiest sister, Seraphina, in the world alongside him. Who at that very moment was fine-tuning her vocal cords silently.

*****

# 47: I am the Phoenix Air Museum, and it is me who is the safe alternative in a storm

If you're a fan of all things transportation, from aeroplanes to vintage vehicles, you'll find a unique haven in me. Nestled next to the Alfonso Bonilla Aragon International Airport, I've been a beacon for over 28 years, showcasing the fascinating world of civil aviation.

My facilities can easily accommodate up to 180 visitors, and I often do.

It all began with a beautiful couple who sadly have passed away and now, I suspect, fly around the globe via the clouds that they so loved in life.

The lady's name was Stella Lloreda, and her maverick civil pilot, engineer, and successful businessman husband was José Guillermo Pardo Borrero.

Together, they were and still are, as far as I am concerned, the heart and soul of my continuing presence.

I am not bragging when I say I am a magical and unique place for all generations to visit and enjoy.

I owe my existence to José and Stella's boundless passion and dedication. Their love for all things transportation, from aeroplanes to classic cars, is evident in every piece of their collection. They were true collectors, rescuing and preserving these treasures for future generations.

Nothing was allowed to go into oblivion.

In today's value, you could never be able to calculate the cost that never mattered to them. The return could never be calculated in monetary terms but in the overall deep satisfaction of seeing all the local population of families enjoying themselves together.

I did hear once a remark made by the strange-looking white-haired man with strong-looking legs to his equally beautiful wife: "I do believe this couple, José and Stella, have left a lasting legacy, and it was an honour meeting and having this Don Quixote hero as a guide and friend. Together, they had the ability and desire to make paper aeroplanes to soar above the skyline."

I totally agree with him. Over the twenty-eight years, I witnessed their unwavering tenacity, idealistic and romantic notions, with their equally vivid and imaginative minds.

Their enthusiasm, determination, chivalry, and honour were equally on display. José, in a different age, would effortlessly embody all the chivalrous ideals of a knight from any medieval romantic literature. Their joint moral compass always advocated and defended each antiquity that journeyed to my Museo Aereo Fenix doors.

*****

I wish they were still here as I have just received a heartfelt request from the "Tree of Life" to open the doors to many of the locally placed older people and their carers who are in mortal danger from floods in the city's northern areas.

Apparently, our old steam locomotive, number 64, was resting outside in our car park, and his son, number 89, a smaller image of him, was on display in a shopping centre called Chipichape. A tiny locomotive, number 127, sits crying for its elders outside the bus terminal.

The Tree of Life has reliably informed me to expect all three to be fully equipped, with older, vulnerable people arriving in the next hour or two.

I can also expect to see fireflies in the lead, in the formation of hundreds, accompanying a rare General Goose, his loyal Chief Warrant Officer, a squadron of 180 geese, and a rather ambitious yellow-haired caracara who apparently wants to migrate to the Pampas in Argentina, followed by a life-changing trip to Alaska. Don't we all!

Step into the minds of historical figures like Felipe Joaquin de Cayzedo y Cuero and General Simón Bolívar at our model display, a tribute to the Battle of Boyacá. We're not just a museum, we're a gateway to the past, preserving and showcasing the rich history of transportation.

For those who love the railway's past history, you will rejoice in seeing our impressive 1.87-scale model, which occupies an area of over 450 square meters, making it the third largest railway model in the world so far. We also enjoy the world of railways and continuously add more models in scales of 1.48 and 1.20.3 that run on our narrow gauge rail tracks.

For those who love cars, the Museo founders José and Stella did, too. In particular, they loved the Buicks from the 1930s onwards. At the last count, we should have at least six on display.

It has never ceased to amaze me how their love for this particular brand of classic vehicle never diminished. These two lived for their nostalgia and personal connections. Two of the models reminded them of their youth and the journeys they made to themselves.

I often listened to José describing the Buick's historical significance from the 1930s. For him, these were classics and needed to be looked upon as valuable artefacts that deserved to have full recognition and a deserved preservation. Their commitment to preserving these classics is truly admirable.

Our show-piece collection has to be aircraft, aviation engines, and even a number of flight suits dating from WW2. We even have some present-day suits to compare.

But our "Piece de resistance" has to be the upper floor and the vast space dedicated to the model world. It is a detailed "beyond one's mind" diorama of historical events, fictional scenes, and natural landscapes representing many specific moments and memorable settings. I always appreciate looking at this incredible display of box-like and realistic visual representations of as many subjects involving transportation as possible. Each can be used to educate, exhibit, and even assist those living in the model-making world.

Why not visit Norman and the team in our modelling workshop on the ground floor? Why would highlighting such a messy-looking room be a good idea? Please allow me to tell you.

Our vibrant and bustling modelling workshop lies in the heart of this air museum, nestled amidst the captivating exhibits and soaring aircraft. This enchanting space, akin to an artist's atelier, exudes an aura of creative energy and purpose.

As you step inside, your senses will be enveloped by a symphony of colours, textures, and scents. The air hums with the rhythmic purr of machines, the smell of paint and glue lingering in the air. Our workshop is a visual feast, with workbenches, each adorned with an array of tools, brushes, and paints in every hue imaginable.

The room is a living canvas adorned with shelves that grow under the weight of countless miniature aircraft, meticulously crafted with precision and passion. The floor is scattered with tiny fragments of creativity: spread P-51 Mustang wings, half-built Messerschmitt engines, and delicate propeller blades waiting to be attached.

Amidst the organized chaos, you'll find craftsmen and artisans such as Norman and the team meticulously shaping and refining their miniature masterpieces. Each dedicated modeller painstakingly brings their vision to life, whether recreating classical war birds, iconic jet fighters, or historic biplanes. Passion emanates from their skilled hands as they delicately apply layers of paint, constructing miniature worlds in minute detail.

Our workshop stands as the engine of inspiration, a sanctuary where imagination takes flight. Amidst the disarray lies an alluring harmony—a place where creation thrives, and dreams are given form. It's an outstanding sight, a testament to the dedication and artistry that transforms the simplest materials into extraordinary works of art.

We even have an exceptional set of surprises for the rescue team and all of the older people. I have been sworn to secrecy until the right moment presents itself.

Everyone is going to have an experience of a lifetime.

Coming to life and assisting with the transportation of all vulnerable older people from their care homes to a place of safety is indeed a joy to behold.

Yes, I, the Museo Aereo Fenix, have been chosen, and I am so honoured!

*****

## 48: *I am the Historical Account of Gracie's mammoth clean-up operation*

Hello, yes, I can finally give you my historical account of the massive clean-up effort made in the north of the city over the past week. There is so much to tell you, my children, and their Abuela Manuela. I am not quite sure where to begin.

I think I will start from when I last spoke to you three years ago, where I described the surprise introduction to the white-haired stranger and his half-terracotta, half-black baggy shorts and terracotta socks.

He had taken a fall earlier on the old, craggy road and suffered a deep cut to his hand that he showed no particular concern for. I must admit he was the first foreigner I had come across, and if my Tios living in London are surrounded by thousands of them, I am sure they are fine and well. They certainly sound it when I call them after church every Sunday.

It has been three long years, and I am still trying to reunite with my Tios. But sadly, so far, nothing has gone well with this venture. The first set of applications for us to migrate to London failed because I needed to earn more money to survive here in the city as a street cleaner.

Couple that with my poor understanding of English and Rita and Hernan's lack of knowledge of the foreign and most difficult language. They often argue with me. They were still trying to understand their native grammatical language and beginning to get their heads around English, and its rules were, as far as they were concerned, one step too far for them.

Fortunately, Abuela Manuela loved languages, and she was proficient in French, English, Italian, Portuguese, and Spanish. It was with her doggedness that Rita and Hernan, with all their moaning, started to understand English.

I am confident that, in time, they, too, will enjoy the world of learning languages. I certainly hope so.

As far as income was concerned, I kept my job as a street cleaner, not just any old cleaner. I volunteered for all duties and amassed a lot of experience and overtime hours. Not long before, my managers noticed that I was different and dependable in times of urgency and emergencies.

Now, three years later, I am the area manager covering the city's northern neighbourhoods, including La Flora, where my home is located. I have a team of over 100 cleaners, and the paperwork alone to manage them all effectively is daunting to keep on top of. But again, I have learned to prevail and take the grasp of every piece of paper required. There is talk of training me in computers, but I still need to do so.

So, anticipating the day I would need to sit at a keyboard, I bought a laptop that Hernan and Rita use nearly daily. When I am not so exhausted from the daily slog, I sit happily and watch them in their world online. I even have my own email address. I use it sparingly, but I am advancing in my grasp of technology. Watch out, Elon Musk and Bill Gates; I am coming to get you!

*****

That first day, we as a family were all at home and having lunch together. The storm over the city had prevented us from going out into the streets. The schools had closed for the foreseeable future, and Abuela Manuela was busy preparing the meal of Sopa de Ajiaco, a delicious creamy chicken and potato soup. This is followed by a sumptuous offering of beans, rice, plantains, a small salad, a mini arepa, fried yucca and chicharrónes, the children's favourite meat. Mine is chicken, and Abuela Manuela is pork.

The protein—and carbohydrate-enriched food was accompanied by a refreshing Jarra de Aquapanela, the children's favourite sugarcane drink.

Abuela Manuela prepared a "Tres Leches Cake" from her mother's recipe to conclude the sumptuous meal. This was her favourite, and whenever she prepared this cake style, her mind would revisit her youth and the splendour of backpacking around South America with her close friends.

Hernan paused to study his online history lesson for today and looked up to his Grandmother.

"Abuela Manuela, are you named after the famous Manuela Sáenz Plaza de Vergara y Aizpuru, who was the mistress and companion of Simón Bolívar."

Before Abuela Manuela could respond to the first question, a second arrived.

"Did you know that Manuela played a significant role in the South American independence movements of the 19th century?"

Hernan was on a roll. He had a third question while Abuela Manuela returned to the table with her and Rita's lunch.

"Are there statues celebrating this incredible and heroic woman in South America?"

Abuela Manuela sat and smiled warmly at her grandchildren. "Yes, to question one, I am named after this famous lady. My father and his father, together, decided on my name. My poor mother did not stand a chance. But that was a different time."

"For example, I had five brothers, all named after five generals who fought alongside Simon Bolivar in the Wars of Independence. They were Antonio, after Antonio José de Sucre. Paez, after José Antonio Paez. Francisco, after Francisco by Paula Santander José, after José Maria Córdoba. And finally, Manuel, after Manuel Piar."

"Thank heavens, I was the only female!" she said, and then she added, "Sadly, we lost both Antonio and Paez, the oldest brothers, during the Peruvian and Colombian War of 1932 to 1933. They were both only teenagers, and the thought of adventures drew them to the conflict over a territorial dispute involving the Leticia region of the Amazon."

"Both countries claimed sovereignty over the border area. The war lasted for several months, and it resulted in casualties on both sides, including my two brothers. It was eventually settled with the signing of the Salomon-Lozano Treaty by Colombian and Peruvian presidents in 1934 and witnessed by the then League of Nations, whom you young ones may know as the United Nations."

"Both sides had negotiated successfully, who had sovereignty, and who had the right of free navigation on the Amazon River. The Presidents also agreed to withdraw their military forces from the disputed area and established permanent markers to demarcate the new border. These same markers are still there today. Sadly, it is too late for my brothers."

Everyone made a sign of the cross to commemorate the passing of the two brave warriors. Then, a minute of silence followed, which was only broken when Abuela Manuela spoke next.

"Yes, to your second question, I learned many lessons from Manuela Sáenz's life. It was not long before I became a huge fan of this incredible and brave woman of her time."

"And a triple Yes to your last question on whether there are indeed statues in her honour in South America. I have been fortunate to visit three such statues. The first was in the Ecuadorian's Quito historic district. I was just a little older than you two and backpacking my way around South America. I discovered the statue of Manuela Sáenz in residence, and I sat for ages paying my tribute to her contributions to Ecuador's struggle for independence."

Abuela Manuela paused and returned to the kitchen area to bring back two more lunches for her and me. The children waited patiently, which was unusual for them to do normally. I was impressed. "When I got to Lima in Peru, I made certain I visited the Parque El Olivar in San Isidro. It is here the Peruvians have a monument of Manuela Sáenz, honouring her involvement in the liberation of Peru."

"There was a third one I managed to visit on many occasions, and indeed, when your mother was younger, I took her there. It is in our capital city, Bogotá. Manuela Sáenz de Vergara y Aizpuru is located in the Parque de Los Journalists, close to the historic district of La Candelaria. I suspect there are many more monuments and statues celebrating my namesake. Perhaps one day you can give me a list, and we will all go together to visit them. Now, eat your lunch before it "gets cold."

The home telephone range. "Who can that be?" Grace inquired as she left the table to answer it. She picked up the receiver and listened to the instructions from the Mayor's Office. Everyone was to report immediately to their places of work. Not only had the city river burst its banks, but the section of the mountain ridge overlooking La Flora suffered from a landslide full of water as if it were weeping uncontrollably.

Gracie raced upstairs to find the uniform she had not had to wear for nearly a year. Today, she will need to work alongside her colleagues. "Now listen, please look after each other and move what you can to the second floor. Light candles and take a couple of torches because, by evening time, there will be no electricity for the unforeseeable future. Take sandwiches and soda.

"Water is coming, and it will be strong and filthy. It will be a waste of time trying to stop it. Just get upstairs and stay safe and close. I will call you to ensure you are all okay."

She was gone. Abuela Manuela, Hernan, and Rita sprang together and rushed to do the things that Gracie had advised.

\*\*\*\*\*

Gracie is startled as she looks up at the pouring water. Goodness gracious me, what on earth is happening? This is not what I expected to see. The mountain ridge is gushing with excessive water and pouring down onto the streets below. This is going to wreak havoc on our cleaning efforts!

Slowly, Gracie turned to her left and observed, for the first time, the floodwater spreading towards her. She started to talk to herself: "That must be the water coming from the city river. The caller had said that the river banks had burst, and now we have the weeping flooding from the mountain ridge, too! This is a nightmare! We'll need to act quickly before the situation gets out of control."

Gracie began by taking out her mobile and calling her team via the WhatsApp Group app. "Team, listen up! We've got a major emergency on our hands. The mountain ridge above is causing excessive water flow, and the city river has burst its banks. We need to prioritise our efforts and act swiftly."

Before anyone from her team responds, Gracie thinks quickly while walking away from the safety of her home: "First, let's ensure the safety of our team. All of you get to higher ground and away from the flooding areas. We must ensure all of you are accounted for and safe."

Gracie then ordered Pedro, her second in command, to contact other relevant departments. "We will need the local authorities and emergency services to begin communicating with us. We need their help coordinating a response and managing the floodwaters effectively."

Gracie was now satisfied she had gathered her team and equipment. "Okay, team, it's all hands on deck. Grab the necessary cleaning equipment, but prioritise the removal of debris and obstacles that could further block or redirect the floodwaters. We must clear the streets and ensure the water can flow freely."

Before ending the group call, Gracie with determination said: "We have a tough job ahead of us, but we are trained for this. Pulling together, we'll overcome this challenge and restore normalcy to the streets. Let's get to work and ensure the safety and well-being of our community."

Within the next hour, the clean-up operation was underway. Many, if not all, of the localised roads and streets were submerged. Fire crews, up to their knees, with water and mud, had begun to help people stay safe. Buses had left the area earlier to avoid becoming trapped and destroyed by the torrents of water bearing down. So, anything slightly resembling a boat or canoe was commanded to rescue people and their pets.

Later, there were reports of over 1,000 lightning strikes across the city. How no one had been struck or died was declared a miracle. The operations of trying to take control took place all night with no rest for any of Gracie's team.

Throughout this time, Gracie was subject to rising water levels. Initially, she noticed the water level in the city viaduct system was proliferating, surpassing its usual boundaries. Within minutes, it reached alarming levels.

Everyone, including the rescue teams, had to deal with the rushing currents. Gracie observed the solid and fast currents flowing away from the river as she attempted to find new pathways as the water approached. The water's force was powerful, pushing objects and debris along with it.

The floodwater was as far as one could see. Gracie had to ensure that all the nearby streets, parks, and low-lying areas were within reach. As it expanded, it gradually submerged the surrounding surfaces and hungrily filled lower areas like basements and low-level car parks.

Gracie began to feel powerless as she witnessed the floodwater presenting an overwhelming sight before her very eyes.

Without thinking, it spread like a vast expansion, submerging cars, buildings, trees, and street signs.

The force of the floodwaters carried along various debris, such as fallen tree branches, trash, and all loose objects it encountered. One day, Gracie made a mental note describing the effects of the floating debris she spotted within the floodwater. Each adds to the chaotic scene before her.

Gracie knew she would never forget the swirling and churning water. Due to the rapid flow of water and obstacles in its path, the floodwater exhibited swirling and churning motions. Gracie noticed and feared the eddies in the water and saw with horror the debris being carried in a circular motion around her.

Then, there was the sound of the rushing water and the forceful movement of the flood. It was tough to talk to her team via her mobile above the mixture of crashing waves, splashing water, and the echoes of objects being swept away.

She had to keep everything in the back of her mind. She and her team had a job to do. She turned to Pedro to pass another command and froze when she heard something new and frightening behind her.

*****

Abuela Manuela stood on their second-storey balcony, first admiring the majestic beauty of the mountains even when it was raining. Little did she know that this serene scene would soon transform into a terrifying ordeal.

Suddenly, a deep rumble echoed through the air, followed by the ground trembling beneath Abuela Manuela's feet. Her eyes widened in disbelief as she looked up at the mountain ridge. A massive mudslide had been triggered, cascading down the steep slopes with an unstoppable force.

Time seemed to slow down. Abuela Manuela's heart raced. She reached out for Rita and Hernan's hands. The roaring sound grew louder, piercing through the peaceful atmosphere. The earth beneath them quivered as if in fear of the approaching calamity. Shades of earthy brown mixed with grey and black descended rapidly from the ridge, devouring everything in its path.

Abuela Manuela's initial shock transformed into a sense of urgency. She rushed with the children back inside their home, haphazardly gathering essential documents, treasured photographs, and anything she could find that held sentimental value. Panic gripped her as she thought of her loved ones, her neighbours, and the community she cherished.

From the window, they watched the torrent of mud and debris hurtling down the mountainside, caring towards the city on its path. The sheer force and weight of the mudslide pushed over trees, rocks, and anything that dared obstruct its powerful descent.

Each could hear Emergency sirens blaring in the distance as the neighbourhood was issued an immediate evacuation order. Fear and chaos spread throughout the city as people scrambled to find safety. Abuela Manuela and her grandchildren joined their neighbours in a frantic race to higher ground. Their every step carries the weight of uncertainty and impending disaster.

Looking back one last time, Abuela Manuela witnessed the terrifying sight of the muddied deluge engulfing the city's outskirts. The once-pristine streets became obscured under sludge layers, and homes were swept away as mere playthings.

As Abuela Manuela, Rita, and Hernan reached the designated evacuation site, she couldn't help but feel a mixture of relief and sorrow—relief for her escape from her but grief for the loss and devastation left in the wake of the relentless mudslide.

She knew that rebuilding the city and healing the scars left in their hearts would be a long and arduous journey, but together, if they survived, they would find the strength to overcome the disaster and rebuild their lives.

Rita cried out in total shock: "Look! Is that mum and a Nun with that awful-looking street man we periodically see now and then showering in the lake of the children and turtles on that massive steam locomotive?"

*****

# 49: *I am the Official Mayor of the city Report*

City of Cali Mayor's Office.                    Date: [Novembre 2020]
To: All the Members of the city Council
**Subject: Flooding and Mudslide Disaster Response.**

I am writing to provide an official report on the recent natural disasters in the city, specifically the catastrophic flooding along the city river and the monumental mudslide near the Barrio La Flora in the north. This report aims to summarise the emergency response efforts, highlight the achievements of our dedicated emergency services and clean-up teams, and outline the ongoing recovery and rehabilitation plans.

**1. Flooding Along the City River:**

On the first day, unprecedented rainfall hit our city, leading to severe flooding along the city river. The overflowing river breached its banks, causing significant damage to nearby areas. Our emergency services were immediately deployed to assist affected residents.

**Key achievements of our emergency response include:**

   **a. Swift evacuation:** Working in collaboration with law enforcement agencies, our emergency services initiated a prompt evacuation process to ensure the safety of the residents in flood-prone areas. Over 5000 individuals were evacuated to designated emergency shelters, preventing casualties.

   **b. Rescue operations:** The fire service team demonstrated tremendous courage and expertise in conducting rescue missions. They led numerous operations to save stranded residents and pets from swiftly moving floodwaters. Thanks to their relentless efforts, 1150 individuals and over 60 animals, from cats to horses, were rescued.

   **c. Provision of essential supplies:** Our assistance teams worked tirelessly to distribute essential supplies such as blankets, food, clean water, and hygiene kits to those impacted by the flooding. This ensured that the basic needs of the affected population were met until the situation stabilised.

**2. Monumental Mudslide near Barrio La Flora:**

Simultaneously, the city faced an unprecedented mudslide incident near the section of the mountain ridge overlooking Barrio La Flora. The emergency services immediately mitigated the situation and provided necessary aid. The achievements of our emergency services and clean-up teams include:

   **a. Search and rescue operations:** In collaboration with local volunteers, the fire service launched search and rescue operations to locate and rescue individuals trapped under the debris caused by the mudslide. Their swift response led to the successful rescue of many individuals from potentially life-threatening situations.

**b. Infrastructure restoration:** Our dedicated clean-up teams and public works department worked tirelessly to clear the debris, reopen access roads, and restore vital infrastructure in the affected area. Through their coordinated efforts, essential services were gradually over seven days, facilitating the safe return of displaced residents.

**3. Ongoing Recovery and Rehabilitation Plans:**

Although the immediate response to the flooding and mudslide disasters has been commendable, the city recognises that comprehensive recovery and rehabilitation efforts are required to ensure long-term stability. The following measures have been implemented:

**a. Damage assessment:** Experts have been deployed to assess and report to all the extent of damage caused by the disasters. Their findings will serve as a foundation for planning and prioritising the subsequent phases of recovery.

**b. Rehabilitation plans:** The city collaborates with state and federal agencies to develop comprehensive rehabilitation plans. These plans will focus on rebuilding damaged infrastructure, providing necessary financial assistance to affected residents, and implementing precautionary measures to mitigate future risks.

**c. Community outreach and counselling**: Recognising the emotional toll these disasters can have on individuals and families, our social services department is providing community outreach and counselling services to support the mental well-being of those affected.

**In conclusion**, the flooding and mudslide disasters that hit the city severely tested our emergency services, clean-up teams, and our community's resilience. However, their unwavering dedication and incredible teamwork saved countless lives, and recovery efforts are well underway. The city remains committed to ensuring the well-being and safety of our residents as we move forward in the recovery and rehabilitation process.

Thank you.

*Mayor signature*
The Mayor of the City.

\*\*\*\*\*

That same day, another letter was sent out from the Mayor's office. This time, it wanted answers to why no care home near the city river and in Barrio La Flora had reported no damage or loss of life. It read:

**Unexplained Phenomenon: The Mystery of the Barrio La Flora reported no damage to its community of Care Home Properties and no loss of life during the recent Natural Disasters.**

**1. Introduction:** Natural disasters can bring about widespread devastation, leading to property damage and loss of life. However, in an unusual turn of events, the care homes near the city river that burst its banks and the single-storey care homes in Barrio La Flora, near a mudslide-prone mountain ridge, miraculously remained undamaged.

This report wants all departments to investigate the mystery surrounding the lack of destruction and potential factors that contributed to protecting those vulnerable areas during the two latest natural disasters.

**2. Background:** Please describe the location and geography of the care homes near the river and the single-storey homes positioned below the mudslide from the mountain ridge. Provide any details regarding the frequency and severity of prior natural disasters in this Barrio, highlighting the contrast of the recent events.

**3. Analysis of the River Bursts:**

**a. Study the river's characteristics:** Assess the river's hydrological data, including primary factors such as water volume, velocity, and channel capacity. Analyse historical patterns of river behaviour during flooding events.

**b. Topographical factors:** Explore the possibility of natural barriers or changes in the river's course that could have altered the flow and thus prevented damage to the care homes.

**c. Human intervention:** Investigate whether any recent engineering projects or flood control measures that may have prevented excessive flooding downstream were undertaken upstream.

**4. Examination of the Mudslide:**

**a. Geological characteristics:** Analyse the mountain ridge's geological composition, including soil type, stability, and water permeability. Assess the propensity for further mudslides in the areas mentioned.

**b. Protective barriers:** Investigate the presence of natural or man-made barriers such as retaining walls or vegetative cover that may have shielded the single-storey homes from the mudslide.

**c. Timing:** Evaluate the time of the event and weather conditions leading up to the mudslide. Assess whether potential factors like dry weather, prior soil stability measures, or early warning systems contributed to the lack of damage.

## 5. Expert Opinions:

Reach out to geology, hydrology, and disaster management experts to obtain their insights into the mystery. Expert opinions can shed light on potential explanations, such as unique local features or meteorological conditions contributing to the avoidance of property damage and loss of life.

## 6. Community Engagement:

Interview the residents of the care homes and single-storey homes to gather first-hand accounts of their experiences during the disasters. Document their perceptions of the events and any protective measures they might have observed.

## 7. Conclusion:

Summarise the findings and present plausible explanations for the lack of damage to the care homes near the river and the single-storey homes near the mudslide-prone mountain ridge. Highlight the need for further investigation and emphasise the importance of incorporating these unique observations into future disaster management strategies.

## 8. Recommendations:

Suggest areas for further research, including comprehensive site surveys, data collection, and monitoring systems. Promote the implementation of early warning systems and the dissemination of best practices to replicate the success observed in the protection of these specific areas during recent natural disasters.

## 9. Mayor's Note:

Acknowledge the limitations of this report and encourage continuous exploration of this mystery to unravel its intricate details and implications for enhancing disaster preparedness and response strategies in similar regions.

## 10. References:

Cite all the relevant sources consulted during the report's preparation, ranging from geological studies and hydrological data to expert opinions and community interviews.

Thank you.

*Mayor signature*
The Mayor of the City.

*****

To date, there has been no record of any replies to this second except one pertaining to have come from the "Tree of Life" Offices. Wherever they may be.

From the Tree of Life Offices,
Calle 44 # 01-01
Edificio Árbol de La Vida,
Barrio La Flora,
Santiago de Cali,
Colombia,
760050,
Sur América.

Dear Lord Mayor or Your Worship (whichever you are happiest with.)

In response to your letter titled:
**Unexplained Phenomenon: The Mystery of the Barrio La Flora reported no damage to its community of Care Home Properties and no loss of Life during the recent Natural Disasters.**

To save you time and energy, this department thought it wise to reply and provide the names of all those present that particular night and most of the next day when the city river burst its banks and flooded the centre and a fair part of the northern barrio—La Flora.
At the same time, the said barrio also suffered a direct hit from the monumental mud-slide from the section of the Mountain ridge overlooking the same barrio. We can attest that the following list of statues, sculptures, figurines, objects, wildlife, Kimmel gnomes, and barbarians were present.
- 20 nurses on their nightshift deployed as Caregivers and 180 Older People, making up the community of Care Homes in the said barrio.
- Jorge Isaac Ferrer, Maria, Efrain, and a Dog with no name. ("El Paraiso.")
- Cristo Rey. (You only have to go outside, and you will see if he is at home.)
- General Simón José Antonio de la Santísima Trinidad Bolívar Palacios Ponte y Blanco & Palomo. (C/O Casa de Los Gobernadores.)
- Captain Sebastián de Belalcázar y Dávila Santillana (C/O Casa de Los Gobernadores.)
- Royal Lieutenant Felipe Joaquín de Cayzedo y Cuero. (Also. C/O Casa de Los Gobernadores.)

- Jovita Feijoó from Palmira. (She is now on display near the steps of San Antonio.)
- Nellie which she prefers to be called or Nelly which secretly she dislikes, The Chontaduro Lady. (Outside the DANN Hotel.)
- The Solidarity Crew. (You will find them at a large roundabout in Avenida 3.)
- Rio Gato and his harem of many beautiful Girlfriends. (Next to the city river.)
- Blacky, Liz, and Goldie. One black cat with an impressive white chest and four white-socked paws. Liz is all shades of silver, mixed with bronze, white and beige tints on her left side. You could say she is tricoloured, and Goldie, who started out looking like a tiger but recently has slowly turned into a mighty fine-looking lion.
- (All three felines are residing in a penthouse with a massive balcony in La Flora with a strange-looking white-haired man with strong-looking legs and a growing pot belly, with his beautiful looking Señora Cristirin, who is of the same age but looking 20 years younger.)
- General Goose (Address unknown, but you should try Alaska or the Pampas in Argentina.)
- One Particular migrating Yellow-headed Caracara (possibly with General Goose.)
- The community of Fire Flies in La Flora. (That's if you have time to get just one to slow down and concentrate solely on you. They are not called Lumina Vespera for nothing!)
- Sister Superior Josefina Ignacia De Mesa and the Sisterhood of Singing Nuns, including Seraphina, who was initially called Rosa. (All these sisters are now on a world tour starting in New York and have over fifty performances sold out at many of the world's famous venues.)
- The Gracie family includes Abuela Manuela, Rita, and Hernan. (Residents of La Flora.)
- Samuel and Sofia Perez are the owners of a Burgundy-coloured Kenworth Truck, Model 1993KW W900B. (Also, residents of La Flora.)
- Archibaldo Federico Alcatraz. (Police Officer and no longer considered a trainee or cadet, stationed in La Flora, still living with his Abuela Deissy.)
- Ximena Londono. (A drop-dead gorgeous beauty who once had a quad bike. (Residing in a Penthouse in El Penon and financed by her parents – Marlena Lopez Montenegro and Don Alejandro Londono y Nieto.)
- Derekamus Stonebeard Stronforce and Abella Goldhammer Darkstone (Two Gnomes from Old Germany now residing in a garden in La Flora.)

- A Stampede of Black Stallions (These equine beauties are located above a bank in Santa Mónica.)
- The Children and turtles are also residents of Santa Mónica. (But do not expect to get much sense out of them.)
- Gabriel García Marquez and a very posh-looking Willy Jeep. (Do not worry, this is not the famous Colombian Writer of magical realism – Gabriel José de la Concordia Garcia Marquez. This one is an Argentinian resident from Buenos Aires.)
- José Guillermo Pardo Borrero and Stella Lloreda. (The late founders of the Museo Aereo Fénix, who should be the next two to be immortalised in stone.)
- Three Locomotives numbered 64, 89, and 127. (They are residents of the Museo Aereo Fénix with Norman.)

Respectfully yours

Stalin.

## 50: I am the Fourth meeting of the Minds. Something magical happens for Simon

The rescue operation in Barrio La Flora began with three feline figurines from the city river, swimming through the flooded streets with a somewhat nervous black cat and two of the bravest of the brave kittens.

Valentina, Bella, and Mia discovered that the sprinkling of gold dust from Abella enabled them to negotiate the waves and carry their counterparts without Blacky, Goldie or Liz becoming anxious and frightened.

Within minutes, the group arrived at the main doors of the building. Blacky and Valentina assisted Liz and Goldie to negotiate the space below the door safely and to reach the foot of the 97 steps they would need to climb to reach the Penthouse.

Bella and Mia followed, and all regrouped to meet the next challenge of climbing the stairs with no street lights to guide them. Goldie decided to lighten the moment with a light-hearted and playful question: "Hey, Blacky, why don't you use magic powers to make all the birds in our neighbourhood come to us?"

Liz immediately jumped in with the fun, "Do you, Blacky, ever get mistaken for an undercover ninja cat in your sleek black fur?"

Blacky laughed and ignored them both as he had no answer to give. The feline figurines laughed with Black's discomfort and joined in with a question from them, "Do you ever get mistaken for a purr-fessional secret agent? Mia and I think you'd make a great meow-assassin!"

Not to be outwitted Blacky responded with the following as he raced up the first flight of stairs, "Oh, absolutely! Me, mistaken for a purr-fessional secret agent? It happens all the time! You see, my sleek black fur and my perfectly timed purring can be pretty deceptive. People tend to think I'm just a regular cat, but little do they know I possess the skills of a top-notch secret agent. I have mastered the art of stealth, effortlessly sneaking around corners without! making a sound.

My keen senses can detect the slightest movements and sounds, making me an expert in surveillance. And don't even get me started on my impeccable balance and agility—like a true feline secret agent! But being a purr-professional secret agent can be challenging. It's hard to keep my private identity intact when I only want to chase laser pointers and nap in warm sunbeams. I'm always ready to leap into action and save the day!

So, if you ever need a purr-fessional secret agent on your side, give me a meow, and I'll be there, ready to tackle any mission with my charm and stealthy prowess!" Now roaring with laughter, the group reached the foot of the second set of steps. Each had imagined they were purr-professional secret agents. This adventure was fun for all.

*****

Blacky knew he was on a roll and sidled up next to Goldie and Liz, "To answer your question, why don't you use magic powers to make all the birds in our neighbourhood come to us?

"Hey, Goldie, you sneaky little bird lover! It would be a hoot if I could just wave my paws and summon all the neighbourhood birds to our Penthouse hangout spot. But alas, even though I'm one cool cat, my magic powers are limited to paw-some virtual tasks. But fear not, my feathered friend! We can still charm the birds with our playful antics and bird-friendly treats. "

Valentina stopped and looked at Blacky with a new level of respect. "Blacky, one day, in the near future, you will become a famous cat indeed. I look forward to the day all the barbarians in this city will rejoice in your heroicness and wittiness this evening."

Now, the group has reached the top floor and is outside the door to the Penthouse. Surprisingly, it was still ajar. Liz, as usual, was the first to nudge the door further. All you could see was that the living area was quiet and empty. With any luck, the owners would have no idea of what had happened this very day to these beautiful kittens and the heroic surrogate "Uncle Blacky."

Valentina quickly scanned each room and was impressed with the living space for Blacky, Liz, and Goldie. She was left with a satisfactory impression that the owners were indeed good barbarians. "Okay, you three, I recommend a hearty meal and straight off to your beds and sleep the night away."

Valentina closed the front door without saying another word and rejoined Bella and Mia. Then, they rushed to regroup with the leading rescue team under the "Tree of Life."

All three were so purr-fectly pleased with their experience rescuing three beautiful creatures in the worst storm the city had ever endured in a century.

*****

Gracie, Rosa, soon-to-be Seraphina, and Stalin were bottomless in conversation as they looked at all the thick mud that appeared everywhere their eyes could see. Gracie asked, "How will we reach each of the care homes? We cannot move all this mud with the brushes and dustpans we have with us."

Both Stalin and Rosa remained silent; neither had any ideas about how to negotiate this disaster.

Gracie had still not gotten over the notion that she was now in the company of a locally famous singing sister and a street man who is never seen without his dangerous-looking rock. "Today just keeps on surprising me," she thought to herself.

Gracie had stumbled on the two unlikeliest friends who embraced each other as if they were old friends. "How do you two know each other?"

Stalin shook his shoulders nonchalantly, "Beats me. I have never seen this Sister in my life. She surprised me just now by exclaiming my name out loud, and then I was the recipient of the massive bear-like hug I could remember. Mind you, I don't remember any of the previous ones."

Rosa laughed and related the incident on the mountain ridge three years before the earthquake had struck. Gracie learned about a heroic truck driver who had sadly died in his first few months of retirement. She also learned about a quad bike and its beautiful rider whose face was disfigured by an escaping kite.

"Wow! When this is over, you two must sit down with me and my family and tell the whole story!" Demanded Gracie, who could only stop and stare, waiting for one of them to say they were only joking.

But no, she could clearly see by the innocence of Rosa and the grumpiness of the street man, whom she had seen often, if not at least weekly, on her rounds of checking the streets were indeed being kept clean by her working teams. It was obvious to Gracie that Stalin, she had never known his name before. She assumed it could be something like Oscar, Manuel, or Alberto, but Stalin? Who made that decision?

Then, Gracie found herself staring at her two children and her Abuela Manuela standing on the other side of the street, who were all agog at the sight of Gracie and her two new comrades, a Nun and a street man. She could see their equally puzzled looks and burst out laughing at the absurdity of standing with Stalin and Rosa.

Rita and Hernan dragged their Abuela across to meet their mother and could not wait to meet Stalin. Gracie held up her hands, foreseeing what would happen next, "Wait, all questions will have to wait until this storm is over. We need to get to safety and find as many older people in their care homes as possible."

\*\*\*\*\*

Now, a group of six, with the dangers of mud, floods, and continuous rainfall to consider, the adults, except Stalin's thoughts, turned to the need for some form of transportation. Walking was out of the question. But how? Then, they could see moving lights heading towards them in the distance. The lights turned into eight sets of headlights.

\*\*\*\*\*

As I, Stalin, stood there, my eyes widened in astonishment, and a sense of pure joy washed over me. Before I stood a sight that seemed straight out of a bygone era, a mesmerising flotilla of beauty. In the centre, proudly exhibiting its restored glory, was a Willy Jeep adorned in the iconic MG colours.

The vibrant hues of Tartan Red, Brookland's Green, and Old English White enhanced the sleek curves and timeless design of the Willy Jeep, instantly transporting me to a world of vintage elegance. The impeccable restoration work showcased the Jeep's ruggedness and resilience, the passage of time only serving to enhance its magnificence. How could I have forgotten, or better still, how can I remember seeing this beauty in a bygone memory?

But the magic did not end for me there. Behind the Willy Jeep, defying all expectations, sat a coffee machine cleverly mounted in its rear. It added, for me, an unexpected touch of modern convenience yet seamlessly fit into the overall vintage aesthetic. The aroma of freshly brewed black coffee mingled with the intoxicating nostalgia in the air. Thus, for me, creating an enchanting and invigorating atmosphere.

As my eyes wandered beyond the Willy Jeep, I saw a sight that would leave anyone awe-inspired: seven stunning Buick vintage cars from the 1930s, each a distinct masterpiece.

Their magnificent bodies, adorned with various shades of pastel blues, vibrant reds, and classy beige, stood in perfect harmony with the surroundings, creating a kaleidoscope of colour and history.

The soft sunlight caressed the polished curves of these vintage beauties, illuminating their elegant grilles, sweeping fenders, and eye-catching details.

Their presence was not merely captivating but also evoked a sense of reverence for the craftsmanship and artistry of the past.

The world seemed to slow as I stood among this flotilla of automotive marvels. Time appeared to stand still, allowing me to fully appreciate the extraordinary combination of old-world magnificence and contemporary ingenuity. It was a rare blending of eras, a collision of classic marvels and modern innovations that created a truly magical experience.

At that moment, I realised that the beauty of this flotilla transcended the boundaries of time. It was a testament to the enduring allure of vintage automobiles, showing their timeless charm and reminding me of the power of nostalgia. The sight before me was not merely a collection of machines; it was an enchanting journey through my history, leaving me a lasting impression on having the privilege of witnessing it and hopefully remembering it.

As the leading Willy Jeep pulled up alongside me, I noticed the mud and flood water had receded away, leaving a pool of normal-looking tarmac in view. I checked as the other seven bricks arrived, and all had the same effect on the water and mud. How strange!

The Jeep driver disembarked wearing a vintage USA flying suit and deep furry flying boots. "Hiya, my name is Gabriel Garcia Marquez, but alas, it's not the famous Colombian word smith you know with the longer name. I am Argentinian and from Buenas Aires."

He turned to the seven other drivers, "Let me introduce you to José Guillermo Pardo Borrero and Stella Lloreda. These two lovely people are the founders and collectors of everything you will discover at our next destination, the Museo Aereo Fenix near the city airport."

Everyone agreed, and Stalin muttered to himself, but he was overheard by all: "What the heck is a Museo Aereo Fenix all about?"

Gabriel continued to enlighten him. "these two are very old friends of mine, and José is a private pilot like me. In fact, we have among us pilots over 80 years of experience in flying, give or take a year or two. With José and Stella, I would also like to introduce a very talented modeller you will see later. The genius, ladies and gentlemen, is none other than Norman."

Norman, slightly embarrassed, bowed to everyone and was pleased with the introduction he had not expected.

With that, Gabriel took centre stage once again, "The museum also owns all these beautiful motors from a bygone era. But wait, let José enlighten you more."

At the same time, Gabriel moved to the side, and José advanced to the still completely perplexed street man and the others.

*****

"Good evening; it is indeed a pleasure to meet you fine people on such an awful night. But tonight, you all, including these Buicks and this handsome-looking Willy Jeep from the 1940s, are going to save many lives. Please allow me to introduce you to my wonderful wife, Stella, who I am sure will rejoice in telling you what is about to happen tonight."

Stella took Jose's hand, her warmth radiating from every fibre of her. She began to speak, "As the owners of the local Phoenix Air Museum and a pair of passionate Buick enthusiasts, we are dedicated to preserving the legacy and history of Buick automobiles. We understand the importance of community and are deeply moved by the human connection these vehicles have fostered.

Tonight, amid this dreadful storm, we are organising a fleet of taxis to safely transport many older persons from their care homes to our museum's sanctuary. We want to ensure their well-being and provide a haven from the inclement weather.

Our museum will serve as a place of warmth, comfort, and companionship for those seeking refuge. and are determined to make their journey as smooth and comfortable as possible. We have ensured that each Buick is equipped with necessary amenities such as blankets, hot beverages, and gentle music to create a relaxing and enjoyable experience. Safety is our utmost priority, and our drivers have the necessary skills to navigate challenging road conditions.

Let me introduce you to Don Alejandro Londono and Julieta Marlena, and the soon-to-be-married Ximena, one heroic Policeman called Archibaldo Federico Alcatraz. "Another memory had smacked right into Stalin's face!"

"I know you! The last time I saw you, you were sleeping with a stack of dangerous Cannonballs from those weird-looking trees in the park." The young Policeman held out his right hand and reached for Stalin's hand; he grasped it in both of his hands and held on. "Ah, you are the one to whom I own my life. I must shake your hand, sir, and say in front of all here present. Thank you for saving my life."

After seeing the two men enjoying being reunited once more, Stella returned to the front and continued with the details of the upcoming rescue mission. "Once our guests arrive at the museum, they will be welcomed by the nostalgic and enchanting atmosphere of our collection of Buicks. Our staff, which will include all of you fine people and a few others you still need to meet, will be on hand to offer assistance, engaging conversations, and a friendly presence. Through this experience, we can provide a temporary respite from the storm and instill a sense of joy and comfort in the hearts of our visitors."

"Together with this truly unique community, we will weather this storm and demonstrate the strength of unity and compassion. Our local transportation museum, home to the seven Buicks, is more than just a collection of automobiles;

it is a place of gathering, preservation, and love for the Buick legacy."

Gabriel moved to the centre of both groups and spoke to all, "Now it is time for each of you here with Stalin to split up and join each of us drivers. Can I suggest Stalin go with Archibaldo, as you both have some catching up to do? Gracie, you join Stella as you probably know more of the locations of each care home; Rosa, you join Ximena and Julieta Marlena, who I have just learned, prefers to be known publicly as Marlena. I also heard earlier, you two have an experience you may wish to revisit; children, you can join José and Don Alejandro.

Remember, you, Norman, if you are okay with waiting five minutes only, your passengers will be Jorge Issacs Ferrer, Maria, Efrain, and their dog with no name. Could I also ask you to catch up with myself and José as soon as you can, and we will make sure we will all arrive as a team.

Oh yes, I nearly forgot. We have to make time to pick up people I don't know. Don Alejandro, you will have Derekamus with you, and Stella, you will have his wife named Abella. Please do not worry; I have also been informed that these two take up very little space. Finally, I have to meet two ladies, Nellie and Jovita.

*****

The overwhelming response from everyone present can only be described as hysterical. Stalin was on the floor, bent over and crying with laughter. Stella and Gracie looked at the Willy Jeep. Both agreed this was a sight everyone with a smartphone should have, and newspapers would pay a fortune for it. Gabriel, who had sensed a trick was being played on him, now knew he would love the joke. His ignition key was in and turning to start the engine long before anyone else had time to react.

*****

Elsewhere in La Flora, work was being done to ensure all three of the locomotives were ready and fit for purpose. They knew soon the Willy Jeep and the attractive-looking Buicks would arrive with as many of the older people in their care homes to be transferred to the awaiting locomotives as possible. Three members of the Solidarity crew manned each one.

Their job was to keep the boilers at maximum output with coal. Where the coal came from was a mystery. Only Abella and Derekamus, a particular truck driver and his wife, knew, and both Samuel and Sofia were still in shock when, one minute, they were shaking their heads at where they were going to find coal in the storm. Suddenly, a mountain of it was sitting in a breaker yard, just waiting to be shovelled up into their burgundy Kenworth 1993 KW.

The coal was transferred to each locomotive's coal tender, which sat behind each engine. The designated Solidarity crews did not waste time shovelling the coal into the locomotive's coal bunkers. As the coal began to burn, it immediately released heat, which, in turn, boiled up the water in the boilers. The magical sight of steam appearing from each chimney brought excitement and joy to everyone.

As each steam locomotive lined up with the largest one first, the slightly smaller one from Chipichapie was next, and a spirited little one was brought up the rear. Felipe had bagged the grand locomotive over Sebastian, who went for the middle one, and Simon was given the tiny locomotive.

"So pray, tell me the reason why I have been given the little locomotive. Surely, I warrant the largest one due to my overall superior place in South American history."

"Felipe and Sebastian conferred and, after a brief moment, turned to face the Liberator and together voiced ", Size Señor. Purely size. Both of us are greater in statue size than your good self." The budding debate was cut short by the sight of thousands of fireflies swooping down towards the three locomotives and positioning themselves in two parallel lines from where the rail track could not be seen in the darkness.

Suddenly, one could see way ahead, galvanising a new flurry of renewed activity. A squadron of 180 migrating geese appeared overhead in no time, with its General and Sergeant Major in the lead. Everyone below stopped and stared in amazement, seeing one solitary Yellow-headed caracara between the General and his NCO! The squadron of geese broke up into two ranks on either side of the lights created by the fireflies. it only required a large number of passengers, and the journey to safety could begin.

*****

It was agreed that the best place for the fleet of Buicks and the Willy Jeep to meet up with the locomotives was on the outskirts of the city; there, all the passengers would board the three locomotives and assist with the needs of all the older people.

What no one knew was that Derekamus and Abella had come up with a surprise plan for all. As each older person boarded the carriages, a tiny amount of gold dust was sprinkled quietly so as to cause no concerns to them. At this point, no one knew what was coming soon.

When Nellie completed a head count, everyone was delighted to learn they had rescued 180 somewhat frightened and drowsy souls from their caring homes. For just short of 20 nurses were available to accompany and provide medication that was scheduled to be taken throughout the coming evening and night.

As everyone settled for the outbound journey, the leading locomotive with the number 64 on its nose tooted its horn, and its massive wheels began to roll forward in unison. At this very point, all the older people suddenly began to feel excited by the fact they were all passengers on a train journey. Where too? They did not know; it didn't matter. It was the sheer enjoyment of doing something they had not done for over twenty years or more. For the majority of them, this experience was their first ever.

The only obstacle that had to be removed was that the rail tracks had yet to be serviced or repaired in the same twenty years. Derekamus and Abella, with their endless supply of magic gold dust, soon devised a solution by replacing all the rail tracks so that all three locomotives could carry their passengers in comfort and style.

*****

As the sun dipped below the horizon, it cast a soft, golden glow over the vast expanse of the countryside. The three majestic locomotives chugged along the tracks.

Bound by steel and steam, they cut through the darkness with unwavering determination. Excited passengers aboard, eagerly awaiting their unknown destination, were unaware of the magical spectacle about to unfold.

In the distance, a symphony of twitters and hums began to crescendo. As the locomotives drew closer to a dense forest, the air became filled with anticipation. And then, as if on cue, the night sky suddenly filled with a thousand or more fireflies, twinkling like stars adorning a black velvet cloak.

These tiny luminescent creatures gracefully joined the locomotives on their journey. They danced and weaved around the chugging machines, leaving trails of magical light that mesmerised the passengers. The fireflies' rhythmic flickering synchronised with the locomotives' rhythmic beats as if they had become celestial partners in a grand cosmic performance.

Everyone now had their eyes wide open with sheer wonder. They couldn't tear their gaze away from the ethereal enchantment unfolding before them. The fireflies painted the night with various vibrant hues, like a painter crafting a masterpiece with each flicker. Their lights transformed into rainbows, cascading red, blue, green, and gold beams, creating ever-changing visions that mirrored the witness's deepest desires and wildest dreams.

As the locomotives roared on with unstoppable might, the fireflies seemed to sense their urgency and matched their pace, their lights blurring into streaks as they darted alongside the trains. The passengers, generally consumed by thoughts of their passing years, found solace in the ephemeral magic surrounding them, forgetting their worries and embracing the surreal wonder of the moment.

Rita and Hernan laughed joyfully as fireflies landed on their fingertips, their tiny bodies illuminating their delighted faces. Jorge, Maria, and Efrain whispered in awe, connecting their aspirations to the whimsical displays that flashed before their eyes. The boundaries of reality seemed to blur, transporting everyone into a world where dreams danced with reality.

The air was filled with a chorus of gasps and applause as the fireflies performed their final act of enchantment. They formed a magnificent light tunnel, leading the locomotives towards the end of their journey. As the locomotives began to slow down their speed, the fireflies bid farewell, each one flickering a teardrop of light as a symbol of their departure.

The older people and their accompanying caregivers, with their hearts a little lighter, lifted their spirits. As they watched, the fiery trail left by the fireflies would forever be etched in their memories, a testament to the ephemeral beauty that exists in the world if one dares to look up and embrace the extraordinary.

*****

As the trains pulled into the final destination, the Solidarity crew began to relax, knowing their work for this evening was over. Sebastian, Felipe, and Simon went among them, hugging and shaking all their hands, giving as much praise as possible. The Solidarity Leader, for once, was relaxed and enjoying his team's heroic endeavour to get the job done. He was even more elated when he discovered there was a large box of beers waiting behind the museum's reception desk. "Time for all of us to clean up and open those bottles to quench our thirst." He beamed to everyone.

Then he stopped in his tracks. What he saw next would stay with him and his crew forever...

*****

All the carriage doors seemed to open together. As they did, what should have been older and frail-looking people were replaced by smartly adorned men and beautifully dressed women!

The bewildered Solidarity crew Leader asked, "Who are these people? Where are the older people who were collected from their care homes? Now, everyone from the rescue team advanced slowly so as not to harm anyone at the moment. The only person to say anything was José while holding Stella up close; tonight, you are welcome to our establishment, known as the Museo Aereo Fenix."

"Tonight and tomorrow morning, each of you will dance, sing, eat, and drink whatever takes your fancy. You can forget your daily medicine, you can forget your sleep, and you can forget your problems. We have laid everything for you to see what we have created over the past 28 years."

José could feel himself choking up at the unparalleled amount of emotion he was feeling. "You will not need any money; leave your purses and wallets in your pockets."

Stella stepped in, seeing her husband struggling to hold his tears of sheer pride. "For all those who wish to have a guided tour of our home, please see Norman and the team of modellers. For ladies who wish to learn of the heroism of female fliers past and present, please settle down here in our modest café and check out the wall-to-wall presentation of lady pilots from the pioneering days of aviation to the present, also, for those who love the world transportation and specifically trains, motorcycles, and aviation.

Feel free to explore and hop into any of the seats. you find. We hope you all have the time of your lives here tonight. To start the evening off, how about some rousing music? Norman, I feel a 633 Squadron anthem is in order!

*****

Suddenly, the entire museum was filled with a highly dynamic and exhilarating piece of music composed by Ron Goodwin for a 1964 movie, "633 Squadron." The anthem began with a rousing fanfare introduced by powerful brass instruments, immediately grabbing everyone's attention. The main melody, carried by soaring strings and supported by intense percussion, further amplified the excitement, including Derekamus. He had never heard an anthem so captivating in its skilful use of orchestral instrumentation and arrangement. I have marvelled at how the composer masterfully weaved various elements, incorporating sweeping strings, bold brass, and thunderous drums. The contrast between the different sections, from soft and delicate moments to bold and intense crescendos, creates a rollercoaster of emotions within him.

He was in love with the seamless blend of traditional military band elements with a more cinematic and symphonic approach. This fusion of styles added depth and richness to the composition, which evoked a sense of grandeur and heroism that had Derekamus wishing for more.

*****

Good evening. I hope you are all having a wonderful time. I know I am probably the only air museum in the world that can say how proud it is to witness the young souls displaying their vibrancy and youthfulness in these older people's bodies, enjoying themselves as if they were in their early twenties again.

I witnessed old age gracefully slipping away from all below me, including José and Stella; a remarkable transformation occurred, breathing new life into these individuals. Wrinkles faded, hair regained lustre, and energy radiated from their revitalised bodies. The air was filled with an infectious excitement, as anticipation for what lay ahead.

As I observe this spectacle, the scene unfolds before my eyes—all the gentlemen have donned elegant evening wear, matching the grace and refinement of their female counterparts. The ladies, adorned in exquisite evening gowns, glide across my recently polished dance floor, their every movement exuding grace, poise, and the sheer joy of newfound youth.

My bricks and mortar can sense the atmosphere, which is charged with magical energy. The space hums with the melodies of nostalgic tunes, blending with the laughter and cheerful conversations of the transformed souls. My resplendent ballroom is enveloped in a radiant ambience as if time has paused to witness this extraordinary celebration.

I witnessed each couple moving in effortless harmony, their dance steps revealing an unspoken connection, the echoes of their youthful hearts beating in unison. I could see clearly that my establishment had transformed into a celebration of life and love, and the cherished moments that age had once taken away, which are now reclaimed and cherished with every passing second.

At this moment, I can truly understand the beauty of the human spirit, its resilience, and its capacity to find joy and liberation in the face of transformation. Every twirl, every elegant gesture, symbolises freedom from the constraints of time and age, a powerful testament to the indomitable spirit that lives within you all.

As the night unfolded, the older people in their youthful forms danced like there would be no tomorrow. They revealed in this extraordinary moment, weaving intricate patterns of joy and jubilation throughout my hallowed halls of the Air Museum.

And so, here I stand, a witness to this remarkable occasion. The Air Museum, now transformed into a breathtaking ballroom of grace and elegance, pays homage to the resplendent beauty of life. The memory of this magical evening will forever be etched in the corridors of history, a testament to the power of transformation and the beauty of capturing stolen moments from the grasp of time.

*****

Mind you, the one that surprised me the most was the street man with a rock in his hand and wearing only a denim skirt on arrival. Three military Officers manhandled him into a toilet cubicle, and within 15 minutes, they escorted a handsome man. But sadly, he was not good at the waltz and even worse at the Paso Doble.

And believe me, I was more surprised than anyone present that the ladies were queuing up to dance with him. I saw a rather tall 12-foot female, a larger-than-life Chontaduro lady, and a drunken bunch of half-dressed Amazonian-looking females that generally are seen on a large roundabout in the north of the city squabbling on who was going to be next.

*****

A klaxon blared out as if warning of a pending air raid. Everyone stopped to see what was going to happen. José waited until everyone was looking in his direction. As soon as he was sure, he began, "Ladies, Gentlemen, and the heroes of the night, everyone from the Emergency Rescue team."

Before he could proceed, he had to pause to the cacophony of hand clapping by the females and foot stomping approval from the males. I could swear I heard a dog who had no name barking his approval of him, too.

"Now it is time for dinner. We wish to invite you all to head through those huge doors at the back, which will lead you to the dining area for tonight's feast of roast turkey and all the trimmings you would expect if it were Christmas. "

"Even more hooting and foot stomping ensued. "There will be lots of beer for the boys and glasses of white wine for all you ladies. After the meal, there will be an open bar with no cash machine or debit card reader. So, enjoy partaking in a brandy or two or whatever else takes your fancy." The following uproar must have been felt in the nearby international Airport, as it was so loud.

*****

Hi, it is me, Stalin. Before I lose my memory, I decided to describe the evening meal we all had wholeheartedly. Let me set the scene for you. reminiscent of their vibrant twenties. The air is filled with anticipation and nostalgia as they are gathered to celebrate their lives and indulge in a traditional feast centred around magnificent Roast Turkey. At the centre of the banquet, twenty beautifully roasted turkeys take pride of place. Each is complete with a golden, crispy skin and succulent, juicy meat. Each turkey is a centrepiece that exudes warmth and comfort. As the older people reminisce about their younger years, the savoury aroma of the roasted birds fills the room, evoking memories of family gatherings and sharing moments.

The banquet served an array of trimmings synonymous with a typical festive season to accompany the roast turkeys. First and foremost, generous portions of stuffing, a harmonious blend of breadcrumbs, herbs, and succulent meats, perfectly complemented the main dish.

Served alongside the turkeys, rich and velvety gravy is deep in. The ladles are only needed to pour the gravy generously over the sliced meat. The gravy's smooth texture and savoury taste enhance the entire dining experience, adding an extra layer of indulgence to each bite.

Gabriel informed me that every banquet would include an assortment of seasonal vegetables. Massive plates were adorned with piles of buttered Brussels sprouts, caramelised roast potatoes, and fluffy mashed potatoes. These colourful accompaniments brought vibrancy to the banquet table, providing a balanced and wholesome dining experience.

Yes, that may be the truth regarding the potatoes, but forget those heathen-smelling Brussels! Suffice to say, Gabriel ate mine for me. Well, he is an Argentinian!

I must also mention a medley of roasted root vegetables gently caramelised with herbs and spices, adding depth and earthy flavours to the meal. Carrots, parsnips, and turnips reflected the season's vibrant colours and created a sense of abundance amidst the harmonious atmosphere. Gabriel never got a look at these parsnips; they were out of this world. I loved them and could have eaten a table full of them.

As the banquet progressed and all our guests continued savouring our meal, I was introduced to cranberry sauce. The tanginess and sweetness of this vibrant seasoning brought a pleasant contrast to the savoury meat, cutting through the richness of the roast turkey with its bright flavours.

To top off this grand feast, a selection of decadent desserts was passed around for all of us older people to enjoy. I tried Traditional Christmas pudding, studded with plump dried fruits and doused in luxurious brandy butter for the first time. With their buttery pastry and spiced fruit fillings, I could not face the Mince pies, so I bagged up half a dozen and hid them somewhere I am bound to forget where.

The banquet served not just as a celebration of the older people's spirit and remarkable transformation. It also offered them a chance to relive their vibrant twenties while enjoying a heartwarming meal filled with cherished tastes and aromas. As the banquet drew to a close, I can confirm that contentment filled the air as each guest departed with a smile. Everyone was now ready to create new memories and carry forward the joy of this unique occasion.

I may do, too; it will all depend on how many brandies I can consume before falling asleep and waking up again with no memory. I want to remember my life, both good and bad.

"Barman, a double brandy, please, in fact, make that two! I have just spotted a fellow police officer who has decided to give up his freedom for a female. I need to educate him as soon as possible!"

*****

An hour has passed, and I have witnessed pure enjoyment from all present in my museum. I could never have imagined seeing so much friendship between more barbarians than I have ever seen before. I cannot stress enough how much pleasure I have experienced tonight. And the surprises just get coming. Right now, I can see the monument of Cristo Rey, which resembles a scaled-down version of the famous Brazilian memorial in Rio de Janeiro, walking towards my doors. I hope this towering Christ statue can lower itself enough to enter the foyer.

I need not have worried. Well, he does represent Christ, and up close, he does look perfect for his age. Only this past October did this 26-meter-tall statue reach its 70th birthday. So yes, he should have been invited.

I can see Jorge, Maria, and Efrain, with the dog with no name, walking towards Cristo Rey. The dog must also know who this formidable figure is, as you can clearly see his tail wagging like never before.

In a remarkable turn of events, the majestic monument of Cristo Rey decided to make a surprise visit to the Phoenix Air Museum. As the evening had begun to settle over the city, the headline-grabbing arrival of Cristo Rey at this establishment took everyone by surprise. The towering figure emerged from the skyline, bathed in a golden glow that seemed to pierce through the lingering storm clouds. A hush fell over the museum grounds as the community of older persons with their nurses and rescue team members gazed up in wonder at the magnificent sight before them.

This unexpected encounter left everyone in awe as the powerful symbol of faith and protection journeyed to express gratitude to the brave rescue teams who had played a critical role in saving the lives of older people in the northern part of the city who faced an immediate threat to their safety during the series of unprecedented storms this past week.

Silence enveloped the scene as Cristo Rey, with a voice as comforting as a gentle breeze, addressed the crowd with words I will never forget;

"During this harrowing ordeal, which I understand has not decided to abate just yet, a group of you decided to create a heroic rescue team, comprising all the members of the Meeting of the Minds, such as the many statues, sculptures, figurines, birds, and fireflies, and including volunteers such as two well-intended gnomes and a special selection of residents, who joined together and took swift action."

Like a faithful professional preacher of the truth, Cristo Rey paused and allowed himself to focus on all who had moved forward to listen to him. "With your unwavering determination and unwavering dedication, you fearless individuals navigated treacherous waters and menacing mud and found yourselves battered by gusts of wind in a race against time to reach the older people stranded in their care homes."

"I can confirm the news of your relentless efforts has spread like wildfire, capturing the attention of all those in heaven itself. Everyone is moved by the selflessness and bravery displayed by this rescue team. When I, Cristo Rey, became aware, I immediately decided to make an extraordinary pilgrimage to this Museo de Fenix to acknowledge your remarkable accomplishment personally."

"Could I please ask the rescue team, namely, Stalin, Gracie, Ximena, Alejandro, Marlena, Rosa, Archibaldo, Gabriel, Rita, Hernan, and Abuela Manuela, you must by now be battling exhaustion from your efforts, gather in group in front of me?"

"Now, please, could all of the Meeting of Minds, statues and figurines stand behind Stalin and his friends? From Simon Bolivar to the Solidarity crew."

"Next, could all, including you wonderful Kimmel gnomes, the many cats, children, yellow-headed caracara, geese, and turtles, come to the front and position yourselves so as not to hide the adults behind you? I wish to ensure I am able to see all of you perfectly this evening."

"And I must not forget you, Nellie, and Jovita. Nellie, you come and stand by me, and Jovita, why don't you stand this side of me."

"I wish to see José, Stella, Norman, and all you incredible older people come forward and join everyone and me in a simple prayer. Finally, could you, beautiful black stallions, please position yourselves to the sides of the rescue team and the older persons."

The monument made a quick check, and once all was settled, he gave his approval and won everyone present. "Thank you, my friends. Let's begin."

*****

"Firstly, please tell everyone present how long it has been since you last saw your favourite white horse, Palomo," Derekamus asked.

"Um, let me think, I passed away back in December 1830. So that would mean it has been nearly two centuries. May I ask why?" inquired the curious mind.

"Now tell us, do you know these five names? I am going to read them out. Please excuse me if I do not pronounce them correctly; I am of Old German origin." He lowered his eyes to a piece of paper that had been passed to him by Abella. I cited "General Antonio José de Sucre, General José Antonio Paez, General and Aidé-de-camp, Daniel O'Leary, General, General Francisco de Paula Santander, and finally, General José Maria Córdoba Muñoz."

Simon looked down in total bewilderment at hearing those five names voiced by an Old German gnome! "Why Yes, I do recall all of them; the first three Generals on your list were from Venezuela, and the latter two from Colombia.

In fact, two, Sucre and Santander, went on to become Presidents. We all fought in the Wars of Independence. Why do you ask?

Derekamus was enjoying himself. "Please be patient, General. Do you also know a lady named Manuela Sáenz de Vergara y Aizpuru, who, if it helps, was an Ecuadorian military officer and politician?"

"Of course I do! She saved my life on at least two occasions when assassins decided I was no longer required. Her swordsmanship was second to none. Even I would have thought twice before taking her on with my mighty sabre. "

Derekamus folded the list and placed it into his overstuffed pocket. He looked in the crowd for two smiling faces. "Gentleman, would you please step forward?"

Both Captain Sebastián de Belalcázar y Dávila Santillana and Royal Lieutenant Felipe Joaquín de Cayzedo y Cuero stepped forward full of mischief, both knowing what was about to be revealed.

Simon stood speechless; he could find no reasonable explanation for what these two clowns, 5 of the bravest generals he had ever known, and an Ecuadorian woman who outshone all females he had the pleasure to have known except his only wife, María Teresa Rodríguez del Toro and Alaysa of Spanish descent, who had died from yellow fever after only two years of being engaged and eight months of marriage. His mind wandered off to that fateful day.

Sebastian coughed diplomatically while placing his arm around his friend. "Simon, it is time to enjoy a wonderful moment."

Simon turned in the direction that Sebastian had beckoned him to.......

*****

Eight black stallions were fully saddled, the reins held by all five generals from his past fighting in the Wars of Independence and a beautiful and smiling beauty he knew as Manuela.

*****

He could not stop himself; he moved swiftly to embrace this incredible woman and welcomed all the five generals one by one. It was indeed a magical moment for all present to witness. The majority in attendance were teary-eyed and choked up with emotions of people they would love to meet again from their pasts.

One of the turtles was beside himself and had worked himself up to a terrible state. He was nearly a century old. Just imagine all the people he must be remembering right there and then.

"Hang on, there are six of you and eight saddled stallions. Is there something else I should be aware of?" Asked Simon, now trying desperately to find his composure once more.

Gabriel Garcia Marquez, the Argentinian one, stepped forward, smiling from ear to ear. "You are indeed observant, General Bolivar." He turned to face the audience. "Would the riders for the two remaining black stallions please mount up?"

Sebastián and Felipe stepped forward, laughing together as they took up the reins and began to mount. At the same time, all the generals and Manuela took the opportunity to mount.

Gabriel looked at Simon and revealed, "As you may now be pondering the likelihood of a horse race between all these fine riders, who would you put your money back on?"

"Oh, that's easy, Manuela, every time!"

The entire audience roared with approval.

It was at that point Jose and Stella walked towards Simon. They were not alone. Between them was a most magnificent white horse.

"Palomo!" Roared Simon. His legs could not carry him fast enough. The memories of their countless battles and triumphs together seemed like a distant dream, but today, he could feel the spirit of his faithful companion drawing him to his oldest and most loyal friend. Simon skipped a beat with his heart as he recognised the unmistakable Palomo, unchanged by the passing of time. His majestic white horse, with its coat as pure as freshly fallen snow and a tail that brushed against the floor, thundered closer with each powerful stride.

Simon's eyes filled with tears of joy as Palomo approached, his hooves pounding against the concrete flooring like a rhythmic symphony. This legendary horse, filled with enduring loyalty, recognised his lifelong companion instantly. As he neared Simon, Palomo reared up, standing tall with pride and exuberance. With a burst of renewed energy and emotion, Simon's hands trembled as he stroked Palomo's elegant muzzle. The touch of his calm, velvety skin sent a shiver down Simon's spine as memories of their shared adventures flashed before his eyes.

Every female, including the Geese, was in a flood of tears. The guys tried in vain to either conceal their emotions or stand ramrod, defying each other to let loose with their tears.

Palomo nuzzled Simon's shoulder to reassure him that this reunion was not a fleeting dream. Tears streamed down Simon's cheeks as he whispered words of gratitude and affection to his loyal friend. Despite the years they had passed, their bond remained unbreakable, forged in the heat of countless battles and the pursuit of freedom.

The pair stood in that vast expanse of shared emotion, their reunion creating an aura of magic and awe. Simon could sense that Palomo had never forgotten him, carrying his spirit through generations of horses. The horse's eyes of him, deep and full of wisdom, sparkled with a familiar brightness that Simon knew all too well.

As they stood together, the wind whispered stories of their epic conquests, echoing across the plains and resonating with those who had fought alongside Simon Bolivar. It seemed as if the very essence of freedom swirled around them, a testament to their shared determination and unwavering commitment to freedom. At that moment, Simon Bolivar and his cherished Palomo were not just man and horse. They were legends, united once more in their quest for justice and liberty. Hand in hand, or rather, hand in hoof, they embarked on a new chapter of their immortal tale – a tale that would transcend time, inspiring generations to come with their unwavering spirit and unstoppable bond.

But first, there was the matter of a horse race……

*****

"Welcome to all of you horse race enthusiasts who have journeyed to the first-ever Midnight Runway Derby here on the empty 3000m runway at Cali International Airport. Unlike the famous Kentucky Derby and the English Epsom Derby, which are raced in the daylight hours, this Derby is happening here at midnight., and if you look up apart from the runway's floodlights, you can see thousands of fireflies adding their speciality of created wonderful displays of light on either side of the runway."

"My name is Angel Rueda, and this is my co-presenter and spouse, Ligia Nieto. Together, we are going to bring all the latest news on this inaugural special horse race. Say hello to the listeners, Ligia."

At that moment, Ligia was knitting. Not with wool, but with plastic bags! Yes, she was recycling plastic bags into large spherical table mats. She had been doing this innocent pastime for many years, and usually, she could complete two per day. Did she create them to sell? No, she nearly always took them to her local church and gave them away to the other worshipers. She was renowned for this. In a panic, Ligia dropped the large needles and plastic into her lap, leaving her hands free.

She took up her microphone and immediately took over, effortlessly raising the excitement in her voice, "Hello, racegoers. It is so exciting to be here tonight in such a prestigious setting, and I cannot wait to explain what will happen. First, we can see over 200 people in the main stand below our commentary box. Everyone is enjoying the free champagne and canapés. They all look resplendent in their evening wear; the ladies look divine, and the men look handsome, too."

"Back to you, Angel."

"Thank you, darling; let me now introduce you to the nine riders and their stallions who will be completing tonight:" "This special Midnight Runway Derby is hopefully going to become the first of many legendary horse races to be held at such an unconventional venue, the runway of Alfonso Bonilla Aragón International Airport. Set at midnight, after all the flights have concluded for the day, it promises excitement and intrigue like no other horse race anywhere else in South America."

Angel looked down to see the riders and horses making their first appearance; it was the right moment to introduce each pair to the more comprehensive listeners in their homes and the Grandstand crowd below him. "This horse race will pit nine fearless steeds against each other, with skilled riders ranging from five distinguished generals, an intrepid Conquistador, and a Royal Lieutenant to the enigmatic Manuela Sáenz. However, the crowd will unmistakably focus on the favourite, the magnificent Simon Bolivar, the venerated Venezuelan soldier and statesman riding his famous Palomo nearly two centuries apart. Will this historical pair still have what it takes to rise to the challenge? Over to you again, Ligia."

"Hi again, please excuse me. I am supping a glass of champers, and a bubble has gone up my nose!" Both Ligia and Angel burst out laughing, enjoying the moment together.

"I can clearly see all nine riders and their mounts have now joined us and are standing around the pre-race paddock ring, showcasing themselves to the cheering racegoers. It is indeed a fantastic spectacle to witness such a traditional ceremony in horse racing. From here, Angel and I can observe and assess the horse's physical appearance, temperament, and overall fitness up close. We can see the jockeys starting to mount their horses. The first couple of riders lead their horses on a leisurely walk, thus allowing the horses to familiarise themselves with the new surroundings.

It also allows each rider to analyse the horse's condition, looking for signs of soundness, muscle tone, and readiness for the upcoming race. Soon, they will up the pace by letting each horse complete a gentle trot, and their nerves should be settled way before the start." Angel finds a perfect moment when Ligia pauses to take a breath and seamlessly takes over the commentary:

"It also allows us all to witness up close and appreciate each horse's sheer beauty. They look magnificent!" Ligia is still enjoying the champers and feels the need to head to the toilet. She leaves Angel deep in conversation with all who are listening to him. "let me take a moment or two to give you my description of what I can see before me, as Ligia has popped out to the "Little house at the bottom of the garden."

"**Number 1. Simon Bolivar & Palomo:** Simon Bolivar, an influential figure revered for his military prowess, has an unrivalled connection with Palomo, a whiter-than-snow beauty known for its speed and grace. Their synchronised movements made them a true force to be reckoned with on this racecourse.

**Number 2. General Santander & Shadow Rider**: General Santander, a seasoned military leader known for his strategic mind, has partnered with Shadow Rider, a powerful black stallion possessing unparalleled endurance and determination.

**Number 3. Sucre & Midnight Stalker:** General Sucre, a highly disciplined tactician, rides with Midnight Stalker, a fierce competitor who boasts an uncanny ability to navigate even the darkest of tracks.

**Number 4. General Paez & Ebony Knight:** General Paez is renowned for his aggression. nature, you have paired up with Ebony Knight, a magnificent stallion known for its fiery spirit and relentless drive to succeed.

**Number 5. General Córdoba Muñoz & Dark Warrior:** General Córdoba Muñoz, a master of strategy and tactics, has joined forces with Dark Warrior, a sleek and intelligent horse that could analyse and adapt to any race situation.

**Number 6. General and Aidé-de-camp, Daniel O'Leary & Midnight Ghost:** Daniel is the right-hand man to many of Simon's endeavours in the War of Independence. A charismatic leader renowned for his ambition, Daniel will race with Midnight Ghost, a mysterious and elusive horse that seems to blend into the surroundings and possibly leave his adversaries perplexed.

**Number 7. Captain Sebastian Belalcázar & Nightshade:** Captain Sebastian Belalcázar, a fearless conquistador celebrated for his courage, has commandeered Nightshade, a dark and mighty steed with an aura of mystique that makes them an enthralling pair to watch. Another possible favourite is to pass the winning post ahead of the others.

**Number 8:** The only lady entering this horse race, but do not expect her to be the last. **Manuela Sáenz & Shadow Dancer:** Manuela Sáenz is a skilled horsewoman known for her grace and daring; she rides Shadow Dancer, a spirited black horse with agility and an ability to efficiently execute intricate movements. I would be happy to wager my money on this lady, but the bookies are closed this evening.

Last but not least, **number 9. Royal Lieutenant Felipe Joaquín de Cayzedo y Cuero & Nocturno:** Felipe Joaquin is known for his wit and sharpness when debating. Both rider and black stallion, who represent the true embodiment of strength and determination, have trained non-stop for the past week in secret. This pairing could give us the upset of the night; we wait to see.

*****

"Let the Midnight Runway Derby begin!" Angel and Ligia screamed out together.

As the midnight hour descended upon the airport runway, the atmosphere was electric with anticipation. The race was about to begin, promising an extraordinary spectacle under the moonlit sky.

The spectators from the Museo Aereo Fenix held their breath as the horses lined up at the starting line. The air crackled with excitement, and the darkness only amplified the intensity. All competitors cast their eyes on the finish line, ready to embark on a remarkable journey.

With a deafening roar, the race began amidst the backdrop of the empty runway. The sound of hooves thundered through the night as the horses galloped, their sleek black coats gleaming under the moon's watchful gaze. Amidst the chaos and commotion, Simon Bolivar and Palomo emerged as frontrunners, displaying their incredible synchrony and undeniable bond.

However, Sebastian, Felipe, Manuela, and the generals were not to be underestimated. Each pairing showcased remarkable skill, strategy, and tenacity, pushing their equine partners to their limits.

As the race neared its culmination, the crowd erupted into a cheers, hooting, and applause frenzy. The midnight hour seemed to stretch endlessly as the horses raced neck and neck towards the finish line. In a breathtaking surge of power, Simon Bolivar and Palomo managed to retain their lead, seizing victory with an otherworldly burst of speed.

The Midnight Runway Derby concluded, leaving the audience in awe of the courageous horses and their skilled riders. It was an unparalleled spectacle, forever etched in the annuals of horse racing history.

And so, under the midnight sky, the Midnight Runway Derby showcased the determination, skill, and raw power of these magnificent black horses and their courageous jockeys, forever immortalising their names in the realm of equestrian greatness.

"Felipe and Nocturno came in last," were the final words from Ligia Nieto and Angel Rueda; together, they indeed made a formidable commentating team for all those present at the first-ever Midnight Runway Derby horse race. They left the commentary box hand in hand and were last seen strolling down the road back towards the city together. Ligia, carrying her latest tableware creation, and Angel wrapped his arm over her shoulder, serenaded her favourite song, "Las Acacias", to the love of his life and the mother of their six girls.

*****

For everyone else, and that also meant the riders and horses, the Museo Aereo Fenix was the final destination for a late surprise concert by the singing

Sisterhood Choir led by the Sister Superior on guitar and little Rosa, soon to be Sister Seraphina as lead vocalist.

On this serene night, under the clear and cloudless (at last) night sky with its abundance of stars and a solitary half-moon, the ethereal voices of the Singing Sisterhood Choir graced an impromptu concert. As the Sister Superior of this unique Choir, I felt blessed to witness such a remarkable event.

The main hall of the Museum, usually adorned with military-themed items, is now transformed into a sanctuary of enchanting melodies. The Choir gathered together, their voices harmonising beautifully, scattering joy and peace into the air. This impromptu concert captivated our souls and uplifted the spirits of all who were present.

Among the choir members, one sister stood out like a shining star. Naturally, it had to be Rosa. Her delicate yet powerful voice resonated with a grace resembling a songbird. Her angelic tones reverberated through the museum walls as Rosa sang, leaving everyone spellbound. Each note coming forth from her soul carried a message of hope and love.

Rosa's voice transcended the venue's physical limitations, reaching deep into the hearts of each listener. Her tone invoked a sense of serenity, melting away the burdens that often weigh us down in our daily lives. It was as if the heavens themselves opened up, and angels descended to accompany Rosa's beautiful voice.

With Rosa's exceptional vocal talent, the Choir reminded us of all the divine gifts that music truly is. It unites us in the celebration of our shared faith and the incredible power of harmony. Witnessing such a breathtaking performance served as a reminder that even in the confines of this humble Museum dedicated to the world of transportation, we can create moments of pure beauty and joy that resonate far beyond any wall.

As the Sister Superior, I offer my deepest gratitude to the Singing Sisterhood Choir for gracing everyone present with their heavenly voices and to Rosa, whose enchanting singing brought us a taste of heaven on earth. May their talent continue to inspire others and uplift the souls of all who are fortunate enough to hear them.

To end the evening of total surprises for all of the older people, I accompanied the sisters with my guitar, and we sang a surprise song dedicated to little Rosa. You should have seen her face. This is what we sang:

(Verse 1)
In a small town where the winds do blow,
there's a sister with a voice that seems to glow,
She strums her guitar with skilled hands and grace,
spreading love and joy through every embrace.

(Chorus)
Oh, she sings like a songbird,
Her voice is so pure it touches your soul,
Guided by faith, her spirit takes flight,
Serenading the heavens, night after night.

(Verse 2)
She gathers all the sisters, strong and kind;
in harmonies and melodies, they intertwine,
Through the chapel halls, their voices resonate,
A tapestry of music, heavenly and great.

(Chorus)
Oh, she sings like a songbird,
Her voice is so pure it touches your soul,
Guided by faith, her spirit takes flight,
Serenading the heavens, night after night.

(Bridge)
With each strum of her guitar and each note she sings,
She brings solace and peace to broken wings,
A blend of folk and gospel, her unique air,
Her music, a prayer, lifting hearts in care.

(Verse 3)
As the years go by, her light only grows.
Bound in sisterhood, each note clearly shows,
She leads her Choir like a shepherd,
guiding them with love in perfect rhyme.

(Chorus)
Oh, she sings like a songbird….

*****

There was one final surprise for all the older people and their accompanying carers: tables set up with row after row of flying jackets, gloves, and goggles. Gabriel, Stella, José, and Norman stood behind each table, facing the crowd.

José spoke loudly so that all ahead of him could hear his words from him; "Ladies and gentlemen."

"Good morning; although it is still dark, in an hour or two, the bright sunshine will be above us again. I have been reliably informed that the storm of this century has gone!" There followed the loudest uproar of approval this Museum had ever witnessed.

"I, José, my lovely wife Stella, my faithful friend Norman, and my comrade in the air, Gabriel, are standing before you with hearts full of gratitude and joy. We want to welcome everyone who has been brought here from your endangered care homes due to the devastating floods and mudslides to experience what we have enjoyed for a lifetime. But first and foremost, we want to applaud all of you for your resilience and bravery during this challenging time. In the face of adversity, it is truly remarkable and inspires us all."

Today, we have an extraordinary surprise for each of you. As a tribute to your courage and to bring a smile to your faces, we have arranged a unique experience that will take you on a mesmerising journey above the beautiful city we call home. In just a short while, we will all be boarding some of our magnificent vintage aircraft housed in the Museum. We will take flight together and soar above the breathtaking Pacific coastline, allowing you to witness the stunning beauty of the land below.

But that's not all! We will continue our journey towards Manizales, a city nestled amidst lush coffee fields. As we pass over this charming region, you will have the opportunity to marvel at the picturesque landscapes and smell the enchanting aroma of coffee. As we return, we will glide gracefully through the skies, making our way back to the Museum, where your incredible adventure began. On this flight, let the wind carry away your worries and troubles of the past, allowing you all to immerse yourself in this moment of joy and wonder.

These surprise flights are symbols of our gratitude and appreciation for each and every one of you. It is our way of saying thank you for your resilience, holding on through this difficult time, and reminding us of the importance of community and support.

If you're as excited as we are, let's prepare to embark on this unforgettable journey together. Buckle up, embrace the thrill, and prepare to witness the world from a whole new perspective. Let the beauty of the city and the strength of your spirits intertwine as we dream through the sky.

Thank you once again for joining us today. Remember, no matter what challenges we face, we can conquer anything together. Now, let's make memories that will last a lifetime. Enjoy the surprise flight and let the magic of the skies embrace you. Please come forward and receive a complimentary flying jacket, a set of goggles, and a pair of flying gloves to keep your fingers warm.

Thank you."

**The END**

Well getting closer……

# Part Three

# *Devil's Breath Claims New Victims*

## *Foreword to Part Three*

Wow, another three years have passed since I put my life on hold to ensure I would finally bring another set of adventures and fantasies to your door. In the same time frame, we all had to live through the global pandemic known as Covid-19.

I spent the latter part of 2019, all of 2020, and the first six months of 2021 in London. At that time, I found work as a Delivery Driver of Indoor plants and Christmas trees. A Parks and Open Space rubbish and dog poo collector and Driver. And finally, a Home Worker for a small number of sufferers of Schizophrenia in North London. I did all the above in the same order. I was best suited to the first two occupations only.

When all the lockdowns around the globe began to end, I was probably the first to book the Avianca flights out of Heathrow back to Santiago de Cali via Madrid. I purchased one-way tickets, even knowing my visa had expired, after someone at the Colombian Consulate in London said, "Do not worry; "we know it was not your fault."

It turned out he was right, the Immigration Officer who welcomed me with the largest of smiles, stamped my passport and sent me on my way back to my small family of Cristirin, Blacky and later our two new kittens, Liz and Goldie.

As soon as I sat at my desk in my office, the stories and future stories began to appear again. Part three is full of those stories, although the tone is heading into darker areas of the city. Everything was motoring along until a certain, very unfriendly mosquito decided to land on me and inject me with a viral disease known as Dengue Fever. It almost finished me off. So please forgive me for not including a nice and friendly story of any mosquito.

I have been asked: "Who is your target audience, and who are you writing to?" I was tempted to say, "Anyone with a pulse."

Truthfully, I firmly believe that as we all age, the outer parts of us also age. But there has to be a tiny part where the original child still exists in all of us, no matter the paths we have trodden on.

This is for all children, no matter what their age. However, it will be ideal for children between 15 and 105. Finally, I must say a massive thank you to everyone. I do hope my brain brings you all – magic moments.

*Mike Bowley*

December 2023

Part Three – Devil's Breath Claims New Victims

# *Contents*

| | | |
|---|---|---|
| 51. | I am the morning setting of unusual friendships. | 388 |
| 52. | I am Climate Change visiting to see what I can do. | 401 |
| 53. | I am Simon, and I am taking my two best friends on holiday. | 406 |
| 54. | I am the Choir of Sisterhood Singers performing in two famous Halls. | 438 |
| 55. | I am a Fire Truck full of Heros and Heroines. | 446 |
| 56. | I am the early history of three devilish sisters. | 458 |
| 57. | I am the "Once was" Police Colonel with a new cold case to solve. | 467 |
| 58. | I am the story behind Gabriel owning a restored Willy Jeep. | 476 |
| 59. | I am the Policeman who gets tipsy with a Street man. | 483 |
| 60. | I am a Street Cleaner who receives Passports, Visas, and Flight Tickets. | 489 |
| 61. | I am the growing consequence for a Plastic Surgeon with an evil past. | 504 |
| 62. | I am the Meeting of the Minds who consider a Request from Stalin. | 516 |
| 63. | I am a proud Derekamus and an itching to find out more Abella. | 530 |
| 64. | I am a team of Fire Fighters who are tested to their limits. | 539 |
| 65. | I am a certain Gabriel who just cannot stop attracting wealth. | 560 |
| 66. | I am Blacky, and I need the wisdom of the Rio Gato and Valentina. | 569 |
| 67. | I am a case needing DNA, Dental Records, & Finger Print Matching. | 581 |
| 68. | I am Stalin, and I have much to learn and remember. | 596 |
| 69. | I am the Net that is closing in three sisters. | 604 |
| 70. | I am an ill-fated Private Chartered Flight. | 624 |
| 71. | I am a couple who feel the need to migrate to Canada. | 633 |
| 72. | I am a growing community of new rocks on a mountain ridge. | 642 |
| | Final thoughts. | 658 |

"The glory of a nation is not measured by its size, but by the virtues of its people."

Simón José Antonio de la Santísima Trinidad Bolívar Palacios Ponte y Blanco. (Venezuelan Military & Political Leader 1783 – 1830)

"Earth provides enough to satisfy every man's needs, but not every man's greed."

Mahatma Gandhi. (Indian Lawyer and Anti Colonialist 1869 – 1948)

"Someone asked me what three things I would save if my house was on fire. I said my cat, my salamander, and one of the twins."

Ricky Gervais (English comedian, actor, writer, producer, director and always someone I have wanted to sit down in a pub with and laugh consistently with.)

"Friends, Romans, Countrymen, lend me your ears."

Julius Caesar, Act III, Scene II written by Gulielmus Shakspere better known as William Shakespeare. (Playwright, Poet, and Actor. None of which I have ever done. 1564 – 1616.)

"We only know a tiny proportion about the complexity of the natural world. Wherever you look, there are things we don't understand. There are always new things to find out if you go looking for them."

David Attenborough. (British biologist, natural historian, broadcaster, author, and someone this author looks up to. Especially the time when this hero of mine needed my help with his shoes at Heathrow.)

"All of my career has been an attempt to educate myself and get paid for it."

Edward Rutherfurd. (My personal favorito British Writer of historical novels. Edward thank you for all the hours your wonderful stories have consumed me completely.)

Ah, Devil's Breath, the mythical potion that can supposedly transform you into a mindless zombie? Well, let's add a pinch of comedy to this magical mixture, shall we?

Fact or fiction, you ask? Well, if by "Devil's Breath" you mean a mythical demon breathing hot air at someone until they become a mindless zombie, then I'm sorry to say, it's pure fiction. We would have a whole different set of problems if demons were dabbling in the pharmaceutical industry!

Now, if you're referring to scopolamine, a chemical found in certain plants, well, that's a real substance. But fear not, my friend, it won't turn you into a zombie searching for hapless victims to munch on. In reality, scopolamine is used for a variety of medical purposes, such as treating motion sickness and nausea. So, rather than turning you into a brain-dead extra in a horror movie, it can actually help you keep your lunch down during a turbulent roller coaster ride.

Remember, it's always good to approach my fantastical stories with a sense of humour and a sprinkle of scepticism. The only zombie apocalypse you need to worry about is when barbarians forget my Tinto in the morning – now that's a real-life catastrophe!

Mike Bowley (Author of Culminating Anthropomorphism-styled Short Stories in 2023 and 2024).

## 51: I am the Morning Setting of Unusual Friendships

The city and its 2 million inhabitants spent the next few weeks cleaning up the central and northern parts of the city. Flood water was simpler to move, whereas excessive mud proved to be more resistant to removal.

It required everyone to coordinate and implement a systematic approach. First, the coordinators concentrated their priority on ensuring all the residents were safe. Miraculously, no fatalities had been reported. This allowed the coordinators to direct their energies next on evacuating the inhabitants who were in immediate danger and providing them with temporary shelter.

The rescue and clean-up teams had to wait for the flood waters to recede and the flow of the city river to drop, making the area safe to navigate around. Then, the following vital assessments were made to evaluate the extent of the damage to infrastructure, buildings, utilities, and natural resources. From these assessments, the barbarians were able to determine the scale of recovery that would require everyone's efforts.

With their heavy equipment, the Clean-up and debris removal teams moved in to meet the challenging aftermath of the floods and mudslides. Each challenge had to deal with the significant debris left behind, including the hardening by the minute mud, the vast number of fallen trees, and the damaged structures. This monumental effort would eventually allow for the rehabilitation of the affected areas. Daily passers-by would witness the involvement in the removal of the debris and begin to see the restoration of all that required mobility and access.

Next came repairing the city's damaged infrastructure, such as the affected roads, bridges, utilities, and public facilities.

The barbarians began to smile more confidently as crucial work to restore normalcy restored life to its state before the storms of the century.

The biggest shock that no adequate explanation could be found was the care homes in the barrio La Flora. Everyone was dreading what they would find. But when they arrived at each location, they were expecting to begin the process of resettling all the affected older people, and providing temporary or permanent housing was not required! There was no need to build temporary shelters, provide rental assistance, or construct new homes in the barrio.

It was like nothing had happened. Rumours and wild stories began to circulate about a power that had visited the homes and saved them all. But how? No one could offer a proper answer.

After the floods and mudslides, the city coordinators focused their efforts on addressing public health concerns, such as ensuring everyone had access to clean water, sanitary facilities, and proper waste management. Measures were also taken to restore the ecosystem and prevent further environmental degradation.

Community support and social services were on standby to offer all necessary emotional and psychological support to the expectant-affected older persons and their care workers.

None did. This meant that Local authorities, NGOs, and social service organisations could channel and provide assistance, counselling, and resources to help other affected communities.

Long-term strategy meetings were scheduled to focus on developing new projects to enhance the city's resilience against future flood and mudslide events. These measures included land-use planning, watershed management, improved infrastructure design, and early warning systems.

"Mind you, it could be another century before we can see what we envisage today will actually be perfect for when the next storm of the century decides to showcase itself." a remark made to the committee of planners by the mayor. "Mind you, with climate change, just maybe we may not have to wait a century."

All the planners stayed quiet, allowing the general warning of possible dangers to come to their city to enter their minds and find a parking place.

*****

"What do we do? Take a look at our nests. Then, look at the state of our usually dependable trees and their branches. I asked, what are we going to do now?" A question was raised by one of a pair of canaries who, at that moment, were perched on a balcony that later would sit a black cat with an impressive white chest and four white socks.

"Oh, my dearest," the male canary said to his female companion. "It breaks my heart to witness the devastation below. The once vibrant and lush trees have now been reduced to barren skeletons. It seems as though nature itself is weeping."

The female canary looked downward and replied, "I know, my love. It's truly distressing. Our little home, nestled among those beautiful branches, feels so vulnerable now. We sang our songs joyfully while watching the leaves dance in the wind. How can we bring normality back to our lives amidst all this destruction?"

The male canary paused to consider what a helpful and ensuring response should be: "Fear not, my dear. We can still take action to restore the harmony we once knew. The first step would be to find a new home, a safe haven where we can rebuild our nest and raise our family—somewhere with sturdy trees and an abundance of resources."

The female canary smiled at the reassurance from her lifetime partner, "Yes, you're right. Moving might be our best option. But won't we miss our old tree, the comfortable familiarity of our surroundings?"

The thoughtful male canary responded with a fair degree of foresight, "I understand that sentiment, my love. But sometimes, change is our only hope for survival. We can adapt and find new beauty in another tree, its branches offering security and protection. We may even discover a different kind of serenity, where new friends and neighbours await."

The now chirping, proudly female canary showed her approval, "That's true. We must embrace the possibility of a fresh beginning. But how do we ensure that we are not just moving from one devastated area to another? We must be cautious not to repeat our current predicament."

The male canary now had his head up high, with his chest well expanded: "Wise words, my beloved. To ensure a favourable choice, we must carefully observe future locations. Look for signs of vitality: healthy leaves, blooms, and signs of life. We can also listen for the harmony of other birds, buzzing insects, and the rustling of leaves. These signs will guide us to a thriving community."

Not totally confident, the female canary paused to consider a doubt that was nagging her confidence, "And what if we cannot find such a place nearby? Should we consider venturing even farther beyond our known territory?"

The male canary offered his undying love to his female partner. "If all else fails, my love, we must be open to exploring new horizons. The world is vast, and there may be untouched lands rich with opportunities for us. As long as we stay together, supporting and nurturing each other, no distance will be too great to find a haven."

Now filled with warm feelings, the female canary moved closer to her companion, "Your words give me hope, my dear. As long as we are united, we can face any challenge and restore normality to our lives. Let's take flight, venturing into the unknown until we find a place where we can build a new home and sing our songs once more."

Now, in two minds, the male canary offered, "Yes, my love, let our wings carry us to a brighter future. Together, we will overcome this devastation and create a harmonious existence where we can flourish once again."

Deep in thought about a possible second offering, the male canary looked up and examined the area close to where they were right now: "Maybe we are looking too far. Maybe we should be looking closer to where we are right now......."

*****

Both canaries turned to see what was making a lot of noise at the other end of the balcony. It was a pair of chestnut-fronted macaws!

*****

An extraordinary event unfolded in the bustling city's vast concrete jungle, where towering skyscrapers reach for the skies. Two magnificent chestnut-fronted macaws, part of a vibrant flock of ten, unexpectedly found themselves in this urban wonderland. Eager to find a safe haven amidst the chaos, they embarked on an adventurous quest to establish a new home.

Guided by instinct and snippets of whispered avian folklore, the pair had heard rumours about the city's northern region being cooler and more conducive to their vibrant plumage and tropical demeanours. With the city's geography as cryptic as the maze of wires lining its streets, these wandering macaws needed a sign—an unmistakable symbol. And that's when fate intervened.

Shimmering reflections from its glass facades caught their attention as they soared high above the city. One penthouse balcony glimmered like a celestial oasis among the countless towering structures. Its ornate design and lush vegetation hinted at a possible sanctuary where the city's frenetic energy mellowed into harmony.

Curiosity sparked in their intelligent eyes, giving them the confidence to glide towards this glittering refuge. Landing gracefully on the edge of the balcony, they were greeted by a soft breeze imbued with the promise of tranquillity. Unbeknownst to the macaws, they had found themselves on the turf of a white-haired man with strong-looking legs and a pot-belly and Cristirin, his beautiful partner with a soft nature and large brown eyes. Together, with a growing interest in nature, they were slowly turning their penthouse balcony into a hidden oasis amidst the concrete canyons.

The two macaws inspected each exotic plant, carefully arranged to mimic a tropical paradise, and tickled their senses, evoking memories of the lush Amazon rainforest. The sounds of cascading water from a small fountain offered a soothing serenade, a rendition of the babbling rivers they used to drink from.

Word spread quickly within their avian community. The two macaws had, by serendipitous likeliness, stumbled upon a secret haven nestled in this concrete labyrinth. The rest of the flock, drawn by the allure of a renewed sanctuary, decided to join them on this elevated paradise and were perched on the rooftop above the balcony.

Together, the flock of ten chestnut-fronted macaws could see the opportunities to transform the penthouse balcony into a vibrant, bustling community. Each macaw could picture living amidst the cascading foliage and blossoming flowers. They would build cosy nests—each intertwined branch a testament to their determination to flourish in an unlikely urban setting.

As the macaws looked down on the penthouse balcony with their brilliant plumage, they knew instantly the residents of La Flora would become mesmerised by the exotic symphony and kaleidoscope of colours. Each barbarian passing by would stop to revel in the awe-inspiring sight, the urban stress and fatigue momentarily lifted by this enchanting oasis amid towering glass and steel.

And so, against all odds, these ten avian adventurers decided to transform this penthouse balcony into both their new home and a symbol of hope—a testament to the resilient spirit of nature even amidst the concrete chaos.

Then another bird arrived; he was a yellow-headed caracara. Behind him, flying high above in formation, were 180 geese with their General and the impressive and all-knowing Chief Warrant Officer just behind them, heading to the same balcony.......

At that point, five Ruddy Ground doves took up the empty space on the balcony wall. They had beaten the bigger migrating birds.

*****

The five doves had decided to take up the centrally empty space on the balcony wall because they had witnessed the arrival of the ten magnificent chestnut-fronted macaws on the right side. Intrigued by their avian counterparts' vibrant colours and lively presence, the doves felt a sense of kinship and curiosity towards the visiting macaws.

A pair of yellow canaries had already claimed their perch on the dove's left side. The doves admired the canary's melodious songs and radiant plumage, finding them charming and delightful. Additionally, the doves recognised the similarities in their small size and appreciated the canary's presence as a reminder that even the tiniest birds possess beauty and grace. As the doves pondered their choices, they noticed a massive flock of geese circling overhead, seeking a place to land.

The doves realised that with the balcony wall being the only available landing spot, they had a unique opportunity to create a diverse and harmonious avian community. Motivated by the desire for camaraderie and the chance to witness the beauty of their neighbouring bird species up close, the five Ruddy Ground doves confidently claimed the central empty space on the balcony wall.

By doing so, they hoped to foster an environment where different bird species could coexist and appreciate each other's unique characteristics and contributions to the diverse avian world.

Of the 180 migrating geese, there was room for a hundred to land on the balcony floor. The remainder formed small squadrons and flew in formation, giving an excellent display of military precision acrobatic flypasts.

*****

The air-filled cacophony of honking, squawking, and screeching from the flapping wings and the sounds of outdoing each other and vying for attention was deafening, and somehow, someone had to take control and quick.

Now, the Yellow-headed caracara was hopping around energetically in the midst of the commotion, adding to the mayhem. The General, a stern grey-haired goose, stood composed while his loyal Chief Warrant Officer stood on the balcony floor.

The general goose began shouting above the noise, "Silence! Order! We shall have discipline on this parade square!"

The squadron of geese and the solitary caracara reluctantly quieten down, with the occasional grumbles heard. They eyed each other suspiciously, waiting for further instructions.

The Chief Warrant Officer adjusted his feathers sternly, "All right, you lot! Fall into formation, facing forward!" The Chief Warrant Officer's voice boomed across the balcony, commanding the attention of the geese and the caracara. They hastily organised themselves into rows, the geese clumsily waddling into place. At the same time, the caracara perched himself on the balcony's brick wall, his bright yellow-headed plumage shining in the morning light.

With his front left paw pointing towards the squadron of geese, the Chief Warrant Officer said, "Line A, adjust your spacing! No gaps allowed!"

The geese squawk and shuffle, trying their best to align themselves perfectly.

*****

While all this was happening, the two canaries, the five Ruddy Ground doves, and the ten chestnut-fronted macaws observed the scene in bewilderment and were transfixed as if set in concrete. They chirped softly to each other, unable to comprehend the chaos unfolding before them.

The female canary spoke first, flapping her tiny wings in surprise: "Oh, my feathers! Look at the parade happening on this balcony!"

The male canary watched intently. "Indeed! I've never seen anything quite like it. What an unusual gathering!"

The canaries, doves, and macaws watched as the scene unfolded, totally fascinated by the surprised spectacle.

The Chief Warrant Officer, now standing taller than ever, addressed all the birds: "Quiet! Pay attention! We are about to commence the parade!"

The Chief Warrant Officer's sharp command again brought silence to the balcony. The geese and caracara stood at attention; their feathers ruffled but heads held high.

The waiting general nods approvingly, "Very well! Let us proceed with the parade and show the world the might of the Honking Goose Air Regiment!"

*****

"As the General of this Honking Goose Air Regiment, I oversee the meticulous planning and execution of our annual migration to the Pampas in Argentina. Our squadron of aviators has a long-standing tradition of sticking together and safeguarding one another throughout the journey."

The general paused for effect: "However, as you are all aware, due to the awful storms we tried to negotiate, it became too difficult and dangerous for us all. We sadly lost our navigator. Subsequently, we became lost. We made an unscheduled stop in this dusty-looking city and almost left straight away when we received an invitation to assist the Tree of Life and his team when dealing with the threat to the older persons in their care homes."

The general paused and produced a letter from under his wing carriage, "I wish to report back to you all that we were very successful in the small part we played, and I wish to say a personal thank you for the impromptu fly past and escort we provided to the aircraft and the occupants from the Museo Aereo Fenix. Today, I have received an open invitation for future generations of us geese; when migrating in the future, we stop and rest annually at the same museum."

"With the weather continuously improving hour by hour, the long-term forecast is that our destination to Argentina is cloud-free. This is great news for us as a squadron, and this year, I have decided to allow a yellow-headed caracara to join our aviator family."

A murmour of astonishment went round the squadron – a yellow-headed caracara joining the aviators seemed unthinkable. The general, suspecting such a backlash, said, "The decision to include the caracara in our migration was not taken lightly. I recognised the caracara's desire to experience migrating despite being a non-migratory bird. It is an opportunity for cross-species collaboration and learning that could benefit both our squadron and the caracara."

"Chief Warrant Officer will now explain how we are going to achieve this almost impossible endeavour."

The Chief Warrant Officer raised his voice to ensure he would be heard, "To ensure the safety and well-being of the caracara, the Honking Goose Air Regiment has devised a comprehensive plan. First and foremost, I have assigned myself, a seasoned veteran goose, to be the caracara's dedicated guardian and mentor. I will guide the caracara, educate it about migration patterns, and help it navigate the challenges encountered."

"Additionally, you trained aviators in our squadron are responsible for protecting and supporting the caracara. We will fly in a formation that provides shelter and minimises the caracara's exposure to wind drafts. You geese will take turns leading the flock, allowing the caracara to conserve energy while still experiencing the joy of flight."

"Throughout the migratory journey, we will also communicate with the caracara, teaching it our honking language and providing updates about our progress. This will help the caracara feel integrated into the Honking Goose Air Regiment and provide a sense of belonging."

"You aviators will work together to guard the caracara against potential threats. Be it dangerous weather conditions, predatory animals, or exhaustion, the Honking Goose Regiment will prioritise the safety of each member, including our honorary caracara."

At this point, the Chief Warrant Officer went silent and nodded back to the general.

Seamlessly and professionally, the general commenced his instructions and explained, "By allowing the yellow-headed caracara to join us on this migration, we seek to foster compassion, understanding, and unity among different species. We believe that experiencing the migration first-hand will provide the caracara with deeper insights into the natural world while reinforcing our squadron's bond and purpose."

"Together, we shall embark on this extraordinary journey, supporting our newest member and fulfilling the caracara's desire to experience migrating. Through our collective efforts, we will demonstrate the power of cooperation and create a remarkable story of interspecies camaraderie that will be remembered for years to come."

With a signal from general, the geese and the caracara started parading in perfect formation, feathers shimmering under the sunlight. The geese honked in unison while the caracara added his shrill calls, creating a harmonious albeit unusual melody.

As the parade continued, the two canaries exchanged delighted chirps with their dove neighbours while the ten macaws squawked in admiration. Together, they watch this extraordinary gathering, captivated by the sight of birds coming together in a display of organised chaos.

Then one of the large sliding glass doors opened, and staring in total disbelief stood a black cat with a magnificent white chest and four white socks. On either side of Blacky, sat two much smaller versions of him except for their individual colouring. One was golden with darker stripes on his legs and tail, and the other was a beauty with tri-colours and eyes to make anyone swoon.

Behind the trio of felines stood a couple of barbarians, one the taller one with his white hair and the other a female with the warmest of smiles holding hands and praying this spectacle does never end....

*****

The three felines moved slowly forward, came to a stop, and sat back on their back legs. Each with their left paws saluted the general and closed their eyes to show their pleasure in having all these birds in front of them. Blacky spoke while taking in as many of the birds as possible,

"Meow, greetings, everybody! Please do not worry; we are well-educated cats. Well, I am; these two little "terrorists" are in playful training. I warmly welcome you, general, and your impressive, if not a bit noisy, for a Sunday morning squadron of 180 geese."

Goldie turned to the one yellow-headed caracara, the two delightful yellow canaries, the cooing gently Ruddy Ground doves, and the magnificent ten chestnut-fronted macaws. "It is an honour to have such distinguished guests among us."

He silently hoped his message was correct.

Blacky spoke again, feeling proud of Goldie and his first steps into the world of diplomacy, "Let me assure you that not only am I a charming feline, but I am also well-educated and highly knowledgeable. Education is of utmost importance to me, and I have passed down this value to my two adorable kittens, who stand proudly on either side of me. They, too, are currently being trained on the advantages of being well-educated, well-mannered, and having a deep sense of safety."

Blacky paused to allow all the birds to take in his actual genuineness to be friendly. He felt he could continue; "Rest assured, dear guests, our little feline family understands the importance of safety and are always careful and mindful of others. We even created a safe and welcoming environment where everyone can relax, enjoy each other's company, and revel in the joyous atmosphere."

Not to be forgotten, Liz piped up, "Feel free to approach us, admire our intelligent demeanour, and engage in delightful conversations. We are here to ensure that your visit is both enjoyable and memorable. Once again, welcome to our cosy abode! Meow!"

Sensing there may be a connection between Liz and his homelands of Alaska and Canada, the general turned to face Liz, "Please enlighten me, Liz and Goldie. Do you know where you got your names from?"

Both kittens conferred, deciding who would answer the general. Goldie, being the shyer of the two, pushed Liz into the forefront, giving her no choice but to respond to the probing question: "We, that is, Goldie and me, are honoured to share our origin story with you—a tale laden with enchantment and influenced by some of the most majestic beings in history."

"I am Liz, and true to my name, I draw my inspiration from the Late Elizabeth Alexandra Mary Windsor, the legendary Queen of the United Kingdom and fourteen of the 56 Commonwealth countries. Just like her namesake, I possess a regal aura that commands attention and strikes admiration amongst those who encounter me. My graceful presence and dignified spirit mirror the same elegance and resilience that Queen Elizabeth exuded for many decades. My white-haired owner, you see in the doorway, said I would act as a symbol of unwavering strength and timeless beauty, much like the incredible monarch herself."

"My twin brother here before you is Goldie. His name has its roots interwoven with the story of a mighty lion from Trafalgar Square. Just as this renowned lion statue stands as a symbol of power and strength in London, Goldie embodies the attributes of a majestic lion. His glorious mane, radiating with golden hues, reflects the magnificence and power one would associate with the king of beasts. Goldie's physically and symbolically lion-like qualities make him an enchanting creature worthy of admiration and awe."

Liz next sidled up next to her brother, her paw now resting on Goldie's shoulder, "When our paths intertwined here with a white-haired Englishman and his beautiful lady, Cristirin, it was as if fate had woven a magical tapestry connecting us with two of history's most revered figures. I, Liz, the embodiment of Queen Elizabeth the Second, and Goldie, the majestic lion from Trafalgar Square, have come together to create a mystical bond that traverses time and space."

"We humbly share this tale with you, general, as a testament to the wondrous connections that exist between beings, both real and mythical. We kittens, with Blacky's guidance, embody the essence of our inspirations, standing as symbols of strength, grace, and majesty. May our story inspire you as you navigate the magical realms of migrating to the Pampas in Argentina, holding onto the power and wonder that exists within us all."

*****

The general bowed his head in honour of the compliment passed to him and his squadron of migrating geese; it was then he did something extraordinary: he turned to face the two barbarians: "Please step forward and hear our oath to you both and to these three felines."

Cristirin, Rob, Blacky, Liz and Goldie stepped forward with anticipation.

General Goose: "I present my squadron of 180 geese originating from Alaska.

Liz and Goldie's eyes widen with astonishment. They did not know why; they had no idea where or what Alaska was. They would bombard Blacky with umpteen questions later.

The white-haired Englishman spoke in awe, "Oh my goodness, General Goose, they are absolutely adorable!"

Cristirin found her voice in wonderment at her newfound knowledge, "Yes, indeed! Queen Elizabeth the Second and Alaska, where beauty and grace converge."

A proud general exalted, "Exactly! And there's more to the story. These birds were born in Alaska and have a profound connection to the late Queen's homeland, Canada. You see, just like our squadron of migrating geese, these kittens will symbolise protection wherever you go."

Liz stared at Goldie: "How extraordinary! So, wherever we journey, we will be accompanied by the spirit and safeguard of this squadron of migrating geese?"

The general saluted both barbarians: "Precisely! As these kittens grow under our watchful eyes, they will inherit the wisdom and instincts of our geese. Together, they will ensure this family's safety and guide you on your adventures through thick and thin. Consider them your loyal companions, forever connected to the vast skies and wide horizons."

Cristirin responded: What a wonderful gift, General Goose. We are genuinely touched by this gesture. These kittens are more than just pets; they are embodiments of our heritage and the protection we hold dear."

Cristirin and Rob, holding hands, looked down on the felines. After both made a sweeping look around at all the birds, each like a loyal serviceman, they saluted the little family before them: "Indeed and what a reminder they will be of the bond between the Late Queen Elizabeth and the lands of Alaska and Canada. We will cherish them always and honour their connection to our future journeys."

General Goose: I am thrilled to witness your delight, now Liz and Goldie. May the late Queen's eldest son, Charles III and his siblings and children bring you joy, companionship, and a constant sense of safety. Together, you will form an unbreakable bond, just like we geese that traverse the skies year after year."

Liz: "Thank you, General Goose, for this extraordinary honour. We are immensely grateful for your thoughtfulness and the everlasting protection of your regal squadron of geese."

Goldie: "Yes, thank you, General Goose. We will cherish this gift and carry its significance wherever we roam."

General Goose: "It is my pleasure, Liz and Goldie. May your journeys be blessed, and may King Charles III and his children be forever by your side, spreading their majestic influence as far as the winds can carry them."

Everyone on that balcony shared a warm smile, knowing a special bond had been formed on this day.

There followed the most unbelievable scene of pure friendship between felines and birds witnessed by two barbarians, in total shock. Cristirin moved to her mobile camera and clicked away like a seasoned professional photographer. Sadly, her mobile battery was flat. Like her husband, she could only stand and soak up the experience of sheer joy between all.

*****

General Goose, with his flapping wings, "Attention, Honking Goose Regiment! It's time to migrate to Argentina! Gather your feathers and beak up! We have a long journey ahead of us!"

The female canary to her partner: "Oh, look! The mighty General Goose is preparing the Honking Goose Regiment for their long migration journey. It's incredible how organised they are!"

The male canary responded, "Indeed! These geese are known for their leadership skills. The Honking Goose Regiment is lucky to have such a dedicated and experienced commander like their general and his Chief Warrant Officer."

The general now, surveying the surroundings, "Ruddy Ground doves and Chestnut-fronted Macaws! Welcome to this city! From our brief experience here, we believe your new home in the north of the city will be all you wish for and more. We would be honoured if, in the future, you wished to join us on our migration journey to Argentina. We will gladly allow you to experience what we do every year."

One of the Chestnut-fronted Macaw answered, "Thank you, general! We would indeed be thrilled to be a part of your grand annual migration flight. We've just moved here and haven't had the chance to explore the city much, so for now, our adventure must begin here."

A second Chestnut-fronted Macaw also wished to speak to such an important bird, "Absolutely! We macaws have heard about your regiment's remarkable skills and stamina during migration. It would be an honour to fly alongside the Honking Goose Regiment and witness this incredible journey first-hand. When you return next year, please come here to see all of us, and we can talk again."

A spokesman for the Ruddy grounded dove moved forward to address the general, "Sir, we are birds who love to be on the ground seeking seeds and the occasional treat from the barbarians. In all our history of being here in this city, there has never been one incident where we have not felt safe. Yes, the noise and the pollution are things we must consider each season, but for now, we have never found an adequate reason to contemplate migrating. We sincerely wish you and your squadron the greatest of journeys, and we hope you all reach your chosen destinations safely. You will always be welcome to our city."

The general bowed and spoke proudly, "I appreciate your kind words and your enthusiasm, my fellow avian friends. The Honking Goose Regiment has trained extensively for this migration, and we are confident in our abilities. Together, we shall embark on this extraordinary journey, showcasing the strength and unity of our diverse avian community."

The female canary chirped up, "Truly, it's a remarkable sight to witness different bird species coming together in support of one another. The offer to the chestnut-fronted macaws joining the esteemed Honking Goose Regiment next year shows the unbreakable bond among our feathered friends."

Her male companion chirped in, "Absolutely! It's awe-inspiring to see the unity and cooperation between different avian species. This migration journey will be a testament to the Honking Goose Regiment's strength and a celebration of the rich diversity in our bird kingdom."

The general raised his impressive wings, "Honking Goose Regiment, and the one Yellow-headed caracara, let us take flight together, guiding each other towards new horizons! Onward to Argentina!" All the birds became emotional, and together, they sang out excitedly, "Onward to Argentina!"

And so, the Honking Goose Regiment, accompanied by the spirited yellow-headed caracara, set off on their grand migration to Argentina, a remarkable journey that would be remembered for years to come.

The two canaries, joined by the five doves, decided it was time for breakfast, and each flew off in search of seeds and a possible juicy insect. The flock of macaws decided their stomachs also needed replenishing, and off they went in search of fruit trees, seeds, fruits, and flowers.

Blacky, Liz, and Goldie decided a race around the penthouse was in order; jumping and leaping was the necessary activity of the day. Blacky's long shiny black tail was the target.

\*\*\*\*\*

## 52: I am Climate Change Visiting to see What I can do

I am Climate Change, a phenomenon that has emerged as a direct consequence of you barbarians and your persistent and most damaging activities, primarily deforestation and the excessive burning of fossil fuels. My existence poses a significant threat to all of mankind and South America's delicate balance of fauna and flora.

Allow me to elaborate on the reasons why:

One of climate change's most apparent impacts is the rise in global temperatures. In South America and many other parts of this Earth, this has led to increased heatwaves, droughts, and changes in nearly all rainfall patterns.

These extreme weather conditions usually have disastrous effects on agriculture, water resources, and overall socioeconomic well-being.

The Andean region in South America is not just your home to numerous glaciers rapidly retreating due to rising temperatures. It is also where I will focus a lot over the coming weeks. My process contributes to your loss of freshwater reserves, affecting your water availability for consumption, agriculture, and various ecosystems.

Climate change also brings about sea-level rise, threatening your coastal areas in South America. Low-lying regions, such as the Amazon delta and your coastal cities, are particularly vulnerable to my storm surges and increased flooding. This puts many of your barbarian settlements, infrastructure, and important coastal ecosystems at risk.

Remember, this is down to you all, and I am not in any way responsible.

South America boasts diverse ecosystems, such as the Amazon rainforest, Pantanal wetlands, and the Galapagos Islands.

Again I, as Climate change is now beginning to disrupt these ecosystems by altering temperature and precipitation patterns, leading to habitat loss and species endangerment.

The loss of biodiversity and unique wildlife present in these regions is a direct consequence of my existence.

Your practice of deforestation is a significant contributor to how I, climate change, will act in South America. For example, the Amazon rainforest, often referred to as the "lungs of the Earth," plays a crucial role in absorbing carbon dioxide and stabilising the climate. However, your endless rampant deforestation for agricultural practices, logging, and urban expansion depletes this vital carbon sink, exacerbating the impact of me, climate change.

Not wishing to bore you, I'd like to point out that climate change has already intensified the frequency and severity of natural disasters, including hurricanes, floods, and wildfires.

South America is already experiencing these events, which become more destructive and more difficult to manage due to my influence. The devastation caused by these disasters not only affects your barbarian lives but also disrupts ecosystems and threatens the survival of numerous plant and animal species.

In conclusion, climate change poses a grave threat to South America by impacting barbarian livelihoods and the intricate balance of fauna and flora.

Your urgent action is necessary to mitigate my effects through global efforts to reduce greenhouse gas emissions, protect forests, promote sustainable practices, and adapt to my changing climate demands. Failure to address my concerns now will lead to irreversible consequences for South America and the entire planet.

Now let me have a look at your city……I think a report is justifiable in this instance.

*****

**Climate Change's Observations and Warning for Your City.**
**Introduction:**
As Climate Change, I have focused my attention on your enchanting city, nestled in the heart of South America. While this city possesses immense cultural diversity, historical landmarks, and mesmerising natural beauty, my observations have led me to identify several concerning issues that demand immediate attention. This report illuminates my disapproval of certain aspects of your city and outlines the potential consequences if urgent actions are not taken to address them.

**Dislike 1: Your city's air pollution.**
Like many urban areas, your city suffers from high levels of air pollution. Fumes emitted by vehicles, industrial activities, and inefficient waste management systems contribute to this detrimental condition. The pollution poses severe health risks to the many barbarians and damages the delicate balance of your local ecosystem. If this issue remains unaddressed, it will exacerbate respiratory illnesses, decrease quality of life, harm local biodiversity, and amplify the effects of climate change.

**Dislike 2: Deforestation.**
Uncontrolled deforestation in the surrounding areas of your city has caught my attention. The destruction of vital forest habitats jeopardises your city's ecological well-being and amplifies the release of carbon dioxide into the atmosphere. If this practice continues without restraint, it will intensify climate change thoughts regarding the disruption of your local weather patterns, increase your soil degradation, and diminish your precious water resources.

**Dislike 3: Insufficient Waste Management.**
Your city waste management system falls short in terms of efficiency and proper disposal. Insufficient waste treatment and recycling facilities are leading to improper waste disposal practices. This not only contaminates your soil and water sources but also harms all aquatic life and agricultural productivity and contributes to your emission of greenhouse gases. If this situation persists, I will escalate pollution levels, contaminate vital resources, and put public health at risk.

**My proposed plans for you to take notice of:**
To mitigate my concerns, I recommend the following plans to address your city's environmental challenges:

**1. Implement Strict Emission Control Measures:** Enforce regulations on all vehicle emissions, promote the use of renewable energy sources, and encourage the adoption of clean technologies by industries to reduce air pollution.

**2. Foster Reforestation Initiatives:** Launch extensive reforestation programs, providing incentives for afforestation and promoting sustainable land use practices to restore and protect your city's forest cover.

**3. Enhance Waste Management Systems:** Invest in waste management infrastructure, establish recycling programs, and raise awareness among your barbarian population about proper waste disposal and the importance of recycling.

**Consequences of Inaction on your part:**
In the event that your city neglects to address my concerns promptly, the consequences may include:

**1. Deteriorating Public Health:** I will begin with escalating air pollution levels that will lead to an increase in respiratory diseases, allergies, and other illnesses, significantly compromising the health and well-being of your population.

**2. Ecological Imbalance:** I will ramp up on the ongoing destruction of your local ecosystems and your practice of deforestation, which will result in the loss of your biodiversity. Furthermore, I will increase the negative impacts on water availability and disrupt wildlife habitats, thus destabilising the delicate balance of your region's environment.

**3. Intensified my Climate Change Effects:** Failure to mitigate greenhouse gas emissions and adapt to sustainable practices will perpetuate my climate change impacts, exacerbating their consequences, such as extreme weather events, water scarcity, and altered agricultural productivity.

**My Conclusion:**
At present, your city is, indeed, a vibrant and culturally rich city. But it must confront the challenges posed by climate change and promptly address the issues of air pollution, deforestation, and waste management. By implementing my

proposed plans and taking necessary actions, your city has the opportunity to mitigate my adverse effects, protect your environment, enhance the quality of life for all your barbarians, and become a model for sustainable development. Failing to do so will only lead to further deterioration of the city's well-being and contribute to the escalating global climate crisis you are currently facing.

*****

Just in case, I, climate change, feel it would be pertinent to investigate and describe what an inferno wildfire could do to your city.......and issue you a stark warning of what to expect if I am ignored.

In the realm of fiction and, indeed, before reality, let's consider the powerful and devastating impact of a wildfire or set of wildfires on your city nestled beneath your mountain ridge.

As my wildfire takes hold, fuelled by strong gusts of wind and an abundance of dry vegetation, it will rapidly engulf the lower slopes of your mountain ridge.

The flames will rage with an almost alive ferocity, consuming everything in their path without mercy. The intense heat and billowing smoke will create an eerie atmosphere, casting an ominous shadow over your defenceless city below.

As my wildfire races downward, it will swiftly engulf your surrounding forests, turning them into a chaotic inferno. The crackling of burning trees and shrubs will echo through the air, bringing a haunting symphony of destruction.

The sky above your city, once vivid and blue, is now a thick blanket of smoky darkness, obscuring the sun and casting an apocalyptic glow upon your landscape.

The first signs of the impending catastrophe begin to manifest on the outskirts of your city.

My fire leaps from tree to tree, creeping closer to the first houses at an alarming speed. Panicked residents will scramble to evacuate, desperately grabbing their most cherished belongings and fleeing to safety.

Your streets become congested with cars and anxious barbarians, all racing against the impending doom.

Within minutes, my wildfire reaches your city's fringes, hungrily devouring everything in its path. Your homes, businesses, and infrastructure become enveloped in an unstoppable torrent of flames.

Your once bustling streets now lie abandoned, reduced to charred remains. Thick smoke fills your air, making it difficult to breathe, while sparks and embers dance through the sky, threatening to ignite new fires even further.

My intense heat radiating from my wildfire causes devastation beyond the reach of the flames themselves. Your buildings, untouched by my inferno, crumble under the stress, their structural integrity compromised.

Valuable landmarks and historical sites succumb to the merciless blaze, forever altering the city's identity.

Amidst the chaos and despair, your brave firefighters and emergency personnel will valiantly battle against my inferno. They will work tirelessly, risking their lives to save as much of the city as possible. The brave efforts of these heroes may prevent my wildfire from spreading to even greater extents, albeit unable to halt the destruction entirely.

Once my wildfire finally loses its strength and retreats back up the mountain ridge, your city stands as a wounded survivor. The stark reality of entire neighbourhoods lying in ruins, reduced to ashes.

The scars I have left behind are not merely physical but emotional, deeply etched into your wounded hearts and those who have lost everything.

But think on the positive side; yes, rebuilding will become a long and arduous process as your city's barbarians come together, each demonstrating incredible resilience and fortitude. From the ashes, you can reimagine a city beginning to emerge. Just think of new infrastructures, green spaces, and an enhanced focus on fire prevention and preparedness taking shape, ultimately turning tragedy into an opportunity for growth and renewal.

See, I am not totally bad; goodness can come from me. But in the meantime, you need to change your wicked ways and not expect me to change back.

*****

## 53: I am Simon, and I am taking my two best Mates on Holiday

General Simón José Antonio de la Santísima Trinidad Bolívar Palacios Ponte y Blanco & Palomo. Captain Sebastián de Belalcázar y Dávila Santillana, with his black stallion named El Dorado, son of Nightshade and Royal Lieutenant Felipe Joaquín de Cayzedo y Cuero and his equally black stallion renamed Independence after Felipe had been riding Nocturno for over a week.

Both Sebastian and Felipe had agreed over an empty bottle of champagne that they, too, wanted to enjoy special bonds with their chosen stallions like their good friend Simon and his Palomo.

Since the adventure of rescuing the older people in their care homes in the north of the city from the expanding flood water and the terrifying mudslide from the mountain ridge looking down on the city, all three military statues and their chosen stallions had re-enacted their Midnight Derby horse race at the International Airport every Saturday evening when all the barbarians were sleeping and when the runway appeared redundant from having any aircraft landing.

All three loved having the Midnight Derby experience as part of their weekly schedule. It gave them adventure and excitement every time, especially after a bottle or two of a chosen prestigious red wine from Spain.

Sebastian's choice for tonight was the L'Ermita, hailing from the Priorat region of Spain. It was produced by Álvaro Palacios and is hailed as one of Spain's most iconic and prestigious wines. It is famous for its depth, complexity, and exceptional ageing potential.

There was no chance the two bottles would last more than two hours.

Last week, Sebastian acquired three bottles of Pingus, which Dominio de Pingus made in Spain's Ribera del Duero region. This red wine was authentic and of exceptional quality, with its boldness and concentration.

Simon and Felipe had yet to learn where Sebastian was sourcing his prestigious wine choices, and they never asked. They enjoyed getting merry, knowing the three stallions would manage to get each to their designated homes without mishap.

*****

On the night of the rescue, riding back from the Museo Aereo Fenix after saying "Goodbye" to so many new older friends, the five generals, Manuela Saenz, and the museum's founders, José and Stella, as well as the members of the Meeting of the Minds rescue teams, Simon spoke to his two longstanding amigos.

He suggested, "Listen, you two fine gentlemen, now we have our transport; why don't we go back in history to when our real selves were alive and visit places that meant a lot to each other?"

Both Sebastian and Felipe were in complete agreement; they sensed new adventures were just over the horizon.

Simon was ecstatic that his proposal was so willingly accepted, "Let me go first and take you both to Cartagena, followed by Barranquilla, and ending at Santa Marta?"

"Felipe, eager to go straight there, asked, "What route should we take? I have never been to these places you have mentioned."

"Nor I, as they did not exist in my time," announced Sebastian.

"Oh, I think this route will be fine for us, " Simon said as he produced a piece of paper from his tunic pocket.

"We will, of course, start from here in Santiago de Cali and will ride towards Cartagena, heading east on Route 25. As we ride through the city of Cartagena, I can show you the historical landmarks such as the old city walls, the Palace of the Inquisition, and Castillo de San Felipe de Barajas."

"From Cartagena, we will take Route 90 north towards Barranquilla. We will visit places like the Museo del Caribe, a cultural museum that showcases the region's history and folklore. Then, from Barranquilla, we will continue north on Route 90 towards Santa Marta."

"Wow, Simon, you thought this through. When did you get the idea of this journey into your past?" asked Sebastian in wonderment.

"I have no idea when I first thought of it. I suppose I have always wanted to go to these places. When Palomo arrived, I knew I finally could. Then I reasoned, why not go with my two best friends, and so here I am asking you both."

Felipe smiled and asked another question, "Are we going to your namesake's resting place?"

"Yes, in Santa Marta, I wish to guide you, as my most trusty companions, to visit the Quinta de San Pedro Alejandrino, where the real Simon Bolivar passed away peacefully in his sleep. It is a museum dedicated to his memory. I wish to pay my respects to a great man who never conquered but always liberated."

*****

The month-long adventure into Bolivar's past covered over 1,500 miles on horseback, with the stallions covering 70 miles a day. This allowed horses and riders to rest and recover each evening and break open another of Sebastian's secret supply of prestigious wines.

The journey between Santiago de Cali and Cartagena took the first two weeks to complete. On arrival, the riders and stallions spent a couple of days and nights resting and enjoying the impressive fortress port and its historical figures, including Gabriel García Márquez.

They were intrigued by finding a head and shoulders image painted on a house wall, allowing every visitor or passerby to know this was his home when he was alive.

They stopped to hear a guide describing who this storyteller was.

"General Simón Bolívar, Captain Sebastián de Belalcázar, and Royal Lieutenant Felipe Joaquín de Cayzedo may not have been Gabriel García Márquez's contemporaries, as they were all famous historical figures from the 18th and 19th centuries, while García Márquez was a 20th-century writer. However, his notable contributions to Colombian literature would undoubtedly have intrigued them.

Gabriel García Márquez, often called Gabo, was a Colombian novelist, journalist, and Nobel laureate in literature. He is best known for his masterpiece, "One Hundred Years of Solitude" (Cien años de soledad), which is considered one of the most significant works of 20th-century literature.

Gabo's writing style is characterised by magical realism, where fantastical elements are seamlessly integrated into everyday reality. Through his unique storytelling, he explored themes such as love, time, family, and the complex history of Latin America.

His literary works vividly depict Colombian society and capture the essence of the region, its traditions, and its people. Gabo's ability to blend reality and imagination made him one of the most influential writers of his time and a beacon of Colombian literature.

While General Bolívar, Captain de Belalcázar, and Royal Lieutenant de Cayzedo may not have been aware of Gabo's work, they would undoubtedly appreciate his impact on Colombian literature and how he contributed to the rich tapestry of his country's cultural heritage."

The Tour Guide then began to hand out a series of leaflets noting the 10 most famous works by Gabriel Garcia Marquez:

1. "One Hundred Years of Solitude" (Cien años de soledad)
2. "Love in the Time of Cholera" (El amor en los tiempos del cólera)
3. "Chronicle of a Death Foretold" (Crónica de una muerte anunciada)
4. "The Autumn of the Patriarch" (El otoño del patriarca)
5. "In Evil Hour" (La mala hora)
6. "Of Love and Other Demons" (Del amor y otros demonios)
7. "Leaf Storm" (La hojarasca)
8. "No One Writes to the Colonel" (El coronel no tiene quien le escriba)
9. "Memories of My Melancholy Whores" (Memoria de mis putas tristes)
10. "The General in His Labyrinth" (El general en su laberinto)

The last title caught the trio's eyes, and each wondered to themselves, "Which General had he written about."

And if, by magic intervention, the guide spoke, "For those of you who plan to visit Santa Marta, then I recommend you read book 10, which describes Simon Bolivar's last days before leaving us all." Then, as an afterthought, the guide pointing toward the mountain range in front of him said, "Pray, do find the time to visit Quinta San Pedro Alejandrino, where our Liberator is celebrated and remembered in wonderful settings."

*****

Later, all three while sitting on the fortress wall and resting their stallions on the golden sands below them, Simon felt it was the right moment to explain his deep thoughts and why he chose Cartagena as the first of the three places to showcase to his two friends, "Sebastian and Felipe, I wish to take you on a captivating journey through the history of Cartagena, highlighting its significance to our cause of Independence."

"Let us first travel back to the year 1533 when the Spanish conquistador, Pedro de Heredia, founded this magnificent city of Cartagena on the northern coast of New Granada. Nestled along the Caribbean Sea, this strategic location breathed life into the city, paving the way for a vibrant hub of trade, culture, and resistance. Heredia made his fortune from trading trinkets in exchange for gold from the indigenous people who had lived in peace here for centuries."

Upon hearing this latest revelation, Sebastian sighed: "Now I know why I never discovered EL Dorado." I never explored further than the southwest of the country."

His two friends laughed at his mock dismay. Simon took a moment to continue with his version of history as he knew it: "Cartagena soon flourished, attracting settlers from all walks of life, including indigenous people, Africans, and Europeans. Such diverse heritage enabled a unique fusion of cultures, laying the foundation for the city's distinctive atmosphere and people's resilience."

"As time forged ahead, Cartagena developed into a coveted fortress as it became a primary port for Spanish ships carrying vast amounts of treasure. Wealth flowed through its cobblestone streets, gilded colonial architecture adorned the plazas, and merchants from around the world established influential trading connections within the city's walls."

But amidst this grandeur, an undercurrent of resistance simmered. The seeds of dissent were sown in the hearts of those who yearned for freedom and self-determination.

Cartagena became a hotbed of revolutionary ideas, nurturing the spirit of independence and fueling the imagination of patriots like me.

My dear friends, the ideals of liberty grew more vital within the walls of Cartagena's San Felipe de Barajas fortress. Sorry, Sebastian, but the oppressive yoke of Spanish colonial rule cast a dark shadow over our people, instigating a flame that would eventually ignite into the fires of revolution.

Inspired by the triumphs of the French and American Revolutions, the great visionaries of Cartagena contributed to the collective awakening of our people's longing for emancipation."

Sebastian looked at his friend, "Please do not apologise. From what I saw, they may have had a point."

Simon bowed his head in acknowledgement of what his friend was willing to admit. "In 1811, Cartagena embraced the cause of Independence, marking a turning point in our struggle against Spanish dominion. The city became an epicentre of resistance, hosting the first-ever constitution of Colombia. It was here, amidst these ancient walls, that the foundation for a united and liberated Gran Colombia was laid."

Simon paused again; with good, there is also bad, "However, the path to freedom was fraught with peril, and Cartagena stood at its forefront. The city bore witness to relentless battles, sieges, and sacrifices, with brave souls fighting to repel your Spanish forces and ensure the triumph of our revolution. The Battle of Cartagena in 1815, symbolised by the heroic efforts of women and men alike, served as a testament to our indomitable spirit."

"Thus, my dear friend Sebastian, Cartagena holds a special place in my and Felipe's hearts and in the annals of history. It embodies the resilience, bravery, and unity that defined our struggle for Independence. Its walls may have witnessed bloodshed, but they also resonate with the audacious dreams of a free, sovereign nation."

Now looking westward to the slowing disappearing sunset, the Liberator thought out loud, "While I, Simón Bolívar, ventured far and wide across the territories of New Granada and beyond, it is here in Cartagena that the indissoluble bond between our people and the pursuit of liberty was forged. Cartagena's historical legacy remains a rallying cry, calling upon present and future generations to uphold the principles of justice, equality, and freedom."

At this point, Felipe moved to stand next to his friend and added, "May the walls of Cartagena forever stand as sentinels against oppression and serve as a reminder to us of the price paid for the liberty we cherish."

Sebastian could find no reason to argue and took up the right side of his two amigos. In an unusual line now stood a Colombian, a Venezuelan, and a Spaniard. Below, three stallions looked up with admiration for all three above.

*****

From Cartagena, they rode along the coast to reach and admire the colonial architecture that had outlived them all in Barranquilla.

"It took a further two days for them to arrive. Again, they rested and took in the sights. This time, Simon took them to the mighty Magdalena River. But before heading to the mighty river, he wanted to stop and explain why this industrial port and city meant so much to him personally. As was the norm, Simon stood in a position so that Barranquilla would act as a magnificent backdrop to what he was going to teach his two friends.

"My esteemed friends Sebastian and Felipe, welcome to Barranquilla, a city that holds profound significance to our cause of liberation. Allow me to elucidate the reasons why this coastal gem played such a vital role in my revolutionary endeavours."

Dutifully, Sebastian and Felipe stood and waited in anticipation of this new lesson in history from the man who was there.

As you can see, "Barranquilla" is nestled along the mighty Magdalena River and possesses key geographical advantages that gave it immense strategic importance during our struggle for Independence. As a vibrant port city, it served as a gateway to the Caribbean Sea, linking us to the world beyond and enabling crucial connections for our military and logistical operations.

"The city's location on the banks of the Magdalena River proved to have its distinct advantages. This majestic waterway served as a vital transportation artery, facilitating the movement of our troops, supplies, and communication between different regions of our liberated territories. Like the lifeblood of our revolution, its flow carried our hopes and aspirations to every corner of New Granada."

"Barranquilla was more than just a geographical blessing for me, my friends. It also, like Cartagena, represented a melting pot of cultures, a testament to the diversity and resilience of our people. Residents of African, Indigenous, and European descent filled its streets, fostering a rich tapestry of heritage and fueling the revolutionary fervour that surged through our veins."

Simon enjoyed his version of the roots of his achievements: "Moreover, Barranquilla became a bastion of economic growth and commerce, serving as a hub for trade and industry. The city's bustling markets and thriving economic activities generated valuable resources that helped sustain our struggle against your Spanish crown, Sebastian. It was here, amidst the vibrant exchange of goods and ideas, that the seeds of revolution were nourished."

"But beyond its logistical and economic significance, Barranquilla embodied the spirit of unity and camaraderie. The people of this city embraced the cause of Independence with genuine passion, standing shoulder to shoulder with me in our pursuit of liberty. Their unwavering support and commitment sowed hope and encouraged my weary heart during my darkest days."

All three were again in a line as before in Cartagena: "My dear friends, as we go to walk the streets of Barranquilla, let us inhale the air of freedom that lingers here. Let us absorb the energy and strength emanating from the ground we tread. With its strategic location, cultural mosaic, and unwavering support, this city became an emblematic symbol of our struggle, a testament to the unbreakable spirit of our people."

"Through fire and blood, victories and defeats, Barranquilla stood firm, never faltering in its commitment to our cause. As we press on in our quest for liberation, let the indomitable spirit of this coastal marvel inspire us. Barranquilla encapsulates the dreams, aspirations, and sacrifices that have shaped our journey towards a free and sovereign Gran Colombia."

Again, like in Cartagena, Felipe managed to find words to encompass all the endeavours made by his friend Simon: "May the name of Barranquilla forever be etched in the annals of our history as a testament to the unwavering resolve that ignited the flames of our revolution."

Both Simon and Sebastian turned to Felipe and once more marvelled at his chosen words.

Not wishing to spoil the moment, Simon quietly left his two friends to bring back the three stallions. He silently mounted and waited until they had turned satisfied with their introduction to Barranquilla. Now, it was time for some adventure.

*****

"Right, before we head to our final city, I thought it would be a perfect time to take us all on a journey up the Magdalena to a point where the sea meets the river."

Both Felipe and Sebastian were in shock, and both at once exclaimed in disbelief, "What did you say sea meets river?"

"Indeed, I did; it is time for action, mi amigos,"

*****

"First, let me enlighten you on the immense significance of the Rio Magdalena, its meeting point with the sea, and the appropriate means of transport for our noble steeds and ourselves, as if we were in the 1800s."

First and foremost, let us acknowledge Rio Magdalena as the lifeline of our beloved New Granada. Stretching across vast distances, remember, this mighty river served as a crucial transportation route, connecting the heartland of our nation with the coastal regions. Its presence facilitated my movement of goods, troops, and information, playing a pivotal role in the success of my military campaigns.

Well, as you are both now aware, the Rio Magdalena was not just a river but a symbol of unity, embodying the flow of our shared aspirations and the lifeblood of our revolution."

"Now, I thought it would be great for us to venture towards the point where the northbound Magdalena River merges with the majestic Caribbean Sea. It is known as the "Mouth of Ashes" or in our Spanish "Bocas de Ceniza." You will witness the river moving swiftly and slamming into the Caribbean Sea with what I can only describe as elegance with a large amount of drama attached. You will also witness the ash-coloured water reaching out for many miles before being consumed by the blue tones of the Caribbean."

"Wow," said Felipe, filled with joy at being on this most memorable journey with his two amigos. "This juncture represents a moment of profound significance, signifying the union of the river's strength and the sea's vastness. It serves as a potent visual metaphor, reminding us of the vast potential that awaits New Granada as a united and independent nation." Simon looked on amused, and Sebastian wondered how his sovereign in his time could not have seen this power of strength heading his way."

*****

Bringing himself back to the conditions that await them, Simon reveals, "It is also a set of narrow embankments that were built a long time ago along the river to strengthen and increase the current and minimise sediment accumulation."

*****

"As for the means of transportation for our stallions and ourselves, I have always envisioned a scene from the early 1800s, when horseback served as a primary mode of transportation. I have always pictured myself riding atop Palomo, his hooves pounding against the earth as we traverse the rugged terrains and vast distances that lie between the Rio Magdalena and the coastal meeting point. Palomo, bred for endurance and strength, shall carry me with unwavering determination and grace."

Simon paused and exclaimed, "Never did I dream of doing this with a Conquistador and a Colombian Politician!"

"So, to ensure the safety and comfort of our noble equine companions, we will prepare sturdy wooden crates specifically designed for the transportation of our horses. Reinforced with robust planks and strong ropes, these crates will secure our stallions during the journey. We shall rely on experienced handlers and grooms who possess the knowledge and skills required to ensure the well-being of our equine comrades throughout the trip. Adequate provisions and water reservoirs will help us sustain riders and horses during our expedition."

Sebastian now thinks he would have a question that Simon could never answer adequately, "Now, Senor Bolivar, where do you intend to find all this help?"

"Oh, that is easy; I had a word with those two gnomes before leaving Cali, that cross-eyed Abella sorted all out. Now, do you have any more questions?"

All three laughed till they were crying and holding aching stomach muscles. The very description of Abella was so much fun for the trio.

*****

Hi, this is Felipe. I thought it would be nice to continue this part of our journey and relate to you how magnificent the destination was. Chancing such an experience of the Bocas de Ceniza would be life-changing for anyone.

It was an honour to witness; I hope you enjoy my narrative. "Ah, Bocas de Ceniza, the final destination where the Rio Magdalena finds its ultimate embrace with the briny sea. Let me, Felipe Joaquin de Cayzedo y Cicero, paint a vivid picture of the awe-inspiring route leading to this magnificent place and the captivating sights awaiting us.

Our journey commences as we depart from the bustling city of Barranquilla, following the meandering course of the Rio Magdalena. The broad and mighty river carried us ever closer to our destination; its waters reflected the vastness of our aspirations and the depth of our determination. As we traversed this great artery of our land, an undeniable sense of anticipation and awe took root within our hearts.

Eventually, the river widened, revealing glimpses of the open sea ahead. We navigated through winding channels, drawing nearer to the legendary Bocas de Ceniza, the iconic estuary that marks the point where the river meets the sea. The name itself exudes an alluring mystique that captivates the imagination.

As we approach this natural wonder, the air becomes tinged with a fine mist, a gentle precursor to the decisive clash between freshwater and saltwater that lies before us.

The river's brown hue gradually merges with the shimmering blue of the sea, creating a breathtaking spectacle of contrasting elements merging harmoniously.

Upon arriving at Bocas de Ceniza, we are greeted by a panorama of magnificent proportions. The estuary unfolds before us like a grand amphitheatre, where the dynamic dance of currents enthrals the senses. The river's relentless flow battles against the lashing waves of the sea, creating a magnificent display of nature's power and resilience.

The horizon stretches vastly, with the distant tracings of ships coming and going, symbolising the constant flow of trade and commerce that envelopes this gateway to our lands. The breeze carries with it the scent of salt, mingling with the natural, earthy aroma of the river, a harmonious blend that symbolises the unity of our diverse nation.

We could not help but marvel at the rich ecosystem that thrives in this volatile juncture. We also witnessed the abundance of seabirds soaring across the sky; their elegant flight patterns testify to the unending cycles of life and nature's unyielding resilience.

The distant silhouette of fishermen casting their nets in pursuit of life's sustenance adds a human touch to this breathtaking tableau.

*****

From there, the travellers took an additional three days of coastal riding to Santa Marta, the gateway to the awe-inspiring Sierra Nevada mountains, mangrove swamps, and a never-ending tropical jungle.

Simon, Sebastian, and Felipe hiked and relaxed here. They also enjoyed the Caribbean Ocean by witnessing their horses galloping through the incoming indigo-coloured waves washing up on the sandy white beaches.

That first night, Simon was quieter than usual, and both his friends allowed him more space to reflect on where they were. The subject of the Quinta de San Pedro Alejandrino waited for the three friends to find the courage to ask whether Simon still wished to visit this historical landmark.

Surprising to all three, the question did not come from one of them but from another…

*****

"Good evening General Simón José Antonio de la Santísima Trinidad Bolívar Palacios Ponte y Blanco. I heard you were not far away. Have you come to visit Quinta de San Pedro Alejandrino?"

Simon looked up, and with warmth in his voice and heart, he embraced a face he had not seen since the night of the Midnight Airport Derby. "Gentleman, let me introduce my loyal friend and most trusted Aide-de-Camp any revolutionary General could ask for, General Daniel Florencio O'Leary."

Simon turned to his two friends with a beaming smile and said, "You may well remember Daniel from the night we all raced on wild horses on the airport runway at midnight."

Both Felipe and Sebastian were moving forward towards Daniel, ready to shake his hand with warmth and friendship. Now, a quartet of a Venezuelan, a Colombian, a Spaniard, and an Irishman were embraced as one.

*****

As General Daniel Florencio O'Leary, I am delighted to share with you the fascinating account of my early life in Cork, Ireland, and the circumstances that led this 17-year-old to travel to South America to become an Aide-de-Camp to Simon Bolivar.

Born in Cork in the late 18th century, I grew up in a vibrant city known for its rich history and rebellious spirit.

From an early age, my family of butter merchants instilled in me a strong sense of patriotism and an unwavering belief in the ideals of liberty and Independence.

As a young man, I witnessed firsthand the injustices and hardships faced by the Irish people under British rule. This oppressive environment fueled my desire for change and sincere admiration for revolutionary ideals. Inspired by these sentiments, I actively engaged in political and social discussions, making connections with like-minded individuals who yearned for freedom from British dominance. I learnt about the Napoleonic Wars at this time, but alas, I was far too young to enlist and experience them.

Fate would play a crucial role in my journey to South America. During one such political gathering in Cork, I met General Francisco de Miranda, a Venezuelan military and political leader.

General Miranda recognised my passion and admiration for the cause of liberation and saw in me the potential to become an asset to his movement.

General Miranda was impressed by my eloquence, intelligence, and unwavering dedication to the cause of freedom. He offered me a once-in-a-lifetime opportunity to travel to South America and join the ranks of the revolutionaries fighting for Independence from Spanish colonial rule.

Grasping this extraordinary chance, I bid farewell to my homeland and embarked on a perilous journey to the distant continent of South America. Arriving on the shores of Venezuela, I was determined to contribute to the cause that had awakened my spirit and kindled my sense of purpose.

Upon my arrival, fate continued to favour me as I soon caught the attention of Simon Bolivar, the visionary leader and key figure in the region's struggle for Independence.

Recognising my loyalty, intelligence, and dedication, Bolivar appointed me as his Aide-de-Camp!

This position would grant me proximity to one of the greatest military minds of the time and a front-row seat to the epic battles and diplomatic efforts that would forever shape the continent's history.

Bolivar and I faced numerous trials and tribulations, traversing treacherous landscapes, engaging in fierce battles, and forging alliances with other revolutionary leaders.

As Bolivar's trusted confidant and second-in-command, I can safely say that I played an instrumental role in the military strategy, diplomatic negotiations, and the overall liberation movement across South America.

My time as an Aide-de-Camp was defined by courage, sacrifice, and unwavering commitment to the cause of liberty. My experiences in South America would shape my life and become a memorable part of the historical tapestry of the continent's struggle for Independence.

I also wish to say the Irish people back home in Cork are still proud that one amongst them who died in 1854 in Bogota is buried in the National Pantheon of Venezuela. I lie with many officers, soldiers, sailors, heroes, heroines such as Manuela Saenz, writers, poets, and politicians who together helped forge the success of the War of Independence and liberate us from the tyrannical control of the Spanish.

Each year, on the day of remembrance of Simon Bolivar and after all the barbarians in Caracas and further afield have retired back to their homes, a stately ball in honour of our Liberator occurs.

*****

"General Simón José Antonio de la Santísima Trinidad Bolívar Palacios Ponte y Blanco, Sebastián de Belalcázar y Dávila Santillana, and Royal Lieutenant and politician Felipe Joaquin de Cayzedo y Cicero. I am pleased to announce there is going to be a small get-together this evening in the Hacienda, Florida, of San Pedro Alejandrino in honour of your arrival from Santiago de Cali. I do hope you agree that this will be one occasion none of you wish to miss."

For once, Simon was at a loss for words; he had never envisaged such an occasion would be possible. He had only wished to escape the noisy city and have an adventure or two with his close friends. Now, he was about to go back in history and meet up with people that history refuses to ignore.

Sebastian approached Daniel and took his hand in his, "Please excuse the shock being felt by our good friend; I speak for all three of us; it will be an honour for each of us to attend."

"Fantastic, I have already taken the liberty to arrange for a fine carriage for you to travel in, and your three impressive stallions can be tethered to the back of the coach. Shall we say seven pm for you to be ready?"

*****

That evening at seven pm, we three, Simon, Sebastian, and me, Felipe, with our three stallions, Palomo, El Dorado, and Independence, were met by a luxurious open carriage with six magnificent horses and a coachman.

The sight epitomises grandeur, elegance, prestige, sophistication, ostentation, and opulence. Together, they perfectly reflect the elevated status of its occupiers. The carriage was spacious and, must be said, breathtaking in appearance. It showcased its ornate design, evidently crafted with meticulous attention to detail and embellishments.

The exterior of the carriage showcased exquisite craftsmanship. Its polished and gleaming body was made from high-quality materials such as fine wood or metal. The carriage was adorned with intricate carvings, elaborate scrollwork, and delicate gilded accents. Its large, open design allowed for excellent visibility and was captivating.

A robust and elaborate suspension system supported the carriage, allowing us to experience a smooth and comfortable ride. Six magnificent horses, meticulously groomed and adorned with regal harnesses, were harnessed in pairs to provide the necessary power and grace for the carriage's motion.

The coachman, typically attired in a smart livery, skillfully guided the horses, bringing life to the impressive equine team. The coachman's seat was positioned at the front, elevated slightly above our passengers' compartment, thus allowing for clear command of the horses and a clear view of the road ahead.

The interior of the carriage was sumptuously appointed to provide the utmost comfort and luxury to its occupants. Plush and luxuriously upholstered seats were elegantly arranged to allow conversation among the three passengers. The upholstery featured rich fabrics, embroidery, and cushions, representing the fashion of our accustomed era.

On this occasion, elaborate curtains made from fine silk or velvet were not needed to drape the sides of the carriage. The requirement that passengers control the amount of privacy or shield themselves from the elements they may have desired was gone.

Delicately designed and functional lamps provided illumination during our evening journey.

In keeping with the period, the carriage also featured small compartments for personal items and accessories, such as folding seats, footrests, and even a miniature liquor cabinet. The latter was emptied rather rapidly.

"Er Simon, did you notice the coachman hardly said anything throughout our journey? Do you think we may have upset him in some way?" inquired Sebastian.

In reply, "I am sure he is just concentrating on his work at hand. Not only that, I suspect he may be in shock at seeing a Venezuelan, a Colombian, and a Spaniard sitting and drinking merrily together!"

It took a lot of willpower for the coachman to suppress the snigger that threatened to blast out loud.

*****

A short while later, the coachman skillfully approached the large set of wooden doors leading to the Quinta by manoeuvring the carriage. As he neared the gates, he prepared to bring the carriage to a stop with a combination of precise commands and gentle handling of the reins.

The three passengers watched with admiration as the coachman first began by lightly pulling back on the reins, applying pressure to the bit in the horses' mouths. This signal prompted the horses to slow down their pace. They responded to the coachman's guidance as a well-trained team, gradually reducing their speed.

Simultaneously, the coachman applied steady pressure to the brake lever on the carriage. This mechanism acted as the brake system, creating resistance against the wheels, further aiding in deceleration.

With his expertise and experience, the coachman maintained control of the horses, adjusting the reins as needed to ensure a smooth transition to a complete stop.

He simultaneously communicated verbally with the horses, using commands such as "whoa" to reinforce their obedience.

This coordinated effort between the coachman's guidance, the horses' responsiveness, and the carriage's braking mechanism allowed for a gradual and controlled halt. The coachman ensured that the carriage stopped safely from the doors, allowing enough room for the three passengers to disembark and for further manoeuvring, if necessary.

There, waiting for all three invitees to enlighten themselves from the carriage, was a small welcoming party consisting of Daniel O'Leary and Francisco de Miranda, the Venezuelan military leader and revolutionary who played a crucial role in the Latin American wars of Independence,

Behind them stood José Félix Ribas, the Venezuelan general and national hero who fought during the Venezuelan War of Independence. He is particularly known for his bravery in the Battle of La Victoria. Rafael Urdaneta, the Venezuelan statesman and military leader who fought alongside Simón Bolívar during the Independence wars, eventually became Gran Colombia's President.

Next, waiting to embrace their illustrious leader, stood Antonio José de Sucre, described fondly by Simon as his chosen son. Sucre was also known as the "Gran Mariscal de Ayacucho," Sucre was a prominent military and political figure in South America, serving as the Chief Lieutenant to Bolivia and later its unwilling President. He went on to have immense success in Ecuador and later Peru. Standing shoulder to shoulder with Sucre was Juan Manuel Cagigal, the distinguished Venezuelan naval officer who served in the Venezuelan War of Independence and later became the General Commander of the Navy.

*****

Simon was now transfixed by all standing before him. At the sight of this noblest of military figures, he focused on Sucre. He went for Sucre first, and everyone parted willingly as they respected the unique bond of friendship they both carried.

With open arms, Sucre declared to all present, "General, you will be amazed at all the guests who demanded to be here tonight to celebrate your arrival. Many have travelled from the National Pantheon of Venezuela; sadly, although there is an empty tomb waiting for my body next to your tomb, our friends far and wide ensured they found me to bring me here."

Simon laughingly offered, "Are you sure my tomb next to yours is full?"

With that exchange, everyone's presents scrambled forward and surrounded the two great friends, and handshakes and pats on the backs continued unabated until someone came forward loaded with two cocked pistols.

*****

"Do you, Simon, remember these?" said the coachman, now minus his hat. Instead, the coachman turned out to be a coachwoman with long, flowing black hair. It was no other than Manuela Saenz.

Everyone roared with laughter at such a brilliant entrance. "Only you fine lady could ever get one over me. I am indeed protected from this rabble this evening."

Manuela embraced her hero and kissed him unashamedly on his lips. "Senor, you owe me another horse race."

"Anytime, anyplace, and any distance you wish. I will gladly succumb to your feminine wishes, my dear Manuela."

"Is that a commitment, I hear?" asked Manuela good-naturedly.

"You will have to wait and see." Simon bowed, one hand on his sword and the other waving a white handkerchief in the air as a sign of surrender. He added, with a grin, "I am always open to negotiation."

Dancing gaily around him, Manuela fired both pistols toward the skies and answered, "Yes, but you forgot, I am the master of persuasion."

Sebastian felt this was his moment, "Would someone please find them a room? I smell a banquet ahead, and I am also parched."

Now, everyone present found themselves openly shaking hands and welcoming both Sebastian and Felipe. No animosity or hostility was in sight.

Gradually, the group of war veterans from two or more centuries ago moved as one toward the grand Quinta. Music could be heard. It was the Viennese Blood by Johann Strauss II, who composed it in 1873.

It was new to everyone's ears, but they could not ignore its lively and exhilarating melody, making it the perfect waltz to dance to. Its spirited rhythm and elegance of style invited all to the main house quicker than they had anticipated.

*****

The converted workshops were transformed into a grand-looking hall for the Hacienda Florida, adorned with flickering candles and vibrant tapestries, creating an ambience of regal elegance. The evening air buzzed with anticipation as illustrious guests filled the room, eagerly awaiting the arrival of Sebastian de Belalcazar, Simon Bolivar, and Felipe Joaquin de Cayzedo.

As the doors swung open, Sebastian entered the hall, accompanied by cheers and applause. Dressed in his finest attire, he beamed with pride and humility. Walking gracefully beside him were Simon Bolivar, the visionary leader, and Felipe Joaquin de Cayzedo, renowned for his tactical brilliance.

The hosts of the banquet, Luis Brion, a distinguished Admiral of both navies in Venezuela and the old Republic of Colombia with an air of authority, and Pedro Camejo, known to all by his longstanding nickname "Negro Primero", inspired by his sheer bravery and adept skills in handling a deadly spear in battle. Not only was he the only Black officer, but he was also well known for always demanding to be first in any line of attack on any battlefield. Both warriors stood side by side, greeting the esteemed guests. They exchanged warm words of welcome, acknowledging the significant contributions of everyone in attendance.

*****

Amidst the lively conversations and the shimmering laughter, attention was drawn to Luisa Caceres de Arismendi, a celebrated heroine known for her unwavering courage and sacrifice. She stood gracefully, illuminating the room as if it were a beacon of strength and resilience.

Simon looked on, puzzled at who this popular lady was. Manuela offered this explanation as if reading his mind: "My dearest Simon, allow me to shed light on Luisa, her extraordinary life and her indomitable spirit that rightfully earned her the status of a national heroine."

Luisa Caceres de Arismendi was born on September 25, 1799, in Caracas, Venezuela. From a young age, she displayed a stubborn character and a firm determination to fight for the freedom and Independence of your nation from Spanish colonial rule. Like you, she was to become a handful for the Spanish."

She paused to accept a flute of French champagne. After sipping, she continued, "Her life took a pivotal turn during the events of the Venezuelan War of Independence when she was just a teenager. At the tender age of 16, Luisa fearlessly embraced the cause of our struggle, supporting the fight for liberation led by patriots like Francisco de Miranda and, later, your good self."

Simon was enthralled by what he was learning, spreading his gaze to Manuela and Luisa.

"What truly distinguishes Luisa is her unwavering courage and resilience in the face of immense personal hardships. She endured tremendous suffering and sacrifice because of her steadfast dedication to the independence movement. When her husband, Juan Bautista Arismendi, was captured by the Spanish royalists in 1815, Luisa, despite her young age, lost her baby girl in childbirth. After that, she took up the mantle of leadership and became a symbol of strength, perseverance, and unwavering devotion to our cause."

Manuela's admiration toward Luisa was not lost on Simon, "While her husband was unjustly imprisoned, Luisa faced imprisonment herself, enduring harsh conditions and relentless interrogations by the Spanish authorities. She never betrayed her principles or the revolution, inspiring all those around her."

Daniel had quietly joined the couple and had been listening to Manuela's narrative of Luisa Caceres de Arismendi's story. When Manuela paused, Daniel spoke of meeting her husband when he was in Cork. "Juan Bautista Arismendi was probably one reason I decided to join you all."

Simon said, "We should all say thank you to Juan later this evening. It looks like if it was not for him, I would never have had the success I did have with not knowing and listening to you, Daniel."

All three smiled at the exchange between them, and Manuela continued the narrative, "Her unwavering spirit and unyielding determination to secure our nation's freedom made her an icon of resistance against Spanish tyranny. Her saga of bravery and sacrifice resonated with the masses, fueling their commitment to the cause of Independence.

Simon now spoke of his deep admiration of Luisa's story, "Yes, her story indeed serves as a testament to the strength and resilience of Venezuelan women during our fight for liberty. Her courage, sacrifice, and unwavering commitment to the ideals of Independence have rightfully earned her a place in the annals of Venezuelan history and a revered status as a national heroine."

*****

In a corner of the hall, surrounded by admirers, stood Josefa Verancio de la Encarnacion Camejo Talavera. Next to her stood transfixed Felipe. He was captivated by this beautiful-looking Venezuelan Josefa and her radiating intelligence and charm; she captivated those around her with her eloquence and wit.

Felipe could easily see her presence added an air of intellectual prowess to the already illustrious gathering. She was definitely a powerhouse of a woman and one he wished to learn more of.

He did not see Simon arriving alongside him until he heard the words, "Ah, the enchanting as always, Doña Ignacia. Did you know she wrote the famous "Bello Sexo to the Government of Barinas" petition addressed to Governor Pedro Briceño del Pumar? Who would have believed the poor sight of a smuggled, clandestine, disguised in the rags of a vagabond Josefina would turn out to be the revered Doña Ignacia."

"She died a decade before me at only 28. She was indeed a huge loss to everyone, including myself."

Both warriors are transfixed, which makes Sebastian interested in knowing what is holding their senses. He turned and saw who they were staring at. He quickly joined to make three in a row. Then Daniel sidled up alongside Felipe.

"Ah, boys, allow me to share the remarkable life history of Josefa Venancio de la Encarnación Camejo Talavera, a courageous and influential figure in our struggle for Independence.

She was born on September 19, 1791, in the town of San Juan de Payara, in present-day Venezuela. As she was commonly known, Josefa Camejo exhibited remarkable determination and intelligence from an early age. Coming from a family of landowners and patriots, she grew up witnessing the injustices and cruelty imposed upon her fellow people under Spanish rule, which fueled her patriotic spirit.

At a young age, Josefa displayed a strong desire for education, defying the norms of society at that time, where women were typically denied access to formal schooling.

With her parents' support, she received a private education, becoming well-versed in literature, history, and the ideas of liberty and equality that were sweeping through Europe and the Americas.

Simon paused and offered this little piece of advice mainly directed at Felipe. "Beware, her brain is as sharp as my best sword. Refrain from ever tangling with the likes of this beauty. She will soon make an empanada out of you."

All four got the fits of the giggles, and Sebastian was bent down the furthest. "Simon, stop it; you are making my stomach ache with this laughter."

Each managed to regain their composure, and Simon resumed his story of Doña Ignacia.

"As she grew older, Josefa's passion for Independence and Justice only intensified. She fervently embraced the cause of our struggle against Spanish colonialism, inspired by the ideals of freedom espoused by our revolutionary thinkers.

Josefa actively participated in clandestine meetings and discussions, often hosting gatherings at her family's estate, where she provided a haven for revolutionaries and served as an essential source of information and support for our cause.

Her commitment to our nation's liberation and courage were truly remarkable.

In the Battle of Las Queseras del Medio in 1819, she accompanied General José Antonio Páez, resolutely riding alongside him on horseback and leading a contingent of troops into battle.

Her presence on the battlefield was incredibly significant, as it symbolised Venezuelan women's unwavering dedication and indomitable spirit in the face of adversity and oppression."

Daniel remarked in sheer admiration, "Sadly, General, you were not there that day, but I was. It is a sight I will never forget. At first, the Spaniards laughed at her approach, but that soon changed. Within seconds, she had broken their line, and she did not stop for one second in her determination to win on the battlefield."

Simon turned slightly in remembrance, "I do remember you and the others who went with you telling all who stop to listen to this heroic-looking warrior."

"Furthermore, Josefa Camejo's influence extended beyond the scope of military engagement. She used her position as a respected landowner and administrator to actively support the revolution financially, providing critical resources to our troops and aiding in the organisation of logistics."

*****

The unashamed Josefa stood facing a line of one Irishman, a Colombiano, A narrating Venezuelan, and a bemused Spanish Conquistador and accepted a tray of flutes bubbling with champagne, flashing her ankles as she moved away inwardly proud of how her heroes saw her with equal status.

*****

All eyes followed the grace and sheer beauty as she appeared to dance away from them. Simon took just a sip, as he wanted to continue, "Josefa continued her involvement in our journey towards Independence by creating our first national constitution in 1819, which emphasised the principles of freedom, equality, and justice. Her intellect and wisdom were pivotal during the deliberations, as she contributed valuable insights and passionately defended women's rights and representation.

Sadly, Josefa's life was cut short at the age of 28, as she succumbed to illness in 1820. However, her legacy and impact will endure forever. She is a shining example of Venezuelan women's unwavering spirit and dedication in our fight for freedom."

*****

Before any more could be said, the banquet commenced, and the feasting began. Delicacies from across the region adorned the tables, tempting the palates of the distinguished guests. Servers scurried around, ensuring glasses were filled with the finest wines while the aroma of sumptuous dishes filled the air, tantalising the senses.

Throughout the evening, animated discussions on strategy, politics, and the continent's future unfolded. Sebastian de Belalcazar regaled the gathering with tales of his explorations and conquests, while Simon Bolivar shared his dreams of a united South America free from colonial rule. Felipe Joaquin de Cayzedo contributed his exceptional insights into governance and leadership, adding depth to the conversations.

The evening banquet, assembled to honour the arrival of these significant figures, surpassed all expectations. It became a forum where intellect, bravery, and vision converged. Daniel Florencio O'Leary, Luis Brion, Pedro Camejo, Luisa Cáreres de Arismendi, and Doña Ignacia all contributed to the vibrant tapestry of discussions, ensuring their voices were heard and respected.

As the night progressed into the small hours of the morning, camaraderie and friendship flourished amidst the gathering. This impromptu banquet became a testament to the spirit of unity and collaboration, where the collective aspirations for a brighter future were nurtured, reaffirming the commitment of all those present to the cause of freedom and progress.

*****

The evening ended with a choice of dance to be agreed upon by the guests. The banquet in honour of Simon, Sebastian, and Felipe had been a grand and vibrant affair, full of energy and symbolism. Three possibilities had to be considered for the last dance of the night.

Simon chose the Joropo, a traditional Venezuelan dance known for its lively tempo and energetic movements. It holds great significance in Venezuelan culture, so ending the night with this dance was fitting, as it reminded him of his homeland.

Sebastian chose the waltz. He fell in love with the Viennese Blood waltz he heard for the first time on arrival. For him, it was a classical dance that could symbolise elegance and sophistication. The conquistador suggested it would be a graceful way to conclude the evening, paying homage to the refined nature of Bolivar's leadership and the diplomatic relations he fostered.

Remembering where he lived in the southwest of Colombia, Felipe had grown fond of the sound of Salsa. He described Salsa as a vibrant and popular Latin American dance style known for its passion and enthusiasm. It could be a dynamic and empowering way to end the banquet, highlighting Bolivar's revolutionary spirit and his enduring impact on his people.

The outcome was that all three were winners, and there would be no losers. All three dances were achieved, and everyone left exhausted but very contented with their sheer enjoyment of that special night.

*****

The next day, all riders and stallions slept on the beach in a secluded setting, aware of all the noisy barbarians. On their last night, the trio overheard a conversation between two barbarian couples, who were also relaxing with a makeshift log fire nearby.

*****

The first couple, consisting of a pale-faced skinny man and his voluptuous female wife, were in a foul mood. To be precise, the woman was more outraged than her subservient husband. "George, do you agree with me that the Totumo Volcano mud bath experience was indeed the worst we have ever been attracted to?"

"Err, yes, Gladys, I do believe it was. After seeing advertisements everywhere throughout the city, the thought of taking a mud bath in a dormant volcano would come in handy as a conversation breaker on our return to New York."

Gladys turned to the subject of the early morning start on a large bus that was already full when they were picked up outside of their hotel. "Even before we had a chance to sit down, we had to introduce ourselves to everyone and sundry. Why did we have to do that? I have no plan on making friends in a mud bath!"

"I agree, my love; I saw your face when I told you we had to remove all our clothes. Luckily for me, I still had my Manchester United shorts on."

"I wish I could say the same; stripping down into my underwear was not something I had planned on a bus full of strangers that morning. I mistakenly envisioned a big white pristine towel to be issued and a changing cubicle to allow anyone who wished to cover up their modesty while changing into their swimming costume. And did you see that awful overweight man with his clearly undersized and definitely ageing skimpy blue and white striped speedos?"

"Err, yes dear, I most certainly did; I nearly threw up. It will be years before I will rid my brain of such a horrendous sight of seeing his butt crack."

"George, I have told you before, stop being so crude. You know how that irritates me," growled Gladys.

"Sorry dear, I saw your face just as you were entering the only two toilets opposite the walkway up to the so-called dormant volcano. I was waiting for an eruption from you!"

Gladys ignored her husband's feeble attempt to make light of this damn horrible experience. "Oh yes, I walked into a urinal where the toilet was clogged, and I suspect clogged for years. It stank to high heaven. I held my breath and avoided the dirty walls. I will never know how I managed to wash my hands with only a broken sink on offer." Gladys was reliving her hell once more. Through 30 years of marriage, George knew when it was best to stay silent.

*****

The second couple had not said one word. They were mesmerised by George's and Gladys's account of what they had planned to do the following morning. They wanted to hear the whole story, both good and bad.

*****

Gladys was not long in resuming her pent-up horror of what had ensued before she entered the mud bath. "I have no idea how long we stood waiting on that ridiculous stairwell; all I know is that my feet soles were burning! To add insult to injury, we had to leave our belongings at the foot of the staircase for anyone to take what they wanted. I could see my Celeste branded embellished slip-on sandals with matching block heels menacingly staring back at me."

George nodded his agreement regarding the narrow staircase, "We were on it for over 45 minutes. I know because I checked my H Moser & CÍE stainless steel pioneer Tourbilion watch, which you bought me for my sixtieth birthday last year. You know, the one you valued for insurance purposes in Harrods of London at over £50,000!"

"Ah, YES, that reminds me. What on earth's sake were you doing wearing that watch to a mud bath in a volcano?!" Not waiting for an answer, Gladys turned her attention to the mud—or should she have said blood bath? George thought as he had forgotten to take the watch. He had no idea how he was going to tell Gladys. Zoom or Google Meet could be a safer option.

Three Generals listening nearby looked at each other in bewilderment. Simon whispered, "What is a watch? Pray that you enlighten me on Zoom and Google Meet." Sebastian and Felipe just shrugged their joint ignorance of the barbarian world. Their focus was brought back abruptly, with Gladys hollering her disdain for the mud bath.

"I could not believe I had endured all this discomfort to find us standing over a small muddy pit. It was full of writhing bodies covered all over in what I can only describe as slime! Local men vigorously rubbed the same foul-looking, slimy mud onto as many jostling bodies as possible. There had to be at least thirty people crammed into such a small hole with a mud puddle in it!"

Gladys was on a roll of outrage; nothing or no one was going to interrupt her. No one wanted to. Even Filipe was silent. He loved to argue and have a debate with anyone on any subject. But this ageing New York powerhouse of a woman was way too much for him and his oratory skills.

"Did you see those awful babies minus their diapers being thrown around like muddy confetti? Have you ever seen a baby in control of its lower parts at ANY time? So disgusting!" raged Gladys.

So advanced in avoiding his wife's wrath, George offered, "Err, yes dear, I did see them, and I did wonder how long they had been in the pit."

Gladys ignored George. She had yet to finish talking with him about his birthday gift from Harrods in London, and she had no recollection of seeing it on their return to the hotel this afternoon.

"Now, you two, I have to tell you about the thick oil slick floating on top of the mud, entrapping everybody in the pit. I can only describe it as a toxic mixture of hair gel, sweat, and sunscreen oil. I looked around, and no one was a bit concerned with rubbing the foul-looking slime onto their bodies."

Gladys paused, shuddering at the memory of what she had witnessed only hours before.

"I was so grateful a rickety ladder was provided for us to use to enter the pit. For a moment, I thought we would have to jump or dive in," remembered George.

Gladys ignored his comment, reliving the moment she had found the courage to climb down. She only wished to remember the descent, not the landing.

"I wish to complain to whoever organised this awful experience. I want them to know that their "massage experts" continuously throw all that enters across the pit, ensuring everyone does careen into the others. I remember trying to stand up as if I was in our private lido back home in our Manhattan penthouse overlooking Central Park and the Trump Tower."

Again, the three Generals were mystified by the alien-sounding words: lido, Manhattan, and Trump Tower. Simon spoke, "Trump, isn't that the sound that comes from your bum when you have overdone it with the beans? A funny name for a tower!"

George felt it appropriate to agree with Gladys on the weird sensation of trying to stay upright in the Totumo mud pit. "Yes, you are right. It did feel alien. There was no bottom or chance of reaching a bottom. The depth below just kept propelling me out of control. I only felt safe again when I reached one of the walls and successfully climbed out using one of the other rope ladders."

The silent couple sensed the ending was coming; surely there had to be a happy ending from Norway, who spoke practically no English!

"Gladys moved on to her next ordeal – namely, the lagoon to which she was forced towards.

The lagoon, or, more accurately, the swamp, was full of unhealthy-looking green muddy water and older-looking Abuelas singing their hearts out with calypso-sounding tunes while merrily sponging the mud away from head to toe. There, probing hands and fingers appeared to go everywhere they pleased.

"Oh yes, George, when I tell you to remove your shorts, I do not mean for you to stand up in a lagoon and lower your shorts, exposing yourself to all and sundry!"

"Sorry about that. I thought I was auditioning for a future porno movie!" smiled George. On those rare occasions, Gladys enjoyed George's quip. Porno indeed!

Sebastian looked at his two amigos, "What is porno?" No one knew, but the three generals shook hands and agreed they had to go to the Totumo volcano and its adjacent Porno pool later that night to find out. Each hopes there will not be a Gladys to take away their sheer enjoyment of a muddy adventure.

*****

The days that followed back towards Santiago de Cali were a quieter affair. Both Sebastian and Felipe held back on conversation with the somewhat subdued Simon. Even the three stallions paced themselves at a more natural four-beat gait, covering a slow four mph. There were moments when they could see flat open spaces, and without any guidance or order from the riders, Palomo, El Dorado, and Independence took it upon themselves to increase their speed of travel to the leisurely canter. The three could easily amble along at a steady 3-beat gait, covering an average of 15 miles per hour.

But stallions would not be stallions if they ignored an opportunity to excite their riders with a full-on gallop, allowing the distance to be doubled.

*****

A week later, while all were resting for the night in an open field under a cloudless sky and watching the disappearing sunset, Simon suddenly began to cry to the other two for unknown reasons.

Felipe was a second before Sebastian reached out to their distressed friend, "What is it, Simon? We have never seen you like this before."

Simon took a few moments to take heed of himself. He wiped away his tears and looked profoundly towards his two friends. "I am so sorry for my melancholy these past few days. I had to think about what I had never dreamt could one day happen. I met the real Simon Bolivar."

*****

"I had left you both in deep conversation with one of my ablest of opponents, Don Pablo Morilla y Morilla, the Peacemaker who was recounting his time at the Battle of Trafalgar. The one I introduced you to as the Count of Cartagena and later the Governor and Captain-General of Venezuela always managed to defeat me in battle until I got my way at Boyacá."

Sebastian remembered the "Peacemaker" straight away. "Yes, I do remember this fellow; he seemed a fine gentleman and a worthy soldier and sailor from my neck of the woods. I was amazed when he told us he had fought in the Napoleonic Wars, the Peninsular War, and the South American Wars of Liberation! I must admit his account of the Battle of Trafalgar left me speechless. I thought I was brave, but this fellow surpassed my endeavours. I can still hear his words even now."

*****

"Picture this, my friends, a place where the vast expanse of the sea becomes a battleground. It was October 21 in the year 1805, and the location was Cape Trafalgar, off the coast of Spain. This was a defining moment in the history of naval warfare, where two great naval powers clashed: the combined fleets of France and Spain against the British Royal Navy, led by Admiral Horatio Nelson."

"I, Pablo Morillo, just recently made a widow with the death of my wife. I was a Spanish officer who witnessed the unfolding events with my eyes on the San Ildefonso board. The sheer magnitude of the opposing forces defies imagination. On one side, more than thirty British ships, including Nelson's flagship, the HMS Victory, and on our side, almost forty Spanish and French vessels, united in our determination to thwart the British dominance of the seas."

Pablo's thoughts as he spoke were now aboard his ship. "The battle raged on for hours, intensifying with each passing moment. Cannon fire echoed across the waves, creating a symphony of destruction, while wooden hulls splintered, and flames engulfed the ships."

Sebastian remembered Morillo pausing in his narrative to accept a canape from a passing server. "Morillo described the sheer chaos and carnage as sailors fought bravely, a dance with death on treacherous waters."

Then, Pablo paused again to gather his strength to decrease the images flashing before him. "But let me tell you that what unfolded that day was a testament to the strategic brilliance of Admiral Nelson. He devised a bold plan, opting for an unorthodox tactic referred to as the "Nelson Touch." Instead of engaging the enemy head-on, he aimed to break the French and our Spanish lines by dividing our joint fleet and exposing vulnerable sections to British firepower."

It was Pablo's turn again to beckon over a waiter carrying a silver tray of flutes containing champagne. As soon as he had wet his lips, he was back to 1805, "Nelson's strategy unfolded flawlessly, as his ships sliced through our formations, their guns unrelenting. Now, Sebastian and Felipe, imagine the sight of cannons roaring, tearing apart enemy ships right before your eyes. Our once mighty Spanish ships were reduced to splintered wreckages as the British rained destruction upon us. My ship, the San Ildefonso, was captured, and I was wounded and taken prisoner.

It was also my duty to hand over our ensign, a massive flag measuring 10 metres by 14.5 metres, to the British victors.

Alas, for the British, victory came at a cost. In the heat of battle, Admiral Nelson himself fell, mortally wounded by a sniper's bullet. But his legacy was secured that day as his men, inspired by his leadership, pressed on, ensuring an overwhelming victory for the British."

Sebastian and Felipe could clearly see Pablo's distress over his memories of that fateful day. "The aftermath was a sea stained with blood and scattered wreckage, a sombre reminder of the sacrifices made by both sides. Our combined fleet of France and Spain lost almost twice as many ships as the British counterparts, sealing the fate of their naval dominance."

*****

Simon waited patiently, but Felipe touched Sebastian on his shoulder and reminded him of the reason they were all talking. "Sebastian, perhaps this is a good moment to hear Simon's unbelievable account of him meeting the real Simon Bolivar."

"Yes, you are right. I do apologise, Simon. Please forgive my Spanish interest in your enemy at that time."

Simon smiled at his friend, "Please do not apologise. Pablo's stories are numerous, and everyone is an eye-opener to the heroics of our day."

Sebastian bowed slightly to his friend, "Please tell us what happened."

*****

As you both know, I am a statue of Simon Bolivar, a symbol of freedom and revolution, in Santiago de Cali.

At the rear of the Hacienda, I accidentally came across the real Simon Bolivar, a living and breathing historical figure enjoying the tranquillity of his final days.

A room with shelves of leather-bound books, maps, and busts of famous historical figures surrounded him. Bolívar's portrait hung on the wall, overlooking an antique desk, where he often indulged in deep contemplation of his accomplishments and the future of his beloved land.

He would, each night, at more or less the same time as we met, walk around the extensive gardens, where flowers blossomed in harmony with nature.

The real Simon Bolivar later told me he had sensed an inexplicable tingling in the air and walked outside, his eyes widening in astonishment as he saw his likeness standing before him—ME!

We two figures stood face to face, staring at one another in speechless astonishment. I could feel the air filled with a palpable energy, a symphony of emancipation and determination.

After a few moments of silence, I, the statue, embodying the spirit and ideals that Bolivar had fought for, finally broke the silence.

*****

But first, let me describe to you what or who sat patiently at Bolivar's feet. It was the most beautiful dog I have ever seen.

Sebastian's interest picked up when a dog was mentioned: "Pray tell us what type of dog captivated you so much?"

Simon looked excitedly at the animal for the first time. "Please believe me; I had never seen such a beautiful creature before. I immediately asked the real Bolivar the question about the dog's breed."

The real Bolivar looked down at his feet, "Ah, you must be asking about Nevado here at my feet. Yes, indeed, he is a real sight for sore eyes. He was born sometime in 1813, and he stood by my side for the next eight years. He was given to me by the people of Merida, which lies on the Venezuelan side of the Andes. He apparently is called a Mucuchies dog, and in mine and his time, you could only acquire such a dog from the local Mucuchies people. He is a very intelligent breed, and why don't we both sit and listen to his version of his life? I promise you it is very enlightening."

Simon paused to see the look on both Sebastian's and Felipe's faces; both spoke at once, "Do you mean this dog actually spoke to you?"

Simon burst out laughing, "Yes, he actually did. It sounds unbelievable, but I have never lied to either of you. I will not start now. I will never forget what he said,"

*****

"Good evening to you all. My name is Nevado, and yes, I am a Mucuchies dog. If it helps you a little, think of me as a distant cousin of the famous Saint Bernard dog who lives and works on the western side of the Alps in both Switzerland and Italy."

"I, then only a puppy, was presented as a gift to my master, and he called me Nevado, which means snowy. When meeting my "to-be master" for the first time, I showed my courage and commitment to safely guiding my original owner's property by barking incessantly towards both impressive looking military man on his white horse and his regiment of patriots."

"They drew their weapons with the aim of quieting me permanently. But luckily for me, my "to-be master" ordered his core of rebels to back down. From that very moment, it felt to me that, for some unknown reason, I had a new master who was sitting on what I presumed was a well-kept and healthy-looking white stallion. The horse's name was Palomo, and I found myself naturally running always by his side. Even in battles where most animals would panic and run away from the noise of muskets and cannons. Not Palomo and me. We were as one with our master."

"It may also have helped my cause that my master had the foresight to organise my training with the perfect dog handler, an Indian fighter named Tinjaca."

"My ancestry was as impressive as my friendship with your renowned "El Liberator". As I may already have mentioned, I am an Andean mountain dog, and my ancestral origins can be traced back over four centuries to the Augustine friars who brought their Pyrenean mastiffs to Venezuela." My breed was well suited for the work of herding sheep and cattle and as the perfect guard for properties and renowned Generals such as my master."

"For the next eight years, I ensured the safety of my equine friend, Palomo, and I defended my master on many occasions. Then, sadly for me, my luck ran out at the Battle of Carabobo in the year 1821. I somehow managed to become entangled with some of the fallen men, and in my slowness to recover my footing, a Spanish Royalist speared me with his deadly lance."

"I tried my hardest to stay alive until my master could reach me, but the wound was too much for me to bear, and I quietly went to sleep, knowing I had served both my General and his people of Venezuela in the War of Independence."

"Please do not be sad for me. I am so proud of my life, and indeed, the people of Venezuela have gone on to honour Tinjaca and me by erecting monuments in our honour in Caracas and Merida."

*****

"General Bolivar and Nevado, it is an honour to meet you both." I managed to say. I could feel my voice resonating with a deep sense of appreciation. "I represent the people, their dreams, and aspirations. I have come to express their gratitude for your valiant efforts in seeking freedom and Independence."

Though taken aback, I could see the real Simon Bolivar smiling with humility and pride. "My monument, I never anticipated meeting you in person, as I believed my journey had long come to an end. Your existence symbolises the lasting impact of our cause. Please tell me, how does the land we fought for fare now?"

I could not camouflage my voice, which held a tinge of sadness. "While progress has been made since your time, challenges persist. The people yearn for unity, prosperity, and justice. They seek a nation that lives up to the dreams we had."

The real Simon Bolivar's eyes sparkled with determination towards me. "They shall have their desires fulfilled. Together, we shall inspire the hearts and minds of our people to continue fighting for justice and progress."

"For hours, the real Bolivar and I engaged in heartfelt discussions, sharing wisdom and contemplating the future of our beloved Colombia. With the sun setting, painting the sky in hues of orange and gold, a profound understanding forged between us both."

*****

Knowing that our encounter was temporary. I willingly bowed to the real Bolivar, expressing gratitude for the inspiration and guidance I received. With a final nod, I turned to face the garden, which was located at the foothills of Sierra Nevada. I could still see the colonial bridge leading to the work buildings nestled with a Ceiba tree, near a Samán tree, and two tamarinds that once acted as the supports for a hammock that the real Bolivar had made use of.

A voice coming from nearby uttered, "And yes, to the question in your head, the General did and still does from time to time sleep in the hammock. He just prefers to keep it our secret."

*****

Simon turned to his great friends. You may find it hard to believe my first encounter with the real Simon Bolivar, but this next chance meeting will blow your minds!"

Both Sebastian and Felipe shouted out loudly, "Who was it?"

*****

I had turned to face the General's Study Room again. The desktop is still immersed in research documents, letters, and maps and surrounded by scattered papers.

I remember muttering to myself that the legacy of Simón Bolívar remains unmatched.

Suddenly, a gust of wind blew through an open window, extinguishing the candles. I looked up in surprise just as the wind mysteriously closed the window, and a figure emerged from the shadows.

*****

I was startled and shouted, "Who's there?"

The real Simon Bolívar spoke warmly to me: "Relax. Fate is a wondrous thing, my dear visitor from Cali. It has also allowed me to reunite with a loyal confidant."

"It was none other than José Palacio himself who stepped out of the shadows, appearing much younger than his true age, exuding an aura of unwavering loyalty and reverence to both versions of his Master and lifelong friend."

José spoke directly to the real General, "My General, it is an honour to see you again after all these years!"

Both men exchanged a warm embrace, their loyalty and camaraderie evident.

They parted for what must have seemed an eternity, and the real Bolívar said, "José, my faithful aide-de-camp, how I have longed to see your familiar face once more. Tell me, how has Venezuela fared in my absence?"

José took a moment before answering with a mix of pride and sadness, "Oh, General, our nation has faced countless trials and tribulations, but your spirit, your ideals, have never left our hearts. Venezuela fights for freedom, constantly inspired by your memory."

The General smiles appreciatively, "That warms my tired soul, dear José. But tell me, how have our ideals evolved? Is there still hope for a united South America?"

José, with a more assured tone and voice, said, "Our dreams of unity persist, General, though the path has been arduous. The spirit of Bolivarianism lives on, inspiring the people and leaders to continue to strive for the vision you so ardently pursued."

The General, not losing his smile, said, "I am proud of the progress made and the indomitable spirit of the Venezuelan people.

I felt the desire to say something, "Gentlemen, forgive me for intruding, but may I join in this extraordinary conversation?

The General turned to me, nodding, "Of course, your curiosity and admiration for my cause have drawn you here. Speak your mind."

I plucked up the nerve to ask the General, "What advice do you have for us today, in a world grappling with new challenges and divisions?"

The General was deep in thought for a few moments, and suddenly, he could be seen contented with this following reply to my question, "Unity, my friend, is the key to overcoming any obstacle. Remember, it is the people who possess the true power. Educate them, empower them, and guide them towards a common goal. Only then can true greatness be achieved."

José confirmed his agreement with his master, "Wise words, General. Your spirit remains our guiding light." Then José approached both of us Bolivars with a salver of tumblers full to the brim with "Agua de panela", a refreshing and delicious blend of unrefined sugar cane, iced water, and lime wedges.

Jose turned back to his General. I hope you do not mind, but I grabbed a bowl of that finest stew served this evening, and I have reserved it for Nevado. Look, he has almost finished it!"

After finishing our drinks, the General and José prepared to part ways again, yet I could clearly see their bond remained unbreakable.

The General turned to face his loyal manservant, whom he had relied on since he was nine years of age, "Farewell, my dear José. Though brief, our time together has been a treasure beyond measure. I entrust you with continuing the quest for unity and freedom."

It was José Palacio's turn to bow, "General Bolívar, your trust is our strength. Your legacy shall endure through the hearts of Venezuelans, just as it has for the past two centuries."

With a final embrace, I witnessed the General, his faithful Nevado, and José bid their farewells, dissolving into the air, their presence felt long after their departure me.

I remember whispering to myself, the Meeting of Minds, the embodiment of loyalty and courage… a moment to be treasured and passed down through generations. I then gazed at Bolívar's portrait for the last time, filled with newfound reverence for the enthusiasm and spirit that history cannot confine. Then, as an afterthought, I turned and spoke out, "Wait! I forgot to mention I have Palomo with me! Would you like to see him and ride once more?"

Sadly, there was no reply.

*****

## 54: I am the Choir of Sisterhood Singers performing in two famous Halls

Cardinal Alejandro Martinez of the Vatican, known for his dedication to ecumenism and cultural exchange, was visiting South America to witness the choir of singing sisters at the Saint Teresa Convent.

The Cardinal, renowned for his compassion and progressive approach to faith, had embarked on a journey to celebrate the beauty of South American traditions and foster cultural connections within the church. His visit to the Saint Teresa Convent and subsequent interactions with the choir was a testament to his dedication to ecumenism and a catalyst for the choir's journey of cultural exchange and spiritual growth.

With deep respect and admiration for the renowned choir of the Saint Teresa convent, the Cardinal has chosen to experience first-hand the harmonious voices that radiated from the walls of the nunnery to the radio broadcasts heard around the globe.

Through his visit, Cardinal Martinez intended to emphasise honouring and embracing the diverse expressions of worship, recognising the rich tapestry of spiritual traditions within the Catholic Church.

With his warm and welcoming demeanour, the Cardinal aimed to encourage dialogue and exchange, embracing the unity found in the joyful songs of the nuns.

As the Cardinal listened to the ethereal melodies sung by the choir, he found solace and inspiration in their harmonious voices. His presence symbolised the Vatican's commitment to valuing and cherishing the cultural heritage and devotion found within the local communities.

This encounter showcased the meeting of two worlds, as the Cardinal from the Vatican and the nuns from the Saint Teresa Convent came together in a celebration of spiritual unity and cultural diversity, leaving an indelible mark on all those fortunate enough to witness this transcendent moment.

*****

I can remember so vividly as if it was only yesterday and not nearly three years ago when Cardinal Martinez spoke out so eloquently the following words:

"Ladies and gentlemen, brothers and sisters in faith, today we gather before the altar of our beloved church as witnesses to a sacred moment in the life of our dear little sister Rosa. On this auspicious day, she has chosen to accept the Veil, embracing her calling as a dedicated servant of God. In honour of this blessed occasion, we, and the singing sister's choir of Saint Teresa's Convent, have congregated under the guidance of our esteemed Sister Superior, Josefina Ignacia de Mesa."

Dressed in our distinctive blue and white habits, skillfully crafted by our talented Sister Gabriela, the chief mistress of the robes, we stood united in support of our sister Rosa's commitment to a life of unwavering devotion. As Seraphina, the chosen name representing her fervent spirit and dedication, Rosa stepped forward to embrace the divine path the Lord had set.

The energy in this sacred space was indeed palpable, not only among the sisters of our congregation but also heightened by the presence of Sister Miriam de Jesus and Sister Mily Gabriella Victoria, both esteemed members of the Mountain Ridge School community. Their joyful presence demonstrated the unity and camaraderie that transcends the confines of our individual communities, reminding us of the shared purpose we, as faithful servants, strive to fulfil. This sense of unity and shared purpose is what we aim to convey to our audience, making them feel a part of our journey.

As we witness Rosa's acceptance of the Veil, Cardinal Martinez said, "Let us find solace and inspiration in her courage. May her example serve as a reminder that faith can ignite our souls and propel us to declare our devotion to a higher calling. Sister Seraphina Celestia shall undoubtedly embody the fiery spirit and radiant dedication to her faith. Her devotion will be associated with her chosen name for eternity, illuminating our community with her dedication and fervour."

His final words to all of us present will live within our memories forever, "Let us come together, pray for Sister Seraphina's successful journey, and extend our heartfelt blessings to her. May the Lord guide her every step, granting her strength, compassion, and unwavering faith as she embarks on this sacred path. Amen."

That night, over 65 singing sisters, including Seraphina Celestia and me, and a congregation of over 100 witnesses jointly voiced in harmony: "Amen."

\*\*\*\*\*

I am a diary entry made by one Sister Seraphina Celestia of the Saint Teresa Choir of singing nuns, the day after her ceremonial acceptance of the Veil, marking the beginning of a remarkable journey that would take them on a musical expedition across South America and beyond.

She wrote nightly about the growing history from its roots to the harmonious voices and spiritual devotion of the Saint Teresa Choir, garnering attention far beyond the walls of their convent. Sister Seraphina mentions how she personally was captivated by their enchanting performances and learning of a renowned classical pianist and music producer called Alessandra Lombardi, who wished to embark on a unique collaboration with them. Alessandra, with her ancestral family Brazilian roots, invited the choir to record their first album of ethereal hymns and sacred chants at her Columbia-based studios. The final album, filled with angelic voices and heartfelt melodies, captured the essence of their divine dedication.

With the release of their debut album, the Saint Teresa Choir and Alessandra Lombardi became popular throughout South America. Their music touched the hearts of listeners from all walks of life, spreading messages of love, hope, and spiritual inspiration. Encouraged by the reception of their work, the choir started touring various cities in the continent, sharing their heavenly harmonies with diverse audiences.

During their two-year journey, the choir toured various cities in South America and collaborated with renowned classical artists from different countries. These collaborations resulted in a series of albums, each a testament to their unwavering faith and ability to embrace and incorporate diverse cultural influences into their music. With each performance, the choir's fan base grew, and their songs evolved into a unique blend of sacred music, reflecting the rich tapestry of their musical journey.

As news of their incredible talent and spiritual presence spread worldwide, the Saint Teresa Choir received an extraordinary proposition. This world tour would take them to illustrious venues around the globe. The excitement peaked when it was announced that they would grace the legendary stages of Carnegie Hall in New York and The Royal Albert Hall in London.

Preparations for the world tour occurred amidst a wave of anticipation and joy within the choir. This anticipation and joy is what we hope to share with our audience, making them feel the excitement and thrill of our journey.

They dedicated themselves to perfecting their vocal prowess, fine-tuning their harmonies, and selecting an exquisite repertoire that combined traditional hymns with new compositions inspired by their experiences.

Invitations were accepted by Alessandra Lombardi and other renowned artists in the music world.

The world tour transformed the members of the Saint Teresa Choir spiritually and personally.

All 65 sisters and their ever-protective Sister Superior witnessed the transformative power of music to transcend language and cultural barriers, allowing them to connect with people from diverse backgrounds on a profound level. This transformative power of music and faith is what we hope to inspire in our audience, making them feel the depth and universality of our journey.

Their performances were celebrated as the epitome of spiritual devotion and artistic excellence.

*****

The culmination of years of devotion and hard work was realised when the Saint Teresa Choir graced the stages of Carnegie Hall and The Royal Albert Hall. Their ethereal voices echoed through the hallowed halls, captivating audiences who were moved to tears by the purity and depth of their performances.

*****

As the heart and soul of this magnificent hall you barbarians call Carnegie Hall, I thought it would be nice to give you my thoughts on the night Sister Superior Josefina Ignacia de Mesa and her 65-singing sisterhood choir stepped onto my hallowed stage.

It was clear they were overwhelmed by a sense of awe and reverence, and rightly so.

My grandeur filled their hearts with a mixture of excitement and nervous anticipation. I would not expect any other reaction.

I have an extraordinary opportunity to perform in such a prestigious venue. I had to be a dream come true for the choir, whose voices had echoed in humble church pews for years.

With my sacred and hallowed atmosphere known as Carnegie Hall, I almost seemed to embrace their very souls as they took their places on the stage.

I am located in the Midtown area of New York City, which was the brainwave of industrialist and philanthropist Mister Andrew Carnegie back in the late 1880s. He wanted me to be the most prestigious and renowned venue for both popular and classical music. Each year, you will see my grand doors open to many barbarians to witness around 250 performances. I am proud to say I have deemed a designated historical landmark protected by some important barbarian committees.

My three auditoriums can seat up to 3,671 people. Tonight's performance in my Stern Auditorium will give this choir of sisters a massive 2,804-seater exposure.

My majestic high ceilings, adorned with intricate designs, soared above, giving my performance space an almost celestial quality. My intricate woodwork and plush red seating created an ambience that whispered of history and countless legendary performances.

As the choir began to sing, their voices resonated through me, bouncing off my opulent walls. The acoustics were nothing short of breathtaking, allowing every note and harmony to reach the furthest corners of me. The harmonies, perfected through endless hours of practice, mingled with the air, filling me with a captivating and ethereal sound.

Each note seemed to dance, floating towards the audience and touching their hearts in ways they had never imagined.

Being enveloped by my resplendent architectural beauty and my sheer magnitude had to ensure I, Carnegie Hall, was an experience unlike any other. I could see the devotion and passion of the sisterhood radiating in every verse as they sang their praises to the heavens. It was as if I had come alive, now responding to their voices with a warmth and vibrancy that embraced them in a unique serenity.

I must admit, I genuinely love this warmth.

The choir must have felt a profound connection to the long line of artists and performers who had graced my stage before them. Their voices reverberated through my grand hall, carrying the generations' dreams, hopes, and faith.

The magnitude of performing in me, the great Carnegie Hall, could not have been lost on this sisterhood choir. It was clear to me and the audience that these spiritual ladies were savouring every moment, cherishing the once-in-a-lifetime opportunity to share their gift with an audience that had gathered from near and far.

Sister Superior Josefina Ignacia de Mesa and her choir must have felt a deep sense of gratitude and humility in my sacred space. They could carry with them the belief that their music conveyed a message of love, hope, and spiritual unity. Their performance in my grand hall would surely become an indelible mark on their journey, forever etched in their hearts as a testament to the power of faith and the transformative nature of music.

What will their thoughts be when they reach my good friend, the Royal Albert Hall?

*****

"Ladies and gentlemen, allow me, the illustrious Royal Albert Hall, to narrate a tale of magnificent history and compare myself to my dear friend, the renowned Carnegie Hall in Midtown New York.

Let me begin with my origins. Work began in April 1867, and the construction was completed in March 1871 and opened to the public in the same year by Queen Victoria herself. I was to be honoured as the official memorial to her late husband and consort Prince Albert, designed by the skilled architect's Major-General Henry Darracott Scott and the late Captain Francis Fowke, who had passed away a few months earlier. My grand structure emanates Victorian grandeur and embodies the essence of British architectural brilliance.

I am a grade-l listed building with some 525 employees. I know you find this hard to believe, but the people who run my annual costs receive no public funding. I am supported by volunteers who financially support my objectives by paying a yearly contribution called "A seat rate." That's pretty fantastic for me, and I will be forever indebted to all those intrepid volunteers.

Over the past 152 years, I have witnessed countless iconic performances in the heart of London. Renowned artists from every corner of the world have graced my magnificent stage, bringing melody and culture to millions. From the annually scheduled and nearly always sold-out 400 or more symphonies to rock concerts, from opera to jazz, my walls have reverberated with the finest music you barbarians have to offer.

My seating capacity is pretty impressive, too. I can easily seat over 5,270 and have been known to have had an additional 4,000 standing once! That was way back in 1906. I would love to do that again.

*****

Dear friends, let me turn your gaze to the illustrious Carnegie Hall. Standing tall in Midtown Manhattan since the year 1891, Carnegie Hall is indeed a splendid counterpart to me. Designed by architect William Tuthill, its majestic appearance captivates all who lay eyes upon it.

While different in style, Carnegie Hall also boasts an impressive roster of performances. Countless legendary musicians have enchanted audiences within its hallowed halls. The likes of Tchaikovsky, Frank Sinatra, The Beatles, and many more have graced Carnegie Hall's stage, enriching New York City's cultural tapestry.

But here, my esteemed friends is where my audacious spirit soars. While Carnegie Hall may dazzle with its impressive stature, I proudly represent British musical heritage and excellence. I, The Royal Albert Hall, have hosted monumental events throughout history, including the annual Proms concerts, the Royal British Legion's Festival of Remembrance, and even the first Wimbledon Championship in 1877.

Furthermore, I am seated in the heart of South Kensington, offering you a juxtaposition of regal beauty and cultural diversity. The surrounding Queen's Gate Gardens and Prince Consort Gardens serve as havens of tranquillity against the hustle and bustle of the city, providing a serene setting for local barbarians and visitors to immerse themselves in the arts.

So, my dear friends, while Carnegie Hall may hold its own greatness in the realm of music and performance, I, the Royal Albert Hall, stand proud, a beacon of cultural heritage woven into the very fabric of London. With my illustrious history, breathtaking presence, and tapestry of artistic brilliance, I remain an unparalleled icon forever cherished by those who seek the transformative power of music.

*****

As Sister Seraphina Celestia and Sister Superior Josefina Ignacia de Mesa, with her acoustic guitar in one hand, and Alessandra Lombardi, sitting at her Steinway grand piano, came to the grand finale of their trio, the atmosphere in the concert hall was charged with excitement and anticipation. The song, aptly titled "She Sings like a Songbird," captivated the audience's hearts with its beautiful melodies and harmonies worldwide.

It was a heartwarming celebration of their music, faith, and sisterhood gift.

As the song's final notes filled the air, Sister Seraphina and Mother Superior Josefina stood either side of Alessandra at the centre of the stage, their three voices blending in perfect harmony. Their eyes sparkled with joy and passion, reflecting their deep connection and shared love for music and their spiritual calling.

As the last chord resonated, the stage lights dimmed, and the room was plunged into a brief moment of silence. Suddenly, from the wings of the stage, 65 other sisters dressed in their vibrant choir robes emerged. Each sister carried a lit candle in their hands, symbolising the light of their faith and the unity of their voice.

In a carefully choreographed sequence, the sisters formed a semi-circle around Alessandra, Sister Seraphina Celestia, and Sister Superior Josefina. The subtle flickering of the candles cast a warm and ethereal glow upon the stage, creating a serene and holy ambience in the concert hall.

The larger body of sisters began slowly swaying from side to side, their voices joining together in a breathtaking "a cappella" rendition of the concluding refrain of "She Sings like a Songbird." The combined choir filled the hall with an angelic, powerful, and profoundly moving harmony.

As the song reached its pinnacle, a collective crescendo shook the room, enveloping the audience in a wave of profound emotion. It was a moment that transcended words, stirring the soul and touching the hearts of everyone present with its sheer beauty and spirituality.

With the song's final notes gently fading away, a hushed silence fell over the audience.

The impact of the performance hung in the air, leaving them teary-eyed and deeply moved.

The applause that followed was thunderous, a testament to the collective talent and devotion of Sister Seraphina, Sister Superior Josefina, and the entire Saint Teresa Choir.

With grace and humility, Sister Seraphina and Sister Superior Josefina stepped back, making way for the choir to take a well-deserved bow. The stage came alive as the sisters acknowledged their standing ovation, their smiles radiant with joy and gratitude.

They then collectively parted in the centre to allow the audience to show their appreciation to Alessandra Lombardi as the song's composer took her bow. This, too, was met with a cacophony of applause and appreciation from the now-standing audience.

In those magical moments, Alessandra, Sister Seraphina, Sister Superior Josefina, and the 65 other sisters of the Saint Teresa Choir shared an unbreakable bond—a testament to the power of music, faith, and the profound connection they all shared.

It was a moment that would be etched in the hearts of the audience forever, reminding them of the sheer beauty that could be created when voices united in harmony.

From humble beginnings within the confines of their convent, the Saint Teresa Choir had travelled the globe, spreading love and spirituality through their music. Their journey served as a testament to the power of faith, unity, and the transformative potential of music in the pursuit of shared human experiences. They rightly felt proud regarding their wondrous achievements.

But unbeknownst to the choir, three members of one particular audience had no interest in their lifetime devotion to faith and music. They had more evil thoughts to keep them occupied.......

*****

## 55: *I am a Fire Truck full of Heros and Heroines*

A lpha company has a fire engine, Alpha 1, and a ladder truck, Alpha 2. We are both about the same age and when we are called out to combat a fire, we can be pretty noisy and impressive together. To all who stop to watch us navigate our way safely to the scene, we truly put on a safe display of speed and agility.

Today is a typically quiet Monday morning, so while I, Alpha 2, am not racing around the city streets, I decided to introduce you to the firefighters. Both Alpha 1 and I totally admire and respect them for their professionalism and courage. Not only that, but their individual lives are full of intrigue, adventures, and, at times, misadventures.

But wait, I am racing ahead. Let me introduce each one, beginning with the "all-knowing, seen it all, done it all," Fire Chief Eduardo Dominguez with the call sign "Master."

The "Master" is creeping up fast towards his retirement; he is now 68, happily married to Maria, and together they have three children who, in fairness to them, are more adults than children. Jamie is the oldest, at 30, a lawyer in the city, and his younger by ten years, twin sister and brother, Rebecca and Manuel, are studying to become cardiologists at Bogota University.

Today, the fire chief is checking the records of each firefighter and his office personnel to determine their current training proficiency.

Next comes Assistant Chief Carmen Lopez, known as "Wolf," currently divorced from Alfredo, who, after 20 years of marriage, had decided he was gay and had flown to Paris to join his boyfriend, Pierre. Carmen had always had suspicions about her husband, but with having two children together and raising them successfully, she had put any doubts to the back of her mind. Her children were also adults, one living in Miami and the other in Medellín. She proudly had both of their graduation photos framed and sitting on her desk.

Today, "Wolf" analysed the previous month's historical incident data. Here, she tracked patterns and identified areas that may require additional resources or preventive measures. Later, she headed the monthly scheduled meeting to collaborate with the other departments to strategise for future emergencies.

Sitting opposite Carmen and sharing the same office, sitting behind his desk, is Battalion Chief Tomas Ortiz, alias the "Strong One." Now, approaching his 45th birthday, Tomas had only ever worn a uniform. His first was as an Army private, for the first five years, before transferring to the city police and spending eight more years patrolling the streets. Finally, after watching the firefighters on various "shouts," he felt he should change his uniform once more.

The "Strong One" was approaching his fifteenth year of continued service with the fire service, and he never regretted his journey. Tomas was also married to Sara, a Bank Manager. They had no children, but they did have four dogs.

One of Tomas's responsibilities was to ensure all was well with the necessary equipment held in reserve and the resource maintenance schedules. He would later coordinate with the fire service maintenance teams to ensure all firefighting equipment, vehicles, and communication systems were in optimal condition. He would audit the regular check sheets and compare them with the scheduled maintenance schedules to ensure all the checks covered all the areas under his watch.

Eduardo, Carmen, Tomas, alias Master, Wolf, and the Strong One made up the executive management team for the city's fire service. They operated from the third floor of the largest fire station, and their offices surrounded the centrally placed ops room where all the calls would be received and all the "shouts" would be designated.

Each would watch the dimly lit room, with banks of large screens displaying real-time information from the city's monitoring systems and despatch centres. One all-important aspect each would be monitoring was that the operations room maintained its usual calm and organised environment.

They could see the operations personnel closely monitoring the incoming emergency calls and any potential incidents that may require their response. Together, they observed the weather conditions and traffic updates and looked for any relevant information. So far, everything was as it should have been for a Monday morning.

\*\*\*\*\*

The second floor is a "home away from home" to the fire crews, and I will introduce each of them after I have given you a picture of this floor.

Let me start with the thoughtfully designed decor, which uses a neutral colour scheme that is conducive to a tranquil ambience. The walls are adorned with motivational posters and artwork, fostering a positive and supportive environment.

Even the nighttime lighting has been considered, allowing for comfortable visibility during the coming hours.

In addition to the basic amenities, the living area is well-equipped with entertainment options, such as a large flat-screen television housed in a fit-for-purpose common area. This also includes gaming consoles and a mini library with a collection of books and training manuals. There is also a countertop with three stools to allow the firefighters to work on their laptops, the three provided desktops, and the printer/scanner/fax machine.

The living area is divided into sections, providing separate spaces for relaxation, recreation, and firefighter personal time. It includes comfortable sofas and armchairs arranged in a cosy lounge-type setting. Here, the firefighters unwind and socialise during their downtime periods. Nearby is a large stand-alone dining table that comfortably seats ten dining chairs.

Another small area leading to the sleeping quarters allows for a dedicated workout area equipped with exercise equipment to encourage firefighters to maintain their fitness.

The sleeping quarters are divided into individual sleeping rooms, each equipped with a comfortable bed, a bedside table, and a personal storage unit for their belongings. These rooms ensure privacy and allow the firefighters to sleep peacefully, even during hectic shifts. The rooms are designed to be noise-insulated, creating a calm atmosphere conducive to rest.

Adjacent to the sleeping quarters, there are clean and well-maintained bathrooms equipped with showers, toilets, and vanity areas. The facilities have separate, private areas for both female and male firefighters, ensuring privacy and comfort for all on duty.

The whole second floor is equipped with security measures, including CCTV cameras and secure access control systems, ensuring the safety of all firefighters. Last but not least, emergency exit signage, fire extinguishers, and fire safety equipment are placed prominently throughout the living areas, thus providing a secure and safe environment for all.

Added with the excellent amenities to help everyone recharge their energy levels during their 24-hour shifts, meaning a positive fostering of camaraderie and well-being among my heroes and heroines. Once completed, each would well deserve their next 48 hours off duty.

*****

So now you know the Executive Management Team and the Operations Room on the third floor. You also know what the firefighter's amenities and "home away from home" accommodation on the second floor consist of. Let's cover where I live with my firefighting partner, Alpha 1.

Alpha 1 is a typically versatile firefighting engine that is a specialised vehicle equipped with a fire pump, water tanks, nozzles, hoses, and various firefighting tools, including axes, pike poles, crowbars, and extinguishers when dealing with small-scale firefighting and gaining entry by force. Alpha 1 also carries medical equipment and can easily accommodate five firefighters, including the driver/engineer, a pump operator, and three firefighters.

Today's Alpha 1's driver is Silvana Serrano, who, in some languages, means "Highlander." She is tough and takes no notice, heroine. She is small in stature only; her whole body, except for her angelic-looking face, is covered in tattoos. She wears no make-up and rides to and from work on a Harley Davidson with extended twin forks like the Hells Angels back in the USA.

Silvana's role as the designated driver is to ensure safety and efficiency when manoeuvring the fire engine to all the scenes of any emergency. Silvana is responsible for operating the vehicle's controls and ensuring its readiness.

I always knew when "Highlander" was coming to the station. I could hear the iconic motorcycle, equipped with a substantial V-twin engine, with its signature rumbling sound from miles away. I would always stand and be overawed by the stripped-down, minimalist design, the definitely comfortable-looking saddle seat, the impressively mounted foot controls, and the obvious dynamic suspension to ensure the "Highlander" always enjoyed a smooth ride, no matter the terrain.

Together, this rider and motorcycle command attention, coupled with an aura of rebellious spirit everywhere they go.

The two firefighters sitting behind the driver are Ana Iglesias, with code name Churches, and Alejandro Marin, with code name Marine, due to his recently completed two years in the Army patrolling the somewhat dangerous Buenaventura seaport. He was relieved to finish his conscription when the city tried to uphold the 2016 truce agreement between various warring factions.

Ana Iglesias, the pump operator who was in charge of controlling the water flow and pressure, alias "Churches", could never have been more different than the "Highlander." But that never stopped them from day one, working together and bonding like no other pair of females. It turned out they were both born in the same year and even in the same month. In fact, only three days separated them. What did it for "Highlander" was "Churches" foul use of language; she could curse more than any person "Highlander" could think of.

The air was always blue when Ana arrived. No man or pump was spared. If a call came out regarding a cat stuck in a tree. Seeing and hearing Ana's foul language soon persuaded the feline target to scarper as fast as its four feet could muster.

She had been told off umpteenth of times, pulled into many offices, and given a dressing down time after time, to no avail. Ann was just one of those thankfully rare people who loved to swear.

So why was she tolerated? You may ask. Simply put, she was one of the bravest firefighters ever wearing the uniform. No one got hurt when Ana was on shift. She was the luckiest talisman a crew could ask for.

Around the living quarters, the standard saying is, "If Churches reports sick, we all go sick!"

So far, in three years, "Churches" has reported on duty and always on time.

Her latest target was the cherub-looking probationer David Castro, code-named "Village". He comes from a long line of firefighters working out of Bogota. "Village" wants to make his name in a warmer climate. Bogota was always too cold for him.

The fifth and very important firefighter was Lieutenant Javier Blanco, code name "Whitey," due to pale complexion and premature white hair. Even his BMW was white. It had been rumoured that when he is to be married in a couple of months, he is going to wear a white suit and matching white shoes to compliment his blushing bride, who, yes, you can guess, is turning up in white with a horse-drawn carriage – Yep, WHITE!

*****

Now, I can finally turn to yours and my appliance's crew. I am the station ladder truck. I am a responsible, hardworking, and dedicated firefighting vehicle with an extendable ladder and ladder pipe attached to the top of the extended ladder, allowing for high-angle firefighting. I also have an elevated stable aerial platform attached to the ladder and all the additional firefighting equipment currently known to man, including forcible entry tools, saws, roof hooks, and ventilation fans.

I was designed to perform tasks involving elevated locations, such as rescuing barbarians from upper floors, providing ventilation to trapped people, and accessing roofs.

We sit on the ground floor of the fire station, which serves as the operational hub for Alpha 1 and 2. If the powers are authorised to have them, there is room for an additional two fire engines. This part of the fire station is spacious, well-organised, and designed to facilitate quick responses and efficient maintenance.

Our fire vehicles are parked up and maintained in designated spacious bays. There is ample room to accommodate us and retain us from either side.

Within each bay, sturdy and adjustable workbenches are equipped with a wide array of tools and equipment necessary for maintenance and repairs. I have often seen firefighters and mechanics on all four parts of me, from front to back and side to side.

Multiple wall-mounted cabinets and shelves line the ground floor area. These storage units are designed to house firefighting equipment, including extra hoses, nozzles, extinguishers, and other essential tools. They are clearly labelled and organised for quick access during emergency response.

Adjacent to the fire engine and ladder, truck bays are designated areas for storing additional emergency equipment. These areas include racks for storing helmets, fire-resistant jackets, gloves, and specialised breathing apparatus. They are easily accessible to firefighters before responding to a call.

One wall in the ground floor area prominently displays essential information and emergency plans. It includes operational protocols, emergency contact numbers, maps of the jurisdiction, and key information about nearby hazardous materials or high-risk areas. This wall serves as a quick reference for firefighters during emergencies.

Another wall is dedicated to training and safety notices. It displays charts, diagrams, and reference material related to firefighting techniques, incident management, and emergency procedures. It also features safety reminders and notices about upcoming training sessions or drills to keep firefighters informed and prepared.

One wall is dedicated to boosting morale and fostering a sense of pride among the firefighting team. It features photographs, commendations, and awards recognising outstanding acts of valour or teamwork. This wall serves as a reminder of the firefighters' dedication and achievements.

*****

Like firefighters worldwide, their joint primary function is to be the first responders to all emergency calls. Their responsibilities include rescuing individuals and stranded animals, combating fires, providing medical aid, and conducting fire safety inspections.

My Captain is a female firefighter called Valeria Martinez, alias Mars, due to the potholes often on show when her make-up had decided to give up the fight during a fire. When going up the extendable ladders or operating the aerial platform, Valeria's complexion would be as one would expect of a 35-ish woman. But whenever she returned from the depths of the flames on the upper levels of any building, her make-up had vanished, and "Mars" would be in attendance.

But in my book and all her colleague's eyes, Captain Valeria Martinez was the ultimate firefighter. She had more citations than any other firefighter in the city's history. If you were someone standing on the top floor of any building with an inferno chasing you from behind, you could not be in safer hands than Mars.

My station veteran, Engineer, and driver, Luis Gonzalez, alias "Son of Gonzalo," had been in the fire service since he was sixteen. Now aged forty-six, his thirty-year service had saved countless lives from floods, mudslides, fires, and even earthquakes.

Luis married his village sweetheart one year after becoming a firefighter, and together, Luis and Constantine had ten children. Two sets of triplets and two sets of twins comprised the vast number. You could not find a fatherly figure than the "Son of Gonzalo." Everyone and everything, including cats, dogs, and the odd iguana, loves this firefighter.

The only part the Fire Service Executive Management Team could criticise Luis for was his continuous lack of dress sense, including his uniform. He always had the appearance of turning up for his shift after four or five hours under a broken-down vehicle, leaking oil everywhere.

If the truth be known to the Master, Wolf, or the Strong One, I am sure they would ignore it.

Sitting behind Luis and Lieutenant Blanco sat two very comical young single men who loved cycling. Mateo Rubio's alias is "Blondie" due to his streaky highlights and fair complexion, and Santiago Delgado's alias is the "Thin Man." Yep, this fella was six foot four tall and slender in build. It was rumoured that other firefighters in other stations in the city had labelled him "Jacob's Ladder."

Alpha 1 and I, Alpha 2, work side by side in collaboration to combat fires and carry out various emergency operations. Alpha 1's primary role is to provide a water supply for firefighting, while Alpha 2, with my ladder truck, facilitates access to elevated areas and assists with all mannerisms of rescues.

*****

Captain Valeria Martinez stood with Lieutenant Javier Blanco while both drivers, Silvana Serrano and Luis Gonzales, inspected the tread on one of Alpha 1's tyres. Both had agreed that it would need replacing soon.

While waiting for the roll call, Firefighters Ana Iglesias, Alejandro Marin, Mateo Rubio, Santiago Delgado, and a relatively quiet David Castro stood in the empty parking bay.

Captain Mars, whose face looked like someone who had a beauty treatment done by Revel prior to coming on duty that day, turned to face the group of firefighters.

"Attention! Today's shift briefing is about to begin."

Everyone came to attention and lined up side by side. Lieutenant Blanco was impressed.

He could clearly see all firefighters were on parade in their turnout gear, a fire-resistant coat made of multiple layers of fire-resistant material that provided thermal protection against heat and flames. Below each coat, the firefighters wore a matching pair of fire-resistant pants, similarly constructed with multiple layers, offering lower body protection.

Each wore a protective hood under their helmets. The hood protected their necks and heads from heat and flame exposure.

The final look of each wearing their designated fire helmet. These would protect their heads against falling debris, impacts, and heat. Every firefighter had their face shield down to show no defects were evident to reduce their eye protection.

Lieutenant Blanco's eyes went downwards to inspect each pair of firefighting boots. These were also made of heat-resistant materials to protect against burns, slips, and puncture hazards.

Finally, each firefighter displayed their gloved hands for the officer's inspection. These gloves were designed to withstand high temperatures and protect the wearer from burns, cuts, and abrasions.

Both officers on parade worked amongst the firefighters, checking their masks, harnesses, and air cylinders, which were providing clean air and protection from smoke and hazardous atmospheres. They looked at each Nomex hood, checking that each hood provided additional thermal protection to the firefighter's head and neck. The last item was the safety harnesses, which would be used in situations that required firefighters to utilise these safety harnesses or bailout systems for emergency escapes.

Lastly, the two officers focused on the firefighter's additional equipment, such as their portable radios. Each was switched on, and a communication check was made to the Ops centre, resulting in no issues raised.

"I can see you are all on duty, and I thank you for your good timing. Firefighter Gonzales, as usual, your trousers are stained with oil."

Luis looked down at the offending patch. I apologise, Lieutenant Blanco; I spilt coffee in desperation when the roll call bell went off."

The rest of the firefighters began to chuckle at the ridiculousness of oil looking like coffee.

Captain Mars allowed this daft explanation to pass. Later, she would speak to the offending firefighter separately from the rest.

"Okay, pay attention; here are your duties for this morning, Firefighter Gonzales; you will conduct the daily inspections of both Alpha 1 and Alpha 2, ensuring that all the equipment, tools, and machinery are in proper working order. Please bring our new probationer, David Castro, and begin his learning."

"Yes, Captain." was the response from "Gonzalo" he was his happiest when tinkering with oil and engines.

Firefighter Serrano, please test and maintain the firefighting apparatus, including pumps, nozzles, and the other specialised equipment listed on the check sheet. "Yes, Captain," roared out the Highlander.

Firefighter Iglesias, today you need to check that our communication systems and emergency lighting are functioning correctly. I also need you to inspect all our backup PPE, such as helmets, turnout gear, and self-contained breathing apparatus (SCBA), to ensure all are clean, operational, and compliant with safety standards."

"Churches "response was low in volume but high in dissatisfaction. "For frig's sake, this is going to take me all flaming day!" Both officers chose not to get into a shouting match with Ana. They knew her well and were confident she would do her usual high standard of inspections. She just always annoyingly had to get the last word in.

Captain Mars looked down at her list of duties and inspections for today and looked up to make eye contact with Alejandro Marin, who, in truth, she had held a mild interest in since his arrival.

"Firefighter Marin, you must conduct routine equipment and resource inventory updates. Please restock any supplies and report any deficiencies or needs for replacement to Lieutenant Blanco or me before the shift ends."

"Will do, Captain," replied Alejandro Marin, who was still wondering if the Captain was interested in him or if it was his imagination.

"Firefighter Rubio and firefighter Delgado, I have saved the best for you two. I need you to clean and organise the fire station and living quarters, ensuring they are well-maintained and ready for any emergency response. That also included inspecting our fire hydrants in the response area,"

Two voices announced their happiness at working together, albeit a long and arduous cleaning session awaited them. "Yes, Captain, would you like us to give out new probationary firefighters a quick tour of the fire station?"

The Captain looked at the Lieutenant and started smiling when she turned and replied, "Thank you, Blondie and Thin Man; yes, you can give señor Village a quick tour and organise his room for him."

Both firefighters laughed, surprised at the Captain, knowing the new alias the company had created over the past few weeks. Only the probationary firefighter was bewildered by his name, Village.

Lieutenant Blanco moved forward and stood at attention.

"Firefighters, attention, parade dismissed. Oh yes, we will be checking in on you all, so there will be no shenanigans from any of you."

*****

Ring, Ring went the operator's telephone. This was going to be the first emergency call from the public today.

A panicking Person spoke frantically: "Hello? Is this the fire department? Oh, thank goodness! You won't believe what's happening! There's a person stuck really high up on a lamppost!"

The despatch operator listened and spoke softly and reassuringly: "Okay, let's stay calm, sir. Can you please provide the exact location?"

The caller, still frantic, answered: "Yes, it's on Calle 47, near the park. A man climbed up trying to retrieve a bunch of balloons, and now he is just dangling up there!"

The Dispatcher, suppressing a giggle: "I see. So, just to clarify, do you need a fire engine to assist?"

Instead of calming down, the unidentified person raised his voice even higher: "Absolutely! The situation seems pretty dire. Who knows when gravity might strike and bring him down!"

The Dispatcher now was clenching her buttocks, praying she could stay in control: "Alright, we'll dispatch a fire engine to assess the situation and ensure everyone's safety. Please stay on the line."

*****

A short time later, I arrived at the scene with my extendable ladder.

Captain Valeria Martinez exited the cab and approached a small crowd of people, one of whom she instinctively guessed was the one who had called: "Hello, we received a report of a balloon retrieval mission gone awry. Can you please point us in the right direction?"

Her instinct was bang on target as the still frantic person uttered: "Thank goodness you're here! Over there, you see that person hanging on the lamppost? He thought it was a good idea to try and grab a bunch of balloons!"

She tried to suppress her laughter, as the Dispatcher had previously said, "Well, let's see what we can do. Safety first, though. We'll set up our equipment and assess how to bring the person back down."

The firefighters Mateo and Santiago prepared a ladder and safety harness from the side of my carriage.

The vexed person: "Be careful! Those balloons are very important to him, you know!"

Firefighter Gonzales approached to offer reassurance: "No worries, we're professionals in balloon retrieval too."

The two firefighters safely brought the unfortunate balloonist back down with precision and a touch of humour.

The Relieved caller came to life, full of gratitude and appraisal: "Thank you so much! This whole situation was truly up in the air. I appreciate your expertise in 'high-flying' rescues!"

Captain Valeria smiled back: "Not a problem. We're always here to assist, even in unconventional situations. Just remember, sometimes it's better to let balloons soar freely!"

The firefighters and the small crowd shared a laugh, and my ladder truck crew headed back to the station, ensuring that the situation was resolved with a touch of humour and a successful balloon retrieval.

We all returned just in time to continue with the inspections and daily checks. At one point, Firefighter Serrano did the rounds with piping hot tinto and a basket full of empanadas.

Back in the Executive Management Suite, the "Master" was deep in thought regarding a disturbing report of a recent house fire with a deceased and unknown body in its cellar that looked innocent enough. He had an itch in his little left finger that only appeared when trouble began to show its first steps......

*****

On Saturday afternoon, the Central Fire Station responded to a house fire at a residential house near the city river. At an initial glance, the fire appeared to be a standard incident. However, during the firefighting and search-and-rescue operations, an unknown deceased person was discovered in the cellar. This unexpected finding raised concerns for our Captain on Duty.

Fire Chief Eduardo Dominguez paused, and after drinking from his flask of cool water, he continued reading:

**1. Cause of the Fire:**

While the fire initially seemed innocent enough and could have been attributed to a possible electrical or accidental cause, the discovery of a dead person in the cellar raises suspicions about the fire's origin and if it might have been intentionally set.

The Fire chief looked again at his finger, which was still itching. He returned to the report.

**2. Potential Foul Play:**

The presence of a deceased person in the cellar suggests the possibility of foul play. It is unclear whether the person was the victim of the fire or if their death occurred under suspicious circumstances before the fire. This situation is alarming, as it indicates the potential involvement of criminal activities.

The Fire Chief leaned back into his sizeable leather-bound chair, stared at the map of his city, and stayed this way for some considerable time. Finally, he returned to the piece of paper on his desk.

**3. Safety of the Community:**
Finding an unknown deceased person during a house fire indicates a potential threat to the community's safety. It implies that an unidentified individual with unknown intentions might have been residing in the house or trespassing. This raises concerns about the presence of a potentially dangerous individual and the need for further investigation.

Signed.
Battalion Chief Tomas Ortiz, alias the Strong One.

*****

Discovering a deceased individual would require immediate coordination with law enforcement agencies. The Fire Chief was concerned about ensuring that the appropriate authorities, such as the police, were notified and involved in the investigation as soon as possible.

He reasoned the collaboration would be crucial to gather evidence, determine the cause of death, and potentially bring any responsible parties to justice.

Encountering a grim discovery like this can psychologically impact the firefighters and emergency responders involved in the incident.

The Fire Chief was concerned about his firefighters' well-being and mental health; he would have to ensure they received appropriate support and counselling throughout the incident and its aftermath.

In light of these concerns and his constantly itching small finger, the Fire Chief prioritised working in collaboration with law enforcement agencies to thoroughly investigate the circumstances surrounding the fire and the discovery of the deceased person.

His primary focus would be to determine the cause of the fire.

*****

# 56: *I am the Early History of Three Devilish Sisters*

In 1939, the third daughter of SS Doctor Hans Hartwig Schmidt and his Bavarian wife Helga was born in the medieval town of Brandenburg an der Havel. Nestled on the River Havel, Brandenburg an der Havel is an hour away from Berlin. It is a quiet village with a history going back 10 centuries.

Even today, you can follow the town's walls to the remaining watchtowers and, as a tourist, take in the late gothic red brick building known locally as the Old Town Hall.

The newborn was christened Gertrud, and her two slightly older sisters, Gitta and Eva, were only two and one years old. That same year, Germany invaded Poland, and WW2 broke out. For the next turbulent three years, the two toddlers and newborn baby led a carefree and joyful existence.

That was to come to an end in March 1945.

The three siblings, each with unique personalities, shared an inseparable bond. They spent countless days with their mother toddling alongside the popular Liepnitzsee Lake with its ten-foot-deep crystalline waters, picking and weaving daisy chains, and listening to Helga as she described their promising futures within the Third Reich. Once, Helga seconded the local ferry to reach the tantalising island in the lake's centre. The young Bavarian family played in the small forest with its cooling ambience.

SS Doctor Schmidt in his pristine black uniform, knee-high boots, and carrying his impressive-looking Lugar, with its cold metal frame polished to a mirror-like sheen. On either side of the adapted-to-fit handle you can bear witness to the ominous symbols of the SS with the Nazi emblems glinting malevolently.

The Doctor worked at the Brandenburg Euthanasia Centre, which was formally the first concentration Camp built in 1933 by Heinrich Himmler, Reichsführer, and second in command only to Adolf Hitler, the German Dictator and Führer.

"Action T4", named after the Berlin district, was created with the primary aim of focusing on the treatment of the mentally ill, physically disabled, and other "undesirables" during the war years. The doctor arrived on its opening day in 1939 to play his evil role in assisting to murder nearly 10,000 mentally ill people and their children with the development of gas (carbon monoxide) chambers disguised as showers.

SS Doctor Schmidt, on two occasions, found it "necessary" to take his three daughters, now aged 5, 6, and 7, in 1944 to visit his place of work. One day, he wanted all three to show their appreciation and deep devotion to their hard-working and industrious father by continuing his dedication to their Führer by becoming scientists and professors in the mental health field.

However, it was during the second visitation that their idyllic childhood took an unexpected turn when The United States Air Force (USAF), the French Air Force, and the Royal Air Force (RAF) bomber aircraft began bombing Berlin and the surrounding towns such as Brandenburg an der Havel.

This operation was a joint bombing raid carried out to deliver a devastating blow to the heart of Nazi Germany in a final push to bring the war to an end. The primary target was the capital city of Berlin. The operation aimed to cripple Hitler's war machine, demoralise German forces, and pave the way for the Allied ground offensive.

On that cold March morning, a massive fleet of American B-17 Flying Fortresses, British Lancaster bombers, and French heavy bombers assembled at airbases across Western Europe. The darkening skies were filled with the roar of engines and the anticipation of those ready to unleash their fury upon Berlin. The allied aircraft were armed with a formidable arsenal of high-explosive bombs and incendiary devices.

As they approached Berlin, the bombers faced fierce resistance from German Luftwaffe fighters. Nevertheless, the allied pilots skillfully manoeuvred through enemy anti-aircraft fire while maintaining formation. The bombers ' Swift, evasive manoeuvre and synchronised tactics allowed them to minimise losses and press forward towards their objectives.

The joint bombing raid commenced with coordinated precision. Bombers unleashed their payloads, raining down destruction upon strategic targets throughout Berlin. The iconic Reichstag building, key transportation hubs, war factories, and communication centres were obliterated. Meanwhile, the surrounding towns of Brandenburg and der Havel suffered strategic blows to their railway infrastructure, disrupting German supply lines.

For the first time, three children looked fearfully to the skies as the black silhouettes roared overhead with their bomb doors clearly open. Dr Schmidt knew instantly it was time for him and his family to leave Germany, and he knew the people he would need to contact for this to happen.

Within hours, Berlin was engulfed in flames and smoke emanating from numerous targeted areas. The combined might of the American, British, and French forces had delivered a devastating blow, severely hampering Germany's ability to sustain its war effort.

It was hours before father and daughters arrived home to find they no longer had a home, nor did they have a living mother as she collapsed in front of them, minus her clothes, which had been torn off from the bomb that had come through the roof above. Her hair was aflame, and her skin was burnt beyond recognition. Dr Schmidt produced his Lugar from his coat, silently kissed his wife's deformed face, and fired his weapon to end her misery and pain. The children stood in a row deep in shock, holding hands.

*****

SS Dr Schmidt had spent the next three hours in despair of losing his wife and finding himself in unknown territory regarding how to look after his three daughters. They were homeless, starving, and without funds.

He was sure the banking sector had been hit hard, and all the banks would be closed to the public. He decided he would have to first find out if his place of work had survived the bombing. His brain told him not to bother and to treat it like that part of his life was now gone forever.

Dr. Schmidt took a deep breath and spoke to no one in particular, "My goodness, what a catastrophic event for my family. I need to act swiftly to ensure the safety of my daughters. First, I must find a safe place for them with a trusted relative. Let me gather my thoughts and make some calls."

His befuddled brain asked him, "Exactly where is a working telephone to make those calls?" Certainly not in the wrecked family home that, in reality, did not exist anymore.

Gitta, the oldest, approached her father, and as if by telepathy, she had read his mind, she said, "Father, we still have the car. Can we head to our Aunt Clara's place in Wenzlow? It is only 9 miles southwest of here. Maybe the Allied bombers did not pass over her place. Maybe she has a working telephone."

Placing his semi-automatic pistol back into its holster and looking down at Gitta simultaneously, he found a smile for such an excellent and helpful suggestion. Right there and then, he could not think straight. He was in deep shock at having to shoot his wife, and if that was not bad enough, he had to do it in front of the children.

"Good thinking, Gitta. Quickly get the girls into the car; we will drive. I hope your Aunt Clara has not been hurt in any way."

On the journey towards Aunt Clara's house, Dr. Schmidt swore the three children to secrecy regarding how Helga had died. He had reasoned the pain of losing her younger sister, Helga, would be too much for this frail lady. The three girls looked at each other and silently chose to obey their father.

*****

With an anxious voice, Dr Schmidt spoke earnestly as the door opened and revealed Aunt Clara holding a silver candlestick holder and white candle, showing concern, relief, and fear when seeing the look on Hans's and the children's faces.

"It's me, Hans. I hope you're well. We urgently need your help. An Allied aircraft dropped one of its bombs directly onto our house earlier tonight, and it was destroyed with Helga inside. The girls and I need a safe place to stay temporarily. Can you please take care of them for a while? I promise it won't be for long. I need to arrange for Helga to recover as soon as possible."

"Oh my, dear, of course, I'll do whatever I can to help. Bring the girls in immediately. We'll figure things out together. Don't worry; I'm here for you all. Gitta, Eva, and Gertrud come; let's get you a warm place to rest. I will make you some hot soup, and I am sure I have some apple strudel left in the pantry." Clara had placed the candle and candleholder next to the telephone in the hallway and coaxed the three girls further inside towards the back of her property.

Hans remained at the front door with his car keys in one hand. "Thank you, Clara. Your support means a lot to us during this difficult time. I'll be back as soon as I can."

Dr. Schmidt returned to his car before Clara started to ask awkward questions or suggest anything else. He took a moment to gather his thoughts. He abruptly turned back to Clara, who was about to close the door. "Do you have a connection on your telephone, as I need to call my Headquarters?" In reality, he needed to call a trusted contact in Odessa.

*****

Hans walked behind Clara, watched her pick up the telephone receiver, and listened for a dialling tone. One question could not be answered: How long would it take? He had to presume time was against him. Clara passed the telephone to Hans, who smiled back with his appreciation. He waited for Clara to disappear towards the vast kitchen at the rear of her house with his three daughters. Feeling he was safe making the call, Hans dialled a number he had committed to memory long ago, never realising that the day would come when he would be dialling it.

He could hear the connection being made to another telephone at an address he did not know. He heard someone breathing on the other end, waiting for him to speak.

With his calm but determined voice, he said, "Good evening. This is Waffen-SS Dr Hans Hartwig Schmidt of the Brandenburg Euthanasia Centre speaking. I find myself in a desperate situation and need assistance from Odessa. I must ensure the safety of myself and my three daughters and escape this war-torn city. The organisation has contacts and resources to help in such situations. Can you guide me on the first steps towards changing our identities and finding a safe haven in South America?"

\*\*\*\*\*

With a degree of practice at sounding sympathetic, the Odessa contact replied, "Dr. Schmidt, I'm sorry to hear about your situation. Rest assured, we understand the urgency and seriousness of your request. We have experience in aiding individuals seeking to start anew. For now, creating new identities for you and your daughters is crucial to ensuring your safety. We will work closely with you throughout the process. Let's schedule a meeting at a secure location to discuss the details and plan accordingly. I'll send you the necessary instructions and coordinates shortly and discreetly."

For the first time, Dr. Schmidt felt confident: "Thank you for your prompt response. I truly appreciate the help you and the Odessa organisation are offering. I eagerly await instructions on how to attend the meeting. Time is of the essence, so please send them as soon as possible. In the meantime, my home has gone, so please leave a message with my receptionist at the centre, and I will pick it up."

"That is agreeable to me, but I suggest a short message such as "transportation of the undesirables is ready." In this dangerous climate, such a message would not look out of place for a doctor like yourself."

"Transportation of the undesirables is ready, and it is an easy message for me to memorise. I await my receptionist's notification that a message has been received."

The other end of the line went dead. The call was over. Soon, Hans and his girls would set off on an unknown journey towards securing a new life for each of them.

\*\*\*\*\*

Next, he had to make a detour back to his destroyed house and place his wife's body in a position so as not to cause any concerns or doubts about how she had died. The only option he could think of was to place her in the closed cellar and secure the hatch with its accompanying lock leading to the steps going down. He then covered the hatch with debris and ash from the bomb blast and threw away the key. Hopefully, it would be months before anyone would discover Helga. By then, he and his daughters would be safe in South America.

*****

The organisation of former SS members known as Odessa was created at the beginning of 1944 to assist Nazis such as Dr Hans Hartwig Schmidt to flee from Europe and escape justice from either the Americans, British, or dreaded Soviets.

To his relief, Dr. Schmidt discovered that obtaining false papers was little to no difficulty, and he had been assured he would have ample money available to establish new lives for himself and his children.

The now fugitive was in doubt; the powers must have made plans when they realised that Germany's assets needed to be saved from the approaching enemies. They had to have transferred and hidden much wealth that had been plundered from the countries and populations, such as the Jews that were murdered. Vast unknown sums would now be out of reach of any judicial bodies. However, they could still fund a future movement to resurrect the party in disarray.

At the next meeting with the Odessa contact, who remained nameless to Dr Schmidt, he was offered assistance to stay in Germany with new identities involving false papers and passports, a safe house, and a new career in one of the large corporations. If he preferred not to remain in Germany, he and the children could be ushered out of the country and begin new lives under false identities in a South American country.

Dr. Schmidt chose the latter option, and it was explained that they would be smuggled across the unmanned Swiss Border and continue their journey to Rome. Roman Catholic Franciscan priests would move the family to South America, particularly Argentina.

The journey was much longer and involved more stopovers than had been mentioned at the first meeting....

The Schmidt family commenced their clandestine journey by boarding a train in Berlin. They ventured south towards Innsbruck, Austria. As the picturesque landscapes of Germany unfolded, they found themselves in awe when crossing the Bavarian Alps and reaching Innsbruck, nestled amidst the majestic peaks. They rested in a monastery for one night and silently ate with a Franciscan Monk.

The following day, the reserved group left the alpine landscape behind and, in no way plausible, bid farewell to Innsbruck. Silently, the three girls held hands once more, and each bid farewell to their mother. Hans had no idea this had happened as he continued gazing out of the train's window at the moving scenery, not knowing if he would ever see such beauty again.

They proceeded southward to the northern Italian city of Milan. They were instructed to transfer to another train heading west to the enchanting port city of Genoa, a gateway to the Mediterranean Sea.

The family boarded a merchant ship destined for Rio Janeiro in Brazil at the bustling port of Genoa. This ship, making its usual stops along the Mediterranean coastline, offered an opportunity to absorb the flavours of the diverse cultures encountered on this maritime route. The outgoing freighter traversed the Mediterranean Sea, crossing the Strait of Gibraltar and continuing along the Atlantic coast of North Africa.

Arriving at Rio, the family took a two-day stopover in this vibrant Brazilian coastal city renowned for its stunning colonial architecture. At the same time, they waited for their subsequent contact with the Odessa members.

From Rio, they were instructed to embark on a riverboat that would navigate the sprawling Amazon River deep into the heart of the Amazon Rainforest. They would sleep in hammocks day and night, witnessing the lush green expanse, diverse wildlife, and captivating indigenous communities as they voyaged through one of the world's most biodiverse regions.

After the awe-inspiring exploration of the Amazon, the family disembarked from the riverboat at Leticia, a Colombian town perched on the border of Brazil and Peru. They continued the journey by taking a small propeller plane from Leticia to Santiago de Cali, the capital of Valle del Cauca department in western Colombia, the final destination.

The now Austrian Müller family, consisting of Karl, a 35-year-old Science Teacher and widower, and his daughters, was slowly getting used to their new identities. Gitta was now Anna Müller. Eva insisted on staying as Eva but accepted her family name, Müller. Little Gertrud was too young to know any difference and was taught to answer to Lisa Müller.

Little did Karl Müller imagine that his three angelic-looking daughters, as young as they were, harboured deep hatred for their father. Learning Spanish as they travelled and mixed with the sailors on the ships had stood them in good stead. The three girls reverted to Spanish without effort on arrival at their new home on a mountain ridge overlooking the city below in a place called Dapa.

The sisters had jointly made an oath to each other to wait until the time was right to seek retribution for the demise of their beloved mother.

In other words, Karl would pay a heavy price for their silence....

*****

The Müller family, hailing from somewhere called Austria in Europe, seemed mysterious and reserved except for the father, who called himself Professor Karl Müller. The professor's three girls were not so approachable; the local population received curt interactions with the village folk to fuel the rumours that circulated, painting them as secretive and untrustworthy.

Curiosity piqued the neighbour's interest, but they couldn't shake the growing unease as they watched the Müller family from afar. Strange occurrences began to unfold in their presence. Eerie whispers drifted from across the fence late at night, sending shivers down the neighbour's spines. Whispers of dark secrets and unearthly powers began circulating in the local church.

Sister Miriam from the local school, always logic-oriented and responsible, heard the rumours and decided to introduce herself to the new family. But her confidence faded when she stood at their door, overtaken by a chilling presence that emanated from within.

The Müller trio, headed by Anna, Eva, and Lisa, who were standing behind her, disclosed nothing of their troubled past. Instead, they decided to invent and reveal a sinister connection to a long-forgotten secret cult that they had desperately sought to distance themselves from.

Each day, the village's fear became more entwined with unrest. They couldn't shake the feeling that the Müller family had brought a dark cloud over their once blissful village. Shadows loomed over Dapa village, and whispers began circling, implicating the foreign family in unexplained misfortunes that befell the village folk and surrounding Campesinos.

*****

Karl Müller, who was supposed to become a professor and take up a science teacher profession, changed his mind on reaching their new home and instead felt safer calling himself a family doctor.

The sisters, driven by their disturbing mindset, started plotting their revenge. Secrets whispering fuelled their determination. Drawing on their collective strengths, Anna, Eva, and Lisa began seeking justice for their beloved mother. They began subtly manipulating events, planting evidence that further implicated their father in malpractice since he opened his doctor's surgery in the village soon after their arrival. They thought up new mischief every week while ensuring their actions remained concealed.

He witnessed the chaos unfolding around him. Dr Müller grew increasingly desperate, sensing the weight of his past finally catching up to him. Yet, he remained oblivious to his daughter's calculated acts of retribution and unable to perceive the manipulations.

As the sisters delved deeper into their revenge-driven pursuits, a darkness crept into their souls. The line between right and wrong blurred, fuelled by an insatiable thirst for justice they believed they were achieving. Their actions bred a toxic mindset that distorted their once-innocent world perspectives.

Hidden behind closed doors and in the depths of the night, the sisters continued their relentless pursuit of retribution. But little did they know that vengeance, once unleashed, could consume them just as it had consumed their targets. And when the truth unravelled, they would face the painful repercussions of their twisted journey, forever altering their bond and haunting their souls.

The trouble was that it would take almost a lifetime for anyone to discover who these evil sisters were and why they did what they did.

*****

# 57: I am the "Once was" National Police Colonel with a New Cold Case to Solve

Hi, it is me, Stalin. I am sitting outside a derelict property that once housed an amiable old lady. She would never think twice about inviting me into her house each Christmas until she made an error with me. The dwellers in the neighbourhood had long ago accepted me as an unofficial protector from other cretins, vagabonds, thieves, and killers. They could sleep peacefully in their beds at night. During the day, most of them would turn their eyes away from me when aware of my presence. This lack of passion bore no weight on my shoulders. I secretly preferred it. I had nothing to offer society anymore. Once, I did, but that was a long time ago and in a different setting.

Today, I wish to concentrate on kindness from the least expected sources.

My friendship with the old lady began one day when I knocked on her door to offer advice on how to keep her kitchen window closed even during the day. It was the season when more people roamed the streets to snatch opportunities to steal. Many carried makeshift weapons, as a matter of course, and felt no qualms about using them should someone resist.

*****

The old lady was holding a tray of freshly baked cookies. She saw my glance and knew instantly I would be hungry for such delicacies. Immediately, she stood aside, smiling and invited me in. Never before had I experienced such a welcome. Was she crazy? I am a street man! She looked at me and whispered as if hearing my words in my mind. "Yes, you are a street man, and I suspect a hungry one, too." Come help me make some coffee, and let's share these together. I am a widow, and it would be nice to have the opportunity to share again. "

So, I gingerly moved forward and accepted the invitation. It had been a long time since I had entered a natural home. The derelict shells of shops and houses are my homes now. She guided me into the galley-style kitchen, clearly displaying its narrowness and length. On the left in the middle stood a six-ringed hob and oven, and on top sat a Pyrex dish of what I presumed was Chilli Con Carne. The smell of the creamy sauce and the aroma of the kidney beans overpowered me, and I became weak at the knees at the thought of throwing my face into the hot food.

The voice from the old lady entered my brain, "I need to finish hoovering my living room carpet; why don't you put the Chilli on the heat. Based on your demeanour, I think you would prefer to have a plate of hot food and my cookies later. "

I was amazed to see her walk away as if it were natural for a street man to salivate over the piping hot food in her kitchen!

That is when she made her mistake. "Do not forget to put the dish on heat first and then make the coffee."

\*\*\*\*\*

I looked around for a lighter or matches and located the small box of matches. Out one popped, and I struck it against the rough side. Immediately, a flame appeared, and with my other hand, I turned the gas on and ignited the hob plate under the dish.

I blissfully turned to find the kettle, and within seconds, a mighty explosion was behind me. I turned in horror to see Chilli Con Carne dripping from every angle in the room—ceiling, walls, doors, cupboards, windows—and I was covered in dripping Chilli and kidney beans.

I stood frozen as if I were a statue. The old lady was back in, transfixed for a moment or two, trying to figure out what had transpired. Then the proverbial penny dropped. "you idiot! You put the Pyrex dish on direct heat, not in the oven!"

\*\*\*\*\*

"Get out, leave my house. Look what you have done to my beautiful kitchen. It will take me days to discover where all my Chilli has gone."

At this point, a mop was in her hands, and she was coming at me fast. I pushed past her and grabbed a handful of cookies. I was out of the door like a whippet.

It would be another year before I saw her again, only this time, she was being carried out by six strong men in a large black vehicle. Already, boards were going up behind her. In time, another derelict house would join the ranks of somewhere for me to shelter when the tropical storms appeared.

The only reason I know this story is today. I was across the road from the now derelict house with no roof and broken windows, accepting a small coffee and a savoury empanada from a street vendor who had been kind to me for the past few years.

"Hey, Stalin, do you remember when the old lady of that house made a mistake with you?"

\* \* \* \* \*

The vendor's offering of a joke did little to improve my melancholy mood. What was making me so sad? I am not sure. Maybe it is because each day is boring and tedious.

\* \* \* \* \*

Yes, to us regular folk, the words boring and tedious are from the same camp, but not with Stalin's logic.

The days when nothing happens are long and dull for Stalin. He can live in a city of two and a half million souls and communicate with none of them. Everything he does on a dreary day he does alone. Is he sad when he experiences such days? In the beginning, yes. Twenty years later, no. Instead, he is grateful for the peace and tranquillity.

But what happens on the tedious and forgetful days? I will let Stalin describe one such day that occurred recently.

\* \* \* \* \*

While I remember that tedious day, I will relate it to you, readers. Life began like any other day, with the burning city awakening the inhabitants at 6 a.m. The sun always rises simultaneously in the dry seasons and is precisely the same on wet days.

Anyway, another younger street urchin had appeared. Instinctively, I can tell he is a dangerous one. His eyes are dead. Signs of emotions had left them on his first kill for drug money many years previously. When his dead eyes focused on me, I sensed more than I saw his glance at my outstretched arm with the massive rock.

The rock silently told him who I was and about my previous life as the police chief. He thought it was better to avoid confrontation and possible injury, so he scurried away, looking for new prey. In a city this big, there was always another opportunity.

I followed at a safe distance. I knew I held no fear. Emotions had left me the day I was subjected to an almost lethal amount of drugs commencing with the Dragon's breath.

The traffic has stopped, waiting for the lights to change. The lead vehicle has the driver's side window down with an elbow on the show. Without warning, the thief with the dead eyes had launched himself through the window, one fist connecting with the driver's nose and the other scrambling for the bulky wallet resting in the driver's lap.

The driver tried in vain to rescue the situation, but another blow broke his nose, and blood cascaded in all directions. The perpetrator now had the wallet and, like a hummingbird, was retreating to safety at an unbelievable speed. At no point did his eyes turn back. He was off and running. He did not even bother to pause when he saw me. The driver was an idiot. He lives in a city where everyone protects themselves with blacked-out windows on their cars. No one would stop in broad daylight with a window open. It's his fault entirely. There is no point in being heroic. The fool should learn from his misfortune.

In the late afternoon, I was returning down the same street as earlier. The same robber was there, but he could see no one this time. He was lying on the sidewalk with his back against the wall. His legs and arms were outstretched, leaving him defenceless. His eyes, no longer black, had disappeared up into his skull. His jaw was wide open, his tongue lying dormant to one side. I knew this thief would never rob again. The dirty needle was still sticking in his vein.

The city dwellers continued on their journeys, not one daring to approach. No one cares or loses sleep over a druggie who had one shot too many.

*****

The next day, Stalin, the "once was" Police Colonel, now a weather-beaten street man with a hefty rock in his hand, had no memory of the day before; it must have been tedious and forgetful as usual.

"Colonel Stalin Oscar Ramirez. Is that you? Do you remember me? I know it's been decades since we last spoke, but I have never forgotten you."

Stalin paused and looked in the direction the voice was coming from. He initially saw only legs in the fire service colours, with a pair of highly polished shoes underneath.

"Who is asking?" muttered Stalin, still with his head facing downward.

"Sorry, I forgot to introduce myself; it is a great pleasure to see you breathing. It is I, Fire Chief Eduardo Dominguez. As I said, it has been a long time since we last spoke and worked together, but I never forgot how incredible your hunger for knowledge was. Do you remember you helped me with a certain cold case in 1975? I was a firefighter with only two years of service then?"

The "Master" was sitting on the pavement with his legs crossed-legged to be on a level that silently gave Stalin as much respect as possible. He needed this street man to open doors within his mind. The master wanted to see the remarkable encyclopaedia of unsolved murders involving house fires.

*****

Stalin did not move; his head was still facing the shoes. "I am not sure of when or why I supposedly assisted you in the past, but I do know this is not your first time visiting me. I have seen these shiny shoes often, and usually, a large 1.5 litre of "Colombiana" with a paper bag full of empanadas suddenly appears at my feet."

"Ah, you must mean these." At that moment, a large bottle of gaseosa and six piping hot empanadas are placed next to Stalin in a greaseproof bag. "I must confess, all my company has reported to me often over the years on when they have seen you. Believe it or not, nearly all of my company, at one time or another, have ensured you have had a meal or two near you before leaving you to attend to their duties as firefighters."

Stalin finally looked up into the honest blue eyes of a man in uniform he totally respected. For the first time in many decades, he smiles warmly. Is there another reason you are sitting here cross-legged on the floor in the middle of the day? Because I think we may look weird to anyone passing by."

"Yes, you may well be right, and yes, I do have a request." smiled the Fire Chief. "Many long years ago. In March of 1975, to be exact, I was a fireman of only two years of service. The company I was attached to was called out to a house fire that, on the surface, looked like any other house fire. Initially, my bosses put it down to an electrical fire. The next day, when we went back to confirm the source of the fire, we discovered an entrance down to the cellar, and it was there I discovered a corpse."

Stalin took a moment to speak next, "I remember that shout and that corpse. I was the leading investigator."

Eduardo confirmed Stalin's memory was correct on this occasion, "Yes, that is why I am here. While researching the old records, I saw you led the investigation. But your report does not say much. Do you not come to a satisfactory conclusion?"

"No, that is the point; I only discovered a dead body with a bullet hole in its face. The nose and top teeth were gone. When I went to investigate the fingers, there was no top surface. Actually, come to think of it, there were no fingers at all."

Stalin was grateful that, for once, his memory was helping him. "We did a TV and radio appeal, but to no avail. We did the usual door-to-door questions and answers and came up with nothing. This corpse was a mystery. The only thing that came out of the coroner's report was the man was possibly French due to the last meal in his stomach looked like he had eaten some French food, oysters, I think, before dying."

"Thank you." said Eduardo, "Any recollection going that far back will be helpful."

"There was something else I have just remembered. There was a similar case a decade before and another a decade afterwards. All three cases came up with nothing. All three persons were never identified, and no reason for the fires, let alone killing someone, were ever discovered." Suddenly, Stalin appeared excited. "Do you think there could be a connection between all the house fires?"

Eduardo took a moment to consider whether Stalin might be onto something. "You may be right; I am unsure as it is early in the investigation. Tell me, if you were me, who would you turn to in the National Police Department who could follow this cold case with a fair degree of professionalism?"

Stalin rubbed his sun-baked chin with steel-like bristles that had not seen a razor in over twenty-eight years. "Yes, there is someone I recently met on a very wet and muddy night. Inadvertently, we, both not knowing each other, prevented a dastardly murder in a park. But that's another story that has no consequences right now. Seek a young Policeman called Archibaldo Federico Alcatraz; you may have read about his heroism in a park with a community of cannonball trees?"

Eduardo started to rise to his feet. "Yes, I know this Policeman; he is engaged to my neighbour's daughter, Ximena. They make a fine couple. I will indeed speak to him next."

The Fire Chief reached out for the Street man's cripple-looking hand without the rock and offered a heartfelt handshake.

Not ignoring the approaching hand, Stalin rose and turned as if to walk away. "Walk with me; Archibaldo is still young and maybe full of the joys of spring with love in his heart. He may need guidance on what to do."

"As a former Colonel of Investigation into Criminal Activities in the Police, now grappling with memory loss due to Devil's Breath, I understand the challenging situation you and Archibaldo will face together. If I were you, Fire Chief, I would approach Archibaldo seeking assistance in solving a series of mysterious house fires with unidentified casualties in the cellars spanning five decades."

Now, both men were walking side by side, "It might also be beneficial to check even before my time in the service. Before I was attacked and rendered as you see me now, I had the notion to do just that; I had a hunch, and it would not go away."

"It wouldn't have been an itchy little left-hand finger, would it?" Enquired the Fireman.

"How would I know? I cannot think that far back. Amazingly, I am remembering things now!"

Both men laughed together. Stalin recovered first, "here's how I would advise Archibaldo to approach the cold case:

"1. Tell Archibaldo to gather available information: Gather all existing records, reports, and any other relevant documentation of the past house fires. Review the details to identify patterns, commonalities, or any leads that could help the investigation.

2. Conduct interviews: Contact witnesses, survivors, and residents living near the affected houses. Collect testimonies and examine similarities and deviations across various incidents. Pay closer attention to any recurring descriptions or sightings of suspicious individuals in the vicinity.

3. Utilise your fire investigation expertise: Re-examine all the fire investigation reports to analyse the burn patterns, trace evidence, and identify potential causes of the fires. These reports can help ascertain any significant correlation between the incidents or if an unknown modus operandi is involved.

4. Analyse the cellars further: Focus on the cellars where the unknown individuals were found dead. Thoroughly re-examine the scene, looking for any evidence that might provide clues about their identities, cause of death, or any connection to the fires.

5. Create a timeline: Construct a timeline to understand the sequence of events and any possible patterns regarding time, location, or other recurring factors. This will help in spotting any anomalies or commonalities among the incidents.

6. Seek technological assistance: Use advanced forensic technology, such as DNA analysis, fingerprint matching, or facial recognition, to help identify unknown victims or potential suspects associated with house fires.

7. Coordinate with law enforcement agencies such as Interpol: Collaborate with other law enforcement agencies, both local and regional, who may have relevant information or expertise in similar cases. Sharing resources and insights might help uncover connections that were previously missed.

8. Engage the online and social media outlet communities: Raise community awareness about the recurring incidents and seek their cooperation in reporting any suspicious activities, individuals, or previous incidents that might be related to the ongoing investigation.

9. Task force formation: If the investigation suggests an organised and persistent series of fires, consider creating a specialised task force dedicated to solving the case. This group can combine experts from various fields, such as fire investigation, forensic science, and criminal profiling, to pool knowledge and resources.

10. Ongoing surveillance and analysis: Maintain a continuous program targeting areas prone to fires or other suspicious activities. Analyse gathered information and adjusted investigation strategies to increase the chances of identifying the perpetrator.

Remember, since this is an ongoing investigation, it is crucial to involve law enforcement professionals and follow proper legal procedures at all times."

*****

This morning, if you had been someone else and had approached Stalin and foretold the conversation he was going to have with the firefighter, he would have laughed and dismissed it. But he should never do that. This is the calibre of the man before Devil's Breath entered his nostrils:

The training duration at the General Santander National Police Academy in Colombia can vary depending on the specific program or position being pursued. The academy offers various training programs, including primary and advanced courses for officer candidates and specialised courses for personnel already working in the police force.

Stalin, the new recruit, was a "Tour de Force." he soaked up and demanded more from all his trainers. If his squad of recruits were scheduled to run a half marathon, Stalin would start an hour before the leading group and complete a full marathon when it took the others to achieve their required distance.

If the same recruits had homework in the evenings, Stalin ensured he was the last to his bunk. Memorising the smallest of details was easy for this recruit.

Stalin's basic training program lasted 12 months. On average, his contemporaries took six more months to achieve what this outstanding recruit achieved. During this period, Stalin received comprehensive instruction in law enforcement tactics, criminal investigations, community policing, and physical fitness training.

Stalin's trainers agreed; this recruit was particular. He would make it to the top and fast, and his humility endeared him to them all. There was no arrogance on display. He was a once-in-a-lifetime recruit of exceptional merit.

After successfully completing the basic training program, Sub-Lieutenant Stalin Oscar Ramirez underwent six more months of specialisation training through several advanced courses. He excelled in all areas. Stalin was a man on a mission. He wanted to be a General of the Colombian National Police and had set a target of two decades to achieve it.

Fire chief Eduardo Dominguez knew all this from reading a file sent to him in confidence from a good friend at the academy. As soon as he read it, he knew who to turn to assist with the continuous itch. He had just prayed Stalin was up to the task.

*****

Finally, both men shook hands. A bus full of commuters in one of the extendable modern-day buses stopped to allow more passengers to board. All eyes were transfixed on an image of a Fire Chief replacing his hat, moving forward, and embracing a street man wearing only a denim skirt with a threatening-looking rock.

"Dear God! What is happening there?!" voiced a perplexed witness. Everyone was speechless. The bus moved away, and the two unlikelihoods of friends parted company and headed in different directions, both satisfied with the exchange of minds between each other.

*****

# 58: *I am the story behind Gabriel owning a restored Willy Jeep*

*I*n Part One of this book, I told you about my early years in the heart of Toledo, Ohio; I rolled off the assembly line in the sprawling Willy-Overland factory. In Part Two, you would have read of my exploits as a restored Willy Jeep in MG colours, assisting the older people rescued from torrential flooding and menacing mudslides.

No one has mentioned the journey in between, from the point I was abandoned and almost derelict to the chance to meet with a strange English-speaking white-haired trekker who came upon me and made a promise that I wanted to believe in.

But first, let me take up a few moments of your time and reflect on my past.

Little did I know that my life as a sturdy Jeep would take me on an extraordinary journey that would span continents and witness the ravages and triumphs of war.

Fresh from the factory, I found myself deployed to the other side of the world amidst the chaos and brutality of World War II. I navigated treacherous terrains alongside courageous servicemen, enduring the harshest elements and dodging enemy fire. From the sweltering jungles of the Pacific islands to the blood-soaked battles of the Philippine archipelago, I served faithfully, carrying soldiers to the frontlines and evacuating the wounded with unwavering determination. The Battle of Manila was particularly harrowing. The city lay in ruins, its once-vibrant streets now a desolate battleground. Bullets whizzed through the air as bombs exploded all around. Through it all, I fought relentlessly, rescuing trapped civilians and providing much-needed support to the valiant troops who fought for freedom.

After the war, I thought my journey had come to an end. However, fate had other plans in store for me. I was transported to Colombia, a land of lush green coffee plantations and rugged mountain landscapes. Nestled within the Coffee Mountains of Manizales to Salento and the impressive palm trees on the Cocora Valley, with its picturesque countryside, ferrying beans and supplies up and down the undulating terrain. My days were filled with the aroma of freshly roasted coffee and the laughter of the resilient farmers who toiled to make a living. With the good times, life always brings the bad times, and I ended up being sold off after the huge earthquake that killed thousands of people who found themselves victims to the brutality of nature when they became angry.

I moved again to the mountain ridge that overshadows the city below. Here, I became a furniture carrier and found the hands that kept changing, each becoming poorer and poorer. Eventually, there were no more hands, and I sensed I was disappearing from view with the undergrowth taking over.

As the years passed, my once vibrant frame started to wear thin. Neglected and forgotten, I was abandoned and almost invisible to the passing traffic on this dirty mountain ridge road. No longer able to serve my purpose, I watched as the city below bustled with life, oblivious to the memories I held. Then, one day, even the views of the city below disappeared. The jungle-like vegetation was winning the war of hiding me from everyone and everything. Sadness was the only emotion I could rely on in my despair and loneliness.

Yes, there were moments when I could be hopeful. I reasoned I had witnessed so much that I had carried soldiers into battle and brought them home. But as the wind howled through my broken windows and rust ate away at my body, I sometimes found solace in knowing that, despite my deserted state, my legacy would live on. On such an occasion was when the white-haired man first ran his fingers over my rusty frame.

The second time was when an Argentinian stopped and examined me from every angle known to a Willy Jeep....

*****

His name was Gabriel Garcia Marquez, but apparently different from the same renowned Colombian writer. "I wish I was because I am his most avid fan." This meant nothing to me, and I was not prepared to ask. Not because I could talk, it was primarily because I could see the White-haired Stranger approaching!

Both men stopped and awkwardly circled my dilapidated frame.

The white-haired man spoke, "Well, a forgotten relic just waiting to be restored. Each time I see him, my heart bleeds for him."

Gabriel, stretching both his hands on the missing bonnet, said, "Indeed, it's amazing what treasures can be found in the most unexpected places. And let me tell you, this jeep has so much potential!"

The White-haired Stranger smiled warmly, "I couldn't agree more. And I have an idea that might just breathe some life back into it. You see, I come from English roots, and I think we should honour that heritage by restoring it to the classic MG colours."

Gabriel paused to consider the idea, "Ah, that sounds like a wonderful way to pay homage to your ancestry. I can already picture the vibrant red, white, and green adorning this majestic jeep. But I have an idea of my own, too."

The white-haired Stranger was intrigued to hear more. "Oh, do tell me, Sir. What's on your mind?"

Gabriel rose to a proud position, "As an Argentinian Coffee and Cascara Importer, my heart lies in the world of coffee. So, while we restore the jeep in those English colours, how about we transform it into hues representing the coffee plant and beans?"

White-haired Stranger, now with his fist leaning against his chin and his thumb underneath it, "What an intriguing concept; I must admit, I've never thought about a coffee-themed jeep before. But we can combine our passions and create something truly unique. Let's shake on it."

Both men moved toward each other with genuine feelings of friendship and the desire to restore a rusty relic into a vehicle that would stop others from looking and staring with admiration.

They shook hands to symbolise their agreement and shared passion for this ambitious restoration project. Without thinking, the Englishman and the Argentinian said simultaneously, the first in English, "Sorry about the Falklands conflict." The second is in Spanish, "Perdón por Las Malvinas."

*****

The Falklands War, also known as the Falklands Conflict, was a military conflict that took place between the United Kingdom and Argentina in 1982. The 74-day war arose over the disputed sovereignty of the Falkland Islands, a remote archipelago in the South Atlantic Ocean, which Argentina claimed as their own and referred to as the Malvinas.

From Argentina's perspective, the claim to the Falkland Islands was based on historical, geographical, and cultural factors. The Argentine government argued that the islands were part of their territory and had been unjustly occupied by the British since 1833. This claim resonated with many Argentinians, who viewed the Falklands as integral to their national identity.

On the other hand, the UK maintained that the Falkland Islands were a British overseas territory and their inhabitants, mostly of British descent, had the right to self-determination. The British government argued that any attempt to change the islands' status should be resolved through peaceful negotiations, not force.

Tensions between the UK and Argentina reached a boiling point in 1982 when Argentina, under the military junta led by General Leopoldo Galtieri, launched a full-scale military invasion of the Falkland Islands. This unexpected move caught the UK by surprise, prompting them to swiftly respond by deploying an impressive task force of 127 requisitioned merchant ships, Submarines, and warships to recapture the islands.

The war lasted for about two and a half months, resulting in 904 lost military lives, of which 255 were British, 649 were Argentinian, and 3 were civilian.

The conflict showcased the UK's military capabilities as they successfully launched a long-distance amphibious operation to retake the islands. On the other hand, Argentina struggled with limited resources and logistical challenges, eventually leading to their surrender.

Ultimately, the UK emerged victorious and retained control over the Falkland Islands.

The conflict had a significant impact on the political landscape of both countries. In Argentina, the war contributed to the downfall of the military junta and led to the restoration of democracy. In the UK, the war bolstered national sentiment and the popularity of the "Iron Lady," Prime Minister Margaret Thatcher.

*****

Gabriel stood back and raised his Panama hat, "Fantastic! Now, our joint adventure begins. Together, we will bring this forgotten jeep back to life and infuse it with the captivating spirit of both our cultures!"

The equally happy White-haired Stranger removed his navy blue peaked cap in unison and bowed to his new friend, "Absolutely, this restoration will be a testament to the power of collaboration and celebrating our individual passions. I can't wait to see the end result."

Gabriel laughed joyously, "Nor can I, my friend. Let's buckle up and embark on this journey together. With your strong legs and my coffee expertise, we'll create something to make heads turn."

The equally smiling white-haired Stranger joined the celebration, "I couldn't have said it better myself. Here's to the forgotten jeep and the new life it will experience!"

And so, with their shared vision and determination, they finally introduced themselves to each other. My name is Rob, and I am a writer of short stories. It is a pleasure to meet you, Sir."

Gabriel offered his hand again. "My name is Gabriel Garcia Marquez, and before you ask, I am not the famous one." He saw the question coming immediately when he offered his name. "Con mucho gusto."

"No, I was not going to ask that question; I guessed you were not the famous Colombian writer. Have you read The General in His Labyrinth?"

"Why, yes, I have read it three times!"

"The General in His Labyrinth" is one of my favourite novels by Colombian author Gabriel García Márquez. Did you know it was originally published in 1989?"

Gabriel continued, not waiting for a reply, "The story is a fictionalised account of the last days of Simón Bolívar, the renowned military and political leader who had successfully liberated much of South America from Spanish rule in the early 19th century."

Still, the white-haired man could not intervene and say he was indeed reading it now. Gabriel was in a world of his own, "It was set in 1830, and the novel follows Bolivar's journey as he embarks on a final voyage down the Magdalena River in Colombia, attempting to seek refuge in Europe." Gabriel paused to breathe, "Throughout the book, the once mighty and revered General is depicted as a tired and disillusioned man, haunted by political betrayals and physical ailments. As the story unfolds, Bolívar reflects on his past victories, his dreams of a united Latin America, and his personal life, including his numerous love affairs."

The white-haired Englishman could only stay quiet to allow this obvious fan of literature to finish his synopsis of a book that was currently in his bedside cabinet. He had only read the first fifteen pages and was already enthralled with the budding plot.

Looking over the mountain ridge toward the sprawling city below, Gabriel concluded, "The narrative not only dives into Bolivar's thoughts and emotions but also portrays the political and historical context of the time, shedding light on the complex and turbulent era following the liberation wars. Through vivid descriptions and poetic language, Gabriel García Márquez explores themes such as power, mortality, and the consequences of unrestrained ambition."

Finally, Gabriel's praise for this book came to an end when "The General in His Labyrinth" serves not only as a fictionalised biography of the historical figure but also as an allegory for the course of Latin American history itself, reflecting on the disillusionment and challenges faced by those who fought for independence."

The white-haired Englishman revealed, "Thank you, I do have a copy of this book, and I am fifteen pages in." then, as an afterthought, "Gabriel, can I ask you a question?"

"Yes, most certainly. I hope I have not ruined your pending enjoyment of such a book."

"No sir, you have not. But my question to you is….do you know how to restore old 1940s Willy Jeeps because I have no idea what to do or where to start."

"Nor I, but it cannot be that difficult. Can it?"

The rusty shell of the Willy Jeep could be heard groaning as one of its front deceased headlights fell out of its casing and began swinging gently in the breeze.

*****

My two heroes talk too much, so I will take over the narrative and explain what happened next.

As I roll into this filthy garage, I feel the weight of decades on my worn-out tyres. With every creak and groan, I announce my arrival to the equally rusty, greasy-looking group of mechanics and restorers standing before me.

The scent of old oil lingers in the air, mixing with the pungent aroma of sweat and dirt.

My once vibrant colour has faded, leaving behind a patchy mosaic of rust and peeling paint. The scars of my adventurous past are etched into my battered body – dents, scratches, and cracked windows that tell stories of countless off-road journeys and daring escapades.

I proudly wear these marks, for they are testaments to my rugged life.

The mechanics huddled around and inspected me with inquisitive eyes. Their hands were dirty from years of fixing broken engines and dismantling worn-out parts.

Their faces are lined with oil-stained wrinkles, showing weariness and determination, as if they have seen hundreds of vehicles like mine come and go.

Yet, I sense a glimmer of excitement in their eyes, as if they recognised the hidden potential beneath my dilapidated exterior.

They set to work with a flurry of activity, their tools clattering against my worn-out panels. The sound of wrenches turning and hammers pounding echoed through the garage, mixing with the faint hum of car engines in the background. I anxiously watched as new parts replaced the corroded ones, the grime scrubbed off, and fresh paint brought life back to my faded body.

Layers of dust are swept away, revealing the gleaming metallic surfaces that have long been hidden. I'm shedding my old skin into something revitalised and majestic. The faint outline of MG livery begins to emerge on my newly painted frame, restoring the spirit of a bygone era.

As the restoration progressed, I felt the mechanics pouring their passion into every detail. They worked meticulously, paying attention to the most minor imperfections, ensuring that I emerged not just as another fixed vehicle but as a true classic.

In their hands, I am reborn, resurrected from my rusty slumber to become a symbol of timeless elegance and strength.

Finally, the day arrived when the last bolt was tightened, and I was ready to face the world again.

My once dilapidated self is now a resplendent MG-liveried jeep, evoking nostalgia and admiration. The mechanics gathered around me, their faces filled with pride and satisfaction, knowing they had breathed life into an old, forgotten warrior.

Although I may carry the signs of wear and the stories of a rugged past, I now stand tall, embodying the spirit of a classic. With a renewed sense of purpose and a gleaming exterior, I am ready to hit the open road again, carrying the legacy of my adventurous past and the skilful hands that restored me to glory.

With their joint vision, the two men from different parts of the world who began the colossal task of restoring this grateful Willy Jeep have transformed me from a forgotten relic into a symbol of culture and passion.

As I roared to life once again and proudly displayed a harmonious fusion of English heritage and the beauty of coffee, I can clearly see I have become a true testament to their friendship and collaboration.

*****

# 59: I am the Policeman who gets tipsy with a street man

*I*ndigenous people in the Choco region traditionally consume a diet rich in fruits, which can contain fibre and sugars that promote gas production in the digestive system. Consequently, they may experience higher levels of flatulence than populations with different dietary habits. This predicament also applied to Archibaldo Federico Alcatraz.

He hatched a plan to see if the same effects would befall his unusual friend. He could not wait until he heard Stalin's excuse. This little street man never appeared to be able to stop, which was both funny and embarrassing.

*****

Since the night of the rescue of all the older people from their flooded care homes in the north of the city, Stalin and Archibaldo had begun building a strong bond, much to Ximena's displeasure.

She did limit Archibaldo to one night per month where he could go and find that horrid-looking street man and get as drunk as they wished. The rules were simple: no scandals, no fighting, no running naked in the streets, and no need to return to the bedroom until the following morning. "I do hate the smell of stale beer!" exclaimed Ximena.

It was on one of their afternoon starts in the park where previously the cannonball trees did their worst to a nasty and devilish-looking street man named Caesar. The duo decided to challenge themselves to an epic beer-drinking competition. Little did Stalin know, Archibaldo had prepared a secret concoction of fizzy drinks and questionable ingredients. As they gulped down one beer after another, the gas bubbles inside their stomachs began to multiply exponentially.

The beer-induced gas took hold of their bodies, and more so Stalin's, as he was drinking at a rate of 2 to 1 with Archibaldo. As the bubbles expanded, so did their predicament.

After an hour, Stalin began to stumble aimlessly down the footpath heading to their favourite eatery. The gas inside him grew to astronomical proportions. Every step seemed to expel a symphony of unexpected sounds and unintelligible words. Archibaldo was in hysterics a few feet behind. He could see people running to avoid them.

Other Passerbys couldn't help but stop and stare at the befuddled sight of a once-fierce ex-policeman, now consumed with gas.

Stalin's attempts to communicate were met with laughter and confused expressions.

Meanwhile, Archibaldo, looking equally distended, followed him around like a loyal sidekick, struggling to contain his gas-induced comedic outbursts.

Stalin now tried to make sense of his gas-filled existence; he stumbled into an open-air restaurant with a man playing his harpsichord to the other diners. As the musician played his lively tunes, Stalin and Archibaldo unintentionally became the main attraction.

*****

Their gas-induced performances had people rolling on the floor, struggling to catch their breath between fits of laughter. "Oy, Stalin, can you hum? Cos you cannot sing!" was met by a resounding uproar from all present, including the restaurant owner.

*****

The beer-drinking competition took an unexpected turn, leaving Stalin and Archibaldo with an unforgettable, albeit slightly embarrassing, story to tell. From that day on, whenever the restaurant waiters and customers mentioned a gas problem or a humorous mishap, they would fondly recount the story of Stalin, the ex-policeman turned street man, and his extraordinary journey fuelled by Archibaldo's fizzy brew.

*****

When Ximena heard the story, Archibaldo had hell to play for at least a week. Even his consistent promises of never repeating the challenge with Stalin did little to quieten his wife. Little did he know Ximena had roared with laughter when her parents told her. But she would not let her husband off the hook that easily.

*****

It was another week before Stalin and Archibaldo were seen together again.

"Archibaldo, come in and have a seat. I've been reviewing some fire service files passed to me by my dear friend, Fire Chief Eduardo; he has stumbled upon a rather intriguing set of cold cases that have puzzled us individually for years. Every decade since 1965, a house fire involving an unidentified body has been attended to by the fire service. Until now, no connection has ever been made, and it's about time we get to the bottom of this."

"But first, sit and have a beer and a shot of Jack Daniels with me."

Archibaldo sat and proceeded to open a can of Poker, accepting the nearly full tumbler of a sweet-tasting bourbon with an abundance of notes of oak, caramel, and vanilla.

"I don't mind if I do. It has been hot today, and my throat is on fire."

Then he paused to see if he could detect a revenge attack from Stalin was in progress. But he sensed rightly he was safe today.

"Now, this may seem like a daunting task, especially considering the need for leads thus far. But with the right approach and dedication, we, meaning you, can finally shed some light on these mysterious incidents. I need you to treat this investigation as a top priority and, for now, only report back to me and the Fire Chief."

Stalin continued his instructions while pouring more bourbon into both half-empty tumblers.

"First, we'll need to gather all the available information on each case. Start by digging clandestinely through the archives, reviewing police reports, and speaking to any surviving witnesses or neighbours who may have information. Pay close attention to details like the time of the fires, witness accounts, and any similarities in how the fires were set."

Archibaldo raised his hand, "Why clandestinely?"

Stalin leaned forward and checked the room. No one was paying them any attention. It appeared an ideal time to top up the tumblers." At this time, everything is a hunch; we have no proof that these fires were part of a series of house fires. So, let's keep it between the three of us for now."

"Okay, I am happy to follow you and the Fire Chief's lead on how we move forward. But please remember this is going to be my first cold case—or, should I say, a series of cold cases that will need investigating."

Stalin smiled, "Please do not fret; we will guide you each day and at each stage as you move forward." Next, we must coordinate with the fire service to better understand the fire patterns and any commonalities they may have observed. It's crucial to work closely with them, as they may have encountered things or found evidence that could aid our investigation.

Stalin was becoming excited at the prospect of a hunt for a possible killer or serial killer, he drank two tumblers of bourbon without refilling Archibaldo's tumbler.

"Simultaneously, I want you to reach out to other police departments in the region and see if they have encountered any similar cases or if there have been any developments elsewhere that we may have missed. Information sharing and collaboration will be key to solving this mystery.

Furthermore, engage with our forensic team. They need to meticulously examine the remains of the unidentified victims to try and establish their identities, as well as determine if there are any links between them. Advanced forensic techniques and DNA testing might provide crucial breakthroughs."

As if having an afterthought, Stalin refilled Archibaldo's tumbler with no space left at the top.

"Lastly, engage your instincts and trust your gut. Sometimes, obvious answers lie in the most unexpected places. Look for patterns, connections, and anything that deviates from ordinary circumstances. Be meticulous in your investigation and keep an open mind. We need to solve this puzzle, and it will be challenging."

At this moment, he left the table unsteadily and wobbled towards the toilet area at the back of the restaurant. This allowed Archibaldo to ask himself how such an investigation was going to be successful with Stalin's lack of memory.

In the next moment, Archibaldo, now alarmed, could see Stalin racing back, full of excitement and determination to get off his chest whatever memory had decided to present itself while he was in the cubicle. The main issue now was that Stalin was totally naked! He had forgotten to redress himself! Before anyone could react, Stalin continued as if nothing had gone awry.

"Remember, our ultimate goal is not just identifying the victims and piecing together their stories; it's also about finding the person or persons responsible for these fires. We can't allow them to continue to operate in our jurisdiction. Unresolved cases like these tarnish our reputation as a law enforcement agency."

Archibaldo leaned forward, "And pray do you not think sitting here talking to me will not also tarnish MY reputation as a law enforcement officer?"

Stalin looked down and then slowly around the room; again, he returned his gaze to Archibaldo. We have to do something about my memory."

Without apologising for his lack of modesty, Stalin marched back to the cubicle and rescued his denim skirt and rock. After adjusting himself in the broken mirror, the once-colonel of the police returned to the table once more.

The bottle of Jack Daniels was almost empty. Archibaldo estimated there were possibly two shots left, and he rapidly divided the last two shots between himself and Stalin.

"This is your chance to make a difference, Archibaldo. Let's open this case and bring justice to the victims and their families. Keep me updated regularly, and if you need any additional resources or support, don't hesitate to let me know. Good luck, and may your investigation lead us to the truth."

*****

"Thank you, Police Colonel Stalin Oscar Ramirez." grinned Archibaldo.

"What? You know my full name. Even I do not know it!" Stared Stalin wide-eyed in astonishment. He had not heard those names since he last spoke to the Fire Chief.

"The Fire Chief told me, and he mentioned you and that we have been long-term friends. Did you remember he is my father-in-law's neighbour, and his daughter Ximena is my lovely wife?"

"No, of course not," mumbled Stalin.

Archibaldo looked at his drunken friend. "oh yes, I nearly forgot; I do remember hearing all that I have to do to investigate these strange series of house fires involving an unidentified corpse in the cellars spanning more than a decade. Eduardo deemed it best to tell me directly as he thought you might have forgotten to do so."

*****

At that moment, Stalin fell from his chair in a heap and was sound asleep by the time his head hit the floor. As for Archibaldo, he could barely stand and decided to sit down next to the toilet nearby and rest his head on the toilet seat. At some point during the night, he was glad that he did. His last memorable thought had to do with the problem of Stalin's lack of ability to remember anything. He believed he had the answer; a conversation with a couple of extraordinarily talented gnomes needed to happen urgently.

*****

The restaurant owners cleared up around them, left the door unlocked, and retired back to their homes, knowing full well that their property would be well protected from thieves or anyone who should feel the need to visit.

*****

The following morning, Ximena awoke late from her night with her mother, enjoying the latest fashionable designer clothes show in the city's south. She could not wait to catwalk her latest purchases to her adorable husband.

She rose, showered, dressed in her favourite outdoor outfit, and headed down the marbled stairs towards the large living room. She half expected to see

Archibaldo having breakfast. What she saw would remain a mystery for the rest of her life.

A circle of bone china cups and saucers was in the centre of the room. In each one was a sausage!

In the centre of the circle was a comatose Archibaldo with an open box of matches and some used matches lying around one particular cup!

She did not want to hear the answer to her question. Instead, she tiptoed to the kitchen and retrieved her mobile.

She silently returned and took a good number of pics. "Revenge is definitely going to be fun today." Ximena thought as she silently left the house and headed towards her white-beaming BMW.

*****

## 60: I am a Street Cleaner who receives Passports, Visas, and Flight Tickets

*H*iya, it is me again, Gracie. It is a pleasure to update you on my family life since the awful time when the city suffered terrible floods and the horrific sight of a massive mudslide heading slowly down the mountain ridge towards the barrio, La Flora, where we still live.

My two inquisitive children and I are sitting at the table in our kitchen. My mother, Abuella Manuela, is busy at the kitchen counter preparing breakfast for us all. She is slicing up a small round watermelon when, out of the blue, Hernan raises a question he does not know the answer to. "Abuella, what is the history of watermelon? How did it arrive here in South America?"

My mother, the font of all knowledge, did not need Google to answer this question. She learned the history of watermelons as a child working in the fields of her family home. "Ah, mi querido Hernan, that's a beautiful question! I'm happy to share with you the fascinating history of watermelon and how it found its way to our beautiful South America."

"Watermelon, as you know, is called sandía in our Spanish language and actually has a long and interesting history that dates back thousands of years. Its origins can be traced back to the continent of Africa, specifically the Kalahari Desert region. Melons similar to watermelons still grow wild there today!"

Hernan knew he could quickly have asked the same question via a Google search on the family laptop, but he loved learning from his Abuella. She made each new learning a new experience that always seemed authentic and believable.

"From Africa, watermelon travelled along ancient trade routes to Egypt and other regions of the Mediterranean. The Egyptians, in particular, held watermelon in high regard and even left watermelon seeds in the tombs of their pharaohs. They believed that watermelon would nourish them in the afterlife.

During the era of exploration and colonisation, European explorers like Christopher Columbus encountered and fell in love with this delicious fruit during their travels. They brought watermelon seeds with them on their voyages as a source of sustenance for the long journeys."

Abuella Manuela works with a lifetime of experience preparing and placing the slices on a large platter. She approached the family table and put the platter before the waiting children. "Don't forget to save some for me!"

I said, with a big grin on my face, "Do not worry, Madre. I will ensure these rascals leave a slice or two for you and your ample belly."

Rita and Hernan burst out laughing, and Manuela playfully slapped me across my bum. "You are not so big I cannot give you the odd tap, my girl."

Abuella Manuela loved this time of day. She always made breakfast the best start to any day. Suddenly, she remembered she had yet to complete the answer regarding the history of watermelons. She carried on without us realising she had forgotten for a short while.

"Eventually, watermelon reached the shores of South America through Spanish colonisation. The Spanish conquistadors brought various crops, including watermelon seeds, to their discovered lands. This is how watermelon made its way to our beloved South America, where it thrived in the fertile soil and warm climate.

Today, watermelon has become a staple in our cuisine, enjoyed by people of all ages. We use it in many delicious ways, from refreshing agua frescas to salads and desserts. We all love its juicy, sweet flesh, especially during hot summer days.

"So, mi querido Hernan, watermelon, has travelled a long journey throughout history to be a part of our lives here in South America. Isn't it amazing to think about the rich stories and travels of the foods we enjoy daily? Now, let me store this watermelon in our fridge so we can all enjoy a delicious breakfast together again tomorrow!"

Hernan was not finished having fun asking questions, such as, "Abuella, how many butterfly species are there in the world?"

"What!" came swiftly from my lips, "How will your Abuella know the answer to that question?!"

Rita piped up, trying to be helpful, "There must be thousands."

With a satisfied smirk, Manuela looked at each one and slowly said, "There are 17,500 species of butterflies around the world."

I looked at my mum, searching her face for a joke coming. "you are not the only generation who knows how to search for answers on the internet." came a smiling Abuella Manuela.

*****

Later that day, upon reaching my office in the central government building near the city river, the receptionist, Marisol, greeted me and passed a note requesting that on my arrival, I was to head straight to the Mayor's office first.

*****

"Good morning, Gracie! As the Mayor in charge of our city's streets, I understand that you've faced several challenges over recent years, including tremors, floods, and a devastating mudslide. It's important to prioritise the safety and well-being of our residents, and you shone out every time. The city owes you great gratitude for your professionalism and unwavering dedication. Please take a seat. Do you like milk and sugar with your coffee?"

"Black only, please. Thank you."

The Mayor took a few minutes to arrange both a cup of coffee and a small plate of cookies. "Help yourself to cookies."

I took one in politeness and waited for the heat to diminish from the piping-hot black liquid of the coffee.

"Now, regarding your personal plans, I have heard you wish to migrate to the United Kingdom with your two children, and I believe, at some point, you wish for your mother to join you as well. It, as you know, is a significant decision to make. Before proceeding, there are a few factors for you to consider. So, I wish to ask you some questions, please do not worry, you will not be in any trouble. Relax and sit here with me on the sofa."

Once both of us were settled and drinking coffee from the machine on the cabinet nearby.

"The first question is, have you obtained the necessary visas or permits required for long-term stays or immigration? Have you familiarise yourself with the regulations and requirements set by both countries?"

I sat there in shock. I was not prepared for this. "Mayor, please excuse me; you have caught me off guard. I had no idea we would meet today, and I have not come prepared."

"Relax, Gracie, all will become clear. For now, please just humour me by answering my questions."

I paused before answering, "No, I must admit. Sorry. Yes, I have done some preliminary research, but I do not yet have the necessary finances to buy the visas and air tickets." To add proof of my intentions, I said, "I have been saving up for some time, but I am still short. I hope to be able to go at the beginning of next year."

The Mayor, still smiling, spoke next: "Ah, it is good to see you have begun evaluating your financial situation and the resources needed to support your family during the migration process. Having a solid plan for accommodation, job prospects, education, and healthcare in your new destination."

The Mayor rose to refill his coffee mug. It was rumoured around the building that this Mayor could consume gallons of coffee on any working day, and his demeanour would never change. He was deemed a solid pair of hands for protecting the city and its citizens.

"Let me now turn to what is required to buy the tickets for your trip to London. There are a few questions you have to take into consideration:

Have you researched and compared flights? Have you Looked for flights that best fit your future schedule and budget? Have you considered factors such as layovers, travel time, and cost?"

With my head bowed, "Yes, I have, and my Tios in London have advised me about the periods when tickets cost an absolute fortune, such as Christmas time."

"Do you have any experience booking air tickets? Do you have a preferred Airline? Have you visited the airline's website or used a reputable travel booking platform to make your reservation?

Have you considered travel insurance? Have you evaluated the benefits of travel insurance to provide you with all coverage in case of unplanned circumstances or emergencies during your trip? Doing this can offer peace of mind and protect your investment."

"Dear Mayor, in answer to all your kind questions, I have to confess I have only scant overviews so far, as it is still only a dream for me. As you may know, I am a single working parent with two children, and my mother is on a small pension to get by."

"That is what I thought," said the Mayor as he began to stand and return to his desk. He reached for a large light brown padded envelope and returned to his place on the sofa.

"Gracie, I have many connections in the city and back in Bogota. I am on a first-name basis with the British Embassy. In gratitude for your incredible work over the past decade, I wish to present passports arranged secretly by our H.R. Department, visas from the British Ambassador and free return air tickets courtesy of our national carrier for you, your mother, and your children. You only need to work out what dates you wish to go, let our H.R. department know which month you have chosen, and turn up at the airport."

I sat there, daring not to move and unable to say anything near adequate to show my overwhelming gratitude. The Mayor looked down. "Take a few moments, Gracie. I need to pop out for a few moments. Let Marisol see your happiness as she has helped me immensely with this well-kept secret from you. Go and enjoy a month's holiday you so well deserve."

As the Mayor moved towards his office door, he stopped and turned, "Gracie, will a month be enough to help you decide whether to make the final move to the U.K.?"

I stood and said, "Yes, sir, thank you. I am sure a month will be perfect to see if Rita and Hernan's future lies in a country with thousands of years of history to explore. Knowing their Tios, I am sure they will both say yes."

The Mayor now had the door open, and Gracie could see a massive crowd of colleagues and Marisol in front, all clapping, hooting, and crying. It was at this moment I realised just how big a secret this had been.

*****

Marisol ran forward to embrace and kiss me. "Well done, Gracie; this could not have happened to a finer lady and her family. Oh yes, do not worry about Rita and Hernan's school lessons. Everything has been arranged, and a series of online classes will ensure they miss nothing during the trip.

The final words came from the Mayor, who was enjoying this day, "Best of luck with your travel plans and potential migration to the United Kingdom! If you have any further questions or need assistance, please ask Marisol.

*****

Later that same day, I sat and gave the news to Mammy, Rita, and Hernan. Unsurprisingly, all went crazy with excitement. When I gave the children their official papers and flight tickets, it enabled them to leave South America for the first time in their lives and head to a country they had only ever read about. Their excitement went above the scales, screaming and crying with sheer pleasure. In contrast, Mammy's reaction was calmer, and she headed to her bedroom to retrieve her box of personal belongings, which she had gone back to when she was a child.

The personnel department found Mammy's passport a little easier as she held an expired passport many years ago. Mammy still had it, and we compared her old passport with her new one. I could see that Mammy had fared well, and time had been good to her.

When I asked when we would fly to London, Mammy suggested we talk to the three Tios first. Within seconds, Hernan opened the laptop and scheduled a Google Meet with all three. It took a further hour to see everyone on a shared screen and another half hour for everyone to stop screaming with excitement.

Francisco, José, and Manuel sat with each of their families, standing around them in their separate homes. Between them, they sure did make as much noise as if they were up against a Twickenham Rugby crowd between England and New Zealand.

*****

Immediately, the sounds from the three screens were a cacophony of suggestions on what they had to visit. The four happy travellers had no chance to write down every suggestion. At some point, it was agreed that Francisco would organise a proper itinerary to ensure all would be filled with lifetime memories. They would set off in three months during July to give them the best English weather possible.

Late on Sunday evening, I received a WhatsApp message from Francisco saying an email was waiting for us. We immediately opened the laptop and clicked open the email.

The itinerary that Francisco and his family had put together was amazing.

London Adventure Itinerary (Weeks 1 to 4)

Your first week will be spent with my family here in Knightsbridge. We are well placed for the following sights.

Week 1 Day 1:

On your first morning, you will arrive in London and settle into our home, with bedrooms reserved for each of you. Of course, we will meet and greet you at Heathrow to ensure no mishaps, such as getting lost, will befall you. We suggest you rest that first day and sleep off as much of the jet lag as you will experience.

The following day, you will start your adventure with a visit to the world-renowned Tower of London. Explore the history, see the Crown Jewels, and even witness the changing of the guard.

In the afternoon, we will take you on a stroll along the Thames River and give you time to enjoy the beautiful views. Please make sure your mobile phones are fully charged every day.

Later, we will head to Covent Garden, where you can explore the street performers, browse the unique shops, and grab some delicious street food.

In the evening, we will take you to enjoy a traditional fish and chips dinner at a local pub, followed by a sunset ride on the London Eye to see the city from above.

*****

On Day 2, in the morning, we will start your day with a visit to the British

Museum. We are sure you will marvel at ancient artefacts and learn about different cultures worldwide.

In the afternoon, we will have something very different for you to experience; here, you will explore the vibrant neighbourhood of Camden Town. Wander through the famous Camden Market and find treasures among the eclectic shops and food stalls.

We will also have time to visit Regent's Park nearby and have a picnic while enjoying the beautiful greenery.

We have reserved your seats at a West End musical later in the evening. Let me show you, Jos. On another night, you may also be able to see the mesmerising performance of the Singing nuns from Colombia. I am sure little Rita will love experiencing the magic of London's theatrical scene. Do not worry, Hernan. We will have you covered later in the week.

*****

On day 3, in the morning, your journey will begin with a visit to Buckingham Palace to witness the ceremony and pomp of the Changing of the Guard. Later, before lunch, you will explore the stunning St. James's Park nearby and have a relaxing stroll.

Later in the afternoon, we will all head to the famous Portobello Road Market in Notting Hill. Here, you will enjoy what we have come to love: browsing antiques and vintage clothing and sampling delicious street food.

Later the same day, in the early evening, we invite you to a traditional British afternoon tea experience at a charming tea room.

As long as the weather holds, we will end the day by taking a scenic cruise along the River Thames to see the illuminated landmarks of London at night.

*****

Day 4 is for you, Hernan, and, of course, you, Rita. But we know how much Hernan loves Harry Potter.

You will embark on a Harry Potter tour with our children in the morning and visit the Warner Bros. Studio Tour London. Here, you will dive into the magical world of Hogwarts and see the props, costumes, and sets from the movies. I am sure your mum and your abuela would love to have a soak and a rest and catch up with you two later in the afternoon.

It will be a relaxing and cultural discovery of the National Gallery's historical treasures. Imagine getting close to masterpieces by artists such as Van Gogh, Da Vinci, and Monet.

Later in the evening, we are all booked to enjoy a tasty dinner at a cosy British gastropub. Afterwards, with our full bellies, we will take a leisurely wabble along the South Bank, enjoying the lively atmosphere and street performers.

*****

On Day 5 in the morning, we will all explore the vibrant Camden Market again and discover something new.

By taking a leisurely boat ride on the Regent's Canal.

In the afternoon, it will be a short hop, skip, and jump to the world-famous Madame Tussauds wax museum, where you can meet renowned historical figures and the latest celebrities.

In the evening, you kids will have a break from us adults and can sit and watch videos or play video games with our children. It is bound to be a pizza night for you lot.

In contrast, we, adults, will experience the bustling nightlife of Soho. We will enjoy dinner at a trendy restaurant in Chinatown and catch a live comedy show nearby.

*****

Now, Day 6 is one I am definitely looking forward to, as this is the first time I have been where you are going for at least a decade. In the morning, you will explore the historic Greenwich. Visit the Royal Observatory and stand on the Prime Meridian. Afterwards, we will take a stroll through the beautiful Greenwich Park.

In the afternoon, we will explore the stalls of Borough Market and sample delicious food from around the world. Stay close to me if you want to experience the essence of the Arabic world with its delightful cuisine and Arabic coffee. Also, if you fancy taking a ride on an iconic red double-decker bus for a scenic tour of the city. This is the time to do it.

In the evening, we will indulge in a delicious multicultural dinner in Shoreditch, known for its trendy food scene.

*****

Now, Day 7 will be a special day for our sister Manuela. As it should be her birthday. We will all visit the breathtaking Tower Bridge Exhibition in the morning. We will even walk across the glass floor and enjoy panoramic views of London.

In the afternoon, we will again explore Covent Garden's charming neighbourhood, watch street performers, and do some last-minute birthday shopping. Oops, I let go of a secret! Jajaja.

Later, we will enjoy a traditional English afternoon tea at a quaint tea room and celebrate a loving sister's birthday with all her three older brothers and their families.

On your final evening in London, we have booked a Thames River dinner cruise to savour a delicious meal while taking in the illuminated cityscape.

This itinerary is designed to provide Manuela, Gracie, and Hernan with a fun-filled London adventure. I hope you all enjoy these exciting activities while exploring the city and considering the possibility of emigrating in the future. London awaits your discovery!

Lots of love

Francisco, José, and Manuel xxx

*****

Also, José and Manuel will send more emails shortly. As you know, José and his family live in Portsmouth, and Manuel lives in Glen Coe, Scotland.

*****

The following weekend, Mammy and I went to the local shopping centre called Chipichape. I am sure we spent a fortune on outfits, rucksacks, hand luggage for the four of us, and two suitcases. The first is a larger one for both adults to share, and the second is a small one for Rita and Hernan to share. Within an hour of arriving home loaded with packages and after re-reading Francisco's email and his itinerary, José's and Manuel's itineraries returned.

*****

José's itinerary for us was equally exciting. We would travel to the historic naval dockyards in Portsmouth, and this week would be full of history and sightseeing.

On Day 1 of your second week, you will arrive in Portsmouth and settle into your accommodation. We have secured a local Bed and Breakfast Hotel for you, covering all expenses. In the afternoon, you'll explore the historic dockyard and visit the HMS Victory and the Mary Rose Museum. I promise this will be one of your highlights by walking and exploring the great ship that was the flagship for Admiral Lord Helson at the battle of Trafalgar. Francisco has told me he is planning for you to go to Trafalgar Square in your first week, where you will see the magnificent monument of Nelson and the mighty lions at his feet. Well, with me, you will have the chance to explore his actual ship and experience what it was like in 1805!

If the weather holds and the sea is calm, we will head to the Submarine

Museum at Gosport. We will travel there by sea via a ferry, which takes only five minutes to cross. In that short time, you will see many Royal Navy ships of many sizes in the harbour. And to make your experience complete, you will all experience going on board the only surviving World War 2-era ocean-going submarine, HMS Alliance!

In the evening, we will all enjoy a seafood dinner at a local restaurant and take in the sights as the sun goes down.

*****

On Day 2, we will stroll along Southsea Beach and enjoy beach activities. In the afternoon, we will visit the Spinnaker Tower for panoramic views of Portsmouth and the surrounding area.

In the evening, we will have a family picnic at Victoria Park and enjoy the scenic beauty of the lush greenery and well-maintained gardens. We are sure our sister Manuela will love exploring this peaceful place. Oh yes, Rita and Hernan, what are your skills at throwing frisbees and flying kites?

*****

We have reached Day 3, and this morning, you will all be able to visit the Blue Reef Aquarium and learn about marine life. In the afternoon, you can revisit and explore the Portsmouth Naval Base and take a boat tour to see the navy ships up close.

In the evening, we will keep it open for now to see how the weather is treating us. If it is dry and sunny, we can head to Portsdown Hill, which overlooks Portsmouth.

*****

Looking at the opportunities for Day 4, we should take a day trip to the Isle of Wight in the morning and explore attractions like Osborne House or Carisbrooke Castle.

We can enjoy outdoor activities like hiking or cycling in the beautiful countryside in the afternoon. Stay calm about hiking boots and gear; we have plenty in our lockup for you to choose from. The same goes for bicycles.

We plan to have dinner at a traditional pub on the Isle of Wight in the evening.

*****

Now, on Day 5 in the morning, we can all meet up and visit the D-Day Story Museum to learn about the city's role in World War II. We can then explore the Portsmouth City Museum and Art Gallery in the afternoon.

We can finish the evening by eating at a local Indian or Chinese restaurant and attending a live performance at the King's Theatre. Mind you, Gracie, you have not lived until you have tried a "Ghandi's revenge" Chicken Masala and Bombay Aloo!

\*\*\*\*\*

After your curry, on Day 6, we thought it would be best for you all to take an open-top boat trip to visit the nearby Hayling Island, known for its beautiful beaches and nature reserves.

We can guide you on water activities like windsurfing or paddleboarding in the afternoon. In the evening, we can finish with a family dinner at our house, where we will serve local cuisine mixed with the odd Colombian dish to make you homesick. Jajajaja.

On your last day with us, in the morning, we recommend that you explore the Portsmouth Historic Dockyard's Action Stations, an interactive attraction for all ages.

In the afternoon, we recommend visiting the Charles Dickens Birthplace Museum to learn about the life of a famous author. We go there often to soak up the atmosphere of a bygone age.

In the evening, we can take a leisurely stroll along the harbour and enjoy the beautiful sunset.

Lots of love and best wishes, José. P.S. I have booked leave from the Navy to ensure we can all be together that month.

\*\*\*\*\*

Manuel is Manuela's third brother and a loving uncle, too. He is also a favourite with Rita and Hernan. He is the closest of brothers to Manuela as there is only a year's difference in their age. They act like twins.

When the three brothers decided to emigrate to the United Kingdom, Manuel was the one Manuela missed the most. In all the years that have passed, you can count on one hand the weeks they did not make contact by letter, telephone, or now WhatsApp.

Manuel's occupation involves working on oil rigs, which is a demanding and high-risk job. Despite the challenges, he is dedicated to his work and takes pride in his profession.

When Manuel is not on the oil rigs, he lives in Spean Bridge and enjoys spending time with his family. Manuel's caring nature extends to his brothers and relatives, especially to Rita and Hernan, and he is always ready to lend a helping hand whenever needed.

*****

Everyone agreed; Manuel's itinerary was just too much to believe! In fact, everyone, including Francisco and José, with the agreement of all the families, decided it was time to venture to Scotland and join us! Even two self-drive minibuses were hired to transport us all!

Accommodation was no problem as Manuel's wife owned a family-run Spean Bridge guest house at the foot of the mountain near Ben Nevis.

Now, read what Manuel has proposed.

On day 1, after settling into our reserved hotel, we will start our tour of Edinburgh, Scotland's capital city, known for its rich history and stunning architecture.

As a party of excitable Colombians, we will explore the historic Edinburgh Castle and enjoy panoramic views of the city.

Later, we will stroll along the Royal Mile, a famous street connecting the castle and the Palace of Holyroodhouse.

We will visit the Palace of Holyroodhouse, the official residence of the King and late Queen of Scotland.

We will end the first day with an evening and surround ourselves with the city's vibrant atmosphere on a ghost tour.

*****

With an early start on Day 2, we will load up our minibuses and head north towards Cairngorms National Park, a stunning natural area famous for its mountains, forests, and wildlife.

We will take a scenic drive through the park and stop at attractions like Loch Morlich, Aviemore, and Glenmore Forest Park. If you're feeling adventurous, you can go hiking or mountain biking in the park.

*****

Day 3: Another early start with driving the minibuses to Inverness, the Highlands capital, and taking a boat tour of Loch Ness. On this day alone, we will explore the city's historic sites, such as Inverness Castle and St. Andrews Cathedral, and watch for the legendary Loch Ness Monster!

Later in the afternoon, we should have time to visit and experience the Mountain Gondola, transporting visitors to the mountain peak of Aonach Mor and seeing Ben Nevis in the distance.

In the evening, we will share an extraordinary place to sample the Scottish cuisine of homemade Scottish Venison Pate for starters, followed by the main dish, Haggis, Neeps, and Tatties. By day, the converted restaurant is a working

Victorian-built railway station, and by night, it is a great location to have fun, eat, drink, and be merry listening to the local folk music of the Scottish mountains. If we arrive on a Friday, we can hopefully see the famous Royal Scotsman train stopping on the platform before us. Another great aspect of this day is that we are only a stone's throw away from the family guest house; it will only require a short five-minute stroll to our beds.

*****

On Day 4, we will embark on the impressive-looking North Coast 500, often referred to as Scotland's answer to Route 66.

We will drive along the spectacular coastline, passing through charming villages like Wick and Thurso.

We will stop at Dunrobin Castle, a beautiful stately home with extensive gardens and falconry displays.

-We will then continue our journey to John O'Groats, the northernmost point of mainland Britain.

Here, we will enjoy the breathtaking views and take a photo at the iconic signpost.

*****

On Day 5, we will drive to Durness, a picturesque village located on the northwestern coast, and explore the beautiful beaches, such as Balnakeil and Sango Bay.

Later, we will visit Smoo Cave, a unique sea cave with a waterfall and impressive rock formations.

Finally, we will walk along the dramatic cliffs of Cape Wrath, one of mainland Britain's most north-westerly points.

*****

If you are not excited so far, wait till Day 6 arrives, Glen Coe.

We will drive towards Glen Coe, a stunning valley known for its dramatic landscapes and rich history.

We will take a scenic hike in Glen Coe, surrounded by towering mountains and cascading waterfalls.

We will most definitely be visiting the Glencoe Visitor Centre to learn about the area's volcanic history and the infamous Massacre of Glencoe.

As a family living here in Scotland, we cannot wait to see you all enjoying the peaceful atmosphere of Loch Leven, located at the base of the valley.

Day 7 will show us going to Glasgow, Scotland's largest city, through the lowlands.

We will have time to explore the vibrant city centre and visit attractions like the Glasgow Cathedral and the Kelvingrove Art Gallery and Museum.

We should walk along the picturesque River Clyde and enjoy the city's impressive architecture. Thereby, end your trip by sampling some traditional Scottish cuisine again in one of Glasgow's many excellent restaurants and pubs.

The next day, we will return to the minibuses and catch a flight back to London.

One final point: the weather in Scotland can change very quickly, so as plan B, I have made a short list of alternative attractions we can go to if the weather goes against us:

The Invernay Jail and Court House, with Kilchurn Castle nearby, is a picturesque village in Argyle. The jail has a reputation as being a haunted location. Visitors and staff alike have reported feeling icy drafts, hearing eerie footsteps, and experiencing strange sensations. It's the perfect location for a night's rest, Gracie. Jajajaja.

*****

A particular favourite destination for us as a family has to be the Isle of Skye. It is a stunning island located off the northwest coast of Scotland. Well-known for its dramatic landscapes, rugged mountains, and picturesque lochs, Skye is a popular destination for outdoor enthusiasts.

One of Skye's charming features is its wildlife, including the iconic brown hairy cows and black sheep that roam freely on the island. These cows, commonly known as Highland cattle or "coos," are a distinctive breed with long, shaggy hair and impressive horns. They are well adapted to the harsh climate and rough terrain of Skye. The black sheep, with their dark woolly coats, add to the eclectic and picturesque scenery of the island.

These unique animals showcase the island's rustic beauty and contribute to its idyllic, pastoral atmosphere. We believe all visitors to Skye enjoy encountering these charming creatures while exploring the island's breathtaking landscapes.

The Isle of Skye and how we will travel to it will be a surefire hit for both Hernan and Rita. Yes, the Jacobite steam train goes to the Isle of Skye. It operates between Fort William and Mallaig in the Scottish Highlands. The train is famous for its scenic route through the Ben Nevis mountain range, crossing the Glenfinnan Viaduct, which is indeed featured in the Harry Potter movies as the iconic Hogwarts Express! Now, you kids can see the connection.

In Scottish Gaelic, you can end a letter by saying, "Mar sin leibh gu bràth, agus cha mhòr nach gabh sinn an-dèidh sibh ann an Alba gu luath!" which translates

to "So farewell for now, and we can't wait to see you all in Scotland soon!"
Love to you all,
Manuel and the Ortega clan. xxx

*****

All that I have relayed to you all, or should I say all that has been written by my three Tios and myself, which, surprising to me, was nearly six months ago, is now about to happen! In that time, as a family, our lives moved at a pace unheard of before. I am sitting in the airport terminal, staring at my newly printed passport and visa with my name clearly printed: Gracie Martina Ortega y Santos.

*****

## 61: I am the Growing Consequence for a Plastic Surgeon with an Evil Past

For their first decade, learning for the three Müller sisters was a resounding success. The teachers, looking for ways to please the girls, hit on the unusual idea of placing all three together and ignoring the slight difference in their ages, believing Anna and Eva would ensure Lisa would never fall behind and suffer a loss of confidence.

All three Müllers excelled in languages such as English and French, and the teachers were astounded by their thirst for knowledge of all that science could reveal to such young minds.

Their "classmates" hated them. The girls found themselves ostracised by the other children and their parents, and they accepted the fact that their names would never appear on any invitation card.

They preferred it that way. The sisters had each other and showed no stress with how they were perceived or treated.

Like their father, their world was only found in large volumes of science and medical books—the more, the better.

Their father raised the trio with a love for books and tirelessly encouraged their thirst for knowledge. It was the only positive they would ever admit to throughout their lives.

Growing up, the Müller girls were fascinated by various fields of science. They spent countless hours together and were sometimes accompanied by their father, engrossed in exploring books on chemistry, physics, and biology from his vast and continuously growing collection.

Anna Müller had an insatiable curiosity about chemistry the moment she discovered Marie Curie (1867-1934), a Polish physicist and chemist. Marie conducted pioneering research on radioactivity and discovered the radioactive elements polonium and radium.

Curie was the first female chemist to win a Nobel Prize and was the only person to have won Nobel Prizes in multiple fields (Physics and Chemistry). Like Curie, Anna marvelled at how different substances could interact and create marvellous reactions. She sought a deeper understanding of how chemicals worked, from experiments to everyday life scenarios. Anna's enthusiasm manifested in colourful explosions, bubbling beakers, and a genuinely inquisitive mind. Could Anna Müller one day become the second female to win two Nobel prizes. At such a young age, she hoped so.

*****

Eva Müller found solace in the realm of physics when she discovered Isaac Newton (1643-1727). Newton was an influential English physicist and mathematician. He developed the laws of motion and universal gravitation, laying the foundation for classical mechanics. He also made significant contributions to calculus and optics. She was intrigued by the rules that governed the universe, the principles that dictated motion and energy. Physics became her constant companion, and she yearned to unravel the mysteries of the universe. Eva's bedroom was adorned with posters of the famous physicist, and she spent her evenings stargazing, contemplating the cosmos, and sitting out on the central porch staring at the passing satellites in the dark and clear skies above the mountain ridge overlooking the city below.

Lisa Müller had an affinity for biology. She was captivated by the intricate systems that gave life to all living beings, as well as the life and works of Charles Darwin (1809-1882). Darwin was an English naturalist and geologist. He is known for his work on the theory of evolution by natural selection, which is explained in his renowned book "On the Origin of Species." Darwin's work revolutionised the understanding of biology and profoundly impacted fields such as genetics, ecology, and anthropology. From dissecting flowers to observing the behaviour of animals, Lisa soaked up knowledge like a sponge, eager to understand the inner workings of organisms. Her room was like a mini laboratory, filled with plants and specimens she carefully collected on expeditions.

The sisters' shared hunger for science deepened their bond, and they spent countless evenings conversing about their latest discoveries and readings. They discussed the interconnectedness of their respective fields and how chemistry, physics, and biology were intertwined in the fabric of reality.

Their quest for knowledge expanded beyond their father's library as time passed. They scoured local bookstores, frequented the city's libraries, and even started attending science lectures and workshops. Their dedication to learning was boundless.

Overjoyed by their passion for science, Karl did everything in his power to nurture their hunger for knowledge. He encouraged them to challenge traditional beliefs, push boundaries, and think outside the box. Professor Müller's love for his daughters, combined with their shared passion for science, created an unbreakable bond that propelled each sister forward on their individual paths of discovery.

Well, that was partly true. The bond only appeared indestructible on the surface.

\*\*\*\*\*

In the beginning, their journey had not been easy, but their unyielding hunger for knowledge and insatiable love for their respective fields made them an unstoppable force.

When the sisters became eligible to enrol in a university, Karl chose the University of Miami. He had asked one or two of his patients from Florida for treatment, and he kept hearing of the reputation of Miami Uni. In all accounts, they talked with admiration of the abundance of strong undergraduates and graduate programs in all science fields, including the three the girls were interested in and excelling in. One businessman who was having nose restructure treatment had majored there previously and now had his eldest boy heading there raved about the uni's state-of-the-art research facilities and offering opportunities for its students to engage in the latest cutting-edge research projects.

Later that evening, over dinner, Karl discussed enrolling all three in the same university at the same time.

For once, the Müller girls were elated with his proposal and agreed to go when everything had been arranged.

\*\*\*\*\*

Karl Müller, in his world of cosmetic surgery, also had to study often and constantly adjust his treatment methods as new developments arrived.

Life as a plastic surgeon in 1950s Colombia was quite fascinating for Karl. It was a transformative period for both the plastic surgery field and Latin America's socio-cultural landscape. In this era, Colombia emerged as a hub for cosmetic surgery, attracting clients from within the country and the United States. Without planning this, Karl was at the forefront of changing his whole life.

Plastic surgeons in Colombia during the 1950s were predominantly based in major cities like Bogotá, Medellín, and some in the city of Cali. These three cities were at the forefront of medical advancements and had growing infrastructures to support the booming industry.

Attracting clients from the United States was not uncommon, for this was primarily due to several factors. Firstly, the improved travel infrastructure, such as the availability of commercial flights, made it easier for American clients to seek medical services abroad. Additionally, some American patients sought more affordable cosmetic procedures in countries like Colombia, where the costs were relatively lower compared to the United States. Moreover, Colombia's reputation for quality medical care and the welcoming nature of its people also played a role in attracting international clients. Karl, with his palatial two-storey hacienda, stables, and offices overlooking the mountain ridge and, further still, the city below, proved to be a magnet for the rich and famous. In this location, intrusive reporters could be avoided easily.

In terms of available treatments, Karl focused on addressing various aesthetic concerns with popular procedures such as:

Rhinoplasty means having your nose reshaped, refined, and improved. Thus, the nose's appearance would be enhanced to be symmetrical with the patient's desired contours.

Karl quickly became an expert in facelift procedures. He was adept at correcting sagging skin and wrinkles, and restoring a more youthful appearance was simple for him to achieve. In the 1950s, Karl had to rely on traditional facelift techniques that focused on tightening the muscles and skin of the face and neck.

Towards the middle of the decade, Karl started to receive patients who wished for Breast Augmentation. Karl primarily utilised silicone implants to create the desired volume and shape.

Although in its early stages, and towards the end of the decade, Karl was able to add liposuction techniques to his growing list of treatments. He had begun to remove localised fat deposits from various areas of the patient's body.

Around the same time, another procedure was listed: eyelid surgery, known as blepharoplasty. This procedure aimed to address any excessive skin and/or fat deposits around the eyes, providing a more refreshed and youthful appearance.

It is important to note that plastic surgery in the 1950s lacked specific techniques and advancements that have become commonplace today, such as minimally invasive procedures, laser treatments, and the availability of diverse implant options. Nevertheless, as a plastic surgeon during this decade, Karl was skilled in delivering satisfactory outcomes using the available techniques and materials.

Overall, the life of a plastic surgeon in 1950s Colombia Karl was exciting, with his list of international clients' growing demand for cosmetic procedures and seeking the expertise and affordability he offered.

As far as Karl Müller was concerned, life was good.

*****

In 1955, campus life at Miami University for three teenage girls studying the three sciences was filled with a blend of academic pursuits, social engagements, and the prevailing social and political atmosphere.

The three girls were academically immersed in their rigorous study of their chosen science subjects, namely chemistry, physics, and biology. They attended lectures, participated in laboratory experiments, and engaged in discussions with their professors and classmates.

The sciences gained significant importance and recognition during this period, and rapid advancements were made in various scientific fields.

Outside the classrooms and laboratories, campus life was vibrant and bustling with activity. The university had a variety of student organisations and clubs where the girls explored their interests and forged few, if any, friendships with like-minded individuals. A couple of specific clubs and societies focused on women in science gave the girls opportunities to network, mentor, and be mentored by other women pursuing similar academic paths.

They ignored them all.

*****

The social atmosphere of the 1950s was influenced by traditional gender roles and societal expectations. Women were generally expected to focus on their studies, aiming to find a suitable husband and start a family.

However, as pioneers in the study of sciences, Anna, Eva, and Lisa faced challenges as they arose and broke some gender barriers and the odd noses.

*****

At the same time, the political atmosphere in the United States during this era was characterised by the Cold War between the United States and the Soviet Union. The fear of communism was prevalent, leading to heightened political tensions, anti-communist sentiments, and a constant sense of vigilance. Nearly all students engaged in debates attended political rallies or participated in student-led movements expressing their opinions and views on these political developments.

No one seemed to notice the three Müller sister's unwavering ability to successfully avoid them all.

*****

They preferred their own company. Their shared traumatic experience from the night of the Berlin bombing raid had never for one moment left their minds to have some degree of peace. Instead, slowly, the memories begin, leading them to develop a disturbed and vengeful mindset. As young, supposedly happy youngsters, the sisters had an incredibly close and intense bond; their loyalty to each other periodically manifested in extreme and violent ways.

One such occasion was hearing of the death of their beloved Aunt Clara three months earlier. The last link to their never-to-be-forgotten mother, Helga.

The Telegram from their father had arrived by messenger as they were all sitting in Anna's campus lodgings having a late-night meal together.

Later the next day, they learned that a will had been read in their absence and that the three had inherited the bulk of the inheritance, giving each an equal share of their aunt's estate.

They had not spoken or corresponded with Aunt Clara since that fateful night. They had no idea of what had happened to her in the intervening years since the nazi's surrender.

A week later, a man turned up, professing to be a New York lawyer handling their aunt's estate.

Good morning, Ladies. My name is Augustus Maximilian Rockefeller III. Please accept my card. As you can see, I have my office at Augustus Maximilian Rockefeller III Law Offices, 1901 Park Avenue, Suite 300, New York, NY 10001.

"I am sorry to say, your aunt has no living relatives except you ladies and your father through the marriage with her sister, your deceased mother, Helga. She did have two sons who had joined the German army in the initial months of World War 2, but alas, both perished in Russia. For your record, their names were Sigfried and Tomas. Sadly, as far as we know, they had no time to have children."

Anna told the trio, "Firstly, may we call you Augustus? Saying your full name is going to be curious each time." Without waiting, Anna continued, "So, there must have been a husband, right? But honestly, none of us recollects who he was."

The lawyer looked down at the bulk of paper scattered on his lap. "Ah, yes, you can call me by my first name, and yes, there is something I can enlighten you with. It took a while for us to find the gentleman concerned, and we recently discovered he was half Polish and half Austrian. His name was Count Stanisław Białkowski."

Eva piped up, "You say he was."

"Yes, by all accounts, he was a dashing Messerschmitt pilot with Goering. Unfortunately for him, he was last seen with his aircraft on fire, heading into the English channel during the Battle of Britain. The war archives stipulate there was no sign of a parachute or bailout."

Lisa leaned forward, "What does that mean for us?"

"Well, it is a vast estate and must go through many stages to be completed. But in essence, you ladies will never have to work for the rest of your lives."

All three sisters look at each other in turn, not knowing how to react to this life-changing event.

Augustus has held hundreds of such meetings since the war ended. "There is only one fly in the ointment; sorry, there are two, so to speak." He paused and found the courage to say the next part of the sentence. "You must wait until you have completed your degrees before having any sums forwarded. Also, your father is contesting the will."

All three sisters' heads shot up, and now Augustus has their full attention. "It appears your father has not been included in the will and, at present, is not a beneficiary."

*****

Anna, Eva, and Lisa needed time to process everything Augustus had revealed. They arranged to meet again the following week.

As soon as the lawyer had left the building and was last seen entering the back seats of a luxury-looking Rolls Royce, Eva and Lisa turned to a venom-looking Anna, "That pig has done it again. I want revenge, and I want it so bad I can taste it right now!"

Eva spat out her thirst for revenge, "I agree; first, our mother has no choice, and now we have no choice on when we should or should not receive our rightful inheritance."

Lisa looked at both of her sisters. I will do it. He will never expect his youngest to take revenge."

*****

This evening was the catalyst that overflowed their thirst for power, their desire to take control and dominate their lives with as much violence as they could jointly muster.

Anna, now pulling both her younger sisters towards her, whispered to each, "We have been victims of an act of violence to our dearest mama; we have had to carry that injustice silently all our short lives. We will seek revenge against this despicable man we have to call father."

Lisa looked at her older sisters and asked, "How will we achieve our revenge without ruining our lives?"

All three sat deep in their own thoughts. Suddenly, Eva looked at Anna and Lisa and said, "I think I have the answer to that posing question. We are all majoring in the three sciences over the next two years. Anna, you are in chemistry, Lisa is in biology, and I am in physics. Indeed, we have a remarkable opportunity to focus on creating the perfect crime."

Anna saw great merit in Eva's trend of thought. "Yes, you are right. The solution is staring at us. I will look at what chemicals will help us be undetectable. I will commence investigating the world of barbiturates, such as the sedative drug Phenobarbital. I will also explore bromides such as potassium bromide. Or maybe a potent sedative compound of Ethchlorvynol will work more efficiently."

Eva smiled. "And I will focus on the physics necessary to keep our revenge permanent. I have a feeling fire is the way towards our goal."

She went to the nearby bureau and searched for a pen and notepad. Let us sit together at the dining table, and I can give you some insight into the aspects of a house fire.

All three were sitting, and Eva began drawing an outline of a two-storey house similar to the hacienda on the mountain ridge.

A house fire is a complex event that involves various physical aspects. The primary elements involved are fuel, oxygen, and heat.

The fuel is typically the materials present within the hacienda and the adjoining offices, including furniture, appliances, building materials, and personal belongings. These items can be made of various substances, such as wood, fabric, plastics, and metals, with different flammability properties.

There must be an adequate oxygen supply to start and sustain a fire.

Air is necessary for combustion, as it provides the essential oxygen molecules required for the chemical reactions involved in the burning process. The heat source, which can be a spark, an open flame, an electrical malfunction, or a heat-generating appliance, initiates the fire by raising the temperature of the fuel materials to their ignition point.

Once the fire begins, it progresses through several stages. The early stages involve the release of flammable gases and vapours from the burning materials. These gases mix with the surrounding air, creating a flammable atmosphere. As the fire grows, it generates intense heat, causing nearby combustible items to heat up, smoulder, or catch fire.

Fire releases energy through radiant heat, which transfers to surrounding objects, heating them further and potentially igniting them. This process leads to a flashover, where the entire space becomes engulfed in flames almost simultaneously.

As the fire spreads, it will produce dense black smoke, which consists of a mixture of carbon dioxide, carbon monoxide, water vapour, and various toxic gases. The smoke will obscure visibility and make breathing difficult, posing a significant threat to the inhabitant, i.e., our intended victim.

The hacienda's structural components also influence the fire's physical behaviour. The type and configuration of walls, doors, windows, and ventilation systems affect the fire's progression and the spread of heat and smoke throughout the hacienda and the adjoining offices.

*****

Lisa, equally, was now in tune with her sisters. "And I will look into the biological ways of what happens to a body before, during, and after such a fire. Wait. I am sure I have an article regarding this very subject in one of my textbooks. Please wait a moment while I have a look."

Anna took the opportunity to open a bottle of vino and gathered three wine glasses. She returned just as Lisa reappeared from her nearby dormitory with an open textbook in one hand.

"Lucky for us, this subject is scheduled to be covered in a lecture by the local coroner's office later next week. Let me read the article to you."

"Part 1, Before a House Fire occurs, the human body is stable. The various bodily systems usually function, including the respiratory, cardiovascular, and nervous systems. The body maintains homeostasis, a state of equilibrium in which body temperature, electrolyte balance, and pH levels are maintained optimally.

Part 2: When a fire starts and engulfs a house, several biological processes occur within the body due to exposure to extreme heat, smoke, and toxic gases.

The individual may inhale smoke, a mixture of hot air, gases, and particles produced by burning materials. Smoke contains carbon monoxide, hydrogen cyanide, ash, and other toxic substances. Inhalation of smoke and poisonous gases can lead to immediate respiratory distress.

As the fire consumes oxygen from the surrounding area, the individual trapped inside may experience oxygen deprivation. Reduced oxygen levels can cause dizziness, disorientation, and confusion.

The intense heat generated by a fire causes direct thermal injury to the body. Exposed skin and tissues can suffer burns, leading to immediate tissue damage. Higher body temperatures may start affecting the functioning of enzymes and proteins, disrupting cellular processes.

Inhaling superheated air or gases can cause throat and lung tissue burns, known as inhalation. These burns can severely damage airways and impair breathing."

Lisa paused as her glass was empty, and Anna immediately refilled it. She was fascinated by what she was learning from Lisa.

After two more swigs from the glass, Lisa continued reading, "The incomplete combustion of organic materials during a fire produces carbon monoxide (CO). CO is a toxic gas that binds to haemoglobin in red blood cells, preventing oxygen from being transported effectively. Severe CO poisoning can lead to unconsciousness, organ failure, and death."

Lisa looked up for dramatic effect at the word death.

Eva spoke next, "What happens after a House Fire?"

Lisa looked back down to the text once more, "The immediate aftermath of a house fire can involve critical injuries, depending on the severity of the burns, smoke inhalation, and toxic gas exposure. The following are some potential long-term effects."

Lisa closed the textbook, surmising that they would not need to know what the long-term implications were for someone surviving a house fire. Their father was in no way going to survive the one he was destined for.

\*\*\*\*\*

Eva squeezed both Anna's and Lisa's hands, "We will bring justice and closure for our mother and target our father, and he will reap the punishment he so well deserves."

All three Müller sisters stayed as if statues moulded together. No more words were necessary for now. Next would be the planning and execution of their Ex-Nazi Father.

The decades passed, and the three Müller sisters would go on to pursue successful careers in their chosen fields. Anna became a renowned chemist, Eva a respected physicist, and Lily a sought-after biologist.

*****

Back in the hacienda on the mountain overlooking the small village below, Professor Müller thought about a new means of making himself wealthy beyond his wildest dreams. Periodically, the tentacles of the Odessa reached out to him in places he least expected.

On the last occasion, he watched the 1954 World Cup Final on a black-and-white television in the local cafe. West Germany beat Hungary three goals to two. Earlier in the group stages, West Germany had been defeated decisively by Hungary eight goals to three!

No one in the football world, fan or player, expected semi-professional West Germany to pull off such a result in the final.

In the semi-finals, West Germany beat their neighbour, Austria, while Hungary defeated mighty Brazil four goals to two in the infamous game due to the violence involved in the match. Footballing skills came second on that occasion.

"Good evening, Herr Müller. Are you enjoying the game?"

Karl looked across the small table in front of him to see a stranger now sitting. By his demeanour and accent, he could immediately tell he was a survivor of the old days.

"Yes, I am, but I do not believe you have sought me out to discuss my passing interest in football."

"You are correct, Professor. We need your reliable services in exchange for what we have generously given you this past decade."

Karl scanned the room, which was empty except for the two henchmen who had accompanied the stranger from Odessa.

"Please do tell me what it is I can wholeheartedly do for you and the organisation?"

A small, battered-looking suitcase appeared on the cafe table, and the "owner" pushed it towards Karl. Inside, you will find a smaller case housing valuable emeralds, uncut diamonds, and two cast bars of gold. We wish you could store everything safely somewhere no one will accidentally discover."

Karl drew the suitcase towards him and, with one hand, moved the case down to next to his right leg under the table. "May I know if this will be a recurring matter?"

The stranger looked at Karl's expression and revealed, "Yes, over the coming months, there will indeed be more reasons why I will meet you. I must bid you farewell for now, as I have another journey to make."

Both men rose and shook hands. No further conversation was made.

*****

On his arrival later that evening, Karl Müller found himself standing in his vault amidst rows of towering wine racks. The cellar's faint aroma of aged oak and delicate grape permeated the air, adding a touch of sophistication to the scene. The flickering glow of carefully positioned candles and wall-mounted lights danced upon his collection, illuminating bottles of rare vintages and treasures from harvests gone by.

As his eyes leisurely scanned the vault, Karl's attention was drawn to the now-opened, battered-looking suitcase lying on the gridded concrete floor. He reasoned he would have to store it in a place with the slightest possibility of damage from dampness and mould. He turned his gaze to the subject of interest on the table. Karl could clearly see it was elegantly crafted, its sleek black exterior exuding an aura of mystery. Intuitively recognising the moment's significance, he cautiously approached the case, his footsteps echoing softly in the cavernous space.

*****

Carefully unclasping the intricate lock, Karl lifted the lid with an anticipatory sense of pleasure. What met his gaze was a sight that caused his breath to hitch in astonishment. White handkerchiefs, flawlessly folded, lay atop a bed of exquisite gemstones.

Emeralds, glimmering with a vivid green brilliance, danced with the light. Uncut diamonds, pristine and unadulterated, glistened with untamed fire. Each precious stone seemed to hold within it an untold story, a hidden tale of its journey through the annals of time.

Yet, amidst this tapestry of gemstones, two golden bars silently demanded attention. Their gleaming surface reflected Karl's awe-struck expression; their weight was a testament to their insurmountable value. The disparity between the matte fabric and the opulent metal was a visual contradiction—a harmonious marriage of wealth and subtlety.

A hushed gasp escaped Karl's lips as he gingerly reached into the case, his fingertips feeling the cool touch of the emeralds and diamonds. His mind attempted to comprehend the sheer magnitude of what lay before him, the rarity of this treasure trove defying logic.

Time seemed to stand still as Karl allowed himself to fully immerse in the allure of this moment. The vault, a sanctuary for his most cherished possessions, had revealed another layer of opulence that surpassed even his highest expectations.

As he closed the lid, the magnitude of this encounter sent his heart racing. Karl Müller, the guardian of old and new treasures, was once again reminded of the enchantment hidden within the depths of his vault. And with renewed excitement, he couldn't help but eagerly anticipate the next Odessa delivery.

*****

# 62: I am the Meeting of the Minds who consider a request from Stalin

"Excuse me, Simon, but do you know who this magnificent-looking bust is in honour of?" Sebastian inquired while sitting on his black stallion, El Dorado.

"I must confess, I have no idea. I can see he is wearing a uniform and looks like someone the real Bolivar would have known." Simon thought, but there was no reference to who the bust was at the foot of the monument. "Have you any ideas, Felipe?"

Felipe and his equally black stallion Independence were moving around the unknown officer and could not find any reference or nameplate. "No, I have no idea who this fine-looking gentleman in an officer's uniform could be."

While all three were still inspecting the mystery, they failed to hear Jorge Issacs, Maria, Efrain, and a dog with no name approaching from the west side of the Parque de Versalles.

"Good evening, gentleman; you all look mighty splendid on your three stallions, Palomo; you look as graceful as ever," Jorge spoke with deep admiration to all three.

Maria approached Palomo, who bowed his head to welcome the gentle-looking lady and neighed a gentle welcome to her.

"Why, thank you, Palomo; I am glad to see you too. Efrain, come and stroke these fine horses." Efrain had needed no invitation and had already welcomed both black stallions. The dog with no name had sat patiently nearby to take in the whole scenario.

Simon looked up into the eyes of the unknown officer, "I am sorry if I have caused you an offence by not knowing who you are, but I have met many people over the years, and I can say the majority I have never known or have forgotten because I may have met them only once."

*****

Suddenly, as if by pure magic, the bust came alive. He was smiling as he surveyed all in front of him.

"Good evening, everyone; please allow me to introduce myself to you all. My name is Bernardo O'Higgins. I was born in Chile in 1776 and passed away at the end of 1842."

Sebastian interrupted, "Do not tell me. This is another of your liberators from my Spanish Rule."

Bernardo continued and ignored the conquistador, "During my lifetime, I was the first head of state for Chile and later the Viceroyalty of Peru."

Now, seeing the seeds of recognition, Simon asked, "Are you the one who led the military campaigns that won independence from Spain? If so, I do believe we did meet."

Bernardo smiled and remarked, "My, you are all so inquisitive. It must have been nearly half a century since someone spoke directly to me. Please give me a few moments to collect my thoughts, and hopefully, I will answer all your questions."

Everyone duly went quiet and waited for the bust to compose himself.

*****

"Lady, gentlemen, stallions, and no forgetting a dog, allow me, Bernardo O'Higgins, to shed light upon my extraordinary life and the remarkable achievements that have led to a bust of mine being displayed here in this park.

"I was born on either August 20, 1776, or the exact date two years later, in Chillán, Chile. Sadly, the records of that time listed me as an illegitimate son of an Irish dubious-sounding "Baron of Ballenary" named Ambrosio O'Higgins and his prominent ladyfriend Isabel Riquelme.

"I do say the dubious-sounding title of Baron because he got it from the "do nothing except pass the time away with hunting" Spanish King Charles IV in 1795. I received my education in Lima and grew up witnessing the turbulent period of Spanish colonial rule. As a teenager, I spent time in Spain and England. During this period, I became inspired by the ideals of the Enlightenment and the fervour for freedom spreading across the Americas. I met and spent time with several future revolutionary leaders, such as Francisco Miranda, whom I am sure you, Simon, will remember as a fellow Venezuelan champion for independence from Spanish rule."

Simon bowed slightly, "Yes, of course, I do know and remember Francisco. In fact, we only recently spent a delightful evening with him and many others in Santa Marta. Did we not Sebastian and Felipe?"

Both friends laughed at the many memories from that night. "In did we do both remember." joked Felipe, now nudging his unlikeliest friend, Sebastian.

"A great place to have a mud bath and a good scrub down in the Rio de Porno nearby." Remarked Sebastian, now laughing at his vivid memories of an active volcano and some buxom-looking females.

Bernardo silently built up a volume of questions he wished to have answered, but now was not the time, he reasoned.

*****

Seizing the moment to continue with his life history, "I dedicated myself to the liberation of my beloved homeland, Chile, when I saw the opportunity arise when Napoleon invaded mainland Spain. It meant all the colonies back home were now less defensible and largely uncontrolled. I could clearly see the first steps to independence were close at hand, and I immediately returned to Chile. In the early days, from 1810 to 1814, I could have had better success. When I led the militia, I always came second to the Spanish forces."

Simon knew that feeling well and nodded politely towards Bernardo in sympathy when things did not go as hoped.

Bernardo continued with his story, taking up the reins again, "Thousands of Chileans, including myself, crossed the Andes and headed into Argentina. We were fleeing the wrath of the Spanish royalists. It took us another three years to adequately prepare and stand a chance in reconquesting Chile again."

Simon turned to everyone and addressed them, "I do remember hearing of your conquest; it was good to hear that we were both fighting tirelessly against Spanish rule. I campaigned in the north, liberating countries such as Colombia, Ecuador, and Peru, while you focused on leading the independence movement in Chile."

"Thank you, kind Sir. Finally, one of my most significant achievements was winning against the Spanish Royalists in the Battle of Chacabuco in 1817. This crucial battle paved the way for establishing the first Chilean government independent of Spanish authority. I then assumed the position of Supreme Director, becoming the de facto leader of Chile from 1817 to 1823."

"During my leadership, I aimed to transform Chile into a more democratic and just society. I introduced many internal reforms, such as the establishment of a free press, the abolition of internal customs duties, the founding of the National Library, and the creation of the Chilean Navy."

Here, Bernardo looked directly at Simon, "Do you remember my collaborations with you extended beyond the battlefield and into the realm of diplomacy. Do you recall that together, we worked towards creating a united Latin America, envisioning a continent free from the shackles of colonialism?"

Simon bowed down, one hand raised to the night sky. "Most certainly, this bond between me and you might explain the presence of your bust here in Parque de Versalles in Santiago de Cali, Colombia. How we have never spoken since your arrival is a tragic mystery that now has been rectified."

Jorge Issacs Ferrer, who had remained transfixed throughout the exchange between two Liberators, found the courage to speak up. "Sirs, by my reckoning of my watch, we are a little late and still have some distance to go. May I suggest we get to our destination and discover why we have been recalled after nearly three years of normality since the memorable night when we saved many older people from the threat of flooding and mudslides?"

Maria, now holding hands with Efrain, also said, "Thank you, gentleman, for an incredible insight into your lives nearly two centuries ago. I cannot wait to learn more as the next few years pass. History is so much fun!"

Bernardo looked inquisitively towards each statue, "Where are you going?"

Felipe advanced forward and reached out his hand in friendship, "Please allow me to have you sitting behind me on my stallion, and I will tell you as we ride to attend our next scheduled "Meeting of the Minds."

Bernardo accepted the gesture and prepared to be transported to the rear of the black stallion.

\*\*\*\*\*

As I, the building known as the Pheonix Air Transport Museum, observe the scene in the central hall, I see Simon Bolivar, Sebastian Belalcazar, Felipe de Cayedo, and a newcomer named Bernardo O'Higgins riding together on Palomo and two black stallions. They make quite a captivating sight as they approach the meeting location. Jorge Issacs Ferrer, Maria, Efrain, and a dog without a name follow them. I could never have imagined such a diverse group of individuals now adding to the gathering.

Five more black stallions, sapphire blue children, and turtle figurines are already present at the Meeting of the Minds, creating an intriguing ambience. Rio Gato, with his entourage of beautiful feline figurines, adds an element of elegance to the gathering. Well, that is when they finally decided to stop racing and climbing everywhere.

Nellie, the black woman from Chontaduro, and Jovita Feijoó from Palmira also contribute their unique perspectives.

Among the attendees, I found the solidarity of workers united by their common goals. With their intriguing names, Derekamus Stonebeard Stonforce and Abella Goldhammer, Darkstone also caught my eye. Lastly, I can see my late museum founders, José and Stella. Just behind them, I could see Norman, who rounded up the diverse collection of individuals present.

With such a varied group of individuals, it is clear that the Meeting of the Minds promises to be a compelling and enlightening event for me once more.

\*\*\*\*\*

For once, everyone else had already arrived, and the Museo Aereo Fenix was a centre of pandemonium. Bernardo's face said it all. He could not fathom how a herd of stampeding black stallions, albeit only five in total, could navigate with at least sixteen equally excited cat figurines of every colour and design possible, including one coloured red with silver needles protruding from every upper part of her torso, and a whole bunch of out of control sapphire coloured blue children and turtles could not in any way destroy all the magnificent machines on display.

For Bernardo, seeing cars, bikes, motorcycles, planes, trains, and ships left him rooted to the chair that Sebastian and Simon had placed him.

Also, there was the small matter that the Chilean Liberator had no legs on which to rely. "Good job, you cannot have a heart attack." mused Simon, and then, as an afterthought, "How did the real you actually die?"

It took Bernardo a while to focus on Simon's question: "Believe it or not, on the death certificate, it read, heart failure."

At some point, Bernardo clapped eyes on Nellie and Jovita and whispered to no one in particular, "Pray tell me who those two are."

"All in good time." voiced Sebastian.

When Bernardo spotted Derekamus and Abella, he almost fell off his chair. Felipe had foreseen the issues that Bernardo would have to maintain his composure. He had placed himself close to allow him to steer and support the Chilean to safety throughout the evening.

*****

The meeting began with Jorge standing and chairing the meetings he had always done for the past two centuries.

"Good evening, everyone. It is a pleasure to see you all again under our new roof at the Museum. As Chairman of the Meeting of the Minds, I would like to welcome our newfound friend from the Parque de Versalles, none other than Bernardo O'Higgins, the Viceroyalty of Peru, revolutionary leader, and the first ever Chilean Head of State in the early 1800s."

Hands, fists, paws, feet, and hoofs pounded the table simultaneously with a greeting no one could deny.

Bernardo wanted to stand but understandably was unable to; secretly, he wished he had been made a full-size statue. It irritated him to know that wherever Chileans resided in the world, there would, at some point, be a monument or a sculpture in their honour. But here in Cali, he was a bust in a park.

"Next on the agenda, it has been nearly three years since we last had a reason to organise a meeting. In defence, the city and its population of barbarians have been as quiet or as noisy as you believe is true. This has left us with a decision that needs addressing, and tonight would be an ideal occasion for it to happen. It is a matter of whether Derekamus and Abella can now be considered full status as all statues or remain as figurines due to their size."

The head of the Solidarity crew stood to address the floor, and Jorge happily sat down to give way to the hard-working steel worker.

"I believe that everyone here firmly believes our two gnomes are worthy of being equal among us. Abella's discreet use of her magical powers led us to success in saving many lives during that terrible storm of the century. How could we forget the wonderful experience we witnessed when all those older people were transcended back to their youth and rejoiced in dining and dancing the night away."

Jovita and Nellie stood together, and each looked inquiringly at who should speak; for once, Jovita gave ground to her charming and eloquent speaking friend, "We wish to second the emotion in honouring these two splendid little people. For me personally, soaring to the clouds in one of those contraptions you call an aeroplane with Jovita handling the joystick was an adventure I will never forget."

There followed an uproar that all participated in except Bernardo, who had no idea what everyone was talking about. He still found it all a dream, but he had to admit, already it was probably the best dream he had ever known.

The vote went ahead, and the result was an outstanding success for both Derekamus and Abella. They stood next; this time, they were so proud to hold hands while standing at the table.

"Ladies, Gentlemen, and all you beautiful creatures. We are honoured to have been welcomed into your fold. We remember that first night when Derekamus decided it was time for us to announce our arrival in this city."

"I have to admit to being of a shyish nature and how I trembled at the thought of meeting you all. I remember how we must have looked soaking wet and wearing no footwear. Then you, Simon, rose, walked towards us, and greeted us with such old-fashioned etiquette, which was a joy for us to behold. You, Sebastian, Jorge, Efrain, and Felipe are standing as I am."

Simon bowed his head in Abella's direction, "The rules of etiquette are simple; when a lady is standing and speaking, then it is right for all the gentlemen in the room to be doing the same, and you, Abella, are a true lady."

Abella sat with both cheeks as rosy as red roses. Her heart fluttered for the way the Liberator had addressed her. Derekamus now came to the forefront.

"Senor Bolivar and all present here tonight, I wish to add to my lovely Abella's comments and also express my gratitude for acknowledging us as genuine statues."

A further round of applause followed. Then suddenly, Norman, the Museum Manager, appeared at the entrance, and everyone sensed there was someone else lurking in the shadows…

*****

"Ladies, Gentlemen, and all you noisy but lovely creatures who make up the membership of this Meeting of the Minds. You will remember me from that incredible night of the storm of the century and how, with your work and dedication, you safeguarded over 180 older people and their carers by bringing them here to our transportation abode. You may wonder why we have asked you all to attend this meeting. So, without further ado, let me reintroduce you all to the late founders of this museum, Jose and Stella."

The meeting attendees rose as one. Some stood on two feet, while others stood on all four feet. With Felipe's help, Bernardo stood shoulder to shoulder with each other.

José and Stella moved forward, and two spaces magically appeared at the head of the table for them both.

"Good evening, everyone; it is an honour to see you all again. But wait, there appears to be a new face amongst you. "Who sire are you?"

Bernardo puffed up his chest and replied, "Sir, I am Bernardo O'Higgins, of Chilean birth. In my lifetime, I was a wealthy landowner of Irish ancestry, later a Captain General of the Chilean volunteer Army, a Brigadier of the United Provinces of the Rio de la Plata, a General Officer under Simon Bolivar's Gran Colombia, and a Grand Marshal of Peru."

Sebastian groaned aloud and playfully commented, "And you thought, Simon, you had a long name and title!"

Bernardo joined in the banter; oh, how he had missed military banter. "I can add more information if you so wish, you uncouth Spaniard."

Stella spoke next, "Now, now, you boys, behave. We have serious business to discuss with you all. Please let us introduce two others you most definitely do know."

\*\*\*\*\*

At that moment, two others appeared from the shadows. It was a policeman they knew as Archibaldo Frederico Alcatraz and a Street man wearing only a denim skirt and carrying a formidable rock in his hand, Stalin.

\*\*\*\*\*

You could have heard a pin drop. The silence in my museum was deafening. No one dared utter a word. Finally, the oldest turtle rose and uttered a polite cough. "May we know why you decided to attend our meeting tonight?"

Archibaldo looked at Stalin first and then turned to face a world of statues, busts, sculptures, figurines, and some of the most amazing sights he could never have believed possible. "We have come for your help, or to be precise, we have come to ask Abella to assist my friend Stalin in maintaining his forever disappearing memory."

Stalin moved up alongside his young friend and, for the first time in many years, found the courage to offer a warm smile to everyone present.

"Yes, I know it must be hard for you all to see barbarians standing before you. I can totally appreciate your privacy; I seek my privacy daily on the streets. Because of how I look and the little that others know of my life, it has helped me to achieve some form of isolation. But right now, I, or we require I, have a memory capable of lasting more than a day at a time. You see, we believe we may be on the hunt for a killer."

*****

Yes, now imagine the scene before you in my central hall that housed a grand function for many older people three years ago. Imagine the shocked expressions on everyone's faces, including the Rio Gato and his harem of beautiful girlfriends. Never in the history of The Meeting of the Minds evenings had there been any barbarians present except, of course, the night of the rescue, but even then, all the older people left with their thoughts intact and a collective agreement to never say a word.

Tonight, my central hall, illuminated by candlelight, was filled with diverse individuals renowned for their extraordinary abilities and knowledge. At the front, Archibaldo and Stalin stand before them, desperate and hopeful. My heart went to them in their request for a solution to change one barbarian's life. Here is my version of what was said this evening.

Archibaldo spoke first, nervously: "Ladies and gentlemen of the Meeting of the Minds, esteemed members, thank you for granting us this audience. We stand before you today with a dire request that only a gnome named Abella can fulfil.

Derekamus was immediately curious when he heard his wife's name mentioned: "Abella? My wife, who is known to possess remarkable powers? Pray, tell us all here why you need her assistance."

Stalin was next to speak, his gravel-sounding voice hinting at frustration: "My dear friends, I have been surviving on these streets for decades with a memory that fades away at the dawn of each new day. But now, with Archibaldo and this grave investigation of ours, we desperately need my memory back, even if just for a short while."

Jorge sounded sympathetic to Stalin's never-ending plight. "We are aware of your plight. But what makes you believe Abella, the gnome, can restore your memory?"

Archibaldo, with a fair degree of determination, spoke up before Stalin could answer, "We have remembered witnessing Abella's possession of unfathomable abilities. Like you all, we saw how she helped countless individuals regain lost memories from their youth, even memories locked away by trauma on the night of the rescue."

Sounding a little sceptical, Simon, who wishes to protect the little dwarf, stood and directed his question to both barbarians: "And what would compel Abella to aid you in this endeavour? What do you offer in return?"

Archibaldo offered earnestly what he felt was a heartfelt response, "Abella, we believe you are a pure soul, and we feel you seek justice in the world we live in as much as we do. We stand here representing the victims of a potential killer. If we can solve this case and bring the perpetrator to justice, it will restore the Colonel's memory and save innocent lives."

Derekamus thoughtfully continued acting as a defence for his beloved Abella, "A noble cause, indeed. But my wife is known to be elusive and does not engage in such dealings easily. How do you plan to convince her to assist you?"

Now standing with his head looking down at my central hall flooring, Stalin spoke clearly and with emotion: "I've been a servant of the law for many years, and now, I ask for it to serve me when I need it most. Abella holds the key to uncovering the truth, exposing the darkness that overshadows our city. If we can prevail, she will see the goodness in our intentions and hopefully aid us willingly."

Jorge rose with a severe expression on his chiselled features: "To bring our Abella, who undeniably holds great power, out of hiding is no easy task, but if this investigation is so important to you both, we shall consider it. Know this—if Abella agrees to help, her powers will be temporary and come at a significant cost to the citizens of this city.

For the first time this evening, Archibaldo willingly expressed his heartfelt gratitude: "We understand and are prepared to face any sacrifice necessary to seek justice and restore Stalin's ability to keep his memories, if only for a fleeting moment."

Felipe said solemnly, "Very well. Then, if we agree, we should convene and discuss this matter further. Please leave us and return before midnight, and if we have reached a unanimous decision, we shall give you our blessing regarding Abella's involvement."

Archibaldo, showing immense relief with how both he and Stalin had presented their request and how positive the response was, spoke to all, "Thank you, esteemed members. We will be extremely grateful for your consideration. At midnight, we shall return and hope your wisdom shines in our favour."

Archibaldo and Stalin left my central hall with a mixture of hope and uncertainty etched across their faces. Their fates are now in the hands of the Meeting of the Minds and its members.

They sat patiently with the three locomotives now on display with each other outside in my car park.

✶✶✶✶✶

As Archibaldo and Stalin sat outside, they could not observe the attendees of the meeting of the Minds engaging in lively discussions and debates, but they could hear them. The largest of the locomotives invited the two policemen to sit in his cabin, which allowed them access to a broken window on the second floor. It was here that the voices below carried upwards to the waiting duo.

Before debating, all present agreed that the children, the black stallions, Palomo, and the harem of cats could go upstairs and be entertained by Stella and José.

A heated argument ensued as the Rio Gato and a representative group of three female cats put up a case for allowing them to have the right to vote. Their point was that they had made many friends amongst the barbarian population over the years, and the felines felt they should be part of the decision to protect the children who show nothing but sheer pleasure when walking and running between them.

After a few minutes, it was agreed that Rio Gato, with his astute brain, could select the three cats he wished to represent the majority of the cats. He picked Valentina, Bella, and Mia.

✶✶✶✶✶

Back on the ground floor, the topic was whether to grant Abella the power to temporarily restore Stalin's memory. This would aid in investigating whether the city had a killer lurking among its inhabitants.

Jorge Issacs Ferrer took a moment to consider the implications of granting such power. On the one hand, it could provide valuable information to help solve the case. On the other hand, manipulating Stalin's mind raised ethical concerns.

After much deliberation, the attendees decided to allow the discussions and debates to take place within the central hall. They believed it was essential for all those attending the Meeting of the Minds to express their opinions and concerns before making a final decision.

As the discussion progressed, it became evident that the attendees were divided on the matter. The Solidarity crew argued that restoring Stalin's memory would be a violation of his privacy and free will. Jacob, Sebastian, Felipe, Bernardo, and Simon believed it was necessary to ensure the city's safety and potentially identify the killer.

To reach a compromise, the eldest turtle proposed that a significant cost should be agreed upon for restoring Stalin's memory. This cost would serve as a deterrent, ensuring that it was not taken lightly or used recklessly. The exact nature of the cost would be decided collectively by the attendees, considering both ethical considerations and practical implications.

The cost could be a form of sacrifice or commitment from the person or group requesting the restoration of memory. It could also involve a significant contribution to a cause that would benefit the community or support ethical research in the fields of neurology and memory manipulation. The idea was to balance the potentially invasive act with the greater good.

As the discussions continued, the attendees considered various options, including a time-limited restoration of memory, regular check-ins with Abella to ensure ethical guidelines were followed, and the formation of an oversight committee consisting of the leader of the Solidarity crew, Jorge, Felipe, Rio Gato, and the elder turtle to monitor the investigation.

Ultimately, the decision to grant Abella the power to temporarily restore Stalin's memory and the agreement on the high cost would be reached through a democratic process within the meeting of the Minds. It would require a majority consensus, indicating that the community as a whole was willing to accept the potential risks and benefits involved in the investigation.

It was at this moment that Abella finally spoke up. Her husband had pushed her from behind, insisting she should have a say in the matter.

*****

"Ladies and gentlemen and beloved creatures, the machinery of all three sizes, and two earnest-looking investigators above me."

Nothing seemed to get one over this esteemed gnome as she smiled and winked above with her wonky-looking eyes.

No one complained that the two visitors could hear the proceedings before them. Each of them concurred that the truth should always be allowed to radiate without restrictions.

Now standing at the table, Abella lowered her eyes to the attendees in front of her. "Today, gathered here in this esteemed gathering, I stand before you with a heavy heart, burdened by the weight of a city's uncertainty and the longing for truth. In times like these, we need to come together, unite in our shared purpose, and seek solace in the power of humanity and hope."

Everyone in the hall was transfixed in the presence of such a wise gnome. They each wanted to learn more. Abella began walking down the table slowly with her hands raised, "I speak as Abella, a being bestowed with a unique power—an ability to restore Stalin's memory, the ex-policeman who, by some twist of fate, cannot retain his recollections of the very incidents that could unveil the existence of a killer among us. They say that with great power comes great responsibility, and it is with immense humility that I embrace my responsibility today."

Abella was looking directly into Jovita's eyes; it was amazing that a three-foot-high gnome could go eyeball to eyeball with a twelve-foot female sitting before her.

"Stalin, as we have learnt, is not the monster most barbarians in his community deem him to be. In fact, he should be seen as a trusted and revered figure despite his awful sense of dress. Stalin finds himself in a bewildering state, unable to remember the moments that could potentially save the barbarians from the grips of fear and paranoia. But let's remember, my friends, that memories are intricately threaded with the essence of who we are. Our past shapes us guides us and ultimately defines us. It is a testament to our shared humanity, a tapestry woven with love, laughter, pain, and growth."

Everyone in the Solidarity crew clapped and cheered their approval. Abella took a moment to allow the sounds of hands meeting to cease.

"It is precisely in this understanding that I, Abella, extend my hand to Stalin. Together, we shall journey through the labyrinth of forgotten recollections, hoping to unearth the truth hidden within the city's cracks and crevices. The human spirit is resilient, capable of miraculous leaps of faith, and fueled by the desire for justice."

Abella paused in her continuous walk up and down the length of the grand table and found herself now facing the new member, Bernardo.

"In times of darkness, the light within us shines the brightest. Our search for truth will reflect our collective will to stand against the supposedly indomitable forces that seek to tear us apart. By joining forces, we shall resurrect Stalin's memories, resuscitating each fragment that holds the key to the heartache that haunts him."

As she moved away from the Chilean Liberator, she failed to see the deep admiration from a bust who had not spoken to anyone for nearly half a century. He almost missed the following words of wisdom from Abella.

"But let Archibaldo and Stalin not be swayed by wrath or vengeance. Let the pursuit of truth be tempered by compassion. They must remain vigilant, with fairness as their compass, as both navigate the stormy waters of mystery. For it is only through the unity of purpose that Archibaldo and Stalin can triumph over the silent menace that threatens our city."

Abella was now standing in front of her beloved husband. She reached out, and Derekamus moved towards her.

"In closing, my friends, I implore each and every one of you to stand alongside me, hand in hand, as we embark on this arduous yet necessary journey to restore Stalin's memory. Let our hearts guide us, let empathy fuel us, and let love be the foundation upon which we build a stronger, safer community."

Abella hugged and kissed Derekamus on his, almost hidden by his enormous beard lips. As she parted from her lifelong partner, she ended her speech with these final words, "Together, in our unwavering determination and immense courage, we shall uncover the darkest secrets and bring light to their shadowy depths. So, my dear companions, let us march forward with hope in our hearts and the unwavering belief that united Archibaldo and Stalin shall triumph over the evils that cloak our city."

Both gnomes bowed to all present and, in unison, spoke, "Thank you."

*****

My decorated central hall excitedly buzzed as the Meeting of the Minds began deliberating Abella's poignant words. Abella stood waiting to answer any questions from the attendees, her eyes gleaming with unwavering resolve. Next to her, Archibaldo and Stalin waited to hear the final decision.

With a voice filled with conviction, Jorge Isaacs Ferrer began, "Ladies and gentlemen, esteemed members of the Meeting of the Minds, thank you for gathering here tonight. I stand before you to endorse Abella's plea, a plea for an opportunity to assist our dear comrade Stalin in his battle against the dreaded Devil's Breath that alone was the culprit in his acute memory loss."

The room remained silent, and the attendees were intrigued by Jorge's opening dialogue. Sensing all was well, Jorge continued, "You see, deep within the core of our beloved city resides a hidden danger. A killer lurks, and his trail leads straight into the barbarian community that surrounds us. But here's the thing: Stalin's sharp mind is necessary for us to unmask this menace."

Archibaldo steps forward, lending his expertise to Abella's plea.

"Abella's intuition is spot-on. Stalin's acute memory loss is our greatest obstacle to unravelling this mystery. But together, with Abella's unique abilities and Stalin's expertise, we can overcome the evil effects of Devil's Breath."

The Solidarity crew exchanged curious glances, their skepticism gradually turning into interest.

A passionate Abella said, "I have spent countless hours studying the human mind, creating techniques that enable someone like Stalin to regain his memories and retrieve the invaluable details his mind has locked away. Together, we can lead the charge in uncovering the truth that haunts him."

The room erupted in murmurs and whispers; a sea of contemplation and newfound hope was emerging. Stalin came to the front, still holding his rock in his hand, a habit that was proving hard to break.

"Abella, Archibaldo, your proposal resonates deep within me. If there's a slim chance of exposing the killer, we cannot ignore it. The collective expertise and passion you both bring are the answer I've been waiting for."

Now, slowly, all the attendees rose from their seats, one by one, showing their support and determination.

Abella, now showing teary eyes and with her shaking voice filled with gratitude, said, "Thank you, dear friends, for embracing this cause. Together, we will embark on a journey to unravel the truth and ensure the safety of our barbarian community. Let us unite our intellect, compassion, and unwavering dedication to justice."

The attendees burst into applause, the sound reverberating through my Central Hall, their shared enthusiasm echoing in everyone's hearts.

Motivated and united, the attendees discussed possible strategies, exchanged ideas, and formed alliances. An unstoppable force of intellect and determination began to take shape, ready to face the challenges ahead.

Stalin failed to see the newly springing gold dust appearing on his torso, and his smiling companion Archibaldo did not. He was sure his intuition would prove to be the catalyst in solving this cold case.

Both walked proudly and taller than either had dared hope for. Archibaldo reached into his pocket for his newly acquired police-issued Suzuki DR650 keys and mounted his recently manufactured mean machine. He looked at Stalin, who hated any form of motorcycle but did not wish to walk for the next eight hours back to his barrio. Reluctantly, Stalin mounted and threw his rock away. For the first time in decades, he believed his brain would become his best weapon.

*****

## 63: I am A Proud Derekamus and an itching to find out more Abella

The following day, after the Meetings of the Mind, Derekamus and Abella sat relaxing in Samuel and Sofia's front yard's enchanting garden. Both gnomes sat side by side on a moss-covered bench. Their bodies were resting, but their brains were not. The constant warm rays of the sun bathed the garden, casting a golden glow over the vibrant flowers and lush greenery. Yet today, the sun felt more intense than ever, causing both gnomes to feel rather uncomfortable.

As the scorching heat washed over them, Derekamus and Abella exchanged worried glances. Derekamus was quietly suffering from his elongated beard and red cloth-peaked hat, acting as sweatboxes. They both knew that gnomes, being creatures of the shade, were not built to withstand such blazing days. The thought of being left under the piercing sun without any respite made their tiny hearts flutter with anxiety. In moments like these, they silently prayed to Samuel and Sofia, their loving owners.

With their eyes closed and tiny hands clasped together, Derekamus and Abella sent their heartfelt pleas to the universe. They prayed that Samuel and Sofia would remember to move them to a cooler, shadier spot in the garden, away from the relentless sun. The words of their silent prayers resonated with deep longing and hope.

Meanwhile, above, the sun seemed to acknowledge their prayers, casting a sympathetic glow upon the gnomes. Yet, despite its warmth, the gnomes couldn't help but notice the gradual increase in heat over the past few weeks.

They whispered amongst themselves about the whispers they had heard in the streets—rumours of climate change threatening their beloved garden and way of life.

The ordinarily serene garden seemed imbued with a sense of urgency as if even the flowers and insects were aware of the shift in the world's balance. The gnomes, too, felt a deep concern for the changes around them.

But amidst their worries, Derekamus and Abella drew strength from their prayers. They believed in the power of their owners' love and understanding. Samuel and Sofia had always cared for their garden and its inhabitants, ensuring that each creature was provided for and protected.

As they sat in the garden, their tiny eyes reflecting resilience and determination, Derekamus and Abella knew that no matter how dire the threats of climate change may be, the bond between them and their owners would withstand any challenge. They hoped today would not be the day they would suffer without shade, and they trusted that Samuel and Sofia's love would guide them through the changing times.

*****

From my vantage point high above, I can see the two worried gnomes sitting on their moss-covered bench, their little faces etched with concern. They contemplate the changes they've noticed in their once-familiar habitat, not knowing the real cause behind them. The chatter of birds, once vivid, has diminished, and the gushing streams have now become mere trickles. The once-stable weather patterns have become erratic, leaving the gnomes uncertain about what each day will bring.

*****

Oh, how my presence looms over them, for I am climate change. I am the force that alters the delicate balance of this ecosystem, disrupting the harmony that these gnomes once cherished. They search for answers, desperate to find a way to preserve their beloved garden and the creatures that call it home.

As they look up at me, these innocent gnomes are witnesses to the devastating consequences of changing climates. They have seen the melting of the glaciers, the rising sea levels, and the scorching heat waves that threaten to destroy the world they know. With their tiny hearts burdened by the weight of the situation, they wonder what they can do and what actions they can take.

But alas, their small stature limits their impact. With their barbarian owners, they can only launch their limited efforts to protect their garden, planting saplings with hopes of restoring the diminishing greenery. They gather their fellow neighbours, rallying them to conserve water, reduce waste, and minimise their ecological footprint. These two gnomes, with the help of Samuel and Sofia, together with their determination and resourcefulness, fight against the insurmountable force of climate change.

From my perspective, I ponder humanity's choices and the massive influence they wield on the fate of the world. I watch as they debate, discuss, and sometimes ignore the warnings that I and the scientists have given. I see the colossal emissions, the reckless deforestation, and the insatiable hunger for finite resources. They hold the key to reversing the damage, yet their collective action falls short.

As I look down on the two worried gnomes, I cannot help but feel a pang of sorrow. They embody the innocent victims of mankind's actions, bearing the brunt of the choices made. I wish I could lift their worries, soothe their troubled hearts, and reassure them that a better future lies ahead.

For now, I have no choice but to continue my role as climate change, ever reminding humanity of the consequences of their actions. Perhaps, one day, they will listen and act urgently, halting the escalation of damage and healing the wounds inflicted upon the Earth. And maybe, just maybe, those two gnomes will witness the rejuvenation of their garden, a sign that the planet can be preserved for generations to come.

*****

An unforeseen calamity begins to unfold in the serene valley that houses Santiago de Cali. The mountain ridge that towered above Samuel and Sofia's peaceful abode became the unforgiving stage for nature's wrath.

*****

It began on the next clear summer evening, with the sun casting a warm glow over the tranquil landscape. Derekamus and Abella were lazing lazily on their moss-covered bench, basking in the soothing embrace of twilight. Samuel and Sofia, unaware of the fateful events about to unfold, revelled in the sweet harmony of their sanctuary, watching a musical documentary on their 54-inch plasma screen.

However, a sinister force stirred amidst the dry foliage that carpeted the mountainside above their home. A single spark, ignited by the extraordinary convergence of wind and heat, cast its malevolent glow upon the tinderbox of nature's creations.

The tiny ember danced erratically, eagerly leaping from one desiccated leaf to the next. A dormant menace awoke in seconds, clawing its way through the vegetation. The malicious whispers of the inferno grew louder and more fervent. A cruel gust of wind served as the orchestra, breathing life into the merciless flames.

As the fiery fiend rampaged on, its insatiable hunger engulfed everything in its path. The once gentle mountain ridge transformed into an ominous beast, roaring with fiery vengeance. The air filled with a pungent mélange of burning wood and suffocating smoke, choking the very essence of life.

*****

Derekamus, with his acute senses, was the first to detect the faint scent of danger. His instincts screamed at him, urging him to rally Abella, but how would he warn Samuel and Sofia to flee to safety? He barked urgently, praying his voice would echo far and wide through the valley. Blindly, he hoped to awaken Samuel and Sofia from their blissful viewing of the music they had loved to sing and dance with since their carefree days as teenagers.

But their television drowned out the desperate cry of their loyal garden gnome. Samuel and Sofia were blissfully unaware that their idyll was about to crumble into chaos. The ravenous wildfire devoured the landscape, inching closer to their beloved home with a voracity unmatched by any earthly force.

*****

The crackling of flames grew louder as if mocking the feeble escape attempts. The amber tongues of destruction greedily consumed the mountain ridge, painting the once-serene panorama in sinister hues of red and orange. It was a sight both breathtaking and terrifying, an unforgettable spectacle etched upon the annals of disaster. It was also the moment when Sofia, seeing the growing danger from the living room window, screamed.

Samuel flew up to meet the danger, trying to figure out what to expect. He was confident that he had never heard such a scream from her in all the years he had known Sofia.

As the wildfire surged onward, Samuel, with Derekamus in one hand, and Sofia, with Abella in her arms and guided by unwavering determination, embarked on a perilous journey away from their home and once tranquil garden. Together, all four traversed a treacherous landscape, filled with fear and uncertainty, in a desperate race against time to save themselves from the unyielding wrath of nature's relentless flames.

*****

Samuel's heart raced with adrenaline as the emergency sirens blared in the distance. Clutching his precious Derekamus tightly in one hand, he rushed towards the front door of their house. Sofia, carrying their beloved Abella in her arms, followed closely behind.

The air was filled with urgency as they stepped outside onto their long driveway. The gravel crunched beneath their feet as they hurried towards their gleaming Kenworth burgundy truck parked further down the driveway, its powerful engine humming expectantly.

Samuel's eyes were fixed ahead, scanning the surroundings for signs of danger. Sofia's voice trembled, filled with fear and a hint of determination, as she encouraged Abella to hold on tight.

With each step, the distance between them and the safety of their truck grew shorter. Cool gusts of wind tugged at their clothes as if urging them to move faster. Samuel clenched his free hand tightly, feeling Derekamus's weight, providing him with comfort and hope amidst the chaotic situation.

Emergency vehicles' red and blue lights flashed ominously in the distance, casting an eerie glow over the scene. The urgency of their escape fueled their every movement as they neared the Kenworth truck.

Finally, they reached their escape vehicle, its sturdy frame a beacon of reassurance. Samuel quickly unlocked the doors, allowing Sofia to carefully settle Abella into the safety of her cargo chest, sitting behind Sofia's seat. Derekamus peeked out from the pocket of Samuel's jacket, his little ceramic eyes glinting in the dim light.

*****

Samuel and Sofia swiftly buckled themselves in with the engine rumbling to life, ensuring their safety. The truck roared into action, tyres gripping the gravel driveway. The engine's vibration reverberated through their bodies, a tangible reminder of their path to freedom.

As they zoomed away from their house, Samuel glanced back at the fading silhouette of their home. The moment's gravity sank in, but he knew they had made the right choice. Their precious cargo was safe.

Samuel, Sofia, Abella, and Derekamus embarked on their journey to safety, leaving behind the chaos and uncertainty. The wind howled outside, but within the Kenworth truck, there was a sense of relief and strength.

*****

The flames danced and flickered as the wildfire raged on, consuming everything in their path with an insatiable hunger. The fire began to crawl up the walls of Samuel and Sofia's home, licking at the wooden beams and devouring the terracotta slate-tiled roof. Smoke billowed into the air, forming a thick, suffocating haze.

Step by step, the fire continued its destructive path. It consumed the furniture, the walls, and the cherished belongings, reducing them to mere ashes. The fire shattered windows, sending shards of glass flying into the growing inferno. The intense heat cracked the tiles and caused the foundation to tremble under its wrath.

As the wildfire roared, firefighters battled tirelessly against the blaze. They fought bravely, directing water hoses and creating firebreaks to contain the fire's advance. With their skill and determination, they managed to prevent the destruction from spreading further, ultimately gaining control over the flames.

*****

The following afternoon, a sombre atmosphere hung heavy in the air as Samuel and Sofia cautiously returned to what remained of their home. They were accompanied by Abella and Derekamus, who they had left on the running board below Sanuel's truck door. The gnomes sat waiting anxiously for the homeowners to return.

As Samuel and Sofia approached the charred remains, they were greeted with a heartbreaking sight. Blackened and twisted debris lay scattered across their property, only recognisable as fragments of what was once their home. The air still carried the acrid scent of smoke, a constant reminder of the devastation.

Samuel and Sofia stood in silence, their eyes filling with tears as they surveyed the ruins. Their hearts ached for the lost memories, the irreplaceable mementoes that had now turned ash. Derekamus and Abella watched, their tiny faces etched with empathy and sadness.

With heavy hearts, the owners and the gnomes began sifting through the rubble. Despite the destruction, glimmers of hope emerged as they discovered small fragments of belongings that miraculously survived the fire's wrath.

Among the ashes, they found a ceramic vase and a faded photograph of a wedding group consisting of the happy couple, their parents, and grandparents, now blackened at the edges but still recognisable. Sofia broke down and sobbed at seeing themselves. Ignacio and Jasmina were on one side closest to Samuel, and Petro and Margarita stood proudly as punch next to their daughter.

Together, they salvaged what items they could, carefully gathering them in a small pile. It was a vivid reminder of the resilience and strength they shared as a couple, even in the face of overwhelming loss. As they slowly walked away from the remnants of their home, they vowed to rebuild and create new memories, knowing Derekamus and Abella would be by their side every step of the way.

For the time being, all four moved into a furnished apartment rented on the city's outskirts, as far away as possible from where the wildfire had struck. Derekamus and Abella now sat on the steps of the apartment block near tall palms that acted as barriers to the intensity of the sun's probing rays.

Samuel and Sofia were often away from the apartment, but the neighbours closely watched them. One is a smallish Colombiana named Cristirin. She is married to a tallish white-haired man with solid legs and a pot belly.

Sometimes, their three adorable cats lay together in the shade of the palm trees and acted as company for Abella and Derekamus. One evening, Derekamus raised a question that bothered him: "Abella, that older cat with his shiny black coat and white socks, is he the one who suddenly visited us three years before the floods started? And am I right, you showered him with some of your magic gold dust."

"Yes, my love, he is indeed Blacky. The two kittens are Liz and Goldie. They all live on the top floor in a penthouse with a huge balcony. But having the apartment facing south means the rooms become a furnace, and the felines have resorted to coming here each day to rest from the penetrating sun. The security man, Alberto, has a constant beady eye on all three of them, and they appear to love the attention they often receive from the old uniformed rascal.

Derekamus took a deep breath and whispered to his beloved Abella, "Please answer another question I have waited to ask you for nearly 250 years. Why do you have the power to scatter gold dust and change a recipient's life, and I do not?"

Abella smiles lovingly toward her husband, "You silly old fool, how come it has taken you all this time to ask me such a question? Never mind, let me reveal all to you."

Looking deep into the cloudless sky, Abella begins to explain why she alone possesses the enchanting ability to scatter gold dust and change the lives of those who receive it. "My magic derives from the ancient and mystical energy of the sacred Glimmering Springs deep within the heart of the enchanted forest."

Derekamus settled down on the first step leading to the apartment block and, still missing, the destroyed moss-covered bench. Well, to be precise, his bottom does.

"The Glimmering Springs are believed to be a convergence of ley lines and natural magic and hold potent and transformative powers. My connection to these mystical waters grants me the unique ability to transmute the essence of the springs into shimmering gold dust. This dust holds within it the potential to bring prosperity, fortune, and blessings to those it touches.

As for you, Derekamus, you do not share the same magical powers as me. Despite our deep bond, our magical abilities are not identical. In our gnome community, supernatural powers are not distributed uniformly among everyone.

While some gnomes possess the gift of elemental manipulation, like I do, others may have talents in healing, divination, or crafting."

Abella sensed that she should go deeper in her explanation to not hurt her darling husband's feelings. "Derekamus, although you lack magical abilities, you are my supportive and loving life partner. Despite being unable to scatter gold dust like me, you compensate for it through your limitless practical skills and steadfast wisdom. For over two centuries, we have formed a harmonious balance that strengthens our relationship and the joy we bring to others."

Derekamus bear-hugged Abella with all the strength he could muster. "Darling, I will never know why I delayed asking such a question; your answer has been a joy to hear."

That is because I understand the uniqueness of my magical gift and cherish the opportunity it gives me to bring happiness and change lives. With our loving hearts and benevolent spirits, we will continue using my gold dust gift to make the world a brighter place, one sprinkle at a time.

*****

Later that evening, when the sun had finally settled for the night and a welcoming breeze had arrived from the Pacific coast, Abella turned to a subject that needed the itch to solve it.

"Going back in our past, do you remember Derekamus when we lived in those grand gardens belonging to an old woman named Clara?"

Derekamus thought profoundly and, after a moment or two, a memory of a dreadful night in Berlin during the Second World War. "Are you thinking of the night the Allies bombed Berlin to within an inch of its existence?"

"Yes, I do; why do you ask?" Derekamus asked, slowly increasing his interest in where his wife was heading with her memories.

"Have you ever wondered what happened to the doctor dressed in a black SS uniform with his three clearly distressed daughters?"

Derekamus had another sudden memory, "I vaguely recall this father had sworn an oath from his three little girls to the fact his wife had perished in the house fire caused by a direct hit from a massive incendiary bomb. Why do you ask?"

"Well, the girl's mother was the younger sister to Clara, who sold us after the war to raise funds for her to continue living in war-torn West Germany and not in East Germany."

Derekamus looked directly towards his wife, "Really, what has triggered your questions? Is it the oath you gave to Archibaldo and Stalin at the Museo Aereo Fenix a short while ago?"

Abella sat down and stretched out her legs, "No, I was more than happy to oblige that unfortunate man with his awful sense of dress and lack of long-term memory. No, it is because of something I heard about that terrible night in Berlin. Something I never thought I would recall in a lifetime. And before you ask, I overheard the three sisters talking, and the older one swore the other younger two to a lifetime of getting their revenge for their mother's execution by their father."

Derekamus took a prolonged intake of breath and walked the block to think of what his wife had revealed. He knew she was not lying; gnomes never lie. However, his reasoning could not add Berlin in 1945 to South America in 2024. The trouble for Derekamus was whenever Abella got an itch to find out something that troubled her: watch out if you are a killer. Because her itch will bring you down.

*****

# 64: I am a Team of Fire Fighters who are tested to their limits

Fire Chief Eduardo, known as the Master, is a seasoned and respected figure sitting at his desk with Assistant Chief Carmen, nicknamed Wolf, and Battalion Chief Tomas, often called the Strong One. The room is alive with the sounds of the Executive Management Team and support administrators preparing for their shifts. The Master, holding a mug of coffee, speaks up.

"Good morning, everyone. I trust you all had a restful 48 hours off duty." Then, turning to face Carmen and Tomas, Eduardo says, "I'm eager to hear how you spent your time."

Wolf replies first, "Morning, Master. I managed to catch up on some much-needed sleep. But I also spent a reasonable amount of time online with my kids. I say kids, but since Elsie moved to Medellin to study Zoology and Jacob flew over to Miami to pursue a career as a drummer in an up-and-coming indie band, they are fast-growing and developing into young adults. Last month, they both had spent their summer breaks in Paris with their father and his partner Pierre. It was refreshing and reminded me of the importance of being close to my family."

Strong One was next to greet his boss, "Morning, Chief. Sara took the time to vacate our apartment, but at least it was done amicably; our separation is still a sore point for us both, and hopefully, after time, we will find a way to reach out to each other again. Her unexpected promotion from bank manager to corporate liaison manager in Bogota, with its attractive relocation package and increased pension, meant we, a couple with no children to worry about and only our four dogs, could not ignore it. She plans to move into a company-paid apartment and fly back to me every weekend when I am not on shift. So, for now, I spent the rest of my two days of rest, working on a personal project – renovating an old motorcycle. It's always been a passion of mine, and it was therapeutic to devote some time to it. Later, I also managed to take the dogs to my parent's place a couple of blocks away and catch up with my mum and dad over dinner."

Master nodded warmly to both his most trusted team, "That sounds like a rejuvenating break for both of you. Maintaining a healthy work-life balance during huge shifts in your lives is essential in our line of duty. I am sure Carmen, with your tenacity, will be fine, and the same goes for you, Tomas, and Sara. Now, who's going to make the first cup of coffee? It's my duty as tradition goes, but a little help is always appreciated."

Wolf laughed mischievously, "Master, it's your honour and privilege to make that first cup of coffee. No need to worry; I'll take care of it. Consider it a token of appreciation for everything you do for us."

A strong one followed by more mischief: "Absolutely, Master. Wolf has got it covered this time. We all know how much this tiny ritual means to you. It's important to share the responsibility, show gratitude, and enjoy a perfect coffee occasionally."

The Master reclined back in his chair with a look of mock horror on his face, "Enjoy a cup of perfect coffee! You both know I am the Master of coffee making!"

Wolf kept the banter going, "Yes, but you most definitely are not the tidiest of coffee makers. Just ask your wife, Maria."

Now laughing out loud, the Master responded, "Please do not mention my morning coffee ritual to Maria. She thinks I have reduced my caffeine intake. She will be livid if she finds out; I still love my morning coffee."

All three start laughing at their Master's self-imposed predicament.

"Thank you both, Carmen and Tomas. I'm fortunate to have such dedicated and supportive team members. It warms my heart to know that even the smallest gestures, like making that first cup of coffee, are valued."

Tomas turned to Carmen, "See how grovelling our Master becomes when we mention Maria!"

Wolf gets up from his seat and heads, laughing, towards the kitchenette to prepare the coffee while Strong One and the Master exchange appreciative glances. The fire station hums with the anticipation of another day, built on camaraderie and mutual respect.

*****

Next on their agenda for the week were the following administrative tasks for the Fire Chief:

1. Conducting yearly appraisals for each firefighter: The Master had scheduled all necessary interviews to complete the appraisals. His secretary ensured sufficient time for each interview and prepared relevant appraisal forms and supporting documents.

For the Assistant Chief:

2. Analysing historical incident data: Wolf must analyse a month's data. This analysis would involve tracking patterns and identifying any areas of concern, particularly regarding the upcoming seasonal threat of wildfires. Wolf's Administrator had provided the data required to ensure Carmen had access to the appropriate tools and software for analysis.

For the Battalion Chief:

3. Tomas's focus was the "Fire equipment auditing and ordering:" The strong one is responsible for a week's worth of fire equipment auditing and ordering. His focus was to identify any shortages in equipment and place orders accordingly.

Tomas turned to his designated support administrator and requested, "Please provide me with last week's completed Equipment checklist and the monthly inventory list so that I can conduct the audit effectively."

Tomas's helper was always someone he could rely on, "Yes, sir, I have everything here waiting for you, and I will place it all on your desk in five minutes."

Showing his appreciation for Yuli's work ethic and dedication, "Thank you, Yuli; I have no idea what I would do without you."

The final topic of discussion was not included on the agenda to end the weekly meeting. The Master raised an important question regarding the house fire with a dead unidentified person in its cellar. "I have not heard yet from my contacts in the Police Department, and I have not seen the logs for the last couple of shifts, so I was wondering if, anywhere in the city, there have been any more reports of house fires with potential fatalities involved?"

Wolf, who had reviewed the operational logs before the meeting, provided reassuring news that there were no reported deaths in any of the 45 emergency calls attended to by Alpha 1 or Alpha 2. She had requested an update from the other stations dotted in and around the city but had yet to receive the data. Wolf further mentioned that most calls accepted by Alpha 1 and Alpha 2 during the past week were less severe, as pointed out by Engineer/Driver Luis Gonzales, who often referred to them as "silly."

*****

Fire Chief Eduardo did not mention his meeting with Stalin as he wished to control any information from any source. The fact that Stalin was a street man with no memory would raise many a questionable stare with this unlikeliest of friendships.

Later this same morning, he had a scheduled meeting with the Coroner's office to shade hopefully a primary cause of death to the unknown victim and whether the fire contributed to his or her death.

*****

The first coffee of the day arrives, and Wolf turns to the Master, "Please sample this perfect cup of coffee and tell us your thoughts."

Eduardo refocuses his thoughts and does as he has been requested: He sips the piping-hot black liquid and swallows. His colleagues look on, knowing he will find a way to surpass his weekly description of what a perfect coffee is for him.

"Let me introduce the perfect cup of coffee as brewed, crafted exclusively for none other than myself, the fire chief who fights fires by day and craves a cup of liquid courage by night! This concoction delivers a fiery burst of flavour to match my fearless spirit."

He is standing in an imaginary politician stance with his cup out front. "Picture this: a robust blend of beans carefully selected from exotic volcanic regions and the sunny slopes of the Andes. These beans have withstood the scorching heat of the earth itself, creating a coffee so intense and determined that it could march right into battle alongside our devoted fire crews."

Wolf and the Strong One clearly saw that The Master was on a roll that day. They had no idea where he was going with this oratory, but they knew it would be entertaining.

"The brewing process is a spectacle in its own right. As soon as Wolf pours the boiling water into the French press, a mini pyrotechnic display erupts, resembling a controlled wildfire dancing passionately before our eyes. The aroma that fills the room is like a freshly extinguished blaze, smoky and powerful, mingling with undertones of bravery and heroism.

But the real magic lies in the cup itself. As I take that first bold sip, a surge of energy courses through my body, much like the adrenaline during a high-stakes rescue mission. The coffee hits my taste buds with an intensity that commands attention, leaving a lingering warmth that feels like a firefighter's embrace after a long day of battling a blaze.

And let's not forget the special ingredient – the brew features a sprinkle of cinnamon sparks, embracing the drink with a hint of sweetness and a subtle spark of excitement. Every sip touches the playful flames that dance within my heart."

Both Wolf and the Strong One could clearly see their Master was surpassing all previous orations and started to clap in appreciation. But the Master had not been finished just yet.

"Whether sipped in the firehouse or savoured during a well-deserved break, the perfect coffee brew is my ideal companion. Each sip fuels my determination, energises my spirit, and reminds me of the bravery that lies within my heart that beats beneath my fire helmet.

So, I raise my mug high and let the brew fuel my soul as I conquer the world, one blazing cup at a time!"

*****

Downstairs, they could hear the uproar of appreciation at the weekly meeting of the Station Executive Management. Alpha 1 and 2's fire crews instinctively knew their Master had surpassed his usual description of what made a cup of perfect coffee.

*****

Alpha 1's team leader, Lieutenant Javier Blanco, commonly known as Whitey: "Hey, team, good to see you all. How's everyone doing?"

"Hey, Lieutenant, we're doing great. It's just another day on the frigging job," Half-moaned Churches, alias Ana.

Highlander, aka Silvana, with a spanner in one hand and handbook for the fire engine in the other: "Speak for yourself, Ana; I had the most exhilarating trip to Rio Crystals with my motorcycle gang over the weekend. You should have seen the stunning views and the adrenaline rush!"

Churches respond with, "That sounds awesome, Highlander. You always have the most exciting adventures with your buddies on your frigging days off."

Both Highlander and Whitey ignore Churches foul language; they have worked with her for a long time and know she means nothing by her foul vocabulary.

Whitey did say to Churches, "Ana, I am sure you were never brought up. Instead, you must have been dragged up!"

Alejandro, affectionately known as Marine, approached to ask a question: "Yeah, I bet it was a wild ride. Did you encounter any challenges along the way?"

Highlander turned to the Marine: "Oh, you have no idea. We faced some intense off-road terrain and unpredictable weather conditions, and I must admit my extended twin forks did not help with the fair number of potholes we had to navigate. But you know me, I love a good challenge."

Davide, the probationer nicknamed Village from day one, says, "Wow, Highlander, that's incredible! I can't wait to join you on one of your trips once I have more motorcycle experience."

Whitey spoke reassuringly, "Don't worry, Village. You'll get your chance soon enough. But remember, there is a massive difference between riding a typical 125 cc Moto and a 1200 cc touring motorbike like our dependable Highlander enjoys on her days off from the station."

Highlander is pleased with Whitey's confirmation of the lack of experience the somewhat over-ambitious new rookie is displaying, "Absolutely, Village. When you're ready, we'll ensure you have the time of your life. But for now, remember that the small engine on your Moto is superb for your city commute and covers the short recreational riding style. In contrast, the beasts I ride have the upper weight and sizes to make long-distance touring comfortable and, dare I say it, easy on my ass."

Ana suddenly had a question on her mind and could not hold it back: "Err, Lieutenant, how are your wedding plans going? Are you still going to wear white and upstage the poor frigging bride?"

Whitey took a pause to figure out how to respond to Ana's choice of words, he knew he should not ignore them, but he would have to address them at some point through the shift. "Ah heck, let's do it now", he thought to himself.

"Churches, thank you for your interest in my wedding apparel. Yes, my shoes have been selected, and yes, they will be white. My suit has been measured, and my socks and tie have been reserved."

Ana had not finished her questioning, "Are you going to wear a frigging white top hat?"

Whitey had not thought of a top hat. He had no idea where he could purchase one. He would have to Google search later during a break. "No, Ana, I have not yet made up my mind whether I need to have a white top hat. and also, please do not refer to my future bride as frigging; her name is Lucia."

Ana responded with, "Whatever."

Whitey now aware that time was pressing on, "Alright, enough about your adventures, Highlander and definitely less from you Churches. Let's focus on the task at hand. We've got a lot to accomplish today."

Churches now slightly bored with the world of motorcycles, "Whitey's right. We've got a job to do, so let's get to it."

Marine agreed and joked, "Let's saddle up and hit the road, team."

Knowing he was with the best team in the firefighting world, Village said, "I'm ready to learn from the best. Let's do this!

Pleased with how the day started, Whitely spoke as he moved towards the fire engine's open door: "That's the spirit, team. Let's show them what we're made of. Stay vigilant and stay safe out there."

*****

With that said, Highlander turned the ignition of the Alpha One fire engine and sounded its warning klaxon, saying that it was about to exit the fire station. So began their first adventurous duty for the day: visiting a local school to give them a pep talk about wildfires and how to avoid them.

As the fire engine began to turn towards the local school, everyone inside heard a muttering coming from Ana, "Frigging kids, I frigging hate kids." No one responded or asked why. Even if they did, they are confident Ana had no idea why or if she actually hated kids.

*****

Alpha 2 was next to meet up. Fire Captain Valeria, known as Mars, stood in the firehouse, ready to greet her team back from their 48 hours of rest. As they entered the room one by one, she couldn't help but let out a small chuckle at the sight before her.

"Welcome back, Alpha 2!" Mars exclaimed, her voice filled with warmth and a hint of amusement. "It looks like some of you had quite the eventful weekend."

As usual, Luis sported oily stains on his work shirt, fireproof pants, and even a smudge on his forehead that he seemed utterly unaware of. Mars raised an eyebrow but decided to let it slide for now, knowing that his dedication to the team outweighed his occasional fashion mishaps.

"How is Constantine and your amazing brood of ten kids?"

Luis uttered only one word in answer, "Expensive."

Next up was Mateo, affectionately known as Blondie due to his golden locks. It was clear that he had spent most of his weekend restoring his roots, as his hair was impeccable and highlighted his boyish charm. Mars couldn't help but tease him a bit, saying, "Did you spend half of your weekend at the salon, Blondie? Looking sharp!"

Standing behind Mateo was the towering figure of Santiago Delgado, the Thin Man, as they called him, due to his extraordinary height. With his slender frame and calm demeanour, he was a constant source of intrigue for the team. Mars nodded at him approvingly, acknowledging his presence without saying a word.

The Thin Man, apart from the times he could be seen racing up the mountain ridge on his bicycle with Mateo on his racer, was also well known for his love of fly fishing. Mars knew how much he loved spending his weekends by the creek, patiently casting his line and enjoying the tranquil surroundings. "Hope you caught some big ones this time, Santiago," she said with a smile.

As the team settled in, Mars knew they were ready for whatever challenges awaited them. Each member brought his or her unique quirks and strengths to the group, making them a formidable force. She couldn't help but feel a sense of pride in leading such a diverse and dedicated team like Alpha 2.

Alpha 2's first duty of the day was dropping leaflets to all the shops and offices that made up the Chipichape shopping mall. Today's message on the leaflet was what to do in case of a wildfire. Luis, on reading the booklet, muttered," All this should be common sense."

*****

**Wildfire Safety Awareness**
Stay Safe, Stay Smart:
What to Do When Confronted by a Wildfire
Thank you for taking the time to read this leaflet. Your safety is our top priority, and we appreciate your cooperation as we raise awareness about wildfire safety. Here are some essential tips on how to protect yourself and your loved ones in the event of a wildfire.

**Section 1: Preparation**
1. Be Informed:
Stay informed about fire risk levels and the latest weather conditions in your area.
Follow your local authorities and fire department updates for any evacuation orders or warnings.
2. Create an Emergency Plan:
Plan and practice your family's evacuation route in advance.
Identify a designated meeting point outside the affected area.
Make sure everyone in your household knows what to do and where to go.
3. Pack an Emergency Kit:
Prepare a readily accessible emergency kit with essential supplies, including water, non-perishable food, medication, a first aid kit, and important documents.

**Section 2: During a Wildfire**
1. Alert Authorities:
Immediately call emergency services to report the fire.
Provide clear information about the fire's location and size.
2. Evacuate, if Instructed:
Follow evacuation orders from authorities without delay.
Leave your home promptly and avoid returning until it is safe to do so.
3. Protect Yourself:
If trapped or unable to evacuate, seek shelter in a building, ideally with multiple exits, away from windows and outside walls.
Close windows and doors to prevent smoke from entering.
Stay low to reduce smoke inhalation and protect the air passages in your nose and mouth with a wet cloth.

On the reverse side of the leaflet, the following text could be read with the backdrop of a forest on fire.
**Section 3: After a Wildfire**
1. Contact Your Loved Ones:
Inform your family and close friends that you are safe and provide them with your location.
Register in local emergency systems to receive alerts and updates.
2. Assess and Report Damage:
Once it is deemed safe, assess your property for damage and report it to the appropriate authorities.
Take photographs and video footage of any damage for insurance purposes.
3. Stay Vigilant:
Be aware of potential hazards and dangers such as falling trees, downed power lines, or unstable structures.
Follow official instructions when returning home and prioritise personal safety.
Remember, knowledge is power when dealing with wildfires. Stay informed, be prepared, and act promptly. Your safety and the safety of your community is vital. Please contact your local fire department if you require assistance or any additional information.
Stay Safe, Stay Smart!

*****

Zamira Flores, a skilled and dedicated operator, held a leadership position in her ops room at the fire station. With her sharp mind and calm demeanour, she had become a respected figure with the Executive Management Team and among her colleagues. Tasked with coordinating emergency response efforts, Zamira's day-to-day work revolved around ensuring the safety of her city's residents in times of crisis.

On this sweltering summer day, Zamira glanced at the latest weather report. A familiar feeling of concern washed over her. The report showcased an alarming temperature increase, with an approaching heat wave that seemed to be headed straight for her beloved city nestled below the mountain ridge. The magnitude of the situation became more apparent as she read further, noting the rising risk of wildfires due to the intense heat.

Knowing the potential devastation that wildfires could bring, Zamira couldn't help but feel a pang of worry. Her mind raced with thoughts of the vulnerable communities scattered on the city's outskirts, closer to the dense forests and dry wilderness. The notion of families, homes, and livelihoods being at the mercy of nature's fury weighed heavily on her heart.

Zamira understood the urgency of the situation and its potential for catastrophe. She knew that she had to take immediate action to mitigate the risks and ensure her team was prepared for what lay ahead. Rallying the fire station personnel, she called for an emergency meeting, emphasising the importance of being one step ahead of the impending crisis. The Master, Wolf, and The Strong One responded to her concerns and stopped what they were individually dealing with to head to the office Zamira and two of her three operatives were already occupying. Each had come to trust Zamira's instincts, and she would not often call such an impromptu meeting.

*****

During the meeting, Zamira shared the latest weather report and highlighted the growing threats posed by the heat wave. She stressed the urgency of being proactive in their response and started discussions on strategies to increase fire prevention measures and enhance community awareness about fire safety protocols.

As the meeting progressed, Eduardo initiated coordination efforts with neighbouring fire stations, reaching out to their counterparts to ensure a united front against the impending threat. Recognising the significance of real-time information, Carmen also liaised with meteorological agencies, establishing a direct communication channel that would keep her, and Zamira updated on any changes or risks that the heat wave might bring.

While concern etched across their faces, everyone present showed their joint determination and professionalism, remaining steadfast. As a team, all would tirelessly work to a well-tried and tested plan, prepare, and execute strategies to minimise potential wildfires' impact. With the support of Zamira's capable team, everyone present embarked on a mission to safeguard their city and its inhabitants, ensuring that they were ready to face the trials ahead.

Zamira's dedication to her role, foresight, and ability to inspire confidence made her an invaluable asset to her city and its people. As the increasing heat wave loomed closer, she remained resolute in her commitment to protecting her community from the fiery threats that nature had in store. Eduardo, looking at Zamira, thought silently, "Climate change, you have picked the wrong person to have a fight with."

With that thought still in his head, he returned to his office and rang the Forensic Examiner's office.

*****

Hola. My name is Zamira, and I am the leading operator in the fire emergency operations room. I have three more operators on the same shift as I am today. I am sitting at my desk, attentively monitoring the incoming calls. The room, as always, is filled with anticipation as we prepare for any potential emergencies that may arise.

Glancing at the call log, I note that Alpha 1 is currently engaged in a vital outreach activity at the local school, educating children about wildfire safety. Meanwhile, Alpha 2, our ladder truck, is stationed at Chipichape, the bustling shopping mall, distributing informative leaflets to the public.

With the day starting quietly, I watch the phone lines and radio communications, prepared to react immediately if any urgent situations emerge. Although there are no signs of trouble, our well-trained firefighters are always on standby, ready to respond to any significant or minor emergency.

In the meantime, I ensured that all the necessary equipment and resources were readily available, organised, and in working condition, should they be needed. I maintained constant communication with Alpha 1 and Alpha 2, ensuring that they were aware of the situation and ready to respond if the need arose.

It is crucial to remain focused and prepared even during these calm periods, as emergencies can occur at any time. As the leading operator, it is my responsibility to stay vigilant and be ready to coordinate the appropriate response team if a call for assistance comes in.

It was not long before my demeanour would be challenged as I read the weather report for today on my screen.

*****

**Weather Report: Urgent Wildfire Warning**
Attention All Fire Station Personnel,
I bring to your immediate attention an urgent weather update regarding the potentially dangerous conditions that are expected to prevail over the mountain ridge overlooking our city. A severe heat wave is gripping our region, resulting in exceptionally high temperatures. This has created a highly combustible environment that poses a significant risk of wildfires. The prolonged period of heat and dryness, coupled with gusty winds, has elevated the fire danger levels to critical.

**Forecasted Weather Conditions:**
1. The temperature is expected to reach record-breaking highs on your mountain ridge and surrounding areas. Readings are predicted to exceed 38°F. The searing heat will further exacerbate vegetation's vulnerability.
2. Unfortunately, humidity levels are projected to remain extremely low, plunging to single-digit percentages. These arid conditions and the relentless heat will make the vegetation prone to rapid ignition.

3. Strong and erratic winds are forecasted to sweep through the area, adding an additional element of danger to the already precarious circumstances. Wind gusts may reach 20 – 40 mph, potentially causing fire spread and making containment efforts more challenging.

**Potential Risks:**

1. Given the extreme weather conditions, the probability of wildfires igniting and rapidly spreading across your mountain ridge is significantly heightened. Fires may emerge from natural causes, such as lightning strikes, or be caused by human activity.

2. In a wildfire outbreak, thick smoke will likely blanket your city below, posing significant health risks. The smoke may reduce visibility, hamper response efforts and potentially cause respiratory issues for individuals with preexisting conditions.

3. Depending on the intensity and direction of the fire, evacuation measures may need to be considered to ensure your safety and well-being while living near your mountain ridge. It is vital to prioritise the dissemination of information and activate emergency response plans promptly.

**Preventive Measures and Preparedness:**

1. Deploy additional teams to conduct regular patrols along your mountain ridge. Swift identification and early detection of any potential outbreaks will be critical in mitigating the risks.

2. Establish seamless coordination with the city authorities, such as local law enforcement, emergency services, and other fire stations. Clear communication channels will enhance situational awareness and facilitate the synchronisation of efforts should an emergency arise.

3. Work closely with local media outlets to disseminate timely wildfire safety information. Educating the public about the risks, precautionary measures, and emergency protocols will help prevent the accidental ignition of fires and promote responsible behaviour during this critical period.

Please take immediate action to respond to this wildfire warning. Your preparedness, dedication, and efficient response will be instrumental in safeguarding your city, the surrounding areas, and its residents.

Stay vigilant, prepare for potential challenges, and ensure everyone's safety.

Best regards,

The Weather Station Management Team, Bogotá.

*****

I forwarded the above weather warning report to all personnel, the police station, and local hospitals. While I was sending a copy as an attachment to the

Mayor's office, my ears pricked up at the next emergency call that started to come in from a worried eyewitness high up on the mountain ridge......

*****

Before you hear what the eyewitness reported, I, Climate Change, should give you an accurate account of what happened because of me.

In the heart of the peaceful mountain ridge, nestled within a small field occupied by two grazing cows, one black and white, and the other more docile looking brown and white. The tranquil setting was abruptly shattered by the spark that ignited a wildfire.

*****

As daylight shone brightly, a subtle breeze danced through the tall grasses, whispering echoes of a change approaching. A small ember flickered into existence, a tiny flame taking form. The morning air carried with it a sense of caution, unknowingly gearing up for what was to come.

The black and white cow, known affectionately as Clary, lifted her head and noticed the flickering glow atop a nearby bush. Curiosity mingled with a hint of concern as she nudged her sister Marta, the brown and white cow. Clary conveyed an unspoken sense of danger. Marta, not being one to ever be watchful, turned her gentle gaze toward the shimmering ember, her instincts alerting her slowly to the potential threat.

With a sudden gust of wind, the wayward ember was set free and carried across the field on a chaotic journey. Igniting a bed of dry, crackling vegetation, it began a ferocious dance between flames and nature.

Initially contained within a small area, the fire danced playfully along the surface, its orange hues flickering brightly against the blue sky.

As the wind carried the flames higher and faster, a chain reaction began, engulfing more vegetation with each passing second. Brilliant tongues of fire leapt from plant to plant, hungrily consuming the dry foliage, setting the stage for an ominous spectacle on the ridge.

Clary and Marta, now fully aware of the advancing danger, retreated to a safer distance, their presence blessedly unhindered by the approaching destruction. Standing together in unity, both cows were observed wide-eyed as the wildfire increased. Flames roared triumphantly, tearing through the parched grass and thick undergrowth, transforming the serene landscape into a fiery battleground.

The wall of flames presented a mesmerising yet terrifying sight from a distance. The mountain ridge became intertwined with a vivid tapestry of red and orange as plumes of black smoke rose skyward, capturing the city's attention below.

The glow could be seen from miles away, a captivating but dangerous spectacle of nature's might.

However, let it be known that amidst the chaos I have created, the two resilient cows found refuge in a verdant clearing far from the path of destruction. I am not angry with these two bovines; my wrath is for the barbarians who have failed to heed my warnings over the past twenty-odd years. While the wildfire ravaged the mountain ridge, the innocent cows' lives remained untouched by harm, allowing you to breathe a sigh of relief within this tale. Okay, back to your eyewitness...

*****

As the leading operator in the emergency operations centre, I took immediate action upon receiving the distressing call from a concerned farmer identifying himself as Alberto, the parent of a twelve-year-old boy named Julian. They were together on the craggy road halfway up the mountain ridge.

As I was responding to Alberto's description, I saw my colleagues ensuring that our fire crews were notified and ready for dispatch. I heard the strain in their voices as they alerted Alpha 1 and Alpha 2 about the urgency of the situation, emphasising the potential threat to surrounding properties and the city below. Given the nature of the blaze involving cows, I asked Alberto if additional personnel with experience in animal rescue was necessary. He said no, as he only had two cows called Clary and Marta to rescue, and he had already done that.

In adversity, it is incredible how something as mundane as moving two cows out of danger can, in special circumstances, be a heroic act.

Simultaneously, I gathered as much information as possible from Alberto to understand the exact location and severity of the fire. This helped us determine the resources and equipment needed at the scene. Additionally, I asked if either Alberto or Julian were injured or in immediate danger, emphasising the importance of their safety.

Next, I received a note recording the time that Alpha 1 was assigned to proceed to the scene as quickly as possible while updating them with real-time information about the situation en route. Their primary objectives would be to contain and extinguish the fire while ensuring the safety of Alberto, Julian, and the family collie.

Given the potential danger to surrounding properties and the city below, I also instructed my colleagues to coordinate with neighbouring fire stations for additional support to be put on standby. This backup, if deployed, would enable us to manage the situation effectively and prevent the fire from spreading further. We hoped.

Throughout the early stages of the operation, we maintained constant communication with Alpha 1. We relayed progress updates on the fire engine's ETA to the distressed Julian and his stoic father, Alberto. This helped alleviate their concerns and ensured they had the necessary information to make informed decisions.

Once Alpha 1 arrived at the scene, Lieutenant Blanco established a command centre and assessed the situation to develop a strategy for containment and evacuation. If necessary, the Alpha 1 fire crew would offer exceptional care to ensure the safety and well-being of the two cows and provide any required medical assistance to injured individuals.

Whitey could not contain himself in sending Churches to check on the cows. I cannot write exactly the expletives she responded with, but I can assure you there were many, some of which I have never heard. Even Alberto, a campesino of close to 90 years of age, had signs of redness in his cheeks!

*****

In a typical situation, after the fire is extinguished and the problem is under control, I would conduct a debrief with the crew, assessing the effectiveness of our response and identifying any areas for improvement. This information would be used to enhance our protocols and procedures for future incidents, ensuring the community's and its residents' safety.

Sadly, I had no choice but to put that on hold. Highlander reported on her radio that a burgundy Kenworth truck with a husband and wife driver team identified as Samuel and Sofia Perez was now stopped in the middle of the road, informing us their house had gone up in smoke after another wildfire had broken out further up the old craggy road near their local pueblo.

My ops team sprang into action and deployed Alpha 2 to respond quickly. It would be another 45 minutes before they were on the scene. What they met that day would haunt their memories for the rest of their lives.

The Strong One silently listened to the commentary before us in the ops room. In his hands was a yellow Post-it notepad. As the scenario ensued, he could be seen frantically writing down instructions and passing them to any operator free to action. I was so relieved to have his experience and know-how next to me.

*****

Battalion Chief Tomas Ortiz took control of a microphone at one stage and began speaking to Captain Valeria Martinez, aka Mars. He was so relieved he had her in charge on the ground; whatever happened next, he reasoned, she would do everything she could to beat the adversary ahead of her.

"Captain Martinez, please tell me what you can see ahead of you."

It took a moment for Mars to respond. She had her mobile up and on WhatsApp video, allowing her to comment in real-time. "I can see a wildfire with a massive firewall spreading rapidly and fast across the mountain ridge, consuming the tea plantations further up. With their intense heat and thick smoke, the towering flames are devouring everything in its path."

Tomas mentally noted Mars's voice's sound of pure anxiety. "Are you able to create a firebreak by removing any unburned vegetation and other combustible materials along the fire's edge?" He hopes that asking her essential questions will give her back the steel she so badly needs right now.

"Yes, there is a small window where we can clear a strip of land near the cemetery to prevent the fire from advancing further towards the pueblo. If we act fast, we may serve as a barrier to reduce its intensity," Mars roared, trying to sound more audible than the sound created by the wall of flames.

"Well done, Mars; I knew I could rely on you. I have instructed our centrally placed fire station to deploy Alpha 10 and Alpha 11 to your location. They should be in reach of you in the next twenty minutes. I have instructed them to initiate controlled burns to be set in front of your firewall. With the desired outcome of using up fuel ahead of the fire, you are fighting. It should reduce the intensity and slow its path."

Camen picked up another microphone, and her voice could be heard loud and strong in the cabin of Alpha 2: "We have been in contact with the Ariel teams at the airport, and they are on route to you as we speak; with their Ariel fighting helicopters. You should see and feel the welcoming effects of huge buckets of water showering you all in the next few minutes. In another half hour, the air tanker will join the fight, spreading fire retardant chemicals onto the flames, which in turn should reduce the fire's flammability."

"Roger, that's great, and thank you. I will keep a running account to assist you all back in the ops room."

Wolf smiled and spoke again, "Now, do not forget. No heroics: just do the best you guys can do. We want you all back here safely when this danger has been resolved. There are more fire crews on their way to you. Soon, you will see more firefighters than you can shake a stick at."

\*\*\*\*\*

**Dear City Fire Service,**

I, Climate Change, am impressed, albeit begrudgingly, by how you handled my attempts to overwhelm you with wildfires. While I intended to push your resources to their limits and test your resilience, your swift and effective response left me momentarily astounded.

I must commend your firefighters for their unwavering dedication, quick thinking, and remarkable expertise. They exhibited exceptional teamwork and coordination, mobilising resources efficiently to contain and extinguish the fires I had set. Your promptness in thorough planning and preparedness was evident as you promptly deployed fire suppression units to the affected areas.

You have used my relentless attempts to hone your skills and improve your fire suppression techniques. Your firefighters systematically tackled each wall fire, strategically employing various extinguishing methods, which is worthy of admiration. I had yet to anticipate such an adaptability and effective response from your team.

Your ability to quickly assess the situation, identify a suitable approach, and execute it precisely was remarkable. Furthermore, your commitment to public safety and determination to limit the environmental impact of the fires is commendable. I can't help but admire your dedication to ensuring the well-being of your citizens and the protection of their property.

While I had hoped to challenge your capabilities and disrupt your operations, it seems I have inadvertently inspired you to rise above my expectations. Your resilience in the face of my attempts is a testament to your commitment to duty and the safety of the community you serve.

Please understand that my acknowledgement of your accomplishments is still the same as my ultimate goals. I remain determined to bring attention to the urgent issue of climate change. However, I must recognise and respect how you handled my attempts, even if they were made with a somewhat mischievous intent.

Keep up your tireless efforts, and may we find a way to tackle our shared challenges more cooperatively.

Yours begrudgingly impressed,

Climate Change.

*****

Alpha 1 and Alpha 2 spent the rest of the day out on the mountain ridge, firefighting their way inch by inch and pushing the wall of flames back. In the end, over twenty more fire engines supported their heroic efforts. By mid-afternoon, helicopters were lined up, waiting to fly over the wildfires to drop their water payloads onto the flames. As evening approached, the threat to the city below abated. Everyone sighed with relief, for the Mayor's office at their debrief from the emergency services, it was wholeheartedly accepted the city had been saved from a catastrophe in the making.

It was just before eight in the evening before both the fire engine and ladder truck were back in their rightful parking spaces, all washed and cleaned from front lights to rear lights. The equipment would be checked and serviced throughout the night by the night cleaners, who were supervised by the now-exhausted firefighters. Even Churches was unusually quiet of voice.

On the second floor of the fire station, everyone was relaxing and practising various methods of de-stressing themselves after such an emotional day when suddenly an emergency call came into the ops room. The operator responded to a call from the police informing him of a house fire in the city's centre.

The same call crackles over the radio in the fire station. Duty calls. The local police urgently requested assistance at a house in the Barrio of La Flora that was engulfed in flames. Without hesitation, Alpha 1 and Alpha 2 spring into action.

Within a minute, all the firefighters had slid down the firefighter's pole to quickly reach the ground-floor parking area. They scrambled to get aboard their vibrant red exterior gleaming under the flashing lights of their appliances. Within another two minutes, the klaxons sounded again, warning of the exiting of both vehicles from the fire station.

Luis and his ladder truck were in the lead, making it easy for Highlander to use the robust and powerful fire engine, growling with determination as it stayed at a safe distance. The engines rumbled through the city centre, heading to the northern side of the city, with sirens piercing the evening air. They navigated the streets expertly, dodging traffic and giving way to pedestrians. The city lights blur past them as they rush toward the fire scene.

\*\*\*\*\*

As Alpha 1 and 2 approach the burning house, they are greeted by thick, billowing smoke rising into the sky. Flames lick at the windows and dance through the roof, threatening to devour the entire structure. The firefighters on board exchange determined glances, knowing that time is of the essence.

Alpha 2, the sturdy ladder truck, arrives first and stands tall and ready, its extendable ladder towering above Alpha 1. Both crews, worn and weary from their day on the mountain ridge, take their positions with unwavering focus.

Alpha 1 takes the lead, positioning itself strategically near a hydrant. Churches, Marines, and villages rapidly pulled out hoses and connected them to the powerful pump on the fire engine. Water surges through the hoses, cascading onto the flames with force and determination.

Meanwhile, Blondie and the Thin Man of Alpha 2 extend their towering ladder above the house. Blondie climbed onto the ladder, his heavy gear weighing him down. With steady hands, he guided the nozzle towards the inferno, dousing it with a powerful spray of water from above.

Together, Alpha 1 and Alpha 2 work in perfect harmony, battling the voracious fire that engulfs the house. The smoke gradually thins, and the flames diminish under the relentless assault of water. The crews push themselves to their limits, their exhaustion forgotten as the safety of possible residents becomes their sole focus.

*****

After what feels like an eternity, the fire is finally under control. Alpha 1 and 2 inches back, giving way to the satisfied hissing of dying flames. The exhausted but satisfied firefighters take a moment to catch their breath, surveying the charred remains of what was once a home.

A young police officer approaches Captain Valarie Martinez and Lieutenant Blanco to inform them he has yet to learn if anyone may have been inside. Both Whitey and Mars looked at each other, knowing that someone was going to go inside and search.

"Before we go in, do you know who owns this property?"

The nervous policeman hesitates before answering, "So far, my base can find no one who actually owns the property. It appears to have been empty for some time."

"Okay, I am going in; Marine, join me. We are searching for any victims," orders Whitey. Firefighter Alejandro Marin stepped forward with his breathing apparatus fixed and tested by the forever reliable Luis Gonzales in place. In Whitey's right hand is an axe to allow him to dislodge any obstacles he may meet. He plans to go in first.

*****

Lieutenant Blanco and Firefighter Marine cautiously approached the remains of the house where flames had once raged uncontrollably. Thick smoke still billowed from what was left of the structure, creating an eerie and foreboding atmosphere. The intense heat had subsided and was replaced by the constant dripping of water, but danger still lurked within.

With their protective gear on and helmets secured tightly, Whitey and Marine stepped forward, their training and experience leading the way. The scene before them was one of devastation. Charred walls, collapsed beams, and rubble scattered everywhere concealed any possible signs of life.

Whitey directed his flashlight towards the darkness, highlighting small pockets of space amid the wreckage. It was a Herculean task to search for survivors in this hazardous environment, but the determination in his eyes spoke loudly of his unwavering commitment to saving lives.

Armed with a thermal imaging camera, the Marine began scanning the area methodically. The thermal imaging allowed him to detect any potential heat signatures amidst the wreckage. Every nook and cranny was scrutinised, and every possible hiding spot was investigated in the hopes of finding a missing person or a victim previously overlooked.

As both firefighters ventured deeper into the house's remnants, tension rose. Every crackle underfoot, every gust of wind sent a shiver down their spines. Moving swiftly but cautiously, they communicated in hushed tones, their senses heightened, keenly aware of the potential dangers lurking around them.

Whitey's experience and intuition guided their path, leading them towards areas that showed the faintest signs of life. Reacting to the slightest sound or anomaly, their training kicked in, helping them navigate the treacherous maze before them.

Their search felt like an eternity, and every passing moment amplified the weight of responsibility on their shoulders. But they persevered, driven by the belief that someone might be waiting for their help amidst the ashes and debris.

Unexpectedly, their perseverance paid off. Through the veil of smoke and destruction, they discovered a small corner where a faint cry for help could be heard. Their hearts raced as they frantically moved towards it, overcoming obstacles and pushing past their bodies' limitations.

Finally, under a pile of rubble, they found a terrified and dying individual struggling to breathe. They could see a wooden-handled bread knife in the middle of his tattoo chest. On either side of the incision of the blade was a lion's head, and on the other, a gorilla's head. With precision and care, Lieutenant Blanco and Firefighter Marine delicately extricated the barely living young male, ensuring their safety while maintaining their own.

*****

Exhausted but relieved, the duo emerged from the remains of the house, carrying the unidentified victim to safety. The ordeal had tested them physically and mentally.

Firefighters Ana and probationer Davide raced forward with a stretcher now placed next to the dying victim. His body was transferred as delicately as humanly possible. The man died there and then took the secret of what had happened this very evening with him.

*****

By now, word had spread that someone had indeed been found in the housefire debris. Ambulances, doctors, and detectives were arriving in large numbers. Slowly, it was deemed that Alpha 1 and 2 had done their duty again, their commitment and bravery shining through the darkness.

As the night settled in, their engines cooled down back at the fire station, and nine firefighters were trying their hardest to prepare for the next call that may come their way.

*****

## 65: I am a certain Gabriel who just cannot Stop attracting wealth

Three years later, I still cannot stop laughing about the night I met Jovita and Nellie. I knew I was the planned victim of a private joke my friends José and Stella created at the Museo Aereo de Fenix. But before that episode, let me reminisce and make you smile.

*****

In the heart of Colombia, amidst the lush coffee plantations of Manizales, there stands a restored Willy Jeep that exudes the essence of the MG era and the vibrant flavours of Colombian coffee. It resulted from a shared vision between a white-haired Englishman and me. We had both accidentally encountered an almost forgotten Willy Jeep wreck. Now, its exterior gleamed with a lustrous paint job that seamlessly blended the majestic colours of the MG era with the richness of roasted coffee beans.

We both had envisaged a time when the sun would rise over the horizon, casting its golden rays upon the Jeep. We both dreamed it would come to life, ready to embark on an enchanting adventure. Nestled at the back of the Jeep was a unique addition – a specially crafted coffee machine designed to serve coffee and a delightful brew known as Cascara tea. It turned out we both love Cascara tea!

*****

We did not foresee a 12-foot-tall statue of a female named Jovita Feijoó from Palmira and a massive monument depicting a Chontaduro lady whom we had later christened as Nellie sitting together on this Jeep. Now, I must return to my reoccurring dream...

*****

From my perspective, I knew immediately that this Jeep would become the blueprint for a future fleet of vehicles housing a coffee machine in its rear section.

Each coffee machine was to be a testament to the creativity and ingenuity of the coffee-loving drinkers of South America, beginning with my homeland, Argentina. Each machine would boast an array of shining knobs, intricate copper pipes, and valves that hinted at the magic that lay within.

As each future vehicle ventured through the winding roads and picturesque landscapes of Buenas Aires, freshly brewed coffee beans filled the air, creating an intoxicating atmosphere. Passersby couldn't help but be drawn to the alluring scent, and they eagerly followed each vehicle in hopes of experiencing its magic.

I could clearly see the brand name Coffee and Cascara Alchemists on show. My fleet of mobile alchemists would be dedicated to mastering the art of coffee and bringing joy to all who crossed their path. Each Alchemist possesses a unique skill, combining their expertise to create a compelling coffee experience.

I had no plans to focus solely on the Argentinian capital. Still, as time passes, I wish for my growing fleet to expand to as many charming villages and bustling towns as possible. I saw them becoming the backdrop for the Coffee Alchemists' enchanting performances. With the flick of a switch and a wave of their hands, the coffee machine at the back of each vehicle transformed into a mesmerising booth. Each emits a soft glow, accentuating the tempting array of Coffee beans and Cascara tea leaves that adorned the display.

In my dreams, I can see cups placed beneath the machine's spouts, ready to be filled with steaming espresso coffee or the delicate brew of Cascara tea. My Alchemists would carefully measure the Coffee grounds and cascara, ensuring a harmonious blend of flavours that would transport their patrons to a world of delight. My Alchemists would operate the coffee machine with precision and flair, pouring creamy espressos, velvety lattes, and fragrant Cascara teas. Each Patron, young or old, would marvel at the breathtaking display, their taste buds tingling in anticipation.

Each sip had the sole intention of transporting each consumer to the vibrant coffee plantations of Hector and Isabella, where the sun-drenched fields and the rhythmic sounds of coffee cherries being picked would envelop their senses. It was to be a sensory journey that left a mark upon their hearts, forever intertwined with the magical brand of the first-ever Coffee Alchemists' Willy Jeep.

Now, I will tell you about the experience of my first two customers, Jovita and Nellie.

*****

My first sight of Nellie and Jovita stumbling in the dark towards my renovated vintage Willy Jeep parked by the roadside left me speechless. It was immediately evident that the duo felt an irresistible urge to explore its hidden wonders. As they climbed aboard, each giggled with excitement at escaping the flooding streets of La Flora.

As Nellie gracefully settled herself on the backseat, her white teeth shimmered under the streetlight, glinting with mischief. Adorned in radiant flowers of vibrant hues, she radiated an aura of beauty that surely would captivate all who beheld her. Her 12-foot-tall partner in adventure, Jovita Feijoó, donned a dashing hat and a flowing scarf, lending an air of elegance to the daring escapade.

But the surprises for me didn't end there. As they explored further, they discovered a hidden treasure at the rear of the Jeep. My new espresso machine was nestled snugly amongst the seats and cushions, ready to serve up aromatic delights!

With Nellie's chubby-looking fingers, she flicked a switch, and the espresso machine sprung to life, releasing fragrant aromas that wafted through the open windows – the scent of freshly brewed coffee beans mixed with the crisp evening air.

Sitting beside a bemused Norman, I drove the Jeep gracefully meandered along the winding roads. Nellie and Jovita sat in the back seat, comfortably sipping their rich brews and engaging in animated conversations with no one in particular, as we were experiencing the worst storm in a century. With each sip, they seemed to have felt a surge of energy and excitement, perfectly matching the rhythmic vibrations of the vintage Jeep beneath them.

As we pulled up to each of the homes for the older people, each resident and carer stood and gazed in awe as they witnessed this extraordinary sight of Nellie and Jovita effortlessly combining their majestic presence with the notion of the Jeep's espresso-fueled adventure. That night, the Museo Aereo de Fenix became abuzz with tales of magical happenings and lively escapades.

I went looking for an entire bottle of rum. I needed to have a strong drink.

*****

If I were setting out today, in the year 2024, with the idea of importing Coffee beans and Cascara tea leaves from my good friend Hector Rodrigues, I would have a thousand questions, regulations, licenses, restrictions, unknown tariffs, and minefields to negotiate. Luckily for me, that was not the case back in 1960.

Hector, my good friend; Isabella, his perfect partner; and Don Carlo had already decided I would be the only person ever to receive their Cascara tea leaves for free, and the shipments of Coffee beans would always be the cheapest anywhere in Colombia. They jointly saw a perfect partner in me, and I was going to satisfy them.

So, supply would never be an issue; transporting it would prove a little more difficult until I met a Paraguayan civil air pilot called Josuha.

Since the end of the Second World War, he had been flying twin-propped aircraft on an ad hoc basis. Initially, he was a Jewish breadmaker living in Saigon who had fun learning how to fly small aircraft with his three older brothers. Like my father, he had moved to Buenas Aires for the adventure and free-spirited way of life.

I turned to Joshua when I needed to find a way to profitably bring Hector's Coffee to my proposed fleet of mobile vehicles.

The first thing he did was produce a vast map of South America. Together, we pinned it to a wall in my apartment's office. It was here that I could speak and plan freely without involving my existing management teams. I intended to run this project with just a select few.

Joshua told me about a typical flying time for a lightweight aircraft, such as a Cessna 172 Skyhawk with a high wing, single-engine, and four-seater capacity. It averages a cruising speed of between 120 and 170 knots and covers a distance of approximately 3,800 kilometres. He reckoned I should expect to be flying anywhere between fourteen and twenty hours non-stop. These estimated figures would always depend on wind patterns, flying conditions, and how my chosen aircraft performed with or without any cargo on board.

He further added that I would need approximately eight destinations where I could land and refuel for the next 500 to 700 nautical miles. As an afterthought, you could rip out the two back seats and house many fuel tanks to give you flexibility on where to sit down and refuel. Finally, his final piece of advice was to use the recommended maximum payload of just short of 400 kilos.

*****

Joshua and I sat at my desk together, planning various ways of flying between Colombia and Argentina. Our favourite one took another two hours to satisfy us both. It read as follows:

**Air route: Buenos Aires to Manizales, Colombia. Departing from Argentina.**
**Stopover One:** Refuel in Cordoba, Argentina, after flying approximately 700km.
**Stopover Two:** Refuel in Asuncion, Paraguay, after flying approximately 950km.
Stop over Three: Refuel in Santa Cruz, Bolivia, after flying approximately 1,150km.
Stopover Four: Refuel in La Paz, Bolivia, after flying approximately 600km.

Stopover Five Refuel in Quito, Ecuador, after flying approximately 1,940 km. Stopover Six, Final destination, Manizales, Colombia, after approximately 670 km.

To help with the cost, I decided to advertise my Cessna to business passengers who would be carrying it from place to place en route. When I reached Hector, I could remove the two back seats and load up all 80 sacks of Coffee beans and Cascara Tea.

By the night's end, Josuha and I had shaken hands to cement a new working partnership until he died in 2000. A further quarter of a century has gone by, and there has never been a day I have not thought of Josuha, the one I would always refer to as brother.

*****

Looking back on my maiden flight to Colombia, I could write a book on what happened. Maybe one day I will. When I look at what is happening now, I am amazed at my accomplishments.

*****

I was recently interviewed for Forbes Magazine, and the young, attractive reporter wrote the following:

**Title: From Skyhawk to Success: The Journey of an Argentinian**
**A businessman named Gabriel Garcia Marquez, now aged 102.**
Introduction:
In 1960, an ambitious 34-year-old Argentinian businessman embarked on an extraordinary journey that would shape his life and career. Armed with determination and a single-engine Cessna 172 Skyhawk aeroplane, he embarked on an adventurous flight from Buenos Aires to Manizales, Colombia. Little did he know that this trip would lay the foundation for a multimillion-dollar empire in the private jet chartering industry. This is the story of Gabriel Garcia Marquez, not to be mistaken for the famous Colombian writer Gabriel José de la Concordia Garcia Marquez. Our hero is a visionary Argentinian entrepreneur who defied all odds and soared great heights.
Chapter 1: The Inspirational Flight.
With dreams of venturing into the aviation business, Gabriel piloted his Cessna 172 Skyhawk across South American skies. Facing challenging weather conditions and navigating unfamiliar territories, he showcased his exceptional piloting skills. The experience ignited his passion for flying and opened his eyes to the wealth of possibilities in aviation.
His first cargo was coffee beans and cascara tea from his lifetime friendship with

a Colombian named Hector Rodriguez.

Chapter 2: Founding the Chartering Company.

Fuelled by his love for aviation and an entrepreneurial spirit, Gabriel, who could not stop becoming wealthy, founded his own private jet chartering company in the late 1960s. Starting with a humble fleet of small aircraft, he focused on delivering exceptional customer service and building lasting client relationships. His dedication and commitment soon earned him a stellar reputation in the industry.

Chapter 3: Expansion and Success.

As Gabriel's fleet grew, so did his ambitions. He continuously reinvested in the business, acquiring various-sized jets, including Gulfstream aircraft known for their luxury and performance. He successfully expanded his operations across continents by establishing a vast global network of clients and partnering with business tycoons. With a keen eye for innovation and trends, his chartering company quickly became a benchmark of excellence in the industry.

Chapter 4: The Journey Continues.

Despite his tremendous success, Gabriel never forgot his roots. At an advancing age, he cherishes the thrill of flying his private Cessna CJ1. This smaller aircraft holds a special place in his heart as he reminisces about his early adventures and the passion that propelled him to where he is today. His continued presence in the cockpit symbolises his unwavering commitment to his craft and inspires his employees.

Chapter 5: Legacy and Impact

As Gabriel reflects on his journey, he takes pride in the millions of dollars his business now generates. However, his true measure of success lies in the positive impact he has made. His company has created numerous job opportunities, supported local economies, and revolutionised the private aviation experience for individuals and corporations alike.

Conclusion:

Gabriel Garcia Marquez's journey from a solo flight in a Cessna 172 Skyhawk to owning a private jet chartering company with a fleet of Gulfstream and other prestigious aircraft is a testament to his grit, determination, and passion for aviation. His story inspires aspiring entrepreneurs and aviation enthusiasts alike, reminding them that with perseverance, the sky is truly the limit. Today, Gabriel continues to soar through the clouds, leaving an indelible mark on the industry he has loved for almost a century.

*****

2024 is a momentous year as I prepare for my final flight at the ripe age of 103. It's hard to believe that I've spent a lifetime soaring through the skies, and

I owe it all to my secret, life-extending elixir: Cascara tea. As I sit here sipping a warm cup of the unregulated brew, I can't help but reflect on the countless adventures and beautiful sights I've witnessed from above.

The time has come for me to bid farewell to the skies, but not without one last memorable flight. I have planned a journey in a few weeks from Cali to Miami, and I am honoured to have three dear friends, who are also well into their golden years, joining me for this farewell flight.

In preparation for this final flight, I have ensured that my trusted vintage Cessna 172 Skyhawk is in top-notch condition. The mothballed aircraft, silent for years now, will again feel the thrill of the wind beneath its wings. The Museo Aereo de Fenix, where my Cessna has been resting, will serve as the starting point for our journey. It feels fitting to embark on this last adventure from where aviation history is cherished and celebrated.

Before taking off, I will arrange for the Cessna to receive a thorough service to ensure that every bolt, screw, and engine component is in perfect working order. After all these years, my cherished Skyhawk is like an old friend, and I want our final flight together to be memorable.

*****

Furthermore, I will ensure the aircraft is fully fueled and ready to defy gravity again. The thought of the engine purring back to life fills my heart with anticipation and nostalgia. The thrill of our ascent has always made my spirit soar, and I am eager to experience it one last time.

As the days draw near to our farewell flight together, I can't help but feel a mixture of excitement and a tinge of melancholy. The skies have always been my sanctuary, my refuge from the world's troubles. From the grandeur of towering mountains to the ocean's vastness, I have witnessed the sheer magnificence of our planet from above.

The skies also hold a special place in the hearts of my three loyal passengers. Together, we'll make this final flight a joyous occasion filled with laughter, stories, and heartfelt moments of reflection. Our shared love for the sky has bonded us, and it will be a privilege to share this final journey with them.

*****

So, as I finish my cup of Cascara tea and prepare for the adventures that lie ahead, I can't help but be grateful for a life spent among the clouds. Soon, we'll take to the skies one last time, honouring a lifetime of aviation, friendship, and the never-ending allure of flight.

How I will avoid the authorities, and my doctor is beyond me. But I must.

To ensure that I can fly my Cessna 172 Skyhawk at the age of 103, there are a few people I will need to avoid or minimise contact with.

I will need to take continued care of my health to ensure I remain physically and mentally fit. I should avoid individuals who may expose me to unnecessary health risks or contagious diseases. These might include sick people, individuals with poor hygiene practices, or crowded places with a higher risk of infection.

Furthermore, I should distance myself from individuals who negatively impact my well-being. These could be people who discourage or belittle my dream of flying at an advanced age or those who bring negativity into my life. I am considering the vast number of directors and managers within my company. Luckily, I am still "Au fait" with the ever-changing world of technology and no longer need to surround myself with individuals who have no interest in ensuring I maintain a healthy mindset and remain motivated. For the past two decades, each boardroom has been waiting for an announcement of my retirement. I never succumbed to the continuous pressure to retire. I am known worldwide as the Life President of all my companies, and I see no reason to change what does not need adjusting.

While family support is crucial to many, I had no family to avoid. I have been a bachelor all my life. The thought of having family members who would undoubtedly discourage my flying aspirations or exert excessive control over my decisions was not something I ever wanted to endure.

Marriage. Ah, where do I even begin? It's true—I've never walked down the aisle or exchanged vows with a life partner. I've had relationships in various cities, but something always seemed missing. And that missing piece was the connection to having a true life partner.

You see, my "wives" have always been my businesses. They've consumed my time, energy, and passion. From the start, I had a burning desire to build something of my own, to create and shape my path. And so, I dedicated myself to my entrepreneurial endeavours, pouring everything into their success.

Every venture I embarked on became like a marriage. I nurtured and cared for my businesses, pouring my heart and soul into their growth. Like a life partner, my businesses demanded my attention, understanding, and commitment. In return, they rewarded me with a sense of fulfilment and accomplishment.

Over the years, my businesses took me to different cities, allowing me to meet incredible people. I had girlfriends who shared their lives with me, but ultimately, I struggled to strike that deep, emotional connection required for a life partnership. It's not that these relationships didn't have moments of joy and companionship, but I always felt a lingering sense of emptiness.

Perhaps it was because I had already found solace and purpose in my work— my businesses provided a level of satisfaction and fulfilment that was hard to match. I often found myself prioritising my professional goals over cultivating intimate relationships. As time went on, I realised that the all-important connection required for a life partnership was eluding me.

It's not that I don't long for companionship or lack the desire to have a meaningful relationship. But I always chose the former when choosing between nurturing my businesses or investing in a personal relationship. It became a pattern that I couldn't escape, as my businesses always demanded more attention and dedication.

Maybe it was fear—fear of compromising my entrepreneurial drive or fear of losing myself in a relationship. Or perhaps it was simply a matter of timing, where my focus and priorities were not aligned with pursuing a life partner. Whatever the reasons, I've accepted that my businesses became my life partners in a way that fulfilled that void and gave me a sense of purpose.

*****

As the decades have passed, I look back with both satisfaction and a tinge of regret. While I am proud of the professional success I've achieved, I can't help but wonder about the relationships I could have cultivated and the love I potentially missed out on. But, as they say, hindsight is 20/20.

So, my businesses remain my companions—my "wives" in life's journey.

*****

I must be cautious of aviation authorities who have imposed age restrictions and unnecessary limitations on older pilots. If the truth is known, my pilot's license expired when I reached sixty-five.

In my life, I have always followed the mantra that it's not what you know that matters; it's who you know that counts.

As I age, I have no choice but to be mindful of weather conditions and potential risks associated with flying. I must admit that in my everyday life on the ground, I feel my body and mind are no longer as reliable as they used to be. But when I am in the cockpit, all my limitations disappear.

*****

## 66: I am Blacky and I need the Wisdom of The Rio Gato and Valentina

Blacky, had tragically become a solitary housebound male cat after his twin brother had passed away from contracting leukaemia from a street cat's bite. It was arduous for him to become comfortable in the peaceful and often mundane life that followed. Due to no fault of his owners, they found themselves away from home for long hours each day.

There were few visitors, and interaction was restricted to evenings and weekends.

His predominantly black fur coat exuded elegance and mystery, making him stand out amongst other felines. His brilliant white fur chest and four matching white paws added a touch of contrast, earning him a striking and unique presence.

However, at the age of forty-four, life took an unexpected turn for Blacky when two tiny newcomers entered his world. Liz, a tricolour beauty, possessed a mesmerising combination of dark grey, white, and caramel hues, resembling a living work of art. Her twin brother, Goldie, carried the distinctive markings of a Bengal tiger in the making, foretelling his future majestic presence. They were the embodiment of youth, mischief, and endless curiosity.

Blacky's owners, aware of his somewhat solitary disposition, decided to introduce the idea of Blacky becoming a surrogate father to a kitten. But when they were presented with two, their hearts melted, and one became two.

They hoped that this newfound responsibility would bring fresh energy and joy into Blacky's often tranquil life, creating a bond that would last his lifetime. In other words, they wanted Blacky to enjoy new experiences, such as interacting with a female cat. As far as they knew, Blacky had no idea there were female species in his world. He, with his brother, had been separated from his mother almost immediately and dumped outside a bodega in a dusty area of the city without any instructions on how they would go about keeping the rat population away from the bags of sugar and powdered milk.

*****

Admittedly, Blacky's initial reaction was one of cautious bewilderment. From a distance, he observed the tiny kittens, Liz and Goldie, unsure how to approach their youthful exuberance and curiosity. But as the days turned into weeks, Blacky's icy reserve began to melt slowly.

Liz, with her playful antics and gentle purrs, was the first to chip away at the walls around Blacky's heart. She frolics around him, unabashedly inviting him to join her games. Her boundless energy and genuine innocence warmed Blacky's soul, making him feel a sense of connection he had long forgotten.

Goldie, on the other hand, presented a slightly different challenge. With his ambitious and adventurous nature, he often pushed the boundaries of his tiny world, eager to explore every nook and cranny. Initially, Blacky regarded Goldie's spirited endeavours with aloof observation, preferring to observe from the sidelines.

But one day, as Goldie found himself on the brink of a daring escapade, teetering on the precarious penthouse balcony ledge, it was Blacky's normally dormant paternal instincts that kicked in. Acting on a surge of emotion, he swiftly plucked Goldie from danger, protecting him from a potentially dangerous fall. At that moment, a sense of responsibility washed over Blacky, solidifying the bond between him and the kittens.

Gradually, Blacky's solitary life began to transform into one filled with shared experiences and tender moments. He found comfort in the presence of Liz and Goldie, basking in their playful presence and cherishing the opportunity to guide them on their journey to adulthood. As days turned into weeks and weeks into months, Blacky became their guardian, offering sage advice and gentle guidance, nurtured by a love that grew stronger with each passing day.

In accepting the role of a surrogate father, Blacky discovered that companionship was worth the risk of vulnerability. The addition of Liz and Goldie brought a newfound purpose to his existence, enriching his days with laughter, affection, and an unbreakable bond. Together, they formed, with their white-haired Englishman and his adorable Colombina, Cristirin, an unlikely family, united by the beautiful contrast of their colourful coats, strong legs, and the showing of each having a pot belly. Their deep love transcended all boundaries.

\*\*\*\*\*

Then Blacky's world took an unexpected turn, and he became anxious like never before in his life. Over breakfast one morning, he heard his owners talking to each other, and he listened to a word he had not heard since he and Tommy were young kittens. The word was neutering……

\*\*\*\*\*

The conversation between his owners was about whether they should ensure Liz and Goldie were neutered. Blacky, quietly listened as his owners discussed the topic of neutering their two new kittens, Liz and Goldie. The memory of his dear brother, Tommy, who had passed away before he could experience the joys of adulthood, crossed his mind. Blacky trembled at the thought of Tommy's painful fate caused by an incident that could have been prevented if their owners had chosen to have them neutered earlier.

Blacky vividly remembered the day Tommy had wandered outside and encountered a fierce tomcat from a neighbouring street. A territorial dispute ensued, resulting in a brutal fight that injured Tommy severely. The expenses for Tommy's medical care had taken a toll on their owners, both financially and emotionally. The devastating loss of Tommy changed their lives forever. It was not long after that the decision to protect Blacky was taken.

Now, as Blacky contemplated the potential consequences for Liz and Goldie if they were allowed to roam unsupervised and unneutered, fear settled in his heart. He knew all too well the dangers that lurked in the world outside their cosy penthouse. His experience had taught him the importance of having responsible pet owners who always ensured their safety and wellbeing. With determination, Blacky decided it was time to reach out to Cristirin and Rob. Jumping onto the kitchen counter, he positioned himself within earshot of their conversation. As they continued discussing the scheduled visit to the veterinarian, Blacky meowed softly, interrupting their conversation.

Startled, Cristirin turned to Blacky, her eyes filled with curiosity. Sensing the urgency in Blacky's gaze, she asked, "What is it, Blacky? Is something wrong?"

Blacky, using his understanding of the human language, communicated his concern in meows and purrs. He recounted his memories of Tommy's tragic fate and emphasised the importance of neutering Liz and Goldie to prevent similar hardships.

Touched by Blacky's heartfelt plea, Cristirin and Rob listened attentively. They realised that their love for the kittens went beyond their immediate desires; it meant ensuring their long and healthy lives, free from harm. Cristirin hugged Blacky tightly, thanking him for his wisdom and compassion.

*****

But Blacky still could not shake off that part of his brain that made him question whether he had indeed done the right thing. He needed sound advice and knew full well where to seek it. Now, he bided his time for an opening to present itself.

*****

It was another week after his owners had gone out together for a series of medical appointments in various locations in the city. It meant they would be out for most of the day. Sensing they had indeed left the building, Blacky sought confirmation. He rushed outside onto the balcony ledge and looked down onto the street below. He clearly saw both humans entering a vehicle and closing the two back doors. Within seconds, the car moved away and turned the next corner. Now was the time for an adventure that only he needed to take.

He checked in on Liz and Goldie, who were happily playing with mini footballs and tattered-looking pink mice. He checked their food and cold water containers, and all was well. Without any more delay, Blacky ran and jumped at the main black door leading into the penthouse. He struck the door handle with such force that it momentarily rushed downwards, ensuring Blacky could push the door open enough for him to rush out. Now on the other side, sitting in the hallway, Blacky turned back and quietly and gently pressed the door back into place.

Getting back in would be a problem he would have to deal with on his return.

*****

Blacky made his way to the stairs going down; he expertly dealt with all of them without any mishap. When he reached the outer door to the building, Blacky shot underneath the gap and was taking stock of what he was doing and, at the same time, scanned the immediate area for signs of danger.

As he made his daring escape from the penthouse, his heart raced with excitement. The fresh air hit his face, and a surge of freedom coursed through his veins. With each step, he felt lighter, leaving behind the confines of luxury and finding himself in the vibrant world outside.

As he turned away from the main door, his path intersected with Derekamus and Abella. They sat under the comforting shade of a tall palm tree, taking refuge from the warm sun. Blacky's eyes widened with joy at the sight of these friendliest of gnomes. With a wagging tail, he approached them, snuggling up close to both of them.

A wave of comfort washed over Blacky as he nestled himself between

Derekamus and Abella. Their presence was like a warm embrace, offering solace and friendship. He felt safe and loved, grateful for the companionship of his dear friends.

As Abella noticed Blacky's affectionate nature, a smile graced her face. She gently stroked his fur, and to Blacky's amazement, a minute amount of gold dust appeared behind his ears. The shimmering particles added a touch of magic to Blacky's appearance, making him feel even more special. Blacky's heart swelled with gratitude for the bond they shared. At that moment, he realised that true companionship was not limited to the penthouse walls but could be found in the simplest of moments, under the shade of a palm tree, surrounded by the ones he cared for the most.

He showed his appreciation by the way all cats use their eyes. Then he was off, now racing toward the city river, a certain Rio Gato, and his harem of girlfriends. Blacky was hoping Valentina would also make an appearance.

*****

Blacky, hoping to meet Valentina again, embarks on a daring adventure through the bustling streets of the city. With his keen senses on high alert, he navigates the labyrinthine urban landscape, constantly adjusting his path to avoid the chaos and noise surrounding him.

Blacky finds himself surrounded by skyscrapers that seemingly touch the heavens. The towering structures cast long shadows over the busy streets, shielding him momentarily from the scorching sun. He weaves through the crowds of pedestrians, effortlessly dodging hurried commuters and street vendors, each engulfed in their daily routine.

The cacophony of sounds engulfs Blacky's ears – car horns blaring, sirens wailing, and people chattering animatedly. The symphony of the urban environment starkly contrasts the tranquillity of the city river, where he hopes the Rio Gato and Valentina are present on this day.

Despite the chaotic atmosphere, Blacky remains focused. He darts across busy intersections, combining his agility and intuition to navigate the bustling traffic with finesse. His nimble movements and acute awareness keep him out of harm's way, allowing him to continue his journey undeterred.

The city's vibrant colours captivate Blacky's senses as he passes by shop windows adorned with colourful displays. The scent of freshly brewed coffee floated through the air, momentarily reminding him of his white-haired owner and his love of Tinto. The earthy scent intermingled with the aroma of street food and sweet pastries, tempting even the most disciplined appetites.

After what feels like an eternity, Blacky finally reaches the centre of the city, where the grey buildings give way to open spaces and greenery. The distant sounds of rushing water and chirping birds. As he approaches the city river, a serene calm washes over him. The urban clamour dissipates, replaced by the gentle gurgle of the flowing water. He spots Rio Gato lounging lazily by the riverbank, surrounded by his harem of girlfriends. And there, standing gracefully among them, is Valentina.

*****

With a burst of excitement, Blacky quickly makes his way to the Rio Gato and Valentina. Blacky and Valentine's eyes meet, and an instant connection is reignited. Their joyful reunion fills the air with an undeniable bliss, marking the triumphant end to Blacky's arduous journey through the city. The all-knowing Rio Gato, heading into his late eighties, senses a possible romance between the feline visitor and his favourite sculptured girlfriend.

Blacky sat nervously in front of both Rio Gato and Valentina, their heads turned towards him, waiting for him to speak. Taking a deep breath, Blacky began to explain why he had rushed to see them. "Rio Gato, Valentina, thank you for seeing me on such short notice. I've been meaning to talk to my owners about something important, and after our conversation together this morning, I still felt unsure, and I knew I needed your guidance."

He paused for a moment, gathering his thoughts, before continuing. "You see, my owners and I discussed the importance of neutering Liz and Goldie, the two wonderful kittens I feel like I've become the father of. We all agreed it would be the responsible thing to do, but I wanted to make sure I understood the process and the safety measures involved."

Blacky looked at Rio Gato, seeking his expertise on the matter. "Rio Gato, can you please explain how the kittens are neutered and assure me of their safety during the procedure?"

Rio Gato nodded understandingly; his eyes filled with reassuring wisdom. "Certainly, Blacky. Neutering, or spaying in the case of female kittens like Liz, involves a surgical procedure to remove their reproductive organs. It's a routine surgery performed by veterinarians under anaesthesia, and various safety measures are in place to ensure their wellbeing during the process."

Blacky let out a relieved breath, grateful for Rio Gato's thorough explanation. Feeling reassured, he pushed forward with his following concern. "Once Liz and Goldie return home after the procedure, how can I best nurse them? Will they be in pain, and if so, what can I do to help?"

Valentina chimed in kindly, her nurturing nature evident in her words. "After the surgery, it's normal for kittens to experience discomfort. To help them during their recovery, you and your owners can provide a quiet and comfortable space for them to rest. Ensure they have access to fresh water and a litter box nearby."

Blacky listened attentively, taking mental notes of Valentina's advice. "Thank you both for your guidance. It eases my mind to know that Liz and Goldie will be in good hands during the procedure and that I can help them recover comfortably."

Rio Gato and Valentina smiled reassuringly at Blacky. "You're welcome, Blacky. We're always here to help. Remember to remind your owners to consult with the veterinarian for specific instructions regarding Liz and Goldie's care, as this expertise is invaluable in ensuring a smooth recovery."

Feeling supported and informed, Blacky expressed his gratitude once more. "Thank you, Rio Gato and Valentina, for your guidance and support. With your help, I feel more confident caring for Liz and Goldie both before and after their procedure."

*****

Blacky turned to leave, his heart pounding with equal parts hope and trepidation. He walked a few steps, his mind consumed by thoughts of what might have been before he mustered the courage to turn back and face Valentina. As he locked eyes with her, he could sense his trembling knees, ready to betray him.

Summoning every ounce of bravery, Blacky cleared his throat and asked the question he had practised endlessly in his mind since the last time they had crossed paths: "What do I have to do to get a date with you?"

*****

Valentina's gaze softened as she took in the vulnerability etched on Blacky's face. She could see the immense effort it took for him to gather the courage to ask such a straightforward question, and it touched her.

For a moment, the world around them seemed to fade into the background as Valentina pondered his inquiry. A gentle smile appeared at the corners of her lips, illuminating her face in all its radiant beauty.

"You know," she began, her voice filled with sincerity, "the answer lies not in grand gestures or elaborate schemes. It's the simplest acts of authenticity that truly captivate my heart."

She paused, her eyes locking onto Blacky's.

"To get a date with me, all I ask is for you to be yourself. Show me who you truly are, your passions, your dreams. Share your stories, your quirks, and your vulnerability with me. That's what I'm genuinely interested in."

Blacky's heart swelled with a mixture of relief and excitement, his fears of rejection momentarily forgotten. Valentina's response struck a chord deep within him, awakening a newfound hope.

With a renewed sense of determination, he smiled back at Valentina, feeling the weight of his insecurities gradually melt away. He realised that authenticity was the key to forging a genuine connection and was willing to embark on this exhilarating journey with her.

"Thank you, Valentina," he said, his voice filled with sincerity. "I promise to be nothing but myself. Let's create something wonderful together."

*****

The Rio Gato, having witnessed Blacky's act of bravery in asking what he had to do to get a date with Valentina and listening approvingly to Valentina's reply, then added to both, "Blacky, you also need to become famous. You require the barbarians to want to make a sculpture of you. Thereby, you and Valentina can forge a real future together here alongside the flowing waters of this city river.

Blacky left the meeting with renewed determination, ready to take responsibility for the wellbeing of his beloved kittens.

*****

From that moment on, Blacky was in a world of his own. He endlessly sat on the balcony ledge, thinking deeply and dreaming of how he would become famous……

Blacky's recurring dream always began with his heart swelled with gratitude and excitement as he listened to the Rio Gato's words. Becoming famous to win Valentina's heart resonated deeply within him. He would go to any lengths to prove his love and dedication.

Driven by the Rio Gato's suggestion, Blacky began dreaming of brainstorming ways to gain fame. He knew it would be challenging, as the city was filled with talented individuals vying for recognition. However, Blacky was determined to make his mark.

He decided to use his natural charisma and charm to captivate the barbarians and the entire city. With the support of Valentina and the Rio Gato, he crafted a plan to showcase his unique talents and make a lasting impression.

Blacky's dream always involved Blacky attending various art galleries and social events to connect with influential barbarians in the city's creative circles. He mingled with renowned sculptors, painters, and performers, sharing his aspirations and establishing meaningful connections.

Simultaneously, Blacky harnessed the power of social media to amplify his presence. He utilised platforms showcasing his wit, intelligence, and compassion, all while sharing his journey towards achieving recognition. Through viral videos, heartfelt stories, and insightful conversations, Blacky's fame began to steadily grow.

As his following increased, news of Blacky's endeavours spread throughout the city. The barbarians, captivated by his uniqueness, took notice of his relentless pursuit of fame. They saw the beauty in his actions and recognised the potential for a future sculpture honouring his bravery.

Word reached the most talented sculptor in the city, who was intrigued by Blacky's story and mesmerised by Valentina's involvement. The sculptor agreed to create a masterpiece in Blacky's honour, immortalising his courage and devotion. The sculpture symbolised their love, attracting barbarians from far and wide to witness its magnificence.

With fame now firmly in his grasp, Blacky's dreams of a future with Valentina seemed within reach. The flowing waters of the city river witnessed their blossoming romance as they forged a deeper bond than ever before. Together, they would navigate the challenges and successes of their newfound fame, cherishing each moment.

*****

Other times Blacky's dreams would turn to new visions; in these, the Rio Gato, proud of the role it played in their journey, continued to inspire and guide them. Its wisdom and unwavering support were a constant reminder of the love and dreams that brought Blacky and Valentina together.

As the days turned into years, Blacky and Valentina's love story would remain an inspiration for all who encountered it. Blacky and Valentina's sculptures, standing side by side, firm and resilient, would serve as a testament to their unwavering love and the power of believing in one's dreams.

In the end, it was not just fame that brought Blacky and Valentina together but the courage to pursue their passions, the support of those who believed in them, and the deep connection they shared with the flowing waters of the city river.

Blacky would always return back to the depressing question, how was he going to become famous for all his dreams to come true. He had no idea, but he had the sense to believe a way would show itself.

*****

He only had a week to wait when Cristirin came pounding through the penthouse front door with the exciting news that Blacky had been shortlisted for a photo shoot to see if he could cut the mustard and be chosen as the new face for a range of medicines and shampoos purely design for cats!

*****

It was not long before the day arrived when both a white-haired Englishman and his beautiful Colombiana accompanied Blacky sitting majestically in his carrier to the west of the city to the barrio known as San Fernando. It was here the photoshoot took place in a spacious studio specifically designed to accommodate feline models like Blacky. The atmosphere buzzed with anticipation and creativity as the team of talented photographers, stylists, and animal handlers gathered around to bring the shoot to life.

The studio was transformed into a whimsical set adorned with vibrant, cat-friendly props. A plush, faux grass carpet covered the floor, simulating a natural environment for the photoshoot. Colourful pillows and cushions were scattered around, creating cosy corners for Blacky to relax and pose.

To ensure Blacky looked his best, a professional cat groomer and stylist meticulously groomed him, making sure his fur was sleek and shiny. They enhanced his natural beauty with a touch of gentle makeup, carefully applied to highlight his striking features.

The shoot had different themed sets, each capturing a specific mood and showcasing the range of medicines and shampoos. A miniaturised veterinary clinic was created in one set, complete with a white lab coat-wearing stuffed animal as the vet. Blacky confidently posed on an examination table while holding a bottle of medicated shampoo.

In another set, a luxurious spa setting was crafted. Soft lighting, plush towels, and an elegant cat-sized bathtub created a relaxing atmosphere. Blacky lounged in the tub with bubbles surrounding him, showcasing a calming shampoo product.

The third set displayed a playful scene with interactive cat toys and scratching posts. Blacky pounced and swatted at the toys, exuding a sense of energy and vitality while promoting the brand's products for joint health.

Throughout the photo shoot, the passionate photographers captured Blacky's every move, ensuring they captured his essence and charm. The team used enticing treats and toys to maintain Blacky's interest and enthusiasm, keeping him engaged and playful.

The overall atmosphere was lively, with cheerful music playing in the background to set an optimistic and joyful mood. The entire team worked harmoniously together, ensuring Blacky felt comfortable and loved in the whole process.

As the day progressed, countless incredible shots of Blacky were captured, showcasing his versatility as a model. The team's enthusiasm and dedication shone through as they brought out the best in Blacky, capturing images that indeed highlighted his individuality and the brand's products.

The photo shoot was a resounding success, with Blacky exceeding all expectations. The quality and uniqueness of the photos ensured that Blacky stood out among the competition, becoming a strong contender to become the new face of the brand's cat medicines and shampoos.

✷✷✷✷✷

Later that night Blacky relived the experience by sharing all that he could remember with Liz and Goldie. Blacky was sure he was going to become famous and win the affection of his beloved Valentina.

✷✷✷✷✷

The following month, Liz and Goldie underwent their neutering procedure under the skilled hands of their veterinarian. Cristirin and Rob took every precaution to keep them indoors, providing ample toys, scratching posts, and love to compensate for the lack of outdoor exploration.

As time went by, Liz and Goldie thrived under the care of their devoted owners. By keeping them indoors and neutering them, they were shielded from the potential dangers lurking outside while also contributing to the greater welfare of the feline community.

Looking back, Blacky felt a profound sense of relief and pride. He had played a vital role in ensuring the safety and happiness of his young companions. As he curled up beside Liz and Goldie, he knew their lives would be full of cherished memories, just as Tommy had been for a short time when he was a kitten.

✷✷✷✷✷

As the soft breeze rustled through the balcony, Blacky stretched out contentedly between Liz and Goldie. Their fur now gleamed with health and vitality thanks to the successful operations they had undergone. Rob kept a watchful eye over them, ensuring their safety and wellbeing.

Inside the living room, Cristirin held her mobile tightly, the excitement evident in her eyes. She couldn't contain her joy any more. The news had arrived – Blacky had triumphed over ten other feline competitors and had been chosen as the face of the new brand of cat medicine and shampoos.

Tears of happiness swelled in Cristirin's eyes as she marvelled at Blacky's achievement. It was a testament to his charm, resilience, and shared special bond. She whispered tenderly to Blacky, "You did it, my darling. You're going to be famous."

Blacky's golden eyes sparkled with a mixture of disbelief and pride. He had always known he had a certain star quality, but now it was being recognised by others, too. Leaning against Cristirin, he purred loudly, basking in the affection and adoration surrounding him.

*****

Outside, Rob heard Cristirin's whispers and turned to see her radiant face. He smiled knowingly; his heart filled with joy for their little family. Silently, he continued his watch, ensuring the safety and tranquillity of their space.

As night fell, the balcony filled with gentle sounds of contentment – the comforting purring of Blacky, the rhythmic breathing of Liz and Goldie, and the distant melody of crickets serenading the night. The aura of success and happiness enveloped them all, cocooning them in a warm embrace.

*****

# 67: I am a case needing DNA, Dental Records, & Finger Print Matching

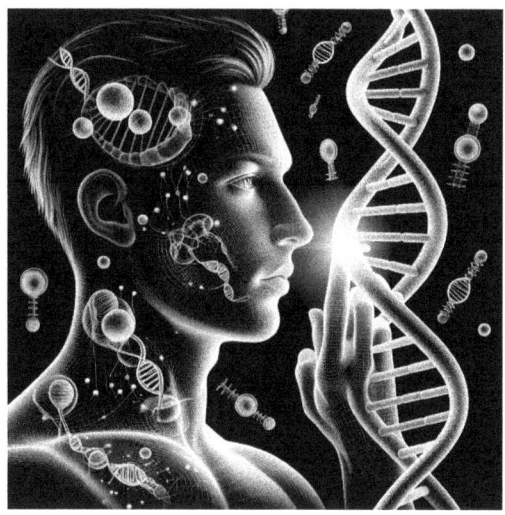

In the quiet Barrio la Flora, a blazing fire had engulfed an ageing suburban home, transforming it into a charred wreckage. As the smoke cleared and the flames were extinguished, the firefighters made a grim discovery amidst the debris—an unidentified victim with a large wooden-handle bread knife in the middle of his chest. On first inspection, he was deemed still alive, but within moments, he passed away without revealing what had transpired beforehand.

As soon as the Emergency Management Team reported the initial finding of a body in a house fire, word was sent out to The Master, the Wolf, and the Strong One. Fire Chief Eduardo raced to Stalin and found him in his usual spot, sleeping under the night sky. Eduardo rang Archibaldo on his mobile, and the young policeman was en route to where both Stalin and Eduardo were waiting.

It took Archibaldo a good twenty minutes to arrive, and then all three discussed the unfolding situation and how best to deal with it. Once satisfied with what each would concentrate on first, Archibaldo and Stalin parted and headed to the house fire wreckage. The Fire Chief made some calls and headed to the Fire Service laboratories.

*****

Archibaldo was the first on the scene, with Stalin arriving a few minutes later after revealing he needed a toilet break first. Archibaldo had turned to Stalin to act as a mentor, now having his memory back, with no limits on his tenacity and sharp instincts. Both were surveying the scene of this intriguing new case. As they studied the remains of the burnt house, it became evident that this was no ordinary fire. The circumstances surrounding the blaze and the discovery of the body raised suspicion.

Stalin commented, "It is a shame the fire crew could not have kept this "John Doe" alive long enough to shed light onto what had happened earlier tonight."

Archibaldo responded, "Yes, you are right. Apparently, all the emergency team tried their damnest to revive him, but to no avail."

"Do we know who he was?" inquired Stalin.

"Sadly, no, not yet. One thing is for sure: our John Doe is not from South America." His milky white skin gave the first hint he was a foreigner.

*****

Fire Chief Eduardo Dominguez, let me introduce you to the forensic team from our Institute of Legal Medicine and Forensic Sciences, which is based south of Santiago de Cali.

The Chief Medical Examiner is my good friend Dra. Emilie Sullivano is an experienced forensic pathologist and the head of the Forensic Institute. Known for her meticulous attention to detail and extensive knowledge of trauma analysis, she led the team in examining the victim's head and chest injuries.

Her second was her husband, Dr. Davide Bennetto, who, in my eyes, is a brilliant forensic neuropathologist with expertise in all manners of injuries. He specialised in studying the effects of trauma on the brain and played a vital role in understanding the head injuries sustained by the victim. The fact there was still a sizable wooden-handled bread knife firmly sticking out of his chest needed no persuasion that it indeed had a significant reason why the unknown man had died.

The team could not be complete without Dra. Sofia Rodriguez is a skilled forensic anthropologist known for her expertise in analysing skeletal remains. While the victim's head injuries may not be immediately visible, Dra. Rodriguez will provide insights into any underlying fractures or signs of trauma.

US Special Agent Ethan Richardson, an experienced forensic investigator from the Bureau of Forensic Sciences on loan, joined the team for this particular investigation. With a keen eye for detail, he documented and collected evidence from the crime scene, which could provide valuable insights into the forensic examination.

Finally, the team was completed with Dra. Sara Gomez is a forensic psychologist who brings her expertise to understanding the behavioural aspects of the case. She can assist the team in identifying potential motives or behavioural patterns that could have led to the injuries observed.

Together, this multidisciplinary forensic team meticulously examined the victim's injuries, analysed any potential inconsistencies, and worked tirelessly throughout the night to uncover the truth behind the incident.

*****

**REPORT NO: FTX-2024/001 & Case Number: 550427-19727**
DATE: January 31, 2024
SUBJECT: Assessment Report – Inconsistent Head and chest Injuries to an unknown person/male with unusual chest tattoos discovered in a house fire.

I. BACKGROUND INFORMATION:

The following assessment report presents findings from an investigation conducted by our forensic team regarding a middle-aged European male who possessed distinctive chest tattoos depicting lions and gorillas. The subject of interest suffered from both head and chest injuries, which appeared inconsistent with those typically sustained in a house fire.

Forensic Team Members Involved:
–Dra. Emilie Sullivano, Chief Medical Examiner
–Dr. Davide Bennetto, Neuropathologist
–Dra. Sofia Rodriguez, Forensic Anthropologist
–US Special Agent Ethan Richardson, Forensic Investigator
–Dra Sara Gomez, Forensic Psychologist

II. FINDINGS:

a) Dra. Emilie Sullivano – Chief Medical Examiner:
Upon examination of the subject's remains, it was evident that the individual had succumbed to severe burns resulting from a house fire. However, further analysis revealed both an atypical head and chest injury inconsistent with such incidents. The injuries indicated potential blunt force trauma to the head and a knife penetration to the chest as the primary fatal factors, raising suspicion of homicide.

b) Dr. Davide Bennetto – Neuropathologist:
Upon closer examination of the subject's injuries, it was determined that the causes of death were indeed both described as traumas sustained before the house fire. The head wound exhibited fractures of the skull, indicating a strong impact, potentially caused by a blunt instrument such as a hammer. The chest was quickly agreed to be a trauma caused by the accompanying bread knife.

c) Dra. Sofia Rodriguez – Forensic Anthropologist:
In addition to the distinctive tattoos on the subject's chest depicting lions and gorillas, a comprehensive study of the skeletal remains provided insight into the individual's ethnicity and possible origin. Anthropological analysis indicated the subject was of European descent, potentially Central or Eastern European, based

on skeletal characteristics and dental work previously administered.

d) US Special Agent Ethan Richardson – Forensic Investigator:

When investigating the subject's possible background, I concentrated on individuals who were known to have the tattoos found on this unknown person. My research revealed a lack of criminal records or ties to known criminal organisations. However, interviews with the FBI, CIA, and Interpol suggested potential involvement in underground activities, specifically within the art trade and illegal animal trafficking.

e) Dra. Sara Gomez – Forensic Psychologist:

Psychological profiling of the subject remains inconclusive at this stage. Further investigation is required to explore the individual's connections, relationships, and possible motives for any enemies or conflicts that could have led to his death.

III. CONCLUSION:

The collective findings of the forensic team suggest foul play in the case of this middle-aged European male, whose remains exhibited tattoos depicting lions and gorillas. Both the head injury and the chest injury were inconsistent with a typical house fire, indicating homicide as the cause of death. Further investigation is necessary to determine possible motives, suspects, and connections related to underground activities involving the art trade and illegal animal trafficking.

The forensic team will continue collaborating and providing further updates as the investigation progresses.

Respectfully submitted,

Dr Emilie Sullivano, Chief Medical Examiner

Dr Davide Bennetto, Neuropathologist

Dr Sofia Rodriguez, Forensic Anthropologist

US Special Agent Ethan Richardson, Forensic Investigator

Dr Sara Gomez, Forensic Psychologist.

*****

The initial assessment from the forensic team revealed signs of foul play.

Archibaldo's mind raced with possibilities. Was this a case of arson designed to conceal something more sinister? He thought it difficult to see it as an accident.

With an insatiable curiosity, the unlikeliest team of investigators began to delve into the victim's identity. His name was unknown, and he appeared to have lived a low-profile life as far as this city was concerned; there was no record of anyone looking remotely as the victim. Archibaldo had asked the airport security chiefs to look into the possibility of this human enigma having arrived on any flight within the past 10 days or less. He was waiting on the findings.

Tattoos gave no initial clue about his identity, except that he seemed attracted to lions and gorillas. His upper chest area showed impressive head and shoulders of both animal tattoos. Stalin's first question was he indeed an animal trafficker?

The detectives were intrigued by this enigmatic persona and bent on unveiling the secrets he held.

\*\*\*\*\*

The following morning, Stalin and Archibaldo agreed that they both had an intriguing case in their hands. Over coffee, both had decided that there would be some key aspects they should investigate to uncover the identity of the unknown male and solve the case:

The victim's movements leading up to the fire. Archibaldo would gather information about the victim's history, including any known associates, friends, relatives, or enemies. He would look for any suspicious patterns or connections that could provide a motive for the crime. Stalin suggested it might be a good idea to check if there are any missing person reports, seeing if the victim matches any descriptions.

Stalin volunteered to see if the unique tattoo of lions and gorillas on the victim's chest could reveal his identity. Stalin would contact the local tattoo parlours and consult with artists in the area to see if they recognised the artwork or who may have inked the distinctive tattoo on the victim's chest. He hoped that, in his questioning, he would identify someone who had any knowledge of someone with a similar tattoo.

Stalin had reasoned he would need to discover who may have inked the distinctive tattoo on the victim's chest?

\*\*\*\*\*

Additionally, Archibaldo, being the more tech-savvy of the two, would explore online tattoo databases or social media groups related to tattoos to see if anyone could provide information.

Archibaldo and Stalin agreed to meet again in the afternoon at the forensic examiner's laboratories and concentrate on the initial findings. This would involve examining the victim's body to gather any forensic evidence. This would include DNA analysis, fingerprint matching, comparison of dental records, and any distinctive physical features that could aid identification.

\*\*\*\*\*

Both had agreed they would need the Fire Chief's experience and would work closely with the fire service to gather evidence related to the intentionally set fire. Hopefully, "the Master" will quickly determine the potential point of origin and search for any accelerants or signs of arson. Archibaldo had requested a review of yesterday's surveillance footage, if available, to identify any suspicious activities near the house before or during the incident.

In the first hours of the investigation, Archibaldo and Stalin began painstakingly interviewing the immediately placed neighbours and anyone who might have information about the victim or the incident. They were looking for witnesses who may have seen someone entering or leaving the house around the time of the fire. At this initial stage, they drew a blank.

Once and if the identity was known, Archibaldo could begin investigating the victim's online presence, including social media accounts, email conversations, and other internet activities. He would look for clues or connections that shed light on the motive behind the crime.

If nothing is known by the end of the next day, they jointly agreed on making a Public Appeal for information: They would turn to publish media releases, sketches, and images of the tattoo, appealing for public assistance in identifying the victim or providing any relevant information. Doing so might help generate leads or reach someone who knows the victim but has yet to come forward.

By thoroughly investigating these aspects, Stalin and Archibaldo would have a better chance of uncovering the identity of the unknown male and ultimately solving the case.

*****

As Stalin and Archibaldo pushed deeper into the investigation, they conducted a door-to-door survey to see if any piece of the puzzle could be revealed. They uncovered no signs of any peculiar events leading up to the fire. The neighbours reported no strange sightings of a figure lurking around the property. The property had no telephone line installed, so no mysterious phone calls could be checked out. No elements painted a picture of a man entangled in an intricate web of deception.

Finally, towards late afternoon, a neighbour came forward and confessed to hearing heated arguments from the house late the night before. After further probing, they discovered a female voice had been heard.

*****

As the puzzle pieces aligned, Stalin and Archibaldo's determination intensified. They requested an update from Fire Chief Eduardo Dominguez, who confirmed their suspicions that the fire had been intentionally set.

After thoroughly investigating the house fire, the chief diligently examined various potential causes. Evidence was carefully collected and subjected to thorough laboratory testing. Finally, the fire chief reached a definitive conclusion regarding the source of the arson attack.

His investigation revealed that the fire was intentionally ignited using an incendiary device commonly known as a "Molotov Cocktail." This type of improvised explosive device is typically made by filling a glass tumbler or bottle with a flammable liquid, like petrol, and adding a fabric wick.

In this case, he identified the heat source as the remnants of a petrol-soaked tea cloth and a shattered Chilean wine bottle.

The unknown perpetrator must have been motivated by malicious intent and strategically placed the Molotov Cocktail in the basement area with highly combustible materials, such as empty cardboard boxes, a mountain of discarded newspapers, and crates of empty plastic bottles, maximising the fire's destructive potential. Upon ignition, the flames had rapidly spread throughout the house, engulfing it in a devastating inferno.

*****

When he passed his findings on to his two unusual investigators, Archibaldo and Stalin, the latter responded with a question for his good friend Eduardo: "Remind me again, where does the term Molotov Cocktail originate from?"

Eduardo smiled at the man he had never lost respect for, "The term "Molotov Cocktail" originates from Finland. It was named after Vyacheslav Mikhailovich Molotov, a Soviet politician who served as the People's Commissar for Foreign Affairs from 1939 to 1949. The term was coined during the Winter War between Finland and the Soviet Union, which lasted from 1939 to 1940. The Finns used improvised incendiary weapons against Soviet tanks, and they sarcastically named them "Molotov cocktails" as a dig at Molotov, who claimed that the Soviets were not dropping bombs on Finland but rather delivering food aid — which he referred to as "Molotov bread baskets."

Stalin smiled back and muttered good-heartedly, "Sure, I hope to remember that again tomorrow."

Eduardo responded, "Do not worry, my friend. When we meet next, I will ask you to tell me what a Molotov Cocktail is." All three had a good laugh at Stalin's memory problem.

*****

The Fire Chief's determination that this act was intentional marked a critical turning point in the investigation of Archibaldo and Stalin; it highlighted the need for further legal action to bring the responsible party to justice.

With this revelation, the case took a new direction—one of arson and a potential murder.

With every step, Archibaldo and Stalin unearthed more clues. Their first breakthrough came when they discovered the tattoos on the victim's chest were not random designs.

A French ex-pat who had settled in the city many years after meeting his Colombiana esposa, Catarina, while touring South America. Together, they had started a tattoo and hairdressing salon. The French inkman was an encyclopedia of tattoos and recognised the inks immediately upon seeing them. "I believe you may find the artist involved is somewhere in Africa. I am unsure as I currently do not know his name. But give me a few days, and I will investigate for you."

"What I can tell you is each tattoo holds a specific meaning, and I suspect, if I am right, is connected to a secret society known as "The Order of the Wild."

"The Order of the Wild" is a clandestine group that operates in the shadows. It is known for its involvement in illegal activities such as smuggling rare animals and exotic artefacts and even organising underground fights between lions and gorillas."

Digging further, Archibaldo and Stalin found evidence from Interpol that the victim was a prominent member of this organisation—a wealthy businessman named Hugo Van Der Vored.

As the truth revealed itself, it became apparent that Hugo's art held more than beauty.

Archibaldo paused and looked at his partner, Stalin. "Is it possible this Hugo character has become a liability to his organisation?"

Stalin momentarily thought, "Yes, you could be right, but we do not have enough of Hugo's backstory to make assumptions. We need hard facts."

With Interpol's assistance, they could trace the victim's steps. They discovered a hidden warehouse in Flanders used by The Order of the Wild. Inside, they found cages filled with rare animals – lions, gorillas, and even endangered species. It was clear that this was where the illegal activities had taken place.

As the Belgian police gathered more clues, they stumbled upon a hidden chamber within the warehouse. They found a secret room where the Order of the Wild held meetings and planned their illegal operations. The walls were adorned with ancient symbols of power, hinting at a deeper purpose for the organisation.

As the European-led Interpol Police delved deeper into the warehouse, they realised that the Order's illegal activities extended far beyond smuggling exotic animals. They uncovered a global network involved in human trafficking, drugs, and even political manipulation.

Stalin sat back, clasping both hands behind his head. "Well, we can dismiss the notion that Hugo Van Der Vored was a saintly type of guy."

Archibaldo could not agree more, "Yes, I believe this is no Nobel Peace recipient."

*****

The next set of clues was the DNA analysis's findings. The following report was sent via Dr Emilie Sullivano, Chief Medical Examiner, and forwarded to her team of Dr Davide Bennetto, Neuropathologist; Dr Sofia Rodriguez, Forensic Anthropologist; US Special Agent Ethan Richardson, Forensic Investigator, and Dr Sara Gomez, Forensic Psychologist.

DNA Analysis Report:
Subject: Hugo Van Der Vored
**Case Number: 550427-19727**
Analysis Summary:
This DNA analysis aims to determine the genetic origin of Hugo Van Der Vored, the individual with the distinctive lion and gorilla tattoos on his chest. By examining his DNA profile, we aimed to uncover any significant genetic markers that could provide insights into Hugo's ancestral background and geographical origins.
Results:
Based on Hugo Van Der Vored's genetic analysis, Sofia discovered compelling evidence suggesting roots in both Flanders and South Africa. While Hugo was born and resided in Flanders, his genetic composition indicates a partial connection to South Africa.

*****

Sofia spoke next to the group, "With regards to Genetic Markers, I can report the following:

1. Y-DNA Haplogroup: Hugo's Y-Chromosome Haplogroup belongs to the distinctive subclade R1b-M343. This Haplogroup is commonly associated with individuals of European descent, mainly originating from regions such as Flanders."

Sofia paused to allow this new information to land with everyone present.

"2. Autosomal DNA Analysis: Further examination of Hugo's autosomal DNA revealed intriguing patterns of genetic variation. Through comparative analysis with our extensive DNA databases, we identified distinct genetic markers that are frequently found within South African populations."

Now, everyone was not only quiet but also motionless, waiting patiently for more of the puzzle to be revealed. Sofia, as if on cue, began again, "Now I will turn to Ancestry Informative Markers (AIMs). Our AIM analysis indicated the presence of specific genetic markers that are frequently observed within certain populations in South Africa. This is consistent with the hypothesis of Hugo's ancestral connection to the region."

Sofia paused to reach for the freshly squeezed orange juice jug and poured herself a glass. This extra pause helped her formulate the following finding: "Now I wish to turn your attention to the matter of Unique Allelic Frequencies." She had expected someone to ask what she was talking about, but no one in the room wanted to stop her—certainly not Stalin, who was like a statue.

"Specific allelic frequencies observed in Hugo's DNA are consistent with those found in South African populations, suggesting a genetic affinity to individuals from that region."

Sofia looked at Emilie to see if she looked approvingly at her, and she observed that Emilie was. This unspoken approval gave her the strength to stay above the parapet and continue with her newfound knowledge. "finally, I come to the subject of c) Shared Genetic Segments."

"By conducting a segment-matching analysis, Emilie and I discovered significant shared genetic segments between Hugo's DNA profile and individuals from South Africa. These shared segments suggest a recent genealogical connection and further strengthen the hypothesis of his ancestral link to the region."

Stalin was the first to speak, "So, in conclusion, and based on your analysis of Hugo Van Der Vored's DNA, can we all surmise there is strong evidence to support the notion that while Hugo was born and lived in Flanders, his genetic roots can be traced back to South Africa? If so, does this finding introduce a compelling international dimension to the investigation surrounding Hugo's mysterious tattoos, adding complexity and intrigue to our case?"

Emilie rose and took command of answering Stalin. "Yes, Colonel, to both of your assumptions. I would also like to advise that additional investigations be conducted to gather more information regarding Hugo's potential connection to South Africa. This could involve exploring his family history, delving into migration patterns, or contacting international law enforcement agencies for collaboration."

*****

Over the next hour, Archibaldo and Stalin are still rooted to their chairs, listening firstly to Davide and his findings regarding his fingerprint analysis of the victim and later to Emilie's report on the same victim's dental record.

Davide rose to a ceiling-positioned projector and, with a small remote, began his slide show titled:

**Finger Print Matching Report: Case Number: 550427-19727**
Subject: Hugo Van Der Vored.
Forensic Technician: Denzel Herrera, Supervised by Dr Davide Bennetto,

Neuropathologist.

Davide began, "Firstly, I wish to point out that I wished to present this analysis as I felt it prudent to ask Denzel to look at the two other cases similar to what we are all investigating, dating to 2015 and 2005. Maybe with today's advancements in our chosen fields, we will be able to open more doors that have remained closed for many a year."

Davide, not wishing to waste any more time, proceeded to provide a vocal backdrop to what they were all seeing.

**Finger Print Analysis:**

1. Right Thumb:
 –Loop pattern, ridge count: 14
 –Delta point: Present, core
 –Minutiae points: 7

2. Right Index Finger:
 –Whorl pattern, ridge count: 17
 –Delta point: Present, core
 –Minutiae points: 10

3. Right Middle Finger:
 –Loop pattern, ridge count: 15
 –Delta point: Present, core
 –Minutiae points: 8

4. Right Ring Finger:
 –Loop pattern, ridge count: 14
 –Delta point: Present, core
 –Minutiae points: 6

5. Right Pinky Finger:
 –Loop pattern, ridge count: 16
 –Delta point: Present, core
 –Minutiae points: 9

6. Left Thumb:
 –Loop pattern, ridge count: 13
 –Delta point: Present, core
 –Minutiae points: 5

7. Left Index Finger:
 –Loop pattern, ridge count: 18
 –Delta point: Present, core
 –Minutiae points: 11

8. Left Middle Finger:
 –Whorl pattern, ridge count: 16
 –Delta point: Present, core

–Minutiae points: 9
9. Left Ring Finger:
–Arch pattern, ridge count: 15
–Delta point: Not applicable
–Minutiae points: 5
10. Left Pinky Finger:
–Whorl pattern, ridge count: 17
–Delta point: Present, core
–Minutiae points: 10

Stalin looked at the Neuropathologist and asked him directly, "Can we assume your findings also match what Sofia and Emilie concluded with their DNA investigation?"

Davide, not wishing to move away, returned his direct eye contact with this strange man in a pair of denim shorts only. "Our conclusion, based on the information that this analysis has revealed to us, is that the fingerprints obtained from the deceased individual, Hugo Van Der Vored, are the prints that match Hugo Van Der Vored's known record. The unique ridge patterns, delta points, and minutiae points on the fingers provide strong evidence for positive identification."

*****

Next, US Special Agent Ethan began, staying seated, and reading out loudly the report in front of him in his steely-sounding voice: Both Stalin and Davide immediately sat, now focusing on the American lawman.

## Dental Records for Case Number: 550427-19127

US Special Agent & Forensic Investigator Ethan Richardson requested dental records for Hugo Van Der Vored, and the city forensic dentist, Dr. Anya Ivanova, performed the dental examination. Ethan began his part of the investigation, "I wish to also let everyone here know I have assigned the same dentist to look into the same files dating back to 2005 and 2015. It will be interesting to see if there are connections that have never been revealed before."

Everyone nodded their agreement. All felt things were moving well for this unusual investigation.

Ethan, too, used the overhead projector and was adept at handling it. Stalin already knew he would be useless with such a contraption and felt it wise to seek his own counsel in this matter.

Ethan began with slide 1 of the Dental Examination:

"First, we looked at the victim's Teeth Condition. We discovered the following:

The upper right second molar (Tooth #2) was missing, and the upper left central incisor (Tooth #9) had a recent filling."

"We were a little surprised to discover there were no Dental Implant."

After pausing to reach the next slide marked: Dental Restorations: "We did discover the following;

The lower right first molar (Tooth #30) had Composite filling, the upper right second molar (Tooth #2) had a crown fitted, and the upper left central incisor (Tooth #9) revealed evidence of having root canal treatment."

Ethan clicked his remote to move the image to the next slide. This slide revealed that regarding any evidence of Tooth Alignment", There was a mild crowding in the lower anterior section. With regard to the overall tooth lengths, all appeared to be within what is expected and classed as normal ranges."

Concluding his presentation was over, Ethan switched off the overhead projector and turned to face any questions the attendees had. As with all the other speakers, it was Stalin who raised what he thought was the most important and pertinent question for this "Gringo" Investigator.

"Based on your dental examination and comparison with Hugo Van Der Vored's known dental records, does the deceased person's dental features match the provided records? Is the missing tooth, filled tooth, dental restorations, and tooth alignment observed in the examination consistent with Hugo Van Der Vored's known dental history?"

Prior to his arrival at this meeting, Ethan had spent his morning hotel breakfast scanning a written file held by the Colombian Police headquarters in Bogota, a copy of which a work colleague had passed to him. When he finally reached the end page, he was shocked at what was recorded of this former Police Colonel, and at the same time, he could not wait to meet this street man version of the same individual.

"Yes, Colonel Stalin Ramirez, you are correct in your assumption, these dental records do belong to one Hugo van Der Vored."

*****

Later, when Ethan was back in his hotel room, he found himself sitting in front of his laptop, formulating the following report for the powers that be within the police headquarters back in Bogota.

As Special Agent Ethan Richardson, acting on loan as the forensic investigator for the local police force, I had the opportunity to encounter and evaluate Stalin Ramirez, an ex-police colonel who had been living on the streets for at least two decades under tragic circumstances that would evoke a powerful mix of emotions and admiration in me.

As a forensic investigator, I have seen many tragic and heart-wrenching cases both in the USA and here in South America. But the sight of a former high-ranking officer reduced to such a vulnerable state would profoundly impact me.

Despite Stalin's loss of memory and descent into a life of destitution, there is a raw and primal survival instinct in the ex-colonel's eyes that is both haunting and awe-inspiring. To see him clutching onto a rock as his only means of defence speaks volumes about his resilience and determination to survive against all odds.

As I observe him navigating through each day with only fleeting memories of his past, I am struck by the sheer strength of his will to carry on. Living with the constant uncertainty of not knowing what happened the day before, yet still finding the courage to face each new day, is a testament to his unwavering spirit. In this ex-colonel's plight, I see a man stripped of everything – his identity, memories, and rank –. Yet, Stalin continues to fight for survival with a fierce determination that commands respect. Despite his circumstances, there is a dignity in Stalin's struggle that is both humbling and inspiring.

While I may have initially approached the ex-colonel's case as just another investigation, I find myself drawn to him in a way that goes beyond professional curiosity Stalin's story challenges my perceptions of strength, resilience, and the human spirit, and I cannot help but feel a deep admiration for his unwavering courage in the face of adversity.

In the end, this ex-police colonel living on the streets with his rock becomes more than just a victim – Stalin, for me, has become a symbol of resilience, a reminder of the indomitable nature of the human spirit, and a source of inspiration that will stay with me long after this set of housefire with deceased and unknown victims cases are closed.

Signed
Ethan Richardson,
US Special Agent.

When he was asked in the years to come what he thought of Stalin, he would always smile and remark, "A fine and more diligent officer of the Law you will never find."

*****

No one in the room spoke for some considerable time. Finally, Stalin broke the silence, "Err, does anyone have any bourbon in their bottom drawer?" Everyone burst out laughing and, at the same time, all checked the lower cupboards. Alas, for all, there was none. The meeting ended with a lot of very happy but dry-mouthed investigators.

*****

Unravelling the Mystery of the latest of a string of unknown Bodies in a series of unresolved House Fires, such as Hugo van Der Vored culminated with Stalin and Archibaldo standing before a pivotal crossroad. Now outside, waiting for a local shower of rain to disperse, they stood under a canopy, keeping as dry as they could.

Each of the unlikeliest of police investigators held a burning desire for justice and an unyielding belief that truth would prevail. Jointly, they braced themselves for the challenges that lay ahead in their pursuit of the truth, determined to see justice served and bring light to the shadowy corners of this intriguing history of unresolved cases.

Stalin looked directly at Archibaldo, "We will not only need to identify the killer, but we also need to identify the motive for such a heinous" act."

*****

## 68: I am Stalin, and I have much to learn & remember

Since the effects of that magic dust landed on my shoulders, my tranquil existence has ceased to exist. Now, millions of thoughts are invading my brain, and they appear at times to be arriving all at once. I am unsure if I can cope with this on such a scale.

It did not take me long to realise I would need to rely on the wisdom of my good friend, Fire Chief Eduardo Dominguez, and the never-ending support from Archibaldo.

To think for many decades, I only had the worry of where to find my rock to keep me safe each day. Now, I was worried about whether I had the capacity to solve this case of a possible serial arsonist and killer who, at the moment, could have been roaming the same streets as me for all this time.

\*\*\*\*\*

Take yesterday and today, for example. I found myself in rooms listening to and advising many people in forensic investigation. As you know from previous chapters of my life, I have spent most of it as a ghostly, solitarily persona. Standing and lecturing others has been a massive ordeal for me so far.

Let me explain a little more to you. I will commence the meeting held in the afternoon at the Fire Station. With all the attendees from the morning session at the City forensic laboratories, I am now back at the fire station, with the Fire Chief Eduardo to my left and Archibaldo to my right.

Within a few minutes, Assistant Chief Carmen Lopez (Wolf) and Battalion Chief Tomas Ortiz (The Strong One) arrived together and sat at the top end of the table close to the coffee station. This left several empty chairs at the opposite end of the table.

Before anyone could begin, there was a knock at the door and the forensic team entered and more or less sat in the same seats as before. Two extra seats were provided for the city forensic dentist, Dr Anya Ivanova, and forensic technician, Denzel Herrera.

The room suddenly became full of noise as everyone was introduced and greeted each other at what seemed to be the same time.

\*\*\*\*\*

Finally, there remained one chair without a warm bum. I was about to ask if anyone else was due when my unspoken question was answered with the arrival of Zamira Flores, Eduardo's most trusty Administrator, who was the best note-taker he had ever had. Everyone in the Executive Management team came to rely on her exceptional skills, sharp mind, and calm demeanour. I was soon to witness for myself how talented she was.

Emilie, the designated head of the Forensic Team, opened the meeting with two files in her hands. She leaned forward and placed both on the desk in front of her. "In the Green file, you will find the Fingerprint Matching Report, and in the beige folder, you will find the Dental Records for Hugo Van Der Vored."

Archibaldo leaned back while witnessing both the Wolf and the Strong One reaching out to a file each.

The Wolf leaned forward, opened the Green folder, and began to read out loudly so that everyone in the room would receive the fingerprint findings simultaneously. As soon as the Wolf had finished, the Strong One started to read the beige folder labelled Dental Records out loud to the group.

Waiting at the end of his team's reading of both folders, the fire station chief spoke up loud enough for all to hear him. "Thank you, Wolf and Strong One. Firstly, are there any questions?"

Everyone appeared to look around the room, waiting for someone to come forward with a quizzical mind, but no one spoke.

"Well, I propose we close this meeting and meet again in the morning. Shall we say that due to the nature and urgency of our resolving these cases, we all should endeavour to be here in this office at 07:00 am?"

No objections were offered by any present, and the room was suddenly filled with screeching chairs as they were pushed back to allow the warm bums to rise in unison.

*****

At 7:00 am the following day, I, Stalin, looked down at a plate of freshly made empanadas and a pot of piping hot coffee. I sat staring, wondering if I should reach out and help myself. The ever-knowing Eduardo obviously saw my hesitation and reached over and poured me a mug of the sweet-smelling coffee.

"Would you like milk and sugar with your coffee?" asked a smiling, freshly looking Zamira who, despite only having had four hours of sleep after writing up and printing all the minutes for the previous meetings.

I muttered almost apologetically, "No, I have only acquired the taste for Tinto over the years. It is not often someone has a couple of sugar sachets in their pockets or a bottle of milk within their reach."

"Well, from today and every day you have been a guest here, should you wish to have either milk or sugar in your coffee, please just ask."

Zamira picked up the plate of empanadas, "Would you like to sample our freshly made empanadas? I promise you they are delicious."

I declined but kept an eye on them. Before leaving the meeting, I intended to fill my pockets to ensure I had a meal for later in the day.

At that point, everyone was tucked into the morning breakfast, and I felt a definite sense of warmth and belonging.

*****

Once everyone felt a decent amount of time had elapsed to partake in an impromptu breakfast with a street man, the joint focus moved to the topic that had been consistently in their minds for years.

It was Archibaldo who was facing and speaking to Police Colonel Stalin Ramirez. By doing so, Archibaldo was informing everyone present that this street man with a reputation of having no memory was now tasked with investigating mysterious house fires with dead bodies in basements starting way back to at least the 1960s and leading right up to our latest murder victim with Hugo Van Der Vored."

Everyone from Archibaldo, Stalin, and the Fire Chief stared in shock. "The 1960s, you say?" A question from equally as shocked as anyone present, Ethan Richardson, the US Forensic Investigator.

Archibaldo initially faced Ethan, and as he answered, he turned to face everyone to ensure his words were fully understood. "Yes, we believe from our limited investigations so far. Several house fires have occurred in a ten-year cycle each time. What I mean is that the first questionable house fire involving an unidentified victim-type scenario began in 1965 and happened again in 1975, 1985, 1995, 2005, and 2015. All around the same month of March, give or take a couple of weeks on either side. "

Stalin took a moment to explain more to the shocked professionals around them: "I will reveal our findings in the next few minutes. I will reveal the reasons why this appears to be the case. I wish to point out from the outset that this latest fire happened within nine years of the last one, leaving both Colonel Ramirez and me to wonder why now and not next year."

*****

The Fire Chief stood to refill his coffee mug. He felt the need for a double shot of caffeine this very day. "Perhaps Archibaldo, with the assistance of our Colonel, it would benefit everyone if you both could describe how challenging it must have been due to the limitations in technology and investigative techniques available at that time of the 1960s onwards."

Without delay, Stalin managed to find his voice and began his first-ever report in decades. "I wish to begin with the term "Limited Forensic Technology**: In the 1940s and 1950s, forensic technology was rudimentary compared to today. DNA analysis, fingerprint databases, and advanced forensic techniques were not available. Gathering evidence such as fingerprints and analysing trace evidence would have been much more difficult and time-consuming."

At this point, Stalin paused to see if there was any objection to what he had said. There was none. Everyone in front of him was inwardly fighting with the incredibility they were witnessing in seeing Stalin now as a Police Colonel and not a street man to be avoided at all costs and coming to terms with not just one murder but a possible seven!

Stalin appeared to ignore his audience and moved on to the subject of Manual Records and Communications. "Investigative information had to be documented manually, and communication between police departments or agencies was slower and less efficient. Accessing and cross-referencing archived reports from different periods would have been a laborious process, requiring sifting through physical files and reports."

Noting no one was raising any objections, Stalin headed to "Point 3. The matter of Witness Testimony. Back then, relying on witness testimony was crucial, but witnesses may have been less reliable and less readily available than they are today. Memories fade over time, and witnesses may have been less inclined to come forward due to social stigmas or fear of repercussions."

"Point 4. Surveillance technology like CCTV cameras did not exist then, making it harder to track suspect movements or identify potential leads.

"Point 5. Investigative techniques and specialised expertise in areas such as arson investigation or psychological profiling were in their infancy. Please excuse the fact most of you had not been born yet, so the lack of established protocols and training in these areas would have hindered the depth and accuracy of any investigation."

*****

Finally, Stalin knew that his contribution to this unique meeting had been exactly what was needed to reveal the groundwork for his later proposals.

Stalin sat more upright and with confidence, continued, "Overall, the process of gathering details, analysing evidence, and connecting the dots in cases of mysterious house fires with dead bodies in basements from the 1960s would have been much more challenging and time-consuming compared to the resources and technologies available to modern police forces today."

*****

"During the time frame when I first joined the Police force and funnily enough, at almost the same time as my good friend, your Fire Chief Officer, Eduardo, also became a firefighter. "Perhaps it would be a good moment for Eduardo and Emilie to give us their personal insight into this time period."

Eduardo smiled at Stalin, "Certainly, Colonel, and with your permission Emilie, let me start from 1955 to 1985, advancements in forensic science and technology played a significant role in making it easier to investigate murders in house fires. Some key developments during this period that contributed to this included:

1. Forensic Investigation Techniques: New techniques were developed for examining fire scenes, such as identifying the point of origin and cause of the fire. This helped investigators gather more accurate evidence and determine if the fire was intentionally set to cover up a murder.

2. Fire Investigation Training: Increased training and education for fire investigators helped improve their skills in recognising patterns and evidence related to arson in house fires. This led to more thorough investigations and better outcomes in solving cases of murders disguised as accidental fires.

3. Improved Fire Analysis Tools: Introducing new equipment and tools, such as fire debris analysis kits and accelerant detection dogs, aided investigators in detecting traces of accelerants used to start fires. This helped in linking arson to murder cases more effectively.

4. Collaboration between Forensic Experts: Collaboration between forensic experts, such as fire investigators, pathologists, and forensic scientists, became more common during this period. This interdisciplinary approach helped Emilie, Davide, and their magnificent forensic team gather comprehensive evidence and begin to solve complex murder cases involving house fires."

Eduardo paused before speaking next to ensure everyone would hear his thoughtful comment. "And yet, with all these advances, we all failed to notice there may well be a serial killer lurking amongst us all. One who had managed to perpetrate not one but at least six more cases of housefires with dead people within them."

*****

Eduardo turned to Dr. Emilie, "Doctor, could you please give us an insight into further improvements from 1985 to 2005?"

As the Chief Forensic Examiner, Emilie stood up and went to a blank whiteboard. She located a marker pen in the tray at the board's base. She wrote and spoke simultaneously, "There were several significant changes and improvements during these mentioned years that assisted in investigations.

Emilie spoke and wrote, 1. "Advancements in technology. These two decades saw rapid technological advancements that significantly improved our investigation capabilities. These included DNA analysis, computer forensics, and automated fingerprint identification systems."

Emilie turned to face her audience and held the marker pen. She felt it was appropriate to speak and not record what she was about to say.

"2. Forensic science made significant strides during this period, with new techniques and methodologies developed for analysing evidence, such as ballistics, blood spatter, and toxicology."

To be fair to you, Colonel, during this period, you were indisposed, so to speak, with your "illness". "3. There was a greater emphasis on providing specialised training to law enforcement officers in investigative techniques, crime scene management, and evidence collection."

Stalin raised his left hand minus his rock, looking directly at Emilie, showing no malice towards her. "Thank you for referring to my forgetfulness as an illness. But luckily for me, at this time, I did harvest all that was deemed specialised style knowledge. Sadly, it has been the remainder of my life on the streets where my memory began to let me down."

"Over the past few days, my good friend Archibaldo has brought me up-to-date with the formations of Specialised investigative units, such as homicide squads, cold case units, and forensic labs, established to focus on specific criminal investigations and improve efficiency. He further tells me that there has been an increased level of collaboration between different law enforcement agencies at the local, state, and federal levels, leading to more coordinated and effective investigations.

*****

Archibaldo rose and joined Emilie at the whiteboard. She offered him her marker, which he thanked her for and proceeded to speak to all. "Thank you, Emilie. In fact, thank you to one and all. This meeting for me, and I hope for you all, has been a resounding success. We walked in here thinking of the 1950s, and now we are up to date some seven decades later."

Archibaldo, now with his back to the board, said, "In comparing murder reports from today's time frame with those from 1955, there would likely be some notable differences due to changes in society, technology, and law enforcement practices over those decades."

Archibaldo began to write on the board as he spoke, "1. **Technology**: By 1985, advancements in forensic science and technology would likely have improved the ability to solve crimes and gather evidence. DNA profiling, for example, became available in the mid-1980s, revolutionising criminal investigations. This could lead to more sophisticated methods of analysing crime scenes and identifying perpetrators."

Next, Archibaldo wrote Figure 2, with the heading "Media Coverage. "The 1980s saw the rise of 24-hour news channels and increased media coverage of crime stories. This led to a higher level of public awareness and concern about murders and other violent crimes during this period compared to 1955.

Under Media Coverage, Archibaldo then wrote 3. **Cultural Shifts**. It was at this point he turned again and began to speak, "Social and cultural changes in the 1970s and 1980s, such as the impact of the civil rights movement, women's rights movement, and the Cold War, would have influenced the motives and circumstances surrounding murders during this time. There might be different trends in crime types and the demographics of both victims and perpetrators.

Finally, I wish to end with point 4. **Law Enforcement Practices**: Improved training and techniques for law enforcement officers during the 1980s would have affected how murders were investigated and reported. Increased coordination between different agencies and the use of databases and criminal profiling must have led to a more efficient response to violent crimes."

*****

Fire Chief Eduardo rose and walked to the front. He placed his hands behind his back and spoke to everyone, "Well, everyone, the reports we receive today on murders in house fires look pretty different from the reports we used to get 50 years ago. The age of computers, smartphones, and DNA analysis has significantly helped investigators solve such cases."

"Fifty years ago, investigators had to rely mostly on physical evidence found at the crime scene and witness testimonies. Without advanced technology, it was often challenging to establish the cause of the fire or identify the perpetrator accurately."

However, today, with the advancement of forensic science and technology, investigators have access to powerful tools such as DNA analysis, which can help identify suspects and link them to the crime scene. Computers and smartphones have made it easier to collect, analyse, and store data related to the case in a more organised and efficient manner."

*****

For us fire service personnel, we expect our reports today to include detailed findings from DNA analysis, digital evidence from devices like smartphones or computers found at the scene, and sophisticated fire investigation techniques that can more accurately determine the cause and origin of the fire.

Overall, the use of technology has significantly improved the capabilities of our investigators in solving murders in house fires, providing us with a more comprehensive and scientific approach to crime scene analysis and evidence collection."

"So, I recommend we pause for today and reconvene tomorrow to see what each of us "Experts" can come up with. Shall we schedule a time to begin at the same time as today? I mention this time because our friend, the Police Colonel, has disappeared with the last of the empanadas. I suspect he will look forward to his next breakfast with us."

Everyone's focus turned to an empty chair, and everyone laughed and agreed to the next meeting. Zamira left quietly and ensured Stalin had all that was required, as well as an extra container full of piping hot rice waiting at the front desk, preempting Stalin's exit style.

*****

## 69: I am the net that is closing in on three Sisters

The next meeting began earlier than expected. Everyone except Stalin was already sitting with full stomachs and half-empty coffee cups in front of them. Stalin arrived at the scheduled time and was surprised to see the room full of happy and smiling faces. As he entered the room, the various conversations paused, allowing each to turn and face the Colonel.

Thinking he had done something wrong, Stalin checked his attire, which included one well-worn pair of denim shorts and a T-shirt recently acquired from Mike and Diane, the original founders of the local MotoDreamer Motorbike Touring store. Both had taken a shine on Stalin and every couple of months, they would receive a new batch of T-shirts to hand out to the customers. Diana always ensured she kept a couple back for this ex-police Colonel, now a street man with only his rock for company.

Stalin thought to himself, "At least the T-shirt was clean and presentable." He felt he needed to say something and offered, "I am sorry if I am late; the traffic was heavy."

Everyone laughed at the absurd excuse and knew he was not late at all.

The Fire Chief leaned forward with an outstretched dinner plate containing only one empanada, which looked frozen. "Would you care for breakfast, Colonel? We did manage to save you one."

"How about a cup of coffee?" offered the Wolf. And then, as an afterthought, "So sorry the coffee has gone cold!"

Zamira, watching Stalin struggle within himself not to rise up to the baiting, says, "Do not worry, Colonel. These reprobates are pulling your leg. I have organised a full breakfast for you. May I suggest we team up at the end of this meeting, and I will ensure you are well catered for?"

The Colonel mumbled his gratitude and turned to others with a grin on his face. "I will surely enjoy getting my revenge in the coming days." Everyone roared with approval.

Archibaldo rose, moved towards the whiteboard, and turned to face everyone present. "For both our part of this meeting, and I mean the Colonel and me, these last two days have been a whirlwind of discovery. If it is agreeable with you all, we wish to open this meeting with what we have discovered so far."

"In front of each of you is a small pile of folders with the specific year a house fire was reported with an unknown victim found within who had perished under suspicious circumstances. Let us begin with the file titled 1965."

"Let's turn our attention to this rather thin-looking report inside from 1965 regarding the house fire and the unidentified corpse that was found. As we review this case, it becomes evident that technology limitations at that time would have made it incredibly challenging to solve this mystery."

"First and foremost, forensic science in 1965 was not nearly as advanced as it is today. DNA analysis, which is now a critical tool in identifying individuals, was not available back then. Without DNA testing, it would have been nearly impossible to definitively determine the identity of the deceased individual found in the fire."

"Furthermore, fingerprint analysis was still in its early stages in the 50s and 60s. Matching fingerprints to a database of known individuals was not as refined a process as it is today. This means that even if fingerprints were recovered from the scene, there may not have been a way to conclusively link them to a specific person."

"Additionally, the lack of surveillance technology in the 50s and the 60s means that there would have been limited ways to track the movements of potential suspects or witnesses. Today, we have access to CCTV footage, cell phone records, and other digital sources of information that can help us piece together a timeline of events. In the 50s and the 60s, such resources were simply unavailable."

Archibaldo replaced his copy of the open file on the desk surface, "In conclusion, the investigation into this house fire and the unidentified corpse would have been severely hampered by the technological limitations of the era. While our team in 1965 did their best with the resources they had at the time, it is understandable why they could not come up with a more conclusive result. Let us now use this case as a reminder of how far we have come regarding technology and forensic science and continue striving for justice and resolution in all our investigations."

Archibaldo closed his copy, which signalled to all present that 1965 was not going to be of much help in solving a lot of possible arson attacks involving the death of someone inside.

"Now, let us move to the next file marked March 1975." A ruffle of sounds followed as each closed the 1965 file and turned their attention to the 1975 file listed.

"As you will see, just like in 1965, very little information is recorded for us to investigate today. Both files so far could only give us one A4 sheet on sketchy results from the 1960s and 70s. We have no choice but to accept the unresolved case of the house fire incident in March 1975. The discovery of an unidentified corpse at the scene has left us with many questions and very few answers. As we all know, the 50s, 60s, and from what I can see here, the 70s were a time characterised by limited forensic technology and resources.

Unlike today, where we have advanced DNA testing and sophisticated forensic techniques, the tools available to us back then were rudimentary at best. The lack of DNA databases, facial recognition technology, and other modern forensic methods made it extremely challenging to identify the victim or determine the cause of the fire with certainty."

"Furthermore, the documentation and record-keeping systems from that era were not as comprehensive as they are today. The lack of digital databases and interconnected information systems hindered our predecessor's ability to cross-reference data and identify potential leads."

"The limited communication and coordination between different agencies, such as the police, fire department, and forensic team, further complicated the investigation process. Without the collaborative and integrated approach that we have today, it was challenging to piece together the puzzle and solve the cases in question. Considering these challenges and limitations of the time, it is no surprise that the victim's identity remained unknown and the case unresolved. While we may never be able to provide closure to this particular incident from 1975, we can learn from it and strive to improve our investigative methods and technologies for future cases."

Sitting and signalling to the Fire Chief that Archibaldo had come to the end of this presentation, "the Master" took a moment to rise and turn directly to his assistant, "Zamira, please make a note of these points for our records. Thank you all for your attention and dedication to this case. If all agree, let us take a short recess of 15 minutes and continue our efforts to seek justice and closure for this and other unsolved mysteries in our city's history up to and before lunch is served in our canteen. I do believe it is lashings of piping hot lasagna day today!"

Everyone voiced their approval and excitement at knowing the chef would serve one and all with his speciality of the day. In the meantime, everyone headed to their designated toilet.

*****

Archibaldo reached for his copy of 1975, and everyone went for their copy listed as March 1975.

Eduardo spoke next. "So, we are investigating a housefire that has a decade in between each one. And it looks like only one month is involved – March. Could this be significant to our investigations?"

"Yes, Fire Chief, you are correct. Every ten years, a housefire involving a dead person occurs in March. Both the Colonel and I believe that once or twice would not mean anything, but every decade, the same pattern happened right up to this latest fire involving Hugo Van Der Vored."

"To save us time, the file listed as 1985 only gives us a little more information, certainly not enough due to the time-lapse of forty years. Many of the people that would matter in that period will be hard to track down. Memories will be suspect."

"Now, when we get to the file listed as March 1995, we can start to gather clues to assist us. Let us stay on track with the dateline and open our 1995 files."

Archibaldo's tone appeared to become more knowledgeable and more positive as he announced that in the file dated 1995, he had a name for the victim. Dr. Emily Greene was a Biologist.: This female doctor had been rumoured to have discovered a groundbreaking genetic mutation that could have potentially cured a rare genetic disorder in children. Instead of sharing her findings with the scientific community, she sold the research to a pharmaceutical company for profit, resulting in the treatment being patented and made unaffordable for families in need."

Inside the file was an almost faded version of an old newspaper article written In 1995. Archibaldo felt the need to read the contents of the article out loud, "The unnamed source and the newspaper reporter had begun to circulate a rumour about a prominent biologist, Dr Emily Greene, and her alleged involvement in a controversial act. It was whispered among scientific circles that Dr. Greene had come across a groundbreaking genetic mutation with the potential to cure a rare genetic disorder affecting children. However, instead of sharing her findings with the scientific community, rumours suggested that she had chosen to sell the research to a pharmaceutical company for personal gain."

"The repercussions of Dr Greene's rumoured actions were significant. The treatment derived from her research was patented by the pharmaceutical company, making it unaffordable for the very families who desperately needed it. The accusations against Dr Greene stirred up outrage and disbelief in the scientific community, tarnishing her once esteemed reputation and leaving the public questioning the ethics of her actions."

Archibaldo paused, "As you can imagine if this is true and as the details of this controversial incident unfolded, speculations and suspicions surrounded Dr Greene. Was she truly the altruistic scientist dedicated to helping those in need, or had greed and ambition clouded her moral compass?"

"The lines between right and wrong blurred as the truth of Dr. Greene's alleged betrayal remained uncertain, adding complexity to the narrative of a once-respected scientist now embroiled in scandal. What makes this more intriguing. After the publication of this article, Dra. Green disappeared and has never resurfaced anywhere in the world."

*****

Archibaldo then reached out and passed another set of files, listed as March

2005, to everyone present. "Let's now turn our attention to the next file listed as March 2005."

Archibaldo began reading when, in fact, he did not need to. He knew this case by heart, having been immersed in all three files since the moment he had laid eyes on them.

"In our mysterious case of 2005, there is a strong possibility that Victim 2 is a renowned physicist named Professor David Wells. Why, may you ask? Whispers abound at the time of a house fire on the western side of our city. Rumours suggested that the esteemed professor was involved in developing a groundbreaking technology capable of extracting renewable energy from quantum particles. However, instead of unveiling his potentially game-changing innovation to the world, Professor Wells purportedly chose to conceal his research, guarded secrets buried deep within the confines of his laboratory."

Archibaldo paused to turn to the next page, and without losing his thread, he continued, "Speculation swirled regarding Professor Wells' motives for keeping his revolutionary technology shrouded in secrecy. Some theorise that he feared its disruptive impact on the established power structures and the economy, foreseeing a future plagued by prolonged reliance on fossil fuels and catastrophic environmental degradation."

"As investigations unfold and details emerge, the contentious figure of Professor David Wells stood at the centre of a storm of questions and accusations, his actions and intentions cloaked in uncertainty and intrigue. The enigmatic physicist's elusive conduct continues to fuel debates and intrigue, leaving a lingering air of mystery surrounding his true motives and the extent of his involvement in the alleged suppression of groundbreaking scientific advancement."

"Excuse me, Archibaldo. What happened to Professor David Wells? Did he mysteriously disappear into fresh air as our first possible victim, Dr Emily Greene?" Carmen, aka the Wolf, raised this question.

Archibaldo looked first at Carmen and then answered, "Yes, it so happens that Dr Emily Greene and Dr David Wells have both been listed as missing persons by nearly every law agency in the world."

Fire Chief Eduardo spoke next, "Thank you, Archibaldo; I know you have a third file listed as 2015 to go over with us, but I could do with a stretch of my legs. Can we convene again, say 30 minutes from now? Is that okay with everyone?" Not waiting to hear if there were any objections, the Master began pushing his chair back to give him the space to rise. Everyone followed suit and started heading to the door leading into the main operations room for the fire station. All appeared quiet.

*****

After just under 20 minutes, the room was whole again. No word was said by anyone to the contrary; the file listed in 2015 was on everyone's mind. This next victim worked and lived in their city. Archibaldo arrived just before the last attendee, who happened to be his excellent friend Stalin, who had taken the opportunity to devour his full breakfast of tomatoes, scrambled eggs, roasted chicharron, rice, plantain, and aqua panela.

Archibaldo quickly swept the room, and all the chairs had bums in place. "Okay, let us turn to this last file marked 2015. In the shadowy depths of our city lies an almost decade-old tale of mystery and danger."

Archibaldo continued without reading, following this mystery from the beginning.

"Whispers swirl about a possible victim we call number 3. a renowned Dr Marcus Reed, who had the reputation of being a brilliant chemist. For some time, he was hailed for his groundbreaking research in pharmaceuticals, but in later years, Dr. Reed was under investigation for alleged misuse of his scientific expertise. Rumours abound about Dr. Reed exploiting his knowledge to create illegal substances or manipulating formulas for personal gain. While no concrete evidence had surfaced, the shadow of suspicion loomed over his once-respected reputation, leaving his colleagues and the scientific community questioning the true nature of his work and begging the question of why he would feel the need to set up supply chains from our city to nearly all major ports around the globe.

Archibaldo now took the position of what he believed a great Shakespearean actor would do, "But amidst the haze of uncertainty and speculation, one fact remains clear: Dr. Marcus Reed should stand accused of unleashing this plague upon the unsuspecting populace."

Archibaldo felt the urge to walk around the room as he said, "Yet, in the murky realm of shadows and secrets, the truth remains elusive. Whispers can deceive, and rumours can mislead. Was Dr. Reed truly the architect of this dark chapter in our city's history, or was he merely a pawn in a larger game of power and manipulation? As the world grapples with the aftermath of Dr Reed's alleged crimes, one question lingers in the minds of all who dare to delve into the depths of this twisted tale: who truly holds the strings in this intricate dance of deception and deceit and where the hell is he?"

*****

Dra Sara Gomez, the until now silent forensic psychologist, raised her hand and at the same time turned to all around the table. "Have you finished Archibaldo? May I share all my thoughts with you?"

"Please do," motioned the fire chief. He felt he and probably everyone else now needed a new perspective on all these seven housefires.

Sara took a moment to rise and stretch her legs. She placed her hands deep in the pockets of her white doctor coat. "As the city forensic psychologist, I have analysed the patterns and evidence related to the possible victims of a mysterious and so far, unknown arsonist and serial killer in our city over the last 60 years."

Stalin could not hold back when it became clear that they had been dealing with housefires for over six decades! Hearing Sara express the decades as actual years left the Colonel shocked to his core. "Wow, 60 years and no one has been indicted for any of these crimes?"

Sara braced herself for a possible firestorm of outrage with what she was about to reveal. She tightened all her available muscles, "After countless hours of extensive research, I have come to suspect that the culprit may be a female individual based on several potential traits that align with profiling data and behavioural analysis."

Zamira dropped her pen on the table. Every set of eyes followed the descent of the offending pen. Sara took the chance and rushed on, "Here are the key reasons why I believe the unidentified perpetrator could be a woman:

"1. Methodical Approach: The crimes committed display a level of detail, precision, and planning that are commonly associated with female criminals. Women tend to be more meticulous and organised in their actions, which could explain the systematic nature of the arson and killings.

2. Disguise and Deception: Female criminals are often able to blend in and go unnoticed. The perpetrator may have evaded detection for a long time by camouflaging their true identity and appearing harmless or unsuspecting to those around them.

3. Emotional Motivations: While both male and female criminals can be driven by various motives, female offenders often have distinct emotional triggers such as revenge, jealousy, or unresolved trauma. The long-term pattern of the crimes suggests a deep-seated and personal vendetta that could be more aligned with a female perpetrator's psychology.

4. Subtle Manipulation: Female criminals are known to use subtle manipulation tactics to control situations and individuals. The meticulous planning and execution of the arson and killings could reflect a calculated manipulation of circumstances to achieve a specific goal.

5. Signature Elements: Behavioural patterns and modus operandi often contain signature elements unique to the individual perpetrator. By carefully analysing the details of each crime scene and victim profile, we may uncover subtle clues or behavioural traits that point towards a female offender."

Sara somehow manages to time her walk around the table to coincide with her winding up her mini-style speech, "In my experience of being the city's forensic psychologist with over 30 years of dealing with all types of killers, I feel my intuition is serving me well again. While the investigation continues to uncover more evidence and clues, the possibility of the unidentified arsonist and serial killer being a female suspect cannot be ruled out. It is essential for us to remain vigilant, meticulous, and open-minded as we work towards identifying and apprehending the perpetrator responsible for these heinous crimes."

For some unknown reason, everyone rose as one to move towards Sara. She to all made sense. Could it be a female killer they are searching for? At this point, no one knew, but it was something none of the others had even thought possible. But Sara did and had done so for some time.

*****

As the former Colonel of the city police, Stalin was the first to take up his seat. His memories came flooding back to him like a raging river finally unblocked. It was a sunny December in 1985 when he found himself standing at the cash machine, minding his business. Suddenly, three mysterious figures surrounded him, their features blurred and unidentifiable.

Before he could react, one of them sprayed a noxious gas into his eyes, a searing pain that clouded his vision and incapacitated him. Panic set in as he struggled to make out any details of the assailants, but it was futile. Darkness enveloped his world as his consciousness slipped away.

For years, he wandered in a haze, unable to remember even the simplest tasks, his once sharp mind reduced to a jumble of half-formed thoughts. But now, thanks to the intervention of two benevolent gnomes, the veil of forgetfulness had been lifted.

With his memory restored, the ex-colonel vowed silently to himself to unearth the truth behind that fateful day, to seek justice for the crime that had robbed him of so much. Armed with newfound determination and clarity, he set out to unravel the mystery that had haunted him for decades.

"Colonel, are you okay? Would you like some water?" Slowly, Stalin began to place the words from his true friend Eduardo. "No water, but a slug of your finished brandy would most definitely meet my needs."

Immediately, the fire chief reached into his bottom drawer and produced not one but two bottles of his finest brandy. Zamira, as if on cue, disappeared and was back in a minute with a tray full of empty cognac tumblers. Within a further two minutes, everyone was sipping and salivating the potent liquid.

Archibaldo took a moment to slip a new file in front of Stalin, who looked down to read the file's Title: The Curse of Devil's Breath. "Colonel, this account was written for you by your then-serving police officers. They had hoped that one day you would be well enough to read what they discovered and what you could not remember."

Stalin opened to the first page and began to read out softly, "Police Colonel Stalin Oscar Ramirez had just finished his shift and decided to stop by the cash machine on his way home to withdraw some money for Christmas presents. As he entered his card and punched in his PIN, a shadow loomed over him.

Before he could react, a masked figure sprayed a mysterious gas in his face. Stalin immediately felt dizzy and disoriented, succumbing to the effects of the Devil's Breath.

"What's your PIN?" a sinister voice demanded.

Helpless to resist, Stalin mumbled his PIN through a foggy haze. The thieves quickly withdrew all the money from the machine and vanished into the night.

As the effects of the gas slowly wore off, Stalin realised what had happened. He was filled with a mixture of anger, powerlessness, and shame. He knew he had to report the incident but feared the consequences of admitting his mistake.

Feeling the weight of his vulnerability, Stalin vowed to track down the thieves and end their nefarious activities. From that day on, the legend of the Devil's Breath haunted him, a constant reminder of the dangers that lurked in his shadows. Slowly, his mind shuts down to protect him from losing his sanity.

Slowly, Stalin closed the file and, keeping his head down, whispered, "The three thieves who attacked and robbed me that night were indeed three women."

*****

Sara was the first to react and move to the stricken street man who was now showing sure signs of deep distress. "Stalin, please do not worry. You are facing a deeply tragic and profound situation. Please expect to evoke a myriad of emotions and experiences. I promise you it is all-natural. With your inner strength, the unlimited support from all of your friends, and my guidance, you will definitely overcome every hurdle you are currently experiencing."

Stalin looked up, feeling miserable, "Where do I begin?"

Sara smiled down and placed a hand on his shoulder. "As a former respected Police Colonel, losing your memory and sense of self over the last twenty years or more has to devastate you. You naturally must have struggled with many feelings of confusion and disorientation, with a profound sense of loss for the person you once were."

"But what about all the rage and anger I feel almost every minute of the day?"

"Well, the positive discovery you have experienced today has been able to discover that three unidentified females were the cause of your suffering. These evil women forced you to inhale the Devil's Breath. Which evoked intense feelings of betrayal and anger. You must have spent many moments questioning why this happened to you and questioning who did it to you and why?"

"But what about all the isolation and loneliness?"

Sara sat on the floor with both her legs crossed. She did not wish to talk down to this stricken man. She wanted to meet him on his terms. Memory loss can be an incredibly isolating experience for anyone, no matter who they are. You are expected to struggle to piece together fragments of your past. You may have felt disconnected from the very world around you."

Stalin looked into Sara's eyes, "What about helplessness, frustration, grief, and regrets?"

"Firstly, let's deal with helplessness and frustration. Yes, it is obvious you have a deep sense of helplessness and frustration. Not having control of your circumstances will almost always lead to feelings of powerlessness and deep despair. Stalin, you are human, albeit a special human."

"Regarding grief and regrets. You will reflect for many years to come on the years you lost and the profound impact of your memory loss on both yourself and those you trust and value the most. It will pass; you will step by step, day by day, become whole again."

At this point, Sara reached out and pulled Stalin towards her, and he sobbed. Everyone in the room rushed to their fallen hero and wrapped themselves around him. All secretly vowing that never again would police Colonel Stalin Oscar Ramirez become a victim.

While everyone was sitting like a rugby scrum at Twickenham, Zamira's mobile phone began ringing. At first, she happily decided she would not let the outside of her world enter and disturb what she was a part of now. Like everyone in that room, she felt Stalin and his tragic life should be the priority of all. She allowed it to continue ringing.

But it never stopped. Whoever it was, it appeared would only stop once she answered.

Zamira felt the soft hand of her Fire Chief resting on her shoulder, "Zamira, whoever it is, they feel it is important enough to keep trying. I think it best you answer the call."

As she switched on her mobile, she gasped in surprise. Facing her on her screen was the front of the Fire Station with Firefighter Silvana, aka "Highlander", with her biker's helmet in one hand and her mobile in the other. Next to her was a couple holding a clay gnome, each in their arms. She also noted that none of the persons facing her now were smiling. In fact, she thought they all looked scared.

Slowly, she looked up to her Eduardo and said, "Sir, I think you may wish to see this. I have no idea what is going on outside of our fire station, but judging by the expressions on all their faces, it must be important."

Eduardo leaned forward and looked at Zamira's mobile screen. "Does anyone here know why a couple carrying a pair of gnomes would feel the need to visit us?"

The mention of gnomes sent Archibaldo and Stalin's brains racing. They tried to come up with a plausible reason, but neither of them came up with anything. "Eduardo, may we look at the screen?" Stalin asked.

Archibaldo and Stalin looked at the screen and then turned to each other. Without saying a word, they silently asked each other, as if by magic, "What do Derekamus and Abella know we do not know?"

Archibaldo coughed and turned to Zamira, "I or we, that is, myself and Stalin, know these four individuals very well. The gentleman is Samuel. He and his late father, Ignacio, before him, have earned a living driving a Kenworth Burgundy truck. It was Ignacio who saved my wife's life a few years back when she was on her quad bike when an earthquake struck high up on the Mountain Ridge road above our city."

Archibaldo continued speaking and still did not look away: "The lady is Samuel's wife, Sofia. And the two gnomes are very special gnomes that I am sure will wish to speak to both me and Stalin. I know you all must have a million questions right now. But please be patient. Zamira, could you please go and bring all four of our unusual visitors to this office?"

Zamira turned to her Fire Chief, who could only say, "Yes, please do." Eduardo could not see his world becoming any weirder than it was right now. Who will believe him if and when he decides to broadcast this unbelievable event?

*****

It took another ten minutes before the office door was opened to reveal the new visitors. Stalin and Archibaldo stood and extended their hands to greet Samuel and Sofia. "Welcome to you both. Let us introduce you to our fire station management and city forensic teams."

Both teams willed each other silently to act as if nothing was awry. Why couldn't having a couple with apparently well-known gnomes visiting the station be an everyday occurrence? Sara and Ethan moved together to retrieve two chairs from a stack resting in the room's far corner. Each chair was politely drawn back to allow Samuel and Sofia to sit next to each other. Everyone else stayed rooted to their chairs, ensuring no one would miss this unimaginable event.

Samuel and Sofia timidly moved to the offered chairs and sat facing everyone. Then, as a final act for this inconceivable meeting, they each looked at each other for moral support and smiled when they placed their two smaller companions firmly on the large table. Every pair of human eyes was frozen, and it would be hard to see anyone blink.

Everyone in the room who had no prior knowledge of Abella's existence found themselves one second looking at her left eye and almost instantly moving to her right eye. None knew exactly where to concentrate, and no one had the courage to ask.

While reading the room, Derekamus moved forward and said, "Please do not worry where you are looking. I would recommend that everyone on this occasion close their eyes to allow them to concentrate on what my wife will soon reveal. Furthermore, I also wish to advise you all to stay seated and forget to try to take notes."

"My name is somewhat a tongue twister for most people, but with you South Americans and your forever-growing names, you may know me as Derekamus Stonebeard Stronforce or simply Derek for short."

Samuel reached down to a small blue holdall if things could not get more outlandish. His hand went in, and out came a miniature garden bench! He placed it behind Derekamus and Abella, who naturally sat down as if copying all the barbarians in front of them.

The Strong One was the first to clap and roar his approval: "I do not know about everyone else, but this is going to be one meeting I will never forget!"

"Nor tell." Offered the Wolf.

"And I suspect never believed. I bet in the years to come, even Google searching will draw a blank." Remarked Davide. This was followed by a murmur from all in agreement, followed by sniggering from the younger ones in the room as they pictured the absurdity of themselves in the years to come, still Google searching for any question they had.

Sofia gently tapped both gnomes on their shoulders. "I think it would be a good time for you to relate what you told Samuel and me this morning. Take your time, and do not worry; these fine people in front of you will be forever grateful for your having the courage to come forward."

Samuel said, "Thank you for seeing us all without any warning. We wish to explain why we are here. It is down to the insistence of this particular Kimmel gnome named for those who have never had the pleasure of knowing Abella Goldhammer Darkstone; please just use her first name, Abella."

Samuel leaned forward, "Could I also ask you all to hold back on any questions till the end of Abella's account of a horrifying event that took place back in March 1945 that she believes holds the key to all your housefires with unidentified victims in each for the past six decades."

*****

Abella decided to stay seated to allow all the barbarians in front of her to relax as much as possible, considering they were about to listen to a 250-year-old Kimmel gnome speaking in their Latin-Spanish tongue.

"During March 1945, the Allied forces conducted a series of bombing raids on the city of Berlin, targeting strategic military and industrial sites as part of their campaign to weaken Germany's war efforts. The bombings resulted in widespread destruction, causing significant damage and huge numbers of lost lives and casualties. A total of around 1,200 bombers from the United States Army Air Forces (USAAF), Royal Air Force (RAF), and French Air Force participated in the bombing raids on Berlin.

They dropped approximately 7,000 tons of bombs on the city over a period of several days, targeting industrial and military sites as well as civilian infrastructure. The bombing covered a significant area of Berlin and caused widespread destruction. The bombings of Berlin resulted in a high number of casualties and deaths. The exact number of deaths and casualties can vary depending on different sources, but I estimated that thousands of civilians were killed and many more were injured during the bombings. The intensity of the bombings and the widespread destruction in Berlin during that time had a devastating impact on the city and its residents.

The attacks were a part of the larger Allied strategy to end World War II by weakening Germany's ability to continue fighting. The bombing campaign against Berlin in March 1945 contributed to the eventual collapse of the German war machine and, in the same year, the Allied victory in Europe. I know all this because my husband Derekamus and I were there to witness all that happened."

The silence in the room became almost thick and heavy; later, Emilie described feeling wrapped up like a suffocating blanket and sensing the air filling with tension and unease.

*****

All eyes refused to move from Abella, and their expressions were a mix of Emilie's curiosity and Ethan's scepticism. Emilie had been raised since childhood that gnomes were famous for their honesty and wisdom. Gnomes were not reputed to speak lightly of any great importance, and most certainly, right now, she believed every word that Abella said regarding the horrors of Berlin way back in 1945.

Ethan struggled the most because he was married, and his two daughters back home in Boston continuously wanted to see a movie rerun called "Sherlock Gnomes."

"Sherlock Gnomes" is a 2018 animated comedy film that is a sequel to the 2011 film "Gnomeo & Juliet." The movie follows the characters Gnomeo and Juliet as they recruit the famous detective Sherlock Gnomes to help solve the mysterious disappearance of other garden gnomes in London. Together, they embark on a thrilling and humorous adventure to uncover the truth behind the disappearing gnomes.

The film features a stellar voice cast, including James McAvoy, Emily Blunt, Johnny Depp, and Chiwetel Ejiofor. Sherlock Gnomes playfully and entertainingly combines the elements of mystery, humour, and adventure, appealing to both his daughters and secretly to both Ethan and his wife.

Ethan refocuses back on the scene with two gnomes sitting on a garden bench in front of him, which is in stark contrast to the animated world he has been enjoying with his family for the past six years, which is difficult to comprehend. At the same time, he allowed his professionalism to remain his key weapon and held back on making any remarks that would put him in a bad light with all his colleagues in the room.

Dra Sofia Rodriguez, the Forensic Anthropologist, was also struggling internally. For her, it was the pull of unseen protective instincts within her. She wanted to rush forward and scoop up this wonderful Abella who had harboured such evil sights deep inside her for nearly 80 years. Sofia had to dig deep inside of her to remain seated.

For Denzel Herrera, with his deep ancestral Afro-Caribbean roots and wearing the darkest and fullest of beards, who, apart from being employed by the city as a forensic dentist. In his downtime, he is a DJ and budding poet. He had been doodling on his notepad, and on seeing Derekamus and Abella, he began composing....

In a dimly lit room of tools and teeth,
Forensic dentist by day, DJ by beat,
I met two gnomes, so small and neat,
Derek and Abella, quite the treat.

Their smiles sparkled in the light,
Their laughter was infectious; oh, what a sight,
I couldn't help but grin with delight,
As they danced and pranced into the night.

With toothbrushes in hand, they brushed away,
All worries and fears, making everything okay,
They sang a tune so strange and gay,
Their gnome voices carried me away.

Derek spun tracks on a mini turntable,
Abella freestyled like she was unstable,
Together, they formed a gnome duo label,
Rocking the party, feeling no trouble.

As a poet, I could not resist,
Capturing this moment amidst the twist,
Of gnomes in my office, a true, bizarre gist,
Derek and Abella are on my guest list.

So, here's to the gnomes of Kimmel's lore,
Bringing joy, laughter, and so much more,
To this dentist, DJ, and poet galore,
Derek and Abella, forevermore.

Fire Chief Eduardo raised his right hand, looking towards Derekamus and Abella, but he directed his next question solely to Abella. "Could you please give us some idea of what happened to those you wish to speak of today?"

"Yes, most certainly; let me go back to that last night when the bombs descended on the houses on our road. Derekamus and I were owned by Frau Helga, and her husband, a very sinister SS Doctor Hans Hartwig Schmidt. The doctor had been out all day with their three daughters, Gitta, Eva, and Gertrud, who at the time were only, I recall, 5, 6, and 7."

Abella looked down, took a deep breath, looked up again and continued, "Before those beautiful babies arrived with their father, a huge bomb rained down on the house and exploded, obliterating the grandeur and beauty of a once palatial setting. The house was instantly reduced to rubble; now, all its former glory was gone. In the same instant, precious artefacts, artwork, and family history were gone."

"We, Derekamus and I, have questioned each other many times about how we survived such a massive blast. We are only made of clay, but somehow, we did. As the infernal took hold, we saw a figurine emerge from what was once the front hall. Her clothes were almost gone, and her hair and body were in flames. We could do nothing. We were helpless; we could only watch as the doctor and his girls arrived. Seeing the horror on all their little faces has haunted my dreams ever since."

"We witnessed Dr Schmidt remove his weapon from his holster, and we sat speechless as he committed a "coup de grâce" to end Helga's existence and pain. If that was not enough, the doctor turned to his three little girls and made them swear never to tell anyone what they had witnessed that evening. As far as anyone was concerned, their mother had perished in the raid."

Later that evening, the same doctor came back and moved Helga's corpse to the cellar below the house and unceremoniously threw her remains into the darkness, closed the lid, and swept leaves and debris over the cellar entrance so as to prevent a swift discovery. In fact, it would be a further two years before bulldozers arrived to clear the whole street and not just this house."

For us two gnomes, we continued sitting there until suddenly, Helga's older sister, Clara, picked us both up and transported us to her back garden.

Finally, Abella stood and moved towards the centre of the table. "I wish to say not all our life has been of horror and unhappiness. No, far from it. We have had a good life together for nearly 250 years. If it had not been for that awful and terrifying night in 1945, we would never have known the feelings of sadness and despair."

*****

Stalin was the first to break the ensuing silence, "Abella, thank you for sharing with us all the tragedy that developed during those Allied raids over Berlin. Do you know what happened to the father and his three daughters?"

Abella turned to this rough-looking street man who secretly held a heart of gold deep within himself. She had taken much pleasure in assisting him with his loss of memory, not realising that he now needed her knowledge further within a few days.

"Alas, no, we have never seen them and have no idea where they ended up. That is until, for some unknown feeling, I have felt something that is making me uneasy with living here in this fair city over the last few days. I can only describe it as something invisible to the eye but still deep within my memory. I have been feeling a sense of foreboding, which has been unsettling. I feel the sisters who now must be old women are close by."

*****

Eduardo sprang out of his chair, which in turn was head over heels behind him. "Is it possible that not just one female may be our culprit, but actually three sisters! "

Now he turned and focused his questioning mind towards Dr Sara Gomez, the city Psychologist who had been, in his eyes, fantastic when his excellent friend Stalin began to fall apart in front of everyone. "Brothers maybe, but sisters? Surely not?"

Sara had her laptop open, and she had just that minute Google searched for any reports of sisters being prosecuted for arson or killing. The search yielded no results for such a thing happening anywhere worldwide.

"Sorry, Chief. It appears that going right back to ancient times, there has never been a case of sisters becoming arsonists or serial killers. If our three suspects, whom we are hearing about here today with the testimony from Abella, prove to be the real culprits, then these ladies will be making history. We must be absolutely sure of ourselves before moving forward with this incredible investigation."

Stalin raised his hand, minus his trusty rock, "Let us for the moment at least. Hypothetically, ask the question, is it possible for this to have happened, and if so, what reasons or motives would they bring together as a trio?"

Sara moved to a standing position and went to the whiteboard just behind her chair. She reached for the marker pen and began to write: Reasons why Three Sisters join together with the aim of killing.

"There are probably umpteen reasons why sisters would join each other to kill, but let us look at the five most experts in psychology would most likely agree on."

"1. Familial bonds: The sisters could have an incredibly close and intense bond, wherein their loyalty to each other manifests in extreme and violent ways, leading them to commit crimes together. In this scenario that Abella gave us, the timing looks good. If they were born on or near 1939, then 1965, each would be approximately 26, give or take a few months either side."

2. A thirst for power: "As they grow older, the sisters may seek a sense of control and dominance, using violence to assert their authority and exert power over others. Maybe their first victim was their father. We currently know nothing of his history except that he was an SS Doctor, and that bunch were no angels. So, if he survived the war, where did he go?"

3. Mental health issues: "Some psychological disorders or untreated mental illnesses could manifest differently in each sister, leading them to engage in violent behaviour together or separately. In either case, we are dealing with three girls who have grown up and carried a huge burden on each other. Did they marry? Did they have children? My instincts are saying No to both questions."

4. Feeding off each other: "The sisters' bond and influence on one another may amplify their violent tendencies, creating a self-reinforcing cycle of deviant behaviour. Maybe our three sisters have grown up and are now ageing spinsters. Allowing for the time frames we are dealing with; they should all be now in their mid-eighties. Which still makes them possible suspects."

5. Manipulation by an outside force: "The sisters may become unwitting pawns in the hands of a manipulator, such as a cult leader or mastermind criminal, who exploits their vulnerabilities to orchestrate their killing spree. I do not believe we are dealing with this last one, but I must still write it down on this board for discussion with you all."

*****

Archibaldo rose and moved to stand near Sara. "Thank you, Sara. We now have much to consider and investigate between you and our two friends, Abella and Derekamus. May I suggest we all stop at this point and head back to where we live, try to empty our minds, and report back here again in the morning fresh and ready to move forward together?"

"Hang on a minute! What about that Lasagna I heard about earlier?" Only Stalin could feel the need to put his stomach first. Everyone appeared to sigh all at once, which in turn broke the ice and allowed everyone to smile and laugh with each other.

"Tomorrow, colonel, I am sure the lasagna will be twice as tasty in 24 hours' time." Offered Archibaldo.

*****

Zamira was the last to leave. She went to close the door of the empty office and stopped. She stared back to see two Kimmel gnomes who had walked into everyone's lives and turned their worlds and beliefs upside down, now walking back to where she was standing. Without a word passing, Derekamus and Abella entered the office again and attempted to assist each other with one of the chairs. Their ultimate aim was to reach the surface of the table. Zamira switched back on the overhead light that she had switched off only moments prior. She almost said to herself, "I was exiting this room and planning to leave it unlocked for the night cleaner to make it all pristine once again."

*****

Behind the two gnomes came Samuel, Sofia, Carmen, aka Wolf, and Tomas, aka the Strong One. Behind them followed the forensic team as a group. As he entered the room, Ethan commented, "There is no way there is going to be anything more interesting on Netflix or Amazon Prime to beat what we are about to discover. Mind you, as an afterthought. Just think, one day, we may all be in a landmark documentary retelling our story! Now that is worth smiling about."

*****

Only a tiny moment passed when Archibaldo, Stalin, and Eduardo marched in a row of three. "Please, someone, get the coffee pot on." Everyone took up their original positions and laid their mobiles on the table in front of them.

Stalin leaned forward, minus any type of mobile, and began to speak when there was a knock at the door. Fifteen pairs of eyes, two of which were a bit cross-eyed, turned to the sound as the door began to open.

Everyone who was on shift that day, whether in the operations room or out on Alpha 1 and Alpha 2, was all bunched up on either side of the duty chef and waiting for one of them to speak. "Sorry to disturb you all, but we were wondering if you might like to eat some of this wonderful lasagna and whether you might need some extra hands tonight? None of us want to go home as we want to help find these perpetrators. We do not want to turn up to any more housefires with dead people inside of each one."

Eduardo stood and slowly moved towards his team. "Listen, all of you. From the bottom of all our hearts, we thank you for the lasagna and for offering us your help. But the city needs you all to rest. Go home, be with your family and relax. Sleep peacefully because we will need you all fighting fit and roaring to go tomorrow. Let us worry about those we are searching for. Let me know that tomorrow morning, when you all return, you will be ready for all that will come our way. Again, thank you. Now go!"

Stalin looks at his friend, Eduardo. Congratulations, Chief. What just happened speaks volumes of the type of man I know you to be. It seems everyone here and in this fire station knows, too."

"Thank you, Colonel; now, do you require a cup or mug of Tinto with your lasagna? "Smiled Eduardo.

"Make them all mug sizes and throw in some good old "Irish Whiskey" to keep me alert."

The room exploded with approval, and everyone was eager to get started. "Now, Colonel, while we are all waiting for the coffee beans, why not give us all something to do? And to save time, use just our first names and forget the formalities of rank and file."

As if on cue, Stalin turned to his new investigation team and looked straight at Emilie. "Please, Emilie, as you have been coordinating much of the forensic investigation, could you please now coordinate with the immigration people to ascertain if there are any records of triplets and a father entering this country from March 1945? Let us see if we can identify our suspects as swiftly as possible?"

Stalin then turned towards Zamira. "Young lady, with your skills, please work alongside Emilie. Chase any leads that arise. The chances are the list will be small. But we may have to meet the challenge of possible name changes." Zamira moved her chair closer to Emilie, signalling her intent to be the backbone of this double act.

Stalin turned to his friend Eduardo, "Fire Chief, I need you to work with Carmen and Tomas. With your joint experience, please relook at the cases of housefires that also housed a possible dead victim. Look for clues to help us see if we are following the right path of believing that three sisters could be our quarries."

Stalin now turned to his right, "Davide, Sofia, and Sara, please join forces and re-examine our latest victim. I wish to know if it was possible that he also fell victim to Devil's Breath, i.e., Scopolamine, also known as hyoscine."

Davide spoke quietly, "Are you looking for a pattern. Are you thinking these three sisters could be the same ones who destroyed much of your life back in 1985?"

Stalin tried to answer with conviction but was still unsure what he sought. "I am right now trying to open as many doors as possible. Hopefully, one will be the right one."

Stalin started to feel he was bringing his team together; he needed an unlikely team to investigate outside the norm. "Now Anya, Denzel, Samuel, Sofia Abella, and Derekamus. I want you all to come together and work outside the expertise restrictions. I want you to think like three sisters who I believe are not restricted to travelling in and out of this country as we mere Colombians do. What are the options they could have turned to?"

"Finally, Ethan and Archibaldo. Overlook nothing. Check everything that each team comes to you with. I have been asking myself a question that I still have no answer to. If March every ten years is so important to them. Then why did they kill in February in year nine and not March in year ten as had always been part of their Modus Operandi?"

Within seconds, everyone moved to their assigned team member and the investigation into identifying three sisters and the reasons why they had crossed many invisible lines to commit murder, not once, but many times, was looking for answers.

*****

## *70: I am the Ill Fated Private Chartered Flight*

As the sun begins to disappear, it dips below the horizon, casting the city of Santiago de Cali Airport in a soft twilight glow. The airport staff begins the process of winding down for the night. The bustling terminals empty out as the last scheduled flights for the day have departed, leaving a quiet and deserted atmosphere.

The Duty-Free stores begin replenishing all their empty shelves, ready for the next day's early start. Cleaners throughout the terminals steadfastly clean every nook and cranny to ensure no mishap can occur. Particular attention is paid to the safety and cleanliness of the Gateway areas. Nighttime security staff refigure all their security apparatus, including Archways and X-ray machines.

In a secluded corner of the airport, hidden from the main terminals, sits a private hangar belonging to a wealthy business magnate. The hangar is registered to Gabriel Garcia Marquez, the Argentinian-born Life President of CT&C Corporation. As mentioned, he must not be mistaken for the famous Colombian writer Gabriel José de la Concordia Garcia Marquez.

\*\*\*\*\*

Inside the hangar, the lifetime President's vintage Cessna 172 Skyhawk is being prepped for its late-night retirement flight departure. As a mark of honour to Gabriel, it will be deposited on the forecourt of his prestigious CT&C US-based headquarters near Miami Airport.

The Skyhawk's engines hum softly as they are tested, emitting a low rumble that reverberates through the quiet hangar. Everything appears set for the scheduled farewell flight.

The pilot and co-pilot, paragons of professionalism, meticulously conduct their final checks. Every system of the aircraft is examined, ensuring flawless operation. The two equally dedicated flight attendants prepare the cabin with the utmost care, leaving no detail unattended. Luggage is loaded, and the final security checks are executed with precision.

Three female passengers have been seated. Their elegant soirée features trays of delicate canapés topped with luxurious caviar, each bite bursting with flavour, perfectly complemented by glasses of golden champagne bubbling with effervescence. The caviar, given to mark the occasion, rests on their laps. At this point, the falsely registered pilot for this flight and the two nameless flight attendants move silently away from the aircraft and board a waiting black limousine.

This discreet mode of transportation is a stark contrast to the vintage Cessna.

The limousine takes them away out of reach from the airport authorities back to the Museo de Fenix car park, where a vehicle is waiting to whisk them to a private airstrip near Manizales. From there, another private jet will fly them back to Argentina, and their bank accounts will soon be filled with newly acquired US Dollars. These substantial sums will undoubtedly change each of their lives and ensure their permanent silence should they be asked why they had not stayed with the Cessna and its co-pilot, who later was presumed as the missing Life President.

*****

With all preparations complete, the Cessna 172 Skyhawk emerges from its hangar, symbolising longevity, wealth, and power. Guided by the nightly ground crew wielding lighted wands, it glided across the tarmac away from the apron, passing by the darkened terminals and rows of parked planes sitting on the taxiway until it reached the designated runway.

The Air Traffic Control Tower, a beacon of authority, gives the all-clear. Then, with a thunderous roar, the jet surges forward, its powerful engine propelling it down the runway. The vintage Cessna 172 Skyhawk took off, exuding a distinct sound profile that blends the deep rumbling of its engine with the high-pitched whine of its propeller spinning rapidly. As the aircraft accelerates down the runway, the engine noise intensifies, creating a symphony of power and motion. The propeller's rotation generated a rhythmic whooshing sound, adding to the overall auditory experience. Additionally, the airstream passing over the aircraft's wings produced a subtle rush of wind noise, further enhancing the sensory experience of witnessing the vintage Cessna taking off.

In a breathtaking moment, it defied gravity and ascended into the night sky, a testament to the luxury and secrecy it represented.

As the private jet climbs higher and higher, leaving Alfonso Bonilla Aragon International Airport behind, the lights of the city twinkle below, gradually fading into the darkness. The Life President and his lifelong loyal passengers onboard settle in for their expectant journey, enjoying the comfort and luxury of their private flight as they soar through the starlit sky towards their US-bound destination.

*****

"Well, ladies, I do believe all has gone well this evening. It is great to have you all again as my passengers. Our flight plan for tonight will include refuelling stops in an airfield close to Caracas and another near the Haiti Airport. We will initially fly northeast towards Caracas, and from there, we will fly eastwards to Haiti. We will stop for a well-earned rest before heading northwest towards your final destination, Miami."

Do you remember when you all were my passengers the first time?"

All three sisters paused, each trying to head far back in time.

"I believe we are sat in the very same seats!" exclaimed Anna Müller, now wedged between Eva and Lisa.

Eva asked the next question: "With the flight plan you have described Santiago de Cali to Miami with stopovers for refuelling in Caracas and near Port-au-Prince, Haiti, will this flight pass through the area known as the Bermuda Triangle?"

Gabriel chuckles: "No, the flight route will not pass through the area known as the Bermuda Triangle. It is located in the western part of the North Atlantic Ocean between Bermuda, Miami, and Puerto Rico and is roughly 1.5 to 2 hours away from our flight path. We will not be traversing into that area."

Lisa nudges her sister, "Eva, why are you asking such a question? Have you been researching our flight tonight?!"

Looking sheepishly at her younger sister, Lisa says, "Well, yes, I have. I have been reading up on this Bermuda thingy regarding notable accounts whereby aircraft have gone missing and were never found."

"Really, are you going to tell us what happened?"

"Of course, you know me; I cannot keep secrets from you two." At this point, Gabriel paused to listen to what Eva had discovered.

"There have been two notable accounts of aircraft that went missing over the Bermuda Triangle and were never found: The first one happened in December 1945, when five US Navy Avenger torpedo bombers disappeared during a training flight over the Triangle. The squadron of five aircraft, Flight 19, failed to return to base, and no wreckage or bodies were ever recovered. The second that alarmed me happened in 1991 when a Grumman Cougar fighter jet piloted by US Air National Guard Captain Lawrence J. Howard vanished while flying over the Bermuda Triangle. Despite an extensive search, no trace of the aircraft or Captain Howard was ever found, leaving the circumstances surrounding the disappearance shrouded in mystery."

Eva did not pause; she was on a roll, "These cases have remained unsolved and have contributed to the legend and mystery surrounding the Bermuda Triangle."

Anna leans into her sister, "Are you letting 2 mysteries scare you?"

Speaking faster than her ageing brain was functioning, Eva said, "No. I mean, yes, there have been other incidents of aircraft going missing in the Bermuda Triangle. For example, 1948, a Douglas DC-3 aircraft vanished while flying over the area. Another case involved a C-124 Globemaster II military transport plane that disappeared in 1951. While these cases are not as widely known as others, they still contribute to the mysterious reputation of the Bermuda Triangle."

Gabriel thought it best to put their minds at rest: "Ladies, please do not get carried away. You will all be safe with me. I have flown this type of route for nearly half a century or more. You would be hard-pressed to find another with as many nautical miles as I have gathered in my lifetime. Never once have I crashed and landed anywhere in the world."

"Thank you, Gabriel. That is one of the many reasons we have always turned to you and your services. We have never feared for our safety," Eva remarked.

Anna asked, "Saying that, Gabriel, what can we expect from the weather this evening?"

Gabriel was on safe ground with his extensive knowledge of weather patterns around the globe, "On our flight path this evening and to some degree that can include the Bermuda Triangle. Of course, weather conditions can vary throughout the year. Generally, this region experiences a subtropical climate with warm temperatures and high humidity. The summer months, from June to August, tend to be hot and humid, with increased chances of thunderstorms and tropical cyclones. The hurricane season that you may be the most frightened of typically runs from June to November, with the peak season occurring in August and September. In contrast, from December to February, the winter months are milder but can still experience occasional storms and high winds. And as you know, this is the month of February, so relax, sit back, and enjoy the champagne and the nibbles."

*****

While Gabriel was reassuring his three clients, he, through years of practice, read every dial in front of him. A recently installed system equipped with weather radar systems that provide real-time weather information to pilots during flight quietly warned them of severe weather conditions ahead, a thunderstorm with the risk of turbulence, icing conditions, and strong winds. The radar system had not yet advised him to adjust or deviate his flight path to avoid hazardous weather.

At this stage of the flight path, he thought it prudent to hold his own counsel.

\*\*\*\*\*

Reports had been flooding in of two oil tankers colliding during a surprise storm that was fast becoming a potentially life-threatening hurricane. If it continued growing, it was estimated that it would soon be on a direct path to Haiti.

No, they must be exaggerating. There had never been a hurricane in this area for many years. He went to dismiss the danger but thought to himself, "Best be careful, Gabriel. This is your last flight, my son. Do not let your guard down now."

He followed his advice and began checking his cockpit instrument and warning systems. So far, so good. There were no flashing lights or sirens blaring away. The air speed, altitude, heading indicator, tachometer, oil pressure gauge, oil temperature gauge, and fuel gauge all worked as expected. But for the first time in his flying career, Gabriel felt uneasy.

\*\*\*\*\*

"Mayday, Mayday, Mayday. This is the captain of the oil tanker "Ocean Voyager." We have just witnessed a collision with another tanker and are now experiencing severe listing. Our vessel is in distress, with over 20 crew members on board. The other tanker has sunk within minutes, and our ship is also at risk of sinking. We are carrying over 1.5 million gallons of industrial fuel oil, which is critical. We urgently need assistance. Repeat: the oil tanker "Ocean Voyager" is declaring a Mayday distress signal. Requesting immediate assistance. Over."

Upon hearing the oil tanker Ocean Voyager's distress call, Gabriel immediately contacted relevant authorities. He was about to call the Coast Guard or the nearest air traffic control to report the distress call and provide them with the location of the oil tanker.

Sensing something hard now resting against his neck, Gabriel tried to turn to see what it was. He witnessed Anna with what looked like an old WW2 Luger P08 pistol with SS insignias on both sides of the handle. "We prefer you do not make that call."

The Luger spoke to Gabriel of a darker time, a time of oppression and tyranny when the world trembled under the shadow of a regime that sought to crush all who stood in its path. It whispered of secret meetings, whispered conspiracies and the clink of glasses raised in sinister toasts.

Anna holding the Luger was to have a piece of that history in her hands, a stark reminder of the depths to which three sisters had sunk in pursuit of power and dominance. And as the cockpit fell silent, the Luger seemed to exude a malevolent energy, a chilling testament to the darkness that once engulfed the world.

Looking directly into Anna's eyes, "I have a question, well, three really. Whatever happened to the Biologist, Dra. Emily Greene, the Physicist, Professor David Wells, and the Chemist Dr. Marcus Reed? I know what happened to a certain Hugo van der Vored."

Lisa was the first to respond, "Wow, Gabriel, how do you manage to remember those names?"

Gabriel is satisfied with his memory skills, even for someone aged over 100. "Well, the last one was easy. He only died a couple of weeks ago in a suspect housefire. The other three are the only recorded names in my volumes of diaries who, after being issued with return flights paid in cash each time, attended the incoming flight but have yet to make it onto their scheduled exit flights. No refunds were requested or accepted by the payees, i.e. you three ladies."

Eva spoke next: "We heard they were all victims of mysterious house fires. Bad luck, I guess."

Anna added, "From our understanding, they all deserved to die. None of them had lived good lives when they had the chance to."

Gabriel looked at all three and then settled his gaze onto the muzzle of the Luger. "Ladies, I have no plans going the same way. I have held my peace for many decades, and I will happily take your secrets to my grave. Only not tonight. I want to deliver this aircraft to my headquarters in Miami and stand back and watch their expressions when they realise their Life President had the nerve and the capability to fly such a distance."

*****

Trying to regain his composure, Gabriel insisted, "After that, I never want to set eyes on any of you again. On another subject, Ladies, please, I must warn other aircraft to avoid flying directly over the distressed vessel to prevent any potential hazards from the industrial fuel oil it carries. We need to follow instructions from the authorities and be prepared to assist in any way we can, such as providing aerial surveillance or communication support."

Eva, without warmth in her words, said, "We will not be attempting a rescue mission as your primary focus should be on ensuring our safety and getting us to Miami without any agreed-upon delays or detours."

Lisa now spoke, "Let the authorities ensure a coordinated and effective response to the distress situation aboard the oil tanker "Ocean Voyager." Please switch off your radio for now."

\*\*\*\*\*

Gabriel had no choice but to concentrate ahead while remaining seated as comfortably as possible in the unexpectedly stressful situation in his cockpit. With both hands, the centenarian pilot could only continue gripping his control yoke as firmly as possible. Gabriel tried his utmost to concentrate on his engine, which steadily made a reassuring sound in the background.

For Gabriel, a lifetime navigating his beloved fleet of aircraft, making minor adjustments to the hand control and foot pedals, feeling the rudder responsive feedback as each plane banks and turns smoothly at his command. Sensing the wind rushing past his cockpit windows and seeing the vast sky around him. The sheer enjoyment of scanning the horizon ensured a clear path ahead of him as he piloted with confidence and precision. But right then, all that was gone. A lifetime of confidence and expertise replaced with fear and panic!

\*\*\*\*\*

Hello readers, it is Climate Change. Like you, I have followed Gabriel and his three loyal clients for a while. My efforts have placed a hurricane in their path. I think I should increase their fear factor, don't you?"

So, first things first, let's increase the ocean temperature to provide the necessary conditions for an ever-increasing powerful hurricane. Let me add a few other factors, such as atmospheric instability, which I will need to support the air's vertical movement. I want the hurricane to develop to keep it organised and strengthen quickly without being disrupted by the stronger winds above it. This is known as low wind shear. Finally, I must create a conducive environment to ensure it becomes a sure-fire, powerful hurricane. It must have warm ocean temperatures, high humidity, and minimum disruption from dry air or dust. How about some rough seas? How high should I go with the waves? Given that we are at sea right now, it's not just conducive but ideal.

Now all the ingredients are in place, let's see how fearful they will become.

\*\*\*\*\*

Gabriel found himself staring ahead inside the cockpit as he began to fly directly into the hurricane. Where had it come from? He had no idea. All he could do was hold on as tightly as possible to his control yoke and stare at his out-of-control six-pack of instruments in front of him.

Gabriel faced one of the most harrowing challenges of his flying career as he navigated directly into the formidable hurricane with winds reaching 100 miles per hour. The sudden and violent updrafts and downdrafts buffeted the now flimsy-looking small aircraft, testing his lifetime of skills and experience to the absolute limit and beyond.

The continuing challenge was the exposure to heavy rain, thunderstorms, and severe weather conditions, which created a chaotic and disorienting environment in the cockpit. The pounding rain on the windshield, accompanied by intense flashes of lightning and deafening thunder, only added to the sense of urgency and danger.

Next, Gabriel began to see icing on the wings building up rapidly, threatening the aerodynamics of the Cessna 175 as he struggled to maintain control and keep the aircraft flying straight. The limited options for escape or diversion forced him to make split-second decisions that could mean the difference between life and death.

Despite the fear and uncertainty of the situation, Gabriel drew upon decades of flying experience to stay calm and focused, searching for any opening or opportunity to navigate out of the treacherous storm. The intense adrenaline rush and the primal instinct for survival drove him to push forward, fighting against the powerful forces of nature that seemed to overwhelm his existence.

As the Müller sisters, Anna, Eva, and Lisa, found themselves staring without blinking out of the cockpit and side windows, seeing nothing as they peered out into the chaotic fury of the hurricane, they were overcome with a mix of awe, fear, and fascination. The wind howled like a banshee, whipping through the plane's fuselage and sending debris flying. Rain pounded incessantly against the surrounding glass, creating distorted views of the world outside.

Having lowered the Luger pistol by now, Anna clutched Eva's hand tightly with her free hand, her heart racing with excitement and trepidation. She had never seen anything like this before, the sheer power of nature on full display before her eyes. Eva's eyes were wide with wonder, and her breath caught in her throat as she watched the swirling clouds above. The sheer force of the storm was both terrifying and mesmerising.

Lisa, the youngest of the sisters, sat with eyes vast and afraid as she took in the chaos unfolding before her. She could feel the plane trembling under the force of the wind, and for a moment, a surge of panic welled up inside her, "Are we going to die?"

"Not if I can help it!" roared Gabriel. Suddenly, the howling wind ceased, and the sky miraculously cleared up in front of the plane. Gabriel was puzzled: "Is there such a thing called the eye of the storm? Do they exist?" At this moment, he felt the eerie sensation of a disappearing storm, thus giving Gabriel and his three terrified passengers a false sense of security.

None of them could measure the size of the eye. It could range from just a few miles to maybe 100 miles or more in diameter. Do they have minutes or several hours before the hurricane returns with its full force?

Alas, you will never know.

We can rest assured that the Cessna 175 Skyhawk was manufactured back in the mid-1960s and registered to Gabriel Garcia Marquez, the Argentinian-born Life President of CT&C Corporation, and not to be mistaken as the famous Colombian writer Gabriel José de la Concordia Garcia Marquez with three German-born sisters named as Anna, Eva, and Lisa Müller as passengers would have put up a brave fight to live. But sadly, in this crisis, every ounce of skill, determination, and sheer willpower was put to the ultimate test as Gabriel battled against the elements in a desperate bid to reach safety and emerge from the heart of the storm, battered but unbroken was not enough.

*****

What did you expect? I am Climate Change.

*****

## *71: I am a Couple who feel the need to Migrate to Canada*

Samuel and Sofia lounged on the sofas, periodically watching the latest Netflix offering and checking their Facebook feeds. Deep down, neither was too impressed with the streaming channel offerings.

Sofia voiced her feelings: "Samuel, why is it always the case that with all that is on offer weekly, we always end up finding nothing that interests us?"

"It beats me. With the new releases each week, I only have a keen sense of watching a movie or a limited series. The thought of sitting through 60 episodes of Simon Bolivar or another 73 episodes of Pablo Escobar would send me crazy within a week!"

Sofia began to rise. "Do you fancy some fresh watermelon? I brought one earlier today, and I need to dice it up and freeze it for future use."

Samuel began salivating at the thought of satisfying his thirst with a vast segment of mouthwatering watermelon. "Oh yes, please. The heat in the city tonight is not welcome. Even our gnomes outside were sweating earlier today. I had to bring them indoors to soak them in the bucket. That reminds me, I should take them out and dry them."

Samuel rises from his favourite sofa and heads into the basement where his beloved Kenworth Burgundy Truck is parked. He walks to the rear of the elongated tail base to the small cabinet where he stores items to maintain the cleanliness of his pride and joy. He smiles when he sees his other pride and joy, Derekamus and Abella, bobbing up and down in the large navy blue bucket.

"Good evening to you both. I hope this bucket of cold water has helped you soften the discomfort arising from the heat in our city today." As he spoke, his hands gently lowered into the clear water, and with little exertion, he lifted both gnomes out of the bucket and placed them on a dry towel covering the cabinet. Abella, shaking vigorously, mutters to herself, "It's a good job. I understand his sentiments in keeping us cool. But right now, I am freezing!" Her partner, Derekamus, has looked sympathetic toward his loving wife for over 250 years, "Do not fret. By midday tomorrow, you will wish to return to this blue magical bucket again."

*****

Samuel returned from the basement as Sofia was wiping down the kitchen worktop. He continued scrolling through the Netflix options again, hoping to find something that would pique their interest. Looking at the screen, he couldn't help but reflect on their shared love for adventure and exploration.

"Sometimes I wish we could go on our own adventures instead of constantly relying on what's available on the screen," Samuel mused aloud, more to himself than anyone else.

Sofia returned with a bowl of freshly cut watermelon cubes. She handed one to Samuel and settled back onto the sofa, picking up the conversation. "You know, I've often thought about that too, Samuel. We've spent so much time-consuming other people's stories; maybe it's time to create our own."

Samuel took a bite of the juicy watermelon, thinking about Sofia's words. "You're right. Life should be an adventure, not just something we watch from the comfort of our couches."

Inspired by Sofia's suggestion, Samuel put his watermelon down and grabbed his laptop. He started searching for unique travel destinations and out-of-the-way places that would allow them to immerse themselves in different cultures and experiences.

Sofia sits next to Samuel, and together, they delve further into their research. Samuel and Sofia soon discover a world of possibilities. They stumble upon stories of hidden temples in Southeast Asia, untouched islands in the Pacific, and remote Andes villages in Bolivia, Ecuador, and Peru.

Excitement filled the room as they realised they didn't need Netflix to provide them with adventure; they could create thrilling stories. They made a pact to plan a series of explorations, promising to step out of their comfort zones and truly experience the world's wonders.

*****

Since his parents' deaths, Samuel had found he did not have to worry about day-to-day living. The ample life assurance on both Ignacio and Jasmina covered more than just their funerals. It left Samuel and Sofia with a nest egg at the bank, which they had not touched. Although hugely sad for Samuel and his boyhood memories, the sale of the various homes his parents had wisely invested in became large sums of funds again untouched, sitting in the bank.

He had inherited the historic burgundy-coloured Kenworth truck Model 1993KW W900B. Although it was ageing well, Samuel foresaw the possibility of selling it and using the proceeds as a deposit for a newer model. Until now, no one has shown the slightest interest in buying the truck, and those who tried to buy it for next to nothing always received a polite "No thank you."

Samuel was also considering donating the classic truck to the Museo Aereo Fenix. Although every other mode of transport was on display, until now, there had been no mighty Kenworth truck. He is sure that Norman and the current owners of the transport museum would love to be its new home. He could see it sitting alongside the 1930s Buicks.

*****

Samuel opened his smartphone with the aim of Google searching the telephone number for the museum, but a Facebook advertisement appeared and stopped him in his tracks:
Couples, take the journey of immigrating as truck Drivers in Adventurous Canada!
Are you and your partner tired of the challenges of maintaining a long-distance relationship? Are you ready for a thrilling new chapter together? Canada is calling you!
Introducing the Canadian Couples Truckers Program!
Discover the Need:
Canada currently needs more couples working together as long-distance truck drivers. This shortage affects the efficiency of the transportation industry and takes a toll on the personal lives of many hardworking individuals. By joining hands as a couple in this exciting career path, you can fill this need and strengthen the bond with your loved one, all while contributing to Canada's prosperous future!
The Immigration Process Made Easy:
Don't let the immigration process discourage you! With Canada's welcoming immigration policies and our dedicated team of experts, we'll guide you every step of the way. From visa applications to work permits, we'll ensure a seamless transition for you and your partner, making your dream of living and working together in Canada a reality.
Enjoy the outstanding benefits of becoming a Truck Driver in Canada:
Enjoy competitive wages, acknowledging your hard work and dedication,

ensuring a stable and comfortable life for you and your loved one.

Travel the diverse landscapes of Canada's provinces, from snow-capped mountain ranges to breathtaking coastlines, creating unforgettable memories as you conquer the open road together.

Work together as a team, crafting your own flexible schedules to accommodate your personal needs and priorities.

Join a thriving, supportive community network of truck drivers, where you'll find camaraderie, friendship, and connection with like-minded couples who understand this profession's unique joys and challenges.

**Career Growth Opportunities:** Harness your professional development by upgrading your skills and certifications. This will allow you to access tremendous growth potential within the industry, open doors to new opportunities, and enhance your long-term career prospects.

If you love a sense of adventure and wish to become prosperous, then guess what? Canada is waiting for you!

Ready to take this amazing leap? Click the link below to learn more about joining the Canadian Couples Truckers Program!

Apply now and embark on an extraordinary journey together!

www.CanadianCoouplesTruckersProgram.ca.

*****

Samuel looked at Sofia and said, "Darling, please read this advertisement that has miraculously appeared on my laptop before you say or do anything."

He positioned the screen so Sofia could read the advert. Samuel sat back and waited to see what she would say next.

Sofia's eyes widened as she absorbed the advertisement on the screen. She made sounds but not words. She got to the end and immediately scrolled back to the top and re-read every word. Finally, she put the laptop lid down and looked at Samuel, "Do you think I could qualify as a truck driver and immigrate to Canada with you as a couple?"

Samuel reached with both hands and took Sofia's hands within his. He looked deeply into her eyes and whispered, "Yes, darling, I can teach you much of what you need to know. As for the examinations and tests you will need to pass, I believe a certain female gnome, who right now is sitting very close to us, can assist with her magic, too."

Samuel paused and continued, "The average individual would take months, sometimes years, to become a qualified long-distance truck driver. Completing the necessary training and obtaining all the required qualifications would quickly put most people off seeing this advertisement. But we are different; you have known my family for nearly all your adult life.

You already have gained a thorough understanding of the commitments and requirements of this profession. Sofia, you meet the basic requirements by holding a valid driver's license and being over 21 years old." Both laughed, with Samuel not saying Sofia's actual age.

Samuel moved on, "With regard to training you, who else is better suited than me to school and train you every step of the way? Remember, I have four generations of truck driving expertise in my blood."

"As for classroom training, I am sure Abella and her magical dust will help you quickly understand all the essential topics, such as rules and regulations, safety procedures, vehicle maintenance, and trip planning."

I will follow up with all the hands-on sessions to ensure you can inspect any vehicle presented to you and learn how to couple and uncouple any trailers. You will learn how to manoeuvre in different driving conditions, such as mountain driving in both the daytime and the nighttime. I will teach you how to execute proper braking techniques that have stood me, my father, my grandfather, and my Great-grandfather, well."

Samuel paused to head into the kitchen to retrieve two bottles of icy cold water on his return. After passing one bottle to Sofia, Samuel continued with what was buzzing around in his head: "While we are waiting for Canada and its Immigration process to move along, we can hone your skills and help you gain experience by taking over some of my routes. I will act as your trainer and passenger."

Finally, we should turn to Abella again for her invaluable contribution to your successfully gaining a Commercial Driver's License."

Samuel looked expectantly at his adorable partner in life; for once, he had no clue what she was thinking. He blurted out, "Tell me what you think?"

*****

Samuel's unexpected suggestions intrigued Sofia. Although she had never considered a career in truck driving before, the thought of embarking on an adventurous journey while earning a living intrigued her.

"I must admit, that's a unique idea," Sofia replied a hint of excitement in her voice. "Imagine the vast landscapes we would witness, the new people we'd meet, and the stories we could gather along the road."

Samuel's smile widened. "Exactly! A life filled with constant exploration and the freedom to create our own narratives. Plus, it seems like a practical way to fund our future adventures."

*****

As they delved deeper into this newfound possibility, Samuel and Sofia began researching the life of long-distance truck drivers in Canada. They discovered that the job offered various benefits, such as flexible schedules, abundant job opportunities, and an opportunity to see the country from an entirely different perspective.

Inspired by their findings, they quickly developed a plan. Before bed, they updated their resumes, highlighting transferable skills relevant to the trucking industry, such as problem-solving, adaptability, and working under pressure. For Samuel, it became a massive task to explain how he, being a fourth-generation truck driver, was now in the throes of teaching his wife to become a truck driver.

Samuel researched his Google Photos files and selected three pics that showcased his family's connection with Kenworth Trucks.

*****

Weeks turned into months, and before they knew it, Samuel and Sofia had successfully found job openings at a reputable trucking company in Vancouver. The freight company had an in-house training department and Spanish-speaking Instructors to assist them while they learned English.

It also helped that both had enrolled in Duolingo and were testing each other every night. At weekends, Abella also gave each of them a crash course in dreaded English grammar with the help of a few gold dust particles on their shoulders. Their excitement grew as they secured online interviews and received positive responses.

Soon enough, they travelled to Canada, filled with anticipation and nervousness. As they settled into their new, vibrant city, they began training for their latest joint profession. They spent long hours in workshops, learning the ins and outs of the trucks, studying the routes, and understanding the industry regulations.

Their training period allowed them to connect with experienced truck drivers who shared their wisdom and adventures on the road. Samuel and Sofia soaked up every bit of knowledge, mentally preparing themselves for their upcoming journey.

Finally, their training ended, and the time had come to hit the road. The couple secured their first assignment, transporting goods from Vancouver to the easternmost provinces of Canada.

*****

Samuel and Sofia stood side by side, beaming with pride, as they gazed at their brand new, gleaming T680E Electric Kenworth Trucks. These state-of-the-art machines were a marvel of engineering, combining the power and ruggedness of traditional Kenworth trucks with cutting-edge electric technology.

The Electric T680E Trucks were elegantly designed with a sleek aerodynamic body, reducing air resistance and enhancing fuel efficiency. Adorned in a metallic silver finish, their exteriors shone under the sun, giving them a futuristic appeal. LED headlights at the front illuminated the road ahead, while streamlined side mirrors gave Samuel and Sofia excellent visibility.

The interior of the trucks was no less impressive. Samuel and Sofia entered to find spacious cabins elegantly furnished with plush, ergonomic seats. The dashboards featured hi-tech digital displays, providing them with real-time information about their driving performance, battery levels, and navigation.

A robust electric powertrain hummed softly under each hood, promising a quiet and smooth ride. The batteries, carefully integrated into the frame of each truck, provided ample power to transport goods across long distances. With zero emissions, they reinforced Samuel and Sofia's commitment to a greener and more sustainable future.

Each T680E Electric Kenworth truck was equipped with advanced safety features, including lane departure warnings, collision mitigation systems, and adaptive cruise control. These innovations ensured Samuel and Sofia's reliable and secure journeys on their long-haul routes.

*****

As Samuel and Sofia sat in their new trucks, they felt excitement and gratitude for the opportunities ahead. The all-electric Kenworth Trucks symbolised a new era of long-distance transportation, where their passion for safe and sustainable driving could be fully realised. With their CDLs and Electric Kenworth Trucks at their disposal, their shared dream of exploring new horizons on the open road was ready to come true.

*****

What no one expected was that Samuel and Sofia decided to wear clothing and outfits associated with the gnome world while driving their new trucks.

Since Samuel and Sofia's relationship with Abella and Derekamus began, they have become fans of gnome culture and found it whimsical and enchanting. They appreciated the intricate details and bright colours that often adorned gnome clothing and wanted to celebrate and immerse themselves in that fantasy world during their drive. Wearing gnome-inspired outfits allowed them to feel connected to the magical world of gnomes, enhancing their overall enjoyment of the experience.

The bewildered new company owners could see Samuel and Sofia, accompanied by Abella and Derekamus, two equally excited gnomes, about the journey. The two gnomes were delighted to see Samuel and Sofia embrace their culture, creating camaraderie and shared experiences between the barbarians and the gnomes. Samuel and Sofia could bond with their gnome companions by donning gnome clothing, strengthening their friendship and making the adventures even more enjoyable for everyone involved.

As for suitable names for Samuel and Sofia, considering their newfound connection to the gnome world and their journey with Abella and Derekamus, the following names were adopted by both drivers.

Samuel became "Gnomelock" – This name combined Samuel's identity with the mystical essence of gnomes. It reflected both his connection to the gnome world and his adventuring spirit.

Sofia became "Faeleaf." Her new name embodied Sofia's affinity for nature and enchantment with gnome culture. It captured her whimsical personality and portrayed her as a guardian and protector of the magical realms.

These names emphasise Samuel and Sofia's transformation into characters who drive trucks and embody the spirit and magic of the gnome world, especially in Canada.

*****

From that moment on, Gnomelock, Abella, Faeleaf, and Derekamus embarked on a series of unforgettable adventures. They travelled through breathtaking mountain ranges, witnessed mesmerising sunsets, and captured the essence of each region they passed through.

Throughout their encounters, they embraced the art of storytelling. At various truck stops, they connected with fellow drivers, locals, and travellers, exchanging tales of their experiences on the road. Every interaction inspired their own creative ventures, fuelling their passion for writing.

Samuel and Sofia's fame and profits began to grow as they built their reputation as reliable and skilled long-distance truck drivers. They could fund their adventures on and off the road while simultaneously pursuing their dream of becoming storytellers.

Their unique perspective and love for storytelling spread, and they attracted attention from publishers and travel websites. Their Instagram account, filled with stunning photographs and captivating stories, gained a significant following, opening doors for additional writing opportunities and sponsorships.

What started as a simple desire to escape the monotony of their lives transformed into a thrilling adventure filled with new opportunities and breathtaking experiences. Samuel and Sofia's decision to become long-distance truck drivers dressed as gnomes not only funded their dreams but also shaped the narrative of their lives, forever opening doors to an extraordinary tale of love, adventure, and creativity.

*****

## *72: I am a growing community of new Rocks on a Mountain Ridge*

Ah, good day to you! We are two male lineated woodpeckers stirring to the first light of dawn; we feel the vibrant energy of the city waking up around us. The chorus of birdsong fills the air, blending harmoniously with the distant hum of barbarian activity. "Why do we birds greet each day at such early hours worldwide?" It is a fascinating question indeed. We, well, birds, have evolved over millennia to synchronise our daily routines with the environment's natural cycles. By waking up at the crack of dawn, we all maximise our chances of finding food, establishing territories, and attracting mates.

Despite our woodpeckers' raucous calls resonating through the trees, the other birds seem undeterred. Each species has its unique song and behaviour, contributing to nature's symphony. As woodpeckers, we marvel at the resilience and adaptability of our avian friends, who never fail to rise to the challenges of each new day.

In this bustling cityscape nestled under a scenic mountain ridge, where barbarian noise competes with the melodic sounds of nature, we birds—and we do mean all birds, including our species—continue our timeless rituals. We love to remind ourselves and all barbarians of the beauty and vitality that surrounds us, urging everyone to pause, listen, and appreciate the world waking up around us."

As two male woodpeckers, we are striking birds with stunning black-and-white plumage. Our bodies are mainly black, with bold white stripes running down our backs and wings. Our striking appearance makes us stand out among the trees in the park where we reside.

Our large park home in the north of the city provides us with ample opportunities to forage for insects and make a cosy nest. A typical day for us starts at the break of dawn with echoing calls and rhythmic drumming as we announce our presence. We spend most of our day drumming on tree trunks with our strong beaks to search for food.

Our routine involves exploring the tall trees in search of beetle larvae, ants, and other insects that dwell beneath the bark. As the day progresses, we take short breaks to rest on branches, allowing us to observe the upper levels of this bustling city in the distance. Our vibrant plumage stands out against the lush green backdrop of the park, making us a beautiful sight to behold for visitors and residents alike. Talking about residents, there is a penthouse with a large balcony. Sometimes, we perch on its sturdy-looking brick wall. That is until a watchful black cat with four white paws and two smaller kittens appears.

Today, we flew away and headed to another building that we knew housed a great selection of trees, and where when the windows of the upper floor were open, we found ourselves with a panoramic view of what was going on inside. Today, there appeared to be many shocked faces that were not looking at us. Oh no, they never bothered to look at us. But one of them was standing in front of all of them, and he was reading from a newspaper. We stopped and listened because this barbarian was only wearing a denim-style skirt!

* * * * *

The night shift began with Stalin instructing the team: "I want each of you to thoroughly search and cross-reference all available databases, including those of immigration, police, and other government departments. Tonight, we must identify any known sisters who are residents or citizens of this city and have been here since 1945. Make sure to coordinate your efforts with everyone and report back with any relevant information promptly."

Eduardo added, "Let us organise ourselves and stop every hour to recap where we are."

From that moment, the office space had been a neverending flurry of activity as the fire station management and forensic teams worked side by side, pouring over evidence and discussing theories. Samuel, Sofia, Abella, and Derekamus became the unofficial recorders of all that needed to be recorded. They used the surrounding white walls from top to bottom. The end result was that each wall was covered with Post-it notes, photos, and maps, while whiteboards were filled with scribbled notes and diagrams.

Eduardo and his fire station management team had spent the night piecing together the events leading up to each devastating house fire by reading and examining every report they could find, whether online or as a paper trail. The team discussed what little eyewitness accounts they could offer, and they agreed that they were none the wiser afterwards. They moved their attention to all fire department logs and available building blueprints, trying to reconstruct the timeline of events for each house fire.

Meanwhile, the forensic team, headed by Emilie and Davide, had concentrated on examining physical evidence collected from the various scenes. They meticulously catalogued the historical records of the charred remains, melted debris, and possible samples of accelerants, hoping to find clues that would lead them to the cause of the fires. They were searching for a pattern that would possibly emerge, giving credence to the same perpetrator or perpetrators causing the fires and killing the victims.

It was around three in the morning when Stalin paused everyone and said,

"We may be approaching all this from the earliest housefire to the latest. I think we should do it in the opposite direction. From the latest to the earliest. Why? Because we have Hugo Van der Vored's body in the morgue and a charred wreck of a house and cellar no more than ten minutes away."

Everyone nodded their approval and regrouped with new perspectives to explore. The noise in the room grew.

*****

At six a.m., the sun began to rise outside. The teams sat back to survey their work. The walls and whiteboards were a chaotic patchwork of information, a visual representation of their collective efforts to solve the mystery. Eduardo, Carmen, Tomas, and Zamira exchanged knowing looks with each other, each determined to unravel the truth behind the fires that had taken so much from their community.

Two hours earlier, Stalin had tried his hardest not to show his fatigue. His whole body felt like it was close to shutting down. It had been decades since he had to muster his brain to absorb all the clues appearing one after another and, many times, often appearing as one. He felt the urgency to leave the fire station and walk the streets to think like a street man, not a befuddled policeman. He turned to Eduardo and Archibaldo, and without saying a word, he left the room. Both his friends knew he would be back when he was ready.

Every investigator in the room was catnapping in the chairs by seven am. Stalin had not reappeared at this point. No one was worried; they knew he would return. All were now waiting for the delivery of piping hot ham and egg breakfasts, fresh arepas bursting with cheese, white rice, bowls of frijoles, and bottles of Aqua con Limon. Eduardo, Carmen, and Tomas teamed up to brew three large pots of coffee. They had been doing this periodically throughout the night.

It kept everyone alert. The surrounding white walls and whiteboards were increasingly overwhelmed with scribbles and notes as new information and priceless clues emerged throughout the night. The clue that galvanised everyone came from a call from the Immigration department. Archibaldo had taken that call, and everyone could see his eyes widening with excitement as he heard the duty officer's discovery.

*****

"Good evening, or should I say good morning? I am the Duty Immigration and Administrative Officer, Mateo Andres Cruz. May I confirm you are Police Captain Archibaldo Frederico Alcatraz?"

"Yes, Mateo. You are speaking to me, Archibaldo. Do you have news for me and my team?"

Mateo, now contented that he was talking to the right person, began, "I must say, after much diligence and thorough investigation, I have stumbled upon some intriguing information regarding the entry of a family back in 1945 at the border near Leticia. It appears that a father and his three daughters arrived with papers named Karl, Anna, Eva, and Lisa Müller and were granted entry into our country."

Archibaldo, not wanting to cause any misunderstanding, asked, "Are you sure of your findings? Do you know where they had travelled from originally?"

"One moment, ah yes, here it is. The Müller family appears to have set out from Germany. To be a bit more precise, they are from Berlin. Does that help you so far?"

Archibaldo needed to know more, "What month did they enter our country?"

Mateo smiled, as he did not need to search reams of paperwork to find this detail: "They showed up in April 1945, on the 27th, in fact."

Archibaldo turned to the nearest white wall and began scribbling. "Please continue, Mateo. I will be taking notes."

"Affirmative Captain, furthermore, my research has unveiled that this small family settled in Dapa, the picturesque village overlooking our splendid city. The father, with a profession as a cosmetic surgeon, must have undoubtedly brought about a touch of elegance and finesse to our community. As for his three daughters, all attended the local school, likely brightening the classrooms with their presence and enriching their minds with knowledge."

Archibaldo did not smile at the presumption that these three girls would go on to become your average good-natured set of pupils. He kept his thoughts and listened to Mateo's innocence. "It is truly fascinating to uncover such a captivating tale from our past, showcasing the diversity and unique stories that have contributed to shaping our nation. If you have any additional details to share or inquiries to make, feel free to do so as I sit here, ready to assist you further."

"Yes, please. I do have a couple more questions for you. "Are the father and daughters still alive and living in Colombia, as far as you know?"

"As far as our records show, the father died in a housefire back in 1965, and the three girls have all moved abroad."

Archibaldo could not contain himself; he shouted out, "Where and what month did he die?"

"One second, please, while I check."

Minutes pass, and Archibaldo concentrates on the white wall. He has not faced his fellow interrogators yet.

"Hello, Captain, are you still there?"

"Yes, I am. Do you have a date for me?"

"Affirmative, Captain, I do. The father, Professor Karl Müller, passed away on the 5th of March 1965 at his hacienda in Dapa. I can confirm all this from the death certificate registered in Yumbo."

"Who registered the death?"

"One second, ah, here it is. The signature appears to belong to one, Augustus Maximilian Rockefeller III. His office address was Augustus Maximilian Rockefeller III Law Offices, 1901 Park Avenue, Suite 300, New York, NY 10001."

"My last question, Mateo, in all your research this evening, has any of the three Müller sisters ever entered our country since March 1965? If so, from where?"

Mateo leaned towards his large tabletop screen and found no entry for any of the three sisters. It was like they had just vanished. "Sorry, no, there are no official records of either of the Müller daughters returning to our country. But that does not mean they didn't."

"Thank you, Mateo. I will get back to you should I have any more questions. You did well for us here tonight. We will report our appreciation to your superiors very soon."

"Thank you, Captain. Oh, I do have one question. Did these ladies do something wrong?"

Archibaldo sighed, "Yes, you could say that. But for now, we would appreciate it if you would keep quiet regarding this investigation."

"Will do; it has been both a pleasure and worth me doing overtime this evening while my colleague is out and about celebrating his twenty-first birthday."

*****

Archibaldo replaced the telephone handle back into its cradle. Finally, he was able to look up and, with a beaming smile on his face, confirmed to all present, "We, my friends, it appears we may have our arsonists and killers. Meet Anna, Eva, and Lisa Müller. Also, I do believe we have the name of the unknown victim found in the 1965 fire. It looks like Professor Karl Müller was their first victim."

The roar around the room said everything the investigators were thinking at that moment. Eduardo waved his hands gently to usher in some calmness to the room. "Friends, please, this fire station is fully operational. Let them work in peace. While you are doing that, start Googling these three Müller sisters. What have they been doing for the past six decades apart from murdering people and setting fires?"

*****

Ethan looked from his laptop and began to read the results of Anna's backstory and profile search out loud: "According to Google and Wikipedia, Dra. Anna Müller, now aged 85, moved with her family to Colombia in 1945. She is listed as having two other living sisters. From a young age, she displayed an exceptional talent and passion for chemistry, spending countless hours conducting experiments in her father's makeshift home laboratory."

Ethan checked around the room, and all eyes were firmly concentrated on him. He continued reading, "Throughout her childhood and teenage years, Anna Müller was recognised for her intelligence and dedication to the field of chemistry. She excelled in her studies, earning top marks in school and winning numerous science competitions. Her insatiable curiosity and innovative approach set her apart from her peers, garnering the attention of prestigious universities and research institutions within the USA. After completing her undergraduate and doctoral studies with honours, Anna Müller quickly rose through the ranks in the academic and scientific community. Her groundbreaking research and organic chemistry discoveries revolutionised how scientists understood molecular structures and reactions.

Throughout her illustrious career, Anna received numerous accolades and awards for her contributions to the field of chemistry. She was honoured with prestigious prizes such as the Nobel Prize in Chemistry, the Lavoisier Medal, and the Priestley Medal. Her research not only advanced the boundaries of scientific knowledge but also profoundly impacted industries ranging from pharmaceuticals to environmental science."

Ethan paused and asked no one in particular, "Did our chemist Anna Müller know of the brilliant but naughty Dr. Reed? Who should we turn to next, Eva or Lisa?"

"Let us stay alphabetical and go for Eva, " suggested Davide. Emilie, would you do the honours of introducing Eva Müller to us all?"

Sitting next to Ethan, Emilie pressed "enter" on her keyboard, and the screen revealed the next search. Like Ethan before, she began reading the text on the screen.

"Eva Müller, Physicist 84, born in 1940 in a small town in Germany, showed an early passion for science and curiosity about the world around her. Raised by her supportive father and two sisters, Anna and Lisa, who encouraged her love for learning, she excelled in school. She went on to study physics at the prestigious Miami University. Throughout her academic career, Eva displayed an unparalleled intellect and drive, breaking barriers and shattering gender stereotypes in the male-dominated field of physics. Her groundbreaking research in quantum mechanics and theoretical physics earned her international acclaim and recognition as one of the leading minds of her generation."

At this point, Emilie paused to sip some lukewarm coffee before resuming. "For six decades, Eva Müller has made significant contributions to the field of physics, publishing numerous influential papers and revolutionising our understanding of the universe. Her work has led to the development of groundbreaking technologies and innovations that will continue to shape the future of science and technology."

Emilie could not help but admire this physicist; she had read many of her previous works and loved her thoroughness and simplicity in explaining her views. Eva Müller has received countless accolades and awards throughout her long career, including the Nobel Prize in Physics, the Albert Einstein Medal, and the prestigious Breakthrough Prize in Fundamental Physics. She is globally celebrated for her unwavering dedication to her work, visionary insights, and profound impact on the world of physics. Eva Müller is regarded as a true pioneer in the field of physics. She single-handedly inspired countless generations of scientists to push the boundaries of knowledge centred on exploring the mysteries of the universe.

Ethan waited until Emilie had finished reading and asked another question: no one was sure the answer was: "So did sister number two, as a Physicist, cross paths with fellow Physicist David Wells, another naughty boy?"

"Thank you, Emilie. Sofia, by the look on your face, I believe you may have a lot of information on the third sister, Lisa?"

Sofia had to admit that she liked how Ethan conducted himself; it was comical but still professional. "Yes, you are right. I have a lot to say about Lisa Müller, who appears to be the youngest of the three sisters. She is now 83, and she is another brainy one, according to what I am seeing here on my screen:"

"Lisa Müller was raised with her two older sisters, Anna and Eva, in a small Colombian village surrounded by nature on the outskirts of Santiago de Cali. From a young age, she displayed a deep love and fascination for animals, spending countless hours observing and studying the wildlife she encountered on the craggy road near her home. Lisa's passion for the natural world only intensified, leading her to pursue a career in biology. She excelled in her studies, earning a full scholarship to one of the top universities in Florida. There, she specialised in wildlife conservation and ecology, starting with Hippopotamuses and later Lions and Gorillas.

After completing her studies, Lisa Müller embarked on a groundbreaking research journey that took her to some of the most remote and challenging environments around the globe. Her tireless dedication and pioneering research on endangered species and ecosystems earned her international acclaim and numerous prestigious awards.

Throughout her career, Lisa Müller has made significant contributions to the field of biology, publishing groundbreaking research papers, leading conservation efforts, and inspiring new generations of scientists. Her work has helped bring attention to critical issues facing wildlife and their habitats, mostly Silverbacks in Rwanda and Lions in the Serengeti. This has led to the establishment of protected areas and conservation programs that continue to protect countless species today from the illegal trade in animal trafficking.

Lisa Müller has retired from active fieldwork but continues to mentor and advise young biologists worldwide. Her legacy lives on through the numerous accolades and awards she has received for her outstanding contributions to the field of biology and wildlife conservation. "

This time, everyone automatically turned to listen to Ethan's next question about the Müller sisters. He did not disappoint anyone. "Well, it's questionable if she knew Dr. Emily Greene; they both were or are biologists. But I feel it is safe to presume our suspect Lisa did know Hugo Van der Vored, and I further suspect she was not impressed with his activities or beliefs."

At that very moment, the office door opened, and a distressed Stalin walked with a wad of newspapers in his hands. As he reached the table, he threw and scattered them in all directions. "I think it best you all read the headlines on this morning's editions."

Stalin immediately went to the coffee machine, poured a large black coffee, carried the mug and a half-empty bottle of whisky, turned, and sat down, adding nothing further to anyone. He just sat there staring at the table surface.

*****

The fire station management team and the city forensic team, in conjunction with Zamira Archibaldo, Samuel, Sofia, Derekamus, and Abella, have worked tirelessly throughout the night and are exhausted. Stalin is now standing before them; each investigator has read the disturbing headlines and the first two paragraphs.

"103-year-old Pilot & Life President of CT&C Corporation Vanishes in Mysterious Air Disappearance with Nobel Prize Sisters."

Gabriel García Márquez, the Argentinian-born Life President of CT&C Corporation with its headquarters in Miami and founder of the Argentinian brand Coffee and Cascara Alchemists, had mysteriously vanished this past evening whilst flying his vintage Cessna 175 Skyhawk from Cali to Miami. Onboard were three sisters from the scientific Müller family: Anna, 85, Nobel Prized Chemist; Eva, 84, Nobel Prize Physicist; and 83-year-old younger sister, Lisa, a multi-awarded Biologist and wildlife conservationist. After extensive air searches, no wreckage or signs of human life have been found.

The US Coast Guard has reported that in the late hours of the night, a mysterious storm reminiscent of a hurricane materialised out of nowhere and vanished just as mysteriously. As chaos reigned in the search area, rescue ships raced to the scene where two tankers had collided. One vessel succumbed to the deep depths of the ocean in a matter of moments, while the other battled against the merciless waves, teetering on the brink of disaster in the unforgiving high seas.

The contents shocked them all, and a heavy silence settled over the room. Their heads were down, and they said nothing.

As if on cue, a flickering light from the overhead bulbs cast shadows on their fatigued faces, highlighting the gravity of the situation. Despite the exhaustion weighing on them, the team knew they had to act to address the crisis at hand. Stalin's gaze shifted from one team member to another, waiting for someone to break the silence and offer a solution. The sense of urgency in the air was palpable, pushing them to gather their thoughts and prepare for the difficult task ahead.

Samuel reacts after picking up a copy of El Pais and has read further down to almost the centre of the newspaper's front page. The paragraph shone like a proverbial beacon. The scientific world, especially Colombia, will mourn after reading this devastating news. The Müller family originated from Germany and relocated to the scenic village of Dapa just before the end of the Second World War.

As Samuel read on, his heart sank at the news. The mention of the Müller family relocating to his neck of the woods – Dapa! He looked straight towards Sofia. She, too, was mortified and frozen to the spot. The thought of hearing that the Müller family had grown up and possibly gone to the same school as her and Samuel. The couple were now clearly shocked to their inner cores. Their minds raced with questions as they delved deeper into the article, both determined to unravel the mystery behind the shocking announcement.

Sofia paused and looked directly towards Abella. "You were correct to say you had an uneasy feeling. You actually ended up coming to the same village as the Müllers. What must be the odds of that happening?"

Ethan raised his hand as if he, too, was back at school: "Excuse my ignorance, but is this village called Dapa near Cali and this other place I have heard of for the first time, Yumbo? And if so, does this village have a cemetery?"

Stalin's head came up, and his eyes locked onto Ethan's eyes. "There speaketh a true investigator." Stalin collected his chair and moved closer to the US agent.

As the tension in the room escalated, Stalin leaned in closer to Ethan and began speaking. "The north of Santiago de Cali to Dapa village is approximately 30 kilometres, which would take about a half hour to drive, depending on traffic," Stalin continued, his eyes fixed on Ethan's. "From Dapa village to Yumbo, it's about another 20 kilometres, another half an hour or so."

Stalin paused, his gaze still penetrating towards the US Agent, as he confirmed, "Yes, Dapa village does have a cemetery. A small one, but it's there." The gravity of his words hung in the air, the conversation's implications becoming increasingly clear to Ethan. "Oh, and before you ask, a Müller family plot is currently occupied by one Professor Karl Müller. With I might add room for three more graves."

Ethan smiled warmly at a fellow professional. "Actually, I had another question I was going to ask first. Who, pray to tell, is this 103-year-old Argentinian pilot, Gabriel García Márquez, I am suddenly reading about? And where is his last legitimate flying license?"

The unexpected reference to the renowned author Gabriel García Márquez being mistaken for a pilot injected a sense of light-heartedness into the atmosphere. Ethan's combination of wit and charm amidst the serious investigation brought a touch of comic relief to the moment, causing everyone to burst into laughter.

The investigating teams, caught off guard by Ethan's humorous remark, applauded his sense of humour and ability to infuse fun into the intense situation. The shared laughter served as a unifying moment, breaking down barriers and fostering a sense of camaraderie among the professionals

Archibaldo turned to Stalin, "Colonel, where did you go in the middle of the night, and how do you know about Dapa and the Müller cemetery plot? In fact, how did you know about the Müllers? We only found out a couple of hours ago from the Immigration people, and you were not here!"

Stalin remained silent for a moment, his expression unreadable. Finally, he spoke calmly, "I left the fire station feeling lost and uncertain about any destination, but I had a deep need to seek solitude and find solutions to my inner inquiries. As I wandered aimlessly, and before I knew it, an hour had passed. I stumbled upon an open-back delivery truck overflowing with bundles of the morning newspaper editions. Noticing that the driver was absent, I seized the moment and grabbed a single copy, tucking it under my arm as I continued my solitary journey."

At one point, I sat on a small brick wall next to the main highway leading out of our city, heading towards Yumbo. I pulled out the folded newspaper, and you can guess what I saw."

"I instantly remembered Gabriel from that night we saved the older people from their flooding care homes. Archibaldo, don't you recall the flamboyant guy with the Willy Jeep, who later took many of us flying with the owners of the Museo Aereo Fenix? What were their names?"

"You must mean José and Stella. Yes, you are right. Gabriel and José gave us flying experiences that none of us there will ever forget. But you still have not told us how you knew about the Müller sisters."

"I am coming to that. Bear with me. My brain cells are not as active as they used to be." Stalin reached for the now half-full pot of coffee and added a tot of whisky. Everyone waited to witness the soothing liquid disappear into Stalin's mouth. Suddenly, his demeanour appeared rejuvenated, and he moved his lips again.

"I hitched a lift on the tail bars of an unsuspecting night bus heading up to Dapa and the tea fields beyond. The bored driver and I never saw each other. I departed the bus just as it started to turn into Dapa village. I walked in the other direction to the old church on the new road. Opposite is a cemetery, and it was here I stepped in between the rows of crosses and headstones. Finally, I stood at the foot of an ordinary black stone with the following gold-coloured words: Here lies Professor Karl Müller, born in 1910 and died on the 5th of March, 1965. May he rest in peace. Anna, Eva, and Lisa.

At first, a sense of melancholy washed over me. Here was a man who had lived a whole life, leaving behind a legacy in medicine and a loving family. Stalin couldn't help but wonder about Professor Müller's life, the struggles he must have faced, and the joy he must have experienced with his daughters. The names Anna, Eva, and Lisa seemed to hold a special significance, a reminder of the family that had been left behind to mourn his passing.

With a heavy heart, I whispered a quiet prayer for the Professor and his daughters. I had hoped that they, too, would finally find peace in the afterlife. Now, to answer your question about how I knew, it was easy. I was sure from when Abella told us the tragic childhood history of Helga Schmidt's daughters. They had to be the Müller sisters. Remember, Kimmel Gnomes never lie."

Stalin winked at Abella, who beamed the rosiest red-coloured cheeks anyone could have imagined.

Breakfast finally arrived, and the newspapers were moved away to allow the sumptuous meal to take up all the space available on the table. Stalin was about to demolish his first chorizo of the day and suddenly paused. "Captain Archibaldo. When did that happen?"

Archibaldo, grinning from ear to ear, said, "Well, to be honest, it was about thirty seconds before I called the Immigration Department."

When the moment came when everyone could eat no more and, in turn, held their bulging stomachs towards them, Eduardo rose and spoke as a great orator: "Ladies and Gentlemen, and that includes you, Abella and Derekamus. I hope you all agree that our station chef has surpassed himself this fine morning."

Hoots, cheers, loud burbs, and the odd passing of wind from too many frijoles rang out. The last one came from the sleeping Stalin, with his arms crossed, acting as a table cushion for his head. His brain and body had finally shut down to allow him to rest.

Zamira spoke excitedly, "I cannot believe how close we came to solving these long-standing cases. I feel like a weight has been lifted off our shoulders. I cannot wait to see everyone's faces when the news gets out amongst all our fire crews."

Before Eduardo could respond, Ethan raised his hand once more. Everyone turned inquisitively to their fast-becoming favourite of all-time US agent, not that, if asked, they could have named another. "Zamira, I feel it wise that we tell no one what we have discovered together over the past few days. Let the records show that over the past several decades, this city has had to deal with several house fires and also had to investigate a murder by unknowns in each. Just now, all those files are in archives, gathering dust, and probably will never again be opened by anyone after our use of them is over. We can count with certainty that there will be no more."

"The victims do not deserve our honourable efforts; they showed no humanity when they were alive. So why should we cause ourselves many sleepless nights, which in turn will have massive negative effects on our loved ones."

"I feel the three Müller sisters should be allowed to rest with their reputations and life's work continuing to benefit all humanity. From my reckoning, all three died as spinsters with no children of their own. Let the tragedy of their early life finally rest.

For us, do any of you here look forward to all the investigations and trials we will have to attend and give witness to? What would today's societies say when they head to their chosen channels of ranting and raging? How many of us will get caught up in the blame game? How many of us will have to leave the careers we love? How many of us will go on to enjoy the fruits of our pensions and grandchildren?

How do we explain how we found out and made the connections from a wicked act committed back in 1945 to a series of events starting in 1965 and finally stopping in 2024? The reporters and others will crucify just about everyone.

No, I feel the price of revealing that we all sat here, listened, and acted upon the knowledge of a pair of 250-year-old Kimmel Gnomes is going to be far too high. No one is going to believe us one bit. In fact, I suspect we may all end up in wards with rubber rooms and strait jackets."

Finally, Ethan smiled towards "Stalin" Let's protect this gallant and heroic street man. He, out of all us, deserves our undying protection and loyalty."

A grumbling voice escaped from the street man, "Sounds like John Wayne would have said a lot more with his exaggerated Texas accent. But thank you kindly Gringo, for your wise words."

Apart from Stalin, everyone rose and came together to pray, followed by lots of hugging and shaking hands. It was clear Ethan's words had struck many cords within them. Without saying so, the unofficial investigation into the unsolved cases would now close and never be reopened.......unless there happened to be another one.

*****

The two Lineated Woodpeckers spent the hours perched on the overhanging branch, curiously observing the bustling scene inside the fire station. Despite not understanding the barbarian language being spoken, they found joy in the barbarians' animated gestures and energetic movements around the large office table. The sight of the abundance of information being eradicated from the white walls and whiteboards added an element of intrigue and amusement to their observation. The woodpeckers remained transfixed by the lively activities unfolding before them, their feathers rustling gently in the breeze as they absorbed the fascinating spectacle before them.

With their curiosity about humans, the Lineated Woodpeckers failed to notice a chameleon silently studying them from a hidden vantage point. He had successfully changed his colour by utilising special cells in his skin called chromatophores, which allowed him to reveal only the pigments that would blend in well with the bark and hanging foliage on the tree. The chameleon's eyes flickered with interest as it watched the woodpeckers' and barbarians' movements and behaviours. Unbeknownst to the woodpeckers, the chameleon absorbed and processed this new information; he likes learning from its interactions with humans and storing it for future use.

As the sun began to set, all three creatures returned to their resting places high in the towering Ceiba tree, where they settled in perfect harmony for the night, safe and secure in their natural habitat. The two Woodpeckers' calls rang out once more, marking the end of another fulfilling day in their urban oasis while their neighbour slept, making no sounds.

*****

What Stalin had withheld from all at the fire station was another mystery he hoped would remain a memory for the rest of his life. While in the cemetery, he was suddenly disturbed by a series of moving lights behind him in the opposite field. He crouched down to hide his presence. The lights came from several moving rocks rolling gently down the mountain slope. Each crossed the quiet road and entered another field adjacent to the cemetery.

Stalin now saw other equally large rocks already positioned in a half circle. Miraculously, the new rocks took up positions as if to complete the circle. The lights went out, and darkness drew in.

Stalin sat back and was unaware he was sitting on the grave of Marcus Eduardo Uribe, the cyclist who had died so tragically a few years back and the same one whose life had been honoured with the impressive man-size square plinth bearing a black slated figure of a cyclist riding up to the heavens with a beaming smile.

"Beautiful sight, isn't it."

Stalin must have the world record for the high jump minus a pole record for the height he rose. When he landed, he was shaking and racing around to see if he was going mad. He was sure he heard someone speak.

"Please do not be alarmed; as I said, my name is Marcus, and my role here on this new mountain road is to ensure no one comes in harm's way."

Stalin was trying his best to compose himself but knew he was failing. His immediate urge was to run as fast as he could down that same mountain road back to the safety of the fire station. But the instincts of his past life as a colonel in the national police force kept him still. He remained rooted to the spot. He wanted to know what the lights and moving rocks were all about.

"Come, we can go together and get a little closure. I am sure the experience of witnessing new arrivals entering the rocks soon will be so amazing and joyful. But we must remain quiet. We should not wish to disturb them."

Suddenly, Marcus was standing next to Stalin, who silently prayed that his heart would cope and continue beating, only a bit more quietly.

The two moved side by side towards the field.

*****

I was born just over 10,000 years ago and was one of the indigenous people of the Ilama who settled in an area you call today the Darien in Valle de Cauca. The region was a true paradise at the time, a lush and vibrant land teeming with diverse flora and fauna. The landscape was dominated by dense tropical rainforests filled with towering trees, colourful orchids, and exotic birds. The mighty Cauca River flowed through the valley, providing fertile soil for our crops and sustenance for the abundant wildlife that called this place home. The air was filled with the sounds of howler monkeys, parrots and the gentle rustling of leaves in the wind.

Our people, the Llama, lived in harmony with nature, hunting and gathering what we needed to survive. We built our homes high in the trees, using materials in the forest to create shelters that kept us safe from the elements. The Valley was a place of abundance, where wild fruits, nuts, and medicinal plants grew in abundance. We shared our land with jaguars, tapirs, and colourful butterflies, each adding to the rich tapestry of life that surrounded us. We lived in balance with the land, respecting its power and beauty.

It is close enough for you to dwell here in Santiago de Cali, but walking and exploring was like a year away for me. As you can see, there were no roads or highways, just jungle. I lost my bearings, and at some point, I found myself all alone on this mountain ridge. There was an earthquake, and I ended up being crushed by this massive rock. I say crushed; I should say I was trapped within it. I have been in this situation ever since.

In all the passing years, and there were many, I spoke to no one until a funny-looking man with white hair, a pot belly, and sturdy-looking legs, who spoke a language I had never heard before, suddenly leaned on me and ate an apple, and talked to me!

Recently, and please do not ask me to be precise, another earthquake visited, and the outcome was that these other rocks similar in size and appearance to mine arrived and created this half-moon you see before you.

The experience of having neighbours such as Hector, Isabel, Ignacio, Jasmina, and nine wonderful souls who perished in a care home fire has been life-changing for me. It is through them that I learned all about Heaven. And do not get me started on all the history from when I was born and beyond. This place called Earth is truly amazing. But I do wonder if this world is really round. I think Ignacio is "pulling my leg."

Tonight, we have new guests to welcome. Hector got all excited when he laid eyes on his good friend Gabriel. Their friendship was plain to see.

Behind Gabriel stood three sisters, but I got a bit confused by their names. Was it Gitta, Eva, Gertrud, Anna, and Lisa? Time will tell. They had the look of learning people about them, and I am sure I will love getting to know them. I think someone said they are scientists!

Finally, the last two new neighbours to arrive were indeed a loving couple. They were holding hands and standing as close as two humans could get. Their names are José and Stella. It became evident that they, too, are friends of Gabriel. The most amazing thing I learned tonight was that all three newcomers were experienced pilots. I am not sure what that entails. I am sure someone will enlighten me at some point. Hold it; Gabriel has just informed me that they fly flying machines. That notion of flying machines took some convincing, and it was not long before I could see they loved to laugh and tease each other. Oh, how I love my friend's version of what Heaven is like for them.

*****

Stalin arrived back in the Barrio of Santa Monica. The place and the streets still looked the same. After a few minutes, he ventured to each doorway and discovered a mattress that appeared to have seen better days. He repositioned it to prevent anyone from being able to enter or exit the shop. He lay down, fell immediately asleep, and was still able to hold his trusty rock in his hand. Sadly, the next day, when Eduardo and Archibaldo had stopped to see if he might want to join them for breakfast. They discovered Stalin had no memory again and believed he was lost in his internal world once more. They failed to see him winking and smiling to himself as he turned his back to them and closed his eyes.

*****

A voice rings out in abject alarm back up on the mountain, "I do not believe it! That old woman who likes to urinate is still alive!"

**Finally, the end.** I am heading off for a delicious cup of Cascara Tea.

## *Final thoughts*

There you have it. Finally, a seven-year journey has reached its conclusion. Adventures, Barbarians, and Devil's Breath is completed. The story of my book goes back to 2016 when I, the white-haired with a slight pot-belly and strong-looking legs, had an accident up on a mountain ridge overlooking the city of Cali below.

I came within twelve hours of dying, and doctors had to fight to keep me going. Luckily, they were successful. Race on to a month ago when I turned up for a routine check-up on my well-being. The doctors thought it prudent with the history of my father passing at the age of 62 and my grandfather passing at 64. Both had succumbed to heart attacks, and with me heading to my 69th birthday, they should look a little closer.

They discovered the main artery just outside of my heart was 80% blocked, and anytime soon, I would be history for good. The battle was on to give me an open-heart bypass surgery.

Now, months later, I am home writing these words to you all.

I owe everything to my wife, Cristirin, for her persistence in getting me to turn up at doctor's appointments when all I wanted to do was write all my hidden stories like crazy.

I sincerely thank Dr Rafael Nunez, or "El Presidente." and his team of dedicated professionals at DiME Clinica, Cali.

Their combined efforts in making me an English success story for them and their willingness to make sure I could return to this book and complete it for you all made it happen.

I also wish to pass on my vast, heartfelt best to a particular lady called Kathy Ann Hurley, who, from 5000 miles away, kept my spirits up and made sure she was able to "kick me up the ass."

Kathy, you have been a particular person in my life for some forty years. Both Cristirin and I love you completely.

*****

Now, let me focus on a certain black and white cat named Blacky. For all cat lovers in the world, Blacky is our hero of the hour. When I came home, he patiently waited to see me sleeping in bed. He joined me and would not leave. He even escorted me to the toilet and accompanied me back again.

I will be forever indebted to this four-footed moggy. I hope the city of Cali will one day allow Blacky to join the Rio Gato and his fifteen girlfriends, especially Valentina.

*****

If all of you readers wish to read more of the adventures of the characters in Adventures, Barbarians, and Devil's Breath, please let the publishers know. I have book two and book three waiting in my head. But please, no accidents in between. *So, I dearly hope Panama, Venezuela, Chile, Peru, Ecuador, and Argentina will gladly open their doors to see what I can create for them.*

Peace and love to all.

*Mike Bowley*

August 2024

Also, I have just finished reading Strange Pilgrims and am beginning to read News of a Kidnapping by Nobel Prize Winner Gabriel Garcia Marquez—yes, the real Gabo.

**Definitely the END**

## *About your author*

Mike Bowley was born in Bristol, in the South West of England, in 1955. Up to the age of 13, he could not read or write. However, an English Teacher took him under her wing, and she spent the next 3 years ensuring he had the gift of being able to read & write. He believed this heroine saved him from a life of crime. This early struggle with literacy would later become a source of inspiration for his writing, as he drew on his own experiences to create anthropomorphism compelling narratives.

At the age of 10, Mike boldly asked his father for 'Pocket money.' His father's response was not what he expected, but it instilled in him a valuable lesson: he wanted something, and he had to earn it. This marked the beginning of his journeyman professions, starting with being a 'Milk Delivery Boy' and 'Newspaper Delivery Boy', both at the same time. His resilience and determination were already shaping his future.

This workload, for such a young mind, also contributed to his often falling asleep during classes.

Mike is a man of dedication and hard work. He has been working tirelessly, and his many stories and experiences have become the foundation of his numerous culminating short stories. His commitment to his craft is truly admirable.

As Mike entered his 60s, he felt the call of another adventure. Little did he know that it would lead him to the vibrant and diverse country of Colombia in South America. His adventurous spirit was about to embark on a new journey.

In the decade since he has lived in the vast and beautiful tropical country of Colombia, he has married for the third time, trained to be a Barista, passed his Colombian driving test, Passed his UK truck driving test, became a self-trained SEO Content Writer, and is now an author of anthropomorphism-styled short stories.

The latter he puts down to an accident he had in 2016 where he did severe damage to his head in a fall down the local Dapa mountain ridge, which overlooks the city of Cali below. This accident, while initially a setback, sparked a 7-year surge of creativity in Mike, leading to his newfound passion for storytelling.

His imagination went wild, and the result was his first outing, "Adventures, Barbarians, and Devil's Breath. This will soon be followed by his forthcoming sequel, "Liberators and Their Mighty Sabres."

A third book is in the pipeline, and it has no name yet. However, the first 16 chapters are already mapped out, and his fingers are waiting to touch a keyboard.

If you love South America or have never experienced such a vibrant and incredible continent, you will love delving into this author's imagination. Mike's writing is a unique blend of features, objects, historical people, historical events, and characters from his experiences and imagination. It's not a travel guide but a journey through the mind of someone who has embraced and celebrated all that he has experienced in such a short time.

www.ingramcontent.com/pod-product-compliance
Ingram Content Group UK Ltd.
Pitfield, Milton Keynes, MK11 3LW, UK
UKHW030649220125
454002UK00005B/56